Scarlet War

Walking Shadow: Book Three
By Jack Fields

Table of Contents

Dedication

For Luke and Elliott, who taught me that brotherhood is just as much about kindness as it is strength.

Acknowledgements

Enormous thanks to my dazzling editors, Michelle Dunbar, Judy Roth, and Dantas Neto.

Heartfelt gratitude to the Legion family, particularly Jez, Chrissy, and Geneva, without whom the ship would have no sails.

Special mention must be given to Brian J. Nordon and Rachel Ní Chuirc, two musketeers without whom I could not claim my current happiness. All for one and one for all!

To the D&D crew, particularly Mr. Matthew Charles Elliott, I am forever and deeply indebted.

Dear reader, I hope you enjoy this finale to a trilogy of scarlet dreams.

Lastly, thank you, Mac Tíre, the wolf who walks the dusky forests of my heart. You know who you are. Know that I love you, and that the moon, the stars, and the softly rustling leaves are yours to command.

Beginning At The End...

In the city there loomed a tower.

In the tower there was an office.

In the office there sat a man.

His hair and beard had once been dark and pure. Now they were well-salted, white-gray bristles tufting amongst the black. His clothes had once been tattered. Now they were tailor-made and well looked after. Of his moth-gnawed coat, which he had always worn with a special affection, there was no sign. Even his face—equine like his father's and foxy like his mother's—seemed stretched somehow. Yesterday he had been nineteen and running from two of the most dangerous people in the world. Wait. No, that was not right. Yesterday he had been twenty-nine, in a hospital waiting room, and he had been waiting to hear if his girlfriend and their baby were all right.

Well, he had not escaped danger.

His girlfriend and his baby had not been all right.

Things had begun badly, and gotten worse. Now and then there'd been good bits. Bright lamps, few and far between, along a road distinct for the thickness and implacability of its shadows. There was a puppet without strings, a butler with a heart of gold, a policeman with a glorious moustache, a ghost who was his teacher and a true friend. So many faces. So many places.

His girlfriend who became his wife.

His new baby who became a monster.

On the office television, footage of the lunar landing played. Grainy images of a gray tundra, unexciting, hostile almost. But people went wild for it. And the broadcaster was enamored with it. So on it rolled.

The man thought about the part he'd played in capturing that footage.

There had been a speech. A rocket taking off, foaming the sky with fire and smoke like an exclamation point. What else? Beehives. The dream of a tree. The great disappearing, reappearing girl. The conversation in a crystal room, and another in a house with three floors. Good bright spots. Bad shadowy clots.

When had it all happened? Over the course of a day? An hour? A moment? Twenty years? When? When?

It was September, a cold, unkind September that took great pleasure in slipping through the slightest gaps in the casing of windows and coming inside and stealing a crumb, a slice, a whole loaf of warmth and comfort to eat. He remembered a woman who ate joy and who laid eggs of swarming, buzzing madness.

To forget, or to try to forget, the man stacked briquettes and threaded firelighters and kindled a good hot fire in the hearth where six dragons of carved stone brooded. He brewed some tea and stood as close to the fire as he could, keeping that thief September at bay. He thought about autumns and lots of other things besides. He perused memories carefully, dotingly—even the ugly ones, the ones that hurt to dwell on. Suddenly he didn't want to forget anything. Yesterday he'd forgotten something important and had the devil of a time settling his nerves.

Yesterday he'd been young.

His name was Hughes.

Act One

Rockabye Baby

Chapter One

On the day he planned to meet Death, Gormon Hughes could not find the answer to one important question:

"What am I going to wear?"

From her spot on the sofa Cate Jubilee shot him a bemused look. "Do you think it matters?" Before Hughes could reply she glanced at the man on the other end of the sofa. The man—Frank Gallant by name—was dandling a baby on his knee. "Does it matter?" Cate asked him.

"No," said Frank.

"Not even a little bit?"

"Not the most miniscule iota of a little bit."

Cate clicked her fingers, plucked the air like she was plucking Hughes' worry right out of him, crumbled it in her fingers, and blew it away like a kiss. "See, my love?" she said pleasantly. "It doesn't matter what you wear."

Hughes grumbled that it bloody well did matter. She could puff away his worries, but they would come back. They were unpuffable worries. To assuage further protests he rushed across the apartment and into the bedroom, flinging off his clothes and tearing open drawers, his heartbeat galloping.

The baby watched him go. She looked at Frank. Frank looked at the baby.

"Your daddy is a worrywart. Thank goodness he's not a wartworry."

The baby honked his nose curiously.

"It's like an anxious person," Frank explained. "Only covered in lumps, bumps, and the occasional toadstool. You find wartworries outside chip shops asking you for bus money. Don't give it to them, kid. They'll only lose it and increase their list of worries. And that's one more toadstool on the wart farm, you dig?"

The baby laughed. It was a fantastically loud whipcrack of noise, so light and merry, it seemed to have taken the holiday season by the breeches and dragged it tinkling into the new year.

Surprised and delighted, Frank crowed his own musical laugh. This made the baby giggle and shriek all the more, which got Frank going again. "Yeah," he wheezed eventually. "Yeah, you dig all right. Hoo damn. My poor ribs."

"Is it a long way?" Cate asked Frank.

"Between where and where?"

"Here and..." Cate found she'd forgotten the name of their destination. Being a mother was proving quite different from fighting. More draining for a start. She couldn't remember the last time she'd had a proper sleep. "Here and wherever you and Hughes are going," she said.

"Dreaming Jija. One of many underworlds where the dead congregate, and where Death herself can be found." Frank removed the baby's pudgy little hand from his nose and walked his fingers from one of her ears to the other, which seemed to greatly amuse her. "Not sure how long between here and there," he said. "I've never been where we're going. Could be a few days' worth of traveling. Could be a few minutes." Frank paused. "Though I doubt it." His considerations were interrupted when the baby grabbed the watch of embossed gold from his pocket, peered at it with suspicion, and put the watch in her mouth. Frank tried to retrieve it without success. "Not for eating, sweetie. Give over."

The baby fixed him with an expression that said, *Well, it could be for eating. Who knows what functions this object might boast, if only your adult brain could fathom them. It's my duty as a child to check. Chomp-chomp-drool.*

Frank looked at Cate. "She going to cry if I take it away?"

"If you're lucky." Cate gave a weary smile. It did not speak volumes so much as entire libraries.

Frank frowned as a trickle of warm spit spilled off the formerly gleaming and now rather damp gold onto the back of his hand. Meanwhile, in the bedroom, hopeful mutterings became grunts of revulsion.

"I've come round on outfit selection. Dress for the long haul, dear," Cate called. "You know the saying: failure to prepare..."

"Prepare to displease the Grim Reaper," finished Hughes irritably. "Where's my hat?"

"You haven't got one."

There was a pause. Hughes emerged into the living room, bare-chested and with a pair of trousers hanging off his arms. He opened his mouth. Closed it. "So I don't. Thank you, darling." He turned and hurried back into the bedroom.

Frank's frown changed. With locks of his hair all bright and dancing with aurora borealis, he spelled out this question: *Is he okay?*

Cate leaned forward and used the floating locks to spell out a reply:

He's been like this since Tinfrost.

At once Frank understood.

It was March the twenty-first. Three months ago, with the help of Estelle Corlum, Mr. Glint, the former Captain Hoshrum Thud (now Commissioner Thud), Desdemona Cauldronpot, and Frank himself, Hughes had put an end to the Spring-Heeled murders ravaging Corinth City. Only a few days afterward, at the annual Tinfrost feast in Redspire, Hughes and Estelle had confronted Lady Wendy Dragontail over Estelle's poisoning and forced confinement. Frank didn't know what had gone on between those three. He didn't know what had been said on that balcony, what had been resolved and left very much unresolved. He knew only that the Perfect Prison had been used for the final time.

Now Wendy was dead.

And the kicker? The old gal was Hughes' mother. Poor guy had only found out when her magic item had recognized his genetic makeup and mingled with it. Had she stuck around to spare two words of explanation? No sir. She'd left her son burdened by too many answerless questions, a frigate doomed to sink in icy water. Frank could sympathize—his own mothers had not exactly been spectacular examples of parenthood.

In his lap, the baby lost interest in his watch. Realizing her daddy was nowhere to be seen, she made a nervous noise verging on panic. Pink roses bloomed in her cheeks. Drool ran down her lips to her little lump of chin; a precursor to tears.

"You know what I wish? I wish bloody Tookus Argyle Vercingetorix of Demeter and bloody Livia Massicordesto of Middlewich had been clearer with us." Hughes stomped out, shirted and trousered and socked and booted, and by some miracle all in the right order. "We've got no sense of the occasion. Could be formal. Could be that formality offends Death. Have I a handle on it? Of course I don't. Neither do you, Frank. I could do with one—I could do with a whole *door!*—but I haven't got one, so that's that."

Now daddy had materialized, but he seemed in some distress. The baby's face was crumpling. Frank's willpower crumpled with it. "Uh. Cate?"

With a sigh she held out her arms. But the baby refused to go to her. She was staring at Hughes, her lower lip making a quivery jut, dark hazel-green eyes watering, pudgy hands opening like seashells, closing, opening.

"Not to mention the meteorology of lands beyond our own," Hughes grumbled, slinging on his coat. "I might well regret wearing this. Roasting sun. Piercing, skin-sopping rain. And lately I've had quite enough snow to last a lifetime. For all I know we could be in for a shower of bewildered hens. You don't have to worry, Frank, you're adaptable. I'm still getting used to Faethe, and the amulet is no guarantee of comfort—only safety, if that! Where's my... here it is." He unfolded a piece of paper. It was red on one side, blue the other. A feeling of implicit magic radiated from it like giddiness from the site of a birthday party. He folded it away exactly as it had been, patted the pocket, and cast around as though searching for something else, though what it was he could not quite remember.

The baby had had enough.

She sucked in a lungful of air and began to wail. Wailing might have graduated to a scream, had not a pair of hands whisked her up.

"A dryad! A girl of the woods born from the leaves, the firs, the foxglove!" Hughes said. His timbre was a mighty bellow, his tone that of wild and noble knight. "Why dost thou weep, nymph of the ninnyish nectarines? Nary has there been a sorrowful sound in these gladed hollows for nigh on a fortnight! Wouldst thou break that streak? Wouldst thou?"

He nuzzled the baby, his nose tickling right under her jaw. She squealed and giggled and wiggled, forgotten tears sparkling on her cheeks.

Cate and Frank sat transfixed. Hughes had changed as quickly as you might flap a tea towel at the smoke alarm to stop its distressing bleating. Worry had flowed out of his face like some warm, unpleasant liquid, revealing a golden fatherliness underneath.

"Dry thine eyes," he said, pulling away so they could smile at one another. "There now. Sunshine. My forest fairy." He darted in to plant a kiss on her brow. "My lovely Evelyn."

Without looking she put out a hand and tugged at his coat.

Hughes pursed his lips quizzically. "You think so?"

Tug-tug.

"Mm. I shall take it under advisement."

He walked to the sofa, handed Evelyn to Cate, and slid off his coat. Under it his shirt was black as tar. He undid the cuff buttons, rolled up the sleeves, and spread his arms wide.

"Better?" he asked.

Evelyn attempted to cram both fists in her mouth, gurgling happily.

Hughes nodded. "Good. Frank, shall we?"

"Abuh—absolutely."

Cate gave a soft jerk of her head; an invitation. Hughes kissed her.

"Off to clear up the big Performance mystery," she said. "Think it'll be Hoochie Mama Nightshade or a Djinn?"

"I'm betting my power comes from the fungal familiar, Clarence."

"The mushroom mate." Her grin was sly and almost achingly beautiful. "The spore specimen."

"Love you, Kitten."

"Be safe, Puppy. Give Death my best. I'm sure she's pleased with the business I've given her over the years. Say 'love you, Dada.'"

Evelyn murble-burbled something that was no doubt very profound.

"Wisdom for the ages," Hughes said. He turned to Frank. "Got the fudge?"

"Course," said Frank.

"Okay. Hoosh. Okay, we're actually doing it." Hughes opened the front door, sparing a glance back at the two most important people in his life. "Back soon. Have a wonderful day."

"We will," said Cate, gently jostling their baby girl. "Won't we?"

Evelyn cooed her agreement.

But they wouldn't.

Chapter Two

He might have known this was where their journey would begin.

"I hope we're not going to wake anyone up to ask directions," he said. Frank grinned over one shoulder.

The cemetery was empty so early in the morning. It was nestled behind the ruin of Saint Mauritius' Cathedral in Polydoros District. From foundations to steeple, the creamy marble and crumbly brick and stained glass had only outlasted demolition by virtue of several property realtors squabbling over who exactly owned it. It wasn't even a vestige of the old church anymore. All sense of being had gone with the collared men and sermons. What remained was a gorgeous building that had been attacked with picks and shovels and glass-smashing hammers. Then, too strong to die but too weak to retain identity, it was left abandoned to amnesiac time, forgetting the resplendence of what had once been. In that way, the graveyard and the Cathedral were in it together.

Clouds bunched in gray groups overhead. A light drizzle peppered the engraved stones. There were no weeds (Corinth's own loamy foundations were rich and fertile—unfortunately early settlers had completely buggered the cultivation of this resource, and now the best things you could grow in the city were infrastructure and alcoholism rates). But thanks to a well-connected groundskeeper who had died a hundred years ago, there were two trees. They were elms.

Frank patted one of them with a friendly air. "Here we are. Take my hand."

Hughes took his hand. He knew better than to ask what exactly his friend intended. Frank Gallant was an ocean of a man—usually it was best to simply let the tide take you where it may.

"Close your eyes."

Hughes did.

"Picture a dream you dreamed only recently. One you've thought about since, maybe wondering what it meant, maybe just luxuriating in the soporific dozy-rose goodness."

"I've got it."

"Hold tight to it."

Hughes held tight to a dream he'd had only three nights before. Not much dozy-rose goodness could be found there, but he'd mulled it over since, that was to be sure. In it he and his mother were on a cruise ship bound for... well, bound for somewhere. Tea was served, and no one wanted them to eat the biscuits, which were precious, but he and his mother managed to sneak a few anyway. It was a sordid business, biscuit thieving, sordid as getting older and forgetting who you used to be—they were in it together. Jaunty music played from a gramophone. And there was something in the water beneath them and surrounding them, something wicked. Wendy kept asking him if he knew who she was. Between mouthfuls of tea and crumbly (stone? No, praline chocolate), Hughes said of course he knew her. It was as if she couldn't hear him. On and on she asked him, and whatever was in the water grew closer and closer.

Every piece of that dream was as colorful and clearly defined as the shards of stained glass clinging to the windows of the Cathedral.

When Frank told him to open his eyes, some boyish part of Hughes expected to smell the salty tang of the ocean, see the prow of the ship, sense the unspeakable thing rising from the depths. The mature side of him expected to see the cemetery. Both were disappointed.

"Soot," he said, and stuffed his nose and mouth into the crook of his elbow to keep from breathing it in. It was all around them, thick as a pall of smog over a factory. Skirts, feathers, and curtains of it—thick as porridge and black as the blackest lump of licorice in a sweet shop. His shirt wasn't well suited to ventilation. His coat would have been better.

Frank was looking at him with a mixture of patience and pity.

"Get us out of here," said Hughes. "Quick."

"Clouds," Frank said.

"Pardon?"

"They're only clouds."

And to demonstrate his appreciation for those drifting buds of cotton, those diaphanous silken streamers, those angry thunderheads which can, of course, look just like soot fresh from the chimney, he changed his suit from a daffodil motif to one that was embroidered with all the clouds you can imagine.

Hughes took an experimental breath. He blew it out. Frowned. Lowered his arm. "Well, it looked like soot."

"Things are not always as they appear," said Frank Gallant. "For example, your baby girl appears to be as ordinary as a red-breasted robin on a snowy scrap of hedge in December."

Hughes made an absent, agreeable sound. He'd listened to Frank but hadn't heard him, not yet. He was looking at the mountains.

The mountains were stubby, like blunted teeth, and as red as the clouds swirling around them were black. All except for one, which was white and fearsome tall. *Not a tooth*, he mused. *A tusk.*

"A tusk is right," said Frank.

Hughes started. Had he spoken aloud? He must have. Though... you never really knew with Frank. A vast ocean of a man, and a mischievous brook too.

They stood for a moment looking at that ridged giant. It was desolate—no trees or bramble thickets or anything.

"Does it frighten you?" he asked his friend.

Frank answered without hesitation. "Yeah. Though 'frighten' doesn't quite frame the feeling. It uh..."

"Unnerves."

"Unnerves me. Exactly. As if whatever was scary about that mountain is long gone, but the tiniest bit of it stuck around. A plaque commemorating a cruise ship that sank a thousand years ago."

"Cruise ship?" Hughes stared at Frank, alarmed. "What makes you say that?"

"I don't know." Frank shrugged. "Sounded right when I said it."

Hughes gave him a dubious once-over, then decided to let it go. He went back to examining the white peak, the huge dark mesh of cloud around them... and as those clouds skimmed and curled, he caught sight of a pass leading through the mountains.

"Look," he said, pointing.

"I see it. Come on. It's closer than you think."

"Deceptive appearances."

"Now you're getting it."

They walked, their bodies brushing and tucking the cloud aside like napkins of coal-colored wool.

After a while, Hughes said, "Frank, I think we ought to have a chat about the word 'ordinary.'"

"Why's that?"

"You said Evelyn appears as ordinary as a red-breasted robin on a snowy scrap of hedge in December."

"Sure did."

"Right. Only that isn't in the least bit ordinary. It's just something people expect. Sort of... filling in the gaps in the real world with what they imagine ought to be there. I can't count the number of times I've passed a branch with a glaze of frost on it and a few clinging leaves and thought to myself, 'Gosh, wouldn't a robin complete that picture? Wouldn't it be perfect?' Like writing yourself a story without words."

"Your grasp of anthropology is dizzying."

Hughes frowned. "So you're saying my daughter appears to be a gap in a real world where people put their expectations."

"Uh huh."

"But really she isn't."

"Yup."

"Oh," Hughes said. And then he said, "Why?"

Frank was peering at the cuffs of his suit. All at once strings snipped out of the sleeves and threaded the cuffs, becoming hard shiny cufflinks shaped like lightning bolts to finish the stormy sky motif of the embroidery. "Listen, man. Everyone thinks that girl of yours used to be the worst serial killer your city has ever seen. They don't know it, but they suspect it, and for some suspicion around an idea is tantamount to its endorsement. Spring-Heeled Jane disappeared in a swarm of butterflies; Evelyn appeared in a swarm matching its description down to the color of their wings. Doesn't take a decorated intellect to draw the link. So people are keeping an eye on her. Fair enough, she's cute as a button today. But what about when she grows up? What then?

"Why am I saying that Evelyn is not a gap in the real world where 'ought' and 'should' are poured heavier than concrete? Why am I saying that she is, in fact, simply a baby? Maybe ordinary, maybe not, but a baby all the same? Just a toddler? Just a little girl? Just a woman? I'm saying it because that's what I'd want people to say if it were me."

Hughes pondered this. He pondered some more.

"You're really quite amazing," he said eventually. "Thank you, Frank."

His fabulous friend shrugged like it was no big deal, anyone could be really quite amazing if they put their mind to it and kept it there awhile.

They had almost reached the pass. Above them the mountains—so distant only a minute or two ago—now sprang in a toothy half-smile. The tallest one, that nasty pale tusk, seemed to tickle the sky, which was as overcast as the ground below it. Nearby, a parade of horses composed of dark cloud matter tramped and stamped and broke into a canter. Hughes wondered how he was only seeing them now, and at the same time was glad he had. They were pretty.

"Just like the lullaby," he told Frank. "All the pretty horses."

***

There was a baby up there where the clouds clumped thickest.

An infant face, impossibly, fantastically huge, both eyelids closed and swaddled in clouds.

When he was done gawping with mingled awe and horror, Hughes said, "What is that?"

"That is Jija," Frank replied. "This is his realm we're in. His underworld, the one he dreamed into existence. We've crossed from the lands of the living into the lands of the dead."

"His... underworld? There are others?"

"More than you'd believe."

The mountain pass had looked long and felt short. Now they were on the other side. No low clouds here—instead the ground was covered in grass, thigh-high and softly swaying. In the sky the clouds were brown-gold tinged with plum, tea-bag suffused by a sunset that seemed perpetual, never giving way to night or retreating into afternoon. Through that fluffy profusion were peepholes of blue speckled with stars. The stars were so dense and closely packed, they appeared to be a crushed diamond paste. And the baby. That huge celestial baby asleep up there in the sky.

Hughes gazed at Dreaming Jija, his wonderment naked and shameless.

Cate had once remarked to him that the face of a baby boy and an elderly man seemed incontrovertibly aligned. She'd gone on to conjecture that it was a comforting idea. To her the mirroring of great youth and great age implied that while people have no idea of their origin or their ending, that place might well be the same. So dying would be like going home.

On that particular subject Hughes wasn't altogether sure. Nice notion though, and mystifying as it certainly was, that plump, slumbery child up there amidst the clouds—endemic to them, he supposed—was rather nice too. *I've become a father,* he thought suddenly. The stark absoluteness of it shrank him; Evelyn and the sky-child were momentarily indistinguishable.

A fragment of hope rose to his lips. Before he could stop them, the words were out. "Is my mother here?"

Frank's expression shaded from one of introspection to one of sad understanding. The shift was automatic—it was clear to Hughes that Frank had anticipated the question.

"Yeah. I'm not sure if she's in this underworld or some other one. But yeah," Frank said. "She's here."

Wendy Dragontail. Out there somewhere.

Knowing her, she had very likely fomented a revolution, dethroned whoever was in charge, quashed any would-be political rivals, and, by now, would probably be enjoying all the meringues she could eat. The dead enjoy a perfect untroubled digestion. The idea gave Hughes a pang of amusement. Sorrow too. Sorrow and regret.

"Did your pop know?"

"Hm?"

"About Wendy," Frank clarified. "Did he know who she was and decided not to tell you?"

There were cramped trees all in a line, about a quarter mile away. The breeze caressing Hughes' throat blew from those woods toward the mountains. He could smell peculiar cloying smells. Bougainvillea and licorice. Weird. Not unwelcome but weird.

"Hughes?"

"Sorry, Frank. Bewitched by our surroundings. No, my dad didn't know the truth. I confronted him, and with harsher words than I want to admit to, but I've got a good bloodhound's nose for lies and he was being straight with me. As far as he was aware, Wendy was a stowaway taking shelter in his love for a while. Somebody poor and lost. He had no money, but my father is a found man, found as I'll never be, because he knows himself from scalp to shoes and back again. But Wendy knew I was her son. She dropped too many hints about it over the years for me to comfortably ignore."

"I'd call that cruel as hell, but I guess she needed to make a game of it. Keep it light so her secrecy didn't weigh heavy."

"I think that's it exactly," Hughes said. "But yes, Dad really had no idea who he was getting involved with. When she left, he assumed it was for greener pasture. The idea that she was going home to effectively take over the sovereignty of the entire city never occurred to him—how could it? This is a man who uses books instead of furniture. Out of sync with the technological world. I had to practically beg him to install a telephone."

"Did he even know her name while they were together?"

"Just 'Wendy.' I can't remember him ever mentioning it, and I don't remember asking, though I must have. And the name Wendy Dragontail wasn't strange to him. There was just... no reason at all for him to think that the Wendy I worked for and the woman he'd loved all those years ago were the same person."

Frank paused. Hughes could tell he was picking his next words with care.

"Look, I can imagine what sort of answer this is going to get, but what sort of friend would I be if I kept my mouth shut? How are you?"

Was that all? Well, no great secret there. The broad, baleful scope of his feelings could be summarized pretty succinctly. Hughes shrugged. "I hate her. I miss her."

Frank cupped Hughes' cheek. His palm was soft as nylon. "When your best friend hurts, you can't help but wish you were Novocain. Love you."

Hughes was touched. "Yeah. Yeah, I love you too, Frank."

They began to walk toward a distant tree line beyond the swaying grasses. Hughes jogged to catch up. They passed a hill covered in wildflowers. It was an odd hill. At this angle, it almost looked like...

"A pig," said Hughes, bewildered. "Under the hill. That's an enormous pig."

"A boar," Frank corrected gently. "Not under the hill—it *is* the hill. Big, right? Taller than a loaded truck and three times as wide. Wouldn't know it to look at him now, but that boar was the guardian of this place."

Hughes hooked a thumb at the sleeping sky-child. "Isn't our friend up there in the firmament guardian enough?"

"Bosses rarely lift the boxes. Poor old Barabala. That was this here boar's name. Used to chop the grass round these parts short as a mowed lawn with tusks sharp as razorblades. Now he's dead and the grasses grow long as a miser's memory."

Hughes looked back at the hill, his pace slowing. "What happened to him?"

"Well now, that is a story. Had it from our mutual acquaintance, Tookus. See, Barabala was a mean old boar. Thought himself the toughest guardian in the underworlds. Maybe he was. Fierce strong, that snout-touting fellow was, and arrogant. Any living folks who wanted to pass him and go into the smoky yonder where not just pretty horses but the deepest dreamers can be found, Barabala would come out of his cave and beat them and string them up by hangman ropes. String them up *alive*, I mean. They hung around until they died and went to their own underworlds, the ones that awaited them. Anyway, when four travelers came one day, Barabala said, 'Your flesh is warm, your heartbeat is as the very drum of vitality. You are yet living. Go back to your home. The pass is not open to you. Go now! I would rather not add your neck to their number.' Your number meaning his grisly trophies, you know. But those travelers had business past the mountains, and one of them stepped forward; a knight. She was a storybook creature, so cool and fine and brave she might have jumped right out of your heart or your head and into the world. Maybe I'll tell you about their fight some other time. But it was some fight, Hughes, and no mistake."

"I look forward to hearing about it," Hughes said, and he meant it.

"Suffice it to say that this knight, she had enough of Barabala's gumption and pride. Socked it to him like a bolt from the rumbling black." Frank turned a wrist, let the dusky light catch his lightning-shaped cufflinks. He smiled. "Even then, I seem to remember Tookus telling me that she was kind about it. Maybe a little like Cate and that Troll in Eurydice, you remember her talking about that?"

"Yeah."

"Now Barabala's pushing up daisies in the most literal sense possible."

"What became of the knight?"

"That I do not know." Right after he said this, right then and totally abruptly, Frank's composure left him. His smile fled his lips. Pallor slammed into his cheeks, which went from looking healthy and lovely to sickly and wan. With his white hair alive with frantic colors—amber, violet, strawberry—he turned to stare wide-eyed and breathless toward...

Hughes didn't know, couldn't see anything out of the ordinary. The grasses swayed. The trees were tall droopy things, the breeze moving in the leaves like hands washing hair; he recognized their species now. *Willows. Weeping willows.*

And... yeah, there was a certain... a certain *malice* to them, he supposed. He bet if he rubbed a sprig of those leaves, they would feel like ownerless leavings on the bottom of a barbershop floor. He bet the wind soughing in that hairy canopy would sound like whispers. And he also bet the whispers would suggest an obvious and harmless course of action; *come closer and part our hair. A touch is all it'll take. Part our hair and see our wooden faces.*

But would it be?

Would it be what?

Harmless.

Sough, went the wind in the greenery. *Sough, sough, sough.*

He felt fear brush along his back. Not with a cold, clammy finger, but with a lock of dry, rustling

(hair)

(part the hair see our faces)

(come and look come and look)

"Frank..."

Somewhere in the woods, a child laughed.

There was not a shred of gaiety in that sound. It sounded wrong, perverse somehow. Like the someone (some*thing!*) it belonged to was in on a joke, and the joke was on them, on the living men trespassing so close to the woods, those hairy scary harum-scarum woods.

He was aware also that... he wanted to obey. The urge had skittered over him, without warning him, indecently, like a woodboring beetle who rudely tunneled and bit and chewed its way into his head as if his skull was made of bark. He wanted quite badly to go into the woods. In fact, it was his idea in the first place. No one had convinced him. Had they? No. Of course not.

Hughes smiled and took a few steps. He stopped. Felt his teeth peel back over his lips in a snarl. He wondered why they should do a thing like that. Turning the hideous expression into a smile, he took a few more steps.

Now the woods, the tumbledown hair, the girlish/boyish laughter, it was close. Had it been close enough to walk into?

A quarter mile, he thought.

No, no, no. Couldn't have been. Could not have been.

Part our hair, said the trees, very near now.

Sough, sough, went the wind.

Come to us. Part our hair. See our faces.

Hadn't he been with someone? Someone of the utmost importance?

Couldn't... be, no.

He was alone and the woods were waiting.

There, he was sure, he would not be in the least bit worried about finding out where his powers came from. Other unpleasant and bothersome things would similarly be left behind, like the fact that he had, since Tinfrosttime, taken up smoking as a habit rather than an affectation, and that he was worried he would not be the father Evelyn needed, and that he had been (at least partially) responsible for his own mother being here

(where)

here in the dead zone, rather than that place the living could call home.

One step. Two step.

Wasn't this fun?

He was within touching distance of a willow.

Three step. Four!

Wasn't this...

And the willow branches, so redolent of long human hair, began to part on their own.

Hot, rippling fear slammed up his back into his neck, shoulders, and throat. It was as if the fright had been taken from the freezer and thrown in the oven notched to top heat. *Run!* he demanded of his legs, but they wouldn't. The leaves were crackling like an evil-minded kid getting ready for the punch line of some cataclysmic prank, laughing-laughing-laughing, and he would see the willow's face *oh God, oh fffffuck, God help me!*

He opened his mouth to scream.

It never came.

Terror cooled in his mouth just at the moment where premonition became sound because something had changed. Some new factor was at work.

Later, Hughes would describe it to Frank like this:

During a particularly stressful day—not only for Hughes but the whole city it seemed—he had been on a train that broke down between stops. Lots of people had gotten on at the last stop. It was stuffy and cramped, and before long there was bickering and ugly blue tempers flaring. The atmosphere was building toward an explosion, you could really feel that. But then something small and yet distinctly powerful had turned the ordeal around. There had been a digital sort of *bing-bong* and a voice had come over the carriage intercom. The conductor spoke to the passengers, and though they could hardly tell each of her words apart from the others—since being sealed up in a package of discontent isn't suitable for good focus—the delivery was so calm and soothing and well-considered that those intimations were communicable. Really, it was hard to feel sore. Tempers were prettier after that, and Hughes saw a pair of formerly rowdy young men offer an old man and a pregnant woman their seats. Then after a very short length of time the train was going again, and everyone was all smiles.

That first scare in Dreaming Jija mirrored this experience almost exactly.

He was on the verge of real trouble. But then a presence—not something he could hear or see, yet which was absolutely THERE—had arrived over the intercom of the air. The malevolence seemed to startle, then cringe, then slink away. In an instant Hughes was under his own control. He took an instinctive pace back from the weeping willow. It made no attempt to stop him. Quite the contrary, its branches were lowered as if they'd never moved at all. Hughes knew better. They had moved, and if that presence... that conductor... had not interfered, he would have seen the tree's face, along with whatever horror lay in its sunken sap-oozing hollows for him. As the reality of that quickened his heartrate and broke him out in nervous, grateful sweat, he felt the conductor leave.

The woods were quiet. No eerie playful laughter. No beckoning whisper from the leaves. The breeze was ordinary.

A hand closed on his bicep.

Hughes yelped.

"Sorry."

"Frank." Hughes exhaled shakily, smoothed a hand over his dry chalky lips. "Holy shit."

"We're okay."

"What was that?"

"Magic. What else?"

"It got into my head."

"Like a woodborer beetle."

Hughes stared, his astonishment plain. "Yeah."

Frank squeezed his arm. "My head too. You felt what came after?"

"The conductor?"

"The what?"

"Nothing, I'll... I'll talk about that in a second. What kind of magic was it? Dreams? Invasive waking nightmares?"

"No."

"Then what?"

Frank glowered at the willows. "The kind of magic that doesn't want us here." His chin tilted so he could look with curiosity over the leafy crowns toward the horizon, perhaps toward their mysterious savior. "And some other kind. Something that wants us here, or at the very least does not want us gone yet. Hmph. Well, no use dawdling. Let's try these woods on for size. I'll wager they leave us alone."

They did. Nothing cropped up, not for the whole journey through the boscage and over the small slopey hills and the smaller river with its bridge all laced in moss. Fat fluffy logs of white stuff drifted down that river. Hughes wouldn't have suspected it was cotton wool until he impulsively turned some ways beyond the chittering banks and saw the word carved into the bridge's arched stone hump. The name facing downriver proclaimed the name of these gently meandering waters: The Woolgatherer. For the first time in a long while he thought of Hughes 2, that fictional version of himself that lived a quiet, unassuming life. What would Hughes 2 make of his very real counterpart, plunging ever deeper into a phantasmal underworld in the company of a child of witches? Probably he would not make anything of it. The extraordinary life is as difficult to grasp by the ordinary one as it is for the excited to comprehend boredom. When you are born in the mud, the airplanes and the satellites and stars seem one and the same. It was a ritual for him. Think of Hughes 2 and his normal life. Reject him. Embrace the romantic, the disturbing, the outright odd.

And the dangerous.

Speaking of...

Hughes listened for laughter, heard none. He watched the trees intently and tried to steer clear of their roots in case they snagged him, hogtied him, hanged him like the guardian boar Barabala had hanged his victims.

He needn't have worried.

Though Hughes' mean aunt of an imagination told him that behind their wigs, the trees were leering at him.

Chapter Three

Outside, things were bedlam. Malfunctioning roadwork signs and lack of manpower to compensate at the nearby mega-roundabout had gridded cars, taxis, trucks, vans, and one very unlucky bridal procession in an impossible game of snakes and ladders. No one could advance or retreat, and the only way to win was to wait, and wait, and wait, and try not to bite through your steering wheel. March rain hissed on grumbling bonnets and windshields fogged from the inside—a steam of seething anger. The traffic stretched like a serpent up R18, coiling round the roundabout, and spread out in a flailing Medusa fringe along the tributary roads of Nikandros District. Close-shaves, scratches, bumper-nudges, and one serious tail-end added to the chaos. Neon news bulletins informed drivers the situation was receiving attention, and the congestion would soon peter out. They must remain calm. Unfortunately, some of these bulletins also malfunctioned, and the moody commuters were subjected to the message that the situation was receiving ten conwoop, and they must remain al. Which, as you can imagine, improved general morale immensely.

Inside the apartment, however, things were easy-breezy-lemon-squeezy. Evelyn had stopped looking around anxiously for her dad and reluctantly accepted Cate as today's caregiver with a magnanimous air of, *Drat. Oh well. You, with the red hair and the boots. You'll do.* The favoritism would cleave the heart out of some parents. Early on Cate had taken a philosophical approach. Now she wore her silver medal with pride, knowing someday it would turn to gold. Kids were fickle. And God help her and Hughes when the girl turned sixteen. They would both wear bronze then, if they were lucky. It would be music, popular vids, boutique fashion, rebellious poetry, renegade outbursts at school, iconic gal-pals, cute boys. All that and more, and more besides. Gold and silver, bronze, brass, corundum— all the medals assigned, and Mum and Dad could climb a tree and jump for all she'd care.

Teenage, skirt-wearing tyranny was a distant prospect, thank merciful God.

Gurgling, nappy-wearing infancy though? Cate could work with that.

It was eleven o'clock in the morning. Porous gray light came through the living room windows, cellular with rain. The warm chalky smell of baby formula wafted in from the kitchen (sometimes Cate yearned to breastfeed, but it was not to be).

Channeling the adventure cartoons of her girlhood, Cate dove behind the cutlery cabinet. She poked out from the cover of its imitation walnut, her jaw jutted forward, fingers poised on her face, drawing the skin taut so she appeared to be as gaunt as a skull. "Clitter-clatter-VROOOM! Rattle my bones over the stones! I'm a Bonemeal Boy! Wheeeeere's.... myyyyy... BIKE?"

Evelyn laughed with a weird, adorably fancy lilt, as if she were an aristocrat at a comedy auction house. That was another thing about kids. They had a million modes of expression. They could put the rug under your feet and pull it away quicker than you could register the fibers.

Cate considered her next move. Had it! A dip, and roll, and she was tucked out of sight under the right arm of the sofa. Evelyn's coos and burbles brought a grin to her lips. Her whole face shone, exerted, collaborative in the merriment and the silliness. If you'd seen her in that moment, you could have mistaken Cate for a girl half her age, sixteen maybe.

Who next, who next. The Bride of the Mists? No. She'd done her. The Shunned Bears of Dunrindel? No, no. Done and dusted. Cate racked her brains for a ghoulie, a creepy, a long-leggedy-beastie.

They were playing Here Are All The Terrible Monsters Mummy Has Absolutely Clobbered. It worked like this: Cate would vanish behind a convenient item of furniture; there would be a moment's preparation, and then she'd appear doing a face and an impression of the monster. Evelyn would then render her judgment. It was an excellent game, probably because unlike traffic-jam snakes and ladders, everyone was a winner.

Inspiration struck. Cate swung her legs over the sofa arm, knees depressing the cushion, hips pivoting, and her back arching, and without further delay she was upside down with her feet in the air. Her hands were over her face, the fingers splayed wide. The effect was apish... or maybe spiderlike... definitely animalistic. "We are the Nightjar Coven," she crooned in a waspish old biddy's voice. "We want our son back, and we're not afraid to turn you into an aardvark to get him." Cate could be quite good at impressions. Combined with her upside-downness and the way she was eyeing her daughter through the bars of her wiggling fingers, this one was perhaps too good.

Evelyn's gummy smile went away. A lukewarm stare replaced it. Then uncertainty replaced that. It happened faster than you can say, "Oh shit." The baby made no sound. Her fidgety hands stilled. Her tiny mouth was a slightly wet, very pink "O."

Oh shit, thought Cate. The rain pattered on the window glass, as if in somber agreement.

They lay and sat there in tableau, Mother and Adopted Daughter, on the cusp of total and complete disaster.

I've got to salvage things. To reverse and turnabout as those cars out there in the jam wish they could. Her body was still rife with little reminders of her escapades in Eurydice. But her mind was a computer banked with honed instincts, and now was its moment.

She launched herself at the curtains, snagged them, and shoved their tassely ends up to her face.

"I am the Troll!" she declared in a loud, and icy, and very noble voice. "I am like a knight from one of Evelyn's daddy's stories, only much colder in the kneecaps and the tush. Frigid regions indeed! And I wouldn't allow those decrepit harridans of the carousel to bother you, Evelyn Hughes. Here, watch me shoo them with a wintry sneeze. AAAAAA-CHOOO!"

Cate doubled over dramatically, the curtain-beard becoming a ludicrous handkerchief.

Evelyn squeaked her approval. A roly-poly noise escaped her.

That almost sounded like, OH. As in TrOHll.

Could babies parrot and mimic so early on in their development?

Cate didn't believe so. But then, Evelyn was no ordinary girl. Regardless, why waste time thinking when the act of doing blew its big bassoon and summoned a new mother to her next impression?

She wallooed and wayehed, cartwheeling and slip-sliding under the coffee table. When she burst from beneath it with her fingers plittering and flowing off her face as if her skin were falling away like raindrops, and moaning uurrrgh, she was Willy Woggle Bingleshim, one of the zombies in Eurydice who was absolutely positively called Willy Woggle Bingleshim, and who was certainly not a faceless minion of Lord Burrows (how could he be, with a name that was definitely real, such as Willy Woggle Bingleshim), Evelyn did not squeak. She laughed a gorgeous, high-pitched laugh like a piano melody.

That's more like it. One more and then Mummy is going to scoop you out of that up-chair and shower you with kisses, and that, little missy, is a promise.

Here it was then. Time at last for her grand finale.

As Evelyn watched attentively, her smile cocked and ready to crescendo into another happy laugh, Cate bolted for the refrigerator. The door opened with a *chump*, concealing her. Artificial cold prickled the left side of her face. There was no need to conjure the monster. She could envision it so, so clearly. Oh the girl would go ga-ga for this one, oh yes!

She contorted her features, anticipation riddling her and fizzing her full.

"Ready?" she asked Evelyn.

She shut the refrigerator door.

The baby was gone.

***

"I hear music," said Hughes.

"Me too." Frank was ahead of him. Hughes couldn't see his face. But his friend's tone was wary. During their forest amble Frank had once again adjusted his suit. He must have been in a chameleon-like mood because he'd exchanged the clouds for leaves. Sycamore, Corinthian oak, fir, camphor, pine, Mysicordelian spruce and sugar maple—fronds of leaf-shaped silk cascaded down his shoulders. Even his tie, shirt, and cufflinks were woodlandlike, deep green, somehow evocative of the spirit of fertility, cherries so lifelike they seemed bulged and ready to burst with sweet tart juice.

The music was coming from a clearing. His brow furrowed as the sound wound out among the willows because it seemed rather a schizophrenic ditty. What sounded pretty quickly became sinister. What sounded sinister rapidly turned pretty. He didn't care for it, that twinning quality, that contradiction.

"We can go around," Hughes suggested quietly. "Give this a wide berth." He gestured to the meadows curling around the clearing.

"We could. But before we get her guidance, we've first got to find Death. Maybe whoever is making that music knows where we might start. How are you with that amulet?" Frank asked, equally hushed. "In case there's trouble, and our unseen benefactor doesn't interfere? I only ask because my power is bound to be unreliable in this realm. Dreams and dreams can't really affect one another, you dig? Like adding iodine to unstarched material."

Unconsciously Hughes' right hand came up, the pad of the thumb touching the spot where Faethe, Amulet of Dragons, hung at his throat. Wendy Dragontail's amulet, now his.

"I'm not so bad with it," he said. Then, wryly, "Not so good either."

"Modesty."

"Honesty." Hughes' disposition grew sunnier. "But I can always use my Performance."

Frank nodded, slowly. "Which works some of the time."

"Yes."

"But not all."

"Y... yes."

"Ah. Well, as the poet said, words will be our shield. And as that same poet also said, thank goodness no one ever hits me." Frank winked, turning his headlight-bright eyes into a single spotlight for an instant. Then he was in the clearing, announcing himself to whoever was there.

Hughes hurried after. Before he'd taken two steps, ducking under a few errant locks of weeping willow hair, he was a changed man. His reluctance now had the look of surety. His posture, creeping and furtive before, was now so ramrod-straight it would make even the cruelest drill sergeant hang up his butt-whooping cord and retire. On his face the change was most severe. Here was a guy, almost thirty, calm and sincere and imbued with all the best parts of being young and none of the worst parts of getting older. A hero, unproud and natural. He could handle anything this dreamworld draped over him. Two steps, and two whole notches divorced from grief and doubt. Not a hint of magic was used to achieve this. Hughes had spent his youth embodying things he did not feel, becoming characters big and small, or making overt that which other people kept hidden or did not know they possessed. He was a production who happened to moonlight as a man, complete with lights, orchestra, set design, and costumes. Which is not to say he was a compulsive fibber (although he was a world-class connoisseur of lies and their wily, wily ways). You'd be wrong thinking that. Cate Jubilee and his own decisions had cured him of self-abdication years ago. But all of this goes a long way to saying that with the theatrical scene in Corinth well-and-truly dead, it found in Hughes a vessel for resurrection. He was a performer. His Performance had nothing whatsoever to do with it.

In the clearing were Frank and two men. One of the men was thin and pale and tremulous. The other was well-covered and rubicund and firm in personality where the thin man was flimsy. This big man was, carefully and unhurriedly, plucking little fairy creatures out of a jar and pulling their wings off. He tossed them away, and bleeding in the grass the fairies cried their loss and pain. Whereupon the thin man gathered them up and whispered kindly to them, and with a wave of his hand, gave them four colorful wings where before they'd only had two. The fairies would plant kisses on the thin man, shoot hateful looks at the well-covered one, and then fly away off into the willows.

Neither of the men seemed to have taken notice of Frank's polite and charming introduction. They didn't pay Hughes' arrival any mind either.

Around and around in a sluggish, sweeping arc, a pair of harps circled the clearing. One had the look of the thin man, and this one played pretty music; the other by contrast looked warped and crooked, and its melodies were sinister lurching things. Both harps played themselves.

"I really wish you would stop," the thin man said.

"What a coincidence," said the well-covered one, seizing a wing, tearing it off, tearing another, and flicking a now wingless fairy up the backside so it cometed through the air. "I was thinking exactly the same thing about you. Why don't you find a downtrodden girl and make her life whimsical?"

"Piss off."

"Verbose as ever."

"At least I can be around girls," said the thin man. "And young ladies and women grown. And boys and men too! At least I can do that."

"Bully for you," said the well-covered man, dipping his hand into the jar where the fairies shrank from his fingers. "However short the acquaintance, I'm sure they get something out of it. You forget that your company is as much reviled as mine is." He selected a fairy, dragged it away from the helping hands of its fellow fairies, and teased the poor shivering creature with fingers like oily sausages fresh from the pan. "I'm fleeting, sticking around for a brief while. Then gone, so they all get to feel relief. You, on the other hand, linger, and when you reveal yourself to be what you are, they feel ever-so-betrayed. At least my interactions bear out well in the end."

"I hate you. Oh stop, can't you stop! Spare that one. Just that one."

"I spare no one," said the well-covered man flatly. He grabbed hold of a wing, ready to rip. "Nor do you, brother."

"Good evening," barked Hughes.

Both men jumped. They turned to stare at him in shock. Frank stared too, only his expression was one of vast approval. Applause, even silent as in this moment, is fuel for the performer's fire.

Hughes stepped forward, the twilight sculpting his frame. In a crisp, authoritative voice he said, "We're looking for Death. That's Death with a capital D, mind. Any idea where we can find her?"

The well-covered man turned to the thin one. "Phantasus. Is this... malodorous reptile of a man... in fact... alive?"

"No!" cried the thin man. "No, he isn't, and you leave him and his friend alone, Phobetor!"

"You *are* alive," the big one told Hughes, cannily, and slyly. To the thin man he glanced again. "Isn't he?"

The thin man sagged. "Yes."

"And did he say, 'Good evening' to us?"

"When?"

"Just now."

"Yes. Yes, I think so."

"To us!"

"Yes brother," quavered the thin man.

"Hurf! I surmised as much." The well-covered man gave Hughes a look that would have stripped paint. "Good evening yourself, and goodbye, and good riddance."

The thin man looked up hopefully at this.

"Whoa now," said Frank, coming alongside Hughes and sending out his strings to form a flute that played referee to the dueling harps. "Let's not barge into rude territory. We're just looking for a steer in the right direction. Maybe we can do something for you in return."

"Do something?" blustered the well-covered man. "What could you possibly do for us?"

"Oh, not much, I grant you. Everything and anything. Dwarf actuality. Capsize fate. Tip untippable scales." Frank shrugged humbly. "That's all."

From the corner of his eye Hughes noticed the flute undergo a change. Frank's strings unraveled and became a moving picture made of twirling nylon. In the picture a jar was snatched from a pair of fat hands, and the winged creatures inside flew free as birds. Frank was subtle with his display. He did it at the right moment when the well-covered man was looking at him and the thin man was looking at the instruments.

But if Hughes' friend had been hoping the thin man would accept their help and help them in turn, he was sorely mistaken.

"No. No, no, no," mewled the thin man. "I agree with my brother—good riddance to you. Get lost! Go! GO!"

Scared, Hughes thought. *Of us?*

"Can't you see you're not wanted? Can't you? Can't you see?"

No, a shrewd part of Hughes decided. *Scared that the universe has handed his brother two new fairies with unplucked wings.*

Frank was trying to calm the thin man—Phantasus, if Hughes had heard correctly—but Phantasus kept overriding him, his voice rising shrill and reedy over the music: "Go, please, you must go now!"

Meanwhile the well-covered man—Phobetor, Hughes remembered, and thinking of the name struck a note of murky recollection in him, one he couldn't quite resolve—produced a lid from his robes. Phobetor screwed the jar of fairies shut, set it down among the tufts of grass, and then regarded his brother the way a hunter might regard a fox defending cubs that are not her own.

"You're sure we can't convince you?" said Frank.

Phantasus goggled at him, dumbstruck by Frank's refusal to gear up and go.

Then both his and his brother's faces went slack as Hughes pushed his Performance.

As ever, the sense of his power gathered in his head like a hundred moths round a campfire. The percentage values were neat and precise as the butler Falstaff, and as fulminating as Cate Jubilee in high humor. But even though he had a pretty good feel for success and failure, he had no real insight into power itself, its origin and construction. Being closer than ever to answers about his Performance galvanized him, made him bold enough to take up Frank's cue and use the power.

But the failure struck him in a mangey alley cat claw swipe; cruel and sharp.

He caught Frank's eye, gave a little shake of the head.

"I wonder," said Phobetor, carrying on as if nothing had happened, "if you two fellows would care for a tiddlywink?"

Very casually he took out an amphora. Hughes blinked at it. It was dusty, baked clay amply curved, one of those antique wine amphoras used in the bodega chains in Jaenqui-Across-The-River back in his world. Also, he was pretty sure the amphora was too large to have fit under Phobetor's robes, which gave the impression that the large man had summoned the wine from the ether.

"A what?" said Frank.

"A drink!" said Phobetor. "A tumty tiddlywink, don't you know."

Phantasus put his head in his hands, trembling all over. "No," he moaned hoarsely. "No."

Phobetor ignored him. He smiled at Hughes and Frank. "A libation to mark our meeting."

Hughes had wondered if the big man was a simple thug; somebody who liked hurting things that wouldn't put up a fight.

Now he thought there was more to it. Now the desperation in Phantasus' voice was contagious.

He did not like that smile. Not at all.

We have to get out of here. Right now.

Maintaining his dulcified composure, not letting even a trace of his fear shine through, Hughes threw up his hands, feigning exasperation with whimpering Phantasus. "Fine. All right, damn it, now will you please shut that racket up? We'll try our luck elsewhere. Come on, Frank."

"Elsewhere? No, no," said Phobetor.

"Brother, I beg you..."

Phobetor closed his eyes, made to swig from the amphora... and found he couldn't. He blinked rapidly—once, twice, thrice. There were strings snarled around the handles of his drink. He stared at them, as if he couldn't for the life of him believe they were there, and then he looked at Frank. Incredulity sizzled. Anger slammed up into his puffy red cheeks, turning them purple.

"You *dare!*"

The strings tightened in Frank's fist. "I do, I do."

"Insolent mortal!"

"That first one I'll grant you."

"Hurf! Let go, you sniveling... you... Never once has a mortal man..."

"Not I."

"Unhand this—this—this *bloody thing* right now!"

"Mister," said Frank. "You must think my friend and I here were born yesterday."

With that he gave a savage yank. The amphora jerked from Phobetor's grip. The well-covered man made a sound Hughes knew all too well; the sound that comes gushing out of anyone who has fumbled something precious, and who can, for a brief second before impact, actually hear the noise that precious thing is going to make. He himself had once labored hard over an anniversary dinner, only to slip and fall on his bottom five short steps from the dining room table. The shatter of the plates and the splat of pork belly drizzled in homemade gravy had been so loud and nasty that his teeth had clacked together painfully in his mouth. A warning shard of migraine had embedded itself in the softest part of his brain. His features had screwed themselves so tight, he had looked like a man in the most unbearable throes of constipation.

The amphora was no different.

For a split-second the whole thing was one big hairline crack with no beginning and no end, every inch of clay spidery and about to... about to—

The dry, somehow earthy crash of broken pottery filled the clearing.

Hughes expected there to be a follow-up, a liquid glurp-glip-glip noise as Phobetor's wine poured out of the clay carcass. Only that didn't happen. Instead a noxious vapor, filthy and blue as exhaust smoke, boiled up from the jagged shards. The effect was a little like cold breath coming through snaggled teeth.

The thought of inhaling that gunk willingly seemed insane, almost suicidal. Why had Phobetor been about to swig a mouthful of something so obviously hazardous? *Unless...* Hughes felt his flesh pebble in goose bumps. *Unless he meant to guzzle it in and then blow it out. Intaking none for himself. Dear sweet God if Frank and I had sucked that into our lungs, what might have happened to us?*

He felt like hugging Frank for his quick reflexes and quicker thinking, but now seemed an inconvenient time to show affection, what with the ball of cartilage in Phobetor's throat working up and down like a dribbled football.

"I'll tell you where Death is," he said.

But Frank was striding past the brothers, bored and irritated, and Hughes only a few paces behind.

"I will!" Phobetor hurled after them. "I'll show you," he muttered, and Hughes got the impression he was no longer thinking about Death. *That brute will show us something all right.* He hurried after Frank, looking back as they neared the trees.

Phobetor stood with surprising speed. He jabbed a finger into his brother's drumstick of a chest. "You don't interfere. If you do, I'll put my foot on that jar and lean. Lean *hard.* Then you'll be gluing wings to dead things like the soft-boiled creep you are. You hear me?"

Phantasus quailed. His eyes, skittish and milky as a cornered animal's, darted everywhere except his brother's face. "Yes, Phobetor. I hear you."

When his brother stormed away, Phantasus nabbed the jar, murmuring sweet nothings of comfort (for himself or the fairy creatures it wasn't clear which), and tried without success to remove the lid. Phobetor didn't follow Hughes and Frank. The last Hughes saw of him he was stalking after his harp, as if he meant to wrangle and strangle the animation right out of it.

Then they were sealed back behind the hairy wall of willows, and Hughes was blind to their bizarre fraternal struggles.

"Their names," he said aloud. That murky association was now crystal clear. Phantasus and Phobetor. Phant and Phobe. "Frank, they wouldn't happen to be—"

Something stirred in the woods. No wind. There was no wind.

But something stirred anyway.

"Take this with a pinch of salt, Frank. A whole heaping, if you like. Only hear me out. You don't think that the name Phantasus might be ah... etymologically related to erm... the word 'Fantasy,' do you?" Hughes licked his lips. They were dry as indoor eucalyptus leaves. The stirring was closer.

Frank was glancing this way, that way, his eyes questing foglamps.

"Only it occurs to me that... well that in the same vein," Hughes continued bravely. "The name Phobetor might be related to ah... to the word—"

"Run," said Frank. He took off.

I'll take that as 'yes' then, shall I?

Hughes broke into a sprint.

Ahead, the trees bowed outward in the middle, almost as if some concussive force—a thunderbomb or a silent banshee scream, something crazy and outside the range of his imagination no doubt—had warped the hard nodules and the scrapey trunkskin of the willows. Down this tunnel of bark and brooding branches they ran, every touch of their clothes or their bare flesh making the willow leaves gossip in snakelike tongues (*rustle, slither, hiss*). The stirring sensation seemed to nip at his heels. He ran faster. Hughes' lungs were breath engines, arms and elbows pistoning, the muscles from his glutes to his calves pumping lactic acid with an efficiency that was almost mechanical. The speed they set was dauntingly, amazingly fast, but he was a long way from sweat and longer still from fatigue. If he had been engineered by his trainers, by Hector and Cassandra and Paris, then he was a project well designed.

Providing him with a consistent source of fuel was something Frank had said: *Dreams and dreams can't really affect one another, you dig? Like adding iodine to unstarched material.* Hughes was, as Phobetor had gleaned, not a dream but a human being. If you add iodine to starch, the chemical turns a ferocious blue-black. It was all too apparent that Frank was not haring through these woods for his own sake. He was doing it for his friend because if the stirring caught up with them, the iodine might detect in Hughes that which it could never detect in the Dream Warrior. In other terms, there might be a ferocious result.

Fallen twigs and dead leaves sent up a chorus of eerie crunches. It was as though the woods admired the tune the two harps had played in the clearing, but it lacked instruments, so all it could do was allow itself to be played by their shoes. An irregular, parched, wilted, *crinkle-crackle* drumbeat keeping time with his heart.

"You know the worst fear a fairy can claim?"

Phobetor's slimy, sluglike voice shuttled and oozed from all around him.

"They fear having their wings taken. What are you afraid of?"

Frank nearby, shouting. Hughes could see his friend's lips move. The words themselves were muffled, garbled incoherencies. Cotton wool language.

Hughes thought, *I may wish it were a nightmare. Dark woolgathering. But it's real, so I'll take hold of Frank's arms like this... I will take hold once he comes closer like that... oh Frank don't move away don't be drawn away from me don't don't I can't do this without you!*

For a moment it seemed like they'd be all right, that the thickening wicked substance, the snail-shell filled with pus that was Phobetor's voice, had fled into the roots and the green-masked faces of the willows. Pressing on his stomach to soothe the queasiness from worsening, Hughes turned to Frank, his mouth daring to smile. He framed the words, "I guess he just wanted to spook us," but never got a chance to say them. A familiar sinister melody stole up on him. It clawed up his legs (he had felt it nip at his heels, holy fucking Lord), and tore him open and wriggled inside. Music blasted through him, turning his whole body into an unwilling radio. It was mixed in with a sound so similar and yet so completely distant from the childish laughter he'd heard at the edge of the woods. This sound straddling the music was a lot less mystical and a lot more dismaying. Phobetor was having himself a giggle. Images of greasy fingers plucking at harp strings came to Hughes. They seemed to float up from the music, which localized itself to a ball rolling along his spine, changing him again from a living radio to something hemmed in and beholden to Phobetor's grotesque jive, like the well-covered man was a jukebox and Hughes was a bowling aisle sieged by a dreadful party—

(*drrrrread, yes, that's what he likes best*)

(*what he savors*)

Darkness.

(*the worst fear, the worst terror*)

FRANK

(*Phobetor his name sounds like*)

FRANK I CAN'T SEE

(*Phobia*)

Out of the dark it padded. It was taller than a rail wagon. Its fur was coarse and gray-white and matted with enough dried blood to fill a jacuzzi, and a room around the jacuzzi, and the lungs of the people bathing there. A smell proceeded it and was reinforced with every tread and step, a rotten sulphureous smell like the gas from the asshole of a man dying of stomach cancer and rotten eggs and old chicken breast left out in the hot sun. Its jowls were nests of slobber, its jaws pits where teeth like moldering fenceboards acted as cages for tongues all swollen and boiled by the bad acids in its throat. It had two heads, one possessed of a cold vulpine intellect, the other frantic and quite mad.

The wolf said, "Is this your biggest fear, Gormon Hughes?"

A woman with a kind face and with one leg missing appeared atop the wolf's back.

"Am I?" said Laurana. "My death because of your choices?"

"How about me?" asked Doctor Artemi Lanmoor, shuffling around from the wolf's flanks. "My office is this way. There's a bag of glass there, and a stapler..."

"So I can hold it all together," Hughes finished. The sound of his own voice in that black canyon of old phantoms brought no comfort. Rather it convinced him that this was all too real, enriching his loneliness and dread. Frank, where was Frank?

The wolf's sane head opened its jaws impossibly wide. Hughes watched as a white-haired figure climbed out of its gullet.

"Are you afraid of me, my lad?" said Wendy. "My bloodhound? My boy?"

"For the love of God, cut it out." He would have raised his hands to shield his face, but he was disembodied. The music was there, an undercurrent. He tried to look for his tormentor, thinking that might offer some clue to escape. Nothing to see. Nothing but past mistakes and the litter of menaces born from the womb of the dark. "Leave me alone, you wretch. Are you like her? Eating up fear? Are screams the gravy? Well, you'll find slim pickings here, fucker. I'm not afraid."

"Like her?" played the sinister tune. "Like who? Like her?"

"Like me?"

Hughes' felt his defiance cremate in his mouth. His tongue and gums and teeth were coated in the remnants. Despair, that was what this newcomer burned him with. Despair, and it tasted like flaky, still-warm ashes.

The newcomer grinned. If he'd been amused he'd have grinned just like that. Identical smiles between identical shadows.

"Bingo," said Jane. "I'm the one. I'm the bottom of the lurid barrel. I'm what you wish you'd never seen, never spoken to, never liked."

"Liked you? You chancer. You... Yes, I pitied you at the end, I'll concede that. But liked you? Never. Not ever."

"What about our guessing game in Sue Dennings' head? You—"

"Shut up."

"—had fun there, oh shut up yourself, baby. Although, although..." The grin widened. "I guess I'm *your* baby now, aren't I?"

"Watch it, Jane. Don't go there."

"Your monarch butterfly princess. Aren't I cute? Little Evelyn? Little bittle Evie Hughes?"

"I'm warning you bitch. I'm fucking warning you, now lay off or I'll—"

"Oh but will I stay that way? Will I stay sweet? Or will I go sour, suddenly, or slowly rot from the inside-out like an infected tooth? What if I start playing with bugs, will Mommy and Daddy—"

"Lay off I said!"

"—will they sigh and scoop me up and say, 'Well, we tried,' and throw me off a bridge?"

"JANE!"

"Will they smash their little girl's brains out?"

"You SHUT YOUR MOUTH!"

"But I love you, Daddy! I love you love you LOVE YOUUUU!"

He screamed then. Screamed his revulsion and his outrage and... and yes, he screamed because he was deeply, helplessly scared of her. She had always had a way with him. A vile touch, but an intimate one. Spring-Heeled Jane. He screamed and she laughed, the high, lunatic laugh of an asylum on vacation.

A presence, soft as muslin, implacable as a summer storm.

If you press firmly on the strings of a harp, it can't be played. Active music is brought to a jarring stop. That happened now, and the giggling (pervasive, going on this whole time like an evil undertow) was snipped cleanly quiet.

"Oh drat. Drat and damn and piss. Must I stop?" Phobetor asked.

The presence moved, scouring the dark like lemon juice over rust.

"At once! At once! At once!" Phobetor wheeled the words out. He sounded completely different, a bully confronted with someone twice his size and a million times meaner. "Here, see? Here we go, acquiescing, making good, making mended. See?"

Jane's laughter stopped. She was enveloped in the dark, they all were, all those ghosts conjured to devil Hughes. Dizzyingly fast, Hughes felt his consciousness going through a tunnel. He felt himself drawn forward along precarious tightropes. And with a final rush of vertigo he was back with the toes of his shoes hooked under a snag of willow root, about to trip. He steadied himself, taking shallow breaths, then deep ones, his nostrils full of pollen and nice mossy perfumes. Around him the dusk of Dreaming Jija sent threads of mellow light through the canopy like emissaries saying, *Welcome back, welcome, welcome.*

"Hughes!"

He looked up at the white-haired figure rushing to him. Not Wendy. Hughes smiled a smile of almost desperate gratitude. "Frank."

They embraced, Frank murmuring, "Where'd you go, man? Where'd you go?"

When they parted and Hughes stood away, wiping a tear from his cheek, he regained the smile. It had been retreating under a sickly nausea. Thinking about what he'd been subjected to. The sheer relief that it was over. *You stay where you are, smile of mine. I'm safe and sound so you stick around, okay?*

"I heard you scream," said Frank. "But I couldn't see you. I'm so glad you're okay, can't tell you how glad..."

"Don't start me off again. The willows are the only licensed weepers here."

Frank's huge toothy grin was a tonic, and it was gone too soon. "That bigger brother grab you?"

"He was tired of pulling the wings off fairies," Hughes explained. "Thought he might try tugging at my sanity. That force put a stop to it. The conductor, the same one from before. It did for Phobetor, scared scariness—isn't that *incredible?*"

"Scared..."

"Yes!" He swallowed, squeezed his friend's forearm and said, "Phobia, Frank. Those brothers were Fantasy and Phobia. Frank, where are we? Dreaming Jija, I know, I know, but... is this an underworld or is this a place where other beings venture to on a lark? Not just the dead but... forces, I suppose you could say... forces beyond humanity?"

"You mean Gods?"

"I don't know what I mean. I feel all rattle and no snake. So shit and beat up and creeped out. Really," he said, his eyes imploring. "Any insight would help me. What do you think?"

Frank nodded, checked behind them, saw they were alone, and then slipped into a meditative silence that lasted almost a full minute. "There are authorities out there, judges and barristers and jurors in the broad unselective cosmos. Maybe better to think of them as ideas given form. Or the form from which ideas come. Hard to tell. If Death is a woman and a woman is Death, then who's to say Sleep and Wakefulness can't have arms and elbows, hearts and attitudes. War and Promethean Fire. Hunting, Cannibalism, Thunder, Mercy. Shapes molded out of a clay you and I can't conceive of because the knowing of it would make us like them. I haven't found many answers to the big questions of my life, Hughes. But life on the road had many a rest stop and junction and superhighway, and each with its own procession of truths like bright headlight cones carving the dark." There were dust motes in one of the bigger beams of twilight coming down through the tangle of branches. Frank put his hand into the beam. The dust motes danced there, little lights riding a weird, crepuscular motorway. "And among ideas, particular power is wielded by emotions, of course. Emotions are wonderful. Wonderful, wicked things. The strongest microscope won't reveal them, but they decide every outcome of our lives. They have a power that makes magic look like a parade of cheap parlor tricks. How often do we hear a man apologize to his wife saying, *It was my emotions. They got the better of me.* How often have I heard two girlfriends say, *I got angry. I want to be motivated. I let go of my grief, I fostered my hopes and my dreams.* I think that means something. Points to something true inside us and outside us. I think that if life were a courtroom, emotions would hold the gavel and pass the verdicts. Perhaps they fight the cases." The dust motes danced over Frank's palm. He folded his fingers up, making a shiny fist. "Perhaps they built the courthouse."

Before Hughes could begin to formulate a reply (not much hope of that, Frank had given him a staggering amount to think over), there was a rattly cough from nearby.

He snapped around, expecting to see Phobetor wringing his hands, an insincere apology curling his pursed, fishy lips, but it wasn't him. It was the brother. His white robes hung from his bony shoulders like a Halloween sheet from a coatrack. Lank hair, so pale it was basically colorless, tumbled over his face. Gray eyes filled with so much desperate hope it reminded Hughes of impounded dogs or starving curbside kittens peering at them between locks of that unruly hair.

"Might I have a word?" said Phantasus.

"You on your own?" said Frank.

The incarnation of Fantasy nodded with a kind of damp water biscuit enthusiasm. He didn't approach, maybe hazarding (accurately) that Hughes was agitated and none-too-well disposed toward strangers at present.

"I'm most grievously sorry for my brother's behavior. I..." He winced. "I *hope* you won't think too badly of him. He's had a very difficult time of things recently, after some rather... sordid and sad business with our elder sibling, Morpheus. We all express our sorrow in different ways, eh?" Hughes and Frank's flat expressions seemed to make a turtle of Phantasus, whose neck crept anxiously into the skinny depths of his clavicle. "I..." he winced again, as though the word caused him physical anguish, "*hope* you'll accept a small token from me. An apology. Once removed from the culprit, if you will, but no less warranted and righteous I think." And with that he reached over his head and broke off a hunk of willow bark. He held it out to Hughes. After a moment's silence, he said, "Won't you take it?"

Hughes examined it from where he was. Unchanged, or so it looked. "What is it?"

"This is a bad wood. Impish and evil. But good emerges where you least expect, and even trees have their dreams." Phantasus smiled a smile of such tired optimism that Hughes felt engaged by it, if only for pity's sake.

He approached, hesitated, then accepted the scrap of willow bark.

"Dreaming trees," he mused.

Phantasus grinned suddenly. "Yes. The saps."

In spite of what had happened to him at the hands of this guy's brother, Hughes couldn't resist. He grinned back.

"Might I know your name?"

"Hughes."

"Why are you looking for Death, Hughes? There's something of the daredevil about you, but no hint of self-destruction."

"No. God no. I don't want to die. My friend here," Hughes gestured to Frank, "thinks she might be able to point me in the right direction. Unless... You wouldn't know where magic comes from, would you?"

Phantasus gave him a puzzled look. "What sort of magic?"

"The kind a shadow of a world might have."

"A shadow you say? I've heard of them, perhaps from Morpheus. My brother was much more knowledgeable than Phobetor and I. Wizened and well-traveled. Phobetor and I are, alas, home birds who seldom fly abroad. I'm afraid I can't help you."

Hughes put the willow bark in his pocket and gave a cool nod to show he wasn't disappointed. "Thanks anyway. Why do you stick with that guy anyway? Fantasy with Phobia? You seem about as well suited to one another as chalk and cheese."

Hughes didn't think it was possible, but the expression Phantasus leveled at him was even more tired. Hughes was reminded of Estelle Corlum, the most effortlessly exhausted person he had ever clapped eyes on.

The superimposed image—one sunken-eyed face over the other—dissolved the instant Phantasus explained his reasons for spending time around his brother.

"Because without me to torture, he would find other methods of distraction." At Hughes' horrified expression, he pulled a blue-collar face and said, "A trying life, but my own. We all express our sorrow in different ways, eh?"

"Hope too," said Hughes and stuck out his hand.

Hearing the word rather than speaking it didn't seem to bother Phantasus. Quite the contrary. He looked grateful, lighter somehow, like a little of his invisible burden had been taken away and shouldered. He shook Hughes' hand gladly, bid the pair farewell, and pottered off to find his brother.

Chapter Four

No one hands you a pamphlet, peers at you over their expensive sunglasses, and says, "Read this and you will be a good mother." Pamphlets claiming this power exist, of course. Books too. But no one takes them seriously, not really, because every baby is unique. There are patterns linking crib to crib across the whole world. Those patterns are useful to know. What to do when the child chokes on something. Why are they making that rather distressing noise when they sleep. What temperature should formula be. How on earth do nappies function. Who the shit produces buggies without adjustable brakes, so we might curse them as we struggle down and up hills, and who the shit invented those little spinning light projectors that the baby is fascinated by at bedtime, so we might thank them forever.

Useful.

But sometimes your baby will do something that you could not prepare for. Despite this, people will offer advice. Not bookish advice. Heartfelt. Sincere. Sometimes good. Sometimes insane. They will pass you warnings and tips with grim faces, like they are handing you the keys to a bomb design kit. In a way they are. Children are possibility given form, infinity smelling of talcum powder. They can be anything.

And always hanging over you is the truth that no one will warn you about.

Yes, children can indeed be anything.

And if you do a bad enough job, they can even be nothing.

Cate stared at the chair where Evelyn had been. She stared at the front lip of the chair where a trickle of errant baby food had stained the white plastic brownish-orange. She stared at the padded seat, the supportive back plate, the chair, the chair, the empty ch—

She lunged for the telephone. Her fingers didn't shake as she dialed the number.

Two rings. Then a voice like old shells and lobster husks in a wretched tin bucket spoke into her ear.

"Yes?"

"Mr. Glint. It's Cate Jubilee."

"Morning to you, Miss."

"Mr. Glint, my baby has gone missing. It happened right now, quick as a lightning flash in a storm. I bet it's magic. You're good at finding people. Could you come over here?"

"Yes."

"Thanks."

"Sound very calm, Miss."

"I'm putting a brave face on it."

Yes, that she was, wasn't she? Nothing for it. Hysterics were fine and dandy provided you had someone else to put in the elbow grease and keep things moving economically and well. If it was all you, then you masked your panic with a brave face. Cate understood that clinically, coldly, perfectly. Inside, her nerves were imploding suns, galaxies in supernova state, white dwarfs, neutron stars, black holes swirling fear of every shade and stripe down the wormhole.

She was right there. I closed the fridge for less than five seconds. Right there. Right there.

"Please come quickly," she said.

"Be round in a trice," Glint promised.

She thanked him again and hung up.

She looked around the room. Scanning for movement. Listening for a telltale noise.

There was nothing. The chair was still empty.

Cate reached into her pocket, took out a scrunchy, and tied her hair up.

Then, in an orderly and businesslike manner that was an excellent credit to her despite the stress of the situation, she began to tear the apartment asunder.

By the time Mr. Glint arrived, somber and dripping rain on the carpet, there was still no sign of Evelyn.

***

There was a town in the forest. Dead people lived there. Some of them preferred the term "differently alive" but calling a spade a spade and a terrier a dog, they were dead, plain and simple. Not zombies. Spirits. Not rotting. Or decomposing.

Or wasting away. They wasted time, but not away. Think of them instead as enjoying a well-earned retirement from the rigors of living. Living can be a chore after all. You can like your work, but it's still work. The dead don't really have things to do. The worst has happened. Now it's about acceptance, and speculation about what comes after the thing that came before, and after this for that matter. There were lots of spirits across the underworlds. It's a matter of being indigenous to the grave. It's a matter of belonging. It's a matter of following once you've been called.

Often the residents of this particular town grew bored, so they held tea parties and games of tag with an elusive figure named Teapot Gavin, who was spry and merry, and, naturally, shaped exactly like a teapot complete with handle and spout. Bored as they generally were, however, the townsfolk even more frequently became possessed of a fancy that could not be shaken. To finally rid themselves of it, the man or the woman, the girl or the boy, whoever, would climb into a machine kept within a manor house in the town, and as the other denizens looked on, the machine would change that spirit from a person into an animal. Cats. Dogs. Microbats with teeny weeny pink snouts. Every creature you can think of. Odd? Well, yes. Dreaming Jija is as Dreaming Jija does is not a saying, but perhaps it should be. It was at that time a realm of change, of flow and flux and mutation, and transmogrification was well within those curvy wobbly lines that passed for the bounds of rationality here beyond the smoke and the fields and the leering willows of the wood.

Hughes' poor brain could just about manage all that.

What it could not manage—indeed what absolutely tore the biscuit—was that this town in the dreamy underworld was called Missicordelia.

"Nope," said Hughes firmly. "Absolutely not. No, I won't accept it."

"Hughes," said Frank. "What is it, man?"

"I refuse, Frank. This town shares the name of a country back in our world? I can stomach boars turning into hills when knights kill them, and I can accept the concepts of Phobia and Fantasy being siblings who torment one another. But this? This crosses a bridge. It is, in fact, a bridge too far."

"Could be a coincidence."

"Oh yeah, right. Pull the other one, it's got bells on."

"Maybe parallels exist all over the universe. Like you and Jane. Mirrors and reflections. Light and dark. Or dark and darker."

"You're not helping, Frank. Not bloody helping one bit."

"What I'm saying is... Well, what I'm saying is *what does it matter?*"

"Matter?" Hughes deliberated. "Well, it doesn't strictly matter, now you put it that way. It's just... weird. I mean two places using the same name? All the sounds and syllables lining up perfectly? And you and I just happen to come across it? It's giving me a very funny feeling."

"Dizziness?"

"For a start!"

The greeting party of Missicordelians, who had emerged from the manor house the moment he and Frank ambled out of the boscage, looked at Hughes as if he were a fish that had just politely informed them to try the water, it's fine. To be specific, they were looking at him with puzzlement, hostility, and a guarded, tight-shouldered sort of fear.

"If it helps," said a young man in yellow flannel and turquoise halfmoon spectacles. "If it, em, helps... this place is named Missicordelia on account of its erm... founder. Her mother and father called her Cordelia—"

"Aye and she's quite the missy," someone said.

There was general nodding.

"Thank you," said Hughes frostily.

Frank smiled, not picking up on the tone. "On firmer ground?" he asked his friend.

"What?" said Hughes.

"On firmer ground. Come to terms with the situation."

"Frank Gallant, I am not on firmer ground. If I were unable to look down at my feet and see the grass, I would assume we were standing on the most slippery surface imaginable. Possibly oiled mongooses."

Frank stopped smiling. "Oh."

"Yes."

"Want to go?"

"No. I want to ask them about Death. Hello," said Hughes, stepping forward. "I want to ask you about Death."

"Yes, we heard," said the spectacled man.

"You did?"

"Yes, you're not very far away."

"From Death?"

"No, from us."

"Um. Marvelous. Ummm, well, here's the thing. We need to speak to—"

"Go away," said the man, his eyes flashing behind his glasses. "Follow the sounds of the bees and get out of here."

Hughes blinked his surprise. "Sorry?"

"He's right." The rest of the greeting party gathered around the spectacled man. An old man had spoken. Now a young girl weighed in. "You've got to go. It's not safe to have outsiders here."

"You seem like formidable folks," said Frank.

"Not dangerous for us," snipped the girl. "For you. Missicordelia is different since our First Resident left. Cordelia kept the place in shape. Now its..."

"Looser," said the spectacled man.

"Looser," agreed the girl. "A flabbiness of the existential type. Soul sag." She gave Frank and Hughes a grave look. "We all want to change and become animals. More and more we want to. Barlow—he was a cat, now he's a man—he keeps us from doing it too much. He says if the moon changed all the time in the living world there would be floods forever, and that people are the same. Some change is nice, but too much is calamitous. If you stay much longer, handsome man and fretful mumbling man, you might undergo a change too. You might like it too much."

"Get a taste for what could be," said the old man.

More nodding. Grim, dour-faced nodding.

"Tell us where we can find Death," said Hughes, trying his best not to fretfully mumble. "Then we'll go quick as anything."

"Too late," said the girl. "It's happening."

She's right. I can feel it. Hughes didn't think it was this beckoning change the townsfolk described. No, it was the presence again. The conductor. It moved over Missicordelia, an invisible hand turning down all the tetchy, querulous dials. There was no room for doubt now—that *was* Death.

She's sensed us like a terrifically omnipotent white blood cell heeding the call of antigens. Hughes wasn't sure he and Frank were invaders to the body of the dead world, not in the nasty fashion that word implied. Rather they were visitors that brought something with them. Hosts for it. Temptation, perhaps. Or... *foreign matter.* He scowled without knowing it. A new year, a healthy daughter, and still his mind thought, hey, let's run that old track, see how it plays.

Never mind that now. Death's here, I can't afford to be elsewhere.

As the presence smothered the town's transformative allure, Hughes watched the girl realize her mistake. A hamster poked out of her shirt's breast pocket. It wore the same expression as the girl and all the rest of the townsfolk: flummoxed amazement.

Hughes proclaimed, "Let the Lady of the black hood and the white scythe come out from where she lurks. Ah. I say lurks, I'm sure it's more dignified than that. We won't take up much time. And we're bothering the local color, that's plain enough. Come out and, ahm, and we'll talk."

Frank nudged him. "The fudge," he urged.

"What's that? Oh, right." Hughes cleared his throat. "We've heard you're peckish for a square or two of ambrosia fudge. As luck would have it, we've got lots of those. Although they might be a bit squashed, it being rather a fraught journey. You understand."

Stillness.

"Oh piss," said the girl, looking at her feet. "You've gone and planted both boots in the bucket, so you have. If you'd only followed the bees you might have found a friendly spirit to take you home. Now, well, oh piss."

Hughes opened his mouth to ask her what she was on about, when all at once he thought he felt himself... thinning.

No, it was perspective playing tricks!

He wasn't thinning, his surroundings were dilating. Sweeping sensations of being lobbed into an engorged pupil, being utterly and completely seen from head to toe and talent to flaw and fondness to loathing. He was a cut stone under a jeweler's screwpoint lens. He was camera-captured fire flickering reel to reel in a documentarian's film roll. Looked at? No, being looked at was a two-way thing, observer and observed, subject and object. This was divorced from ordinary examination by exponential figures. It was a confession made unwillingly and spoken in a language his tongue could not have familiarized itself with, not in a hundred years of cultivated study. A country of widening dark through which an isola of a man is glimpsed, no more impressive or memorable than a comet in the sunfire eye of a galaxy.

Was this what it was like, being peered at by Death?

Dimly, so very distantly, he was aware of the townsfolk hurrying back inside their manor house, of Frank's hair painting itself with eerie shimmers of red, yellow, green, and purple.

Coagulation! Attenuation! All the broadness of that conductive power narrowed into a pinhead.

Out of it came a boy. The boy was seventeen or thereabouts. He looked as though puberty had saved itself up for a rainy day, and that day was today. Spots clustered his nose and cheeks, which were cheesy in complexion and texture. His dark hair hung lank about his apple-shaped head, which was too large for his body. His build was bandy and yet extremely short. His eyes were rheumy and weepy, their wan moldy blue color reminding Hughes of a slice of brie he'd left in the fridge for eleven months during his days as a Corinth City bachelor. Odder than any other element in his appearance, the boy was clad in black robes, and in his hand he carried a staff of nobbly white bone. Also, he was astride what could only be described as the universe's most miserable bear. It was a large bear, brown and paunchy and equipped with a saddle. Its liquid onyx eyes regarded Hughes with the deepest, most intractable sorrow.

"Ooooooh wow. Here I am. Yes?" quavered the boy. "Can I help you?"

Hughes turned to Frank Gallant, whose hair was now a perplexed hue of puce. "I thought Death was a woman."

"She is. Hey, kid. Who are you?"

"Me? I'm Rupert Prindlee, if you must know."

"Nice to meet you, Rupert," said Frank, inclining his head in a display of impeccable manners.

Rupert Prindlee raised a hand. "Cripes, how polite. It's a pleasure, Mr. Gallant."

Frank straightened, his expression curious. "You know me?"

"Not personally," said Rupert Prindlee. "I'm quite good with names."

"How about anthropomorphic beings? Where's Death, kid? I was sure you were her."

"Me too," said Hughes. "Don't tell us that was *you* we felt? That phenomenal, overwhelming presence stifling the willows and constricting Phobetor?"

Hughes was mollified when Rupert fanned his hands in that frantic "no, no, not at all" sort of way.

"Oh cripes and jam pudding, no. No, that was Lucy."

"Lucy?"

Rupert Prindlee nodded. His eyeballs watered with the effort. It really was a disproportional head to body ratio. "Lucy. The Angel of Mercy," he explained. "The Scythebearer. Outwitter of the Tarot Troupe. Lover of Lainey and connoisseur of that most exquisite delicacy, ambrosia fudge. The Dark Pilgrim. The Kindly Reaper. Old Scratch. You know," he said. "Lucy Nowhere. She's... well, Death. You mean to say you haven't heard of Lucy? I thought everyone knew her. Surely you've come across one of her plays, at least in passing acquaintanceship?"

"We just know her as Death," said Frank. "So it *was* her before. And again now."

"A moment ago? No, that was me. Oh bother, it's rather complicated. You see, there's this thing called the Empress of Ice Cream. And it sort of borrows... or rather it permits the borrowing of certain... Well, let's not tarry in the weeds about that," said Rupert Prindlee smartly. He gave them his most helpful smile. Meanwhile his bear groaned mournfully. Rupert pointedly ignored this. He said, in a loud, proud voice that only cracked a little, "Safe to say I'm your Scythebearer today. Hello and good morning to you, Gormon Hughes and Frank Gallant." Distress galloped across his face. "Unless... Is it morning where you've come from? Let me check..."

In a bag slung across the wide bristly back of the bear, Rupert rummaged. From it he produced a pot of honey. He stuck his hand in the pot and drew out a great big dollop. He splayed his hand wide, the clear amber stickiness formed letters like webbing between the fingers. "I see," Rupert said. "I seeeeee. So you're from *there*, are you? A strange world, as these things go. A *sleeping* world." He paused, studying the gooey, dripping mess. "Coming up on afternoon there. Depending on time zones, of course."

Hughes turned to Frank. "Have you any idea what's going on here?"

Frank nodded. "Think so."

"Good for you. I'm lost as a lucky penny in a jar."

"Want me to fish it out? Make all this shiny and comprehendible?"

"That would be lovely."

"Well, if I've got it straight, it's like this: this pimpled fellow Rupert wields a fragment of Death's power. That bony staff isn't complete; I bet with a moment's notice a blade comes pushing out. Which would make it not just *a* scythe but *the* scythe, the one owned by Death herself. More important than that, Rupert has declared himself our 'Scythebearer today,' which implies he's going to be able to provide guidance for us in Death's absence. That pot he's got is a kind of augur. Drawing the honey from inside allows him to divine true things, things like the name of your world of origin. And see the way he's putting the honey back inside the pot and his hand emerges clean and free of gunk? Hear the grumble of the bear's stomach? Poor old bear. No wonder she's in a funk. That magic honey will never be on the menu."

"Right on all counts," said Rupert Prindlee. "Only you really needn't mind this precocious old bear. An ursa minor in discipline, and an ursa major pain in my bottom. I feed her thirteen times a day, and still she isn't satisfied!"

Meanwhile Hughes was trying not to gawp at Frank. "All of that... bloody useful, Frank. Thank you."

His friend winked. In the aurora of his hair a crimson star also winked beyond the green and purple strands of light. "What was it you said? *Really quite amazing?*" Frank shrugged modestly. "Shit, I'll take it."

"Can you take us to the place where my power comes from?" Hughes asked Rupert Prindlee.

"What powers would these be?"

"It's called Performance. I can influence the behavior of those around me. And there's Chimera, which inflicts more substantial, permanent change within the um..." *Target,* his brain offered, a touch sneeringly. He was always in two minds about his power. "The recipient," he finished. Whatever sourness had entered his tone was gone in an instant. He met the boy's open stare with an entreating one of his own. "Look, I'm only a person, Rupert. Where I come from there's magic and all sorts of ways of thinking about the subject of the arcane from top to bottom. But no one has ever conceived of an ability like mine. My ordinariness has somehow become extraordinary. The mystery behind that has become a part of me, so much so that it's indistinguishable from the rest of my basic parts. That said, the time for idling in mysteries, playing detective in more ways than one, is over. Could be that approaching my thirties has made me impatient. Mostly, it's the fact that the horizon has gotten dark, not with twilight but with danger. My world, whose name you've seen in your honey, is being threatened by another. It sent an envoy of its evil, a woman who also had the power to influence others. Jane was her name. She identified herself as the shadow of Eurydice. In that same breath she declared me Iphigenia's shadow. Eurydice and Iphigenia—"

"Are two worlds," said Rupert Prindlee, very quietly, and with none of his voice's former quaver.

"Exactly. I've got to unravel if she was speaking the truth, and if she was, what being a shadow is all about. It's imperative, not just for my own sanity and comfort, but for things of much more pressing demand, such as the safety of people who I care for. And who you ought to care about, since he who fills in for Death must also be furnished with Death's prerogatives, and the untimely demise of so many will undoubtedly result in increased paperwork for you." Hughes grinned a macabre grin, then allowed his malleable features to soften into a look of absolute desire couched in a gentle, coaxing need. "Can you help me, Mr. Prindlee?"

Rupert Prindlee gave him an appraising look. "You're sure you don't simply influence people by speaking like that at them?"

"Positive."

"Cripes. Must be cherries on an already made cake, in that case. Cripes and jam. Lucy herself couldn't have written better. Ah, I tell a lie, I've remembered that she could and has. No offense. Um... What were you asking me?"

"*Can you help me?*"

"Oh yes! Sorry about that." Rupert's smile was like a balloon inflated with sour cream rather than air; flimsy and unfortunate. "Quite good with names, quite bad at everything else, that's Rupert Prindlee for you. Of course I can help you. I am an aide-de-camp to Lucy Nowhere herself, after all."

"Aide-de-camp is a military term," said Frank.

"Is it?"

"Yes."

"Oh. Then I'm..."

"An assistant?"

"An assistant! That's it precisely!" Rupert's apple-shaped face rumpled up with concentration. "Say um... you didn't mention something about being a shadow to Iphigenia, did you?"

"Yes. A shadow to Iphigenia," said Hughes with patience that earned him an admiring look from Frank.

"I *seeeee*. In that case I know exactly where to take you." Rupert scooted forward in his saddle. "Hop on."

Hughes and Frank weren't about to turn their noses up at answers after so fraught a journey. They wasted no time hopping onto the bear, who introduced herself as Daisy.

"I'm Frank," said Frank. "Frank Gallant. Sorry for a lack of introduction. Truth be told, I thought you were a bear."

"I   am,"   said   Daisy.

"Fair enough."

"Where are we headed?" said Hughes.

"To the Willows housing estate in Glasnevin," said Rupert Prindlee.

"Where's that?"

"In Ireland. It's a wet island no one in the universe cares about."

"Oh yes?"

"That's where Lucy hid the worlds, you know. Normally I wouldn't dream of taking you or *anyone* there because it's a preserved secret."

"Ah."

"But my honey pot told me I ought to."

"Right."

"It's got a good read on people, my honey pot."

"Does it?"

"Cripes yes."

"Good for you and it both," said Hughes.

The bear named Daisy began to tramp away from the town of Missicordelia toward the fringes of the dreamy wood. The buzz of either many insects or very large ones became discernible. Hughes wasn't sure if he liked or loathed that sound. It was sultry, almost drowsy. Overhead the cloud child Jija slept his eternal sleep, dreaming this underworld into existence. The group were on their way toward answers long sought after. And it was all thanks to a pot full of divinatory bee vomit.

Somewhere in that parallel universe, Hughes 2 is drinking tea and eating an egg and cress sandwich, Hughes privately lamented. He's thinking about watching a match on the television, or calling one of his work friends for a chat. I bet the sandwich tastes like a simple carefree January day. In this moment Hughes 2 thinks, "Why not be a bit wild." Grinning at his own madness, he puts on the kettle for cup of tea number two. The bastard.

Chapter Five

"So how does one go about becoming Death's assistant?" Frank asked Rupert Prindlee.

"It was an easy thing born out of difficult circumstance," the bear-rider and honey pot consulter disclosed. "I applied."

Hughes was incredulous. "What, like... with a *CV*? I can't imagine what that would be like. Have you got any experience harvesting souls? Bring your own whetstone since the scythe tends to get dull around five o'clock in the evening? The meek, the squeamish, and those averse to a bit of Sunday morning reaping need not apply? Would your previous employers call you reliable, particularly in the event of a mass extinction event such as famine, plague, or overland disagreement?"

"In an oblique way that last part actually was relevant," said Rupert Prindlee. "My world was ending and I wrote her a letter."

There was a morose, intrigued silence.

"Ending?" said Hughes, trying to sound nonchalant, and at exactly the same time Frank said, also casually, "A letter?"

They were in a close, misty place, narrow and transitory seeming. Around them the mist formed into towers, cities, endlessly tall countries of mist. Then they dissembled and flew apart in mushroom clouds, white spores whirling and streaming. The place gave Hughes and Frank the feeling they were crossing a bridge. One that linked Dreaming Jija to... well, Glasnevin, according to Rupert. Wherever in God's name Ireland was.

All the while Rupert Prindlee told them about his world punching its ticket, how worlds come about, and where they go when they die.

"What you might not be aware of is the fact that the worlds used to be spread out in a big wood. The trees were made of cloth and the moss was pearly, and the worldplanter beetle moved from likely spot to likely spot, popping his noodle to the earth and coming back up, and there would be a fresh tree and a new world, right there!"

"So each tree in the clothwood represented a world?" Frank asked.

"Think bigger, Mr. Gallant! A representation and a door and the world itself!"

"We traveled to Jija through an elm," said Hughes.

"Yes, well, you would have had to," said Rupert sagely. "The clothwood is gone, but the principles of growth, decay, and connection remain quite fixed. Lucy wouldn't allow it otherwise."

"But you were telling us about your world," said Frank.

"And the letter," said Hughes.

"Was I? Cripes, so I was. Well, the worlds were content enough, I suppose. As content as worlds can be, what with all the niggling wiggling problems arising from the fact that planning permission is never granted and igloos keep being stolen, and there is only so much oasis to go round in the desert, and so forth. But content, yes, I think so. One day this terrible group of ne'er do goods called the Tarot Troupe arrived. At first they were stronger than Lucy and all her friends and allies put together. One of the Tarot Troupe bore a sword that could cut down the world trees! And he sliced the worldplanter beetle's head right off— lopped it clean away, all that buggish gristle and chitin just as easy as slicing cucumbers! But Lucy was cleverer than all the rest, and it's said she pulled some fantastic tricks on the Troupe during the great war that raged between the forces of good and evil. But in the end push always comes to shove. A fight was brewing, a fight unlike any the worlds had ever seen, and the guardians of each world joined with Lucy. What a pugnacious barney that must have been, eh? And, of course, in the end Lucy Nowhere came out on top. To prevent anyone else from harming the worlds she hid them away."

"In a wet unmemorable place called Ireland," said Frank.

"That's right."

Frank thought about this. Hughes joined him.

They caught one another being ponderous and shared a knowing smile.

"Makes sense," said Frank.

Pugnacious barney, Hughes mouthed, and Frank had to conceal a laugh by coughing into his sleeve.

But the mirth was short lived. Bleakness crept in. Hughes channeled their surroundings, forming a sense of bridginess out of mist and conjecture. "Rupert. Your world was one of those destroyed by the Tarot Troupe."

"Yes," said Rupert Prindlee. "The one with the sword was interrupted partway through the felling of our world tree. They never finished cutting. Still the damage was done. Eventually the tree toppled over, and my world came to an end."

"All at once?"

"Slowly," said Rupert, and if his voice had held a sad, hollow note before, it was sadder and more hollow now by a great deal. "Slowly and painfully. Rare is the world that ends in fire, ice, or instantaneous calamity. More often it's social, cultural, and political. The end comes as a result of jealousy, hatred, and a lack of empathy, all congested and stuffed up into a single block of bad feeling that pulps the reasoning minds and squashes flat all chance of reticence, love, and recovery. I've since learned that bombs are common. In my case, it was gas. A detonation of gas that cloaked the world, so pervasive that it slipped into lead-lined shelters of the paranoid as easily as it snuck into the homes of the unwary and content."

"We're so sorry, Rupert," said Hughes.

Frank echoed the sentiment, his aurora deepening to a commiserating plum.

Where he sat in the saddle, Rupert gave a curt nod. This time Hughes didn't think it was the effort of maneuvering his ample head that made his eyes damp and tricklesome.

"But you wrote to Lucy," Hughes prompted.

The boy brightened. Not much. But a little. "Yes," he said.

"And she responded."

"Yes."

After a moment of silence Frank opened his mouth, presumably to ask what such a letter could have contained and what such a response from so magnificent a figure as Death could have been like.

He felt Hughes' touch on his elbow, bringing him up short.

Hughes gave a small shake of his head.

His gaze—hazel-dark and depthful—informed Frank of the trauma he saw like bolts of heavy steel riveting Rupert's posture. *Gas*, the boy had said. Gas had ended his world. And with that one word uttered he left many others unspoken. Memories better left undisturbed. It was not for Frank and Hughes to prod or inquire, certainly no further than they had done already. It would not be right. All this from Hughes' expression, which anyone—especially a friend like Frank—could discern in a matter of milliseconds. His face was that communicative, like a broadcasting center with cheekbones.

Thinking on his feet, Hughes steered the conversation into safer, more delicate waters. "Did you say that Lucy wrote plays? You don't mean of a fully-fledged dramatical nature?"

Rupert's good humor seemed to advance another few paces.

"Mr. Hughes," he said with a happy quirk in his tone. "Are you a theatre man?"

Hughes allowed himself a furtive smile. "You could say that."

Time passed in an amiable fashion after that (Hughes was too wonderstruck and fascinated to think of checking his magical red-and-blue letter, more's the pity), and at length the mist abated here and became solid there, the cool milk-white city becoming brick, wood, alloyed steel, and glimmering starlit glass.

It was night and the night people were out and about, romantically strolling arm in arm, carrying beer bottle crates to nameless parties, or eating greasy cheeseburgers and chicken wings from takeaway boxes. The trio drove up a long street. There were trees separating the car lanes. It was wintertime, so the trees were stripped of their leaves, except for a few curled-up brown clingers riffling in the wind.

Hughes' brow clouded.

Drive? Don't I mean ride? You don't drive a bear.

He looked around and saw that he and Frank were in the backseat of a car. Frank looked as startled as he felt. The seats were dark brown, comfortable, and their material gave Hughes an odd shaggy feeling as of sitting with his back against fur and the muscle of a large animal beneath. The air inside the car was redolent of skin cream and... something sweet. Hughes cut his eyes to the rearview mirror. An air freshener dangled there. It was a honey pot.

"That's Glasnevin cemetery on the right," said Rupert Prindlee from the driver's seat. His hands were folded in his lap. The wheel turned itself. "We're almost there."

The car went a little farther. Through an iron fence all spiky and foreboding they saw headstones sprawl like a field of gray flowers, and the cemetery monuments pawed at the curtain of cloud above as if scheming to usurp the very night. *From their grave plots, the dead plot our graves*, thought Hughes. A weird, intrusive sort of thought, and false too. He ought to know. He'd met members of the differently alive that very day.

Maybe he was thinking of Cate's encounter with Lord Burrows and the undead horde in Eurydice, an encounter that had nearly cost his beloved her life. Hughes wasn't sure.

The car turned into a housing estate. For a moment a streetlamp—its bulb barely clinging to life like the last of the leaves—gave a shiver of brightness. In golden letters like drizzled honey, two words appeared on the car windshield.

THE WILLOWS

The bulb died. The words vanished.
And Hughes began to feel afraid.

*****

The apartment was in shambles. Total and utter disarray. No baby.
Evelyn's chair stood like a monument to that, a kind of mean testimonial.
A baby? it seemed to goad. *Why, there was one right here*
(there, she was right there)
and that was only recently. Where could that baby be?
Cate didn't know. She didn't know and it was destroying her.
She collapsed onto the sofa. Her body was shaking, something it almost never did, not even in the most brutal climaxes and denouements of battle. Throw her into the frying pan, then the fire, and watch as a woman refuses to burn. She'll crystallize instead, then climb out of the sizzling smoke and break your nose to make up for the inconvenience you've caused her.

But hoh-lee hell, was she terrified. She had not felt like this since the ultrasound room at Saint Wilhemina's maternal hospital, and the house of mirrors before that, when a million ghosts of her father chased a million Cates across the glass, workman's mallet in hand.

"I don't know what to do," she said, her voice a harsh whisper that seemed to teeter between a growl and a scream. "I'm going over possibilities in my mind, the ones I haven't exhausted. And they're useless. I've written to Hughes in case he or Frank can help. No word, nothing, but... they're probably in the company of Death right now, so that's... no good." She giggled, heard the mania like a crooked totem in that sound, and clamped her mouth closed on it. Her lips stretched in a grin devoid of humor and too-wide with revulsion. "I've contacted John Isherwood," she said colorlessly. "He reached out to various peers of his, people who might have heard of a phenomenon like this. None of them could offer anything that helps me. Just speculation. And I thought maybe Desdemona Cauldronpot could um..." A tiny shake of her head. "But she's unreachable. Probably she'd wave some incense and declare my daughter is... who knows where." She looked up, dismayed but not sobbing (only once had Cate ever really given in to tears, although on that occasion it was over the loss, not the disappearance, of a child).

The man she'd summoned to the apartment was standing in her kitchen, smoothing the creases out of his suit with a long-fingered hand.

"Mr. Glint, it's driving me mad. Stark raving mad. Usually my mind offers something, a bit of... something, I can't describe it. Something that guides me. Pushes me this way or that way toward a course of action. More often than not it's the right course of action too. Now that something is dead silent. Silent as a pram with no one inside it. God, I can't believe I said that. What a horrible thing to... I can't believe I'm here at this... this point of fucking drowning in excruciating worry. After all Hughes and I went through to get her. To *have her in our lives*. I... Oh ssssshit. Shit, shit, shit. I do not know what to do. Why am I saying this? Like I expect you to yank a solution out of thin air. Stupid. So stupid. She's missing and I'm useless. I just don't know."

Mr. Glint said something.

She didn't hear him. Locked on Evelyn's baby chair, Cate's eyes had taken on a stunned, vacant look. A ball of helpless dread was rolling back and forth in her belly. *She was there.* The phrase and the ball were the same, a little snippet of despicable truth nauseating her, making her sick with fear for her daughter. *She was there. She was there. She was right there.*

She only acknowledged Glint when he sat down next to her. Cate didn't know it, but at that moment Hughes and Frank were passing by Glasnevin cemetery.

This was one of life's incredible parallels since passing by a cemetery is remarkably similar to being within the vicinity of Mr. Glint.

"Maybe what?" she said. "You said maybe something."

"Maybe thin is the thing," he said.

"What are you talking about?"

"This one time Miss Gleam and I went to a dreamy place. We were gonna scrag your old pot and pan, Mr. Hughes."

Pot and pan. Husband. Cate found herself too listless and miserable to correct this mislabeling of her relationship. She listened as Glint went on in his coffin mold tones.

"In the dreamy place, Miss Gleam saw a world, lovely and spoiled, like a big tapioca what has turned runny and stenchlike on a hot day. I didn't see nothing. A pie crust of nothing going on and on. So I made my jaw wide as wide can be, and I ate that crust, and the filling below, and the bottomy base bit until I found Miss Gleam again in the dreamy place. Only it wasn't a pie I chomped and scruggled down my gizzard at all but my preconscious, conscious, and subconscious mind. I started to remember what it was like. Before the straps. The syringe pricks. Before Mr. Shine and Miss Gleam and Mr. Twinkle and everyone. Then I got to the... luminous bit. In here." He tapped the side of his gaunt head. "Mr. Gallant says that people believe so much is far away. Things they save up credits for. Places they've never poked a foot near. The person that they were before, and before, and before even that. And it makes them droop like droogles on a rainy day, thinking how far away that stuff is.

"But it's all thin. It's all conceptualization pie waiting to be gobbled up. And it's doors too." Glint made his left hand flat. "One side." His right hand joined in. "The other side. Both could be as broad as they fancy." He wriggled his hideous fingers in the space between the imaginary sides. "The door itself? Dead thin, gov."

"You're saying Evelyn is on one side of a door," Cate said quietly. "That she could come back just as easily as she left."

In response Mr. Glint pushed out his hands. A closed door opening.

"But how can you know that?" Cate snapped testily. "Whatever brought her away might operate like an elastic band, first stretching then contracting. It could be akin to a door, it's possible. But it might be a one-way system. She might be gone without any way of returning. Or worse, snatched by some malignant force that means her harm. I can't take that chance."

"Begging your pardon, Miss. What choice you got?"

And to that, Cate Jubilee had no answer.

***

There were houses, a green, a postbox. A few manicured gardens. A few ramshackle ones. No big hedges, only some thorny rose and bougainvillea tangles in the ones that were worse for wear, and the neater affairs were draped in potted plants. There were flowers blooming in those cold winter gardens that Hughes had never seen in his life. Their foreign and undiagnosable beauty made him think of Krys and The Mum. He had intended to ask Death about them. Maybe Rupert Prindlee would do well enough in her stead. Anyway it was a concern for later.

He was scared. More so than he would have believed. It seemed to Hughes that something very bad was going to happen. Or perhaps it had happened already and would strike him like a viper from a thicket of unassuming garden shadow. The idea that this feeling might be related to his girlfriend's predicament, much less Evelyn and her geographical upset, never occurred to him. Why would it? Rather it was a displaced feeling of dread, a soul-deep uncertainty. His rational mind asked him, *Are you sure you want to know what it's all about?*

And another part of him, irrational with cowardice and a responsive bravery fighting that flightful urge replied, *You want to. You've wanted to for as long as you can recall. Now do like your power's namesake and perform, you gutless gormless Hughes. If you can't be the man who faces the truth behind the curtain, then the least you can do is act like him.*

Muscles around his eyes moved uneasily, then settled once more. He drew in a breath. Set it free. Sent his misgivings free with them, and in doing so freed himself from their hold. His jaw set in the liquid concrete of resolve.

"Each of these houses is a world," Frank commented. "Seems unlikely."

Hughes agreed. The Willows estate was small. The idea that it contained every world, that Death had hidden them here somehow, was preposterous. It boggled the mind. Defied logical explication. He supposed Death was supremely powerful, and that allowed her to twist the laws that limited the universe. Even so... each house a world. It was unlikely, that was the perfect descriptor. Stupendously, totally unlikely.

"What would happen if I went in?" asked Frank. "Hopped out of the car, chose a house, and went in."

"You'd meet them," answered Rupert. "Provided you were welcome."

"Meet? You mean the world's people?"

"You misunderstand. The worlds themselves."

"Worlds that think."

This last was from Hughes. His voice drew every drop of attention, including his own. He'd been brooding, the words were unplanned. He almost leaped out of the car seat hearing them.

What's more, they jarred him toward a realization, one that sparked a few embers in the cold hearth of his doubt. Those embers caught, plumed, and leaped to incandescent life.

"No," he said, gazing at the side of Rupert's face. "You're taking me to meet *her*?"

Rupert nodded eagerly.

"Who?" said Frank, puzzled. "Meet who?"

"Iphigenia," said Hughes. "Rupert. You mean to tell me Jane wasn't lying. I'm a shadow, Iphigenia's shadow. You must tell me what that means, please, before we arr—"

"Why not let your caster do that for you?"

"My... my what?"

Rupert turned and fixed him with a guilelessly obliging expression. "Thanks to the light at the center of all things—Life and Death—every world in existence casts a shadow. *She* will tell you all, Hughes. Iphigenia. All that you'd care to know. I'd only make a hames of the explanation and you know it. It's why you've resisted asking me about your status as a shadow until now, despite it weighing on your mind. You know—or sense at the very least—that a better, more reliable reprieve is close at hand. Ooooh *crrrripes*," he squeaked, jittering with anticipation. "A shadow and his world having their first meeting. What fun, eh? Shame I won't be privy to it."

"Pardon?" said Hughes sharply.

But just then the car pulled into a drive. His doubts doused. He looked up at the three-story house. The lowest floor had walls festooned in weeds, flowers, and ivy. The next up had walls trussed in ribbons of rain-swollen vine, and toadish mushrooms poked through the bricks. The tallest floor was grainy and bare, a barren desert of architecture. At the top of the house there thrust a tall chimney, blue-gray brick topped by white. For a moment Hughes struggled to grasp what it reminded him of. The shape, it was so familiar, achingly familiar, it was...

It's...

Mountainous, he decided. *Yes, it would be like a mountain. Iphigenia has three regions: the forest, the swamp, and the moonlit desert. And the mountain looms over all.*

"Wait," he said. "Wait, take us out of here."

"Out of here?" Rupert looked affronted. "But you haven't gone in yet."

"Reverse the car. Take us back to the road."

"Everything okay?" said Frank.

"Frank, don't you see it? *Every* world. Including..."

Frank's foglamp-yellow eyes widened. "Eurydice. Damn, Hughes..."

"Your home world, Frank. The place where your mothers made you. The world that cast Jane as its shadow." Hughes turned excitedly in his seat. Energy, high and sudden, suffused him. "We can go there and do something about her."

"Do something about her?" Rupert did not look affronted now. His apple head was rotten and wormy with horror. "What do you mean?"

Hughes ignored him. "What do you think, Frank?"

"Tempting," said Frank. "Very tempting."

"What do you mean *do something about her?*" insisted Rupert.

Frank looked at Hughes. "Take that kettle in your head off the boil, pour this idea out."

"I'm not pulling away. I still want to speak to Iphigenia. After we speak to Eurydice."

"Oh," said Rupert, deflating. "By do something I thought you meant something drastic like..."

Hughes finally elected to glance at the boy. It was a glance of kindness and condemnation rolled into one. "Like subject Eurydice's people to the same treatment yours got at the hands of the Tarot Troupe? I'm not without my gruff moments, Rupert, not immune to the tidal exertions of my own temper. Even if there was no other choice, I like to think I'd be at least reluctant, and more likely disgusted, by the prospect of damning an entire civilization for the crimes of its sovereign. Some people might say 'oh well, it's for a greater good,' to which I say 'bugger that' for the cold-minded, iced-jelly-hearted bunk it is." Hughes might have said more, for the idea of cold-minded utilitarianism had put him in mind of his mother. But he resisted, biting off further tirade and letting solitary compassion shine from his face to soothe the telling-off he'd just given Rupert. Hughes returned his gaze to Frank, leaving Death's apprentice to stew on what he'd said.

"What I'm thinking about is the invasions. The ones Cate talked about. Eurydice sending her monsters to wreak havoc in Iphigenia, and sending Spring-Heeled Jane to my city. What if we can put two mysteries to rest today instead of one? The power behind Hughes' Performance *and* the motivation behind Eurydice's cruelty. I'll do you one better—what if we can subvert hostilities for good? Say for example Eurydice believes my world and Iphigenia have wronged her in some way. Offended her terrestrial sensibilities. One simple conversation, or even a bloody complex one, might resolve any misunderstanding of that nature, thus saving everyone who might be lost in the badness you and I both sense coming. We can't deny that her actions have pointed to some evil mentality toward what might be called—for lack of a better term—her neighboring communities. Let's curb that animosity now, Frank, if curbed it can be."

"If curbed it can be," Frank echoed. "I hear you, man. And I'll give you two good reasons why we ought to stick with the plan and leave off this idea of gabbing with Eurydice. Push it down the track a little."

Hughes nodded. "Go."

"Imagine you've been spurned, okay? Spurned so nastily you go on a rampage. If you are at that point in things, do you really want to explain the whole situation to some stranger? The stranger in this case being you, Hughes. Isn't it more likely that this stranger would become the new object of that rampage, and be thoroughly, cataclysmically messed up as a consequence? Food for thought, Hughes. That's the first thing. Second thing is this: Maybe it can be done. Maybe you can sell Eurydice on the fact that this whole thing is a misunderstanding—*if* a misunderstanding it is, and that's a big if. Fucking tectonic if. But for the sake of argument let's say she buys it. You're not dealing with what might be dubbed a stable personality. Eurydice as a world and as the feminine representation of that world, shit, she changes in the blink of an eye. You've seen some of that on your trips there and back. If the situation is not handled in the perfect way, every little thing falling into line, then my bet is that the moment things seem like they're going to be okay, Eurydice will do a total turnabout. Then all bets are off. Nothing's been gained. Plenty has been wasted."

Hughes had been listening, his excitement first quelling into a petulant determination, then a somber realization. Now, as he scraped his hand over the coarse bristles of his beard, slowwww rasps up and down the jaw, he made a little grunting noise in his mouth. "Well argued."

"Sorry."

"And I suppose even if I was set on talking to Eurydice, it'd be better to get a feel for her from Iphigenia. I just thought... if it could be resolved, then Iphigenia and I might meet on a more equal footing. She's given me something that's complicated my life, made it worse in some ways, yet so much better in others. I'd never have met you, Cate, Evelyn."

Frank took Hughes' chin and tilted his cloudy face so they were on a level.

His friend said, "Don't mope. Don't get in your head about this."

"I don't know what to do," Hughes replied, and a long way away indeed, Cate Jubilee told Mr. Glint the exact same thing.

"Pretend you do. Treat that black shirt as costume, the sounds of that house as sound effects, my eyes like spotlights, and my good opinion as the audience. Take my applause for granted. Whatever thunder in me is yours forever. Storm the stage now while the storming is good."

For the second time that day Frank had moved him. "Damn it." He sighed, but it was a hopeful sigh. "Okay, Frank. I will." Rallied, Hughes opened his door and got out. "Coming, Rupert?"

"I'm afraid I can't. It's part of the arrangement. Sticky business, but unavoidable."

"See you in a while then."

"I'll be here."

Hughes shut the door and walked toward the three-story house.

Frank joined him. "Still wild for me?" he asked.

"Of course."

"It'd never work between us."

"The lady of the evening has her claws in you."

"Gouge me. Bleed me. Never leave me."

Hughes grinned. "Same old Frank, chasing the interstitial point between excess and harmony."

"A pox on that. A raggedy, buboidinous, rubiginous pox. You are too cool for verse."

"And you for speeches. *Whatever thunder in me is yours.* Come on, Frank."

"Worked, didn't it?"

"Well, I suppose it did." Hughes tried the front door handle. It was open. "Never work out between us. Hmph. We can always dream."

***

Have you wondered who is telling you this story?

Have you guesses about who lives and who dies?

Those might already be percolating for you, here near the outset of our last story. Are they?

That's interesting.

Me? I don't need to guess. I know. I saw all of it play out from my... unique vantage point. When Lucy stuck us here in Glasnevin she didn't bother installing cable. Or streaming. Pretty big oversight.

Oh well. We entertain ourselves. We keep active. Fit. And we fit in too, those of us who know how to play nice. How to follow the rules, such as they are.

And we do that other thing. Endure. We endure. After what happened with those Tarot Troupe creeps, it's the least we can do.

Know me yet?

Yes. You do.

We've met before.

I still remember how he looked when he came into my house in The Willows.

My shadow.

I still remember because I had the good memory before he did. I'm the reason he's got his.

What did he look like? Not much. Just like the only hope I had. That's all.

***

It was stiflingly warm inside.

Hughes rolled up his sleeves, exposing hairy wrists, and sent his silent thanks to Evelyn. She'd given him a sound steer about the coat. He'd brought that, he would have baked alive.

Together he and Frank stood in a hall. The walls, the floor, the ceiling, they were all covered in tiny mosaic stones. The mosaics showed deep roots, tall trunks, and green canopies of leaves like crowns of fairy monarchs. Tart, dimpled, red berries hung like garlands and necklaces from the flowering bushes hunkered like floral dogs snuffling in the undergrowth. Swords of gold sunshine plunged through the branches of the trees and struck the carpet of misplaced leaves, the woods like emerald shale excalibured. Here and there along the hall, little clouds of midges spiraled, evoking those dust motes Hughes often saw occupying slants of sunshine.

His nostrils were tingling. The aroma filling them was mellow, tangy, fresh, luscious.

"What do you smell, Frank?"

Frank Gallant closed his eyes and inhaled deeply. He breathed out, opened his eyes, and gazed at Hughes in naked awe. "Spring in January."

"Me too."

"Where do you think she is?"

"In here," called a feminine voice from the claggy, sweetly-smelling depths of the house. A figure poked their head around quickly, asking, "Neither of you thought to bring Solpadeine, did you? Only I've a migraine you could bend iron around, a real horse-shoer of a headache," before vanishing just as quickly, murmuring, "Oh, but I suppose you wouldn't have. I should have sent a message. You could have called into a pharmacy along the way. Never mind. Won't you come in? You're very welcome."

Hughes and Frank exchanged surprised looks.

Solpadeine? Hughes mouthed.

Frank shrugged—he hadn't a notion.

Following the rumble-rattle of a kettle coming to boil, they came to a kitchen. The mosaics were still present—organic and bursting with rich greens and windblown petals in a kaleidoscope of colors—and there were cupboards of herbs, drawers of spices, decanters, pots, jars, blocks, pans, and cabinets, all scattered higgledy-piggledy under the light of a chandelier. The chandelier was like a flower, the flower from which all those petals in the wall mosaic originated, a nice seamless effect. It was a Jupiter Fly Trap, close cousin of the Venus, and the much larger of the two. A network of veins ran along it from trigger hair to nectar gland, greenish-blue and vermiculate.

Nursing a cup of steaming-hot soup and leaning her back against the kitchen table was a woman. Her hair was strawberry-blonde, verging on true sunset. It was cropped very short, a tomboyish cut. She had huge eyes, not supernaturally large, but fantastically big, soft, and green like the sea in April. Maybe they were starker than they would have been were she healthy.

And she was not healthy. Not by a stretch.

Pencil wrists and a hollow-throated, sylvan neck emerged from her baggy daffodil-yellow sweater. Her cheeks were peaches bitten to the hard seed. Her legs were wasted—her leaning against the table seemed like necessity rather than ease, as though the jaunt from here to the door that led to the hall had taxed her greatly.

Hughes' eye was practiced and subtle. Practically undetectable. But the way she smiled at him made him feel like a gaping fool. Such a knowing smile.

"You filled out, Hughes. I've filled in."

He mistook her meaning. "I'm sorry. I didn't know that a shadow thriving would have adverse effects for its world. Actually, I don't have a clue—"

"Don't be crazy. You haven't done this to me. It's that vile creature. That harpy. Eurydice." The woman's baleful expression evaporated. She put out her hand like a zoologist proffering some brittle specimen. "I'm Iphigenia. It's wonderful to finally meet you."

Hughes shook her hand, very carefully. "Likewise."

"I'm at your disposal. Cross my heart, I'll explain everything. You're hungry. I'll fix you some soup."

"Let me," said Frank smoothly. "You two sit yourselves down."

And so saying, Frank Gallant executed a small performance of his own. He became a fixture of the kitchen, a fly on the wall, an audience sitting unobtrusively in the dark while the show got on the road. Hughes adored him for that.

"I'm sorry about the heat," said Iphigenia. "Lately I haven't been able to keep warm. It's like my weight. I eat and eat and it just falls off me. I've stopped worrying about it. No use worrying. Was the journey all right? I lost track of you when you left Saint Mauritius' graveyard."

"It was fine."

"Really?"

"Mostly fine. We came through Dreaming Jija."

"And something happened there."

It wasn't a question. She could see it in his face.

"We can discuss it later. It's not important," said Hughes. "I want to talk to you."

She leaned back in her chair, rooting in her sweater pocket. "I'm at your disposal."

"So you've said." He paused, not liking how his voice had sounded there. He tried a smile. It came forced, so he added, "Thank you."

Iphigenia took out a cigarette. "That's okay." She held the cigarette over her head. The Jupiter Fly Trap chandelier gave a little fizzle, as though the bulbs inside it were on the fry. The cigarette lit at once. Iphigenia took a drag of it, folded one arm over her emaciated stomach and crooked her other elbow on it. Her fingers with their red painted nails held the cigarette aloft, an image that struck Hughes as terribly familiar. "What would you like to know first?" she said.

This he was ready for.

"What is a shadow?"

It earned a wry curl of her lips. "Good opener. Well, in the sense that you mean, a shadow is a projection of a world caused by the cycles of the universe. Life and Death smash against one another, and like atoms in a reactor they produce energy. That energy has no name—certainly not that I'm aware of—and I've never seen it as you've never seen gravity or magnetism, only the effects of these phenomena. A world is born out of a moment in which that energy reaches a kind of crescendo. There's chance involved. And strong emotion. Fiercely, unimaginably strong emotion. It's complicated. Interesting though. I've thought a lot about it. Anyway, when a world is born it can, over time, develop an additional consciousness. One that splits off from the world and does its own thing. That's what a shadow is." She inhaled, blew a smoke ring, inhaled, blew a flock of smoky sparrows flying through the ring. She indicated Hughes with the smoldering end. "That's what you are."

"And Jane?"

"Yes. Jane told you the truth about that, and about her being Eurydice's shadow. It behooved her to give you a hard time. She enjoyed playing cat and mouse. Too late she figured out the roles weren't quite as she'd imagined."

A tiny twist of pleasure sparkled in those huge green eyes, then it was gone.

Hughes wondered how to phrase his next question. Perhaps simplicity was called for. "Am I a human being?" he said.

"Sure. You can be both."

"What happens when I die?"

"You'll go to your underworld like everyone else, whichever one awaits you. Could be Hades, could be Murimuria or Burotu. Odin One Eye's Mead Hall. Emain Ablach if you're really lucky. There's a thousand and one underworlds."

"And after that? Where do we go after the underworlds stop prolonging our consciousness?"

Iphigenia smiled sadly. "That, I think, only Death herself knows. Maybe not even her. If there is something after the underworld's fall and all things fade, I suppose I'll meet you there. Shadows are about as durable as worlds in the grand scheme of things. The Tarot Troupe proved that long ago."

That troubled Hughes. At the same time it made him light-headed with relief. Being existentially unbalanced had threatened to knock him off the tightrope of sanity and lucidity. He hadn't realized how close he'd come to despair and possible madness until now, when Iphigenia had declared he was a normal person after all. Well, a normal person with a few asterisks, perhaps. In the same region of ordinary living, if not quite the same postcode.

He looked down. Sometime in the past few moments, a cup of soup had been set in front of him. God, Frank was surreptitious. No sign of him about the kitchen now. He might have been there, discreet and hidden with his magical strings. If he wasn't, Hughes suspected his friend would remain close by. That gave him comfort, a useful resource in the thick of strange revelation upon stranger discovery.

Hughes drank the soup. "Good," he said. "Delicious."

"You like it?" said Iphigenia.

"Really good. Coriander?"

"Lots of spices. Some chicken too, for the weight I can't seem to regain. I suppose I do worry a little."

"You said Eurydice is responsible?"

"I did. But I can see you want to ask me about another thing. Is it the Performance?"

"How could you tell?"

"A woman knows her shadow. Especially when his scruffy mug gives away the whole game."

"Can you act through me?" Hughes said, disguising his unease at the idea.

"Indirectly," she said and smiled as he imperceptibly relaxed. Again, he had the sense she was reading his mind. "We'll talk about Performance. That's how I do it."

"Yes, you daintily lift the leg and it's me who does the farting. I see how it is." She laughed. Quietly.

Any louder and you'll come apart, Hughes thought.

"So tell me," he said. "How does Performance work? Why is it all symbology and numerics?"

"The percentage chance and Level Ups and stuff? That was part affectation, part kindness."

"How so?"

"I thought it'd be easier for you. I knew the power would manifest when you were a kid. I thought a little boy would grasp a game."

"So there is no percentage?" said Hughes. "It either works or it doesn't? What decides that?"

"In my view the percentage system is actually pretty good. Somewhere you understood there were lots of factors in a successful Performance, and plenty in failures. Sorry about the Congratulations, by the way. I think I got carried away."

"Yeah, I was going to ask, were you purposefully being mean?"

"No, no!"

"Sure?"

They were laughing together. From his fly-on-the-wall spot, a silent Frank Gallant frowned. Hughes and Iphigenia were so different on the face of things. Just then as they'd been fooling around and joshing, they'd looked not simply like siblings, but identical twins. How could that be?

"Why not send a message that explained it all?" Hughes asked. "Why all the cloak and dagger?"

"Put yourself in my position. I don't want to compare you to an instrument—"

"There's that famous kindness."

"Oh, quit it you."

More laughter. *Dark and light*, thought Frank, observing closely. *Him dark and her light. This is too weird.*

"But if you were to expose an instrument to abrasion, it would stop working."

"Ah, I see. You had to keep me tuned and playing like a prized fiddle?" Hughes asked.

She covered her face, shoulders shaking with embarrassment and joy. "I'm making such a mess of this, aren't I?"

"No," Hughes replied, and he meant it. "No, this is going better than I could have dreamed."

They smiled at one another.

"I'm glad," said Iphigenia.

"What about the night I was with Cate?" said Hughes. "The night in the park when she and I hashed it all out?" He was thinking about Honesty. *The elixir of hope*, his powers had dubbed it.

"That?" Iphigenia shrugged like a thin coatrack coming to life. "Well, it's what I believe. And you? You think it was okay of me to point out?"

"I'm still unspooling that particular ball of yarn. Was it okay? I think so. Anyway, I understand now. You gave me Performance and made it like a game so I could understand it to some degree without becoming overwhelmed. Now I've seen so much and accomplished and lost, I'm ready for the truth."

She nodded, slurped the ends of her soup, apologized for slurping (further charming Hughes), and stubbed out her cigarette.

"I think I'll have another. Would you care for one?"

"Please."

They sat together in the kitchen in the house in The Willows, smoking and studying one another, and the room, and one another some more. Not making a secret of it. It was fine. Better than fine.

"Where were we?" said Iphigenia. "Aheh, yes. The internal whatchamacallit. Processes, I guess. Performance works exactly as you understand it. You push out and cause a change in other people. Sometimes it's what you might call a superficial adjustment. Other times the change is deeper."

"Chimera."

"Mm. Yes. Like it?"

"The name?"

"Yes."

"I suppose I do."

"The sword I gave you was only the signature. A little exclamation point to mark the occasion."

The sword you gave me...

Feeling as though a seismic shift were happening under his feet, his heart going staccato, threatening to stop, and his skin rashing out in gooseflesh, Hughes knew where he'd seen those red-painted fingernails, that cigarette. He had seen them before, many, many times throughout the course of his adventures. In the most spectacular instance, he'd seen them emerge from the chest of a two-headed wolf in...

His eyes widened.

She looked at him. She knew his mind.

A woman knows her shadow. I've been hers this whole time.

Under her auspice. Her protection. And beneath that frumpy sweater, he knew what her arms would look like. Long and too-trim.

Long arms. Red fingernails. Cigarette smoke.

Puzzle pieces scrambled, tucking together smartly and without hesitation now that he was sitting before his benefactor. Those arms had kept him safe from the Nightjar Coven. They had appeared in the hospital when he'd defeated Jane. And, dear God yes, they had burst from the body of the wolf—the two-headed, wormy, slobbering horror that had killed a woman named Laurana

(hooyou?)

and her squad.

Long arms. Red fingernails. Cigarette smoke.

And a smell. Yeah, there'd been a smell. Nourishing and sweet like...

This time his heart really did stop.

Like spring in January.

"Holy shit," he said. The words came in a low, lung-squeezed croak.

"You look unwell," said Iphigenia, all concern. "Ghostly."

Hughes took a moment. At last normal respiration returned. "It's fine. Assembling the fact that you've taken a... what would you call it... a *defensive role* in my life... it's brought back some unpleasant memories."

"I'm sorry."

Quickly, tersely, he dismissed this. "It's all right. I'm all right."

Her eyes on him suddenly felt like rubbing alcohol, a necessary hurt on the way to recovery. And also like an accusation. Absurd but true. And he didn't think she was accusing him of anything, a suspicion that firmed into certainty when she said, "I'm sorry about what *she* did too. Withholding the truth. What she did is *extremely* unpleasant."

The idea that the waifish, sad, beautiful world of a woman could somehow precede him—blatantly predict what he was going to say—hit him a moment after the image of Wendy's body on the balcony.

Hughes stared in open astonishment. It shaded to caution.

Iphigenia shook her head—no, the gesture said, she couldn't see the future.

He had grown up in Leonidas District, a place where survival often meant placing suspicion over trust, so some part of him filed the idea away for further study.

"Thanks," he said. "For keeping me safe."

Another smile as she dragged on her smoke. This one shone from her mouth and lent her whole self an occult mysticism that jarred with the smart, doelike woman he'd been speaking to. *She's entitled to being more than one thing*, he chided himself. *Like the rest of us. After all, this house has three floors and a chimney. You can't have the nice woods without the nasty swamp or the hot/cold desert for that matter.*

"You're welcome, Hughes," she said. "What else tickles your curiosity?"

The time had come for him to learn more about her. He'd indulged the subject of himself for what felt like hours, though it was impossible to tell how much time was passing in this chafingly hot greenhouse of a kitchen.

"Let's get into this Eurydice problem."

She nodded agreement. "Let's."

"How did it start? How's it developed? What's the endgame?"

"It started that day you set foot on my soil."

"With the two-headed wolf."

"Yes. Up until then I'd felt this odd feeling like someone was creeping up behind me, someone who meant to hurt me. I hadn't felt anything like it, and by the time I got around to investigating, it was too late. After that it was a matter of degrees. The wolf was the pebble signaling a landslide, you see."

"Eurydice's invasion."

"First of me, then of your world. For some reason I can't explain, the invasion is paring me down. Diluting me. *Thinning* me. I get headaches. Sick, so violently sick I wish it would all be over. Don't worry, I'm exaggerating... sort of exaggerating. I shouldn't wonder that your world is undergoing something similar."

"Does my world have a shadow?"

"Yes, I believe so. But he's a lazy world, sleepy and given to turning a blind eye. Lazier than you could conceive of! I can't imagine he'll take much of an interest in saving anyone. Even himself. As to where this problem is going to end, I haven't an inkling. Eurydice has gone mad. She's lashing out."

"How can a world go insane?" Hughes asked.

"How do people? Things fall apart."

"The center cannot hold."

Iphigenia blew another smoke ring and sent smoky bees bumbling through it. "It was William Butler Yeats who said that."

"Hm?"

"That things fall apart. He was Irish, you know. Born not far from this estate. Not around the corner, mind, but not far as these things go."

"How would a poet in my world have written the same thing?" Hughes asked, baffled.

"Things do fall apart but they also endure. Sometimes they get so strong as to cross thought and time. I think that's how ideas live and die, by traveling."

"Hm."

That was all he could say, hm. What else was there to say to that notion? It was too big to fit inside a tired head, especially one that was already full to bursting with new information. Hughes let it go. He puffed at his own cigarette, enjoying the way the end winked orangely like a piece of morse code from hell.

"So Eurydice has gone gaga," he said. "That fits with Jane being so scattered and rotten-to-the-bone. Caster imitates shadow and vice versa. What can be done? Will Death or any of the powers that be help us? Do they give a shit?"

"Lucy cares. But in order for things to continue smoothly around here, she has to care a little to the left."

"That indirect approach again."

"Uh huh."

"How come?"

"There you and I are both indisposed; I really don't know. If I had to guess, I suppose I'd say it's part of some ineffable plan."

"Hm."

"Hm."

Another swift grin at one another across the tabletop. A girlish grin; its boyish echo.

"Either that," said Iphigenia, "or it's basic nature."

Cate's battle mantra slipped from his memory to Hughes' tongue. "You try to kill me. I try to kill you."

Iphigenia was looking up at the chandelier now, tracing its contours. "Eurydice tries to kill us. We try to kill her. No interference lending strength or deliverance to one side or the other."

Which means it's up to Corinth City, Hughes thought dolefully. *It's up to us and every other city and town and hamlet to get our acts together. It means we're going to war, and God help us.*

"You won't need God," Iphigenia said. Her eyes—wide and green as springtime without end—were bright. "I said *we,* didn't I?"

Chapter Six

Time does not pass in The Willows. Not conventionally. It strobes. Blink, and something aesthetic or vital has probably changed.

During his time with Iphigenia, Hughes took note of that. Using the amazing collection of herbs in her kitchen he brewed her his favorite tea, cardamom and fennel. She pronounced it yummy. When he sat back down opposite her, Hughes saw that the room's mosaic had changed. The chandelier too. Now that glass fixture overhead was an egg rather than a flower. The egg was broken, the shell splayed wide. Those same vermiculate lines took on new meanings to suit the new shape—cracks in the speckled shell. Instead of leaves and petals, the mosaics filling the kitchen walls are aflutter with birds. Larks, tanagers, owls of barn and tawny plumage, peacocks, crows, sparrows, on and on, wings swirling round the chandelier egg like they were born from it. Also that mellow forest smell had become freer, more open and less sweet in his nose. Still redolent of spring, just in a different fashion. The perfume of a wind laden with gorgeous birds in endless migration.

Over time Hughes would come to associate this rapid strobing effect with his baby girl (more on that later), but right then he thought, *Is this how Iphigenia sees time?* He believed so. *It makes sense. A world lives so very, very long. Isn't the length of a human blink sufficient time for many insects to mature? By the time we go to sleep and wake up, who knows how many creatures have lived entire lives. To Iphigenia, people like Cate and I must be the most fascinating things. So intent and purposeful. Then—blink—and all our seasons have come to a too-swift close. Blink, and the dance that seemed so important while we danced it is over.*

Eventually the rigors of lively conversation took their toll on his host.

Claiming exhaustion Iphigenia announced she had better go upstairs and rest. The claim's currency spent well with Hughes. The woman looked five whole steps beyond fatigue, not to mention the illness gnawing and dissolving her body.

"I feel as though we could talk for a year and not be satisfied." She sighed as she saw her pair of visitors out. Frank gave them respectful space. "Ten years. A hundred. We could natter on till the last cow plods home and the rooster retires his crow. Don't you think so, Hughes?"

"Yes, I think so."

"I've had an idea. Want to hear it?"

Hughes told her he was all ears.

"Let's chat every night. Maybe every night might be impossible... but every chance we get!"

"How?"

"I'll tell you. Right in that space between wakefulness and slumber, NREM I think it's called, try and fixate on a photograph of this house. One your eyes snapped from today. Focus on that picture and I'll open my door to you. I bet we'll have time to ask one another a question or two before you fall into deep sleep."

Hughes said he would like nothing more.

"Splendid!" She laughed, quieter than ever. She held out her arms to him. As they embraced Hughes marveled at those arms. Thin enough to snap like matchsticks. Strong enough to save his life time after time.

Her voice rose to him, slightly muffled against his shirt. "I'm glad we're friends."

"Me too."

"You'll go through with all of it?"

"Yes."

"Even if it makes you unhappy?"

"I'm unhappy about it now."

"Don't be. Shake that wintry mood off like Boochums the dog after running through a snow pile. Are you happy again?"

"I'll get there."

"Good," she said, smiling up at him. "Spring's just around the corner. New opportunities will come up for you. It's an exciting time."

"Yeah, I know," said Hughes. But they both knew that other things were round the corner. Things that lurked. Things that schemed and groped for purchase. Iphigenia was not the only world on this estate.

They said, rather awkwardly:

"Okay."

"Okay."

And then, rather less so:

"Hm."

"Hm."

Last grins like last drinks shared under the wooly Irish clouds. Rain on the way. Or sleet. It was cold enough for sleet.

"See you soon," Iphigenia said, drawing back inside and looking askance at him.

Hughes held up a hand, a gesture that said farewell and please don't go. She went. He got into the car. Frank got in with him.

"So," said a cheerful Rupert Prindlee. "How did it go?"

***

Of course, he replied that it went as fine as he could have imagined.

And in a way that was true.

Only not the whole truth.

"Rupert," said Hughes. "Before we go, I'd like to see Eurydice's house."

"Hughes." Frank's voice, couched with warning.

Hughes held both hands up in a placative, *Don't worry*, gesture. "I just want to see it," he said.

The car pulled out of the drive. Instead of turning left toward the estate exit, it turned right.

There was a little boy with dark hair on the street. Crayons in his chubby fist. As Hughes looked at him, he seemed to be a young man at a typewriting desk, a middle-aged man at a computer, an old man with dictation software. Then the sleet began to fall, heavy and chill, and the boy gathered his crayons and paper and dashed into his house.

"Who was that?" Hughes asked Rupert.

"You know, I'm absolutely top-notch with names," Rupert replied. "And yet I do not know him."

"Even a clock well-run tells times we don't like."

"A riff on the common saying, how nice!"

They drove past houses slowly, steadily, heading deeper into The Willows. Sleet thumped and splashed. The windshield wipers cleared the worst of the mush.

Deeper they went, and concomitantly Hughes sank deeper into thought.

The whole truth was that Iphigenia had tasked him. She had tasked him with work of the highest importance. And there in her kitchen he had said yes.

His superb memory played it out, as it would rerun the scene many times in the days to come.

After she reminded him that she had said, "we," rather than, "you," as in *Eurydice tries to kill us. We try to kill her*, Iphigenia had reached out to him across the table.

He took her hand without hesitation.

And once more, for the sake of old times, she gave him her gift in the old, ludic way.

<table>
<tr><td colspan="1" align="center">Hughes, Shadow of Iphigenia</td></tr>
</table>

Hughes, Shadow of Iphigenia
Level Up! *24 → 25* Max Level Attained! Congratulations!
Secret Ability Unlocked: Menin Your Performance can now draw out the ingredients for magic item creation from the creatures of Iphigenia. No longer will death need be dealt beforehand. From this peace, my shadow, shall we make a most terrible war.
Current Bonus: 51%

Frank later told him that the room had filled with a pale green light, so intense he had been forced to envelop himself in string or risk going blind.

Hughes admitted he hadn't been aware of that. Menin ran itself alongside Chimera and Faethe; snug companions combing the fibers of his being with filaments of exquisite power.

"But the Citadel has hunted them for so long," he said, meaning the beasts in Iphigenia. "Don't um... get me wrong." This with a stunned little laugh. "It's amazing. Just a hard sell. Violence, like these cigarettes we really ought to quit, is a habit. Peace between Corinth and Iphigenia will involve a dramatic shift in thinking."

She favored him with a squeeze of his hand. It cost her effort. Her frailty frightened him.

"That's okay. Soon you'll be in a position to cause dramatic shifts in thinking."

Hughes frowned at that. "What do you mean?"

"Well, the Citadel was founded by a Dragontail. You won't force it to break that habit, will you?"

He looked at her with dawning realization. "You mean for me to lead them?"

"Sure. Gormon Dragontail. Oh no."

"What?"

"You winced. Maybe Hughes is fine."

"Yes, I... think that'd be best. Ahm..." He retrieved his hand, ran it over his beard bristles. Pensive. Distressed. "I don't know about that."

"You'd better know it. And you'd better know that your home country of Corinthia can't hold the fort on its own. You're going to—"

"Hold on."

"Going to need the whole world!"

"That's too far. I won't be a king." His expression was an arrow, his voice the drawback of the string. "Maybe I can stomach being the leader of the Citadel. The city and the tower are one. Stomach it, what bullshit. Even the idea of that thrills me. But it scares me too. The sheer responsibility. Wendy was a tyrant but things *worked* under her rule. The trains ran on time."

"It was all roses then."

Who would have believed it? Biting sarcasm from a world.

"I didn't say that," Hughes protested. "She wasn't perfect—"

"You called her a tyrant."

"And she was, and she was. Listen to me: there is no other kind of meaningful leadership. The difference is democracy. When the medicine is arranged in a neat package, it's easier to swallow. My mother's death has opened the door to that. Only, God, only the other day I heard a rumor about dissolving parliament and holding a vote for a kind of president."

"That'll be you," said Iphigenia. "Hughes, don't recoil at that. I'm asking you not to. Hunch your shoulders if you want. Disconsolately smoke. Here, have another!" It struck his shoulder, fell to the floor. Hughes made no effort to get it. They sat in surly silence for a moment. Iphigenia tamped out her cigarette in the soup cup. "Turn it around, now you listen to me. Eurydice is on the warpath. She's barreling toward something awful. Are you telling me you'll condemn your world and me along with it because of something you believe? You think that's right?"

"No, I—"

"You think that's right?"

"I don't have a fucking clue what's right. I'm a new father to a little girl. Father of a nation?"

"Of many nations."

"Yeah, I'm not cut out for it. I'm not." He huffed at his smoke. Tried to blow a smoke ring. Found she was better at them. His were only a shadow of the real thing. He looked down at his knuckles, that pettish refusal slinking away as his brain turned the matter over. "What eh... What'll happen? Say I don't become president. Unite Corinthia and other places against her. Eurydice."

"You're not a child," Iphigenia said. Her tone was icy, frosty bracken in March. "You know exactly what'll happen."

Hughes said nothing for a long time. Then, without breaking that silence, he put out his hand.

Iphigenia tentatively took it.

He gave her fingers the lightest squeeze.

She broke into a big smile. The insolence was forgiven. They were with one another again.

"I'll think about it," he said.

"Okay," she said.

They both knew there was nothing to think about. No mind reading required.

"What does it mean?" he'd asked her.

"Huh?"

"Menin. What does it mean?"

"Oh," she said. "Wrath. It means wrath."

In the backseat of the car, Hughes chewed the inside of his cheek.

The acceptable truth was that he couldn't cope with being in a position of such total power. Better to foist it on the people. Let them decide which way the compass spun. No more absolute north. Polarity dictated by ballot. Rock and roll.

"There it is," said Rupert Prindlee. "Eurydice's house."

Hughes leaned over to join Frank peering out his window.

"Fuck," he said. Never had the word been so eloquent.

"Fuck is right," said Frank. "Far off from these a slow and silent stream, Lethe the River of Oblivion rolls, her wat'ry Labyrinth whereof who drinks, Forthwith his former state and being forgets, Forgets both joy and grief, pleasure and pain."

"A Mr. Glint composition?"

"Milton."

Hughes had never heard of him. Even if he had, the name might have meant nothing to him in that moment, so harrowed was he by the sight of Eurydice's house in The Willows. He could not for the life of him believe what he was seeing.

"Those slants," he said.

"Those lights," said Frank.

Pale, stricken-faced, and seized with a fit of muscular spasms in his abdomen, Hughes retreated from the window. "Rupert," he muttered.

"Yes, Mr. Hughes?"

"This was a mistake. Could you take us out of this place, please?"

"Of course."

They left The Willows, Glasnevin, and wet, forgettable Ireland.

Hughes tried to get his pounding heart under control.

Frank had his head in his hands. "Fuck," he said.

Hughes grinned anemically. "Fuck is right."

***

The acceptable truth was that he would have to do as Iphigenia asked. No alternative. He could do it his own way, but at the end of the day it would have to be done.

But then, the acceptable truth is rarely the whole truth.

As Iphigenia kept him, Hughes kept the facts within arm's reach.

The whole, raw, complete truth was that the idea of being king sort of excited him.

***

As the car sped away from the forbidding house, a figure appeared in one of the windows. The window frame was just one small piece of the house's horror. Around it sculptures of unnamable birds and other gargoyles were fused in a messy, tortured tangle. Necrophagous white bugs seemed to leak from the stone like maggots squeezing through a coffin lid.

The figure in the window watched as the car turned onto the road opposite Glasnevin cemetery, merged into traffic, and drove away. The figure didn't know who was in the car. She could make a fair guess though.

Things were really moving now. How fun.

A small sound disturbed her.

She turned her attention away from the view to the bundle in her arms.

"Hushabye, Jane. Hushabye."

Looking up into the figure's face, Evelyn smiled toothlessly.

***

Refusing to accept there was nothing she could do, Cate had geared herself into overdrive. Weighing the pros and cons of a bad selection, Desdemona Cauldronpot seemed her best option. She contacted Desdemona's friends. They didn't know where she could be found. Did Desdemona have siblings? No, and no surviving parents, aunts, or uncles either. But there was a cousin who worked in admin at the Sequins Messenger Club, another cousin who was currently in prison for an online larceny racket, as well as an assortment of nieces and nephews.

Calling in a few favors and recruiting Montcrieff (normally Cate would have reached out to Falstaff but the usually dependable butler had been MIA since Wendy Dragontail's death at Tinfrost), she chased these leads down. Eventually her rekindled hopes gathered like a fire around an extremely nervous moth—the perp cousin stewing in the joint. Luck was with her. Before her departure, Desdemona had felt it incumbent on herself to visit this cousin—a greasy, snide fellow named Lenny Caldwell. No love was lost between them, which meant the glass partition in the visiting room was pretty welcome. In exchange for a promise to discuss leniency in his case—something she was not sure she could actually achieve, but right then Cate would have promised him the moon—Lenny told her that Desdemona (Denise, he called her by her old name) had gone straight from the prison to the port. She was going to Jaenqui-Across-The-River on an occult retreat. She was dead set on "opening her mind to the intrinsic fluctuations of the cosmos" or so she told Lenny. "Whatever the shit that means," he growled in Cate Jubilee's ear. "Hey, you'll come through for me about this leniency thing, right? The judge is a real hardcase."

"Sure thing," said Cate and hung up.

Every drop of misery was wrung out of her. The speediness and totality of its effect on her was unnerving, but right now Cate was too preoccupied to give a damn. No one hands you a brochure and says, "Sometimes you will panic. Sometimes being a mother is about diving headfirst into sorrow. A river of sorrow. Then it becomes about building a bridge and getting over it."

The moment she hung up on greasy Lenny Caldwell, she dialed the central telecom depot number.

"Operator, this is Cate Jubilee, Scarlet Citadel code 11Q4. Can you put me through to the portmaster's office in Nikandros? I need high priority status on this."

"Yes, Miss Jubilee."

"Thanks."

A few clicks, then a tone trilled in her ear.

Trill, trill.

Pick up.

Trill, trill.

I swear to God.

Trill, trill.

Pick up the ph—

"This is Janet Rusby, who am I speaking to?"

"Cate Jubilee."

"Miss Jubilee. What can I do for the Citadel today?"

Cate explained the situation, truncated, snappy, fast. Her mind showed her a galling image while she talked: Cate on the apartment couch, shoulders slumped, talking about not knowing what to do. How could she have fallen to pieces like that? It was so unlike her. *Learn and move on,* she told herself. *That was then and this is now, and Evelyn still needs you.*

What choice you got? Mr. Glint had said.

A simple one. Stay blown to bits or put yourself back together.

Baby, hold on. Hold on, your mother is going to find you.

She finished her spiel.

"Give me one moment," said Rusby.

Cate waited.

"You're in luck, Miss Jubilee. That vessel is still in the water. We've sent a message to the captain. The weather's bad but we've got no interference on our end. With any luck, he'll be making an announcement to the crew right at this moment."

"Can you organize a boat for me?"

"Say again?"

"A boat," Cate said, cool and collected. "I'd rather meet them on the water than wait for the ship to dock. Time is of the essence here."

"Miss Jubilee, I'll see what I can do."

"I'll be there in three minutes."

If she couldn't trust her eyes to find suitable reflective surfaces in this muggy, rainy day, it might take as long as five. Her luck was turning though. She'd push it a little further.

She hung up the phone and took off.

Mr. Glint opened the door for her and made to follow.

"You stay here, Mr. Glint. In case that door theory of yours pans out."

With her back turned she didn't see him nod, only heard her front door closing shut, but that was enough.

Cate had just reached the apartment complex elevator, scanning its current floor to see if it would be worth waiting or legging it down the stairs, when she heard it.

Plaintive and squalling.

She thought, *Crying.*

She thought, *Baby.*

Mr. Glint must have been listening for her footsteps because the door swung inward just in time. Cate ran inside.

There, sitting in her chair as if she had never left and crying a "hold me, love me" cry was Evelyn.

When Hughes arrived with Frank two hours later, the tension in the room hit him like a pot of scalding water.

He registered the apartment in an instant, deciding it had the feel of mess that has been well made and then brought back under control. He looked at Cate, who was lying on the sofa with her body and her concentration curled around Evelyn, and Mr. Glint, who was in the process of lifting up the refrigerator in case there was anything interesting under there, since all the excitement had left him rather peckish.

"What's the matter?" Hughes said.

"Little moppet tottled off for a spell," said Mr. Glint. "Back now."

"It's true." Cate's voice drifted up from where she was lying down. "We're sorted and settled. Daddy and Evelyn went for a jaunt, but now they're both back, aren't they?"

Evelyn could sense Cate was speaking to her. She burbled happily, unaware of the alarming flatness in her mother's tone. Hughes sat down next to them. He rested a hand on his lover's jean-clad thigh.

"Kitten. What happened?"

"I wrote to you."

"I'm so sorry, babe. I didn't check it. There's no excuse for that, and I'll be better in future. Promise."

"It's okay."

"You say Evelyn *went somewhere*?" Hughes persisted. "Where? How?"

"I tried asking her but she's been sworn to secrecy."

"Cate, don't joke."

"She disappeared. A few hours later she reappeared."

"I heard you. I'm asking how that's possible."

She gave him daggers. "How would a copper like Thud put it? Oh yes. *We are continuing our inquiries.*" She saw how that hurt him. Softened. Raised herself up to a sitting position. Her lips twitched in a regretful curl. Cate kissed him. "Sorry. Sorry, Puppy. I haven't made any headway on the hows and whys. While she was gone it was terrifying. Now she's back it's... It was like waking up in the Citadel recovery ward. After Eurydice?"

"Sure."

"Surreal. Like all of it had happened to someone else. And she's soaked her nappy, but I'm afraid to change her."

"I'll change her."

"We can't let her out of our sight. She might—"

"We won't."

"—go again, we can't let that happen."

He pulled her to him. Stroked her hair.

He saw Frank whisper to Mr. Glint. They headed out. Frank glanced back, met Hughes' eye, and tapped his wrist with three fingers. *Give you space. Back in thirty minutes.*

Hughes nodded. Good old Frank.

He looked down and couldn't resist a washed-out smile. Evelyn was gumming Cate's little finger as if it were, if not delicious, then at least interesting. She shook one fist toward the window as though admonishing the weather outside.

"That's right," Cate said. "It's dark. And the rain's stopped."

It had too.

Hughes thought nothing of that at the time. He would come back to this moment later, longingly, yearningly.

But he had no idea what was coming, so he went on smiling.

Until his eye snagged on the thing poking out of Evelyn's dungarees. It was in the front pocket. Dull and only peeking out a little, but yeah.

"What is that?" he asked Cate.

"What is what?"

Hughes reached into the pocket and pulled out a letter. It was small and sealed in wax. The wax was a glimmering pinkish color. The seal showed a broken harp. *No*, thought Hughes, his confusion growing. *Not a harp. A broken lyre.*

Cate was right there with him. "I didn't check the pocket," she murmured. "I checked her all over to make sure she was unhurt. But I never checked the pocket, I..." She trailed off as Hughes opened it.

He read the letter's contents. Knotting his insides, confusion turned to anger. Anger thickened to fury. Cate must have seen it because the moment he was done she snatched it from him and read.

Dear Jane,

Thank you for your kind and thoughtful visit. It is So Nice to make a new friend. Although for us new friends might as well be old friends, since I have known you almost as long as I have known myself.

To Gormon Hughes and Cate Jubilee (your mum and dad) I extend a cordial Hello. It is possible that they will burn this letter and you will never read it, my darling Jane. If they do, they will Regret It. Because I bet you will come back and visit me someday (soon, I hope) and maybe by then you will understand the difference between preserving Well-Intentioned Correspondence and destroying it. Maybe you and I will become even closer than we are now. Won't you be PO'ed at Mum and Dad for getting in the way of us?

I know I would be.

If they do not burn this letter, and you are reading it now, then I am grateful to them and you should be too. Give them Big Kisses and Bigger Hugs.

I hope that you are having a wonderful day. The day I wrote this letter was the first time you came to see me, and so for me it was The Most Wonderful Day Of All.

Signed, your Loving big sister,
Eurydice

"Oh my God," said Cate. Her arm, relaxing thanks to Hughes' presence, clutched Evelyn closer than ever.

Meanwhile Hughes was staring out the window into the black January night.

Menin, Iphigenia dubbed his final power. *Wrath. It means wrath.*

Act Two

Frère Jacques

Chapter Seven

At the house of Iphigenia:
"Hello?" said a tentative voice.
"Hughes, you came."
"I did. Will it always be like this?"
"Like what?"
"Floaty. Soupy."
"Of course. Think about it. When you come to talk to me, you're right on the cusp of dreaming."
"I suppose you're right."
"Well, don't just float soupily there," Iphigenia chastised him. "Tell me everything on your mind. We haven't much time." She wasn't really incensed, she was teasing. It was strange being teased by a world, stranger still that he felt as close to her as a friend he had known forever. Perhaps he had.
"I've put out feelers. Gauging the temperature. People are piping hot on Wendy's replacement. As in that there *must be* a replacement. And many are keen that it be... me. Some of the old-guard members of the Citadel are playing it cool, but... Yeah. If there is a frontrunner to take over Redspire, it's me."
"You sound surprised."
"I am. What do they see worth following?"
"I think when they look at you, they see what I see. What everyone can't help but see."
"And what's that?"
"A man who loves his city, while expecting nothing in return," said Iphigenia. "A man who loves his city can keep it the same or change it. People will want you to do both. You'll have to make difficult choices. I don't envy you."
"I feel like I've drunk a flask of distilled jitters."
"Just remember that what people want is for you to go to war for them. Wendy was a peacetime leader. You'll do what's best now that the fighting time has come around with its gloves on, studs on, deal-you-all-the-lumps on."

"There'll be more to fight than just Eurydice," Hughes pointed out. "People are already getting antsy about water shortages. You think this drought will last?"

"Last long? I can't say, Hughes. I really can't say."

"Can't or won't?"

"I'm not your Painted Girl, Krys."

"I miss her. And The Mum."

"And Falstaff, you miss him too."

"The Tower doesn't work properly without him. He up-and-vanished after Wendy died."

"Yes, he did."

"Do you know where he is?"

"My broad view of things comes to me over time. Sorry, Hughes."

"You're my friend, not a dousing rod. It's fine."

"Your friend?"

"My shadow caster. Did I say friend?"

"You did. Oh," said Iphigenia. "I feel you fading away to sleep."

"Wait. I wasn't thinking directly about Falstaff. How'd you know I miss him?"

"Well, it's obvious. When we meet somebody we really care about, they notch us like young people notching their initials into tree bark with a key or a penknife. Just because people come and go from our lives doesn't mean the notches come and go. It's our bark, our skin, our armor, our stuff. You think you can hide those notches? Even a little? You're crazy."

"I'd like to know more about yours," Hughes confided. "Your notches."

"Next time." She hugged him goodnight. "Who knows? By then you might be King."

***

And sometime later, at the house of Eurydice:

"Can you say, 'sister'?"

The baby babbled.

"Sis-ter."

The baby gurgled.

"Can you say, 'Eurydice'? Can you say, 'my big sister, Eurydice'?"

The baby looked away distractedly.

"Sis-ter."

The baby looked back, laughing.

"Sisss-ter."

The baby stopped laughing. She stopped laughing because the face looking down at her was no longer smiling.

"Sisssss-ter. Can you say it?"

The baby smiled, as if trying to show the face how the process worked. Encouraging it to do likewise.

"Fine. Fine. You can't rush a good thing. Go to sleep, Jane. Hushabye."

The baby found herself settled down in a crib. The crib's bars formed shapes. Disgusting shapes. Unspeakable shapes. The woman walked away.

"ssser."

The woman stopped. Hurried back to the crib. Gazed down at the baby. Waited.

And like her father who was never one to miss a cue, Evelyn Hughes said, in a tiny, toddlerish voice, "ssser."

The woman's mouth curled, and Evelyn smiled back as if to say, *There, now we have an understanding.* Like that, here's some more.

"Ssser," she said, abbreviating *sister.* "Ssser. Ssser."

Hughes and Cate would never know it (they would document things in their own fashion), but in that moment they were missing their daughter's first word.

The tragedy of that would never sink into their souls, and that is a mercy.

***

Daddy says I want to keep a diary. I say I don't.

He says yes I do. I do want to keep a diary because it will be good for my brain. It will make my brain big. I say that I'm already eating all my broccoli and peas and fish for my brain. If it gets any bigger, my head will fall off.

He laughs. I say it is no laughing matter.

This makes him laugh more.

Daddy is horrible.

I love him.

***

Today is my birthday. I am six.

Mummy has gone to the Front and Daddy has gone to Ikahagua. Grandad is looking after me. For my birthday Grandad took me to see the jellyfish. He says his grandad was stung by one and he died. But before he died he had a good day because the jellyfish have pictures in their zappers. I asked if I could see the pictures and Grandad said no because then I would die and he would be sad. He smells like tea and old. I like him.

I get letters from Mummy. Grandad reads them to me.

She says she is working hard to keep bad people from coming to our world. I asked Grandad if Mummy meant house instead of world. He says I am sort of right and that I am good at metty-fours. I do not know what metty-four is. Maybe when I am big, I will find out. In her birthday letter, Mummy said that she was very sorry she couldn't be home in time for my candles and cake. She says there is a dragon who is making her unhappy.

Grandad said that the dragon is called Ruthven. He is also a vampire.

I think this is too much and Mr. Ruthven should make up his mind.

I asked for a letter from Daddy. Grandad says Daddy has not sent me a letter, but that's okay.

It is not okay. I became a lump of grump and Grandad tried to cheer me up but it was no use.

I blew out my candles and had cake. When I was eating a big spider came up from the floor and onto my shoe. He had hairy long legs and a fat body. And eight eyes! I counted. I picked him up and played with him.

Grandad saw. He asked if I liked spiders. I said yes, and I like bees and weevils and wasps and grasshoppers too.

He asked if my big sister likes spiders.

I told him no. Eurydice just likes when music breaks.

***

Sometimes in the day with the sun or in the night with the moon I see a house. The house is pink and shiny. If I go in, I will see my big sister. If I don't go in, the house goes away. I like the house. It has lots of fun shapes. I asked Grandad if it is a metty-four. He says probably not.

Eurydice says I should come visit her when I want to.

Mummy and Daddy say that Eurydice is not my sister, only she is pretending to be. She is a liar.

But Eurydice said Mummy and Daddy didn't know about truth and lies. No one does.

I said yes they do.

Eurydice said if I told them a lie, they wouldn't know. If it was a clever lie.

So one day I wrote to Mummy on the magic letter and said I had seen a fluffy white dog. I didn't say purple dog. That would have been a stupid lie.

Mummy said that she would like to see a picture of the dog. I drew him, and she said he probably looked just like that in real life! But I hadn't seen a fluffy white dog.

I told Eurydice, and she said that Mummy believes in the fluffy white dog like some people believe in God. I said no because God makes everything, even jellyfish and cheese and hell. He is not the fluffy white dog. But Eurydice said that there was no proof of God being real. People who said God made things only said that because they were afraid of not believing.

She said I must not believe in anything but Evelyn. That means believing my heart and my eyes and my nose and my ears. And my tongue too. And my brain, which is getting bigger, and will soon make my head fall off.

She said that is the only way for me to pick what is true and what is a lie.

***

Mr. Eight Eyes lives in my drawer now.

It's a shhh.

So no one knows but us.

***

At the house of Iphigenia:

Sometime during their conversations she'd started calling him Hugs and he'd started calling her Spliffy. The story behind those nicknames was hilarious to Hughes and Iphigenia and incomprehensible to anyone else. No point recapitulating it here; you wouldn't get it and that's okay. The best friendships are like that. Outwardly crazy. Inwardly just as crazy, except glowing with happiness. That night's visit got off to a rocky beginning though.

"Spliffy!" He laughed and enfolded her in his arms.

She held him. It was like being held by a bundle of twigs. But her laugh had verve and fire. "Hugs is here! Hide the teabags!"

"What's happened?" said Hughes, going from goofy to somber in two seconds flat.

Iphigenia's grin faltered. "What do you mean?"

"What do I mean? You looked better the last time we spoke. Now it's like you took that step forward and walked it back a hundred miles. You look ragged." A pause. "Shite. I'm sorry."

"I've had better hellos."

"I just got a wee fright. Ah, that's a crap excuse. Can you forgive me?"

"If you're charming from now on."

Hughes told her he could do that.

"I'm eating my soup," she said as they settled down.

"Nothing heartier?"

"Soup is about all I can keep down." Iphigenia gazed at the kitchen window, her eyes close and also very far away. It was a clear evening in Dublin. Halfway to full dark. Stars. "Soup and cigarettes."

"Eurydice's invaded again," said Hughes. It wasn't a question.

"Yes. A big coordinated effort. I don't know where she gets the energy, fighting your coalition all day and night."

"I'll ask Cate what can be done."

"I don't want to be any trouble. Besides I don't expect anything can be done. Not until you've got enough firepower at your back that you can share it around. You mustn't worry. I'll be dandy. Enduring difficult times is part and parcel of being a world. You learn to take the good with the bad." Her voice was not low, nor did she sound very high and bright, which would have come across disingenuous. Hughes thought she simply sounded resigned, and that cut him to the quick. He made to say something but she overrode him. "Let's not talk about it. How are you finding Ikahagua?"

Hughes gave a fraught, tired little grunt. "Speaking of trouble."

"A write off?"

"No, I wouldn't say that. But it's tenuous. We've got a very tense situation here. Ikahagua is a country that can't remember its best times, they were that long ago. Hundreds of years of famine, invasion, linguistic erasure, political corruption, and an extracurricular dose of domestic warfare have resulted in a culture like a bus purchased from a deranged car dealership; huge and complex, all acceleration, no brakes. I don't know. I'm not sure how I'm going to pull off anything worthwhile here."

"I believe in you."

"You and Cate both. I'll give it my all."

"Is magic item production okay?"

Hughes nodded. "On that score, I have zero complaints. The Jolenes are doing some remarkable things, but they couldn't without your creatures playing their part."

That cheered her, restored some vigor to that ashy, limpid complexion. "How are you finding Menin?"

Even though addiction couldn't touch him here in this space between waking and sleeping, Hughes had been about to light a cigarette. Her question forestalled him. He popped the smoke behind one ear and gave her a wary, foxy smirk. "That how it is? Vanity over coffee?"

"We don't have coffee."

"Ah, just the vanity, then."

Iphigenia giggled. Hughes' vulpine grin grew. "Come off it," he said. "You know Menin has changed everything. It's sensational."

"Do I?"

He shrugged. "Suit yourself, Spliffy."

"I'll suit us both, Hugs."

"Mm. It's sensational. Drawing out the power to create magic items while keeping the beastly host alive, not having to exchange steel for spilled blood... It's a revelation. Not that there isn't pushback."

"Still?" she said.

"There was always going to be." Hughes was blithe. The subject permeated his days, soaked them, it was old hat and no big deal. "And a vocal minority can shout louder than the majority can murmur. That's how it feels, anyway. But by and large the people of Corinthia view Menin for what it is: a miracle. A storybook scenario that's as real and tangible as salt and butter with supper."

"I'm glad." Her wanly pleased expression turned mischievous. "Okay, you've shot the breeze long enough."

"Sorry?"

"Hugs, just ask."

Hughes huffed. She had the measure of him. As usual. "I wanted to leave it alone until you brought it up, but I see that impatience is the virtue you're after and that biding my time was a fool's errand."

"Be direct. I like direct."

"Fine. I can be direct. We once spoke about people who are important to us, and the fact that they sort of notch us forever. Leave their mark."

"You're going to ask about mine?" Iphigenia rolled her eyes. "Where do I start?"

"I'm not sure we've got time," Hughes interrupted. "Maybe focusing on the main one will serve for the moment. If I understand the idea behind worlds coming into existence, then you were a human being before. Right?"

"Right." Iphigenia reached across the table with her matchstick arms. Her brittle fingers drew back, holding his cigarette. The light fixture about them fizzled. The end of the cigarette lit. She drew on it, looking at him with a deep reluctant bliss. "I was the princess of Mycenae in a place called Greece. The daughter of a king and queen."

"What turned you into a world?"

"I'm not sure I *turned into a world*. Not with a snap of fate's fingers. I think it was closer than transformation, whatever the word for such a thing might be." She seemed surprised at her own diversion and gave him a wide, self-conscious stare. "The moment the woman I was ended and the world I am began was when my father killed me."

Hughes went cold. "What are you talking about?"

"My father's brother, Menelaus, had lost his wife. She'd been taken to Troy."

Hughes frowned. "The Troy in southern Corinthia?"

"No, no. Remember the William Butler Years thing? Ideas traveling?"

"Yes, I'm with you. So your aunt was kidnapped."

Iphigenia hissed smoke through gritted teeth. She shook her head. "I wouldn't say that. No, Helen went happily enough. Anyway, Menelaus begged my father to assemble the armies of Greece. They'd bring war to the walls of Troy, and death to its people, should Helen not be returned."

"Did your father accept?"

"Sure. And when the armies of Greece stood on the shore by their boats, ready to set sail, and the wind was still, Father sent for me. He asked if I wouldn't mind being sacrificed. To get the wind going."

"God almighty."

Her lips made a thin line. "I certainly thought he was. Which is why I said yes."

"And he went through with it?"

"He got a priest to do it. Stabbed me here." She traced a circle on her stomach. "Then finished it while I screamed that I took it back, I wanted to live, live live..." She stuck out her thumb and ran it across her throat. "I remember thinking, Daddy, you didn't tell me it would hurt so bad. I remember thinking, Blow wind blow. And keep him safe in the war. Such a childish whim to go out on. Then there was this feeling that I was going to sleep and waking up at the same time. Doing both things at exactly the same time, and it was spring. I was sure it was spring and the wind was blowing so sweetly over the woods and the rivers, rushhhhhing, rushhhhhing. I felt my mind and body grow, and even though I was so confused, some part of me understood this was the first spring on the new planet that was me. Plasma pools and rye. Instead of going to my Underworld, I became a world all my own. It took three things: my father offering me up as tribute, the hope and despair I felt as I died, and the inexplicable energy of Life and Death clashing fantastically. It was pure chance." She blew a smoke ring and sent a smoky knife piercing through it. "It was inevitable."

Hughes was looking at her. One hand had curled up. It partially covered his mouth, lips a bit mashed against it, the bristles of his beard tickling his fingers.

At length he said one word, and it was, "Bastard."

"Don't get sore."

"Your father," he said, "was a bastard."

"Don't get sore. I'm happy with it."

"Hurt by your own... how could you be..."

"I get to be a home for a billion-billion lives. I get to find in each of them a trillion homes for me. My father gave me up for his reputation and a favorable gust. That notch slashes me to the core. But I'm a woman as well as a world, and every woman is an infinity." She smiled. "Who's your most important notch, Hugs?"

"Cate and Evelyn."

"Quick answer."

"It required no thought."

"Yes. Slipping away?"

He was. Sleep's talons were tugging at him. "I feel... that you're a big sister to me. That we're co-producing and performing in something. Taking the stage, brother and sister, and the stakes of success are as high as kites on the moon." Flustered embarrassment made him ask, "Do you, ah, take much from these chats?"

"Our talks are like photo albums to me."

He frowned. "How do you mean?"

Iphigenia shucked his chin. "They remind me of a time when I was happy."

***

Daddy has come home from Ikahagua.

He says that lots of people there are sick. I laughed when I thought he said they all had the Penguin Virus. It made me think of everyone turning into birds and being angry because their black and white suits made them too heavy to fly. But it is the Dengue Virus, and it does not turn you into a penguin. If you get it, then it makes you really sick and you might die.

And there will be no jellyfish zappers to show you pictures and make it a good day.

Daddy says the Dengue has been making people sick for a long, long time.

I asked how long and he said as long as I've been alive.

Daddy says he's been trying to help for ages and ages. He says there was a man like a king in Ikahagua called Marshal Eloti (I have checked this spelling and it is good. Also I have learned Parentheses, hurray!). My daddy thinks Marshal Eloti didn't want people to get sick, but when they were sick or scared of getting Dengue, then the Marshal could tell them what to do. And they would because they believed he would help them get well and stop being scared.

I asked Daddy why didn't Marshal Eloti help them get well.

Daddy said it was because Marshal Eloti wanted to be a king.

I asked if my daddy wanted to be a king and not the president anymore. Then he'd get to wear a crown and I could be a princess and Mr. Eight Eyes could be a duke.

Daddy said no, he didn't want to be king. He said a crown often wears the monarch. I am sure this is a metty-four, but I have no proof, like people have no proof of God or lies except their eyes and noses.

When Daddy was away in Ikahagua, he met a nice lady called Kokumo Lugbara (I have checked this spelling. It is good and also pretty). When Kokumo was small, her mummy and daddy worked in Marshal Eloti's cabinet. I asked Daddy how they fit, since cabinets are full of clothes. Daddy said it was a different kind of cabinet. I said okay and listened.

Kokumo's mummy and daddy didn't like Marshal Eloti because he wasn't letting anyone help with the Dengue, like Mr. John Isherwood, who is my mummy and daddy's friend. Kokumo's mummy and daddy left Marshal Eloti's cabinet, and that made him angry. He burned down their house and killed everyone except Kokumo. She went away into the jungle and made friends there with people whose houses had also been burned.

Then, Daddy said, Kokumo got big and strong and clever, and she made a war with Marshal Eloti, like the war Mummy is fighting on The Front (I have learned to give this big letters because it is Important). Daddy says that my mummy is fighting a head-on war while Kokumo and her friends fought a war with gorillas. I asked why she went to the zoo. Marshal Eloti wouldn't be there. Daddy said no it is guerilla, which is not a monkey but a war that is fought all shhh. Quiet and small. Daddy liked Kokumo. So he said he would fight with her. Then, when she was queen of Ikahagua, she could help him by sending people to help my mummy at The Front.

"And did you win?" I asked.

"Yes and no," said Daddy.

"How come both?"

"How can both be correct?"

"How can both be correct?" I said, lumping into a grump.

"We beat Marshal Eloti. But Kokumo isn't going to send her troops to The Front yet."

"Why not?"

"She says her country needs to heal first."

"Her house is still on fire?"

Daddy smiled. Only it was sad. "Yes," he said. "All our houses are still on fire. It's Daddy's job to turn the masses into rain."

"What's the masses?"

"People. Lots of people. Everyone in the world."

"Oh."

"Yes."

"Daddy?" I asked.

"Yes, Evelyn?"

"What's rain?"

***

(Stuck into the pages of Evelyn Hughes' diary is the following poem.)

One morning a blind man asked his grandson to take him to the lake
What color is the lake, asked the blind man
The lake is blue, said the boy
The blind man looked sad.
That is not a color I remember, he said.
Take me away from here, Grandson.

That afternoon the blind man asked his grandson to take him to the tall tree
Growing at the end of his garden
What color is the tree, he asked, and the boy said, hopefully,
Green. Again the blind man looked sad.
That is not a color I remember, he said.
Take me away from here, Grandson.

That night, much in a funk, and low
The blind man asked his grandson to look at a photograph
In the photograph the blind man was a young boy. In those days he could see.
What color are my eyes in this, he asked
His grandson looked at the photograph a long time
Eventually the grandson said, I cannot say. The picture is faded
They could be any color.
But here, Grandfather, listen. At the bottom of the frame
Whoever took the photograph has noted that it rained that day
They must have waited until it stopped to take this picture
You look about as old in this picture as I am today
So I will say that your eyes are the color of my own when I see rain.

The blind man smiled at that.
I will remember, he said.

(The poem was written during the dry, rainless November before Evelyn's seventh birthday by Mr. Glint. That dry, rainless quality was not special. All Novembers had been dry and rainless since her birth. Every month had been, all the world over. The day of the party came. Evelyn read the poem, looked up into the sunken, ghoulish face of Mr. Glint, and to the horror of almost everyone in attendance, she threw her arms around his waist and hugged him tight.)

***

Mummy is nasty.
Mummy is a wolf.
Mummy is the big bad wolf.
She came into my room and asked why I was crying.
I couldn't talk. I pointed at the drawer.
The drawer was empty. All of Mr. Eight Eyes' lovely cobwebs were gone. So was Mr. Eight Eyes.
Mummy said to talk to her. I shook my head. I didn't want to.

She said I must. She only comes to see me once in a blue moon, which is a figure of speech, since the moon is white (or orange or red or yellow, also full, middle, and little). She said I must talk to her. "You have to," she said.

"You killed Mr. Eight Eyes," I said. "Daddy said I could have him."

"Who's Mr. Eight Eyes?"

"My spider, he's my spider and you killed him."

Mummy looked at the drawer. She looked at me. Then she sat down on the floor and said, "Evelyn. When I opened that drawer, I saw a tangle of webs and, at their center, a very large member of what certain people would call the Bathroom Scream species of spider. Are you telling me you were, in fact, keeping that spider for domestic purposes?"

Mummy always talks like that when she thinks I'm angry. She wants me to be calm and relaxed. But I can't be relaxed when she's a big fathead wolf who gobbles up my drawer friend, Mr. Eight Eyes.

"When I asked if you wanted a dog, you said no," said Mummy.

"That's because I don't want a dog."

"Or a cat."

"No."

I wanted fleas. Ticks. Little nibblers, that's what I call them. They nibble everyone just a teensy bit. Not me. Not even when the Citadel had bedbugs. They hopped all the way from the bottom of the tower to the top, where I have my bed. When I saw them hopping on my sheet, I said, "Don't bite me, please." And they didn't. So I gave them names like Barnabel Quilliams and Mrs. Sheila McGovernshire Smith and Fart, and when all the other bedbugs went away in the Spring Cleaning, mine stayed in a shoe. Not shhh, but proper shhh. Secret.

I bet Mummy would have squashed them if she'd found them. That would be just like her.

She knows I like creepy crawlies. And it makes her Menin, which Daddy says is angry only worse.

"Did you bury him in the ground?" I asked Mummy. It would be okay if she had done that. He would find his way to his spider underworld if he was in the graveyard.

"Bury who?" said Mummy.

"Mr. Eight Eyes."

"No."

I had a bad thought. My face felt hot. My eyes burned. "Not the *bin*."

"You said Daddy let you have the spider. That's a lie, honey."

"You didn't put him in the bin, did you Mummy?"

"I sincerely doubt your father gave you permission to keep bugs in your drawer."

"Not in the bin, not in the bin!"

"I do not want you making friends with them anymore."

I barked.

Mummy pulled away. "Evelyn..."

I barked and barked. Then I said, "That means 'go away' in wolf, Mummy. That's what you speak. You're the big bad wolf. Go and blow some houses down."

She stood up. She went. Blew away like bricks, wood, straw.

I hate her. I hate her so much and I miss Mr. Eight Eyes.

I hope when Mummy fights the vampire dragon he sucks all her blood out.

I hope it hurts.

***

My first big holiday is to Champleurs. I am here now. There are buildings in funny wiggly-waggly shapes, not like in my country. Ladies have small handbags. Men have big mustaches and beards. There is a river and boats with movies that play in the smoke from their chimneys. Everything smells like the pastry shop. It is beautiful.

I am here for June and July and August. Daddy is here too. He is talking with barons and counts and duchesses all summer long. Champleurs has pots and pots of nobles, and they all like to talk and fan themselves cool with the help of people who live in smaller houses than them.

Days, Daddy is working. Nights, he is working.

But every afternoon when the sky is going fuzzy-pink and soft, he sweeps into the room and says, "Fawn! Fawn! Harken to me, for there is adventure and merriment to be had." And this is my cue to say, "Lead on, Ser Gardener!" And this makes Daddy happy because his favorite story is about a knight called Gwendle Gardener.

Mummy isn't with us. Daddy and I haven't talked about Mummy killing Mr. Eight Eyes. They write to one another with their special letter. Mummy and I have a letter too, just me and her, but we haven't written to one another since I called her the big bad wolf.

At the gloaming time (this is the name of the soft time I just told about), Daddy takes me walking by the river. We are in Lelepon, which is not the middle of Champleurs, but it is the capital. Some of the boats in the river were drinking the water up in long sticks like straws. Daddy said the straws were purifiers, taking all the bad stuff out of the water and making it good for drinking and showering.

"I've seen them back home, Daddy."

"Yes, you have."

"In the river on the way to Jaenqui. They had even bigger straws."

"Purifying filters. And yes, they were big. Well remembered, Evelyn."

"Are there lots of them, Daddy?"

"The boats? Yes, quite a few."

"How many?"

Daddy looked at the boats sucking up the water and making it pure.

"Not enough," he said.

There were umbrellas and chairs and people sitting by the bridges that went over the river. Some of them smoked cigarettes like Daddy. Some of them had tattoos like Mummy. Only they smoked much more than Daddy and had fewer tattoos than Mummy, who Grandad says is a painting in motion.

By some steps a girl who was older than me played a guitar and sang a song.

Over the roofs there was a really huge steeple.

"Look, Daddy. A church."

"Yes."

"Is that an old church?"

"Oh, very old, I should think. Maybe a thousand years old."

I made a shocked face.

Daddy grinned.

"How do you know?" I asked.

"The stained glass windows are on the front of the church. That was a practice used by architects a long time ago. They stopped doing it because the later schools of thought in the church deemed it impious. That means they thought that having windows on the sides of the church would be less proud and showy, and more holy."

"They thought God would like to see in through the sides instead?"

"No. They thought God would see their simple wooden doors at the front of the church and think they were humble."

"Can we go to church?"

"If you like. There are no holy people there anymore."

"Why not?"

"Because it isn't allowed. You can still believe in God, but you have to do it in here."

And Daddy pointed at his heart.

"Why?" I asked.

"If people are allowed to talk to other people about what they believe, say about God, or other things like that, then they might be angry that other people aren't listening. They might decide not to whisper or speak gently, but to shout. And scared people might be drawn to those shouts."

"They think it's true?"

"Yes."

"Even though the shouting is lies."

"Yes," said Daddy. "Mostly it's lies. Sometimes the worst lies come from the best truths."

"What happens then?" I said. "Do the scared people shout too?"

"Generally. And that can cause other people to shout back."

"And fight?" I said.

"Uh huh."

"I don't like shouting."

"Me either."

"Daddy?"

"Yes?"

"Is it okay if I don't believe in God?"

He nodded straight away. "You've got to believe in yourself. Anything else is a bonus or a detraction. It's up to you to tell the difference."

I wanted to tell him that my big sister Eurydice said the same thing. I kept it secret. I think Daddy hates her. Maybe she is his big bad wolf.

We walked by the girl with the guitar.

I could hear what she was singing.

I turned to Daddy. "What's Pharoah Jacket?"

"Frère Jacques," Daddy said, grinning again.

"Fireman's Jumper."

"Frog-leg Jester."

I stuck my tongue out.

He stuck his out too.

People looked over at us laughing, some of them smiling and some of them wrinkled-nosed and frowning, and one waiter in a restaurant called over that I had a pretty laugh. "*Trés jolie!*" he said, which Daddy said means "very pretty."

I was happy.

"It's funny that she would be singing Frère Jacques," said Daddy as we walked off. "It's a sacred song."

"Sacred?"

"Holy. It's a song about a monk named Jacques. He's sleeping in late and can't hear the bells calling him to matins. Matins are prayers people say in the morning."

The roofs were higher, but if I went up on tiptoe I could see the steeple.

"Now the bells are asleep," I said.

"And the monks will never be late again," Daddy said, and I could tell he was happy with me. (Approving).

"Maybe now the old church is gone, people won't fight and..." I almost said, "and Mummy can come home forever," but just in time I remembered I was Menin with her.

"And what?" said Daddy.

"And you won't have to talk to fops anymore."

Daddy laughed. "Where did you hear that word?"

"Which one?"

"Fops. Where did you hear the word fops?"

"Umm." I smiled cleverly. (Slyly). "In a book."

"Not one I've been reading you. And I'm afraid that people will always find a reason to fight, Evelyn."

"Why?"

Daddy looked at me. Then he moved his hand to say "come on" without talking and started to go over a bridge. I went too. The sun was almost gone. It sat right on top of the river and made the purifier boats look like mosquitos hoovering blood.

"All sorts of reasons," said Daddy. "Some people fight because they like what a king or a queen have said or done, so they'll fight whoever the king or queen hate. Some people fight because other people pay them to, or promise them an education, you know... send them to school so they can get a job. I used to be like that. I needed money because I was poor."

"And because Mr. Glint would eat you if you didn't give it to him," I said.

Daddy jumped. "Who told you that?"

It was Mummy, but I lied and said, "Uncle Frank."

"Hmm. You know Mr. Glint and I are fri..." Daddy opened his mouth and closed it for a bit. "You know Mr. Glint and I aren't enemies, don't you?"

"I love Uncle Glint."

"Which makes you unique among our species."

"Answer about fighting, Daddy."

He went like a lamppost, really straight. "Yes ma'am! Thank ya, ma'am!"

"Daddy!"

He tickled me. I tried to lick his nose for distraction. Daddy boomed his laugh. After, he said, "Well, it's about belief, Evelyn. You fight for what you believe in. And if you don't believe and fighting is still going to happen, then you listen to your gut. When it says sit, you sit, and when it says stand, you stand."

"Isn't it hard, Daddy?"

"Isn't what hard?"

"Not knowing."

"Yes."

I felt sad. I hate when I should be happy and feel sad instead. Champleurs is beautiful but when Daddy said not knowing was hard, I felt ugly inside and outside. "Maybe... we can try to know," I said, wishing he'd say I was on the right track.

Daddy nodded. He said something that I think is ugly and beautiful at the same time. "We can try. But maybe the knowing is for God, or your auntie Iphigenia, and the trying is as close as we can get to that. And if that's our lot, we've got to be okay with it. But if it comes to set-in-stone things, or things that can be set in something harder than stone, then we can tell right from righter and wrong from wronger there, and that's a blessing of our own making.

"Your mother is the best fighter in the world. Want to know what she believes in?"

I didn't say anything.

"Hey."

Daddy turned me to look at him. He was on one knee. The sun was behind him. Red was around him in a line. *Daddy*, I thought. *If you were an angel I'd believe in God.*

"Your mother believes in you snug in bed. She believes in you getting to go to school. She believes in cuddling you and keeping you safe in her big, strong arms. She believes in you being able to choose your friends. She believes in forgiveness. She believes in spiders being buried, not put in the bin. She believes that Mr. Eight Eyes is still going to an underworld, where he will spin webs with tarantulas and angulate orbweavers forever. She believes she loves you, loves you, loves you."

I was crying. I said, "Stop, Daddy."

"Loves you, loves, you, loves you."

"Stop, Daddy, you stop."

He held out his arms.

I put my head on his chest.

"Stop," I said.

But he didn't.

He said, "loves you," until the sun was gone and the gloaming was over, and the city went to sleep with the monk Jacques and the church bells.

No more matins.

I cried and cried.

I'm all cried out. Except I'm not because I'm going to cry again now.

***

Mummy I miss you.

Don't be bloodsucked by the vampire dragon.

Come and cuddle me. Believe in me.

I wrote her a letter.
Your Evie misses you.
Misses you, misses you, misses you.
Loves you.

***

When she came home, Mummy brought me a terrarium.
It is a box of dirt and leaves and moss. Slimy snails and millipedes with lots of feet and sowbugs live there.
Also worms! Earthworms that tunnel. And poo.
Not all animals have good poo, but earthworm poo is good.
I asked Mummy if my poo would help the terrarium.
She said not to push it.
Later, after we had dinner and hot chocolate, Mummy and Daddy and I listened to the radio and danced. It is New Year's Eve. We did The Countdown. When the man on the radio said, "Happy New Year!" Mummy and Daddy had a big kiss. Then Daddy kissed my right cheek and Mummy kissed my left cheek.
Then Mr. John Isherwood came in and said he wanted to speak to Daddy. He looked almost scared but not really. (Nervous).
Daddy asked if it could wait but Mr. John Isherwood said no.
When it was only Mummy and I, she turned the radio to rock and roll. Daddy hates rock and roll but Mummy and I think it is amazing.
I think it is the only thing Mummy and I have by ourselves.
There was a guitar and a fat guitar (bass) and a drum like a big metal heart having a heart attack. And there was a singer. He sang about his beautiful girl and how much he wanted to go for a ride. I asked Mummy if he meant a ride on a horse or in a car, and Mummy said she hoped a car. "Although by the sound of his voice, that singer is a stallion."
That made me think the singer was a horse and I laughed.
Mummy laughed too. I think when we laugh about two different things, and it's okay, that this is what Uncle Frank calls 'being on the same wavelength.' It is like two radios, really different, playing rock and roll together.
Mummy asked if I liked my terrarium.
I said it was my favorite gift.

"This year?" asked Mummy.

"Ever," I said.

Mummy looked so happy.

I said, "You aren't the big bad wolf."

"I can be. That's why it made me sad when you said that to me, Evelyn. Because sometimes Mummy can be a big bad wolf."

I am six now. Too big for carrying. So I hugged Mummy's leg and she put her hand on my head.

"Can I be a cub?" I said.

"You don't want to be a bug? You've got lots of bug friends."

"Mummy?"

"Yes?"

"If you're the mostly good wolf then I want to be a cub."

Mummy was quiet for a long time.

"Happy New Year, Mummy."

"Happy New Year, sweetie."

I howled.

And because she is on the same wavelength, Mummy did not get a fright.

She howled with me, long and loud.

Chapter Eight

At the house of Eurydice:

The delivery came in a heavy box. Evelyn helped her sister bring it into one of the living rooms. Unpackaging it, they saw it was a harp. The harp was tall and wide. Its curves were carved to look as though dogs and wolves were running across the wood in packs. It was very beautiful.

Eurydice went to the cupboard where she kept her tools.

"Jane?" she called. "Come here."

Evelyn came.

Her big sister showed her an implement. "This one?"

Evelyn made a, *We can do better*, face.

Eurydice selected a new one. "This?"

"Perfect."

Eurydice was pleased. Effortlessly she plucked the sledgehammer out of the cupboard. They went back to the living room. Eurydice blew on the strings and the harp began to play itself. Then they took turns hitting it with the sledgehammer.

"Sister?" said Evelyn.

"Yes, Jane."

Eurydice only ever called her Jane. Evelyn asked her not to once, and her sister had grown Menin with her.

Evelyn smashed a section of the harp, sending dogs and wolves of wood scattering. The harp played on, its melody tortured and weakening. "Why do you like it when music breaks?"

Eurydice took the sledgehammer. "You don't?"

"I do!" Evelyn said quickly. "I was just bitten by the curiosity bug."

Eurydice smiled, as Evelyn knew she would. Her big sister liked when she mentioned insects in any context.

"I like when music breaks," said Eurydice, "because I do not like music."

"Why?"

"Why does it interest you? You've never been interested in the why of it before. What makes today different from all your previous visits?"

Evelyn pondered that. She didn't know. The question had simply come to her. Eurydice hooked the hammer head behind several strings. She yanked. They twanged. She yanked harder. They screamed. Gave. Hung in tawdry mutilated tangles. Perverse glee shone in Eurydice's eyes. She laughed.

Their relationship often felt like a beach to Evelyn, with the sand representing stability and kindness and the sea representing less cheery prospects, such as damp melancholy or crashing, foamy rage. Suggesting that Eurydice call her by her real name had brought the tide in. Evelyn had worked hard to push it out again because she loved her big sister when the shore was sandy, warm, and untroubled.

She debated pushing the subject, then decided it would be safer not to.

That hungry old curiosity bug bit her. "Do you like anything made?"

Eurydice looked at her. "Made?"

Evelyn pursed her lips. She'd misspoken. What was the word... Yes! She had it now.

"Do you like creating anything?"

"Of course I do." Eurydice hefted the sledgehammer. "I like creating a mess."

***

Once, on a night like New Year's Eve when I was seven, a night when we were all together, Mum and Dad told me about the Bonemeal Boys. They were skeletons who rode motorcycles. The motorcycles were made from dead people, and the engines burned dead people instead of fuel.

There's a dark, very Mr. Glint word for the Bonemeal Boys. *Macabre.*

And there's a song that uses that name. It's called the *Danse Macabre.* Uncle Frank played it for me on his strings. The song was thin and full of energy. (Spritely). It sounded like skeletons with moss on their bones riding on motorcycles and laughing, and the dead people inside screaming, remembering what it was like to be alive.

When Mum and Dad told me about their adventure, the part that made me feel scared was when Mum was in the Bonemeal Boys' castle. The castle tower fell.

Dad didn't know if Mum was alive or not. He said watching the tower come down made him feel like he was being lowered into a fishing hole in Daethumberland. (The hole is made in the ice.)

The story got better after that, but I thought over and over:

How do the fish stand being so cold?

I thought about that story today because now I am nine years old and I am in Daethumberland.

I am as cold as Dad was when he watched the tower fall, and I know Mum is safe. So it's weather, not fear. Which means everyone feels as cold as I am now. Maybe colder because I have a wooly coat. How do the people here stand it? Back home across the sea, people in Corinth are going for March walks. That's not fair. Can't be fair.

But maybe it's okay.

People may be going for March walks back home, but they're unhappy. You can feel it, see it, almost smell it, which makes that sadness true (at least for me). Here, people are much happier. I am smiled at all the time, wide smiles splitting blushy-red cheeks and fat grins carving paths through the biggest beards I have ever seen. These beards make the beards in Champleurs look like they aren't even trying. They are woven, and braided, and I want one. Dad says if I go into a dark room and think about my chin and then a badger, I will eventually grow a beard. His eyes were twinkling like falling green stars. He is a fibber. But I have learned to find lies funny as well as essential.

Yes, everyone is happier here in the north. Ice is frozen water, after all.

And I suppose water under your feet as opposed to plopping on your head is a silver medal. Second best.

But they have not forgotten the rain. The teenagers and adults. Under their feet, cold and unsure, are children like me who haven't seen rain. We're unsure because you can't miss what you never knew.

And still... on days like today, I do miss rain.

I see something remembered, something like the *Danse Macabre* plucking its laugh/scream strings behind their faces, and then I feel it too, only blurry, like seeing my bald, beardless chin in a block of ice.

When I get this way, I reread that poem Mr. Glint wrote for me on my seventh birthday. It's here, glued into my diary.

It makes me feel better. Warmer.

Not many adults understand, but he does.

***

Dad's not sure what to do.

I can hear him pacing outside my door.

Thump, thump. Pause.

Thump, thump, thump. Pause.

I wonder is he taking pauses because he's getting closer to making up his mind, or because he's getting further away.

His footsteps are quiet on the carpet running all along the room, but I think worry has poured like runny, melty snow into his shoes; they're thumping up a storm. The carpet is heavy, shaggy, and was a polar bear before Jorn Olevsson's spear went into its heart and killed it.

Thump, thump, thump. Pause.

Jorn Olevsson is the man who owns this house. He met our retinue when we came into Kelpavúgor, which means City of the Rime-Encrusted Throne.

We were near the center of Kelpavúgor. It was a square with tall buildings all round. The wind was mean and whippy and bitey, not nibbly like a lovely insect but big and chompy like a hippopotamus with ice for teeth.

We got out of Dad's car and that was when we met Jorn.

"Welcome, President Hughes. My name is Jorn Olevsson." He was wearing a suit and tie, shiny shoes, and a long coat that looked like it was made of owl feathers. There were two huge owl eyes painted on the back.

"Helvr Olevsson. Or is it Jorn Coldlance?"

"Make it Jorn. I dislike my nickname. There is nothing frosty about me."

"Well, it's shorter than *nephew to the high king*," said Dad, shaking his hand. "Though 'Coldlance' makes you sound like you can cure coughs and runny noses."

"Pardon?"

"Never mind. A pleasure to be greeted by a warrior of your caliber."

"Are you Evelyn?" Jorn asked me.

"Yes," I said, shaking his hand. "*Brindev inhr fellim*, Helvr Olevsson." *You have very healthy whiskers, Lord Olevsson.* This is an idiom. It means nice to meet you. Idioms are close to idiot in spelling, but they aren't stupid at all, they're super.

"That was good," said Jorn. "Good pronunciation. You are a smart girl for ten."

"I'm nine."

"Ah, in that case you are not only smart but intelligent."

He had a very deep voice. Not as deep as Mr. Glint, but it's not a competition. And I bet if there was a competition for handsome men, Jorn Olevsson would win gold. His hair was so gold, like a honey jar in a sunny garden.

"I look forward to seeing your uncle," Dad continued. "The prospect of his majesty's wit and charm have been like a portable fireplace these past few hours, keeping this chilly Corinthian toasty warm."

Jorn's face went strange. "You haven't heard?"

"Heard what?"

"I left a note with my secretary. He was to call you at once."

"No, no one called." Dad beckoned to his little group of assistants. They bustled over, listened, spoke amongst themselves, and shook their heads. No call.

"We passed a few toppled pylons," one said. He shivered. "This damn wind got them."

Jorn was looking at my dad.

"President Hughes, I'm afraid I must perforce be the bearer of bad tidings."

"Tell me."

Jorn Olevsson swallowed. "My uncle is dead."

Later, Dad told me he knew from the moment Jorn's expression went strange that his friend the high king was dead. I bet he did. Dad knows what people are thinking just by looking at them. He says people are like theatre. Everything is happening right there on their face, like a stage between their ears. Sometimes I can fool Mum if I want to keep something secret. But Dad? He always knows. I've learned that the only lie you can tell my dad is one he wants to believe.

Like Eurydice. He says I mustn't go to visit her, made me promise.

And when I said I wouldn't, he nodded once, and that was that.

Even though he probably did know the truth about the high king, Dad looked as though Jorn had punched him in the stomach. "Dead?"

"He suffered a cataclysmic stroke at five o'clock this morning. My aunt telephoned the royal physicians. By the time they arrived it was too late."

From the building closest to us, which was pretty yellow and white stone (marble), some men came. Some of them were tall and some were small. All of them had long beards, and their coats were beautiful. Covered in animals. Made from animals. One of them was almost as red-haired as Mum. There was a boar's head on his shoulder, the tusks like swords.

"The low kings extend their invitation to the Vúgorsmoot," he said. "We trust we'll see you there, President Hughes. You and your..." He paused and looked at me. He smiled. I didn't like that smile. "Your bodyguard."

Dad's eyes roamed over the faces of the men. The low kings of Daethumberland.

He said, in a voice that wiped the smile off the red-haired man's lips, "A Vúgorsmoot. You're holding an election? When?"

"Tonight," said the red-haired man. "We thought you'd be pleased, given the urgent tone of your communications with the late high king. We, ah, thought you'd—"

Dad stepped closer. "Tonight. While Isloffir's body is being prepared for burial. Tonight. While his wife gazes down the tunnel of the rest of her life, knowing she will walk it without her husband. Tonight. You will have an election tonight."

"My family has given our blessing," said Jorn Olevsson.

"Under no duress whatsoever," said Dad mildly. "Isn't that so?"

The low kings were all looking down at their shoes.

Except the red-haired man. He gave Dad this toothy glarey sneer.

"Careful. We aren't pansies like your friends in Champleurs. Or thugs like those people you've raised up in Ikahagua. We do things right here in the north. Always have done."

"Always will do," said Dad. "Of course. And it would be right to push the election out a week."

Something happened. I saw the red-haired man's sneer drop. Everything dropped inside him. He was drooped and fallen over inside, even though outside he was standing up. I knew that Dad was using his Performance.

"A week? Yes, that seems proper," said the red-haired man.

The low kings all snapped their heads up. They goggled at him.

"Not sure what I was thinking," said the red-haired man, his face pinched, his fingers making a comb in his beard. "Isloffir's body is only being buried tonight, for God's sake. And his poor wife..."

"Hir helvr," said Hughes. *My Highborn Lord.* "You are the soul of decency. You and I shall have a meeting tonight. One. Two..." He pointed at each of the low kings. "... Five. Six. Six. A perfect number. Each night I'll meet with one of you. I look forward to enjoying Daethumberland's famous hospitality. On the seventh night, we'll all go to the throne hall of the high king and have the Vúgorsmoot. We'll get this whole thing sorted."

"May I offer my house in the city to you and your retinue?" said Jorn Olevsson.

"On the lone condition that you don't mind me accepting. Now," said Dad, "if you'll excuse me, gentlemen. Places to go. Friends to mourn."

He left them like a fisherman who has whapped his caught fish on the side of a bucket. Their mouths opening and closing wordlessly.

He fumed in the car, all the way to Jorn's house.

He seethed, that's the proper word.

I told him I was sorry his friend died.

"Hm?"

"Sorry your friend died. Can I help?"

He seemed to push out of his bad temper. "You do."

"I do?"

"Yes."

"How?"

"I'm not sure," he said. "When you stop, I'll let you know."

"Oh," I said. Then, "What are you going to do, Dad?"

"Feel sad. He was a good friend. We never actually met in person, but it's amazing how conversations over the phone can establish—"

"I meant about the election," I said.

"Oh, that." He shrugged. "I'm going to rig it."

That was six days ago. Dad has met all six of the low kings.

The election is tomorrow.

He's pacing.

Thump, thump. Pause.

Earlier I poked my head out to ask if I could help.

"No, hon. Thank you."

"Who are you going to throw your weight behind, Dad?"

"Either Hanselrolf Torgsson or Ilrak Ilraksson. Ilrak is the man with the boar on his shoulder, the red-whiskered guy."

I scrunched my nose to show I remembered him all right.

"Are they both clever?"

"Clever?" Dad crushed tea leaves while the kettle boiled. It is a thing that makes him chilled out. (Reposeful.) A cigarette was parked in the corner of his mouth. Dad can smoke without his hands. He put the leaves in water and strained them and looked in Jorn Olevsson's presses for honey. "Nah, I wouldn't say either of these men are clever. Opportunistic, maybe. Sly. Like all good politicians and cinema directors, they know their bloody audience."

"You sound like Commissioner Thud, Dad."

"Do I? I suppose I do. Well, I ought to." He gave me a wink. "Thud's a clever man. Help me find the honey."

We looked. We found it. We drank tea. It was delish (Dad's tea is second best in the world after Grandad's, and it is not a competition, although really it is).

"Hanselrolf is a traditionalist. So he believes there should only be low kings and low princes to inherit. He believes that taxes should be very low, so that people can have more money to invest in the country rather than the government. And he believes that Daethumberland could use more spending on the army and wilderland hunting in the snowy mountains that seem to close in like claws near the towns and villages at the fringes of society. With me?"

I said I was, even though I only understood some of it. Dad and Mum have conversations like coloring books—they give me a shape to understand and let me color in the rest myself. (Context.)

"What about boring Mr. Boar?" I asked.

"Ilrak Ilraksson is a neoteric king. That means he believes there should be less hunts and army stuff. More education and scientific solutions to dealing with the environment. Higher taxes because while people can certainly choose to invest in the betterment of their country, he thinks most don't really give a damn beyond their immediate circumstances. And, most controversially, he believes that there should be low queens, with low princesses as likely to inherit as low princes."

I did the scrunchy face again. "Why is it controcommercial?"

"Controversial, Evelyn." His lips twitched. "It's controversial because up until now women in Daethumberland didn't see the point in politics."

"Why?"

Dad sipped his tea. "I expect they were busy keeping their husbands from eating the furniture. Only a joke, dear. Sort of. There's a sort of unspoken code, call it a value, in Champleurs and other civilized places. They think that Ikahaguans love a jolly violent war, Calciferns are fond of a bit of fiscal corruption, people from Jaenqui can't find their own bottom without first commissioning several tapestries on the subject, and let's not even get started on Corinthia. You and I and all the rest of us are hopeless. And in those places, the ones under scrutiny, they've got values too. They say Champleurs can be culturally stuffy and stifling as an attic in July. So it goes. There's values and then there's values. One value that the whole world seems to have ironed out in the last few years is that, aside from the rare moment of natal inconvenience, people are basically the same. The whole world *except for Daethumberland*. Indeed, on the subject of gender, they are not behind the times so much as mining some dank corridor of stupidity several leagues beneath the times."

I gulped my tea and thought about this hard.

"I don't like Ilrak Ilraksson."

"Yes."

"But... I do like... his things."

"Yes?"

"His parrot seas."

"Policies."

I nodded. "Them too."

"Hm," said Dad. He went to take a sip of his tea. Paused. "Hm."

I went to bed to write in my diary. He kissed me before I went. Dad's kisses are warm and Mum's are cold (because of the glass. But they make me warm inside, so that's okay).

Through the door, I hear:

Thump, thump.

Pause.

And very softly, Dad's sound: "Hm."

I am also pacing. Not with my feet. Inside my noodle. (This is slang for head. I like slang and idioms and figures of speech.)

No low queens. I keep thinking of wagging fingers. No, no, no. That's so unfair. All of me is under the blankets. There are six, one for each low king, although by the sounds of it, my blankets would make better kings. At least blankets keep everyone warm, and don't pick who gets warm and who doesn't because they do or do not have a willy.

I hope Ilrak Ilraksson wins. He's a scabby, gross blanket, but he'd go around the whole country, not just the boys and men.

Dad isn't pacing anymore. I wonder if he's gone to bed too.

I'm going to put this away now and say goodnight to the friends I've made in Jorn Olevsson's house. He doesn't know they live here, but they are residents just like he is.

Once, when I was very small, Mum and Dad asked me why I wasn't good at making friends with girls and boys my age. Did I feel strange about them?

I said no, I didn't feel strange.

I just have too many friends already.

Dad got a pinched look and asked me to produce a list of these friends.

I told him about the bugs in my room, and the living room, and the kitchen, and his and Mum's room too. There are bugs everywhere, so close all the time.

Dad's face unpinched. He said perhaps I should keep this little tidbit to myself. It might upset people. Not him and Mum, of course. They love me always.

But Jorn Olevsson doesn't know me, much less love me. So his many cohabitants go about their business under his notice.

Goodnight greeny-blue Daethumbrish butterflies and fat brown moths at my window. Goodnight spiders. Goodnight teeny bugs keeping secret all over the room and house and world.

Goodnight, dear sirs and madams.

Goodnight.

Tomorrow there shall be a new king.

***

Am I a monster?

A man called me that today.

He looked at me with a face so white it looked like the bottom of a fish, and his big lips like seabass lips shivering, and his eyes huge staring black balls like shark eyes, this man pointed a finger at me and said, "*Kuh-kurahak!*"

Later, after the man was taken away and Dad was gone fuming and steaming like a kettle to visit the new king and everything was tight with quiet, I asked Jorn Olevsson what *kurahak* means and he said, "That means monster."

He was looking at the floor, the walls, the windows. Anywhere but at me.

I'm going to write about what happened earlier. I think that will get this sick feeling out of me, like an antidote for poison.

Dad and I left early this morning for the Vúgorsmoot. The thronehall is a room so tall it felt like magic had lifted it up, magic hands of gold and silver that poured their color into the beams and chandeliers. Screens had been put over the tall, curvy windows. The screens showed a winged horse carrying a bloody boy over a field of ice. Dad told me this is a depiction of Astrelseph, the first high king of Daethumberland, who was saved from a gruesome fate by a pegasus. The pegasus told Astrelseph he was destined for great things if he killed his cruel father and married his mother. I asked Dad if he was making that bit up. But no, Jorn Olevsson said that really was how the story went. Astrelseph killed his dad and married his mum. At the very first Vúgorsmoot he carried his wife's favor into a duel, slew his enemy, and became high king.

I told Dad that he mustn't worry. I would rather be eaten by slugs than hurt him. I don't much fancy marrying Mum, either.

He said that was very comforting.

Maybe the nastiness of the whole thing—the bleeding boy riding the winged horse and the story of the gross man he'd become—should have been like a warning for how the day was going to go. Grandad says that bad turns worse at the drop of a hat, and I think he's right.

The low kings came dressed in animal skins, their crowns bright in the blue light of the chandeliers. They made presentations and gifts to these three ceremonial groups called The Three Watchers: old people to watch the past; middle-aged people to watch the present; young people to watch the future.

They also gave some presents to the family of the high king who died. They asked for blessings in return, no matter which of them became high king next.

Jorn Olevsson got a new house and a spotted hunting dog. I think he'd prefer his uncle coming back to life, but when the low kings asked for his blessing, he was kind and strong. (Gracious.)

Ages ago the low kings used to have to duel, cutting one another down in a room. Dad told me at one stage Daethumberland felt that society needed to return to its caveman roots. So they loosed a wolf, an eagle, and a bear into the arena with the low kings. Alliances were made and broken. The man who crawled out of there was probably maimed, but people thought he was either tough or lucky, both good things for a king to be.

Now the low kings duel with words. They make speeches. The Three Watchers, who are elected from their age groups, then stage an election of their own. A new high king is crowned.

I could see the crown on a block of pretty stone. (Plinth.)

It was the color of the sea. Winged horses of metal galloped around the rim, and there were loads of tiny rubies like drops of sparkling blood.

While the low kings talked and talked, I looked at Dad. He was writing a letter to Mum at The Front. I tugged his coat. His eyes slid off the page and lit on me (sometimes his eyes are brighter than they are dark, I just don't know how that happens).

"Tell Mum I want to watch a movie with her when she comes home," I whispered.

He mouthed, *What movie?*

The offices in my head were working, but the name of the film was on vacation.

"There's a giant bird... and... some talking mice..."

You don't want to see another play? Dad mouthed.

Ever since he built The Gate theatre, Dad is mad on plays.

"No thank you," I whispered. There was a pause. "Unless there's another one like Timothy Androgenous."

I should never have taken you to that. It's too violent for a little girl.

"Those were the only good bits. The rest was people gabbing and being stupid. My favorite was when the man baked those other men into a pie and made their mum eat it, and besides it's all ribbons and strings and red food coloring, you said so."

Dad smiled a smile that he didn't want to, I could tell. (Rueful.)

He went back to writing Mum.

The low kings were still going on about why they were best of a bunch. The Three Watchers and all the assembly were listening like it was the most interesting radio program in the whole world. I thought it was interesting for another reason. I knew it was all a lie.

The winner was already picked.

And when The Three Watchers sent an old man, a middle-aged man, and a boy to give the results, they announced that the new high king would be Ilrak Ilraksson, and the whole room went absolutely bonkers.

Jorn whisked Dad and I out of there. He told Dad that his mother, the old high king's sister, wanted to talk to him. We were in one of the palace's function rooms. White cloth covered a table and chairs. The cloth smelled soft, and under the softness the room smelled like lemony air freshener and old wooden things. Also there were lots of woodcuts on the walls.

I asked Dad if I could stay here for a bit.

"No, stay with me," he said. "Tempers are high in this palace."

"She can stay with my cousin," said Jorn. "He has three daughters of his own."

I thought Jorn's cousin looked nice, and I did want to stay, but when Dad shook his head and said that it wasn't wise, I knew he was probably right. As horrible as things were about to get, I suppose they could have been worse if I had stayed in the function room. The cloth would have been ruined, for a start.

Hanselrolf Torgsson met us in the corridor. He had one nostril closed over, curly white hair, and puckered skin on his cheeks. There were men with him.

"Fixer," he called Dad. "Cheat."

My dad said something in Daethumbrish. It only seemed to make Hanselrolf angrier. His men had their hands in their coats.

Dad used his Performance. I saw it go wrong. He said something. Jorn spoke too. I couldn't understand them. But he and Dad were getting ready to fight.

Jorn's cousins were scared, but I wasn't.

Dad wears Faethe, the amulet of dragons. It didn't matter what the men were keeping in their coats. It would take something harder than a kosh to stave in Dad's head. And they might be called quickbolts but he's *quicker*.

That was when three of them took out a quickbolt crossbow and shot at me.

I can't remember what happened next. Too fast, it was too fast for me. I can only guess that Dad did his best, snatching two of them right out of the air.

The third bolt could have hit me. *Would* have hit me if not for the white witch moth. It was massive, its body about as large as a person's two hands put together, and its wings like fuzzy fingers stretched out wide. It made a thump when it fell, and the moment was just like Dad's pacing.

Thump. Pause.

Everyone looking at the moth. Every single eye watching its wings twitch. Twitch. And go very, very still.

The bolt stuck out of it.

The whole corridor was looking hard (transfixed) at that skinny bit of steel.

Except me.

I was staring at the man who had shot at me.

A weird thing happened. I got the feeling that something was standing right beside me. There was no one. But I suddenly knew I could make the man who had shot the moth sorry. I wanted to. The feeling (desire) was so enfolding. It wrapped my chest and throat like fuzzy fingers. Like witchy white wings.

I thought

(come)

and they came.

They danced in from every corner. From under the heavy curtains. From the fibers of the carpet and the gaps in the flagstones. They scurried and hurried and rushed.

Harmless alone. Fierce together.

The bugs.

They climbed over the men with the crossbows. They didn't bite. I wanted to give them permission to (they were waiting, I felt them waiting) but I made myself gentle and calm.

In real life the ribbons and strings and food coloring are people's insides, and hurt is something I don't want to feel, so why would anyone else?

It didn't stop the men screaming. They screamed as if they were being killed. They pushed at their clothes, batting with their hands, peeling off the warm-blooded slimy guys and swiping at their ears and mouths and noses, keeping the creepy crawlies at bay. I wouldn't have let them crawl inside the men. But at the time I thought, *They don't have to know.*

I sent all the spiders in the palace up the trouser legs of the rest of them. Only Hanselrolf Torgsson was left untouched.

I turned to Dad. "He's got a knife in his pocket."

Dad is always so cool. Steady. Not today. Today in the buzzy, oozy, skittery corridor he looked like a breeze would blow him away.

"Dad?"

He made a noise. Not, "Hm." It was more like an animal.

"There's a knife in Hanselrolf Torgsson's pocket," I said. "A midge told me. And knives aren't allowed in the palace. It's banned." I thought about almost being shot. "And quickbolts too."

The men covered in bugs were running away.

Dad looked at me. I saw him come back to himself. He and Jorn made a lunge at Hanselrolf. They all tumbled to the floor, and after Dad broke one of Hanselrolf's fingers he dropped his knife and they pulled him to his feet.

He pointed that finger at me. The broken one.

It was like a crooked wand. A wizard's wand after the wizard has seen something awful and gone crazy.

It was him who called me a monster.

What did I feel next to me? It let me call the bugs. Made me sure they'd hear me and answer.

Is it something else, something smart, or me?

In the dark behind my eyelids, I can still see Hanselrolf's fishy face, whiter than the giant moth's wings. It's a normal moth in the Daethumbrish wilderness, but what was it doing in that corridor? Why did it get shot and not me?

Monster, Hanselrolf called me.

Am I?

I asked Dad and he said no, of course not.

But he didn't answer right away.

And just like Jorn Olevsson, he wouldn't look at me either.

***

At the house of Eurydice:

"You are not a monster."

Quietly, "I know."

"The men who tried to... hurt you... they're the ones who are wicked at heart."

Even quieter, "I know."

"They take all the badness inside them and they spread it around. You do the same with your kindness. You're so good to bugs... the moth... she showed you that they appreciate it. They want to give the goodness back."

Quieter still, "I know."

"No matter how pretty a face, monsters are ugly inside. You are beautiful inside and outside."

Crying now, unable to hold back the tears, "I know."

"I am looking at you."

"Thank you."

"I am looking, and I love what I see."

"Thank you. Best sister ever."

Eurydice looked at Evelyn a moment longer. Then she pulled her in for a hug.

***

At the house of Iphigenia:

They'd tried to quit the ciggies on their own and failed. Together they would give it another go. They had to quit. The logic was sound. A president shouldn't smoke because it increased his chances of lung cancer. A world shouldn't smoke because greenery would fail and the fog and mist creeping along her swamp and forest would develop a tarry aftertaste.

Hughes wished it would increase her rainfall. Over the years they'd discovered Iphigenia could pump up her output of rain as long as it didn't offset the stricture of her seasons. Too many summer storms at the extremities of her equator and she began to get woozy. She also possessed an amplitude of freshwater lakes and rivers. Having direct access to her world through the portal in Corinth had mitigated the drought.

It had helped, though not enough. Never enough.

His world's throat was scratchy and parched. Agrarian settings, urban, every biome drank endlessly, or so it seemed.

The crisis was so wide in scope it simply couldn't be dealt with, merely kicked down the road.

Well, he'd kicked the goalposts of addiction down the road enough. That, at least, he *could* try to take on. Iphigenia's vow to stop huffing and blatting like an exhaust pipe lent him strength. Quitting an addictive substance is a miserable business, and misery loves company.

To take their minds off it they'd started playing scrabble, only stopping when they realized with amused horror that they were constantly lining up words like "chimney" and "filter," "tar" and "ash." They took up instruments as a last resort, Hughes the violin and Iphigenia the double bass. Keep the hands busy, you know. Their logic was ever sound. Their hands were busy, and they played together, and they were so, so crap.

"That's enough for today," Hughes said. "My fingers hurt."

"How are your ears?" said Iphigenia.

"They hurt."

"Mine too. Throbbing their protest. I think our improvement has stalled."

"I'm not sure there was much to start with. Maybe we ought to try those instructional manuals again."

She dismissed that with a wave of her hand. "We've got the basics."

Hughes wondered. Sometimes they sounded halfway okay, the rest of the time like a bat nest undergoing renovation. "We need a teacher," Iphigenia went on. "Someone who can show us advanced techniques. The real stuff."

"I'll speak to Frank. He can really play."

"That's a great idea!"

"Thanks, a Hughes original. I'll talk to him. He's back and forth to the Front with Mr. Glint, but I'm sure he could give us some tips."

They sat down. Hughes was not in danger of falling into REM sleep. With practice he'd gotten better at lengthening his visits to this house of eternal green where the air always smelled like rich flower pollen and tangy fruit. That smell was depthful too. He'd come to appreciate that. It didn't mask a hidden foul smell, as spritzing air fresheners did. That aroma, like Iphigenia's loveliness, was not superficial; rather it went all the way down.

"How's your paper fort?" she asked.

"Complicated," he said. "Never uncomplicated." During his tenure as president, Hughes had found it impossible to keep every detail of his rule straight. His memory was famously sublime, but for God's sake, there had to be a limit. The solution had been a room in Redspire. He'd commandeered it, cleared it, and crammed it full of notes. Notes in books. Notes stuck to the walls with glue. Jars of notes. Pots, cans, and repurposed salt shakes overflowing with notes. Countries and provinces of notes mirroring the countries and provinces of the wider world. Hughes had been born in Leonidas. He was scrappy by nature. A computer would have been too clean, plus it could be hacked. He held the only key to the room (his paper fort as Iphigenia had dubbed it), and it really was terrifically scrappy in there, a suitable match to his temperament, so really there was no question of going digital. On that he and his mother were aligned, for she had used notes when she was queen in all but name.

"Anywhere laying on hell?" Iphigenia wanted to know.

"New problems crop up every day. Its constant."

"Bother you?"

"Nah," he said. "Oh, stop reading my mind and cut the grin. It bothers me a little. It wouldn't if I could smoke."

"Stay on the wagon."

"Wagon with a wagon. Fine."

"Calling me wagon?" Iphigenia was giggling.

"You're healthy as a horse-drawn," he observed. "You look well."

She did not look well, not by a long shot. But today was a good day, so he told her she looked well. On bad days he didn't draw attention to how she looked. It was an arrangement never spoken aloud, yet one they'd agreed upon nonetheless.

An impulse took Hughes. He followed it. "Evelyn's um..."

"Yes?"

"She's stopped going to visit Eurydice."

"When?"

"Recently. I've no idea why."

"She's getting to that age," Iphigenia commented. It was a wry little comment. For some reason it sat jaggedly with Hughes.

"She's not a teenager yet."

"Almost. And girls get a head start on boys. It's a well-known fact."

"Says who?"

"I don't know." She patted her pocket absently, looking for a cigarette without realizing she was doing it. "Everybody. And the Tower? How are things?"

"Hectic as ever."

"That butler of yours not turn up?"

"No."

His mind went to Falstaff less and less often. He couldn't remember the last time he'd dwelt for any length of time on his old friend.

"I'm sure he'll turn up."

"I don't think so. And the war's just as hectic."

"An ecstasy of fumbling."

"That's a vicious little phrase. Apropos," he said. "You?"

She shook her head. "Wilfred Owen. He was in a war in which they used a lot of gas. Trenches, you know."

Hughes' face became a rictus. "Sounds like a war in my world. Cate's dad fought in it. Grim, the whole thing was grim." It was raining in Dublin. It pattered blissfully away on the kitchen window glass. He wished he could bottle the meteorology here and take it with him and give it to his world when he woke up. Bastard drought. "We've tried gas on the undead."

"And?"

"Useless. Their lungs don't function like ours."

"Oh, I see."

"Necromantic respiration. Some shit like that. John Isherwood gave me an earful about it. I was only half listening."

"You're busy."

"Yes."

"Harried."

He grunted.

They sat together, the stillness warbling around their instruments and collecting in restless, anxious circles about both the world and her shadow. It was a good day for Iphigenia. A good day for the war. But circles tightened. And tightened.

Because who knew what tomorrow would bring.

Theirs was not a war of trenches, but it was still fumbling ecstasies. Unpredictable. Mayhem and numb victories.

Eventually Hughes muttered, "I keep thinking about what Hiromi said. More and more I think it's going to become the fulcrum around which the whole thing turns."

"What whole thing?" Iphigenia asked.

"The war," he said. "What else?"

She patted her pockets again. Caught herself this time. "I'm hopeless," she said.

"Don't hog it all to yourself," he said. "Leave some for the rest of us."

"What can we do?"

Hughes looked into those magnificently large eyes of hers. He found the answer in them. Without a word he got up and fetched the instruments.

"We keep our hands busy," he said. "And we don't give an inch. Not to Eurydice. Not to addiction. Not one inch."

***

It's been years since I've opened this diary. Years of school. Years of travel.

The compulsion hasn't been there. Now I feel as if I need to write. The idea that memories are drips of poison that eventually harden into a lump, a lump that must be lanced and drained, has clung to me since I called the bugs to attack Hanselrolf Torgsson's men.

That day in Daethumberland seems so long ago now, like a page from a rumpled old picturebook. But here it is, in these pages. Fresh and new for the version of me who called the white witch moth to protect her.

I was nine then, only beginning to lose sense of my own geography. I think little girls feel perfectly oriented. Their compasses don't point magnetic north, but rather magnetic inward, because as far as we're concerned, we are the center of the galaxy. Then we get a bit older. We stop happening to life and life begins happening to us.

I'm twelve now. I feel so very lost.

I need to find my bearings. Maybe lancing more recent memories with this pen will accomplish that.

Where to start?

I asked myself that out loud just now, holding my pen against the tip of my nose. It made me laugh. The question. The action. Silly.

I'm lost and silly and the truth is that I can only pick this up where I left off.

After the election of Ilrak Ilraksson, the high king met with my father. He pledged to help him. Father seemed pleased. His treaty had almost unraveled with the death of his friend. Now he could console himself with the fact that Mother and her armies would receive the help they so desperately needed.

Help against what?

Eurydice, of course.

My so-called big sister.

No. I can't write about her yet. I amn't ready.

Two years went by. Two more years without rain. More purifiers in the sea. Supermarkets shutting down. Small businesses cropping up and crumbling. Anxieties piling on anxieties. More bitter voices shouting for my father to do his job. More people wondering, *What if?*

What if the war is behind the drought?

What if the magic that unites us to Iphigenia is behind the drought?

What if the purifiers fail?

What if the title of president is really President for Life?

What if the rains never return?

What if Wendy Dragontail, my grandmother and the city's former sovereign, had lived?

Questions like that trigger the ageing process. In those two years Father turned thirty-eight. He seemed to become middle-aged overnight. Along with gray hairs he also sprouted gray attitudes. In the people around him. Watching him. In himself. In his city. Corinth City looks colorful but feels gray. From the tower where I live and its streets I love to walk. Lines of gray pulling everything and everyone, constricting.

We just wish the gray would rise up and thread the sky.

We wish the threads would become woolen clouds.

Even people like me who can't remember overcast skies wish that the clear days would end.

They wish for rain and blame its absence on the man scrambling to make up for that absence.

He didn't resent any of the shouting voices.

He listened. He's still listening.

Maybe that's why they still hate him.

In the first spring of my life in double digits (ten years old seemed special, like I had just exploded into something new), Father took me to Mysicordelia.

I remember the taste of candied eel and saltwater crab, the sun shining on dazzlingly awesome cars, suited men and women in sunglasses, sexy shops, nail salons, boys with odd mechanical umbilical cords coming out of their bellies and connected to sacks of paste floating next to them, signs splashed with crazy colors and writing, holographic giant coy fish swimming above our heads, the whiskers clipping through umbrellas raised for fashion, or in hope that at any moment the careless blue sky would darken and cry for the years spent apart.

Father met Emperor Tanaka at the emperor's prime sushi restaurant. The royal office in Mysicordelia is more of a business than in other countries. No taxation exists there, only credits jumping from one bank account into another.

It was under the mild, rheumy gaze of the emperor that I ate the candied eel.

"Good?" he asked me.

"Excellent, your august majesty, brightest beam of the sun's celestial effluence, and master of the whims of men and beasts," I said.

"Ah," he said, inclining his head politely.

It was the only exchange we had.

Mostly he spoke with my father. Their conversation was two bulls circling one another, refusing to lock horns. I remember the way the emperor lifted his chin and laughed at my father's turns of phrase. Sometimes he played with his sushi, sticks clicking like thoughtful lobster claws. Similarly, I recall Father's tells. President Gormon Hughes and the man I cuddle whenever I have the chance are the same person, and yet so completely different. The president is a less patient man. He runs his knuckles and the ball of his thumb over his beard bristles when he's irritated. They got a good scratching that day, with the hum of sushi stitching the air.

I know Dad only uses his Performance as a last resort. He thinks it's a necessary evil. Eventually, when the emperor dodged Father's request for help in the war for the umpteenth time, Tanaka's face went droopy like a bloodhound's. Father said, "Come, your august majesty, brightest beam of the sun's celestial effluence, and master of the whims of men and beasts. Think of what will happen when we win. Your soldiers, who I intend to outfit with magical weapons and armor, will return home. Who can say what doors such a force might open in times of domestic strife? Who else but a mind as canny and precise as your own."

The emperor came back from wherever the Performance had sent him. He inclined his head, low enough to indicate something greater than politeness.

"If there is a victory to be had, then Mysicordelia will lend its hand to that outcome."

"Corinthia will put a sword in it," replied Father happily.

That happiness turned glum quickly.

It became clear that while the emperor controlled the armed forces, there were other fighters whose loyalty did not fall under the parasol of his rule. These were the syndicates. In manpower they outnumbered the army thirty to one. The main operations were the Long Shadows, the Synthetic Confabulates, the Jammer Wolves, the Ninety-nine Fishermen, the Incarnadine, and the Screaming Mimis.

Negotiations with the heads of the syndicate families made Father feel like a charger amongst matadors. "Matadors with barbed capes," he grumbled once as we went to meet the Incarnadine leaders.

"Didn't Commissioner Thud fight an Incarnadine?" I asked.

"Yes, and Mr. Glint."

"Yes! They told me his eyeballs were flowers that melted anyone they looked at."

"That was before you were born. To think I'm about to meet with the people who sent that man to my city."

"Are you going to use your Performance on them?"

"If I must."

And the oddest thing—odder than the notion of a man with wicked flowers for eyes—is that Father didn't have to use it.

The Incarnadine leaders welcomed us with a grand presentation. A necklace of blood-red jewels was slipped over Father's head, a scepter placed in his hand, a robe the color of fresh blood draped over his shoulders. They escorted him to a luxurious banquet. Between courses, they explained how apologetic they were about the situation many years ago, and moreover how grateful they were that the president's commissioner, then a simple captain of the city streetbeaters, exercised his restraint and mercy. The prompt return of the Incarnadine agent to

Mysicordelia was viewed as an extra sprinkling of sugar on this already sweetened event.

It was only later that my father cleared up the mystery behind this unexpected hospitality. The central figure, the leader of leaders at the heart of the Incarnadine was named Arihabu Saito. He was the flower-eyed man whose life Thud spared all those years ago.

Around this time of bulls and barbed capes, Father and I were introduced to a woman named Hiromi. Aside from being one of the nicest, most polite and elegant people I have ever met, Hiromi is a scientist at MSP, or the Mysicordelia Space Program. Over lunch she told my father about the plight of her company, how they've struggled to gain funding.

"But you can see why," said Father. "Your basic Humdrum Harry is worried about the price of cheese, his daughter's exam results, his hairline. What he is not worried about is the goings-on of the solar system. What, for example, your standard Tuesday is like on the moon."

"You've never wondered what Tuesday is like on the moon?" said Hiromi. "Only it seems a specific thing to say."

Father pursed his lips. "Fair enough. Okay, so maybe I've looked up of an autumn night and played a little game of Are There People Up There And If So Do They Look Down Here And Wonder What It's All About?"

"Fascination with the moon is very common," said Hiromi. "Only at MSP, what you describe is not a game. It is hypothesis, theorization, and plans to uncover the secrets of the moon."

"How?"

"We will engineer a rocket."

"Keen on blowing the moon men up, are you? Think they'll send a surrender notice and a brochure? Come and see the lovely lunar seaside, enjoy a Dark Side cocktail, oh and incidentally please don't send any more high explosives?"

Hiromi smiled graciously. "You misunderstand. Not a magnesium sparkler or a bit of tubing full of saltpeter, charcoal and sulfur. I mean a rocket capable of seating a crew and shuttling them through our world's atmosphere, safeguarding the crew from the Van Irol radiation belt and the cold claws of space."

"That is an admirable goal."

"Thank you."

"You'll never get it funded."

"No?"

"No," said Father. "It's a nice idea, but it's like I said, we've got enough stuff down here to be worried about. The moon might inspire a bit of nocturnal wistfulness, but that's all."

With poised little movements, Hiromi pushed her food aside and sat forward in her seat. "Mr. President, you were not altogether off the mark when you discussed explosive motivations."

"Oh?"

"You see, we would like to blow up people's conception of the universe. Of an autumn night I too look at the moon. Ever since I was a girl of your daughter's age, I have worked hard, saved up, and bought the best telescopes. I have pictured ships landing in the maria, the moon's seas. When I matured, those ships were replaced in my mind. Replaced by the rocket I have described to you."

"The one that'll get past the world's irradiated belt."

"The Van Irol radiation belt, yes."

"Without frying its passengers insides."

"Yes."

I brought over a fresh teapot. Father poured. He watched Hiromi, and I thought of two matadors talking about a mythical bull, one of them not convinced anyone would care if they killed it, and the other doubly convinced they must try.

Hiromi must have been thinking something along those lines because she inched even closer to Father. With the steam fogging her glasses, she said, "Forgive me for speaking boldly, Mr. President. I have heard you are uniting the syndicates of my country toward a single purpose. A man who can do that can drum up funding for my company. He can put boots on the moon." She took off her misty spectacles, sat back as she cleaned them with a cloth, and put them on again, looking right into Father's eyes. "And if he is willing to put his own neck on the chopping block of my country's political system, his cause must be desperate. Desperate enough to require some clout with the Humdrum Harries of the world, who I think you'll find watch the moon of an autumn night as often as scientific girls and kings who do not wear crowns."

Father's gaze roamed hers, exploring it. How often have I seen him do that? He sees you and everything underneath. It's not his Performance, I've learned. It's simply him.

I had no idea what would happen. I bet Hiromi didn't either.

The ball was in Father's court. We waited...

And with a grin that shaved years from him, showing Hiromi and myself what he was like as a boy, my father said, "Tell me, could this rocket of yours accommodate a camera?"

Hiromi's elegance burst into excitement. She matched Father's grin.

"Well, I do not know," she said. "But I would very much like to find out."

When we set out east, Father intended to remain in Mysicordelia for three weeks. We were there for three months.

When we returned Father was flanked by two armies, one straight-laced, the other straight-jacketed and ready to be set loose.

What had begun in Corinthia had spread to Champleurs, Ikahagua, Daethumberland, and onward.

Time passed. My father's work continued. Calcifern, Rhönland, Jaenqui-Across-The-River, Yi-Shi. One by one they answered his call. They've become fledging feathers for Father's arrows, drawn back and loosed into battle by his general, his confidante, his love, my mother.

This year arrived. I think Uncle Frank arrived at the truth before anyone else. Mother and Father have put a third of their lives into the machine of war. I call it the machine because when I talked to Mr. Glint about it, he explained the idea with his usual succinctness. "War goes in," he said. "War comes out."

New Year's came and went. No letters. No celebration as a family.

When that truth of absence struck my parents, I can't say. But Uncle Frank is sometimes as much a prophet as my father's old friend, Krys the Painted Girl. By confiding in me that Mother and Father have devoted themselves so totally to the war effort, Frank cast a kind of secret spell. Not like a wizard might perform. Something uniquely Frank, a dream concealed in an observation.

In February Mother surprised me with a visit. We spent the Monday to Friday doing absolutely nothing but lounging and watching movies and stuffing our faces.

It was wonderful. And on Saturday Father took our beautiful incompleteness and made it whole.

Here, in this private written zone, I can admit that it would be whole without Mother there. I love her so much, but my father brings emotions stronger than love from my heart. When he's gone, I find myself drifting. Staring into space. Given to melancholy. When he's around I'm present and connected. Happy.

He feels it too.

I see it when he smiles at me. Even if sometimes those smiles are complicated, hiding the scope of his feelings as I used to hide insects everywhere I could.

Earlier in this diary a nine-year-old asked herself if she was a monster.

Her twelve-year-old self can answer that with a resounding "no."

I didn't hurt those men in Daethumberland. And there have been times in which I've reached out and my small friends have come in a hurry, times when danger was averted because the hostile party noticed a sudden amplitude of beetles. Still, a girl keeping herself safe does not a monster make.

Oh, I wish it were that simple.

It isn't.

Like Father's smile, it can be complicated.

I suppose I've worked my way up to this sufficiently.

I've got to run to supper now.

When I'm back I'll be ready to write about Eurydice.

***

My big sister is a font of good advice.

My big sister lets me lean on her.

My big sister would never let anything hurt me.

My big sister is my best friend.

My big sister is not who I thought she was.

***

Popped off for a cry. Back now.

It's odd. I didn't cry when I realized the truth.

Eurydice is the place my mother goes to fight. A whole world of murderers.

At the same time Eurydice is a lady. Just the one murderer there. A mother of murderers. A queen.

There was no grand reveal. I remember snippets of chatter from Mother and Father rather than one big conversation in which the curtain was pulled back and my sister's identity became suddenly clear. Over years and years these snippets formed a line of dominoes. I haven't a clue as to what started them falling, but they've been falling ever since, repeating those ideas to me with heavy thudding rhythms.

My big sister is my best friend.

My big sister is not who I thought she was.

In my mind's eye the dominoes look like Uncle Glint's teeth.

Like gravestones.

It's horrible to have enjoyed such an amazing closeness with someone, someone with whom you could discuss your fears of being different. Of being a monster. Only to find out that the person you've grown to care about is the most wicked monster of them all.

I suppose what got me started on all this was her emissary.

That evil little creature who appeared in Father's meeting today, livening up the dull day like mold appearing in stale bread.

Skuggs. That was the creature's name.

Funny, no one had to tell me that. I knew his name already. I think he and I have met before. At the house? I can't remember.

It's been Father's habit to bring me to his meetings ever since I turned ten and could be trusted not to make a complete shambles of proceedings. My education in etiquette has spanned every school of thought from choosing the right words and gestures (Father) to the eight essential rules of charm (Uncle Frank) to not offending your host by eating the other guests (Mr. Glint).

Yesterday Father met with what might be called the usual suspects: Doctor John Isherwood, Commissioner Hoshrum Thud, Frank Gallant, Mr. Glint, Hector and Cassandra of Troy, Father's friend and quartermaster Jolene, the head of communications who is a mumbling, skulking goblin of a man called Montcrieff, and me.

When Eurydice's emissary first stepped out of the shadows there was lots of shouting, calming down once everyone could be convinced that he had come in peace, and at last lots of putting things back in order. During that fuss I couldn't take my eyes off Skuggs. In one of my storybooks, there is a version of the headless horseman with a pumpkin affixed atop his neck stump. The pumpkin is rotten, bits slopping and mulching and oozing from the wrinkly orange skin like greeny-brown wax. Skuggs is what would happen if that pumpkin became an entire person. When he speaks, he has two voices. Two throats. Both of them sound evil.

"Joyous convivilations and apprecitims to you sir-rahs and dame-ahs," Skuggs announced to the tense room. "Oh, but what tarsty tidings have I got. Negotiations. An offer. Yes. A nicest of nicelest offers in my pocket, just for the enemy of my dearest Lady Eurydice."

"I'm sure I won't like an offer of her design, especially when you're her pigeon of choice, Skuggs," said Father. "Still, you've taken great pains to come here. Speak."

"In the last barney, you grabbed a few of our handsome infantry, yeah?"

"We took some of the undead prisoner, yes."

"Right. Guzzlible luck for us because eh... truth be told... you gone and grabbed Lord Burrows' nan."

Everyone was confused.

"Sorry," said Commissioner Thud. "I think I must have misheard you. You said, Lord Burrows' *man?*"

"His nan," said Skuggs. "His dad's mum. His grandmother. His old granny. Haven't any of you buggers got a nan?"

"But he's the master of an undead army," said Hector. "A necromancer supreme."

Skuggs nodded amiably. "Does her proud, he does. Chip off the old gallows."

Father turned to Frank. "Could you and Mr. Glint check if we do, in fact, have Lord Burrows' grandmother in the cells? If she is present, cordon her off."

"Sure thing. Want to come, Doctor John? They're your experiment fodder."

Doctor Isherwood shook his head. "No, I'll stay here. Take care cordoning, Mr. Gallant. The undead go from zero to ferocious gnawing faster than you'd believe."

"Will do."

Uncle Frank and Uncle Glint left. Skuggs watched them go. He watched Uncle Frank particularly closely. *He hates him*, I realized. *Really, honestly hates him. I wonder why?*

"What's your game, Skuggs?" said Father. "Burrows wants his beloved grandmother back? You can't be serious."

"Serious as unguent," said Skuggs. "Serious as a mouth ulcer's pinchy sting."

"In exchange for what?"

"Who, you mean."

Father's hands had been very still. Locked together. Now he began to turn his wedding ring. Round and round. "The cartographers are still alive?"

"Sure are. Locked up."

"Any proof?"

Skuggs leered at us. "Yeah. Got a whole reel of moving picturefilm, ent I?"

The temperature in the room grew colder. There is no technology in Eurydice. It doesn't work even if you bring it from our world, unless it's really clever bio-mechanical stuff Doctor John has made.

"Hm." Father seemed unimpressed. "I won't take your word and forfeit Burrows' relative just like that, Skuggs."

"Everything's got a bit of risk," said the ghastly pumpkin creature. "Play with 'ifs' till you hork up your supperest meat, or negotiate and who knows? You get your scouty map makers and Lord Burrows can rest easy knowing darling Nan is safest and soundly. Everyone wins."

Father considered. "I'd like three days to test Burrows' grandmother."

"Test her?" Skuggs' wretched face squashed tight in a frown. "What for?"

Father only smiled. "Call it caution from the enemy of your dear Lady."

Skuggs had no choice but to give another shrug. "Whatever inflates your balloon, sunshine."

He turned and set off for the shadows again.

"Skuggs?"

The temperature dipped even further. My father's voice was ice.

The creature froze with his back to us. "Uh?" he said.

"You seem confident I'll let you go. The head of Eurydice's communication network has come to me freely. Instead of contenting myself with an exchange of prisoners, I could..."

"Use your Performer-whatsit on me?"

Father didn't reply.

"Or kill me? Is that it? Neither are bloody likely. I got protection from your magic, me. And if you cut me quick and quibblest from my scratch to my knackers, well, who knows what it might do to your pretty girly?"

My belly knotted. What was he talking about? I felt every eye swivel toward me. Cassandra's. Doctor Isherwood's. Silly old Montcrieff's. Father's. It was his that I looked for, his gaze that mattered most in that moment.

But I was wrong. He wasn't looking at me. He was staring at Skuggs. Staring *daggers* and *knives* and *broken-bladed swords* at him.

"Bluffer," said Father. "You know I can't call you on it."

"That I do!" cried Skuggs. And he vented the most sneaky, devious little laugh I have ever heard. "Ahehn-hen-hen!"

It was only after he left that I suspected Skuggs of double-speak, or talking with words of more than one meaning. Was he trying to tell me something? Something about Eurydice?

Well, I don't care. Message away. Transmit from your radio. My ears and heart are firmly shut.

I'm glad I picked up the old diary once more.

Writing this down has helped me realize how closely Eurydice and Skuggs resemble one another. They ought to. He was born in some dark corner of her being. Something like a child she created. Which makes perfect sense, since she is the best I know at creating messes.

Also, writing has shown me how very distant Eurydice and I are now, and perhaps always were. We were never sisters. All this time she was the liar, the cheat, the monster. Everything she warned me against and comforted me from.

I—

Wait.

She's in the room.

She's behind me. Beside me. Surrounding me.

I always knew she was the something that pushed me toward hurting people. People write about a violent voice. She's mine. I always knew I always—

Her fingers on my shoulder. I haven't let her touch me in a long time. One visit when I was nine, I remember, she hugged me, touched me. I was crying, distracted, but for the first time, I thought, *Her skin. It's moving.*

I can feel her breath on the back of my neck. Making the hairs stiffen with fear. And I am, I am so, so afraid.

Why isn't she saying anything?

It's so dark. When did I turn my nightlight off?

I didn't I didn't turn it off she did—

Her fingers are squeezing me, her skin is too hot and busy, moving, moving—

Dad, she's come to take me, I should have built a wall, a huge brick wall in my head to keep her out but now she's here she's here she's—

***

I just woke up. Lying in stickiness. I must have been ill.

My arms and legs hurt. Bruises.

But I'm alone in my room.

She's gone.

Tomorrow morning I'm going to start building my wall. Maybe Uncle Frank will have some tips. He's the Dream Warrior, and when it comes to dreams it's all in the head. And I'll talk to Jo. She's the finest builder ever, and a wall needs to be bricked-up strong right from the start, or else it'll topple with ease. I'm only twelve and thick as clotted cream and I know that.

And I shall tell my father what happened tonight.

Maybe he's experienced something similar. He would have, I'm sure of it.

Because he's a shadow too.

***

Evelyn was right, of course. Skuggs' appearance in Corinth City had indeed been mischievously motivated. His pretense about Lord Burrows' grandmother was not bunk, for Skuggs had been warned about Gormon Hughes' militant capacity for skepticism and detecting lies. But the subject of hostage negotiation, though genuine, had been a disguise.

Eurydice sent Skuggs to convey a message, you see.

Not to Evelyn, but to someone else who was present in the coalition chamber that day.

In his study on the eighty-seventh floor of Redspire, the good doctor Isherwood bent over a sheet of paper with a pen in his hand. During the negotiation Skuggs had spoken a great deal. Some of his words had been accompanied by a buzzing sound, as of a great fly circling a pile of shit. The doctor had known instantly that he and he alone could hear this buzzing.

He wrote down the words, and using a simple yet effective cypher solution technique he took the first letter of each word and put them together. The letters formed the message, the beginning of which was his own first name: John.

He read the message over and over.

John, it said. *Tonight you must sleep with your money.*

He took a credit to bed with him. Sparkling pink quartz it was, and a connection to Eurydice. The crust of that world, and the lifeforce of its creatures, was made of this very substance, this pretty pink stone. How? Who knew. Add that one to the mystery pile, which was immense and reeked more woefully than shit, yet which held for John Isherwood an implacable gravity, and always had.

He stowed the credit under his pillow like a child hoping for a visit from the Tooth Fairy or the Sandman.

He slept.

He dreamed.

In his dream she found him, as he knew she would. She whispered secrets to him and fucked him and whispered some more.

"What would you like to learn today?" she asked.

"Everything." He pecked kisses in the delectable hollow of her throat. His arms were wings trying to close around her and all the things she could tell him. No wingspan was that wide. She was a whole world. He tried anyway. "I want to know everything."

"Then come inside me, my bird," said Eurydice.

John Isherwood went gladly.

Act Three

All The Pretty Little Horses

Chapter Nine

The man who was not called Andrew arrived at *The Pear and Princess* at five o'clock pee-em. It was Sunday, March twenty-third. The days, lengthening since the solstice in December, were now about halfway toward their biggest stretch of the year. The effect was akin to being ferried along by a stubborn caterpillar struggling through a chrysalis of time. Someday not too far in the future it would be a butterfly, spreading large gossamer wings of summer. Whether or not those wings would be dark or light remained to be seen. In Corinth city, summer was no longer a season of charming diversions, otherwise known as honest goofing around. No, not for a while now.

Still, it was Sunday, in that hour which can be classified as late afternoon or early evening. This meant hubbub and clamor for *The Pear and Princess*. It meant constant pulling of taps, coasters frantically slid under pint glasses to prevent those despicable damp rings of moisture on the wood grain, the televisions and sleek portable vid screens tuned to the day's Hippodrome event. It meant a busy kitchen, laughter both wholesome as well as blue-bawdy, and a warm, comfortable atmosphere punctuated by the smell of fish and onions.

It meant that for the friends of Hedley Intrig, table was in session.

It was to this table—perfectly positioned to minimize noise from the wall-mounted TVs and to maximize the chances of regular service—that the man who was not called Andrew made his heading.

Bums and seats were shuffled to make room. There were hellos from all except Marldorp Wilbecomb, who was mid-tirade and not about to let the newcomer's arrival interrupt him.

"All I'm saying," said Marldorp Wilbecomb, "*all I'm saying* is that in my father's day things were done differently."

"Yeah," said Thomas Coats, wiping ale froth from his lips. "Yeah well. Stands to reason, like. Since that were then and this is now."

"I think," hazarded Lilian Dippinswick, "that what our friend is getting at is that, em-em, *different* in this case means, em-em, *better.*"

"Exactly bloody right," said Marldorp Wilbecomb. "Remind me to buy you a pint, Lil. Clarity ought to be rewarded. Look, take this drought, right? I've got a friend, er, friends I should say, the Jurdels. They lived out in the country before signing up for the war. Older couple. Had a daughter. Something happened to her. Can't recall now, anyway—"

"Laurana was her name," said the man who was not called Andrew. "She was a Scarlet Citadel fighter. Died. The Jurdels buried her under a blackberry thicket."

"Yeah. Shame. Didn't know you knew the family, Andy," said Marldorp Wilbecomb. "Anyway, my father was good friends with Mr. Jurdels' father, so we became mates too. Used to have a call with him, oh, once or twice a year. Before and he and the missus left for the Front, Jurdels told me they were up to their necks—their *necks*, mind—in worry. T'were like that for two-and-a-half years. Can you imagine?"

"Worried about the seed sewing?" asked Lilian Dippinswick.

"Among other things, Lil. Among other things. Livestock need watering as much as the fields."

Thomas Coats nodded. "Seeds don't muck as much as cows, but t'end of the day, they're all about what's on the table at breakfast time."

"Exactly bloody right," said Marldorp Wilbecomb.

"It is a rough old shake at the moment," said Lilian Dippinswick. "I'm on the team drawing up the blueprints for more purifiers at the moment. More efficient, you know? We're, em-em, strained. I wish there was more we could do."

Marldorp Wilbecomb's indefatigable grouchiness became momentarily fatigable. "Eh, well. No one's blaming you, Lil," he said. And indefatigable once more, he thumped the table with his fist. "It's the administration at fault. Can't blame a wheel for the car's misdoings. Do you think I blame a single worker if the perfume or cream gets wonkled at my end of the factory? Could do, I suppose, but more likely the problem's administration and oversight. Stands to reason."

"Stands to reason," Thomas Coats echoed.

Hedley Intrig cleared her throat. Everyone shut up.

This attentive silence owed itself to the fact that Hedley Intrig was the de facto leader of this little consortium. She was the principal of The Wimples School For Exasperating Young Ladies. Each of the others had a daughter enrolled there. The four had hit it off at the parent teacher meeting a year ago and had been meeting up for drinks every first and third Sunday of the month since.

"On Friday morning, the school received a letter from the Redspire Irrigation Initiative. They're no longer going to be able to provide the students with clean drinking water. Cutbacks."

The word spun the dial two or three shades grimmer on the table's mood.

"I'm reaching out to a few organizations to see if they can help," said Hedley Intrig, "but if there's any help to be found, it'll be a while coming. Everywhere is going to be hit tomorrow. I wanted to tell you three in advance. The girls are going to have to dip into the family's rations."

"Thin enough as is," grumbled Thomas Coats.

There were glum mutters of agreement.

"Pissing administration," said Marldorp Wilbecomb. "Print-ink smudged tossers. They'll have us drinking it in no time."

"What, print ink?" said Lilian Dippinswick.

"No, Lil. Piss. Our piss, they'll have us gulping it next."

"Oh, I see. You, em-em, really think so?"

"I would not put it past them, Lil. Our president is a man given to flights of the oddest fancy. Why only the other day I happened to be perusing The Times, and I read an article saying that one in every three people now living in this city was born outside the country."

"One in every three?" said Thomas Coats doubtfully.

"One in every three," affirmed Marldorp Wilbecomb. "Can you credit it? Why one in every three's practically... it's practically *half!*"

"Give or take seventeen percent," said Lilian Dippinswick. "I must say I'm pleased with the new influx of culture."

"Culture?"

"You know. New little festivals and parades and ceremonies. Um. Oh! Not to mention we've got a million new options for take-away on a Friday evening." Lilian Dippinswick took a dainty sip of her cocktail, which was flamingo pink and bubbling aggressively. "And with the war on, I feel quite comforted we've got so many allies rallying to the Front."

"Yeah well. Many hands light work, and so on. Share the load. Six spades are better than one," said Marldorp Wilbecomb with grudging admittance. "But a full one in three? That's... Well, it's eh..."

"Practically half," said Thomas Coats.

"Practically half! And they're not all brown or black either. Them I can get along with happily enough. But a heap of these newcomers are *Champleurs*! In my father's day they were the snail-sucking buggers taking potshots at your helmet from their trench. Now we're bezzy mates?"

Hedley Intrig cleared her throat. Everyone shut up.

"I happen to quite like escargot," she said.

"Driving is a fine thing," said Thomas Coats. "Letters too."

Hedley Intrig allowed herself a small smile. "Not ess-car-go, Thomas. Escargot. Snails. Incidentally, did you know we're having this entire conversation in a language that derives itself from Champleurs?"

Thomas frowned, interested. "Eh? That true?"

"Absolutely. Corinthian is a patchwork tongue. About forty percent of the words we use every day come from Champleurs." She took a large, whopping gulp of her cocktail, which was blue and thick as soup. "Not 'bugger,' granted. That word is a Corinthian invention. Snail-sucking too, I wager."

There was a silence. It felt like a pointed finger of a silence, the jagged crescent of nail fixed on Marldorp Wilbecomb, who reddened. He wasn't especially angry; you don't get angry with the woman who dealt with a thousand of the most exasperating young girls in the country, who (mostly) kept them civil and (occasionally) away from vices, and more importantly, who kept them away from their long-suffering parents. Realizing he'd stepped from safe territory into hostile, Marldorp Wilbecomb shifted smartly, hoping to regain some lost footing with the group. "Forty percent of words, you say?"

"Mm," said Hedley Intrig. "Practically half."

Marldorp reddened further. "What's your opinion on it, Andrew?" he managed.

The man who was not called Andrew shrugged. He waved over a server. "I'll get us a round."

"Sound out," said Marldorp Wilbecomb. "And well said, Andrew. All right, enough about Johnny Foreigner. What do we think about this commissioner of ours taking over all the precincts?"

"Oh, I like him," said Lilian Dippinswick. "And I'm not sure he's taking over anything, Marl."

"What would you say, Lil?"

"Uniting, I suppose."

"Granted, granted. What do you make of it, Tom?"

Thomas Coats belched. He did not redden. He didn't even pinken. Not one for embarrassment of any kidney was Thomas Coats. "Hoshrum Thud's a Leonidas boy. He's a hard man. Fair man. My daughter's a sight happier cattin' out at night with him at the helm. Security of mind as well as street, you know. Far as I'm concerned that's how a father takes the temperature of peace in his home and country. Daughter goes out of a night laughing and comes back safe and seeming like she spent that laughter well. Good on Thud. Good on us. Cheers, Andy."

The drinks had arrived. Glasses *clinked*.

"That was lovely, Thomas," said Hedley Intrig. "A lovely way to put it."

Thomas Coats grumbled politely. Not one for compliments of any kidney was Thomas Coats.

"Of course in my father's day a daughter wouldn't be sent off to war," said Marldorp Wilbecomb. "Nor a son. Now all the young people are gearing up for combat. It's the media, I reckon. Showing videos and stills from the Front. Monsters rising up and being smashed down and dead people blazed up in fire or stuck like moldy pigs with magic ice, and that's the least odd method of, ah, disposal, if you take my meaning. Putting it on screens was an odd call. Glamorizing the whole shebang."

"Too gruesome to be called glamorous," said Lilian Dippinswick with a shiver. "How Cate Jubilee and her troops stand it, I'll never know. Oh, but she's so beautiful with her tattoos all over her. Like a watercolor in motion!"

Marldorp Wilbecomb seemed about to go off on how, in his father's day, women with tattoos meant so-and-so and such-and-such, but the man who was not called Andrew spoke up instead. "What do we think about the network broadcasting the rocket launch?"

Their reaction to his inquiry was instant and astonishing.

"*Moo-oo-ooon girl,*" sang the whole table. "*Buy me a ticket... to the white viewin' room. Moo-oo-ooon girl. Come back to me soon.*" Even Hedley Intrig lent her voice to the refrain. That was rock and roll for you. You heard one of its hits roll in from the radio, saw its long haired visionaries and tight-leather-jeaned prophets on the vidscreen, and just like that you were bitten. You had it. The bug. The man who was not called Andrew smiled as the others sang, and it was a convincing smile that you wouldn't have questioned or thought badly of, not unless you too were sour on rock and roll. Its pervasiveness. Its infectious quality. Its bite, bug, and beat. Yes, its beat most of all.

By some twirl of fortune, "Moon Girl" came on *The Pear and Princess'* speaker system. Around the table there were whoops, as though the four of them were soothsayers privy to the haruspeculation of music's whims and wishes, its guts, its glory, its hearty beat-beat-beat.

That was the other thing about rock and roll.

You had it just as much as it had you.

As the song went on and the table lost interest in keeping up with the lyrics and the sharp striking guitar notes, the mood was elevated, that unpleasantness Marldorp Wilbecomb had been peddling quite forgotten, and all was gentle and friendly and sweet.

"I can't tell you how excited I am for it," said Lilian Dippinswick. "The launch, I mean."

"Exactly bloody right." Marldorp chuckled voluminously. "About the only thing that president of ours is doing I'm in favor of and completely behind."

"Brilliant," said Thomas Coats.

Hedley Intrig cleared her throat. Everyone shut up.

"Totally brilliant," she said. "Wimples will be tuning in live, naturally. The girls are in rhapsodies over the prospect. One of the astronauts is a woman. If her, why not them someday, or so runs the logic."

Grins burst onto the faces of the other three.

"My little one would make a good astronaut," said Thomas Coats. "Got a natural advantage. Her head is in the clouds already."

The grins broadened.

"The moon?" said Marldorp Wilbecomb. "In my father's day it was just that. *The moon.* Soon it'll be ours. Brilliant. Eh, Lil?"

"Brilliant," echoed Lilian Dippinswick.

"It's only a hunk of rock," said Andrew.

They all looked at him as if he had spouted twelve additional heads.

"Don't be daft," said Thomas Coats.

"A hunk of rock?" said Marldop Wilbecomb. "A hunk of rock, is it?"

"Ridiculous," said Lilian Dippinswick. "A bit of detritus from a mountain, shoals on a beach, those are hunks of rock. This is the moon we're talking about! The isolated pearl! The white viewin' room, right? Like the song says."

"Daft as a spoon," said Thomas Coats.

"Hunk of rock my eye," muttered Marldorp Wilbecomb. "Sure it's in *space*, isn't it?"

"Yes. And if you're going to be a spoilsport, Andrew, I'll order the next round. We'll soak that cynicism out of you," said Hedley Intrig in her most principally of tones. "Excuse me! Waiter! Ah, there you are. We would like... Let's see now, we would like..."

So the meeting went on.

At length the banter dissolved into goodbyes. Each headed their own way. Outdoors the day had long given up its struggle. Night was well launched, that glittering black rocket detonating dreamily in shades of octopus ink, plum, and pinhole white, the twinkling hue of starshine. There, beckoning, pale and three-quarter bright was the moon.

The man who was not called Andrew watched the moon from the backseat while his driver took him home. As he peeled off his wig, his false bushy beard, and his mustache to reveal cropped, tidy hair and bristles of an entirely different color, and moved on to the removal of his clever facial masking and colored contact lenses, he reflected that the moon was quite like rock and roll in one interesting way.

People were not sure why they liked it yet were utterly sure they did like it.

They liked it so much they wanted more. Rock and roll they could get easily. More and more of these so-called musicians were cropping up daily. The moon though, the trickiness of that goal tantalized. There was no denying it. The evidence was there. People were transfixed by the moon. More, they clamored. More, more. Part the pale veil. More! Launch! Land! The moon, the poet's singer's sailor's gemstone. MORE! Give it to us! Gift us the moon!

So be it. I'll give it to you, thought Hughes.

"You want to listen to some music, Mr. President?" asked his driver.

"Please."

"Station or tune in mind?"

Hughes answered at once. "Anything but 'Moon Girl.'"

"Sir, yes sir."

***

His elevator trip to the seat of Redspire's power was the quiet before the storm. In the clunking-thunking darkness he took long, slow breaths that tasted of stainless steel and anticipation. Eighty-six, eighty-seven...

Eighty-eight—now the doors slid open, and he was a brisk shape dressed in blacks and silvers, his beard silver and black, a thunderhead zooming through the moon-shaped décor of the Lunarlight Wing. Here, the antechamber. Hector nowhere to be seen. Why? Running an errand. Something about purifier security, some toothless faux-terrorist threat there. No matter. Hector was a bulwark, Cassandra a devastation engine, Paris a demon with a bow, and God help any anarchists foolhardy enough to tangle with that sibling trio. The door ahead of him slightly ajar. Prickle of paranoia. Gone. *Me, it was me, I left it that way.* Through the door. The Dragon's Lair. Deprived of its former master, the Last Dragon, it was a shell. He had whiled away more than a decade trying to fill it because if he could fill this office then the wide world would be a doddle. No luck. Fool's errand.

There was a fire in the hearth. Nights could be cold even this far into spring, throbbing his joints with ache. Cut logs crackling, crackling and heat-gouged in red grooves that coughed sparks up the flue, the dragons of stone encircling the flames as though seized with fever, needing to sweat out the sickness of abandonment, purge the sweat and sickness out through their scales, and the desk over there, his mother's desk (*mine now, mine for twelve years damn it*) and the window closed and a feather of moonlight brushing the windowsill.

Hughes went to the desk, snatched up the papers there, read the most important information they contained, and in a rough, severe tone he shouted, *"Montcrieff, can you hear me?"*

"Urk."

"I've got an hour and my city is a rumpled shirt. Let's iron out what creases we can."

"Urk."

An hour-and-a-half later he found Evelyn on the eighty-ninth floor. It had become her sanctum. That suited Hughes. No one was using it. Certainly not its former occupant. He wondered where Estelle Corlum was sometimes, but not that day. Ever since she'd used the Perfect Prison and killed Wendy Dragontail, Estelle had been like a clown at a comedic award show—in other words, completely absent.

The eighty-ninth floor was a complex maze, but Hughes' feet knew the way. He followed them. Evelyn was in Estelle's old room. Shelves groaned humbly under the weight of near eight-thousand books. Here the moonlight was not a feather. It was an entire fan of plumage. The room would have bathed in it had not Evelyn kindled a periwinkle-blue lamp to study by. Jo and Frank were there. Those two were facing toward Hughes as he entered. Evelyn stood with her back to him.

With his arms folded, Frank made a subtle gesture—one finger came up.

Despite its subtlety, Hughes gleaned its meaning at once.

Stall the ball. We're in the throes of progress, so you just stall the ball and hang tight, cotton-hushed and quiet.

Hughes obeyed. Less than twenty-four hours ago, Saturday night, Evelyn had come to him with a confession. She had continued visiting Eurydice years after promising him she would stop. The appalling enormity of the lie was dwarfed only by Evelyn's shame. She hadn't cried, perhaps because she believed he'd be furious with her, and she'd rather take the brunt of that fury all at once rather than an abiding, harsh, fatherly bitterness diluted by tears. He'd surprised and horrified her by not being angry at all.

She'd looked into his eyes and seen hurt. Pure, uncomplicated hurt.

Hurt because she'd concealed the truth from him.

Hurt because he had just now learned he was the kind of father whose daughter felt compelled to keep secrets from him.

It was only when he spoke to her gently, lovingly, that she cried.

Raising a child was a constant lesson in humility. Here he was, a sovereign of fabulous wealth and power, an instrument of change, a conductor, a wielder of magic both unique and exquisite, and he could not stop his daughter crying for twenty minutes. He held her as the sobs wracked her body. Tissues filled with snot and tears. She blubbered incoherencies. When she was coherent, her words frightened him. Each minute had felt like an hour. He told her that she was so brave to tell him the truth. So wise and wonderful. Her idea to recruit Frank and Jo to show her ways to protect herself was inspired. She was okay. A good girl.

Fine, amazing even. He was proud of her. A good girl. It was okay, all okay, all okay, all...

"Okay," said Evelyn. "I can see it. Every mossy brick, just like you said Uncle Frank."

"What color are the bricks?" said Frank.

"Lime."

"Why lime?"

"I like limes."

Amusement flickered over Frank's face. His aurora hair turned lime-green. "Good answer. How about the moss?"

"Red. Red and hairy looking."

"Dry?"

"Wet, it's been raining."

"You've never seen rain outside of vids, kiddo. We want this to be perfect."

"I can see it, Uncle Frank. I swear."

"We'll see."

Frank reached out a hand. It spindled into a network of fibers, thin strings of golden-brown nylon. Hughes had seen this before, many, many times, though not quite enough to dampen the awe that rose in him.

"Jo," Frank murmured. Jo stepped forward.

The strings had but to touch Evelyn's hand and the girl was out like a light.

"Timber," said Frank softly as she fell.

Jo caught her.

Frank's strings circled Evelyn's head, rotating slowly in a halo. Frank closed his eyes. "Brick by brick, the wall comes down. Or does it? Here come the mind mangonels, the thought catapults, here..." Some strong emotion cut him off there. He whistled. His eyelids fluttered and opened wide. "I'll be damned."

The strings retreated, forming his hand.

Evelyn woke up. She seemed on the verge of upset, then a grain of boldness lengthened her and she offered Jo a smile, stood straight, and looked at Frank.

"You broke through," she said. "My wall couldn't keep you out of my head."

"Are you disappointed?" said Frank unbelievingly. "Kiddo, don't you dare. Jo, did you hear me whistle just now?"

"I did indeed, Frank."

"Evelyn, you know why I whistled?"

She shrugged, still fighting that defeated sense of sorrow.

"I whistled because I had to work to bust that lime-green wall with its hairy looking moss so wet and so red. I had to work and that impressed me, and when I get impressed my lips can't help but give it away." Frank whistled. "How do you get to The Hippodrome?"

Evelyn's smile was genuine now. "Practice, practice, practice."

"That's what we're gonna do. Every single day from now on Jo will help you build that wall inside your mind, and every day I'm gonna try and knock it flat. And when you've got a wall inside your mind that could withstand all my might and my mommas' combined, were they still kicking, then..." Tendrils of carmine and burgundy curled in Frank's hair. "Then we're going to build something behind the wall. Something that Eurydice won't like if ever she does break through those lime-green bricks all smeared in wet, red moss. Sound sweet?"

"Sweet as vanilla and honey biscuits, Uncle Frank."

"That is sweet." His lips fluted out a whistle. He started. "See? I can't help myself."

Evelyn laughed. She could give Cate Jubilee a run for her money with that laugh. It was really something.

Frank gazed over at where Hughes stood.

"Look who's joined us," he said, as if Hughes had only now appeared.

Evelyn spun. "Father of mine!"

He emitted a gruff, cuddly sort of noise when she dashed over and threw her arms around him.

"Hello, Daughter of mine," he said.

This formality was an inside joke of theirs. Last night, the night of confession, it had been, "Dad?" Hughes had known there was trouble brewing right away. Modes of address were alarm bells, some small and tinny, others huge clangers, and parenthood made him a host to these alarm bells, a belfry in a church devoted to worship of a goddess who relied on his belief, his support, his patience, his understanding.

She recounted the day's lesson to him in a flurry of words he would not have had a hope putting together, had he not just now caught the tail end of things.

As he listened he hugged first Jo, then Frank, which was like being embraced by a cheerful werewolf and the platonic ideal of a bewitching summer night respectively.

"How's The Foundry, Jo?" he asked in a lacuna between bouts of Evelynish excitement.

"Busy," replied Jo. "Full of monster bits."

"Iphigenia's raw materials for magic items, you mean?"

Jo nodded. "S'what I said."

"And the Foundry is full of them?"

"Yeah, got a delivery this morning, didn't we?"

That was news to Hughes. "How were they delivered?"

"Ah," said Jo sagely. "They arrived in what you would call, technically speaking, a *big sod-off pile.*"

"Right." Hughes opened his mouth to follow up. Closed it. Frowned up at his friend. "Right. Glad we've got that sorted."

"How long have I got you for, Dad?" asked Evelyn.

"I've got a meeting with some delegate or other at eleven. Till then, I'm yours." Hughes turned to Frank and Jo. "Sticking around a while?"

"Can't," said Jo. "Work."

"Can't," said Frank. "Play."

"Play, eh?"

"Making the most of what time I have left here. Catherine wants me back at the Front when Evelyn here has got her wall good and strong."

"Mum hates when you call her that," she said.

"She really does," Hughes echoed.

Frank shrugged languidly. He shook Evelyn's hand. "Stay cool, kid." And with that he swept away. Jo lumbered after him, pausing to murmur an arresting little something into Hughes' ear.

He nodded, gave her a quick hug farewell, and watched her go.

"Let's chat here for a few," he said. "Take in the view where the air is rare."

"There's not much air at all. It's stuffy tonight."

"Crack a window. Not so much." He chuckled. "A crack I said."

"Sorry, Dad."

"No bother. Come here to me and we'll have a chat."

They both set themselves right, undoing what the lively gust of wind had done to their clothes and hair, and sat together on two chairs facing the window. It was dark out, and at Evelyn's insistence they dimmed the periwinkle-blue lamp so the moon could have its due hour. Now they could see the night properly. A few wisps of cloud seemed to wave good evening to them with fluffy cotton fingers. The stars were not so friendly, twinkling for their own benefit it seemed, and Hughes wondered what stars glimmered over not Catherine (she really did loathe being called that) but rather Cate Jubilee. He expected a letter from her any hour now. Developments at the Front. Hopefully welcome ones, but more likely the other kind. Well, add them to the developments at home. Very few things began or ended when you ruled a coalition state. Things persisted or they changed. Developed. There was no end to the developments, so numerous and peculiar that eventually they'd become ordinary to him, as ordinary as this once spectacular view of the night from the eighty-ninth floor.

Fatherhood remained a puzzle though, a puzzle that confounded, rewarded, and occasionally punished harshly. He wondered if all dads found it so, or just silly old powerful old Gormon Hughes, lord of the tower, king of the castle, woopdie-doo-da.

"What did Jo whisper to you?" Evelyn asked him.

"She told me not to worry. You're going to be safe."

"That was all?"

"By and large."

In fact, Jo had said a good deal more. She had in fact said, in a dour voice that jived against her usually jolly disposition, "Hughes, if Frank's wall can stop Eurydice, I'll be a baked banana. Things that know what they are—*really know*—are tougher than tough, and that woman is dangerously mental when it comes to knowing herself. I've seen her work and seeing a woman's work is the same as seeing her. You got to understand, Eurydice is so mad she's not confused about who she is. She's a hundred things at once, and a thousand things at twice, and sure about every single one of them. No, Frank's wall won't matter a tosh. But I'll keep your girlie safe. I got a plan on the go, just you wait and see."

Seeing a woman's work is the same as seeing her.

It struck him as a distinctly Jolene thing to say, a deceptively simple thing that held lots of stuff just underneath like a flaking cellar door over a vault of tunnels.

Thinking about the rest brought that bleak feeling of powerlessness again. Putting Evelyn's wellbeing in the hands of someone else ought to have felt okay. After all, it was her safety that mattered. But it didn't. It felt so utterly wrong, and he needed to get a hold of that before it got ahead of him.

"Dad?"

"Uh?"

"Away with the mushroom familiars?"

"No, I'm here."

She gave him a wise look. It made her look older, sixteen rather than twelve.

"How were Miss Intrig and her friends?" Evelyn asked him.

Why, almost as baffling to me as you are, hon.

"Fine," he told her. "Obsessed with the moon launch."

"So are you, Dad."

"*Touché*, sweetie, but in a different way."

"How?"

"Well, they're excited for the fact of it. They want to see the rocket go up, make the landing—"

"Or explode." Evelyn shied. "Oh. I shouldn't have said that."

"You aren't wrong. It'd be an awful lightshow, but people find they can't look away from such things."

"Because they're macabre."

"Sometimes."

"Anyway," Hughes said, getting back on track, "while most people want to see the whole thing come off without a hitch, finally get to see what the moon is like, I'm... Well, I want to see that too. But I also want to use the moon landing. Use it the way you use tools to keep your terrarium neat and tidy."

"What are you hoping to use it for, Dad?"

"For recruitment, sweetheart. To get more people interested in the war."

She said nothing to that, thinking.

"No," she said, giving up. "I don't see how the launch and the war have anything to do with one another."

"Want to find out?"

Her face lit up. "That'd be interesting."

"Well, I'll give you two options. We go to a show as I'd planned for us. Or we go to the telecommunicog and I'll show you how the launch and war are related."

"The second one!" she chirruped. She realized she'd chirruped. Hughes watched color rise redly in his daughter's ears. God, she was so like him as a boy, it boggled his mind. "You're sure you'd like to show me?"

"Of course I'm sure." The idea pleased him. A show would have involved passivity, giving Evelyn more time to brood on this nasty Eurydice situation. Showing her what he'd put a chunk of his concentration toward for the past three years would allow her to play an active part in her evening. If he were in her place, Hughes knew he would have liked the distraction.

"I've never been to the telecommunicog," said Evelyn as she sleeved herself into her coat.

"Yes, you have."

"When?"

"I showed it to you."

"What age was I?"

Hughes checked the archives of his memory. "Seven and a half."

Her expression twisted up irritably. "I'm obviously not going to remember it then, Dad."

"Really?"

"Of course not!"

He fetched a sigh. "I suppose you can't take after me in every way."

"That's mean."

"Is it?"

Evelyn gave a cross nod. "Lauding your memory over the rest of us is mean."

"Oh."

"And you mustn't be mean."

"Oh?"

"If you are, I shall kick you very hard in the shin. And you'll remember *that*, won't you?"

She stalked haughtily toward the elevator.

Hughes scratched his beard. "Takes after her mother too, I see."

And he followed after her.

***

The telecommunicog was the device responsible for landline calls within the city. It's designer, the very first Jolene, was the same woman responsible for the city's harnessing of electrical energy some time ago. The building it was housed inside had been converted many times to keep up with architectural trends in Ptolema District, but the device itself never received a single alteration. How to improve upon brilliance? Nowadays its home was a rather officious structure, very large and austere with computers, wall-spanning grids full of dead or lively blinking lights, and rather serious people with clip-on ties and aggressively bland trousers, and names like Miriam, Janet, or perhaps that most middle-managerial of names, Nigel. But the telecommunicog itself was a triumphantly exciting device. As you might imagine, it had the appearance of a terrifically large cogwheel suspended in the air with struts. It spun consistently on a rotary cycle, huge metallic teeth plucked from and then eased into gums of galvanized steel. With each turn of the wheel, an invisible string connecting every home and place of business stretched taut, capable of transmitting little blips of phonemic expression, sounds both reedy and righteous, and so the serious building and all its serious people gained an unspoken dimension of gladness and pleasure. The machine of the world must needs turn. Nice to be contributing a little something, no matter how dreary. Such was the prevailing sense, anyway, accompanied by the gentle, continuous grinding noise of the great gear, the locus of chatter and arrangements and emergency and relaxation, the well-oiled emblem, the telecommunicog.

Hughes could not help but smile at Evelyn's reaction to seeing it.

"I *do* remember!"

"Told you," he said.

Hughes brought Evelyn around for a quick tour, introducing her to junior and senior workers alike. They were all nervous around him and giddy because Hughes invariably remembered their names and what they did, as well as the health of their elderly relations, pet names, and in some cases, their gripes with the workplace. These Hughes would carefully inquire after, giving all impression of engrossment and concern.

Sometimes he felt Evelyn looking at him. When he glanced she would look away, embarrassed, her ears glowing like little raspberries, and Hughes would feel aglow himself and carry on as though he hadn't noticed a thing.

Being a father can be a lesson in humility. It can also boost your confidence so enormously you begin to worry about the width of doorframes.

"Mr. President." Approaching them was a man in a white shirt, ludicrously prosaic spectacles, and suspenders that might have been holding up his entire frame from collapsing into sheer puddling mediocrity, as well as holding aloft his trousers. And those trousers—they were the most aggressively bland trousers of them all. The man was of middling height, middling weight, middling features. His hairline was receding, but not too much. His eyes were an uninteresting beige-brown. When they'd first met, Hughes had decided that should this man be offered three wishes, at least two of them would be used to improve global filing systems. "Mr. President, there you are. I hope you'll accept my apologies for the delay. We've had a pylon fall on the crowlines, and—"

"Not to worry, Gail," said Hughes. "This is my daughter, Evelyn. She'll be joining us today."

The man put out his hand. "Gailfax Marmley. Pleased to meet you, Your Worship."

Miss Hughes will do nicely, Hughes thought. *And you'll be Mr. Marmley.*

"Miss Hughes will do very well," Evelyn told Gailfax Marmley, shaking his hand. "And you'll be Mr. Marmley."

Hughes suppressed a grin.

Gailfax led them through a series of corridors and rooms—each one a carbon copy of the last—until at length they came to a private office. The office was much bigger than the others Evelyn had been privy to that evening. More intriguing than the sheer size was the amount of equipment. Wide eyed, she scanned it all: film cameras, digital cameras, tripods and stands, a veritable nest of cables like glossy black snakes, as well as processing paraphernalia Evelyn had only ever seen in documentaries about the making of her favorite movies. Before these, taking up about one half of the room, was a staging area. There were boxes there, large and small, and the only open one was filled to the brim with costumes and props.

"Are we, eh, going for anything out of the ordinary today, Mr. President?" said Gailfax.

"No, Gail," Hughes replied. "I've had an idea, but it's all on my end."

"Hope it works out for you, sir."

"Me too."

Evelyn was frowning at the scene.

"Watch for now," Hughes told her quietly. "I'll explain after."

With an air of someone going through an old and familiar routine, Gailfax Marmley went to a soundproof booth tucked into the corner of the room. He stepped inside, closed the door, and could no longer be seen.

Simultaneously, Hughes pressed "play" on one of the higher-grade digital cameras. He reached down inside himself and took hold of his Performance, as a man who knows his neighborhood may take hold of an opportunity for an evening walk, suburbia by moonlight. Even should blindness strike him halfway along that walk, the man would still know where he's come from and where he's going. So too with Performance, which unrolled in him and lengthened his body and absorbed along the laneways of his mind like so much glowing moonlight.

Moving quickly and with terrific purpose, Hughes stepped into the staging area. He raised a hand, curling the fingers of that hand just so. The biomechanical lights, clever in their response to hand signals, switched on. They were as beige and homely as Gailfax Marmley. Now Hughes raised his other hand, twitching the fingers, and a row of secondary lights began to shine with a light as hazel-green as his own eyes, which of course were exactly the same shade as Evelyn's eyes.

He looked into the lens of the camera, and in a voice so engaging it could have convinced a hen to lay dragon eggs, he said, "When you come out of the booth, you will recognize me, but not my daughter. She will just be a girl who came with the president. You will ask her name and where she goes to school."

Out flew his Performance. He aimed for the lens, and at the same time he envisioned his target beyond the lens. The invisible motes of energy carrying data. The booth, connected via those motes to the camera lens. And the man inside the booth. Hughes pictured him as clearly as you might picture an important task looming on your itinerary—in other words a complex, three-dimensional contemplation. He envisioned all these things and sent the Performance rolling along these tracks of visualization. Now, as the moment moved, he delicately siphoned off a little of the Performance and sent it toward Evelyn. Not enough to root its power in her but enough to involve her in the show.

Audience participation, he thought, bemused.

The doing of this—the siphoning—was particular. A year ago he was sure he could not have managed it. With use, Performance was becoming easier to manipulate. Even first trial attempts of technique, as this was. He thought of Frank's words of encouragement, intended for Evelyn, yet recurring now to her father with a sharp urgency:

How do you get to The Hippodrome?

Practice, practice, practice.

A minute or so later, Gailfax Marmley emerged from the booth.

"Well?" he said. "Did it work?"

"You tell me." Hughes indicated Evelyn. "Do you remember her?"

"Your daughter? Certainly, sir."

Hughes gave a resigned little smile that didn't touch his eyes. Neither of the other two knew it, for they had never met her, but just then he looked exactly like Iphigenia flashing one of her sweet, doomed smiles. "No, Gail. It didn't work."

Gailfax commiserated with a shrug. "I'm sure you'll think of something, sir."

"Yes, I expect I will in time. Thank you for taking the time today."

"Anything for the Citadel, sir."

"You'll refuse my offer of money again?"

"Couldn't take a single credit, sir," said Gailfax. "It'd chafe against my civic duty, sir."

"You will let me know if that ever changes. Come along, Evie."

In the *Eschezmont,* driving home to the tower, Hughes noted a faraway look on his daughter's face. "You've been patient," he ventured.

"Have I?" Faraway face, faraway voice.

"Don't you want to know what all that was about?"

No reply.

They sat, Father and Daughter and silence, silence like a dark cousin filling the car bonnet to boot.

"I suppose I do," said Evelyn. She turned away from the dry black night and looked at him. "Go on then, if you must."

Her tone rankled. Now the silence was his.

"*Well?*" she said.

"Easy, Daughter of mine."

"Are you going to use it on me, Dad?"

"Evie..."

"Use it!" she snapped. Her ferocity shocked him, and worse. It goaded him. "Use it! Use it!"

"*That's enough.*"

"Use it like you used it in that room. I felt it. You pushed it through the camera. You're trying to put your Performance into people through vids. For the rocket launch, I bet, when everyone will be glued to their screens. That's your recruitment drive. Get the whole world watching, and when they are you'll appear and speak to them, and suddenly Mum will have a lot more boots on the ground to fight Eurydice. Very clever. There. Happy?"

He drove. His teeth ground together like little white cogs in his mouth. His grip on the wheel was white-knuckle-tight. His complexion was pale too, and his mood, deathly pale.

From the corner of his eye, he saw his daughter's mouth twist. Not a smile but a dark cousin to a smile. "So sorry, Father of mine. I'm in a strop, you see. Use your power on me and I'll be as compliant and lovely as you like."

When he didn't, she looked angrier than he'd ever seen her.

Her head jerked at the neck, wrenching her face away from him and toward the passenger window.

The speed of the conflict surprised her too. He could read that much from her. Bugger all else. Hell, he was surprised he could parse much of anything. The cloudy maroon letters of his rage were awfully difficult to gaze past. Inside him they wrote the script of lost tempers, a script he refused to read. He had never hit her. Not once. And the fact that he had wanted to just now—almost needed to—jetted that rage full of a helpless loving fear, the fear of a parent who has come close to treating their child like... foreign matter. Like something to be dealt with, possibly excised. Something that you could cherish when you wanted and broken when you wanted.

He had no idea what had brought this on. Which meant he could not resolve it. How to plug up a flood when you can't find the initial leak?

One thing he was convinced of: Evelyn would not guide him. For whatever reason his daughter had gone off him tonight.

Later, his father would tell him this over the phone:

"Son, you see a lot, but you can't see everything. Children, now, they're all about seeing. A baby is all mouth, and a young boy or girl is all eyes. Soon she'll be all mouth again. The teenage years, God have mercy. But for now, she's got her whole self out on stalks, peering at stuff that seemed meaningless yesterday but today is nothing but meaning. I can't speak to what it might be, but that girl has seen something she doesn't like. Her losing her cool with you, that is her letting you know about it."

"I'll give her time and talk to her."

"Give it a go. Don't be aggrieved if she broods a while. Mad for brooding. All eyes and all brooding and all loving, that's bairns at twelve."

"What could she have seen, Dad?"

"If I had to guess," his father said, "I'd say it was you."

"Me?"

"Yup. You see a lot, son. But not everything."

Hughes could only frown at that, wondering if Evelyn had seen something in him he had not noticed. If so, what?

But that was later. For now he turned from one avenue to another. He could see Redspire, a great solemn giant louring over the electric streets.

He wondered if he ought to send Evelyn back to The Wimples School For Exasperating Young Ladies. It was a boarding school, the girls home for the long March weekend. Evelyn had been going there for five years, ever since Cate and Hughes made the decision that she needed a relatively normal education with interesting peers her own age (and you don't get much more interesting than the girls who attend Wimples). Hence Hughes' disguise as a man named Andrew who went for beers of a Sunday with some parents and the school principal; hence, although it was not his sole motivation for attending these meetings, the friends of Hedley Intrig.

Last night, when Evelyn told him about Eurydice, her dreams, and her seizure, he'd made up his mind at once to keep her out of school and at home. Within arm's reach. Now, he was coming round to the idea that the opposite might be best. Frank and Jo could teach her when she finished lessons and before she went to her Wimples dormitory.

How can you entertain that? his kindness said. *You've got to keep her close to you, in case she needs you.*

She doesn't speak to me that way, that cloud of fear and anger in him replied. *No one does. Not anymore.*

She had probably even deduced that the reason Hughes wanted Gailfax Marmley for his experiments with Performance was a matter of scientific awareness. Gailfax was the equivalent of a massive sample size because the man was so ordinary you could feed him letters and call him a postbox. A lowest common denominator in suspenders. If the recorded and transmitted Performance worked on Gailfax Marmley, it would work on the whole bloody world.

Yes, Hughes bet his girl had figured that out as well as the rest. Figured it out and spat it at him like a mouthful of cold stomach acid.

There, she'd said. *Happy?*

With a small yet quietly savage turn of his fingers, Hughes turned on the radio.

From the *Eschezmont*'s speakers came a crabby, crunchy guitar riff, and lo-and-behold, the lyrics. Rock and roll lyrics and a rock and roll voice.

Evelyn hummed along. She was faraway again.

Her humming brought Hughes back to himself completely. That precipice of ugly paternal fury was gone. Evelyn's hum was vague and very beautiful.

It was that and that alone which prevented him changing the station because the song was "Moon Girl."

Chapter Ten

Let your mind's eye sweep down into the depths of Redspire.

See the cavernous space below the tower, the officious people doing officious jobs, totting up calculations, fussing and hurrying because this is war damn it, and war is like gossip (it never stops, so how can they?). The portal of stone and flame rises high over all. It was made by an ambitious man some years ago, a man who listened with both ears at the keyhole of the universe and who heard the universe speak the only way it knows how: in ideas.

He made two doors of fire. He scrawled names next to the blueprints on the little sketchpad in his office. The second was called Iphigenia. That one he built above ground because it was a good door that would only swing as he built it to swing, i.e. one way.

The first door, though, he built underground. That's this one, here in the vast flickering depths. This door does not swing one way. It misbehaves.

One world and another. Back and forth. Us and them. Them and us.

And that means war.

Hear the drums yet? The drums of hate?

No. You wouldn't.

Let me show you.

Go through the door of fire. See the insane, ever-shifting land? See the sky that sneers at logic? See the suns, the moons, the stars? They misbehave, or give the appearance of... call it astral disobedience. But really, it's the world that disobeys the cosmos. She's a rebel. When she can get away with it, she likes to cause a mess.

And she always gets away with it.

This is Eurydice. A woman and a world. She loves when the music breaks. Any music. All music. As the conductor declared approvingly to her orchestra: No notes. No notes whatsoever.

Or else.

There are exceptions. Most rules have those. One such outlier to the melody-killing absolute was the drums, the drums that sound on this soil, Eurydice's soil. Hear them now, close your eyes and listen.

Tum-te-tum-te-tum-te. Boom. Tum-te-tum. Boom.

The drums of two rival sides. Think of them as the home team and the away team. Home wears Eurydice's colors. Away wears scarlet. The home team's drums are necrotic flesh stretched over mildewed bone, tom-toms and goblet-shaped djembes of the most horrible manufacture. The away team's drums are the earth itself. What sticks could pound out that sound? Why, only the leg-shaped trees carrying fortresses called Bettys. Their colossal stride shakes the scenery, beats the rhythm.

Listen. Undead and monstrous versus the living. Home versus away.

Tum-te-tum-te-tum-te. Boom. Tum-te-tum. Boom.

Here the drums of hate go round the clock.

Midnight, and Sunday night became Monday morning in the span of two seconds. Near the center of Eurydice's mutating continent (near, but not too terribly near), a meeting was about to take place.

Skuggs was first to arrive by a fair margin. He ought to have been first. It was his house that was to host the meeting. When he wasn't running communications for the war, Skuggs lived inside the husk of a riddlewood tree. The tree, once a living, thinking, talking, and most importantly riddling thing, had made the mistake of trying to take Skuggs' spot on Eurydice's council. It challenged him to a match of wits, a riddle contest. Skuggs lost. He admitted defeat cordially. Then he went away. While the tree celebrated its victory with a slurp of good rainy earth, Skuggs returned. With him he'd brought a mushroom. He planted the mushroom in a tiny fissure of bark where it wouldn't be noticed, and over the course of three excruciating months, the mushroom spread a fungal sickness through the taproot of the tree. By the time it discovered the source of its malady, it was too late. Skuggs, in the market for a new abode, or a "gaff" as he called it, claimed the dying tree as his home. It was still alive and aware as he filled it with furniture. Now the riddlewood decayed slowly by a cliffside. It had been on its way to throw itself (and Skuggs, or so it hoped) off the cliff and to their mutual destruction, but alas succumbed to pain and died shortly thereafter. Skuggs found the suicide attempt hilarious.

Lord Burrows arrived at five past the hour.

Skuggs heard Burrows' wolf breathing hard—it was a long way from the Front to Skuggs' riddlewood home, and the wolf could not teleport as Skuggs could. They did have one thing in common though: two throats. Skuggs had only the one head, but often it's commonalities that lead to friendship, and Skuggs took care to keep the two-headed wolf as companionable as possible. Truth be told, she gave him the belly-bugles almost as horribly as the last member of the council to arrive.

The front door opened. Skuggs heard footsteps on the stairs.

First came the crown made of rotted beastly teeth. Then the veil and the hair, wafting and white like strands of cobweb. Then the mouth, thin and gray-lipped and scornful. At last, the rest of Lord Burrows appeared, taller than a human being, and clad in robes to match the midnight hour, every stitch chased in gold embroidery.

"That red-haired cretin," he said, "is really beginning to nettle me. I'm talking about deliberate provocation here."

Skuggs, who was enjoying a wormy apple cider by the window, raised his tankard. "Good day to you as well, I'm sure."

The room—located where the trunk of the riddlewood swelled widest—was about as large as a cottage. Nevertheless, Burrows' displeasure brimmed it up full.

"She's got me relying on birds and oozes. Oozes!"

"Who's got you relying on oozes?"

"The birds I can deal with. I like birds. They tick the anatomy checklist, plus or minus a beak of course. And they've got the decency to keep up their end of the conversation."

"Burrows."

"You just try bandying it out with an ooze and see where it gets you. I give them a direct order and sometimes they obey and sometimes they won't. All I get in response when I confront them about it is 'burble-gurble-sclup-blup.' I ask you, what am I supposed to do with that?"

"Yeah, your basic ooze is a narsty sticky-trickle minger. So what?"

"The worst thing is they've proven essential. We can't climb those fortresses of hers without them. It's this machine, you see. She's had her scientists build a machine and attach it to each of the fortresses' legs. What happens is, it sucks in my soldiers as they climb, scrambles them like eggs, strips skin and muscle, pulverizes bone, and... You won't believe this, I barely could, and I was there. The machine refines all of those insides, those pure, necromantically restored insides, into resin. Then it pumps this resin up to wall-mounted turrets and fires my own people back at me! Scattershot style. Rest assured that no matter how many engineers were involved, that bit of devilry originated in her."

Skuggs gulped his cider, his two throats bulging with each swallow. This was interesting gab, all right. Machines that sucked in Burrows' undead and chewed them up and turned their bits into blasting wads of woe? Guzzlible luck, that, and horriblest. But interesting.

"So we've got to deploy the oozes. Ride them up the legs to gain the battlements. My troops can keep hold of their firmer upper sides, and the mucus from the underbelly gunks up the machines."

"Gunge them up, eh?" said Skuggs musingly.

That was clever. Burrows was all about being clever. That was his role in the council: the brilliant commander. Who better to run the drudgery of war than a necromancer? If you took the trouble to raise people from their graves, you could jolly well get them organized afterward. Better Burrows than Skuggs. Skuggs had too wayward a personality for leadership. Happily lonely and capable of traveling along the tectonic plates of pink quartz crust under the earth, he was the ideal messenger.

As for the third member of their council... well, the less Skuggs thought about him, the better. He finished the squirming dregs of his cider. Meanwhile Burrows was still on a tirade.

"It amounts to the fact that with the oozes we've got land power as well as air. The birds, you get me. Flying means avoiding the fortress legs, avoiding the machines. Imperative oozes. What have we come to? They're unnatural. No culture or ritualism. Have they leaders? Basic society? Nothing. Tentatively ask one if they can be brought back from the dead and they gyrate at you. Actually it's more of a disdainful wobble. As if the cycle of life and rebirth were beneath their superior gelatinous consciousness. I swear, I could throttle them if only they had necks."

Skuggs gave his fellow councilor a sympathetic sneer. "Even the thought of it gives me the craggles."

"What?" Burrows reeled on him. "What are you yammering about now, Skuggs?"

"Who has got you relying on oozes?"

"Cate Jubilee." The name dripped from Burrows' tongue like warm seagull crap. "Who else? I swear, Skuggs, darting around as you do you don't see half the troubles in this war. You don't see the tricks our enemy pulls. This thing with the oozes is just the most recent of her wiles. She's lucky. And when her luck runs out she's crafty enough to make her own. It's damaging to morale. She's got my soldiers firing looks at me. Looks! At me!"

"Bloody nerve."

"Bloody nerve is right." Burrows drove a foot into one of Skuggs' thankfully empty booze barrels. It smashed satisfyingly. "And they were meaningful looks too! What's the word... sounds like compliment mashed potato juice... means insubordinate..."

"Contumacious," said a voice. There was something of muslin about the voice, soft and sibilant. At the same time there was something clinically poisonous about it, as though the muslin had been dipped in arsenic.

"Thank you," said Burrows. "Have you heard me, Skuggs? Do you understand? Contumacious looks from my own... my..."

Burrows looked up. Skuggs was way ahead of him.

Ruthven was wrapped around one of the ceiling beams. Very little of the chilly green glow from Skuggs' array of lumenfly lamps could climb so high, and so the dragon's fur, and claws, and rusty surgery kit of a grin, were pitched in shadow. They could see his eyes clear enough. White with red slits, an albino rattlesnake's eyes.

"Oozes and birds. How versatile you are, Burrows. How adaptive to circumstance."

"Thank you," said Burrows.

"And I'm sure Cate Jubilee is doing exactly as you are. Lamenting your genius. Throwing a hissy fit. Oh, but do go on," Ruthven bid them. "Don't mind me."

A shift of movement. A *click-clock*ing sound, very faint, like clothing stands falling on a bed of rotten silk. All three councilors looked toward the southern end of the room. There was something there, something like a man or a woman, only very wide on top. As if instead of a head the figure had an enormous wheel.

Or perhaps it was merely a large pillow concealing their head. After all the figure was lying down. Possibly snoozing. And though the shadows at that end of the room were even more dense than those that obscured Ruthven, and so the details were more suggestive than scary, Skuggs found the arrival of this new and unexpected visitor inspired more dread than a hundred Ruthvens could have.

Slowly, and with as much deference as they could summon, the three councilors bowed to the figure. Skuggs' bow drew his one crystalline eye all the way to his knees, not a very far distance, granted. Burrows' bow was graceful, his black veil shivering. Ruthven inclined his head, his demeanor poised, yet his scarlet-spotted fur betraying his unease, for it was bristly and stiff.

From the figure there was no visible reaction. The quiet raggedy sound was not repeated. Just a shape. Perfectly ordinary.

Aside from the fact that a minute ago, it hadn't been here.

"Perhaps we ought to get down to brass tacks," said Burrows. He selected a chair.

"Cider?" said Skuggs, straightening and waddling over to crack a fresh barrel. Burrows nodded. "What about you, Ruthven? I might have a bubo slug you can suck on."

"No, thanks oh-so-much," said Ruthven, slithering down from the rafters. "I've already eaten."

I bet you have, thought Skuggs. *I just bet you have.*

He handed Burrows a tankard and then it was on to business.

"Let's begin with my number one concern," said Burrows. "It's a pressing one."

"What might that be?" said Ruthven.

"Ground, Ruthven. We're ceding too much of it. Good cider, Skuggs."

"Cheers. Pickled the worms meself."

"Ceding ground is all according to plan," Ruthven pointed out. His slitted eyes darted to the figure enmeshed in shadow. "Ceding ground was ordained."

Burrows was not to be cowed. "And I was all for it. For twelve years I've been for it. The problem isn't a question of losses. We can handle those. We've got the numbers. And I understand that we must lose these battles. That the order of operations is to engage the enemy, fight, and make it look like we're losing... really convince the enemy we're about to break and that tactical retreat is our only option. A policy of brutality, inflicting as many casualties on our foe as we can before tucking our tails between our legs and running like hell. I know that's..." Here Burrows made a conscious effort not to look at the figure. "... I know it's according to plan. Our issue is geographic. Territory, gentlemen. We've simply allowed Cate Jubilee too much of it."

"If you're referring to the Crystal Country," said Ruthven, "I shall stop you there. Our mistress would never dream of compromising her sanctum."

If Skuggs' memory told it true, Burrows never smiled. The closest the necromancer ever got was a small parting of the lips, accompanied by an even smaller gasp. Skuggs thought his own tittery laugh far more jocund, but Burrows' arrogant little gasp always got on Ruthven's draconic tits, which was some consolation for the fact that it also got on Skuggs'.

"I'm not talking about the Crystal Country," Burrows said. "Our changing landscape keeps it out of our enemy's reach. Cate Jubilee and her allies will never find it. I'm talking about the rest of our kin. The ones that have ignored our flitters, or which the flitters cannot find. The ones that have eluded Skuggs."

"Oi," said Skuggs. "I found the Beldames."

Burrows' retort was cold. "And who else?"

Skuggs let that one slide. It was true he'd had trouble finding the rest of their allies. The world was a big place, and though he was an enviable tracker, not everywhere could be reached from the earth directly. One of his tasks, given at the early outset of the war, had been to track down the lot of them: the bigwigs, the meanest and mightiest creatures in the world. Once he found them, he would pass on the mission. The mighty creatures were to cross over into Iphigenia. There they would spread a healthy helping of havoc. Make a meal out of mayhem. Then they were to come back and lend a hand (or indeed a paw, a claw, a talon, or a fin) with the war. Skuggs' list detailing these powerful creatures included the Troll, William o' The Wisps, the Old Stony Crow, the Beldames, Yellow-Eye the Gentler, as well as many others. Things had gone well at first, with Skuggs achieving success after success. Then disaster struck. Now for the life of him, Skuggs was having the pits of a time finding those on his list.

If only he had his crystal compass. If only Cate Jubilee hadn't stolen it, scruggly thieving bint that she was, then Skuggs might have been saved the disapproval of his peers, as well as that of the enigmatic figure at the southern end of the room.

"Are you suggesting that Cate Jubilee might find them instead?" said Ruthven.

"Not suggesting. I'm stating it. She will find them." Burrows set his cider down. "It's only a matter of time. She'll find them and she'll kill them, and our hope of reinforcements will dwindle and be lost."

"Well, that is distressing," said Ruthven, as if it were the least distressing thing he had ever heard. "But unlike you, Burrows, I have a soupçon of that great fortifier: faith. Our mistress will look after her best and her brightest."

The Troll might disagree, thought Skuggs, though he would rather have eaten his own foot than say it aloud.

"The more territory that glass devil consolidates, the greater her chance of stymying our chances of a counter offense," said Burrows.

"A devil." Ruthven laughed. Skuggs was known to titter, Burrows to frown and gasp, but Ruthven's laugh was like the wind rustling and whispering around you before lightning strikes. Also, as with the wind before a lightning strike, most people only ever heard it once. "A glass devil no less. Don't be fatuous, Burrows. I admit, Cate Jubilee has been bothersome for us. Why, a few months into the war she equipped her soldiers with blood packs so I could not drink them into a quick and neat submission. How they keep supplied, I can only imagine. And once, when she made a play for my life, she drugged many of her troops on the front lines with a soporific drug. The moment their blood was inside me, I fell sluggish. For what seemed like hours I thought I'd fall asleep and crash out of the sky. I would have been swarmed and killed. I've been a trifle more careful about who I taste since. Yes, her intellect is keen, Burrows. But Cate Jubilee is only a woman. Our mistress is a woman and a world."

"She'll find our kindred," Burrows insisted with all the stubbornness he brought to bear against the idea of Death. "They might not know there's a war on. Has that occurred to either of you? It's unlikely, but our world is wide, high, and deep. It has corners that even we three are unaware of. If our kindred are taken unawares, Cate Jubilee might take no prisoners. She may err on the side of caution, ambush them, and kill them." Despite the black veil, they could feel his eyes narrow at Ruthven. "Then where would we be? Answer me that, wyrm."

Oh blast, bother, and buggeroo.

Skuggs interceded quickly, before Ruthven could retort and escalate tensions.

"Perhaps our mistress could reach out to our friends and countryfolk?" he ventured. "Wouldn't that save us headache?"

"Skuggs, war has made an amnesiac of you," said Ruthven. "Our mistress would make contact if she could. Of course she would. If only she had her shadow."

"Right, right." Skuggs grew wistful. "Our Lady's shadow. Forgot about her. Oh witchy crumbs and hagskin biscuits, but things'd be all the better if she were back. Such lubbly bugs as never I've seen before or since!" Another thought found itself added into the scrambled casserole of malice that was his brain. "Hang on, hang on, what about the *doctor*? Maybe *he* could get in touch with Stony Crow, Yellow-Eye, and the rest?"

Click-ick-ick.

A sound like fingerbones shaken in a Crock-Pot.

The three councilors looked at the dark figure. The wheel—yes, a wheel, not a pillow to prop their head against—was spinning. It was the wheel clicking so terribly. Bulbous shapes made spokes on the wheel. These were heads. And the mannequin they connected to was woman-shaped. As the wheel spun (*click-ick-ick-ick-ick*) the mannequin tried on different heads. One slid into place upon the neck. There was a definitive *clock.*

The mannequin stood. She came toward them.

Skuggs did not know about Ruthven and Burrows, but as the woman approached, so tall she seemed to fill his riddlewood house, so lissome she was beautiful, and so herky-jerky in her movements that she was terrible, he felt himself cringe and shiver all over. He smothered it when he saw the head affixed to her body was smiling. He felt fresh fear when he saw what kind of smile it was.

"The good Doctor Isherwood is otherwise occupied," said Eurydice. She extended a hand, knuckles facing upward. "Happy witching hour, boys."

They rushed forward, Ruthven nuzzling her wrist, Burrow brushing those dry, ashen lips of his to her knuckles, Skuggs peppering her fingers in kisses that stank of putrid pumpkin flesh. When she retracted her hand they recoiled, as though stung, and then slunk back to their positions in the room, each nursing their own private shame at the indignity, each feeling as though they'd just awoken from a trance so sweet they could not help but yearn to return.

They were quiet now—the messenger, the necromancer, and the dragon—for their mistress was smiling the coquettish smile of a trickster. Who was the joke on?

They did not know. *We love you*, their eyes said, and behind their eyes they whispered, *Please, oh please not me. Let the joke be on anyone but me.*

"Burrows is right," said Eurydice. "Too much ground ceded, didn't you say?"

"Yes, Mistress."

"I put it down to tedium. War is deliciously gruesome but only in snaps and stages. Most of it is long games—waiting, waiting, waiting. Yeah," said Eurydice, tracing the grooves in the riddlewood with a finger. "Too much ground ceded. She's close, boys. Closer to my Crystal Country than you know. What happens if she finds it?"

None of them spoke.

She turned on Ruthven, beckoning him. He slid around her shoulders, a dragon reduced to a mink. Skuggs had to dig his fingernails into his thigh to keep from braying laughter.

"Your Crystal Country is your womb," said Ruthven like a good little wyrmy. "Your womb, your breath, your mind, Mistress. If the enemy gains it, there will be little we humble servants can do for you. We'll have lost the war."

The dragon closed his slitted eyes as she scratched under his chin. Her voice was mellow. "Uh huh." A good sign, that lackadaisical tone, or so Skuggs deemed. A promising sign that the joke was not on them but someone else. Cate Jubilee, he hoped.

"And Cate really is close, you know. Another year, and I think she'd have a shot at it. There, there, boys. You mustn't let it get you down," said Eurydice. "I'd never let things go that far... though I guess I've left it long enough. I've been distracted, you see, I..."

She trailed off. A blank spot. The trickster smile was empty. They said nothing. They watched her every move.

From the wheel there came a brief, ominous *click*.

Skuggs' throats were like dusty pipes. His bowels were growing watery.

Please, he thought. *Please keep tracked and true and changeless, Mistress. Please, pleeeeease—*

She looked directly at him. He smiled at her instinctively, a big desperate smile.

"But it's all okay now," she said.

Skuggs almost relaxed. He thought it would indeed be okay, that they would be spared a shift in her disposition.

She went on, "I've caught the matter just in time. Burrows, do something for me?"

"Name it and it's yours."

"Goad Cate Jubilee to follow you west of the Tailed Cat river. Make for Golgomir."

"Golgomir?" This unwise interruption from Ruthven. The dragon looked at Eurydice. "Mistress, forgive my outburst. But the mountain Golgomir has always overlooked... that is, it has always been very proximal to—"

"The Bloodwood," said Eurydice. "And so it shall stay."

"A battle in Ruthven's home ground?" Burrows sounded intrigued. "It's a prospect, certainly. The terrain will be bad for both sides. It will be difficult for our enemy's fortresses to walk in the mire, but in order for us to make full use of that, I'm going to have to rely on oozes."

Click-ick-ick, went the wheel.

Eurydice's face melted into a mask of amusement. "What do you call an envious ooze?"

"No clue," Burrows admitted.

"Jelly."

There was a thoughtful silence.

"That was terrible," Eurydice said eventually.

"Quite bad, Mistress," said Burrows. "But the delivery was spot on."

"I think she would have laughed."

"Who, Mistress?"

Click-ick-ick. No more amusement. A hollow, toneless expression took its place. Skuggs thought Burrows' waxy skin grew paler.

"Never mind," Eurydice said. "I don't want to think about her. You can't make me."

"Mistress?" said Ruthven. He had gumption, Skuggs had to give him that. "Mistress, about the Bloodwood. I had hoped the conflict would... that is to say, I have been fortunate enough to keep it from the clutches of the enemy till now, and if our policy is still to lose, then—"

"Only this one last time," she replied. "One last time, and then it'll all be over."

"That is truly wonderful news, but my Lady—"

Click-ick-ick, spun the wheel. The first face returned, cunning and mischievous. That was when Skuggs understood. The joke was not on him. It was not on Burrows. Not even on Cate Jubilee. It was on Ruthven.

"Ruthven, my dear," said Eurydice sweetly. "How do you feel about teeth?"

"Teeth, Mistress?"

"How would you describe your relationship to them?"

He gazed at her. Hesitated. "I suppose... you could describe my relationship to teeth as... attached, Mistress. Very much attached."

Eurydice's head tilted slightly. "And would you like to keep it that way?"

"Y... Yes, Mistress."

"Good boy. Burrows, get on that dog of yours and scram."

Burrows was gone in a sigh of frayed fabric.

"What about me, Mistress?" said Skuggs eagerly. "Have you a job for me?"

She regarded him, a woman and a world. "I do. When you went to Corinth City, did you see Frank Gallant?"

Skuggs' brow dimpled with distaste. "Too right, Mistress. Too right, I did. Poxy, manky so-and-so looked down his nose at me."

"That was naughty of him."

"I agree, Lady. I agree wholetartedly."

"He was naughty for his Mommas, and now he's naughty for us."

"Always had time for the Nightjar Coven. Nice sort. Nice, eh, spells and that. And they had a way with animals, you got to hand it to them."

"Yes. You do."

There was no spin of the wheel. Eurydice's lips remained quirked at their awful angle. Only now, Skuggs thought, the joke was not on Ruthven, but on someone else entirely.

"The Coven are twenty-two years in their grave. What do you say," she asked him, "we punish their naughty boy on their behalf?"

"I say *piss on Frank Gallant*," crowed Skuggs happily. "*Ahehn-hen-hen!*"

***

So it was that Skuggs found himself traveling to The Rotunda of The Bell Sir. It was a long way, though Eurydice shortened it for him with her power over the world's geography. Still, it was hard going, shuttling himself by the great quartz glaciers underground. By the time he emerged overground he was very tired. He took a little walk, limbering his body and getting his mind back on form.

It would be taintly stupid, or so Skuggs reckoned, to speak to the Beldames without his full roster of wittissums and clever-clog-capacities. They were not the sort of women you stepped wrongfooted with.

I might wrongfoot no matter what, thought Skuggs. *Me and my guzzlible luck.*

The Rotunda was a huge and lonely building, with clean white pillars at the bottom and a silver dome on top. At some distance Skuggs could see a forest of lynchwood trees, a river, a few wildflower copses all gray and winking orangely like smoldering cigarette ash in a glass tray. No trees near The Rotunda though. The river diverted away from it as well, as if the gradient of the ground were trying to keep the water pure and the dome was some corrupting influence. Why, there was not even one weed that crept toward the building. The bas-reliefs carved in stone showed bells of all shapes and sizes carried by women up, and up, all the way toward the rounded parabola of the silver dome. There was no front door, only a yawning portico that seemed to say, *All Visitors Welcome*.

Not without trepidation, Skuggs bustled inside.

What's that I hear? A song to prick the bones and tickle the sticky plaque flossing my gummy gums. Not a song, no, not a song!

He was right. It was chanting.

In a central chamber, under the skylight of the silver dome, Skuggs found the Beldames. Held high over the tiled floor was a bell of magnificent size. It bore no ornaments, and with its detailed carvings and flat dark color, it was a somber bell if ever a bell could be said to give off feeling. Somber and clairvoyant, like an old man waiting in total stillness for death.

The Beldames were grouped below this enormous bell. They wore robes of roughspun, long-sleeved and hooded. There were eight of them. Or perhaps eighteen. Then again, eighty... no, there could not be so many, not when he'd first supposed eight...

And yet...

Skuggs felt a weariness come over him, nothing to do with his former fatigue, a dazed sense of weightless spinning, rattling... *ringing...*

A voice, penitent and low, said, "On the first day, she built the bell."

Many voices spoke the refrain. "The bell."

"On the second, she chose a man to ring it."

"A man."

"On the third, she knighted him with her scythe of spine."

"A knight, a sir, a man with a charge."

"She gifted him women who would love him and make him comfortable."

"The dames, the dames of the bell."

"She charged the man to keep the bell safe."

"Safe."

"The knight asked, 'What is the bell for?'"

"Sage of him," came the refrain. "A man should know his business."

"And she told him the bell was for autumn."

"Autumn."

"For the last autumn when all things must die and for the winter in which the universe is a museum and all things stand dead for the observation of her and her alone."

"Her and her alone."

"So he must listen and watch and wait."

"Listen, watch, wait."

"And soon," came the voice, "on a fourth and final day in the yonder of experience, the knight will ring the bell."

"The Bell Sir will ring it."

"*Yes*," said the voice, and though it was broadly speaking a voice that was too proud to let emotion in, Skuggs detected the smallest trace of preening exultation in its delivery. "*Yes*. And once the bell is rung, it cannot be unrung."

Skuggs felt as though an ice cube were being teased along his innards as, without ceremony or fanfare, the Beldames turned to look at him.

One of them rose. She must have been spindly as a choking wire under that robe because it hung off her like a frayed coat off a scrap of birch cut up for a coat peg. She approached him, bent down low and lower than low, and he wondered if her back were magic for all the bend it had, until he could see her face in the shadow of the hood. That face was strangely smooth. From brow to chin it stretched longer than a face had a right to.

"Why do they call you Skuggs?" she said.

"'Cause I look like a Skuggs," said Skuggs. He opened his mouth to proceed with his message, then stopped. He looked around.

The Beldames circled him. All of them.

Skuggs swallowed. Two clicks popped in his throats.

"Have you ladies heard of a slimy piece of work named Frank Gallant?"

They nodded. The one who had approached Skuggs first said, "The Nightjar Coven were our sworn enemies. When they died, we held a feast that lasted eight days and eight nights."

"One for each of you Beldames?" Skuggs hazarded.

"No."

"Ah." He foundered but quickly recovered. "You see our mistress... my mistress," he corrected, eyeing the huge bell, "owing to what you might call extraneous circumstances, what with the war and that, my mistress has elected to play a little trick on old Frank."

"A trick?" Now the hoods whispered amongst themselves. The leader straightened warily. "What kind of trick?"

Skuggs told them.

"Yes," said the leader when he was done. And there was no doubt of it now. Skuggs heard joy in that voice. A beatific joy. A crazed, leaping lunatic joy. "Yes, that will do nicely."

***

If you had told her war and motherhood would share more in common than they espoused difference, she would not have believed you for all the glass in the world. Both war and motherhood were, for example, rather distressing...

Cate snatched a look over the side of the crenellations. Up came the oozes, their orange insides sprayed with red like blood in a cup of Jell-O. Atop their gelid backs rode the dead, festersome and stinking and mad. Their musty bellows mingled with the sound of the huge hawkish birds overhead, slitting the air with their wings and talons, rending it apart with their screams.

That was another thing. Children were loud. And they smelled. Sometimes it was an agreeable smell, especially when they were toddlers, a kind of pervasive soft smell that made you love them. Mostly it was the other sort of smells, such as the smell of mushed crayon, sick, wee, perhaps the smell of something that you swore you'd thrown out of the cupboard weeks ago, or hair mixed with mud, hair mixed with yogurt, hair mixed with toilet water, and speaking of toilets, that most singular smell signaling a poo is on the way, or that said poo has been delivered with much fragrant ceremony. At twelve years old, Evelyn was out of nappies and blessedly bored of finding expired things at the back of cupboards. But the loudness and the smells had not gone away. They had merely evolved to suit their new pre-pubescent lodgings. Cate's daughter was quieter now. Motherhood taught you that certain kinds of quiet were louder than screams. Evelyn smelled of baths, and under that she smelled of the reason for the frequent baths, which were earth, and the honest sweat of hard work, and bugs. Lots and lots of bugs.

Then again, being a mum meant you got to try out new and exciting experiences...

"Ella," she said. "Give me a leg up."

Eilandri Titansgrave threw her colossal hammer in a fantastic overhead swing, turned to her commander without skipping a beat, and laced her fingers together. Cate stepped a hobnail boot into their cradle. Then she was flying. The fortress sprawled below her. Other fortresses were visible too, a great phalanx of bio-engineering, an entire offensive wall of Bettys. A glow of pride flickered in her. *My Bettys.*

One of the hawkish birds had been about to plunge down, raking its talons over whatever vulnerable target it could find, and was rather surprised when Cate kicked off its undead rider, dug in her heels, and said, "If you flip over in an effort to shake me off, I'll make you wish you were baked into an omelet as an egg. Fair enough?"

The bird, whose species had survived in Eurydice's hostile skies thanks to an evolved sense of self-preservation, did not flip over.

"Lovely," said Cate. She surveyed the battle, saw that the undead were massing heavily in one particular spot, and steered her new mount in that direction.

In war as in motherhood, you were constantly aware, endlessly alert. You could be tired. Everyone gets tired now and then. But even though you may be asleep on your feet, as much a zombie as the ones on Lord Burrows' leash, that does not slacken the hold your responsibilities have on you. Quite the contrary.

Also, both battle and parenthood introduced you to such interesting people...

The undead surged over the battlements. Some of them charged, others had the wherewithal to take in their surroundings. She landed among them, churning limbs and pungent, maggoty gore. She broke the bird's neck with a twist of her hands, scissored her legs to crush a pulpy undead skull between her boots, and then she was in it. They roared her name in hate. It was music to her ears, a melody of encouragement.

"For Lord Burrows!" several cried. "The glass devil will break!"

"Probably," she agreed and killed them.

Yes, that was right. She'd broken once and she might again. No one went on flawless as a diamond forever. Come to think of it, no one went around flawlessly at all. You had to remember your limitations. She was not a world, only a woman. And a woman is simply an infinity. That's all.

Her own soldiers were with her now, magic weapons hacking, undead fingers pawing, troop-on-troop thunder, the battlestorm playing out along familiar lines. The scarlet force—Cate's force—were fewer in number, and by definition less experienced, their opponents being dead. But their courage held and now there was a new addition, a fresh challenger for the hungry, roiling fray.

From him the undead cowered, as Cate might once have cowered in her girlhood.

"I spy... with my sweet little eye... something beginning with..."

"You!" howled an undead, just before he was eaten.

The newcomer swallowed, nodding to himself. "Good guess."

In war as in motherhood, you also had the opportunity to reevaluate old relationships...

"It's a buffet, Mr. Glint," she said.

He caught two undead trying to run away. "All you can nosh, Miss Jubilee."

Crrrrrack, and his jaw was a gaping portal to a nightmare, that nightmare being whatever constituted the digestive system of someone like Mr. Glint.

Cate let combat whelm over her in its bright, delirious waves. The tide was in. She waded, happy as anything.

Because war and motherhood are simple. In war: you try to kill me, I try to kill you. In motherhood, even simpler: you love me and I love you.

After an interval of time Cate would have been hard pressed to formulate, so intense was survival's narcotic high, she heard a voice cry out in pain. She recognized it.

"Mr. Glint. Will you be all right on your own?"

He grunted.

Cate took to her heels. In the courtyard Xacorca Demon had been overwhelmed. Her squad were twisted shapes all round her, sticky with blood, staring at nothing. The undead had Xacorca pinned, back-to-fortress-wall, her bilious breath sizzling as it clouded, keeping them at bay, but only just, only *just*, and she was terribly hurt. As she closed the distance Cate counted three fingers missing from Xacorca's left hand. One of the dead had jabbed her eye savagely, popping it like a balloon full of melted chalk and raspberry jam. In the wilted-lotus-colored sky the birds screamed their hectoring scream. Blood wept along the lines in the stones under her boots, and the stone was grouted with old blood like a protest for the war, and the war was a drenched drum pounding with the tom-toms and the lichenous trunks of fortress legs, whamming sickeningly in her temples. She hated them for hurting her friend (them versus us, us against everything), and she drove the tip of one boot up into the sodden ribcage of one and sent him scattering in moans, and the songs of her enemy were not musical now but discordant bomb blasts thumping up a mushroom cloud inside her, and Xacorca sliding down the wall now, wincing as the grouted stones bit into her back, why slide? Why slide? Worse than bad. Hurt worse than bad.

Cate would save her. She fought bitterly.

When it was over Xacorca told her she'd been wrong about Cate. She'd been wrong and she was sorry, so sorry.

And when it was really over and the drums were gone and the undead left only their stink and the birds the memory of their screams, a stretcher came and took Xacorca to the medical wing. Cate looked on after the stretcher. No one approached. Cate approached *you*, you didn't approach Cate. Not old Diamond Jubilee, as they had come to call her, no, no.

A general is set apart. If she doesn't set herself apart, the soldiery will do it for her. And she must set herself apart from the harsh realities of war.

Because war is unbelievably complicated.

Just like being a mum.

She saw Eilandri helping with the wounded and hurried to do likewise.

"Another victory, General," said a dying man. "Did you see me? I fought bravely for you."

She hadn't seen him. "Not just bravely," said Cate. "Dare I use the word valorous? I rather think so."

He smiled with what little mouth the undead had left him.

He tried to swallow. It hurt him, she could see that plain. So did speaking. He spoke anyway. "Sorry I'm dying."

The second apology I've received today. Cate liked this one less than the first. "What's your name?"

"Norman. Norman... Pricewell, if it pleases you."

"It does please me, and so have you."

"Will you tell my sergeant I was valorous?"

Cate looked at the man's symbol, pinned to the collar of his uniform. "You're one of Daniel Jurdels' men?"

"Yes, General."

"He'll have a glowing report from me, Norman. Rest now."

"Is it like the president says? The lands of the dead?"

"Yes, it's like my husband says. It'll be an adventure. For now, rest."

Another ruined smile from Norman Pricewell. His breath hitched, as if crossing uneven road. She watched him focus on a spot that was near, and yet unaccountably far away. She watched him die.

He was eighteen, eighteen at most, she thought. *Evelyn is six years his junior. That's not much at all, when you think about it. I've been fighting in this world for twice as long.*

Norman Pricewell's stretcher took him. To the undertaker unit rather than the medical pavilion. The undertaker, and after that the morgue.

Cate touched the fresh glass that had appeared between her knuckles. A large patch on her thumb. Where else? Everywhere, she supposed. Some people got scars to reflect on. Cate had reflections for scars. Funny old world. The other thing too. Awful. Awful old world.

She wished suddenly that dawn would come. It might not come for a few hours, or days. Nothing was ever certain in this topsy-turvy realm. For now, night reigned like a dark queen over the battlefield.

Wife to a dark-haired king, keeper of a host of soldiers and responsibilities, Cate Jubilee went off to do a general's work, the murky kind that arrives after the pure, enviable clarity of fighting has gone.

They were winning the war, and it had been years since she'd felt close to her daughter.

***

Incidentally, if you bet on glass, as Cate's army so often did, you would have won every time. Diamond Jubilee, that's what some called her now, for her value in the thick of battle, and for her skin's propensity to break out in spots and smears of glass, punching through her tattoos like glittering stars through a patchwork of cloud. A silly nickname. But reverent, in its way.

And she knew their victory was artificial. Maybe the rest of them didn't, but Cate did. She held the fact inside her like a furnace keeping one nobbly, crooked coal burning inside it, and that fact was this: Eurydice was letting her win.

Cate knew that instinctually and rationally, the same way you know the moon is shining even when you look up at night and cannot see it.

What she did not know was why. Why lose on purpose?

Because losing achieves something else. It draws us deeper into their territory. As she headed along the bridge connecting one Betty to another, she studied the terraformer as the army engineers secured it in place. *Even as we take that territory for our own. Deeper and deeper into this world. What does that intimate? Yes.* Cate smiled grimly. *To precisely no one's surprise, it rhymes with "ham bush."*

It seemed a solid conclusion. Cate had waited a decade for the guillotine of Eurydice's plot (whatever that plot might be) to fall. It never had. Sometimes Cate could almost convince herself this implied a mechanistic problem in the enemy camp. Trouble in this wicked paradise. Bickering amongst its elite, perhaps, or some other flavor of political unrest. The guillotine blade, gleaming and suspended over Cate's naked neck, would simply remain there until the war was over, whereupon it would be disassembled, smelted, and transformed into an instrument of peace. A waffle-iron perhaps. Or a mirror frame. Yes, she could almost go for that. Jagged glass was pretty right up until the moment it cuts your finger, and pretty ideas were just the same.

You're a cynic, her doubt told her.

Yes, replied her confidence curtly. *An optimist would have died ages ago.*

From her height upon the interim bridge, the terraformer was not particularly large, nor was it particularly impressive. A rhombus-shape, matte-black and brutalist. About twelve-feet by twelve-feet. Elegant but very simple.

If John Isherwood was to be believed, that elegant but simple shape would win the war. Really win it.

In private, Cate had expressed her concerns about the potential ambush many times. Hughes had deferred to John, and the good doctor had insisted that whatever mischief Eurydice had brewing wouldn't matter a damn once the terraformers were deployed.

"It's important to think about it like taming. Eurydice's major ecosystems are in constant conflict with one another," he said. "We terraform her, and it'll be like breaking and shoeing a wild horse."

Taming. That sat poorly with Cate, though she could not have told you why.

She supposed John's words would see themselves actualized soon enough... that, or they would be refuted. According to him, the project would require only one more terraformer deployment. One more victory, false or genuine, it didn't matter. One more win for the scarlet army, and after twelve long years the war would be over.

That sat better with her. Surreal, but better.

She loved fighting with a compulsive passion, but absence makes the heart grow fonder. And in her heart Cate knew that soon she and combat needed to see other people. At least for a while.

One more win. One more.

After half an hour she found Sergeant Daniel Jurdels. He was an older man, sixty-five at least, but trim and exceptionally fit. War weaned you down, turned what was soft leathery and what was leathery into steel, but Dan Jurdels had been a farmer before the war kicked off, thus gaining a physical head start on what seemed an endless host of city boys eager to cut their teeth on Eurydice's fist. Dan Jurdels had been on battlement brigade with the rest of his company. It was a tough night's work tonight, and his cheek was slit almost to the bone. The bandage covering it was of poor quality; field medicine was getting better all the time, though not fast enough, *never* fast enough to keep up with loping, wide-striding war. Jurdels' posture was bad, and there was almost no red left in the hair at his temples and chin, but his eyes were attentive. Speaking of, he fairly snapped to attention when Cate found him sharing a well-earned supper with his troops.

"General in the mess hall," he barked as the company leaped to their feet.

Cate nodded. She was a known grinner, and the sober cast of her mouth told them the empty place at their table was not going to be filled. "At ease, gentlemen. I'm sorry to tell you this, Sergeant, but Private Norman Pricewell is dead. He died fighting. Fighting very valorously at that. A credit to you and your company."

Jurdels took it well enough. "Thank you, General. We'll mourn him tonight. Have a toast and the like." He hesitated. No matter how respected a general is, their presence is never completely welcome. One can't help but feel like one is a little boy or girl in the presence of a teacher. "Would you eh... join us, General Jubilee?"

"No, thank you. I'm off to the medical center, Sergeant. Accompany me."

"Oh no need, General. This bandage will do me well enough."

"Like or lump your bandage," said Cate frankly. "I want a report from someone who had a good view of the battle. That's you, Jurdels."

"Oh, I beg your pardon." She'd flustered him. "Em. I shall er... oh bugger, loosened my belt for supper, give us a tick."

Cate looked away politely. By the time they left Jurdels was red faced, and his men were snickering. But it was only a superficial amusement. Cate knew that the moment their sergeant's misfortune and embarrassment faded, the empty place at the table would accumulate their silence like a wound accumulating infection. A silence of death, louder than screams.

"Poor lad," said Jurdels, picking up on her thoughts by chance. "I saw him dragged over the parapet by one of the dead. Fell thirty feet, thirty at least. You saw him fight, General?"

Cate lied and said she had. Valorously.

"Must have landed on top of the zombie bugger," said Jurdels, frowning. "Tough lad. Good too. Had a way with the company cat. Eh, not that we have a company cat," he said quickly. "Rations being what they are. Couldn't afford to have a cat."

"With rations being what they are," said Cate.

"Yes, General."

"And this cat that doesn't exist. Did someone bring it from home?"

"No, General. Definitely not one of the lads from Rhönland. He did not sneak it here in his pack."

"I see."

They walked the fortress halls. The medical center was about two kilometers away. Everywhere she went she got salutes, murmurs, and space. Respectful, awed space. Cate didn't mind. She was well used to it by now.

"What's its name?" she wondered idly. "This cat that doesn't exist."

Jurdels looked uncomfortable. "Erm. Scrap, General."

"Scrap."

"Short for eh..."

"Yes?"

"Short for Mr. Scrappalotocus née Scrappybum, General."

Cate thought the man's neck would explode, it was so purple with shame.

"Mr. Scrappalotocus," she said.

"Yes, General."

"Née Scrappybum."

"Yes, General. Ah. Sorry, General."

"You learn something new every day, Sergeant."

"Yes, General."

"That cut is going to go green and make your head fall off."

"I worried it might be so, General," said Jurdels. "I was putting on a hard front for the company, as you might have picked up on. Erm. I don't suppose we could stop by my wife's corner of the center? Dab hand with a needle and thread, my wife."

"Why do you think I brought you with me?"

He blinked at her. "For a report, ma'am."

Cate permitted herself a small smile. "I was putting up a front too."

"You were?"

"Yes."

"Oh!"

Their path took them past a group of scientists on their way to test the terraformer. They did not salute Cate, but they did deign to nod. She nodded in return. Jurdels was working his way up to something. It was only as they left the fortress proper and made their way up to the battlements and the interim bridge beyond that he voiced it. "They're a good lot, my company. Private Pricewell was one of the betters, but there was stiff competition, if you take my meaning."

"I do." And now they were alone, and she saw a long look drag his face from firm stoicism to melancholy in less than a moment. "Sergeant?"

"Good boy," he croaked. "Very good. Made Scraps purr and gambol about like no one's business."

Understanding moved in Cate. "Daniel," she said. "Daniel."

He looked at her. His eyes were red. Not wet but red with the effort of keeping them dry.

"You miss her," she said.

He knew who she meant. Years ago, before she had met her husband Hughes, he had tricked his way into a unit of Citadel fighters. They had gone into Iphigenia and encountered a two-headed wolf from Eurydice. Only Hughes had survived. The leader of that unit was named Laurana. Her remains had been sent home to the countryside. Her father and mother had buried her under a blackberry thicket. The blackberry thicket on their farm, the Jurdels family farm.

"I do," said the sergeant. "I haven't for a while. Terrible thing to say, but when you're thinking about a hundred things, your people, how to keep them safe..."

She nodded encouragingly.

"Private Pricewell dying made me think of her. Laurie was brilliant with animals. They'd have been friends, I think, if she were alive and here with her old dad at the Front."

"Does your wife struggle with it too?"

"No more'n I do. Some." His lips slid back, revolted with himself. "General, this isn't stuff to bother you with."

She stopped. Grabbed his arm and turned him. Looked him hard in the eye, not letting him glance away but keeping him grounded in her gaze.

"Life doesn't end at death," she said. "It just changes. Laurana and Norman might be swapping stories now. You've seen the president's vid about it? I promise you, it's not drivel as some people grumble. It's true. Countless underworlds to go to, exciting adventures, and a second post-mortem rest to look forward to. And when you and your wife find your time and it finds you, you'll pass on and undergo that change. Then you and Laurana will drink beer under the shade of trees and cordial under the stars."

Jurdels' face crumpled for an instant, then reformed and was strong once more. "Laurie was fond of a sweet cordial."

This time Cate's smile was not controlled. It was a grin, big and bright, the Jubilee special.

"Blackcurrant," she said. "Come along. Before that sodden bandage of yours attracts flies."

"Aye, General. Eh. Thanks."

She clapped him on the back and, keeping apace with one another, they marched.

After depositing Sergeant Jurdels into the care of his wife, the recently promoted Senior Surgeon Anissa Jurdels, Cate embarked on a search for Xacorca.

She found the Demon being prepped for surgery. Xacorca was unconscious, but the nurses bustling about her were dialed to the most intense level of wakefulness, susceptible to gossip and small talk while their bodies went through the big motions of saving lives.

"Have we the fingers on ice?" said one.

"We do, yeah," said another. "Doctor Rollinson will get them back on in a jiff."

"He did with your one the other day."

There was general nodding amongst the nurses.

"He's good with fingers."

"Eyuh," one replied, sliding Xacorca's arm in a tightening band that checked blood pressure. "Not so good with eyes."

"Might have a donor."

"Nah. Low stocks. Stick of gum?"

"Fish in my pocket."

"Thanks." A pause. One of the nurses, the one taking her blood pressure, was staring at Xacorca's throat. "She's got a pair of bells here."

"Huh?" said another. "Whatdya mean bells?"

"Tattoos. Look."

The others gathered round.

"What's that mean?" said one.

"I think she's one of Cate's Company."

"No shit!"

"I think so."

"Golly," said one.

"One of the... you really think so?"

"Let me check her chart. Xacorca. Yeah! I knew the name was familiar."

"One of Cate's Company. Golly. And here we are—"

"BP's not bad."

"—here we are looking after her. That's kinda like caring for a celebrity, huh?"

"I'm gonna try get a hold of the donor list," said one nurse, hurrying away. "If there's an eye to be had, it ought to go to one of Cate's Company."

"Heard that," another agreed, slipping off the BP band.

The excitable one was so excited she dropped her stick of gum. "Poot," she says.

"Poot?"

"I never swear in front of patients."

"Fuck."

"Hey!"

"There, did it for ya. Get outta here and see what's holding Rollinson up. Our gal here is losing a lot of blood."

The excitable nurse dashed away, chewing busily.

Nearby, unobtrusive and with her hair covering the glassy portion of her face, Cate Jubilee nodded her satisfaction and slipped away unnoticed.

Her body sent a message asking for sleep in no uncertain terms, but for the time being Cate denied it. Lately she'd found exhaustion the only antidote to bad dreams. Those dreams featured Evelyn being in danger and Cate rescuing her. Not beats from the past or soothsayer prophecies of the future (she hoped), but just good old fashioned maternal anxiety.

A shift underfoot, as of an earthquake shivering the Juner Scale. The terraformer was operational. *One more win, Eurydice,* she thought as she sought the company of her least likely friend. *In his letter tonight Hughes revealed you've been keeping our daughter company in secret, that you recently turned on her, gave her a seizure. All's fair in love and war. And I promise to be as unfair as possible if I ever get my hands on you. I swear it. You've got magic but so have I, and the technowizardry of contemporary science. Just you wait. One more win and your ass is mine.*

Mr. Glint was not in his quarters (the coldest, dampest part of Cate's own Betty). Instead he haunted the crenellations. Patrols on their circuit hurried past him, trying desperately not to be eaten alive, or worse. They needn't have worried. Mr. Glint was ensconced in creativity.

"Hello, Miss Jubilee."

He was one of the only people with whom she brooked informality.

"Hi, Glinty."

Similarly, she was one of the only people who could get away with that. A runner came, gave Cate a message about provisions and the latency of the crop gestating in biopods. Cate nodded, gave a return message about relegation of focus, but sparingly since there was little enough focus from the science team to go round, and the messenger snapped a crisp salute and vanished down the steps to the courtyard. It was cold in this part of Eurydice, too cold for march. Cate zipped her jacket closed, rummaged in the pockets, and found two gloves knit for her twelve years ago by Ulf Seamster. Damn good gloves, and no wear and tear. It took people like Ulf to remind you that magic wasn't all about kicking names and taking bottom, or however that saying went. Magic could be cozy and preciously kind too. Thankfully their advance had brought them aways from the site of battle, so the reek of undead didn't foul the air. Indeed it smelled simply cold, that mystic chilly smell of odorless, fertile spring. The sky was pitch-dark but for a streak of lavender. It was not quite an aurora, too wispy and full of swimming cosmic tadpoles (God, this planet was weird), but the presence of the light reminded her of Frank nonetheless. She missed the gregarious ex-puppet dearly.

"Whatchya writing?" she asked Glint, sweeping herself astride the crenellation next to his.

"Little poem."

"Can I've a look?"

"Not done."

"Can I hear *ze starrrt?*"

Glint gave her a look that was all grave, no yard.

Cate yearned for Hughes. Her Puppy always went wild for the old reliable vampire-out-of-water bit.

"Suit yourself," she said tartly. "I'll write a poem."

"Ain't got paper."

"I shall dictate it to the wind."

"Listening."

"Mr. Glint is like a spare jam pot. Good in a pinch, and you can use him to really mess up anyone who dares invade your kitchen without fear of consequence."

Mr. Glint deliberated. "Bad scansion," he declared.

"Hm."

"Not even a poem really."

"Hmph."

"More of a simile with ribbons on."

"Shut up."

He stared at the paper in front on him. He wrote. He said, "Finished."

Cate frowned at him. "Really?"

"Yeah."

"You were just stuck on the last line?"

"Yeah," said Glint. "And your crap poem inspired me."

"Amazing."

"Like a phlegm-and-shit-covered muse."

"Charming."

"Really green drippy phlegm too."

"I preferred you when you were trying to kill me."

Glint handed her the poem.

"What's this?"

"Wanted to see it."

"No, no." She handed it back. "Oration."

He grunted. But she would not relent. She pouted, crossed her arms, and her legs, and exuded crossness. "Only a reading will breach the gap between us. The gap of offense and besmirchment of my rhetorical genius."

"Didn't know there was a gap."

"Yes. Well. There bloody is."

Another malefic grunt from her companion. Then Mr. Glint, great conciliator and mender of offended breaches in fellowship, read his poem:

I have a fear of heights

And your fingers are columns
Your arms tall spires
Your eyes windows through which
Purple cities can be visited
From a distance of a mile
And your smile is
Highest of all in my mind
And there it must stay for
My eyes haven't seen your lips
Curl like the path of comets
In the steepest house of night

I have a fear of never saying
That your face is the one I see
When I think 'What does love
Look like? Really look like?'
Because things left unsaid
Are like those icetail comets
I spoke of before, the ones
At home in the tall, scary dark
Things left unsaid fly by too fast
And are gone forever
My fears are not yours to solve
But know that for you
I will be brave as a comet
Plunging into heights
And wordless black eternity.

Cate could not have stopped her mouth it she had tried. It dropped open.
"Mr. Glint..."
"Yeah, Miss Jubilee?"
"That was *beautiful*. And..." Who did she know with purple eyes? Only one person. "And how long have you been in love with Eilandri?"
His sour mouth grew sourer, his sunken eyes puzzled. "Since ages ago. Tinfrost when Evelyn came from the butterflies."

"Twelve years? No."

"Thereabouts."

"No. Couldn't be. I'd have noticed."

He shrugged. "Ain't exactly secret."

"Come off it. I mean... look, you don't exactly wear your emotions on your sleeve."

"No." He folded his poem into his suit's inner pocket (Mr. Glint always wore suits. Armor would simply slow him down). "The reason being," he said, "because my sleeve is in the way."

"How can a man who wrote that poem be so literal?"

"Mr. Gallant says that linguistically I am an angel on the streets and a freak on the sheets."

"*In* the sheets." Cate giggled. "The phrase is 'a freak *in* the sheets.'"

Glint shook his head. "No room, Miss. On account of the inky letters in them already, see?"

"I see. And if you're an angel on the streets, I'm a..." She almost said shrinking violet and caught herself in time. "A person who isn't like me at all," she finished lamely. "Why don't you tell Eilandri how you feel?"

"Did it the once," said Glint. "Mr. Gallant gave me clips."

"Tips."

"Thanks."

"How'd it go down?"

"Like a ton of rectangular building things, Miss."

"Ah." Cate tried to picture Mr. Glint presenting flowers, chocolates, cinema tickets, or indeed performing any sort of romantic gesture. She succeeded and understood immediately why he had not been successful in his wooing. The man was the polar opposite of romance. He was as sexually alluring as a piranha tank. "When was this?"

"'Bout five years ago."

"That's enough time elapsed for another go, I suppose."

He looked at her. "What?"

"Another go." Now Cate was confused. "That is the point of the poem, isn't it?"

Sourer still grew his mouth. "Course not. Poem's for me."

"But... I don't understand."

"She said no. I asked and she said no." Mr. Glint clicked his pen, popping the ink nib back inside the sheath, and tucked it away with the paper in his pocket. "Must be kind to people, unless they're wicked, in which case I can have their guts for starters. If I can't be kind, I can't be at all. And far as I can tell part of being kind is taking no for an answer. And not asking again, even if the fancy takes me."

"So you're not going to read that to her?" said Cate. "That poem that just melted my heart like butter on a hot pan?"

"S'right. Wouldn't be kind."

Her gaze went from him to the landscape of the inhospitable world and back to him. "Bloody hell," she said at last. "That's... bloody hell."

Glint nodded, morose and terrifying. But then, no more so than usual.

Rapid pattering footsteps up the nearby steps. A runner appeared.

"Message for you, General."

"Give it, soldier."

"Lord Burrows himself has been spotted heading northwest."

The unpredictable terrain of Eurydice meant Cate had no internal map to consult, but she had cartographers. *Northwest, eh?*

"How recent was this?"

"Two hours, General."

"Northwest. He heads for Golgomir," Cate mused aloud. To the messenger, she gave the following instructions: "Direct Captain Cinch to turn us in that direction. I want double-quick pace. Scheduled stops for search initiatives are to cease from here on out. Afford all companies personal downtime with rotating watch. Think you can do a bit of rumor mill work, soldier?"

"General!"

"Get the word going that Burrows has been spotted on his wolf. Tail between its legs. We're after the bastard. Whoever brings the general his head will leap through the ranks like a frog on really, really good amphetamines."

"I'll make it a good rumor, General."

"Bells and whistles. Top points, that man. And it's true, I will promote Burrows' killer." A scrappy glimmer appeared in Cate's eye. "Unless I get to him first. Dismissed."

The messenger took to his heels.

Cate swung herself lithely off the crenellation. "Battle, Mr. Glint."

"Right you are, Miss Jubilee."

"Anything you need before we face the enemy? Could be the last time we fight undead."

"Well, there is something..."

"Yes?"

Mr. Glint smiled dreadfully. "Knife and fork would be nice."

***

How does an assassin prepare?

The answer is simple: you prepare for it your entire life.

Up until the moment you pull the trigger, stab and twist the knife, tighten the garrote, arm the bomb, you are one person about to become another. Like day becoming night. Like a woman setting foot on the moon.

It can be personal. It can be business. Because killing another person has become a fragment of economy as well as anthropology.

In a world that could create people like Mr. Shine, who in turn created people like Miss Gleam and Mr. Glint who take the fundamentals of nastiness and build upon them, surpassing their maker in every way imaginable... in a world that could hold such sorcerers of pain inside it... in a world like that assassination and bin collection and home insurance policy fulfilment are the same thing.

On Monday morning the people of Corinth City got out of bed and went to work.

The assassin did likewise.

Only he was not a paid assassin. No currency or favors of any kind had been exchanged. This was one of those personal cases. Which are always more violent. Always bloodier. Always more brutal than the clinical ruin of murder in the name of the bottom line.

Debts of the heart are infinitely more savage than those of the checkbook.

The assassin got on a train at two minutes to ten in the morning.

On the train a little boy sat next to the assassin. The little boy hummed the words to the nursery rhyme "All Of The Pretty Horses." His feet were bare, crusty with dirt. His clothes were obscenely ragged. He smelled bad, like a public toilet never cleaned. When the ticket collector came, he asked the boy for his ticket. The boy said he had none. He'd hopped on the train illegally. He said it just like that, frank and shameless, and the ticket collector stared at him for a while. Then the ticket collector asked the assassin for his ticket. The assassin showed it. The ticket collector moved on.

It was a clear sunny March morning. Sunlight slid in warm bright bars through the windows. The train car was getting hotter the more people got on. By mid-April it would be stuffy, by June unbearable. But for now, it was okay.

"Are you going somewhere good?" the assassin asked the little boy.

"The distillery on Coriolanus Row," the boy replied. "My brother works there."

"Where are your shoes?"

"Haven't got any. But my brother has an eye on a pair for me. A flat too."

"You want to move?"

"Yes." The boy lifted his foot and flicked away a bit of crisp wrapper clinging to the sole. "We want to move from the street to a flat."

"How did your brother get a job if you're homeless?" asked the assassin. "You need an address to gain employment."

"Distillery owner likes my brother. Says my brother works very hard."

"Has your brother ever mentioned the Welfare Housing Act?"

"Nope."

"It was put in place to eradicate homelessness. There's lots of places you or your brother could stay. Safe places with food and water and well-compensated guards."

The little boy was growing bored with the conversation. He bent and picked up the crisp wrapper foil and fiddled with it. He made no effort to reply.

"Why don't you stay in a place like that?" said the assassin. "There's one not far from Coriolanus Row. Only ten or fifteen minutes' walk."

No answer.

"What do you say, little fellow?"

"No, thank you."

"Why?"

The boy shrugged, as children will do when they don't want to speak about something anymore. But the assassin persisted.

"You should go to the safe place."

The boy looked at his knees, scabby under the thin frayed fabric, not abashed, simply uninterested. "My brother would have taken me already if there was a place like that. It costs money."

"That's what I'm trying to tell you. You don't need money."

"Yeah you do."

"I'm telling you, you don't."

Another shrug. Puzzled, the assassin let it go. The train pulled into the station. The little boy left. The doors shut after him. Through the glass windows on the train doors, the assassin saw the boy pause. The boy turned and gave the assassin a wave. The assassin raised a hand. The boy padded away on filthy bare feet.

When it came time for his stop, the assassin got off the train. He went into the closest office, explaining that he needed to make a telephone call. The front desk staff were quite accommodating. The assassin called the Welfare Housing Department at Redspire, inquiring about the misapprehension of certain members of the populace, i.e. that they must pay to be given quarters on the premises. No, the department official explained, that was not a misapprehension. That was correct. Water pumped from the mains into the shelters was growing scarcer and scarcer. General supplies were actually increasing with the purifiers doing their work, but demand was higher than ever. In order to be expected to provide it for washing and drinking, boarders hoping for sanctuary were required to pay the shelters a "pump fee" to mitigate the rising cost of water. What if they couldn't afford to pay the fee? The department official hesitated, then admitted that though it was a regrettable state of affairs, the shelters were well within their rights to turn such people as could not pay the fee away. But that would mean homeless forced to brave the streets. Yes, it was truly regrettable.

Chagrined, the assassin pointed out that under the previous administration, the city had been coping admirably with the injustice of homelessness. The department official said that was not something they could speak to; they had gotten their job after President Hughes' election. They thought the best of Wendy Dragontail, of course, and could see the fruits of her labor were still ripe and excellent, but Wendy had not been forced to cope with circumstances like the drought, as President Hughes was now.

After a moment the assassin thanked the official and gave a decadently polite farewell because it was his custom to be polite. Only he didn't feel very polite. He felt like cracking the phone like an egg, letting the circuitry run like yolk. He felt a deep, carefully maintained hate within him give off a few baleful steam clouds.

Heading back into the sunny March morning, he looked toward Redspire. Somewhere in that tower a member of the Welfare Department was standing up from their desk, the conversation fresh in their mind, replaying it while they fetched coffee. Somewhere in that tower was the man who gave the orders, the man behind the new fee for shelters, the man responsible for that little flare of callousness and more, much more.

The assassin hurried, keeping the tower centered in his sights.

How do you prepare to kill someone, not for a living but because you believe it is right? How do you justify that to yourself?

You do it by corralling all your pretty horses. By being short on something vital, like your senses, and by being ready for a long, long time.

You prepare by wanting nothing else.

Hughes, the assassin thought, *to think you and I were once friends.*

Act Four

Row, Row, Row Your Boat

Chapter Eleven

The Bloodwood was known by many names.

In their damp tunnels under the ground the slugmen of Eurydice called it Drake's Hollow. From their nests of all thorns, no roses, the birds cheeped to one another about the Sanguine Swamp. The Beldames and the yellow-eyed folk who lived inside the carcasses of trolls called it the Fell Forrest. The lynchwoods creaked their own treeish version of its name deep in their trunks, a noise of sap-chilling fear. Amongst their fractured and mended factions, the undead knew it simply as That Wood, or indeed by its most common moniker of Bloodwood. Very few spoke that name aloud, however. Half-formed superstition tied their rancid guts in knots. For it was said that nothing could live there for any significant length of time, not even the undead.

Furred, spotted, serpentine Ruthven knew it not by any particular name but by a feeling, and that feeling was the comfort you yourself may get when you go to work from a chaotic home. When such a thing occurs, work becomes a home away from home, gaining a place of wistful favoritism in the heart.

Eurydice was Ruthven's home, naturally.

The Bloodwood was his home away from home.

It was where he went when the demands of the war eased. It was where he pursued important things. It was where he'd been born.

It was where, if Ruthven had his way, something new and ever-so-exciting would come to be.

He flew between the trees, and what trees they were! Skyscrapers scratching at the Monday morning. The trees like aspens, thin and white. Only the little chipped brown bits of an aspen were not recreated here. Instead the bark was split by gaping sores. They wept blood. The blood seeped down the grooves in the trees so that an onlooker would think to themselves, "Those trees are weeping blood," and they were, they were crying. But for what? Only Ruthven knew, and he was not telling.

The leaves were something else entirely. Black with a reddish sheen, they lived short sullen lives on their branches, then tumbled to the floor of the wood. The ground there was a morass of dead leaves, not dry autumnal leaves but soggy, coppery-smelling piles. A stew of compost, twenty-feet deep at the shallowest, a hundred at the deepest. A bog of weird, loathsome microorganisms. And over this stomach-churning humus of rot swarmed a million-million bugs, some needle-sharp, others gorged fat like kings on the tannic-tasting vintage of decomposing cellular sludge.

Ruthven's wings disturbed the bugs, riffling them to disarray for a while before they migrated back to their suckling sheriffdom. It was a fast flight, but Ruthven's route was sure. Few leaves were clipped. No branches broke.

He was troubled. A rare thing, that. Rare and unwelcome.

Eurydice. His queen. His mistress. She decreed that the final battle of the war should take place here. Here, of all places.

Only this one last time, she'd told him with insufferable serenity. *One last time, and then it'll all be over.*

When he'd protested, she'd asked him how he felt about his teeth.

Why, I feel attached to them, he thought now. *And you, Mistress? How do you feel about your throat?*

Perhaps the two parties might arrange a meeting: his teeth, her throat.

Ruthven grinned his surgery toolkit grin. *Temper, temper. How would such an encounter end? We are as amoeba under the microscope compared to her. Even a dragon.*

No use in indulging one's vexations.

No, he was going to have to be shrewd about this.

If Cate Jubilee could be led by the nose to the Bloodwood, then Ruthven would simply snare her with a leash of his own. He would keep her army from wandering too deeply into his home away from home. She would not discover what he'd been toiling on. No one would.

The surgeon who takes true pride in his profession does not allow public viewings. He reveals *what* he will, *when* he will. To be sure only after the work is complete.

Around him the trees wept.

Only Ruthven knew why.

And only he could stop the tears.

***

Gormon Hughes, President of Corinth City, wanted a smoke.

Evelyn sulked off to school, Hiromi jabbered and prattled about trajectories and the costs of rocket fuel, and meanwhile the telephone would not stop ringing.

"Your Eminence, I'm sure the ambassador meant nothing of the sort," Hughes soothed the voice at the other end of the line. He gestured impatiently to his butlers. They hurried to get him the document he needed. Suited and bowtied, there were eleven of them, and while he appreciated them for the most part, Hughes sometimes wished they would transform into penguins. They would get roughly the same amount of work done, i.e. bugger all, only with the added charm inherent to the common penguin. The dignitary squawked their fury in his ear. "Indeed, your Eminence? Well, it doesn't bear thinking about. Perhaps the ambassador was referring to someone else's concubine?"

The butlers were fumbling over one another. Documents fluttered like aggressive pelicans.

A hotbox, Hughes' mind whispered treacherously. *Bar the office door. Close the window. A few deep drags, a few long exhales. Make this room a real Dragon's Lair. A real smokehouse, baby.*

This last pronouncement occurred to him with Cate's gusto. God, had he resorted to impersonating her in his head? For a quick blast of nicotine?

"Your Eminence, that will not be necessary. Nor indeed, will it be condoned. Corinth City has not had a duel since the reign of The Tyrant, and by then the institution was so muddled and perverse that both challenger and offender fought with tinned leeks. The only things drawn at dawn will be tickets to the farce. Listen to me. I'll telephone the ambassador and..." He clicked his fingers sharply. One of the butlers, sweating profusely, placed the document into his hand. Hughes continued, "... yes, I have her number here." A pause. "Yes, absolutely. Rest assured." A somewhat weightier pause. "I'm sure Lady Dragontail would have erred on the side of what was right. She always did, after all. Even when she didn't. Hm? Nothing, your Eminence. Just reminiscing on old times. I trust there'll be no more discussion of duels? Good."

He slammed the phone down and immediately began dialing.

Smoke flowing over his desk. Smoke perusing the ceiling overhead. Smoke curling round the stone dragons of the fireplace. Smoke caressing the old gramophone. Smoke in the eves, creeping along the floor, the taste of smoke like evaporated relaxation, the smell, God almighty, the intoxicatingly sleek smell, the full feeling, the kiss the lovely licking the all-powerful the goddess of crushed ends, ashtrays, goddess of relief, goddess of delicious mist, fog, fucking smoke now do it now, do it, DO IT—

He made an audible sound, quiet but firm, of revulsion. He dialed faster. *Keep the hands busy. That's the key.*

The problem was his hands were so busy they had actually started to feel idle. They seemed to insist the activities he was making them perform could only be improved by the feel of a cigarette between each index and middle finger. Hell, between every finger. Make it a party.

(Do it)

"Put me through to Ambassador Kohvolo," he said the moment the call was answered. "President Hughes speaking, code six-eight-zero-zero, fast as you can, there's a good chap. Who's that behind me?"

He slid the phone into the crook of his clavicle, turned.

"Montcrieff, what's the story?"

"Urk."

Hughes read the brief communication he was handed. It was from Hiromi.

Dear Mr. President—so on and so on—supplier conflict—so on and so on—*matter requires resolution or the Laurana Project will stall with immediate effect.*

The receiver was vibrating softly against his neck. A voice speaking, too faint to hear. The ambassador. Hughes ignored her for the moment. He said, "Montcrieff, contact the liquid fuel production facility in Polydoros. They should be in our database under the rocket icon. I want a detailed summary of the supplier of that fuel, including the phone number of its arbiters. I have no use for some Johnny Woodgrain manager type. Get me the top tier mahogany, man. Get me their board."

"Urk."

Hughes didn't even glance up to see if Montcrieff would obey. You relied on your trusted seconds. No man is an island. Delegate or be relegated to the trash compactor of political failures—refuse and be refuse.

(Delegation rhymes with fumigation)

(fumigate: to purify with vapors)

(smoke 'em if you got 'em)

He pressed the phone to his ear hard enough to hurt. "Madame Ambassador, so sorry to keep you waiting." A pause. "Charming as ever, Madame Ambassador. Forgive me for the abandonment of etiquette, but as the man searching for the other half of his sword said, 'I must get directly to the point.' I trust you are aware that, given certain recent remarks concerning certain concubines, his Eminence the Viscount of Île de Colette would like to introduce someone to the business end of a crossbow? Someone in this case being you, Madame?"

The doors to his office flew open. Tommy Fahrenheit strode in.

"It is intolerable!" he declared.

I swear to God...

One of the butlers minced toward Tommy with an air of polite arrogance. "Monsieur Fahrenheit. The president is most busy at the mo—*Oh my good gracious!*"

Without breaking stride Tommy picked up the offending manservant and placed him on the office sofa like a father placing a child's discarded doll on a cushion.

"Do not impede me, pompous executor of manners," said Tommy. He turned to Hughes, who was keeping one ear on this unfolding chaos and the other on the ambassador, who was explaining her precise objections to the viscount, as well as her hopes toward his contraction of several colorful diseases, most of them venereal.

"Security detail?" Tommy spoke the words as though they were also members of the sexually transmitted ailment family. "You would keep me from the Front so I may guard men who smell of the mustiest corner in a café and women who keep spare pencils in their hair? Monsieur President, I must object! I must object most thoroughly!"

Hughes groaned inwardly. "Madame Ambassador, I will call you back. Dwell on this, if you would: the obelisk that your noble family has used for its crest these past hundred-and-forty-years was modeled on the phallus of the Dauphin of Champleurs. If we remove sex from culture and tradition, including political tradition, we shall be left with cold monoliths indeed to rally round. And they shall *still* look a bit penisy. Good day to you." He clapped the phone into its cradle forcefully. "Tommy—"

"Monsieur President, you see this card, *oui?*"

"Yes," said Hughes wearily. "It's blue."

"*Mon triomphe bleu*," said Tommy with real zeal. "This *petite carte* marks twelve years of sobriety. Twelve years divorced from that abusive lover contained in bottles of sensual glass and barrels of aromatic wood. Twelve years *off the sauce*, as you say in Corinth. *Off the sauce* and *on the wagon*. I ask you this: would you condemn me to become weak of resolve in the company of soft-bellied scientists? Will you drive me to drink?"

You couldn't hop off that wagon if you tried, Hughes thought. *The driver is called Chimera, and it would stop you, Tommy. My magic usually fades, but not that. Chimera is for keeps, or didn't you know?*

He decided a gentler course would be appropriate here. "Tommy, Cate always needs more soldiers, that's true. And you are the perfect soldier."

"*Bien sur*," Tommy agreed. "And though you have wisely recruited many troops from Champleurs, there are none who can match my evincing of *splendide*."

"I still don't fully understand *splendide*."

"Nor will you ever. Your belly is firm and hard as steel, but you will always be fundamentally soft." Tommy shrugged without pity. His face became rather steely itself. "Do not divert me, Monsieur President. My form and physique will be a bane to your enemies at the Front. Anywhere else they are wasted potential."

"Even on a task which will determine the outcome of the war?"

"*Quoi?*"

"The Laurana Project," said Hughes. "The Moon Landing."

Oh, but that gave Tommy cause for hesitation.

"It is those scientists you wish for me to keep safe?" he said.

Hughes nodded. "The world is not on our side, Tommy. Much of it remains in contraposition to our stance on Eurydice. They think that when I express my fear and our collective need, I'm masking some agenda of my own. Trust is the currency of international relations, and it spends well with wide-minded people and poorly with the narrow and insular. I've received credible intelligence that there are plots—ongoing schemes I'm talking about here—to thwart our mission to the moon. A mission whose success I believe with a great and growing passion is key to favorable public sentiment for the war. Only last week a man was arrested. In his possession was a bomb of terrible explosive capability. In his madness, he freely admitted to police that he intended to blow up the rocket. 'Before it blows up the world' he is recorded as saying." Hughes smiled without humor. "In a way I understand what he meant by that. Thin lines between sanity and insanity, eh? Perhaps rule has made me mad. What I'm getting at, Tommy, is that advanced security measures need implementing."

"*C'est moi.*"

"You," Hughes agreed. "A man who can move faster than those with..."

"Explosive capability."

"Indeed."

Tommy gave a meditative grunt. "I had not considered it," he admitted. "That the office you meant was... that the flabby, potato-figured paper shufflers you intend for me to protect were those attached to the Laurana Project..."

"You hadn't considered that I value you?" Hughes pulled an expression of mocking outrage. "I must object. I must object most thoroughly."

"You prod me." Tommy grinned. "I suppose it is deserved. Media fetishist."

"Racist bastard."

Tommy's grin widened. He opened his mouth, possibly to compare Gormon Hughes' posture to that of a sexually incompetent lemming, and that was when the phone trilled and, simultaneously, Evelyn Hughes stormed into the office.

"Evelyn," said Hughes, leaving the phone to be answered by one among a host of fumbling bumbling butlers. He came around to the side of his desk. "Why aren't you at school?"

"Where's Uncle Frank?" she demanded. "I want to work on my wall."

"Knowing Frank, he'll arrive when you need him. But you were to attend your lessons and train with Frank and Jo this evening. Evelyn, what are you really doing here?"

"Skiving," she said. "Bunking off. Playing truant."

"Ditching," offered one butler.

"Scrimshanking," said another.

"Teacher was going on about etiquette," said Evelyn.

"Good," said Hughes, hot under the collar now. "You could use the practice."

"I need to know how to protect myself."

Father shook his head at daughter. "You can't train all the time. Think of your mind as a muscle. If you put constant strain on it, something important will break."

"Hector says you took to training like a duck to water," she snapped.

"More like a new bird to a deep pond. Carefully. With instruction."

The butler on the phone said, "Mr. President, there's an urgent matter which requires—"

Hughes overrode her, his gaze lead-weighted and intent upon his child. "I shouldn't have sent you to Wimples. That was wrong of your dad."

"Ahm. Sir?" quavered the butler.

Hughes held up a hand. The butler quailed.

"Head up to your room," Hughes told Evelyn. "I'll send word to Frank. I'm sorry for trotting you off to school. You must have felt restless there. Helpless. I don't—"

"Stop it," she said.

Oh, but she knew how to rile him up all right. "What? What did I say?"

"What I want to hear," she said, and was it his imagination or was there a tremor in her voice? She turned her face from him, her ears reddening, fists bunched at her sides, strands of dark hair plastered to her brow with dried sweat, and to one cheek with... yes, he realized with surprise and a gripping feeling of worry, one cheek was wet with tears. "You never... I'll go to my room, I'll—"

"What?" he demanded. "I never what?"

Her gaze snapped to him, sudden and piercing. "You're like Grandad's furniture: a big pile of closed books. People can read the loose pages on the floor, but the books never say a word, a real word. That's you."

"That's very pretty," he said with terrible hollowness. "Get out."

"I want—"

"*Get out.*"

She didn't pull away. She wasn't stung.

Daughters are so rarely stung. Later, when they talked about bees, Hughes would come to understand that better. For now the way she looked at him, a look of slow honeyed poison, a look so savagely sweet it was bitter, it was all he could do not to pick her up and haul her to her room kicking and screaming, and lock her there, and listen to her batter her fists on the door with a honeyed poison satisfaction, a sense of paternal superiority so brutally nasty it was nice, but he would never, God no, not *ever*, he loved her too much. And that was why the anger boiled so fast and so pure, yes, and... and...

And I need a cigarette.

He was going to have one.

He gave in. Felt himself give in. Falling, falling off the wagon, as Tommy Fahrenheit stood nearby, very much on his own wagon of sobriety and riding strong.

Hughes rubbed at his mouth, his eyes held by Evelyn's. It was like looking into a mirror that showed all the anger he felt inside. Loose red pages next to pristine ones, and all contained in closed books. His temper and his pride looking up at him with her hair in dark horsetails.

Maybe the intensity of that, a father telling his daughter to get out and the daughter refusing to go, maybe that was what distracted him. Awareness is funny. The other thing too. Dreadful. Awareness is dreadful.

A lack of it can get you killed.

On a wall in the office, in the shadows cast by one of the six stone dragons looming atop the hearth, a door quietly opened. No one in Redspire—not even Hughes—knew about that door. A figure slipped inside. Discreetly, hushed as hushed can be, they took out a long tube, very similar to a flute, only in place of holes the tube had a button on its side.

Someone watched this happen. It was a spider. The butlers—bless their lackadaisy—were not diligent about dusting and cobweb removal, and so this particular spider had the run of the space beside the secret door. Or, more accurately, the skitter of the space.

Now the door was open. The cobweb had been shorn to drift in limp sticky ruins, and the spider was extremely affronted. It fixed its eight eyes in reproval upon the figure.

Which meant that Evelyn—connected to insects as she was—saw the flutish tube raised.

She saw it raise and

(*no*)

(*no no NO*)

she saw it swivel and settle on the dark-haired, dark-bearded man at the center of the room's incipient drama.

"Mr. President," chirped the butler on the phone. "There's been an *explosion*, sir—"

Hughes whirled. "What?"

"One of the purifiers, sir. I was trying to—"

"An explosion? That can't be right. Hector and Cassandra—"

"Hector is the one calling, sir."

Words moving fast as the newcomer took aim. The hand holding the tube was soft, powdered. The nails were immaculately well cared for. So noted the spider. So noted Evelyn. She knew where every creepy crawly in the room was. Picture something important to you. Really important. Where is it now? That was the level of clarified knowledge Evelyn had: some internal radar within her was permanently dialed to blip with bugs.

Wish as she might in that moment, there was nothing like the witchy white moth that had saved her in Daethumberland, only tiny fruit flies, spiders, and a teensy-weensy wood-munching beetle living in one of Father's desk drawers. Nothing to intervene. Even if she cried out, it would be too slow. Tommy Fahrenheit was quick and Daddy was quicker, especially with Faethe the amulet of dragons, but no. Nothing to be done.

Except—

The tube whispered as it fired. The spider heard. So Evelyn heard.

But not even she heard the whisper the dart made as it struck her in the throat and sank its poisoned tip three inches into her skin.

The room heard the things that happened next. The thump. The slam. The sigh. The thump of Evelyn against her dad, the slam of the secret door, the sigh Evelyn emits into the stunned silence).

Oh yes.

Her neck felt hot.

A bee, thought Evelyn. Thinking was hard... soupy. Golden syrupy. Honeyhoneyhoney. Commotion. More sound. She was deaf to it, deaf and unbothered. The warmth was spreading from her neck, up and down, spreading. *So this is what it's like to be stung. I wondered, I really did... oh—*

***

Hoshrum Thud arrived just as the doctor was leaving.

For fifty-eight he was in excellent shape (though his famous mustache dwarfed, trumped, and outperformed that excellence handily). In his black-and-white uniform adorned at the breast with its platinum streetbeater boot badge, Thud moved with a sturdy, somehow crafty grace, the kind a canny criminal will take note of should they wish to remain at large, or indeed at small. Despite that grace, there was also a stiff, dazed, hard-done-by quality to the man. In truth he had never quite adjusted to his role as commissioner of Leonidas District. Bearing that in mind, one can only imagine how poorly suited he felt to his elevated position as chief of police for the entire city. He had protested that, and stridently. Fat lot of good it had done him. Damn Gormon Hughes seven ways to hell, but the lad was persuasive. Thud still remembered the clinching argument. Hughes had looked at Thud, very frankly and modestly, and said, "I thought it was yours and you were its?" It being Corinth City, of course. The bugger had Thud there, had him by both badges, the one you could take away and the one you couldn't. The one you could take away was the platinum badge, the one he wore on his breast on duty and carried in his pocket when he was off. The one you could not take away had no color because when you think about it devotion to an idea doesn't have a color either. That idea was Corinth City. The good and the bad. Thud was its and it was his.

Chief of police. An ear-to-the-ground copper like him. How was he to wade through the paperwork and get any bloody work done? Having someone attend to the paperwork for him felt like passing the parcel, something he had never, ever done in his life. Ruddy chief of blasted police. Well, it had pleased his wife, Hettie. That was worth a bit of professional discomfort.

He was hers too, you see.

Thud went into Hughes' private rooms. Evelyn was in bed, fast asleep. The girl looked chalky to Thud's eye but otherwise okay. Still, you never knew with poisons. Poisons were like time: full of unpredictability. Also too much of it will kill you.

Hughes was by his daughter's side. The President of Corinth City looked as pale as she did. No ashtray in sight, and Thud's nose detected no trace of smoke. A surprise, that. Ciggies were the refuge of the addict under stress, and as a cigar man himself Thud knew for a fact that Hughes had been trying to kick the smokes for years now with mixed success.

He's so stressed he's come right back around to being calm, and calm like that is dangerous ground. I'd better tread carefully. Thud said, after some quick consideration, "What was in the dart?"

Hughes glanced at him. "Discharge from a cat's infected ear. An unusual choice of poison but an effective one."

Thud had never heard of such a thing. "Bacteria, like?"

"So the doctor said."

"I'll speak to Tyrae Leborski about it."

"If you can rouse her." The ghost of amusement curled Hughes' lips. By that alone, Thud knew the answer to his next question. He asked it anyway.

"She improving then?"

One of Evelyn's hands lay on her stomach. Hughes touched it with a finger.

"Yes," he said. "The doctor asked to examine the dart. Big thing. On the table there."

Thud went to the table and, using a handkerchief, he put the dart in his pocket. Hughes continued. "Presuming the assassin wanted to guarantee my death, the amount of poison contained within the dart would have had to be enough to take full effect on a man of roughly twice my weight. I know it sounds it, but that amount isn't random. The dart's length and the silo within indicates that such a dose would have been well within reason to administer. Had I been struck, I would have succumbed in five minutes. Sourcing an antidote in that time would have been impossible. Faethe, my amulet, allows me to alter the density of my body. It's powerless against an internal threat. And my status as Iphigenia's shadow means nothing when she's as weak as she is now. Who knows, my death might have killed her too."

"How did Evelyn know our assassin was in the room?" asked Thud.

"There was a spiderweb near the secret door the assassin used. I can only think it was a spider that warned Evelyn of the danger." Hughes' hand took hold of his daughter's limp fingers. "A fatal dose of poison fails to kill a twelve-year-old girl. The doctor, she um... drew blood. Fed it into a portable machine. Took another sample sixty seconds later. The reduction in the levels of poison make no sense. Evelyn's white blood cells are crushing the foreign agent at impossible speed."

"Eurydice is still strong," said Thud, wondering was he treading ice with this line of conjecture, and if so, how thin? "Stands to reason her shadow is strong as well."

Hughes was silent for a short, tense while. He drew a deep breath and let it go and let the tension go with it. "There are times when I forget. I know that sounds ridiculous, but it's true. There are times the *who* overpowers the *what* in my mind. The who of Evelyn rather than the what." Gently, he extracted his hand from hers. Hughes the worrying dad was folded away, and Hughes the avenging father was ready to rumble. "We need to move fast, Hoshrum."

"City's cordoned off. The tower too. No one coming in or getting out."

"Unless he knows things we don't."

"Always a useful assumption, sir," affirmed Thud. "The ticket is knowing that they know we don't know and getting them nice and cocky, sir. Or paranoid as to who knows about the knowing and who might not know all they think they know about the unknown. Sir."

A glitter in Hughes' eye, not amusement this time. Thud knew that glitter well. Hughes was president now, but the bloodhound was still underneath. Its chain was gnawed, ready to snap. The thrill of a hunt would not make it happy, but it would satisfy, and that was enough. "In that case see to the knowing, Thud. Nab him while I run this beautiful shambles of a city. He'll outmaneuver us if he can. Neatly, I'll wager. Have you figured out who he is?"

Thud nodded. "On the drive here, sir. Only one person knows this tower well enough to pull the old 'secret door' trick. The only question is why?"

"Clean the rust and buff the tarnish off your observation, Chief," said Hughes, ushering him out. "First rule of policework. The person you're dealing with has had a motive for twelve years. The question worth asking isn't *why* but *why now?*"

Chapter Twelve

There was a house. Music was broken there.

Not many were welcome inside, but Evelyn was. She had but to ask and its door would open. Its owner was always pleased to see her.

In her naivety Evelyn had been fooled into believing the house was shiny and pink and inviting. Now she knew the truth about its owner and more importantly about herself. When Evelyn was dosed with poison her body cocooned itself in sleep, a sleep that would make her well. In sleep, she dreamt. In her dream she saw the house as her father and Frank Gallant had seen it, twelve years beforehand. She screamed.

She screamed and the house's door swung open.

Two long, feminine arms plunged out of the dark within the door. Evelyn had an instant to register them coming for her (longer, longer, how they *stretched*!) before a pair of hands clamped on her shoulders. "No," she murmured. It didn't hurt when they wrenched her inside the house. They didn't need to hurt. She screamed again, a scream like harp strings destroyed by a sledgehammer.

Then the scream was smothered against fabric.

Someone holding her. Their face against the crown of her head. Evelyn felt their mouth and their breath as they spoke.

"Hushabye," said a familiar voice. "There, there, Jane."

Evelyn planted both hands on Eurydice's chest and shoved. The arms enfolding her gave her up without struggle.

Evelyn didn't demand to go. Betrayal had wrought a maturing in her, the work of years occurring in a few days. A demand involved words, and words were a waste of action time. That age old question sprang into her mind. Fight or flight?

Eurydice smiled at her. "Neither," she said.

Evelyn broke into a run.

Inside the house looked as it always had. She found her way to the main hall. The front door, not far. Her footsteps hammered, outpaced by her heartbeat which was going full gallop. The door was different than she remembered—a small pumpkin-skinned cyclops, a furry, spotted dragon, and a thin man with his eyes hidden behind a veil. All three were carved in the door with its handle in the middle of them.

Evelyn recognized the little cyclops at once. *Skuggs.*

Did she know the other two?

I do. I met them here in this house. The veiled man is Burrows and the dragon is Ruthven.

They're...

Both words occurred to her simultaneously.

(*Enemies*)

(*Friends*)

Her fingers itched for that handle. Grasp that handle, yank it down, pull, and she was a fly in the wind. She would run as if propelled by wings.

The carvings moved. Skuggs clutched his tummy and laughed without sound. Ruthven's muzzle wrinkled in a lupine grin. Burrows pulled up his veil.

Scare tactics, Evelyn told herself. *I won't be frightened.*

She reached for the handle—and drew back.

It was not a handle but a bee stinger. How had she not...

But I did see it. It must have changed.

She heard laughter; raspy chuckles, sinewy giggles, gleeful titters.

She looked up sharply. The three carvings on the door were still. *Us?* They seemed to say. *Not us. Couldn't be us. We're only scare tactics, right?*

With no alternative, Evelyn turned around the face the hallway. If she could find a window...

Like the door handle the hallway had changed. Before it had been a simple hallway full of boxes, with stairs going up and stairs going down, and a plum-colored rug tufted with dust kitties.

Now it was the hallway of the psychedelic jellyfish museum in Corinth City. Cool blue light filtered through glass panels. Slow, frumpy shapes swam in the water on the other side of that glass, their tendrils milky and strange. Over the stereo system a mousy announcer squeaked that you must not hold your hand against the glass for too long. "Who knows? It could be your older sister, Jane. Not Eurydice. The other sister. The one that turned to glass inside your mum. They got it all out, but hey, they wouldn't throw out all the shards! Waste not, want not! She could be anywhere, just anywhere, just—" And then the announcer could not go on, for they were laughing too hard, a crazy zigzag laugh that made Evelyn feel sick.

She closed her eyes and opened them.

The hallway was made of mouths. Fox mouths, vole mouths, anteaters, frogs, lizards, nightjars, hedgehogs, bats, and weird, scaled pangolins. Endless mouths. And before Evelyn's wide, terrified eyes the mouths put forth their tongues. Tongues of every shape and size embarked on wet, salivating quests for that meat that tastes so sweet: bugs.

She closed her eyes and opened them.

The hallway was simply a hallway. In place of the normal boxes and packages, there were mannequins. The mannequins were white and smooth. The mannequins were posed in erotic positions. Blank, featureless faces watched her as they did that thing she was only vaguely beginning to understand.

She closed her eyes and opened them.

There was no hallway. The living room was decked out in Tinfrost decoration. Stockings on the hearth. Tinseled tree. Blinking red-green lights. The whole shebang. In three armchairs were three men; one with a cap covering his eyes, one in dapper gentlemanly furs of white all spotted in red, and one small and missing an eye. Their armchairs were embroidered: Uncle Burrows, Uncle Ruthven, Uncle Skuggs. A fourth armchair was set in the middle of them, the fulcrum around which they turned. Its embroidery called for someone named Jane.

Evelyn grew angry then. Her dark eyes, soft with dread, hardened.

"My name is Evelyn. And you are *not* my uncles. You're monsters." She thought of Mr. Glint and Frank Gallant. "That is... my real uncles are much classier monsters than you. And they don't need to pretend to be something they aren't so I'll like them. They simply are, and I do. Like them. And you all make me want to puke. So there."

The hallway closed its eyes and opened them.

Evelyn was never quite sure how this happened, but that was the impression she had. No time to ponder it. The hallway was restored to its former normalcy, but all was not well, no, far from it.

Eurydice was there. Her big sister was there, and *she was coming for her.* Eurydice was wearing a dress that looked like it had been dragged through every gutter and latrine in the worst medieval city. Flowers of unspeakable ugliness coiled about her feet and ankles like socks darned by devils. Where the dress was torn her legs sawed in and out, in and out, yes, because that weird capering shuffle was not a mere advance, it was a waltz. Eurydice was waltzing by herself, her hair a wild jungle, her smile peeking through like a tiger through a mask of thorns, and she was coming closer, one-step-two-step-three-step-four!

Evelyn stood, paralyzed with fear.

Got to do something, her mind wailed.

One-step.

You must do something now—

Two-step.

Oh, she's almost here, she almost has you, you silly girl, think!

Three-step.

Think, think, there must be something you can—

Four.

"Sometimes little sisters run away," said Eurydice. Her eyes were so wide and full of blood. "I see your mossy wall. In your head. Are you planning on scampering over it? You can. I'll let you. Little sisters run. Big sisters fetch them. That's their job. They fetch them and bring them home. Big sisters are the real mothers and fathers. The only family that counts."

Evelyn was only half-listening. She was thinking of her mother, of a conversation she'd had with her mother years ago, recorded in her diary, preserved, a fly in the amber of written memory. She'd been angry with her mother about a spider, and the reason they'd had to make up was that Evelyn had been hurt, and she'd called her mother...

Evelyn Hughes began to sing. She sang fierce and harsh and desperately.

Who's afraid of the wicked wolf,
The wicked wolf, the wicked wolf?
Who's afraid of the wicked wolf?
Not me, not me, not me.

The effect was both instantaneous and remarkable.

Eurydice's jouissance burst in a bubble of shock. The flowers at her feet withered. Her dress shredded. Putrid fabric spun in weird cyphers over her skin. Filth crusted, cleaned, evaporated. Her hair flew out in a medusa-snake-frisson. Her face crumpled in on itself, starting with the ears and moving toward her brain. The ears shrinking, her mouth shrieking, her hands clawing the air helplessly, all in protest of that hateful sound. Evelyn sang on.

Who's afraid of the biting wolf,
The gnashing wolf, the crunching wolf?
Who's afraid of the red-haired wolf?
You oh you oh you.

Eurydice barely looked human now. She was a writhing mass of human parts, fleeing away from the song down the hallway.
Evelyn roared after her. "My mother is the red-haired, hobnail-booted, big bad wolf and she's coming for you, big sister. *She's coming for you!*"
She spun on her heel. The door handle was back.
Evelyn grasped it, reefed the door open, and was gone.

***

She woke. The curtain was drawn. No blue peeping through. Night then. The same night? No way to know. One thing was sure: this was not her bed. It was too ample. Something crinkled under the pillow as she stirred. She reached in and rummaged under it. It was pages. Pages of a manuscript stuck together to make a blanket.
Just like that she knew exactly where she was.
Evelyn closed her bleary eyes. Half expecting to see the room shift into some nightmare version of itself, she opened them. All was as it had been. Safe then. Relief moved in her like good shadows under a friendly moon. She replaced the pages in their spot beneath the pillow. Her fingers roved up to her throat. Of the dart, and any wound it might have left in her, there was no sign. There was pain though, and a fair helping of it. For some reason it was localized in her head.
Sitting up like this made the headache worse. She lay back. That was better.

By the bed a little reading lamp was dialed to its lowest setting. The red light brushed at the dark and softened it. By that light she saw her dad fast asleep in a chair. Attuned to notice change—a result of her fraught encounter with Eurydice—Evelyn saw that there was something different about Hughes' chin. At first, she had no idea what that change could be. The next moment, as though her realization had given him a gentle shake, he drew in a longer breath and his eyes came open.

"Are you okay?" he asked.

"Yes. Did I sleep long?"

He checked his amulet. He'd had a watch fitted to the back of it years ago. "Three ay-em, so not too long. Get some more."

"More?"

"Sleep."

Triumph at getting away from Eurydice left her then. Drowsiness had cut a swathe through it. Her dad's presence did the rest. Now there was only fear. "Can I have a hug?"

He got up and bent down. His arms closed her up in a ball of love.

She cried a bit. Not too much.

"Bad dream?" he asked when she was better.

"Awful. But it's not that."

"What is it?"

"You could have died, Daddy."

"I'm all right."

"You *could* have."

"Maybe," he said, and he must have seen the gratitude in her face for telling her the truth because he went on reluctantly. "You were okay, and you and I are alike in more ways than one."

"So you would have been all right?"

"I don't know. I can't know. That's the truth. Next time let me find out."

"Don't say that." Her head nestled deeper in the inglenook between his neck and collarbone. "I'll always keep you safe."

"That's not for you to do," he replied. "You worry about you and let me worry for the both of us. That's what I signed up for when your mum and I had you."

"We shall meet in the middle."

"How do we do that?"

"We keep one another safe."

She felt his smile on the crown of her head. She did not dare tell him how much that reminded her of Eurydice because he would not understand the comparison was favorable.

"Okay, Daughter of mine," he said. "You've gotten prim lately."

"Really?"

"I suppose these things come in phases. I like prim, so long as it's kind."

"Is it prim to tell you about something you might not like?"

"No. You can tell me."

"Your beard's going gray, Father of mine."

"I don't think so. I trimmed it this morning."

"Check again."

"I'll do that. Gray?"

She gave a small nod. "I could see it in the red light. Could even be white."

He made a neutral noise that Evelyn did not think was very neutral at heart. She rather liked white hair. But most people seemed not to. It meant they were getting on, as Grandfather would say. Exchanging one season of themselves for the next, and unlike the ones native to the world, the seasons inside people run out.

"I love you, you fartsome, crotchety old windbag," she said, hugging tighter.

"I love you too, fawn of the prettiest forest."

"Noooo." She flicked him gently. "It only works if you're insulting back."

"I'll try harder in future."

"See that you do." There was a pause. "Oh God, that was really prim."

"I wasn't going to say anything."

"Am I really like that?"

"No. Not all the time."

"I'm actually mortified."

"Mortified?"

"Morto!"

They were laughing.

"Sleep?" he asked.

"Sleep sounds good. Will you stay?"

"I've got to work. Things aren't good in the city."

"And you've got to find the assassin," she said grimly.

"Yes."

She didn't ask why anyone would try to kill him. Her father was a powerful man. Even at twelve Evelyn Hughes understood that with visibility came vulnerability. Climb the political ladder high enough and you ran the risk of assassination, as well as loose shingles, slippages, and rogue pigeons.

Instead she asked him if it was going to happen again.

Dad thought about it. "Hard to know. It could. My old neighbor Ernie Wilks used to say that when it rains, it pours."

"I wouldn't know," said Evelyn. "What with never seeing rain."

"You saw. You just can't remember." She heard him scratch his beard. "White?"

"Sorry."

"Hm. Gambling is a mug's game, especially when the stake is life and death. If pressed I'd bet on it not happening again. The assassination attempt, you get me."

"Yeah."

"But I'm going to practice using Faethe even when there's no danger. That way I'll always be invulnerable. The problem is that it takes concentration, and I need every drop of that I've got to keep things ticking over."

An idea occurred. "You could practice with me if you'd like. I'll build my mind wall against Eurydice, and you build your reserves of concentration."

"That's a splendid idea. We'll do that."

"Hurrah!"

"Hurrah?"

"I'm still morto. I've elected to roll with it."

Chuckling, he gave her one last loving squeeze and sat back. "Am I really a closed book?"

Evelyn pecked him a kiss on the chin, right where the fine white hairs sprouted. "Goodnight Dad," she said.

***

The caterpillar of spring struggled on through its chrysalis of time. The question of what sort of summer butterfly it would become was pertinent all throughout Corinthia, and the world beyond.

April arrived hot. May followed, humid and sticky and sweaty. It could get hotter. It *would* get hotter.

A curious soul could check the meteorology records covering weather for the past twelve years. A curious soul who was also sensible and trained would conclude that the drought that now gripped the world had started in Corinth City and radiated outward. Keen historians noted that, at first, the scientific community were at a loss to respond coherently. Understandable. Nothing like this had ever happened before, and scientists, like lawyers, adore precedent. The Now is so much more explicable because there is so much Then to compare it to.

One of the few rational initiatives undertaken in response to the drought had been the purifiers. Their construction was codenamed Project Ogminio after a half-forgotten pagan goddess of the sea. Project Ogminio was formulated by an emergency coalition between the heads of the Calcifern Engineering Guild, the Climate Control Board of Rhönland, the much-lauded Green Hegemony of Yi-Shi, and key scientific minds handpicked from the rather egoistically named University in Corinth City.

Thirst is one of the great motivators, along with patriotic verve and the desire to have sex with radiant young ladies who fate conspires to put on the right balcony at the right time. In order to avoid being torn apart for want of a well, a pump, a cup, a thimble of water, world governments quickly fell in line with Project Ogminio's recommendations. Those that did not were ousted and swiftly replaced with more amenable representatives. The Dengue Virus was not the only reason for an uprising in Ikahagua. Seldom are politics simple, but it does happen, and just as the notion of a moon landing fascinated the world's brain, so too did the notion of drinkable water fascinate its belly.

Why had it happened?

Well, that's always tricky. Acts of God are synonymous with a twiddle of the thumbs and an admission of ignorance. Who could say why?

None. That's who.

But there were those who held suspicions.

Three such suspicious minds were active during late March, April, and the first fortnight of May.

Take Hoshrum Thud. The case for the missing assassin certainly had. The cordon around the city had been erected fast enough that Thud was ninety-percent sure the murderous bastard hadn't slipped the net. That ten-percent was reserved for outlandish circumstances, i.e. say the assassin could rely on a bit of magic. That was Hughes' domain though. Let the bloodhound sniff where he could. During his early days rising through the precinct ranks, Thud had chewed enough criminals to ribbons to earn the nickname the Leonidas Labrador. Say what you like about Labradors, they're straightforward. Magic made Hoshrum Thud uneasy, but he was at his best on the street, and his best was damn good.

Leaving all the bloody paperwork addressed to the chief of police in possibly more capable (and undoubtedly more willing) hands, Thud slid his badge into his pocket, dressed like the tenement boy he had been before he married Hettie and always secretly would be, and started at square one. Ask questions. Who had seen what? When? Could they think of anything else? Anything out of the ordinary? Assemble facts. Where you didn't have facts, fill in the blanks with the plywood of guessing. It'd do in the meantime. Follow up.

One of the laundry crew had seen someone matching the assassin's description. The assassin had been in a hurry, but the laundry fellow said that he was quite sure the assassin had been futzing with his hair. The hair had looked funny. Funny how? Well, the laundry fellow wasn't sure. Just a bit funny. If he had more to tell the officer, could he contact Thud? Sure. And he had, a day later. The laundry man had, at one point, lived in shared accommodation with a young woman who worked in the makeup department of a movie studio. One time she brought back a wig to work on. That was what the assassin's hair looked like. A top-notch wig. The kind that would fool most people but might give a skewed sense of surreality to those familiar with wigs.

Thud checked up with ticket stations, including digital booking centers.

No luck. Okay. Roll things to square minus one, where does that take the picture? Twelve years. Consult the suspect's tickets. Results. A record of a trip out of Corinth City. A paper trail. It came to an end. Where? In a dead end? No, with potential leads, only a call away. O-*kay*. Now he was cooking with charcoal.

He traced the suspect's movements across the continent. Meanwhile he walked the beat, keeping his eyes and ears open. Under the sun the city baked like a potato in tinfoil. Thud knew he was one of the lucky ones. He had something to distract himself with.

More questions. Always more.

Employ the gentle touch. Lean on the rough, no-nonsense copper routine. This Labrador hadn't got fleas but he was hardbitten. Adjust the temperature of tone. Change line of inquiry. Leave no stone unturned. Think two steps ahead and three to the left. Adapt to the interviewee. Kick up a fuss. Kick down the dust. Get things moving. Ask enough questions, you might just get the right answer.

Back to basics.

It's true that you can't teach an old dog new tricks. Equally true is this: you cannot take away his old ones.

Take Cate Jubilee. Loss, leadership, and war had mostly transformed her devil-may-care attitude into an engine that ran on reticence and coughed clouds of smoggy black suspicion. But one engine is not the whole machine, one element not the woman. At the end of the day decisions were her bread and butter. Combined with the fact that her decisions were good ones eight times out of ten meant that she secured maximal victory and minimal loss, and that in turn secured loyalty. Also adding to that fealty were the lozenges, knitted by Ulf Seamster whose power had evolved strangely so that he could not only knit warm, comfortable clothes terribly fast but also delicious lozenges rich in vitamin C and D. Considering the ability for Eurydice to deny her enemies sunlight and fresh fruit, these lozenges were peerless for staving off gum disease, rickets, and generally keeping up morale. Further, it necessitated the hiring of several more army dentists. Soldiers at war can never have too much of a sweet thing.

With a promise from John Isherwood that one more terraformer in the right spot would win the war, Cate raced Burrows for the mountain called Golgomir. Burnished Isaac Lawless and the other scouts informed her that the arena for the final battle would be a place called the Bloodwood. The men were informed of the poor conditions they would be fighting in—the threat of insect bites was particularly troubling for the un-nibbled. Cate addressed concerns where she could, consulted her advisors, and did what she had always done since the onset of the war: she led from the front with an eye to what was behind.

Which was very fortunate for her men because in April, as the Bettys marched toward the Bloodwood, as the strange stars of Eurydice winked in her stranger sky, the murders began. Armies are, even at their ease, immensely busy things full of drama on a small and grand scale, so it was two days before it became clear that the soldiers dying in their beds were not succumbing to mysterious illness but rather being induced to that state by malefic intent. Thorough investigation by the company sergeants revealed no signs of unrest amongst the troops, and besides, autopsy revealed there were no obvious signs of foul play. Cate concluded they were dealing with magic. And while Hoshrum Thud rightly supposed that magic was Hughes' domain of expertise, he ought to have lumped Cate into the mix. In her experience, magic that occupied the real world was divorced from the kind in stories. In the real world there was always a source, an origin from which the power derived. Always.

Following the blueprint set forth by Hughes during his hunt for Spring-Heeled Jane, Cate tried to find a pattern between the dead soldiers. There were more differences than commonalities, and the commonalities were the only thing she had to go on; they were soldiers—of different rank, true!—but soldiers at war. Eurydice, then, she had sent this killer. An agent of the woman and the world.

With news of their magical killer sent out amongst the regiments, Cate could only pace her famous hobnail boots from fortress to fortress and try to think of a solution. Failing that, biding her time was the best she could do. Perhaps a pattern would emerge. She didn't have to wait long.

A young woman came forward one night in mid-spring. She claimed that before her best friend's body was discovered in bed, her best friend had complained of frightening dreams, or what he hoped were dreams. Apparently, the young man had confided that each night for the past three evenings he'd seen a thin woman at the end of his bed. There were no other distinguishing details he could remember in the morning. He could voice only the lingering thinness of the figure. The first two nights he'd screwed his eyes shut and when he'd opened them the thin woman was gone. But the third night she had still been there. He'd opened his mouth to scream, but before he could the woman had melted into the long shadows spread throughout the room. The next day he told his friend all about it. A good friend, the young woman rolled up her bedding, deposited it on his floor, and promised to stay with him so nothing happened. That night he'd died.

Cate acted quickly. She ordered every soldier to report immediately if they received any visitations from a thin figure during the night.

Events took a turn for the worse. As Hughes' neighbor Ernie Wilks had so eloquently said between cackles of hag-like laughter: When it rains, it pours.

Reports of sightings flooded in, which caused quite the panic among Cate's inner circle, who were expecting one report at a time, since there had only been one death every four days. After a bit of digging, Margherita Stranger, one of the original members of Cate's Company, sent word to Cate that there had commenced a game of silly buggers. In other words, people were lying about seeing the thin woman for a bit of fun. Margherita informed Cate that the culprits behind the false reports were a contingent of men from Rhönland, as well as a few Corinthian soldiers speckled amongst their unit.

Twelve years garnished with the heinous herbs of war meant Cate was well-used to bouts of bad discipline in the ranks. But lozenges or no lozenges, the murderer was at large, morale was getting dicey, and these pranking bastards were not helping the situation. She had each of them psychologically evaluated. Those deemed to be thugs were dismissed from duty with none of the usual severance pay. Those deemed to be salvageable were turned over to Jennifer Goblingrin, who reminded each of them what would happen if they played pranks again. These measures were effective, given that what would happen to the offenders would be Jennifer Goblingrin.

During this mess, Cate met the only person who was receiving genuine visitations from the thin woman. She was a career soldier who had fought in the war with Champleurs. Steady and brave, she told Cate that she'd taken a shot the second night the thin woman had appeared to her. The crossbow bolt had struck the back wall, passing through the thin woman as if she were not there.

Desperate to save this woman's life, Cate positioned sentries around her while she slept. She recalled that Spring-Heeled Jane's method of killing involved Jane crawling into the heads of her victims, forcing them to commit horrible acts of violence, then leaving the victims to a life of drooling, fish-eyed stupor. It stood to reason that this thin woman might be doing something similar, perhaps forcing her victims to asphyxiate themselves. On the third night of visitations, the career soldier stirred a little but was overall completely fine. The fourth night, she died. There was no struggle. Only a small, involuntary spasm that put her guards on alert, then death.

The following night, Cate's old friend Lorna Blacktower saw the thin woman.

Evidently the thin woman was finished with the soldiery. For reasons that were her own, she now fixed the more powerful members of the army in her sights. On the third night, the night before Lorna would surely have been killed, Eilandri Titansgrave wrote on one of her little yellow cards and handed it to Cate.

I think you were onto something thinking of Spring-Heeled Jane. Think of an insect laying its eggs, waiting for them to hatch. We can't find the eggs. We can only see their murderous results. But they must exist because otherwise Eurydice would have done this years ago. What's changed?

"I agree that something's changed, but we've tried finding the source. There's nothing in the victim's belongings," Cate pointed out. "We searched every single one. Tore their quarters apart. There was nothing to find."

More writing. Another yellow note.

Then we must look everywhere.

Cate thought of the career soldier, so brave even though death was right around the corner, and she thought of Lorna. In the end, some decisions are easy to make. It's discovering their existence that can be hard.

"Thank God for you, Ella," said Cate.

Unsmiling, for she never smiled, Eilandri winked a lavender eye and left to get the search going.

So it was that from Betty to Betty, from building to building, from room to room, every scrap of furniture, every bag and box, every container, repository, barrel and bed was overturned and checked, inside and out. It was in the courtyard of Cate's own Betty that the stone was found. It was not particularly large, but it was a distinctive shape. Slender and curved. It was shown to Lorna Blacktower.

"That's her," she said. "That's the thin woman."

Cate tossed the stone to Eilandri, who closed her hand and promptly ground the stone to powdery silt. Everyone present—many of Cate's close confidantes and, of course, Cate herself—felt like a coldness seeped suddenly into them, a hateful coldness, and then with a feverish silent snarl that could only be experienced and not heard, the coldness... and the thin woman... were gone.

The happy tidings went out and the army slept its first good night's sleep since March. The question of where the stone had come from plagued Cate. It could have been left there by an undead during one of countless battles. Or by one of the shrieking birds. Or by Skuggs, sneaking around as he did. Or Ruthven, clever as he was. Or it could have simply appeared.

There was no answer. That and their failure to save all the victims made the victory hollow as Cate believed all victories were in this rotten world.

She marched on, excited for only two things: the coming end of the war, and the day after it was over. She intended to put her feet up, order pizza, and kiss Hughes until he forgot he was president.

Before that, there would be battle in the Bloodwood. *With a name like that, Ruthven's got to be in the mix somewhere.* They hadn't fought directly, not since Cate had tricked the dragon into drinking blood from soldiers who were bombed on hard drugs. She had almost had him that day. If he was in the Bloodwood, he would have his own mischief in store. Cate Jubilee would be ready.

Take Gormon Hughes, even more suspicious by nature than Thud and Cate combined. When the leader of the terrorists who blew up one of the purifiers contacted Redspire and demanded to speak to the president on their terms, one-on-one, no tricks, Hughes expected a trap.

On a mercifully cool day in early April, Hughes arrived at an abandoned pet shop. The pet shop could be found in an alley off Blackchapel Road, just another nameless corner in rough, rambling Leonidas District. There were ducks painted on the only un-smashed front window. Hughes saw why the shop had closed. Who on earth had ducks in Corinth City? Sooner find an honest politician than a duck in Corinth City.

"Come in Mr. President," called a voice from inside. "Only me in here."

Hughes stepped inside. On his left the till had been broken into. The phone cord hung limply, the phone itself snicked with scissors and stolen. On his right, all the way from the entrance to the back of the shop, the shelving units were cheap pig iron, rounded into wheels, empty, and glazed in dust like the most dystopian of donuts. In the middle of it all sat a young bespectacled man in a wheelchair.

He gave Hughes a friendly wave. "Nice to meet you, gov. My name's Owly. Really, it's Oliver, but it was Owly for the glasses or rolly-polly-Olly for the wheelchair. Think I picked right?"

"I suppose so."

"The lads have a cruel streak, but they've hearts of gold. Sometimes even a heart of gold has a bit of green on it, eh? Buffing and polishing and that? Take you, for example, Mr. President. You're a Leonidas boy, aintchya?"

"I am."

"Right. And here you are leaving us to our own devices. Oh, you've changed some stuff for the better. People've got more money and things to spend it on. Working week is shorter. Even a few new hospitals 'cause of your... the net thing."

"Nets for Nurses," said Hughes. He remembered that. Net incomes for nurses were through the floor when he'd taken over office. He'd done what he could to point their earnings at the economic roof again.

"That's it. Yeah, definitely some improvements," said Owly. "I bet that heart of yours is good as gold. But it's got green on it, Mr. President. Sorry, but that's the simple truth. That green tarnish is manky. Needs to be buffed out. And if you're not gonna buff it, people like me will."

"What is it you want?" said Hughes.

Owly gave him an impatient look that said, *Catch up, chum.* "Water, gov. Kind that goes in sinks and toilets. Some for a shower to wash our nadgers too, if you'd be so good."

Hughes' face remained calm. "And did you try contacting your local officiaries? You know, before you blew up one of our precious means of getting water?"

Owly rolled his eyes. "As a matter of fact, we did. You know what we were told? Current supplies are at a low point, so sorry, must await further updates. Have you ever had to wait for a drink, Mr. President?"

"No," Hughes admitted. "I haven't."

"Have you ever had to worry about your friends and family?" Owly demanded. "Ever had to look into their eyes when they tell you that they're so damn thirsty, and when they ask you what you can do about it? Because even though you were given bad eyes and worse legs, you always had the best ideas right when it counted? Have you ever had to think strategy and next steps while your throat feels like it's about to enter the chimney Olympics, drier than you've ever thought your throat could feel, so dry you think you'll bite your hand any moment and drink what comes out of the teeth marks, so long as it's wet? Ever been there?"

Ah, thought Hughes. "No, Owly. I went hungry all the time when I was your age. But water was never an issue."

Owly nodded. "The taps worked. Now they don't, no matter how hard you spin them."

"But why attack the purifier?" Hughes wanted to know. "Why not something else?"

"When you make a statement, you got to use the right words," said Owly. "If we can't have water, neither can other people. So we took out the purifier. Build another, Mr. President. Build another after that. No more spending on the war or anything else..." The boy hesitated. "Except the moon launch. Our mum is mad to see that on the telly. Only thing keeping her going, sometimes."

"Lunar lunacy is the reason for the season," said Hughes. "And I assume you want the first supply of water shipped directly to you, is that right?"

"Usually assuming makes an ass of you and me," said Owly. "Only in this case, you're bang on the money."

"I see. And if I don't relegate all available funds to purifier construction?"

"We'll blow up the pipes sending water to Ptolema. Cut off the head of the serpent, like. See how you like the way the slicksters of this city wriggle then."

"You'll condemn people to the same thirst you've suffered."

"And it is not a case of the more the merrier," said Owly, very serious now. "Me and the lads talked about it for a long time, Mr. President. In the end the decision was left to me. We had to make a statement, with the right words, and loud. Loud enough for you to hear. And it worked, didn't it? You're here now."

"I am."

"And alone, well done. Didn't think you'd trust me," Owly confessed. "Had you watched all the way from the tower. Don't get itchy. I really am alone too. Better that way. Leonidas boy to Leonidas boy. One greeny-gold heart to another. So what do you say, eh? We've got a deal?"

Hughes looked around. Smiled sadly. "You used to live here."

"Not much gets past you. How'd you know?"

"When you mentioned your mother, your eyes cut to the till. It was very fast, probably an unconscious look. You were seeing her there, weren't you?"

Owly had the grace to look impressed. "Yeah. Dad worked the stocks, Mum worked the till."

"How'd the business fail?"

"Lots of reasons. Do you care?"

"I'm from around here. So yes. I really do."

Owly adjusted his spectacles. "Lots of reasons," he repeated stiffly. He hesitated. "I tried to warn Dad about the ducks. No one's got ducks, I said. Dogs and cats and hamsters and that. Could have a mouse, if you like them. Snake if you don't. But no. Dad was dead set on ducks. He thought it'd attract 'a better class of people' to the shop. Well now he's gone and I'm here."

"Doing what you think is right."

"Don't mope about all sincere like you know what's going on. You try out this chair, I'll try yours. If you'd stayed a Leonidas boy, if you'd never been sucked up by them at the Citadel, you'd have done the same as I did. Maybe you'd have blown up more than the purifier. Why should some have water all the time and my poor mum gasping for a drop? *If it be denied some, it ought be withheld from you.* Know where I read that?"

"*A Summer Knight's Stroll,*" said Hughes. "Saw it at the theatre, did you?"

"Not me, gov. Too expensive."

"I made it cheap."

"Not cheap enough," snapped Owly. "I read it in your old man's teashop. I heard it was your favorite, so I read it. I used to want to be you. Can you imagine?"

Hughes said nothing.

Owly shook his head, despairing the so-called president for a fool. "Enough carping. I'm thirsty. Have we got a deal or not?"

Hughes took a step toward the young man. Slow. Threatening. His voice turned murky, quite sinister. "You really came alone?"

"Absolutely." Owly was completely unperturbed. "And if you take out that broken sword of yours and ram it into my guts, you can kiss the rest of your machines goodbye. Not just the purifiers, the lads will recruit more lads and it'll be a total blastbox. Fireworks and metally bits scattering down. It'll rain debris, first rain in ages. So stab away, squire. Martyrs are like a pond in a desert, eh? Gather round and drink."

"I'm not going to hurt you."

Owly grinned. "Too right."

Hughes took another step forward. "Can I ask your second name? Indulge me."

"Clufp."

"Clufp?"

"Great-great-grandad was from the countryside."

"Oliver Clufp," Hughes said again. "That's distinctive. I'll remember. And for what it's worth, I'll see that your mother gets that drop. I'll see she gets every drop she can drink."

Owly's amusement had developed a few hairline cracks. "What are you on about?"

"Listen to me closely," said Hughes, and he pushed his Performance.

A few moments later, he dug within the cellar of himself, rooted out Chimera, and used it to twist Owly's personality slightly askew.

And just like that, the anarchist movement brewing in Leonidas lost a charismatic leader and the potential for a martyr. The movement lost momentum, stride, everything. But they gained Hughes' attention, and he would try and make that worth the pivot toward conformity. Even if he resented the way they'd gone about it. Even if the cost of doing so meant using his power in a way that made him sick to his stomach.

Hughes had indeed gone to the pet shop expecting a trap. His.

Aside from quelling that potential disaster, April and the first half of May were reasonably quiet for Hughes. There were hiccups in the army screening process, burnout amongst portal technicians, communication breakdowns across the gamut of his life from personal to political, forest fires in southern Corinthia, other drought related problems that boiled down to making people in crisis like Oliver Clufp feel seen and heard by their president so that another like him did not crop up. Speaking of crops, the planting this year was off to a spectacularly crap start with machinery issues, a shortage of agricultural engineers, Emperor Tanaka's health took a turn leading to a certain degree of instability in Mysicordelia, oh health wasn't it fickle. Hughes himself came down with a fungal infection in his throat, but did he take to his bed, no, of course not because according to Cate's latest report from the Front the final battle was going to involve dealing with too many bugs, so Hughes issued an executive order for as much insect repellant as could be sent through the portal to Eurydice. Also blood donations had slackened because of that utter thorn in the side of delegation, Bad Management, and Ruthven was a factor in this last battle so the troops would need their rapid blood transfusion packs. Thankfully Hughes could rely on the rose in the hand of delegation, Good Management, sorted, okay, ah, now there was an email from Hiromi about the Laurana Project. Dear sweet God, fine, anything, what do you need, extra funding, fine, done, why had he quit smoking, why on earth had he given up smoking, and consultations with John Isherwood about the terraformers and how they would end the war, and bureaucracy, endless helpless, helpful, help me bureaucracy, and Evelyn.

There was Evelyn.

After the assassination attempt she was fairly sweet to him. Kind. Generous. Even goofy, and he treasured that goofiness in her because he didn't think she often got a chance to cut loose. But something simmered underneath almost every interaction they had. She was still cross with him—still patently angry with him—about... what?

In the reasonably quieter moments between reasonably quiet work, he fixed himself tea, stood by the window in the office called The Dragon's Lair, and he pondered the question hard. A Hard Think, that's what his own father would call it.

And at such times his father's words came to him. *That girl has seen something she doesn't like. If I had to guess,* Gormon Senior told his son, *I'd say it was you.*

Me?

Yup. You see a lot, son. But not everything.

He thought about that a lot as the weeks passed.

You see a lot, son. But not everything.

Except I do, Dad. First rule of policework. Observation is the key to unlocking the box of mystery. And first rule of theatrical performance: in order to inhabit a role you must first understand that role. And that means knowing people. Having insight into them. How they think. How that thinking presents itself in the face, in gesture, in the voice.

He was, in short, an expert in seeing. What could Evelyn be looking at that he was blind to?

Less often but no less keenly, something else whispered to Hughes, a memory he'd sooner forget.

The memory spoke in Wendy Dragontail's voice. His mother's voice.

Does it perturb you, Hughes? The fact that we are so adept at observing others and so inept at observing ourselves?

He closed himself to that. And he almost was. Shut of it. Almost. As with most doors, a little light or a little dark crept through. And regrets in the past and worries about the future knock often.

May's sweltering heat was good for his joints but miserable for his city.

Hughes mopped at his brow, Thud at his temples, and Cate Jubilee at the bells tattooed on her throat. In unison their suspicious brains leered at the world around them and identified the chief architect whom they strongly suspected was at the root of woes like the drought, and familial strife, and the war: *Eurydice*, they thought grimly. *Eurydice.*

***

At the exact moment in which three minds were united in suspicion, one mind was interrupted in its search for cosmic enlightenment.

This mind was a rather one-track affair, in which the trains did not run on time or, indeed, ever. Picture instead a kind of on-rails parade float that did not entertain distraction, or even entertain itself, but was rather absolutely obsessed with its forward motion and its attainment of things that harmonized with one another. These included portentous tea leaves, candles that burned every shade except the usual (yellowy-orange) and whose tallow gave off extra ooze, jewels and jewelry affixed with jewels, black cats, ravens, skulls with ravens on them, robes with black cats on them, incense, books on different kinds of ancies (oneiromancy, pyromancy, you get the picture), cats of any kind, actually, and of course tarot cards with interesting pictures on them, such as hexagrams, philters, and men and women in various stages of undress.

Recently, the parade float had begun to veer in odd directions. Directions that involved less objects of manifold synchronicity and more of... well, oneness. You couldn't have many objects at all once you got started on oneness. None at all, really. Not even tremendously fluffy cats.

The interruption, when it came, found Desdemona Cauldronpot in a monastic temple in remotest Yi-Shi. She was in her room, a blank, featureless space that was slightly slanted at the floor in an approximation of... well, in an approximation of the idea of a bed according to oneness. She had sought out the temple after hearing about it from a traveling monk named Brother Yoohoo. Brother Yoohoo had been an extremely disgruntled man, thrown out of his monastic order by the stuffy Abbott because of Brother Yoohoo's tendency to get trollied on sacramental mushi-moshi incense, which made him think he was an elephant trumpeting through the savannah of space, which was pretty enlightening in Brother Yoohoo's opinion. He'd spoken to Desdemona Cauldronpot for twenty minutes before casually suggesting she might seek out the next phase of her journey by finding his old monastery and presenting herself to the kind and beneficent Abbott. That'd show the smug old creep. This foreign woman was round-the-bend bananas.

Thrilled beyond belief, Desdemona had scaled the mighty Polunnhesh Mountains, located the temple, and presented herself to the Abbott, who had not been able to make her go away no matter how hard he tried. This was partially a language issue, for Desdemona spoke not a word of Yi-Shiin, but there was also the fact that, once the parade float of her mind was going along its track, there was no diverting it, no matter how many times you shouted at it while shaking a broom.

Desdemona was dressed not in her usual clobber—a community of adornments that jangled like Tinfrost bells and a dress you could hide a religion inside—but in her Robe of Astral Projection. It was a sackcloth. It itched. But oneness was about being outside the itch. Her feet and arms were bare. All the other monks in the temple were bald, and she hadn't quite been able to bring herself to shave her head. However, since oneness was a state of mind, she had taken to acting as if she were bald, including heaving a sigh whenever the sun peeked through the dense mountain clouds, and looking about for the temple emergency supply of sun cream, which she pretended to apply to the smooth cranial skin she did not have because what she had was, in point of fact, lots of hair. She was convinced this would be sufficient.

Partway through her spiritual ablutions, her eyes rolled to the whites. She fell onto her back from a cross-legged position. After about ten or so minutes, she shook herself awake. She looked around as though expecting to see something there, or perhaps someone.

"Oh good heavens." She stood, trembling, though with fright or delight, it was not clear which, even to herself. "Oh good heavens."

The Abbott was in his holy vestibule. He was fiddling with an incense burner.

When Desdemona Cauldronpot entered, he didn't even glance up. The temple was the holiest place on the mountain, and the vestibule was the holiest place in the temple. Every monk in the Abbott's congregation knew that he was never to be disturbed in the vestibule, not even if they heard him shriek or cry out and beg for help. Also, the jangling sound was a dead giveaway.

"Hello your Supreme Eminence! Not disturbing you, I hope?" Desdemona said as she barged in. She was dressed in her old clothes, bangles and baubles included.

"Ah. Harlot of the distant west. You're here," said the Abbott, who did not understand a word of Corinthian. "The universe sends me a sign." His fingers pried uselessly at the incense burner lid. "I don't suppose you have a screwdriver on you?"

"Most well, thank you," said Desdemona, who assumed the Abbott had asked how she was this fine and fateful day. "Most well indeed. And you? Are you in communion with the spirit of the one true nature of divinity at this moment?"

"When I banished Brother Yoohoo for profaning the mushi-moshi incense by smoking it, I believed I was in the right," said the Abbott. "Your stay with us has convinced me of the error of my ways." He turned the incense burner upside down and shook it.

"Wonderful!" cooed Desdemona. "I'm so glad I haven't interrupted anything. But you see, there has been an interruption, your Percipient Omnipotentship. I... have had... a *vision*!"

"When you came, I asked you to go. You refused. I took a sacred vow of pacifism, as have all my flock here in the temple. Thus we cannot make you leave. Indeed," the Abbott opined, "I am not sure a belligerent approach would have achieved greater success."

"Yes, it's deliriously cool," Desdemona said. "Forgive me for using so vulgar a word, but I can't help it! A vision has shimmied up my chakra, and not only that, your Holiness. A quest to go along with it! An actual vision quest! Can you believe it?"

"Belief is a funny thing," mused the Abbott, flicking the incense burner to see if that did anything, and unaware that, for a moment, their detached conversations had lined up.

"I wish I could tell you all about it. But I lament to tell you that instead, I've got to go. Nothing for it. Has to be done. I know you and the rest of the chaps will wish me well."

"For seventy-five years I have believed that the path to a higher consciousness could be found through divesting myself of all earthly desires. By committing myself to oneness, I could, in actuality, touch God." The Abbott began to slap the base of the incense burner. Good hard slaps. "Since meeting you, you cambion of unending torment, I am quite sure that I do not wish to meet the God who created you. I no longer wish to touch that higher power, in case whatever it has is contagious. My choices and beliefs have led me here, to this moment, and to you, oh sphincter of immorality." The Abbott shrugged. "So I figure, why not mix it up? Perhaps Brother Yoohoo was on to something. If only I could..."

"May I help you with that?" Desdemona compressed two buttons on the side of the incense burner. A hidden catch clicked. The lid came off. A block of aromatic incense fell onto the floor.

"Ah. I am much obliged to you, gristly bacon rind in the clean pan of my aura," the Abbott told Desdemona. "Now, I think I have the pipe and matches I confiscated from Brother Yoohoo around here somewhere..."

"Farewell, dear man! Will you be a saint amongst men... more so than you are already, of course... and give my love to the rest of the chaps. We have had fun, haven't we?"

"Here we are." The Abbott brandished the pipe and matches, then looked at them curiously. "It occurs to me now that I didn't throw them out. Another sign, possibly?"

"This is so dreadfully hard. I must go before it becomes any harder. Farewell! Farewell!"

She left. The Abbott took no notice.

When the other monks went to tell him the good news (that the madwoman had departed the temple), they found that they could not, for he was in the holy vestibule which could not be entered under any circumstances.

There was some debate about whether or not they should do so anyway.

The Abbott was making some rather distressing noises in there. And there was a smell. A familiar smell, as of sacred ceremonies, only just that little bit different.

"What part of 'not under any circumstances' do you not understand?" said one monk.

"You know, I think that's incense," said another. "Do you smell it too?"

"That's it!" said another. "I was wracking my brains trying to remember."

"Incense? Perhaps it is an oracular moment," ventured one.

"Would an oracular moment sound like that?" said one.

They listened.

Muffled by the vestibule door, they heard the Abbott giggling. Occasionally he made vague trumpeting noises.

"Here," said one monk, arriving on the scene. "Has anyone seen the flagellation rod of Master Luzen?"

Down the mountain pass strode Desdemona. Overgrown and wild, it would have been treacherous footing, but she felt much safer traversing the pass with her new stick in hand. In her view, the Abbott wouldn't mind bestowing a parting gift on so devoted a follower of oneness. There were some ugly stains on the stick, but she would have them cleaned at her earliest convenience.

A vision quest! The sheer wonderment of it thrummed through her.

She took one last glance over her shoulder at the temple. Parting was such sweet sorrow, but nothing was sweeter than plans tomorrow.

She set off again. The parade float of her mind was in motion.

After a while she began to sing. Her voice drifted among the clouds, which in turn drifted among the crags of the mountain.

"*Stars shining bright above you...*"

Act Five

Who's Afraid of the
Wicked Wolf?

Chapter Thirteen

The sixteenth of May.

In the midst of a meeting with her military advisors a hand touched Cate on the shoulder. She turned from the map her scouts had drawn of the Bloodwood. Lorna Blacktower murmured a message into her ear. Cate looked at her friend.

"Here?" she asked. "When?"

"An hour ago."

Cate took a moment. Nodded. Adjourned the meeting until later that night.

A few minutes later she arrived aboard on the Thelmas. These juggernauts were the support version of a combat Betty, not equipped for battle but rather for the defense of key assets like supplies, non-combative personnel, and military technologies through near-impregnable fortification.

Below the main deck, in a huge assembly area where engineers tinkered with the last of the terraformers, Cate found the recently arrived head of the science division.

"John!"

"Cate." The good Doctor Isherwood returned the hug she offered.

"I wasn't expecting you," she told him.

"Felt odd taking part in a race from a whole world away. Thought I'd come and run this last leg myself."

"You're going to lead the installation?"

"Yup."

"John, that's great news. You'll see it go off without a hitch."

"I'll keep these pencil pushers humble."

"From the chief pencil pusher himself. What's kept you in Corinth? I feel like I haven't seen you in a year."

"Fourteen months. That husband of yours keeps me busy."

"The drought?"

"Among other things. Hughes has caught the same lunar lunacy gripping the populace."

"Mad for the moon, is he?" Cate's eyes narrowed slyly. "And you're not? Too astronomical for a career biologist?"

John shrugged. "Hey, you can lead a whore to college, but you can't make her think."

Cate laughed. "Keep the dry humor coming, Doc. Dosage is just fine."

"So I gather."

A fantail of sparks caught Cate's eye, drawing her attention toward the assembly station. The terraformer was not quite there yet, some sections of the immense shape separated out like a diagram of a black and totally alien heart. The outer surface was smooth but the insides of the terraformer were glutted with blinking lights, panels, and snarls of fiber-optic cables that reminded Cate of veins.

The structure of the terraformer was astonishing when viewed from above. From below, as she viewed it now, it was...

"What's unnerving?" said John.

"What?"

"You said 'unnerving.'"

"Did I?"

"Yeah." He glanced at the terraformer. "Suppose you meant that. It's certainly unnerving in scale. I tried to make the designs as compact as I could. Prototypic technology is often bulky, shrinking over time as efficiency rises to compensate for sloppiness. Not that efficiency is always the watchword. Sometimes pseudo-wisdom advises the community that if it ain't broke, you better not fix it. Know why cars only started locking themselves once you get out of them last year?"

"Why?"

"Original designer never thought of it. It was assumed that the absence of an automatic lock was intentional, but really the designer was just a guy on a deadline. Shows how attitude informs production. The Jolenes have the right of it. Modern invention is still based in the forge, when you get down to it. Filling out an order sheet with base materials and sweat."

"You sound beleaguered."

"Maybe I am. Tiredness tempered with professional ambition, I assure you. Look at that section there, the one about to be attached. Vast," he said with no small hint of self-judgment and paradoxical pride in his tone. "Vast as hell, these planet-killers of mine."

"Rosemund Valkyrie thinks they look like eggs."

She was looking at the terraformer. If she'd been looking at the good doctor next to her, she would have seen his jaw clench and his spine stiffen.

"Some of your clever scientists think it's beautiful," Cate went on. "Each to their own."

"You're not fond of my design?"

"I like what it achieves very much. But it's austere. If it is an egg, I just hope it hatches when you say it will. This war is like a bout of shingles: I want it over as soon as possible." She turned to him, her expression sweetening from genial to jolly. "Want a beer?"

Natural and so very friendly, John Isherwood grinned. "Do mice shit in the attic?"

They drank on the lip of a crenellation. Above the sky was a waxy jade-green color, with only a large moon like a baleful cataract up there, no sun or stars. Not far in the distance was a mountain range with two much bigger than the others, Gol and Gosuet. Those two spires of stone and snow combined into one larger peak every third day (Eurydice geography was sometimes predictable in its oddness), and so their names were fused together in Cate's scout reports: Golgomir.

Beyond that mountain range, should they be crossed or skirted, lay a short cruel country of wetland. Beyond that, the Bloodwood.

"How long before the battle?" John wanted to know.

"I give it ten days. Could be five or six but I won't risk a trip through the mountains. We'd be toffee apples in a barrel."

"Easy pickings."

"Mm." She sipped her beer. "S'good." She leveled a raised eyebrow at John. "S'good?"

"Tasty."

"Mm." Birds flitting round one of the peaks. Cate smacked her lips, real scorn tickling her thoughts. She'd never had a problem with birds before they'd come swooping out of Eurydice's ever-shifting skies, talons arched and intending to scoop out her throat like dripping red ice cream. Back home in Corinth, twittering was going to bother her. What was it John had said? Among other things.

Post-traumatic stress, warned her doubt. One hobnailed boot step at a time, said her confidence.

Besides, birds weren't all bad.

Take the one drinking with her.

John Isherwood had been a paunchy rooster of a man in his late thirties. At fifty he'd been a slimmer, pear-bellied falcon with a wingspan encompassing all realms of education and scientific pursuit. Turning sixty-four this year, he was a gaunt gray hummingbird of a man. Age hadn't slowed him. Quite the contrary, he worked, spoke, even moved with an uncanny avian swiftness. Most men his age pottered. John Isherwood was like those birds circling Golgomir. He flitted.

What motivations moved a man like him, kept him flitting that way? Cate supposed he'd said it himself. Professional ambition. She understood that. Responded to it, even. *I still count you as a friend*, she realized. It was not the kind of thing she'd say aloud. Not anymore.

"What'll happen?" she asked him. "When this last terraformer is locked in. What'll happen then?"

"I've filed a brief summary with your staff."

"Give me your version."

John Isherwood's spectacles were dipping. He nudged them up his nose, pursed his mouth in an oddly peevish look of introspection, and at length gave her a truncated answer. "At first very little. The terraformers are built like dominos. We've set them up, but it'll take that last one being positioned to get the cascade going. The actual, ah, fall—if you like—might take weeks, even months. But it's a chain reaction. Can't be stopped once it's been started. We might experience some peculiar weather, although what's peculiar here? Hopefully that's all we'll see. I advise a quick exit back through the portal once we're finished with the installation. Anyway, what else... Well, the percentage of certain chemicals in the air may change very quickly. Flora and fauna will exhibit signs of distress. Ecosystems will falter. There'll be seismic activity. Tectonic movement. Earthquakes. Tsunami along coastal regions. Then, once the terraformers have sent their signals all the way to the planet core, it'll be game over."

"Tectonic movements," said Cate. "Like a paroxysm before death."

John nodded. "Pray we don't hear Eurydice's death rattle. That'll be some final breath, I'd wager."

Cate smiled a hideous smile. "Knowing her it'll be a howl."

"Yes, I suppose you're right."

Silence for a while.

Cate took a swallow of her beer.

"Apricot and mulberry." She raised her bottle to him. "The fruits of your labor, John."

He seemed taken aback. That gave way to pleasure. He *clinked* his bottle against hers. "The fruits of yours, General."

***

The formation set some pace. Bettys fairly galloped, their great tree-trunk feet kicking up terrific clods of earth and then slamming down, filling day and night with crashes, crunches, and thunderous booms. Word had spread about this being the last big push and almost everyone was eager for the war to be over. It amounted to the journey taking nine days instead of ten as Cate had predicted.

On the twenty-fifth the Bloodwood rose up out of the horizon like a ghost rising out of a tomb. Soon they were inside it, at a much more controlled speed—and that was the leaves' fault. The gaunt white branches and twigs groping at the army with pale fingers didn't matter. They bent, snapped, and burst just as normal trees would when confronted with the awe-inspiring majesty of a Betty. No, it was the leaves slowing them down. The leaves and the blood pumping in fat teardrops down the trees. All that squelchy compost carpeting the forest floor was like trying to run through festering, stinking manure. Damp smooching sounds erupted every time a Betty stuck its foot down into that mire, and an equally moist sucking sound reached a crescendo when that foot managed to drag itself free. And the bugs, God, the sheer sound of them was incredible, like a humming, burring, buzzing wall, each brick and slop of cement made from a noise that crept up your spine and made it shiver because you had the feeling they were all over you, crawling and biting and pricking and drinking you.

Cate spoke to key members in the regiments. Hughes had his friends of Hedley Intrig, a group of people who acted as a barometer to check the atmosphere in Corinth City, and Cate had her own version. Men like Dan Jurdels and women like Ida Surries, a formerly perky nurse in Taggart House now severe and promoted to head of battlefield surgery. In spite of the ugliness of their surroundings, that eagerness endured. The soldiers could sense home calling them. Cate thought that was to be expected. But she was proud all the same.

The twenty-sixth dawned bright. The sun was a black hole ringed in blue fire. Its light mingled with the red effluvium of the Bloodwood, the air was thick and close and hot, and to a one the troops agreed that it was going to be like fighting in a sticky purple compôte. They were all smiles. Those smiles faded as Eilandri Titansgrave appeared atop the tallest turret of the foremost Betty. With her came their general, her red hair flowing like a banner. The sun glinted off each patch of glass on her skin. Cate wore her steelish armor, originally designed for Hughes by his friend Jo. With Faethe around his neck, Hughes didn't need it, whereas it had saved his wife's ass more times than she could count.

She could feel the attention of the army on her. In her ears their expectant silence was louder than the ceaseless hum of the bugs.

A hatch opened by Cate's feet. A small face was on the other side.

"You're em... you should be live now, General."

Cate nodded. The hatch closed. She glanced up at her second-in-command. Ella's presence gave her courage.

The Pale Giant gave her a wink.

Cate winked back. When she spoke, her voice was broadcast to each and every fortress arrayed throughout the trees.

"Where have your smiles gone?" she asked them. "I saw them shining as I made my way up here. Faces drunk with happiness, vouchsafing that they're bloody glad to be rid of this place and going home."

Laughter rippled up from the ranks.

Cate's mouth curled at the corners. "That's more like it. I don't want to see sober faces. How can we be sober when death is not the end? My husband, your president, has crossed through dreams into the lands of the dead and returned to give us all the good news. I have told that story, hell, too many times. You all know it by rote. And some of you might doubt it, and be afraid, and worse! Sober! Tell you something, I have never been scared to die. But knowing that death is not the bitter pill we must all swallow, that there is second life waiting all of us, intoxicates me with a relief like good beer on a crap Friday full of worse work. And you have worked hard, every single one of you. I've seen it, am inspired by it. You see me down there in the fight today, my hobnail boots lopping the heads off the dead like footballs, you better think: damn, she is not all talk. The woman works! And we showed her how!"

A roar went up. "Cate! Cate! CAAAAATE!"

She rode that wave, her voice growing giddy and bright. "If you hear my laughter, be emboldened by it. If it stops, cut off by who knows what, make some laughter of your own. Be merry, my friends. Smile a while longer. And if you meet the reaper with her grinning skull, grin back all the harder. Now, as they say: Once more, with feeling! Scarlet brother be my shield!"

"Be the weapon that I wield!" they chorused.

"I will be your courage true."

"I will burn like fire for you."

"If I'm laid eternal low."

"We pray that it shall not be so."

"Yes, but if it comes to be?"

"WE WILL CARRY ON FOR THEE!"

"I'm sick of this world, and already sick of these woods. Shitty, dank, scheming place," she told them. "A red place. Let's show it our color, people. One last time, let's show our enemies the real scarlet."

Cheers. Inez Symphony would have played Cate off, but Inez had died before the war started, torn apart by undead. The cheers would have to do, and you know what? They did.

The hatch by her feet opened. "You're... erm... no longer live, General. Let us know if you need anything else."

"A dashing victory and, after that, my husband wearing only a saddle."

"Pardon?"

"Nothing. That'll be all, thanks."

The hatch closed.

Cate turned to Eilandri. "How'd I do?"

Eilandri see-sawed her hand back-and-forth. *Comme ci, comme ça.* Not bad.

"You'd never fancy a triste with Mr. Glint, would you?"

Eilandri's lavender eyes sharpened. She wrote on one of her yellow cards.

"*I would rather triste with a sausage roll.*"

"Yes?"

"*One sold in the Leonidas bazaar.*"

"Oh. One of the shoddy, flaky ones?"

"*No.*"

"Oh!"

"*One of the ones that make you never want to look at a sausage roll again.*"

"Oh. That little of an attraction?"

Eilandri looked at her as though Cate were eating sawdust. Cate raised her hands, mollifying. "Cool your pipes, Ella. I'm not playing matchmaker."

Eilandri folded her immense arms disapprovingly.

"Don't look at me like that. I was only saying."

Those lavender eyes were sharp as needles now.

"All right, all right. You've no interest. I get it."

Eilandri uncrossed her arms and stalked away.

When she was at some distance, Cate muttered that she thought Eilandri would be a supporter of the arts, particularly poems, as well as a champion of the disenfranchised, such as poetic monsters of the Glintish variety.

"You could get him to brush his teeth first. Dab a bit of aftershave under his arms. Better make those splashes actually, just to be safe. Comb his... Okay, he hasn't got hair. String of floss would take care of the worst of the stuff caught in his gums. Scrub his face. Touch of concealer and rouge for his complexion. Bleach his fingernails. You never know. He might spruce up niceleeeeeeOHSHITOHSHITOHBUGGERBUGGERBUGGER—"

Many generals take time before battle to center themselves. Some read the collected works of military doyens, stewing in the lessons of bygone strategic masters. Others meditate, drinking only the finest purifying liquids, supping of the most fortifying elixirs. A select few trust their minds and instead warm up their bodies. General Cate Jubilee fell into this last category.

She spent the buildup to battle running away from her second-in-command at top speed.

***

While Cate hared and rabbited away from the retributive clutches of her best friend, Hughes was expressing reluctance at being peeled from the clutches of his work.

"We can't put it off another day," said Evelyn. "It's been ages. There's got to be pots of honey by now. The bees will drown in sweetness. Now, drowning in sweetness is a decent way to go, I'd wish it on a friend rather than an enemy."

"That isn't how honey production works."

"We know that, but do they?"

"I'm sure the ones that do will tell the ones that don't."

Evelyn became melodramatic, a character in a romance play. "Oh, but to blight their ignorance with destruction, Father! To condemn them to the sticky, orangey-brown gallows for the price of pithy delusion!"

"The bees are not deluded. You are."

"Father, you mustn't be so cruel! I am but a humble protector of the hive!"

"You're ridiculous."

"If only I could take one of their stringers and prick the wickedness from men's hearts! If only I could prick their pricks."

"Evelyn!"

She covered her giggling behind both hands, then shook her head and pretended to weep. "See the brute I've become. It's your influence, sire. Your depraved and rotten example hath led me astray from the pious path!"

In truth, Hughes would have liked nothing more than to go with her. This was prime-grade goonery, the kind he liked best. He didn't know what had come over Evelyn, but her flying form was contagious. He opened his mouth to relent... then gave the paperwork in front of him a mournful look. "I'm afraid I haven't the time, sweetie. You could go with Hector?"

His daughter's blooming humor wilted slightly. "He's in the Embassy. You told him to go this morning."

"Did I?"

Evelyn scrunched her face, puzzled. "Don't you remember? You said that Hector was to sort out the ambassador before she got herself into even more trouble."

"Which ambassador?"

"The swashbuckling one. You told her that if she didn't stop goading people into dueling her you were going to take her up on it and throw down the gloves. You told her that you only had a broken sword, but you wouldn't even need to draw it from its scabbard to teach her a lesson she'd never forget."

That, at least, was familiar. "Ambassador Du Gaquelin. I sent Hector to have a word with her?"

"You really don't remember?"

He really didn't. It disconcerted him.

"But your memory is brilliant, Father of mine."

Yes, that was what bloody well disconcerted him. It wasn't just brilliant. It was peerless. If Hoshrum Thud had a streetbeater badge inside him, Hughes had a script. It detailed his entire lift from when he was very young to the present day. Consulting it was as easy as opening a well-oiled drawer. Tiredness stiffened that hinge, blurred the words of the script, but he could usually make them out if he squinted. Yet now of all small, insignificant moments that flawless memory was exhibiting a flaw. With an effort he gave the internal drawer a yank and vaguely recalled speaking to Hector earlier that day. But his usual clarity was mugged-up, foggy, like a mirror in a bathroom fogging with the steam of a hot shower. Dim, it was dim and hard to... what was the word, he'd had it a moment ago... hard to...

"Dad?"

He forced himself to brush the niggling worry aside. *Tired, I'm just tired is all.* A break would do him the world of good. He favored Evelyn with a smile. "Give me fifteen minutes, Daughter of mine."

Her bewilderment was whisked away. She beamed, planted both hands on his desk (rumpling the pages there), leaned across the desk, and fluttered her lashes on his cheek in a butterfly kiss. "Meet you at the elevator!"

He chuckled, unaware his ears were turning red. "Off with you, girl."

Only six or seven minutes went by before his resolve shattered. He was away from the desk like a shot from a trebuchet, jogging that quick-footed paternal jog all fathers learn in the course of parenthood, his long, exhausted features furrowing with amusement. Amusement with himself because play always felt a little weird after he crossed the threshold of forty. It felt right though because somewhere deep inside the wolf with white beginning to appear in his dark fur was still the puppy Cate Jubilee had fallen in love with, was still, in other words, a boy enamored with the chaos of fun as much as he needed the firm structure of work.

Evelyn thumped the elevator button when she saw him. He had her under the arms in a trice, twirling her through the elevator doors as they clunked open.

"Fawn! Fawn!" he cried. "Harken to me, for there is adventure and merriment to be had."

"Lead on, Ser Gardener!"

The elevator doors closed, muting and stifling sound.

But you could still hear their laughter.

***

Mrs. Hankelminkel's was a meretricious boarding house on Plato Street, one of the busiest streets in Leonidas District and that was saying something. Mrs. Hankelminkel was essentially an architectural beautician. She was very good at hiding just how banjaxed her place was. During the flooding twenty-two years ago the entire house had been washed away and rebuilt from the bits that came back on the tide. In the snowstorms twelve years ago the pipes froze, the windows cracked, and the roof collapsed, and that was before the blizzard hiked up its garters and really began to blow. Now there was a drought and Mrs. Hankelminkel's was at last on a level playing field with the rest of the buildings in crisis on Plato Street. Air conditionless and southwest facing, they were all sweating out the worst of it together, and with its baskets of fake flowers, yellow wallpaper, and tunefully whistling tenants, Mrs. Hankelminkel's sweated prettier than most.

The assassin came in by the back door. He bid Mrs. Hankelminkel a good afternoon and headed for his room, groceries under one arm and a folded parasol under the other. With her daytime television murmuring through its usual beats, Mrs. Hankelminkel watched the man's retreating back. She bit one of her nails and chewed it, her eyes wandering to the watermarked ceiling, her mind picturing the man's room directly above her.

The assassin flicked the key into the keyhole, unlocked his room door, and went in. He paused on the threshold. Very smoothly and gracefully he closed the door, plunged the parasol into the empty terracotta plant pot by the door, and set the groceries on a little end table. The room was an all-purpose space. He went into the "kitchen," if you could call it that, and put the kettle on. "How do you take your tea, Mr. Thud?"

There was silence. Then a sigh. Thud stepped out of the cabinet. "Not sure why I bother. How'd you know?"

"I have made it my policy to detect even the most subtle odor. It might give offense to the wrong nose."

"My mustache pomade? I washed it off specially."

"Alas, to the refined nostril it is still a... distinct perfume."

"Damn. Black, please. Five sugars."

The assassin nodded without so much as a raised eyebrow. The kettle was dancing a polka, steaming like a more sensual dance was on the way. The assassin snatched it off the boil, and in a flash there was a teabag, a cup, and a sugar bowl being put to good use.

"None for yourself?" Thud asked.

"I don't partake in tea. In Jaenqui-Across-the-River, traditionalists advocate that you must never drink the same drink as your enemy. Defining the self by abnegation of the other. How droll and interesting, don't you think? Here you are."

"Thanks."

Thud preferred his tea piping hot. He guzzled, spilling a few drops, noting with some satisfaction the mild wrinkle he saw form in the assassin's brow. *Caught you flinching. Even the best put-together paintings have a few places where the brush missed the mark.* But something the man had said struck him.

"Never drink the same drink as your enemy, eh? Well, Hughes does love a cuppa tea."

"I would appreciate it if you would not speak his name."

"Fair enough. Mind if I ask you something?"

The assassin laced his fingers in front of him. "An interrogation, is it? I presume by your presence here that you know everything."

"Most of it. Have you a coaster for this? I don't want to muck up Mrs. Hankelminkel's counters. Ah, there we go. Right, now what I'm wondering is—"

"Forgive my interjection, Mr. Thud. I wonder if you might equip your truncheon? Being questioned by an unarmed man feels... unfair."

Thud looked at him. "You want me to pull out the kosh?"

"Yes."

"Why?"

"As I said," the assassin replied politely, "it feels unfair."

"Unfair how?"

A pair of neat little lips twitched. "Think of it as... giving up my head start in what is about to transpire. Out of respect for another gifted professional."

Thud hesitated. He gripped the handle of the truncheon and slid it free. He held it by his side.

The assassin gave another nod, as if grateful. "Thank you. And, if it is not too objectionable, I would prevail on you to know how you found me."

"Now who's interrogating who?"

"Very droll, Mr. Thud. Rest assured I shall answer you truthfully when the time for your own questions arrives."

"Right." With his empty hand Thud picked up the tea and guzzled some more. He watched the assassin, never taking his gaze off the other man's eyes. "No secret," he said with a shrug. "Last night I was down at the Maedar. Awful place, but it's a place where people drink and that means it's a place where people talk. I overheard one of your fellow boarders complaining about how some geezer down the hall tidied up his coats. Apparently, he had them in a lovely mess, and here comes some random berk putting them all on pegs and organizing them according to the foulness of the stains, dirtiest to cleanest."

"Philistine," said the assassin.

"Yeah. Gabby too. Bought him a round and he told me all about this orderly bastard. Moved in at the end of March. Our philistine never trusted him. Talked funny. Cleaned up after himself. Made a point of wishing Mrs. Hankelminkel a good morning and goodnight. Mrs. Hankelminkel, who knows her way around a decorative magazine but wouldn't know a doily if you slapped her on the rump with it."

"And you found me out like that? From the drunken testimony of a sot?"

"Matter of fact, I think he's an electrician by trade."

"But that's just luck," said the assassin hotly. "You didn't have to do any policework."

"That's where you're wrong. I had a fistful of leads. You follow those up, and meanwhile you wait for an opportunity to ask the right questions. Opportunity is right place, right time, and that's plain old luck wearing a skirt of handkerchiefs. Accept that you're a pawn of luck, first rule of policework." Thud finished his tea. "Same again, squire."

The assassin refilled his cup and stirred in five lumps of sugar. "I thought observation and instinct were the first rules of policework."

"Hughes tell you that, did he? Back when you and he were bezzy mates?"

Thud's hand snaked out. His fingers wrapped around the assassin's arm in a vice grip. "You might be tempted to throw that tea in my face. Soak my mustache and scald my eyes. Don't, okay? Just don't. Maybe this will go south, in which case I have my truncheon and you've got... whatever you've got that makes you slick and confident. But until then let's keep this mannerly. You're good at that. Famously so. Gonna let you go now."

He did. The assassin handed him the tea. He squeezed the creases from his shirt, which was cream-white and clean as a whistle.

"Yes," he said. "Hughes told me about his policework during the Spring-Heeled Jane case. This was before his election. His *rigged* election."

"Don't be acrimonious. All elections are fixed. Hughes was as honest about that as he could be. Got to admire that."

"No," said the assassin after a time. "No, I think not. Whatever happened to 'best person for the job'?"

"War happened. That's what." Thud held on to his tea. He looked like a cross between a common constable (which he was) and a rich toff (which he was, through marriage). Thinking of Hettie, he sent a little prayer to whoever might be listening. It was a simple prayer, one that arrives in divine letterboxes every day, in every conceivable package. *Let me get out of this alive.* "My turn," he said. "Why now, Falstaff? Why let things lie for twelve years, only to try to take your revenge for Wendy's death now? Answer me that?"

Falstaff ahemed a little, as though clearing something unpleasant from his throat. "I beg your pardon, Mr. Thud. I have not, as you say, been letting things lie. I have been biding my time."

"Twelve years. That's a lot of biding."

Falstaff paused. Again, the perfect façade cracked the tiniest bit. "I saw a newspaper. The headline read, President Of Corinth Claims Moon Rocket Will

Launch In Summer. I had heard Hughes was doing that. But not until then did I know the *name* of the project."

"Project Laurana," said Thud. "An old friend of Hughes'."

The crack in composure widened. "She was an old friend of mine. Not his. Mine. He was the one who got her killed. Hughes is remarkable at getting people who are better than he is killed. It's his legacy. He's got a knack for it."

"First Laurana, then Wendy. Two does make a pattern. Not much of one, but I take patterns seriously as a copper. Murdered them both, did he?"

"He may as well have! How could one man hold so much stupidity inside him? And the most loathsome thing about it? They eat him up. They worship him."

"Who?"

"Who do you think? The people. That newspaper was the last on the stand. Everywhere they were gossiping and grinning at one another. He promises them the moon, and in return they point to their hearts and simper, 'Land here, dear man, land here.' And when asked about Wendy Dragontail, about what they think of her compared to him, do you know what they say?"

"Go on."

"They say, 'Who?' The gall of that. The nerve, the... Have you any idea what that woman sacrificed for this city? What she endured? How she innovated and planned and developed every single aspect of... of... And they ask 'who?' Then they remember and wave a dismissive hand and bleat, 'Oh her. She was all right. But she wasn't a street boy like our current man. Hughes has his finger on the pulse.' That's what they say. Finger on the pulse? Yes, I agree, but only to test the longevity of that pulse, to snuff its rhythm out, to take advantage, advance himself, the arrogant, up-jumped, stupid little man. He..." Falstaff had been shouting, and Thud saw him realize it. The butler turned assassin reined himself back to perfection. He studied the policeman in front of him, so cool and collected, and the only evidence of his anger was the pulse. Yes the pulse in his throat and the vein in his temple, standing out and throbbing with hate.

"I've been doing some digging on you," said Thud. "Calcifern. Mysicordelia. Jaenqui. Yi-Shi. Hasn't all that travel given you a bit of perspective? I've heard of carrying a grudge, but this isn't that. I think grief has driven you mad, mate."

"Travel has certainly informed me of much, including the fact that madness is in the eye of the beholder."

Thud frowned doubtfully. "Isn't that beauty?"

"Not at all," said Falstaff smartly. "Beauty is the eye itself."

There was a thoughtful lull.

"No," Thud said cheerfully. "No, I'm pretty sure you've gone off the deep end. Incidentally, you have the right to remain silent, a right I'm hoping you'll make liberal use of."

Falstaff smiled. "Am I under arrest, then?"

"Right you are sunshine. Hands where I can see them."

"Naturally," said Falstaff. He held out his powdered, gorgeously manicured hands.

Thud heard the click just before the knives slid out of Falstaff's sleeves.

The butler lunged.

Instead of falling back Thud came to meet him, truncheon and teacup in hand.

***

A top-down view of the trees and the undergrowth below them gave Ruthven the impression that the Bloodwood had spontaneously evolved to accommodate several rivers converging on a lake. Getting a little closer, the slow flow of the water resolved itself into rank upon rank of undead. Five-hundred-thousand strong was their number, as large an army as had ever been assembled in Eurydice. They were men and they were beasts, all resurrected by Lord Burrows who ruled over them as lord and master. Ruthven's wings beat a breeze through the stillness of the wood. Any closer than this and Ruthven would start to smell the dead regiments. A moldy, morbid, festersome stench like a fully stocked fridge plugged out and left to sour over months and months. Of course, Ruthven didn't mind in the least. Closer he got, and closer still, until the horde (the lake, as glimpsed from above, was really the main body of the undead getting into position) was within sight, and the Bettys beyond it, though Ruthven took pains to conceal himself as carefully as possible.

Far from the front lines he found Burrows. He found him by following the scent of worms. You'd think that'd be impossible with all that maggoty, putrefying flesh nearby, but its wasn't. Burrows' mount, the two-headed wolf, was infested with the most pungent worms in the land. They burrowed deep into the creature and nuzzled the nerves under its shaggy hair, its molting skin, its eyeballs, ears, and long canine muzzles.

One wolf head snapped and slobbered at the dragon as he arrived. The other peered solemnly at him as he slithered around Ruthven, his own lupine head rearing up so he was eye-to-eye with the king of necromancers.

"You couldn't have delayed them?" Ruthven demanded. "A fortnight you promised me. I count ten days. Cate Jubilee is here. A promise is a bill to be paid, and you are shy ninety-six hours, Burrows. How did this happen?"

"Our mistress ordered me to meet the enemy here and give battle," Burrows replied. "If you take umbrage with my methods, raise your objection with her." The dragon turned its head ever-so-slightly so Burrows could see one milk-white eye slit in a pupil the color of infected blood. Burrows was not immune to the dread those eyes evinced, but he'd be pulped into jelly before he'd show it. Plus he had never seen Ruthven discomfited before. Burrows found he was rather enjoying himself, even though the object behind that discomfiture remained a mystery to him, more's the pity.

"Perhaps if you'd told me more of this secret of yours," he said blithely, "the one you would like to keep hidden from everyone, even our... beloved mistress... then I would have been more inclined to hasten my own advance and stall our enemy's."

If he'd expected further chagrin, he was disappointed. Ruthven was done with the conversation. He slipped away, sinuous and cold as a wintry disease.

One of Burrows' captains had been waiting till the dragon left.

He lumbered forward, his bones creaking and two candleflames flickering in his bony eye sockets.

"Permission to report, m'Lord?"

"Granted, Captain. What tidings?"

"Good, m'Lord. Very good. That idea you had about leading the oozes with whistles was just the ticket. Stroke of genius."

Burrows was pleased. He'd had the idea only recently, having confirmed with Skuggs that the oozes and the whistling wisps had a rich history of war, yes, but also collaboration. It was a gamble (using music to achieve anything in Eurydice was a gamble), but it seemed as though it had paid off. "See that they retain discipline. We aim to retreat here, but I want to inflict heavy casualties on the enemy. And I want Cate Jubilee's head."

"You shall have it, m'Lord."

"What about the... new recruits?"

The captain's candleflames guttered uneasily. "Yeah. Er. About that, m'Lord..."

"I trust they're fitting in well?"

"Not... as such... my liege. Not as such. They keep to themselves. And the troops aren't keen on them, either."

"Not... keen on them?"

"Yes, m'Lord. These things they ah... well, they're like the dragon, if you take my meaning. They..." He trailed off. You couldn't tell what he was looking at, that was one of the worst things about Lord Burrows. Worse would be knowing he was looking at you. Not as bad as Ruthven's gaze, of course. Nothing was as bad that. But you had to mind your words with the king of necromancers. He loved his followers, that was an undeniable fact. But there was gentle love, and there was tough love, and Lord Burrows was partial to a bit of tough love.

"They what?" said Burrows frostily. "The new recruits what, Captain?"

"They give us the craggles, m'Lord."

"They give you... the craggles."

"Yes, m'Lord. A very mild case, of course. Nothing we can't overcome. For ah, for the cause, my rancid and wrinkled king, my liege, my raiser and ruler."

"Shut up."

"At once, m'Lord."

"Commence a charge upon the Agents of the Red Death."

"Yes, m'Lord."

"You lead it."

"Yyyyes, m'Lord."

"Fight dauntlessly. Dauntlessly. Spread that word like a fungus in the damp dark. All are to take courage in the wheel."

The captain bowed. "The wheel of life must spin."

"It must," agreed Lord Burrows as his underling hurried off. He motioned. The two-headed wolf padded to him. With a rustling from his robes and wrappings like mummified papyrus, he mounted up. Today, he would do Cate Jubilee the courtesy of doing as she did. Leading from the front. Let Skuggs have his cider, his pies, his host of petty vices. Let Ruthven have his furtive schemes.

Burrows had the wheel, and whoever had the wheel was more powerful than Death herself.

"Cate Jubilee, in combat there are no speeches, but I will say this to you after you are dead and I have raised you as my servant: you have been a worthy adversary. You have been a nettle. A thorn. A righteous splinter lodged in my craw. I was supposed to lose, yes, but you were not content to simply win. You felt the need to humiliate me. You have, in short, given me hell in a handbasket over this past decade and change. Hell in a handbasket." He spurred the wolf, which broke into a run across the droning bug-covered mulch. "Now, you wretch, I'm going to give you what you have given me. With interest." He could see the forerunner of the enemy fortresses looming in the distance. Cate would be there, he was sure of it. "Interest in spades. Your fiery laughter will turn to ashy screams in your mouth. And that is a promise I intend to keep."

***

Gauging the enemy number, Cate decided to change her plan. She'd told her staff to form a curved line. The Bettys would surround the undead and close in, a killing ring. But it seemed Burrows had managed to conceal the extent of his forces from her scouts. The horde were too many. Her line would falter, then break.

From her position on the battlements Cate turned toward the cockpit of her fortress and brought her fingers together in a triangle. Her hands jabbed then went their separate ways. *Give me a phalanx. We try to punch through the undead ranks head-on. If my vanguard can manage it, the Bettys behind are to enclose the undead as before, only this time using two rings instead of one.* Blinkered lights in a sequence meant the pilot acknowledged and would send her orders to the troops en masse.

She clicked out a pocket telescope and peered through it. Ahead, visible through the warped white trees like something approaching through an enormous, macabre chessboard, she watched the horde lurch and shamble. Some fell and were trampled into the gunge of bloody leaves, only to rise drenched and dripping.

Cate's Responsible Leadership made a final inventory.

Let's see. By now Steffan Cerulean ought to be hard at work with his apprentice hydromancers, thickening the gunk on the forest floor for the enemy and thinning it for the Bettys. Cate doubted it would make much difference. The stuff weeping from the sores in the trees might not even be blood. It might have a lower water content, making it tricky for Steffan to manipulate. She was more confident about Xacorca Demon's efforts. Having made an admirable recovery after the loss of her fingers, the Demon had asked how she might make herself useful. Cate had just the thing. Now, from regiment to regiment, people were grimacing as they uncorked gourds filled with Xacorca's despicable breath. The breath had been diluted using small traces of nitrous oxide, commonly known as laughing gas, so that it posed no risk to people. But the properties of Xacorca's breath were loathsome to insects, including (thankfully) those swarming the Bloodwood. It wouldn't keep them off her troops completely, only a little, but in Cate's experience with warfare a little went a long way.

Anything else... Anything pressing...

Footsteps drew her focus. A man, fit but pouring with sweat in the wood's clamping heat, was there.

"Message for you, General. No sign of the dragon."

"What about Burrows?"

"Headed straight for us, ma'am."

That was a first. Cate had no time to consider the connotations. In fact she believed she knew them instinctually. *Eurydice is going to spring it today. That ambush I've been waiting for all these years. Whatever it is, I've got to be ready.*

"Your staff was wondering if you planned to lead from the back on this occasion, General?"

"Nope. I'm comfy here."

"Only... there are a lot of them. The undead."

Cate's chest swelled with pride. "Yes, soldier. There are a lot of them. Gristly and gnashing and with hearts poisoned to the core. This is what Burrows serves me on a platter. An unconventional menu, I grant you. My boots aren't picky. But how is a woman to know what's good to eat and what isn't?" She snapped her fingers. "I've got it! Send for the military's best taster."

"Ah. Who, ma'am?"

The living dead were negotiating their way closer. She did not need a telescope to pick out individual ones now. Candleflame eyes burning in empty sockets.

Jawbones dangling by strings of sinew. Flaps of flesh going green. The rank refrigerator smell. Closer they marched. Closer. The oozes were with them, having an easier time of the dense, wet undergrowth. The oozes glided, and on their backs came even more of the undead, their smiles oozing too, trickling pus. Underneath her boots, Cate felt the fortress rumble in its foundations as it struggled to charge through the morass.

Faster than the rest of the horde, even the oozes, she saw something furred and strangely shaped dashing directly toward her scarlet army. At first her mind, burning the fuel of thought in every cylinder, mistook that shape was Ruthven. *No*, she realized. *There are two slender wolfish heads there, not one. Well, well, well Burrows. Maybe there is no ambush, after all. Maybe you're just sick of letting me whoop that skinny necrotic breadboard you call a bottom around this world.*

"General?" said the messenger. "Who's this ah, military taster you want me to fetch?"

"My little ears are burning," said a voice like knucklebones clunking in a bucket of cooling tar.

Cate grinned. "Mr. Glint. Punctuality is your middle name."

"Haven't got a middle name, Miss Jubilee. Got an appetite though."

"That, I think, will do very nicely. Messenger, before you go."

"Yes, General?"

"Everyone is aware that the evacuated Betty is to remain evacuated, yes?"

"Course. Those were the orders."

"Good. No harm in checking. Dismissed, soldier."

He saluted and scurried away.

Mr. Glint regarded Cate from sunken eyes. "An empty fortress? What for?"

"Our foes can conjure amazing numbers, Mr. Glint, but we have our own magic to call upon. Mine has... call it *developed*."

"Your jumpy mirrors?"

"Yup. I've been saving it for the right occasion. Maybe I'll play my trick on Ruthven. Maybe on Burrows. We'll see."

Mr. Glint squinted. "He's got a wolf, Miss Jubilee."

"Burrows? Yeah, he does. Are you worried?"

"Knew a girl named Rosey Posey when I was small. Had a dog named William Supposey. When she got phlegmy with rattly coughs... and died... he hadn't a thing to eat. So he gobbled up his mistress."

"Loyalty is super fickle," said Cate. She had been feeling too wired. This conversation was helping to unscramble her, keep her centered. "I like it anyway. Loyalty, I mean. Take Hughes and I. We're steady together even though he could have anyone, and I'm no slouch either."

"No slouch indeed, Miss."

She punched his arm, wincing as her fist felt as though it had struck concrete. "You old softie."

"That wolf, Miss."

"Uh huh?"

"It's... the same one... what almost scragged Mr. Hughes in Iphigenia?"

"No. I see why you'd remember it like that, but no. That wolf died when Hughes used his Performance. This wolf, the one Burrows rides, is like its sibling, or a cousin."

"Member of the same pack, like."

"Yeah."

The undead vanished under the lip of the fortress. They must almost be under the vanguard Betty's feet now, building ladders of their own bodies for their fellow undead to climb.

"That other wolf, in Iphigenia," said Cate. "It killed a friend of mine. Laurana."

Mr. Glint's face became a mask of horrifying concentration. "That bird what the moon project is named after?"

"Well done. Hughes named the project after her because of her freckles. He says when Laurana smiled, the moony freckles on her nose became half-moons."

Silence. Cate could almost hear the gears turn in her companion's head.

When he spoke again, he said something that nearly knocked her flat.

"And he named the project after her... 'cause of loyalty... or 'cause of... atonement?"

"Atonement?"

"Stands to reason. He's alive. She's not. Sometimes I think about Miss Gleam. The fact that she had to go while I got to stay. And I think, 'You've got things to do, Mr. Glint. And you'd better make them count double or triple because even though she was bad she could have been good.' So I do the good like what

Mum and Dad instructed, and as Mr. Gallant guides. Those who go, they get to see the light. People who stay, like you and me and Mr. Hughes, we got to grapple with the darkness."

Cate stood there, her mouth open.

"Just a few bits of butter off my lumpy loaf," said Mr. Glint with a shrug of his gravestone shoulders. "Have a squint and a blink about it, and we can wag chins later."

"A dizzying salvo of profundity followed by a burst of Corinthian rhyming slang," said Cate, laughing a little to dispel how stunned she felt. "You are on form."

"And a good thing too." Mr. Glint took his bald head in his hands and pushed it this way and that. Pops and clicks and crackles more disgusting than the whine of the Bloodwood's bugs emerged from his spinal joints. "Here they come."

He was right. Cate could hear the raspy voices raised in discordant melody.

When he was young his grandma knit
A veil of spider silk so black
She whispered that he must forfeit
His eyes, or she would take it back
He plucked them out, and that was it

So our Lord Burrows came to be
The child became a man so wise
And the dark veil allowed him see
So that he did not want for eyes
Prophet and conqueror is he
And now for you, whom we despise
He comes, you foul red Jubilee

Cate raised a hand and brought it swooping down. About a hundred yards away, Clothilda Toffington—she of the enchanted handkerchief—sniffed from her pepperbox and unleashed a sneeze that, even though its sound was dampened by the compost heap below, could be heard for miles in every direction.

The scarlet army roared their challenge. The undead sang. The two-headed wolf howled. And Cate Jubilee leaped into the fray.

The battle in the Bloodwood had begun.

***

Cate was not as big a reader as Hughes. She loved vids with big stakes, simple, strong emotions, high highs, low lows. She did not think about the world in what you might call a literary way. Probably Hughes described it best when he sat across from Iphigenia during one of their talks that preluded sleep. He said of Cate: *Most of the time she is too busy living to think about what living ought to be about.* Maybe she'd been different when she was younger. And hell, very little is cut-and-dry axiomatic. Even now she could fall prey to introspection—sometimes on the war trail she looked at her body swimming with tattoos. Times like that, she wondered what exactly had happened between her pink girlhood and this inky, glass-smeared womanhood.

But by and large she shouldered the luggage of her past, made sure it was all in order, and forgot about it as she walked forward. Who knew where the path led? Not her. She wasn't in the habit of paying any such path the slightest bit of attention. One boot, then the other. Forward. That was the whole scene.

Combat sort of deepened this fundamental truth about her. When she was fighting, Cate was inclined to forget not only who she was but what she was. An animal. A machine. Lover. Mother. Daughter. These things blended into a scarlet stew not dissimilar from all that bloody leafy shit that made up the basin of the Bloodwood. Now and again a little flavor would come into the stew. Self-preservation was one. Laughter was another, and that was more common. Whatever she was, it was a thing that loved to laugh while it moved and killed. Not in celebration of killing, of course. Cate was no more a sadist than Ruthven the dragon. She laughed because she, like Mr. Glint, got to stay.

Staying and doing good, or what you believed must be good, felt wonderful.

Even to somebody who lost and found themselves all the time.

A bonus, and not an inconsiderable bonus at that, was that it mightily pissed off whoever she happened to be fighting. After twelve years of hearing that happy, almost euphoric laugh, the undead were about ready to burst. And hey, burst, they did.

Those hobnail boots were heavier than they looked.

The battle started out as well as these horrible things can be expected to. People died everywhere. Sometimes they did the dying but sometimes it was us. Mostly it was just people dying. Nothing to be done about that. Minimize the damage. Staunch the flow. Treat the wound by dishing out a couple of your own. Forward. Laughter floating from her lungs. Forward. It went on like that—fraught but okay— until the wraiths appeared.

Thirty minutes of carnage in and Cate was already bathed in gore and perspiration. The sweat was hers. The viscera were not. She could abide that. It was always the same. She would never have believed you could be absolutely enamored with something and totally done with it at the same time, holding those two states equal. That was war for you. Bravery and cowardice. Smarts and stupidity. Skin and glass. It was all one big contradiction. *Pull up a pew because I'm right there with it. Whose skin is this, whose glass for that matter? Whose mother? Whose wife? Whose general?*

What's that?

Forward?

If you say so.

Popping a glittering mirror from a vial onto the fortress masonry, she dragged four undead by the scruff of their necks into a realm of prisms, reflections, and ruin. She gave them a true death, sending them to whatever underworld they were intended for. An instant later she emerged from the pane of a window far above her former position. She liked to do this now and then; use the boots to get a little perspective on the brouhaha. Battle was always lousy with problems too. Too many to solve, and yet she had to solve them all, trying was for despots and morons. Great leaders led. They led kindly if they were good as well as great but no fucking around. Cate got Kpele Cinder's attention. By funneling the undead in endless droves, not being tactical about it, just sending them to kill and be killed, Burrows revealed his hand. He was anxious to stop this vanguard Betty in its tracks. That would be disastrous, they'd be fish in a grotesque barrel.

Cate didn't bother Kpele with that. Instead, she told the firesmith to get a hold of Rebecca Lupine and Rosemund Valkyrie.

"Douse them, Kpele. Bonfire city."

"Burnt black, Cate. *Burnt black.*"

"Go! Quickly!"

Spotting where the enemy clumped thickest along the battlements, Cate squeezed a new mirror from a vial to make the journey there nice and quick, and that was when she saw them.

The wraiths reminded Cate of snub-nosed monkeys. They were semi-translucent—stare at one for longer than a second and she found herself gazing right through them at the space beyond. Robes covered them from throat to ankle, robes that looked stitched from severed monkey paws. No wings sprouted from their backs, and they didn't fly exactly. Rather those specters seemed to drift through the air, their heart-shaped faces edged in orange hair and split with grins that chilled the blood.

Cate had time to think, *Eurydice, is this it? Have you been saving your worst in the wings?* before a voice hoarse with fear cried, "Get away... ohhh shhhhit, get away fr—oh no, *no don't touch me!*"

One of the wraiths had snatched a scarlet soldier. It's hold on him looked tight, brutally so. *Then why can't he break free?* She watched the man's hands sail harmlessly through the monkey's grinning face.

Padhraig Willowfly, veteran of only five battles, but already a distinguished Scarlet Citadel man, tried to fell the wraith with a volley of scattershot arrows, each shrapnel sliver fizzling with magic. The shot was controlled, avoiding the caught soldier. The onlookers watched in dismay as the slivers did not so much as nick the wraith. And when it grinned even wider, first at them and then at the soldier in its clutches, they felt hate overcome their misgivings.

The wraith pulled the soldier kicking and hollering over the fortress wall. Cate expected it to drop him, a brief but terrible plummet to a messy end. But it didn't drop him. It carried him.

Where?

Cate got her answer swiftly enough.

Hauled out of the sludgy murk by scores of undead came a monster. It was round, bloated, wriggling like a leech suckled fat. And yet its face was the prudent, somehow sad face of a gorilla. Out of its hairy stomach, chest, and thighs stretched tendrils. At the end of each tendril was a pair of... Cate's abdomen gave a violent lurch. *Oh my God... are those lips?*

They were. Huge corpulent lips, like the lips of an actress held hostage by her fading career, lips injected full of filler and poised in constant fishy pouts.

The undead hoisted this hideous leech-ape up with hooks sunk deep in its back. The tendrils slid through the air as though searching.

And it was toward one of those tendrils that the wraith brought the screaming soldier.

Cate squashed an ooze, flattened its riders, fought bitterly, thundered orders.

No use. The wraith had brought the soldier away too quickly and too far. She was helpless to watch as the poor man thrashed for a moment and then went completely still as though hypnotized by the lips coming toward his own.

There was a kiss, a sinister, silent kiss. Then the man went limp.

Dead.

Quick as that.

The wraith dropped his body. He fell a long way.

But the horror was not over. It was just beginning. Fresh shouts broke out amongst the regiments. The wraiths were picking and choosing the next offering, the next sacrifices to their flabby, greedy friend. And the leech-ape was greedy, Cate understood that at once. Being married to Hughes had given her insight into expressions, and she had seen satisfaction tug the monster's features. Satisfaction and pleasure as it kissed one of her soldiers to death, like a succubus in a fairy tale.

Cate had seen too much to be outright undone by such a thing, but God... God, was it awful. Unnerving and gruesome and—*and I've got to do something. Right now.*

Smoke billowed up to her right. Wings of a marmalade-gold hue flashed. Moonlight. Terrific tongues of flame lapping and licking down into the undead masses, cooking and charring. Kpele, Rebecca, and Rosemund were busy, but perhaps if she could get the attention of Morvran Oats, she could—

Damn. No, she was out of luck there. Morvran was on another task, one she'd set for him days ago.

She could get herself down into the mire, down to the succubus, but she would be surrounded, five thousand to one. Impossible odds, hopeless. And the succubus was a foe she'd never contended with. Unpredictable. Stupid to rush in alone, even if the shrieks of her people were maddening. Forward, yes, always forward, but sometimes the future was uncertain and you had to tread lightly, even if your boots were heavy.

The undead foamed over the fortress walls. Cate killed them and sifted through possible solutions.

The solution presented itself in the form of a twelve-foot tall albino who swung her gigantic hammer with a sound like a bus falling from a great height.

"Ella!"

Lavender eyes swerved to her. Blood caked Eilandri's face, dripped from one earlobe, painted her cheeks and chin.

"Toffington special? Down to that kissing freakshow?"

Eilandri nodded. No hesitation.

Cate felt a surge of grateful love for the woman. "Come on then."

They fell into a pattern, Cate the anvil, Eilandri the hammer. Nothing withstood them. The undead were crushed, pulverized, sent scattering in a confetti of mossy, brittle bones. Clothilda was right there, only a scant few dozen yards away. With her help they could solve the succubus, solve it savagely.

Cate shouted her name, but smothering it was a pair of howls, one strong and controlled, the other jagged and crazy.

The two-headed wolf cleared the heads of the defenders in a spry jump, landing before the general and her second-in-command.

"Cate Jubilee," leered Lord Burrows from atop its back. "And Eilandri Titansgrave. I've found you at last, the whore and the whoremaster. My sweet spokes on the wheel, my undead! My friends! Behold!" Privy to their master's whims the undead yawped and roared Burrows' name as he reached beneath his veil and drew forth an impossibly long-handled weapon. "Behold and cry bedlam, for the axeman cometh..."

Chapter Fourteen

Hoshrum Thud's wife, the much-lauded new wave fusion funk artist Hettie Thud, was a lifelong devotee of cozy crime fiction.

Often in bed together, Thud would be treated to a series of gasps and giddy little utterings, such as: "Oh my goodness; No, no, it can't be him, there's been a mistake; Getting good now, getting very good now; oh my goodness *gracious*!"

Out of burning jealousy and no small amount of curiosity, Thud had taken it upon himself to read one of the novels. He'd been skeptical for an entire chapter. By the end of chapter two, he was hooked. He read voraciously, nibbling his lunch and flipping pages whenever he had a spare moment. Then came the end of the book. When he finished, he was in bed. He set the book aside and stared at nothing in particular for about five minutes, after which time Hettie began to become a bit worried. She shifted about under the blanket and asked him if everything was all right. "It would never happen like that," he replied tersely.

Hettie got his meaning at once. "Hoshrum, my darling. It's only a bit of fun. Intended to entertain rather than replicate life."

"How would you feel," said Thud icily. "How would you feel if you saw an artist entering the new wave fusion funk movement and being praised by lots of people for doing it, only to discover that what that person makes is paper airplanes."

"Don't be silly, love. Paper airplanes aren't art."

"How would you feel if people said it perfectly captured the field?"

"Yes, but no one is saying that."

"All right, fair enough. What about if lots of people simply believed it captured the field then?"

To this Hettie had no immediate argument. She frowned. "I suppose I'd be a trifle... peeved."

"Peeved is right," said Thud. He jerked a thumb at her stack of cozy crime. "Do they all end like that? With the detective sleuth taking everyone to a parlor and explaining the whole thing, only to have the criminal fess up. Put their hands up.

Say, 'Drat and double drat, you've got me by the short and curlies, oh well, better luck next time'?"

"Well... most of them do follow a certain... pattern," Hettie allowed. "That's why they call it cozy crime, Hoshrum."

"No criminal worth their stolen bag of chips and their haversack of pinched diamonds is ever going to admit to murder. They're going to ask for a solicitor. Criminals, especially the ones smart enough to pull off a scheme like the kind I've just read, know their rights. And even if they don't, they know that someone else will know them for him. Failing that, they'd grab something heavy off the mantelpiece and get to work on the detective sleuth. One murder is as good as another."

"Hoshrum, these novels capture a civilized perspective."

"I'm not saying the story was as good as lavatory paper, love."

"Hoshrum!"

"I'm saying it's as good as a paper airplane. Good for a bit of a glide, but sooner or later it'll fall into the bin. I hope they keep bringing you joy, darling. I mean that. No messing about. Just so long as you know that civilized perspectives don't have a thing to do with policework, no more than a stale digestive biscuit is artwork." He paused. "I liked the detective. Funny little man."

"He's very good, isn't he? *Ze little gray cells.* So shrewd and particular."

"A bit of a Jeeves, but yeah, I liked him."

As he fought for his life against a butler turned assassin, which was the ultimate Jeevesian couplet, Thud was gratified to find his assertions vindicated. If Falstaff of all people wasn't going to surrender himself to the cleverness of a pragmatically solved case, then no criminal in this uncivilized world would.

Now, all that remained was to survive and go home for supper.

They crashed around the room in Mrs. Hinkelman's boarding house.

Thud had managed to get the knives away from Falstaff. In return Falstaff had parted Thud from his trusty truncheon, which had flown out a window. That left the teacup. Thud wasn't sure how much good that would do him, but he was damned if he was letting go of it.

Falstaff punched Thud in the stomach hard enough to drive the wind from him just as Thud laid one on Falstaff's ear. A dirty spot to strike a fellow—if you have ever whacked your ear off an open kitchen cabinet, or by ill luck received a fist to the side of your head, you know how sensitive the human ear is—but Thud was a firm believer in the "smash the plates now, delicately place the dessert spoons later" style of fighting.

Wheezing, he stepped back, studying Falstaff as the former butler nursed his throbbing ear.

May sunshine flooded in through the smashed window, lining both men in late spring gold.

As breath filtered back into him, Hoshrum Thud had one of his moments. They were what Hettie described as the moments in which her husband shifted his thinking, in which he stopped thinking about clues and started clueing about think. If moments like that could manifest a sound that echoed through the wrinkled gray country of the brain, it would be *thud*.

He had an idea. It was a risky idea, one that would probably cost him the very life he was so intent on saving. Before it could be attempted, he had to be sure of the man in front of him, the man who had been scuffling like a crocodile on very good speed and putting up one hell of a fight to boot, and who despite that still managed to look as neat as a pin.

"What's it to be then, Falstaff? Kill me, hide the evidence, then pack up your things here and go to ground somewhere else? Wait for Hughes to put his guard down, then give the old knife in the dark palaver another go?"

"Regrettably, it is the only course of action available," Falstaff replied. "Lady Dragontail must be avenged. Hughes has let this city go to the dogs. You know I met a boy without a home recently? A child without a roof to hold off the rain, in Corinth City. It would never have happened like this. Should never have."

"There aren't any rains. Shut it, I take your point. It's bad," Thud agreed. He saw Falstaff's gaze, still hard and unflinching, take on a note of interest. He continued. "The city's sweat through its clothes. It needs a drink. Not one to numb the pain, one that'll take away the pain for good. It needs water, only there isn't enough to go around. Don't you get it? I bet you do. You're a circumspect thinker. You kept some of the doors in Redspire secret, even from people you trusted. Hughes didn't know about that one in his office, eh? My point is he's doing his best. There isn't enough to go around, but most people understand that he doesn't take baths while people go thirsty. Dear God, man, do you even watch the vids? Hughes' hair is a greasy mop most of the time. He showers in the sink like most of the people in Leonidas. I have it from his wife that he sleeps under the same bits of cutout manuscript he slept under as a child. Does that sound like someone sitting on his hands and twiddling his toes? You think Wendy Dragontail would be better?" Thud snarled. "Are you so stupid that you actually believe she'd be half as good?"

Falstaff glowered. He massaged his ear a final time, straightened, and slipped into a fighting stance. "I shall take the liberty of writing your wife a letter of apology. Have you anything you'd like to tell her?"

"That there'll always be more clay to break."

The butler turned assassin frowned. "Explain."

Thud thought of the detectives in cozy crime novels, so eager to explain their deductions, their process, everything. He grinned. "You know, I don't think I will. How high up are we? Thirty feet give or take a few inches?"

Falstaff's frown was grooved very deeply now. "What are you talking about?"

"You're an assassin. I expect you'll kill me like a gentleman, in a gentlemanly way. But you will kill me. I'm not as young as I used to be, and your travel has done you a whole bloody world of good." His grin widened. "No. Thanks, but no. I shall go out on my own terms. Write that letter to Hettie. Include the bit about the clay, all right? She'll know what it means."

And before Falstaff could reply, Hoshrum Thud charged the window. The truncheon had cleared some of the glass. He took care of the rest. Shards slashed at him, ripping his clothes and skin. Then it was fresh air. Hot, but not unpleasant. He fell.

***

Cate, the anvil. Eilandri, the hammer.

The wolf, the butcher's block. Burrows, the axeman.

The scarlet army and the cavalcade of undead gave the four of them a wide berth, in the same way people tend to avoid eerie ticking sounds coming from beneath a desk and tend to give a respectful distance to actively erupting volcanoes.

The four fought bitterly, with full twelve years of animosity propelling each swing, each dodge, each landed blow. Burrows had been right when he mused to himself that battle was no time for speeches. Taken further, it's generally not good for any communication, except the kind Cate spoke best.

He tried to hew off her head and succeeded in shearing a few red hairs. Too close, that. She gave ground. Burrows pursued. She vanished into a mirror, reappeared, feinted, and then broke his hip to show him she did not appreciate his advances. Delight shot through her in manic tingles to see that arrogant little mouth of his shrivel with hurt. The impact of the kick sang up her leg, booted foot to lumbar. The insane wolf's teeth closed on the offending boot. It would have sliced into her foot, possibly severing a couple toes, but the boot's Jolene craftsmanship showed its grit. The other wolven head, frighteningly sane and deadly, dove to test if her breastplate was as sturdy. Cate cracked it upside the chops with her free boot, but the beast was not to be deterred. It yawned, resetting its jaw with a sound like termite-chewed tinder snapping, and lunged for Cate.

From the corner of her eye she saw Eilandri fend off a slash from Burrows, roll (spry for such a massive woman), and intercept. Her hammer's tiny cuspated points bit into the sane wolf's head. The weight behind the blow crumpled its muzzle in a spray of blood, and the blood squirmed as it painted the scene, for it was pulpy-thick and wormy. The beast stank, a noxious eggy smell, and its insides were somehow fouler. Cate wrenched her boot free. She fell with her hands well-placed on the cold fortress stone, and was backflipping to stable footing in a jiffy.

Burrows gave a sharp whistle of command. The wolf head with the crumpled muzzle raised its head. Burrows slid a thin-fingered hand into the wound. The wolf whimpered but did not recoil. Burrows' hand emerged holding a fistful of wriggling worms. He spoke a word, flung the worms high, and with a crackle they lengthened into a fan of icicles as black as frostbitten fingers. The icicles spread out, seemed to pinpoint Cate, and stilled.

Oh fuck, she thought. *Oh fuck me.*

Ice exploded around her as she performed a series of desperate carnival acrobatics. The blade of Burrows' axe rushed toward her. Split-second reflexes made her jerk aside. The blade curved on, laying open her cheek.

"A mirror with meat underneath," sang the undead at the sight of her blood. "A mirror with meat underneath!"

Burrows had dismounted the wolf. He limped, favoring the side with the unbroken hip. But he was a lithe, lean fiend and those icicles of his kept coming. He gave Cate no quarter as the two lupine heads deviled Eilandri.

Evelyn's voice. She heard it, a memory as opposed to the real deal. Six years old, just a tot with a bug obsession rather than the complicated twelve-year-old Evelyn of today.

Mummy. If you're the mostly good wolf then I want to be a cub.

Burrows swung. A mistime. Cate made him pay for it. She caught the axe along the handle, felt its necromancy lash her with a feeling like she was dipping her hand in a jug of sizzling oil.

"I pray it hurts," said Burrows.

She laughed in his face. "This is a doddle. When your mate Skuggs stabbed me in that hand, that hurt. Where are you going? No, no. Come here."

He was trying to pull away, her laughter washing over him, but Cate was strong. Under her armor the veins in her arms stood out like cables.

"Come here," she bid him. "I've a kiss for you like the succubus down there."

And with that she drove the shelf of her brow into where she judged his nose to be. As it happened, beneath the veil Burrows did, rather unfortunately for him, have a nose.

Cate heard it crunch, heard Burrows make a sound that was half outrage, half agony, and heard herself laugh and laugh.

"You..." She could barely get the words out. "You sound like a goose with indigestion. Oh God that's funny. Oh no, no. Don't go anywhere. I'm not—"

Again she headbutted him.

"—even *close*—"

And again.

"—to being done—"

And again.

"—with you."

She locked a leg around his waist, drew him closer, reared back her body, and headbutted him as hard as she could.

Burrows' head rocked backward. Then it swayed on his neck, lolling back and forth. The stuff pouring from inside his veil and down his chin was a clot of pink-red mush.

The wolf barreled into them both, knocking Cate off the necromancer king.

She lay where she was for a second. Cool stone on the unwounded half of her face. Nice and cool on her cheek. Nice.

Hoh boy. *Holy shit, I'm knackered.*

Clothilda, her Responsibility urged her. You've got to reach her now. Have her blast you and Eilandri down toward the succubus. Kill it. Save your soldiers.

"Yeah," she croaked.

Save them. They're *dying. Get up.*

She groaned and got up. Two icicles were sticking out of her shoulder.

Cate gave these a look of utter bafflement. When had Burrows stuck her with those? She supposed it didn't matter. Cate left them in for the moment. Maybe they'd melt and cool her down. It was seriously balmy, pretty... what was the word? Cramped. War packed you in tight, but the Bloodwood was muggy as shit. *Melt away, ice friends.* Nice.

She looked around, not bothering to plunge through a mirror for a new vantage point on the battle.

Her senses were in overdrive: hot, wet sensation, her face gushing blood, some of her cheek skin hanging in a ragged flap, she could feel it; everywhere there were barks, bugles, glottal screams, scared shrieks; tang of roasted pork (*Kpele's cookout, she needs to turn those fillets*), sulfur, the sickly sweet odor of the Bloodwood's falling leaves like charred caramel, pungent copper so familiar (*blood, old friend, how the hell are ya, haven't seen you this abundant in years*), Burrows' own hum, (*fucker smells like a weed-choked graveyard*), and sweat, always sweat; not to mention the frenzied sights, the tangerine monkey wraiths, the white-and-red of the trees, gray Betty stone speckled in quartzite, Burrows' black veil fluttering (*a gift from his gran, what a hag, what a goddamn crone*), and the haze in the air, like a mirage reified, a shimmer rising off the rhythm of the pounding drums of hate.

"General."

She turned.

"Sergeant?"

Daniel Jurdels looked as bleak as she felt. "Battlement brigade, reporting for duty, General. Looked like you could use the help, if you'll forgive my presumptive arse its presumptions."

"Bum forgive, Sergeant."

"Thank you, ma'am."

Burrows had regained his composure. She'd done a number on him, but evidently the necromancer king was a maths exam. You could do a number on him all you liked, and he'd carry on as before.

Cate made a decision. It was quick, as all decisions in combat had to be. "Sergeant, have your brigade engage Burrows and his wolf."

Bless him, the man saluted. "Yes, General. Those monkeys and that lippy thing down there in the trees are giving us a walloping, General."

"Working on it, Sergeant."

"If I die, give my love to the wife."

"If I die, give mine to the president."

They grinned at one another, the way condemned folk will grin as they tell blue jokes on their way to the rope.

"With me, lads!" cried the sergeant. "Corinthia!"

"Corinthia!" his brigade echoed.

"Ju-bil-ee!"

"Ju-bil-ee!"

Brave bastards, she thought as she dragged Eilandri (and herself) reluctantly away from Burrows and his two-headed wolf. *Beautifully brave. I'll be back to bail you out as soon as I can. Clobber the smug fuck one for me. I'll be back, I swear it.*

Forty-five seconds later there was a concussive blast. A chunk of fortress sailed through the air, headed directly for the succubus. Cate and Eilandri were holding on to it for dear life.

At the launch site Clothilda Toffington dabbed her nostrils delicately with her enchanted handkerchief. It didn't help much. Her handkerchief was always sodden by battle's end. Oh well. War was all about sacrifice.

How she yearned for home. Her partner's restaurant. Little plates with even littler food on them. Now *that* was living.

Sacrifice. Well, their general sacrificed more than most. Inspiration, and so forth. Of course, once Cate had Xacorca Demon on her side, everyone else's loyalty was a given. That was years ago now that they mended their broken bridges. But word was this was the last big fight. Clothilda was ever so relieved to hear it.

She paused, surveying Cate and Eilandri's trajectory. Rather good. Yes, rather good indeed, if she did say so herself.

They were off to fight that malebolginous disaster of a creature down there, the one with the leech body and the gorilla head. Seemed somewhat foolhardy, given the surplus of undead cavorting nearby. It'd be dreadful for something to happen to those two, this being the last battle.

Clothilda fetched a sigh. Must she do absolutely everything?

Meanwhile the block of masonry detached by her sneeze caromed through the Bloodwood. Cate was first to depart, firing a mirror to coagulate on a tree near the succubus' head and slipping into another she'd prepared earlier. Eilandri's approach was somewhat more direct. She crouched, timed her moment, and threw herself at the succubus like a pale lance. The chunk of stone exploded against one of the stupendously tall trees, but Eilandri's aim was true. The head of her hammer gored the succubus, gored it as bulls had once gored matadors in The Hippodrome of Corinth City. Eilandri's weight pulled it down after her, and the succubus squealed as the denticulated hammer opened its bloated belly like a letter packed with rancid sausage. Its tendrils whipped in a frenzy, their murderous lips puckered with pain. Uneasy with the succubus but unable to leave their ally to its fate, the undead began clambering up the trees. The wraiths were much more invested in the succubus' fate. They came as quickly as they could.

Eilandri's hammer snagged in a lump of gore as thick as frozen cottage cheese. The Pale Giant leveraged herself up, stood in the abdominal cavity she'd made, hefted her hammer, and began mining the succubus' insides like a prospector hunting gold.

Tears streaming, the creature's sorrowful apish gaze darted to Cate Jubilee. The general's forehead was purpled with bruise, her slashed cheek in need of immediate stitching, but for some reason the succubus could not reconcile the woman was laughing at it.

It sent its lips to kiss the life from her.

Wraiths rushed for her. The undead clawed at her.

Cate's hobnail boots caught the blue light streaming through the forest canopy. In and out, they went. In and out, clotted with blood and hair.

Inside the luggage of her life a photo album opened. There had been a hammer once. A workman's hammer. That had been clotted with blood and hair too.

Cathy. Her father's voice. *Cathy, give us a kiss, there's my girl.*

The wraiths were disappearing as the succubus died.

Kevlin Paladin and Marcus Angel were tending to the clambering undead. Cate didn't care that they had come to help her. She was simply grateful.

For good measure she kicked the succubus until the toe of her boots scraped the back of its skull. She reeled, her ponytail coming loose so her hair flooded about her face in a weave of carmine and gave the undead her most cheerful smile. "Be with you in a moment!" she said.

Those of them possessed of a granule of sense slowed their climb toward her. Some went still as hares in headlights. Others actually lost their handholds and plummeted.

Dad, Cate thought, shaking brains off her boots and hopping across branches toward those undead lacking sense (soon to be insensible). *Daddy, war took you and gave you back to me broken. A feral moon-eyed animal instead of a human being. You huffed and puffed and blew our house down, and your wife, my mum, with it. Now your daughter is all grown up. She's become the big bad wolf, the nasty wolf, the wicked wolf. I am the nightmare that haunts these people of Eurydice. You mustn't flatter yourself with thoughts of ghosts in the gantry. You haven't haunted me since I met Hughes, since that day we beat the Nightjar Coven. Here's a little missive anyway, since I know you're in an underworld somewhere, hopefully not resting too easy. A little message from your Cathy. My little girl, your granddaughter, is my cub. She is not a mirror of me and I will never, not in a million fucking years, be a mirror of you. Our reflections are non-consummate.* That was one of the great challenges of parenthood, after all. You had to accept that your child was not a better version of you. They were not you at all.

The undead enjoy gossip and news of every stripe as much as the living. They all shivered to hear that the succubus was an empty vessel, a dead sack hanging from its hooks. Suddenly, the promised prize for killing the red-haired fiend seemed less appealing. A march to join their comrades on the front lines of battle, that was surely a more noble pursuit. Those not committed to the climb and the fight hurried away, streaming in their gruesome ranks as fast as they could away from the laughing, which had reached a crescendo, a braying, big bad howl.

Meanwhile Cate gave Kevlin Paladin a bit of respite from the oncoming undead.

"Did Clothilda send you?" she asked.

"Insisted on it." Kevlin was by and large austere, but Cate saw amusement glimmer behind his firm expression. "Apparently Marcus and I were to hurry to your aid, or Clothilda would sneeze us into next Sunday. Her words, mind."

"Good old Clothilda. Ah, here's your lift."

Rosemund Valkyrie landed on an undead, popping its decay-filled body like a boil. She looked tired to Cate's eye, that too-alert quality that radiates from the really exhausted. "Want to come back?" said Rosemund. To her credit she made an effort to sound like she was doing okay.

"A lift would be lovely," said Cate.

"I can take two at a time."

"Start with Marcus and Kevlin. Eilandri and I can hold our own in the meantime."

Kevlin clasped her arm. "Luck to you, Cate."

"You too, Kev."

She watched Rosemund's impressive marmalade-colored wings swooping back toward the vanguard Betty. Alone now, and with the undead in no rush to tussle, Cate waved to get Eilandri's attention.

"Rosemund'll be back for us. Head straight to Burrows?" she wondered. "Or are we needed elsewhere, do you reckon?"

Eilandri held up her index finger. The first one.

"Burrows it is," said Cate. "He's not so tough."

The Pale Giant pointed at Cate.

Cate refused to look. "The two icicles are still in me, aren't they?"

A nod.

"Now you mention it they hurt like buggery."

Raised brows. A question.

"Nah, I'll leave them in. Maybe Burrows has got a certain toughness about him."

Another nod.

"We'll get him."

Cate determined look faded because from her own branch she watched Eilandri's expression go stony. Her lavender eyes blazed like a furnace burning under that stone, and Cate felt a flicker of hot, urgent dread, and she followed her friend's glare, and there he was.

"I heard you laughing," said Ruthven. He was curled around a tree, his wings folded so he looked like a serpent, his muzzle more wicked and wolfish than Cate had dared recall. "I heard your song, Cate Jubilee. I've come to switch the record to its B-side. I've come to make you beg for death."

Cate Jubilee said nothing. Moving with practiced smoothness she unpocketed a vial of instant-mirror, aimed, and squeezed. The gooey substance shot harmlessly up through the gnarled branches, landing on a tree trunk high overhead.

Ruthven did not even have to flinch. "Thinking of vanishing and reappearing through that, are you? Raining down boot-blows on me like the wrath of a flimsy god?" He smiled, and the effect was a shed door blowing open, and the shed's dim insides stuffed with rusted tools. "Really, you are a one-trick pony, General. I—"

But that was as far as Ruthven got. Cate turned tail and ran. Eilandri had a three second head start. Ruthven watched them, a curious pathologist watching subjects caper and dance their dreary dance, unaware that when the time came, he would perform their autopsy with enthusiasm. Historically human beings had been called "the most dangerous game," but Ruthven didn't see it that way. The most *interesting* game, ah, now that he could get behi—

A shadow fell over him.

Ruthven's smile faltered. Aware that Cate Jubilee was laughing again, he looked up suspiciously.

Half a million tons worth of fortress crashed upon him, like the wrath of the mightiest of gods.

***

Let the eye or the ear not linger too long on this next part because nothing exciting happened.

A father and daughter headed to the apiary in Redspire. They spoke with Amiable Winkins, son of Jolly Winkins the groundskeeper. Amiable was someone who can only be described as one of life's nevergivvas, as in nevva givva fuck. He called the daughter by her name and the father by his, despite society indicating that he should not do so. The daughter and the father were more than fine with this. They called Amiable "Mr. Winkins." Amiable gave them bee suits with zippers, gloves and boots.

Surrounded by the bumbling humdrum buzz of the bees, the daughter told the father all about queen bees, how they did their job and how they were replaced by the hive's new queen. Becoming the new queen was a competitive business. There were many potential her highnesses bred on the hive's royal jelly. Things got messy. There were very private wars. Then the new queen rose to the top of the proverbial pot because all the other competitive honey (the other prospective queens) had been scraped away, you see.

The father asked the daughter if it didn't bother her, the females killing one another to become matriarch of the sticky-sweet queendom.

The daughter replied that it oughtn't bother anyone. Supersedure was just something bees did. The daughter said that her mother didn't want to fight a war. Fighting was simply what her mother did, and did better than anyone else. It was only nature being nature, bees being bees.

The father listened. As he listened, he began to feel uncomfortable with himself in a very sharp way. He tentatively asked his daughter if he had ever told her how his own mother had died. The daughter said that yes, he had, didn't he remember?

The father admitted no, he did not. She patted his hand for comfort, but he still wasn't feeling himself. Trying to sound at his ease, he put it to the daughter that you could view what happened to his mother as supersedure. She was a dragon, not a bee, but she was replaced by... well, even if he hadn't wanted her to die, her son had become the new leader of the cit... of the hive.

Surely that made the daughter feel odd.

The daughter shook her head.

"Dad," she said. "Life has enough barbs and stingers for us. No need to sting yourself over something that wasn't your fault."

"I don't know what to say to that."

"Say thank you."

"Well, thank you. You didn't have to say it so kindly. I'm glad you did."

"I... Never mind."

"What?"

"Never mind," said the daughter. "It's silly."

"Maybe it is silly. I like silly. Tell me."

Productive and unmindful of the pair, the bees worked the daily shift. They roamed about the screens and the boards of the imitation hive. Somewhere in there the queen exuded pheromones, and thought queenish beeish thoughts, and did not think about being replaced.

"It's silly," said the daughter.

"Tell me."

"Just speaking of odd, you... you've been looking at me oddly."

"Have I?"

"Yeah."

The father considered this. "Recent or..." he said.

"Ever since I told you about my visits to Eurydice."

"Oh."

"You keep... Dad, can we talk about something else?"

"Keep talking about this for the time being. I want to hear."

"It was a mistake."

"Don't get upset. I want to hear. Am I mad?"

"You don't sound mad."

"Because I'm not. Talk to me."

The daughter gave a snuffle that made her sound young, then spoke about things that made her seem as ancient as the world. "I'm sorry I lied, Dad. Eurydice told me I'd be good at it and I was. I didn't think it would hurt you."

"Did you think that?"

"No," she said. She was crying. "I knew it would hurt. I just didn't think about it. I'm sorry."

"It's okay."

"I'm really sorry."

"It's okay," said the father. "I used to be good at lying too. I still am. Before, when I was young, I felt like I had to."

"You did?"

"Yes. I did. When I met your mother, she told me I'd be better at telling the truth. Not letting go of lies completely because sometimes you've got to lie. I won't fib about that or cover it up. Sometimes I do lie. But only at times when I know it won't hurt. Or because I've been given responsibility, I'll use a lie to hurt someone bad or support someone good. That sounds right, now I say it aloud, but who can judge themselves on any real level? Maybe it's the same for those without what I've got. I don't know anymore. The most important thing is that your mother showed me how to hold close to the truth and to be held by it in return."

"Okay."

"Honesty is the elixir of hope. I believe that. You don't have to."

"I do. I felt so bad after I told you and you looked sad. I'd never seen you look so sad."

"What about these other looks? Are they sad?"

"A bit," she said. "And a bit angry. And a bit... I don't know."

"I think you do."

"A bit... scared."

"Scared?" The father felt like he'd been jolted with electric wire. "Scared of what?"

"Of me?"

"Sweetie, I could never feel that."

"Yes, you could. You were scared of me in Daethumberland. Remember the wintry moth and the bugs?"

He remembered. "I wasn't scared of you."

"But you were scared."

"Yes," he said, and saying it was hard but it was honest. "I guess I was. But not of you. I promise. I was scared of what brought the bugs."

"Eurydice?"

"Yes. And her shadow, Jane. I'm scared of her too."

"So you're scared of—"

"No. You're my stethoscope. I could never be frightened of you."

"Your stethoscope?"

"Yes."

The daughter frowned. "I'm your stethoscope?" she repeated.

"Yes."

"Cold against your skin?"

"No."

"You put me in your ears?"

"What? No."

"Then how am I a stethoscope, Dad?"

He took her hands and put them on his chest. "You remind me that my heart is still there."

The apiary windows were shut, but the afternoon sunshine was most welcome. There was the light, the somnolent drone of the bees, and words.

Nothing exciting to see or to hear.

Only love.

***

Hoshrum Thud fell.

Corinth City did not spread out like an armature below him since Mrs. Hankelminkel's was not a particularly tall building. But the street was there to embrace him when the falling was done. Little shops. Cobblestones. Good old Corinth City streets. One more embrace then, for old time's sake. If you had to go, go out surrounded by your friends and family, or as a silver medal second-place sort of thing, go out doing the job you were born to do. Good old manky, magnificent Corinth City.

Thud closed his eyes...

And then soft, pristine, and most importantly strong hands closed on his shirt collar.

A morose voice said in his ear, "Arms closely tucked against the torso, sir. If you don't mind. Though its buttons look sturdy, your shirt is regrettably damp with sweat, and I don't want you to slip out of it."

Thud did as he was told, still not quite daring to open his eyes. Without much ceremony, but with a certain amount of what Thud suspected was the "pomp" in "pomp and circumstance," he was hauled back into the boarding house and deposited on the floor.

He opened his eyes.

Falstaff was there. The man had acquired tweezers, from where, Thud had no clue. Falstaff's neat little teacup of a face was tight with concentration as he picked slivers of glass out of Thud's hands.

"How did you know?" said the butler.

"Pardon?"

"How did you know I'd stop your fall?"

Thud considered telling him the full extent of his thought process: that you couldn't teach an old dog new tricks, but you couldn't take away his old ones. Falstaff was no old dog, and he had learned a lot in his travels, but the second part of the idea held true. Infuse the finest training and traits of an assassin into one of nature's butlers, and you did not get a pure assassin. What you got was a diluted mixture. You got a butler willing to get his white-and-black attire a bit rumpled, and a bit red.

But telling Falstaff that felt much too close to the end of Hettie's cozy crime novels, too close to the detective sleuth preening as he told everyone assembled in the parlor about The Facts.

Defiance against cliché made Thud's whiskers twitch. He gave a modest sort of grunt and said, "It wouldn't have been polite."

Falstaff hesitated, then went back to picking out glass slivers.

There was a knock at the door.

Mrs. Hankelminkel poked her head into the room. She gave the two men a disapproving smile. How she managed to do that was a mystery to Thud, who was quite finished solving anything strange for the foreseeable future.

"Mr. Thud? There are some... people asking for you."

"Thank you, Mrs. Hankelminkel. That'll be the Leonidas District department. Never there when they're wanted, but if you need them, well... fifty-fifty odds. Send them up, will you?"

"Certainly. Goodness, the room needs a spruce."

"We shall arrange someone to spruce it for you, madam. Thank you for your cooperation."

She flashed that vaguely hostile smile at him again and headed away to fetch Thud's back-up.

Falstaff pinched the last sliver from Thud's thumb, stood the chief of police up, and began dusting him down. "Your cuts are not too deep," he said. "Still, you must have them cleaned and bandaged post-haste. Unless I'm mistaken, I can hear your streetbeaters on the stairs. There's no need for restraints. I won't resist." He sighed down at his own folded fingers. "It's over."

"Look on the bright side," said Thud. "When most people go to prison, they're bound for some strange place they've never been. You're going home."

Falstaff's expression grew wistful. Suddenly he cringed. "Has there been at least... some standards maintained in my absence?"

Thud stroked his moustaches. "Define standards."

"Oh. Oh, dear me."

"Tell you what. When Hughes passes his judgment, I'll put in a word on your sentencing."

"You will?"

"Incarceration accompanied by extended bouts of community service." Thud grinned. "With an extra mop and duster if you behave yourself."

***

Twelve years ago, when Steffan Cerulean had siphoned the water from acres of trees and created a spear of ice to pierce Ruthven the vampire dragon, there had been vast quantities of blood. A torrent. Here's the thing: Steffan's spear hadn't hit anything vital. No arteries pricked. For Ruthven it was the equivalent of a nick, such as you might give yourself when cutting stalks of celery.

So when a fortress named Betty hit him, and pinned him to the floor of his own Bloodwood, and squashed him, squeezed him, pulped him like a overripe fruit, ground him, mashed him, macerated and liquidized him, Ruthven vented a sound that only a dragon can make when they are afraid. Then he exploded.

All the blood he'd ever drunk expelled from his body.

All of it.

This was not a matter of jars and cartons. This was rivers. This was canals. It geysered into the air, a kilometer, no, a mile high. Turning to see, Cate felt a sharp, warm spray of it on her face. It was the prelude to the flood. There was no time to climb one of the crooked white trees. Here it came now, bearing down on her, waves of scarlet plasma foaming like the sea in a book about gods denied their due. That tsunami of blood would whelm over her, crush her along with legions of the undead.

She was aware of them all around her, their fetid legs trying to pump faster and faster, candleflame eyes waxing with dread, and she could hear the Bloodwood's bugs zooming and zipping, the sensitive part of her innermost ear clenching and unclenching in response, and her heart doing the same in her chest, painful cadence, terrified rhythm, and her fingers, yes, her fingers fumbling at the vials in her satchel, looking to her right, Eilandri gone, lost in the dash, cold smoothness against her skin

(a vial!!!)

Something tinkled.

(two!)

She took out the vials. She aimed both at the same time.

Rushing, a rushing sound just behind her. A thunder. A maelstrom. A line from one of Hughes' plays occurred to her: *Who would have thought the old man to have had so much blood in him?* No time to aim, no time!

Go, her doubt and confidence cried together.

The wave crashed...

And somewhere not too far from Cate Jubilee, in a place sheltered from the battle by the Bloodwood's most tangled trees, something young and fairly new to this world of Eurydice felt the wave flow over them. Their senses sampled the blood and pronounced it an excellent vintage: Ruthven orchard, bottle numbers one through seven-hundred-and-twenty million.

Ruthven's secret project opened a pair of slitted eyes, swam to the surface of the blood, climbed a tree clumsily, and shook their wings dry. An experimental flap was tried. The results were deemed satisfactory. Ruthven's secret project took flight.

For the first time in a long, long time, the trees of the Bloodwood stopped their endless red weeping. Ruthven's juices were already seeping into the greedy soil, enriching the mutating muck. Where the blood lake had not reached, the tears dried in the long grooves of the tree trunks. Between those trunks flew the new life of Ruthven's project. A breeze clicked and clapped the branches together. It sounded like grateful applause.

Meanwhile Lord Burrows knew a setback when he saw one. At a surprising and vexing stalemate with Cate's forces on the battlements, he seized the opportunity to make good his escape. As the bloody pimple that was Ruthven burst, Burrows summoned his wolf and made for the legs of the fortress. There, he called as many oozes as he could together. They cobbled their forms into one jiggling mass, and before the tsunami slammed into the ranks of good and evil alike, Burrows and his wolf were safe in a submersible that could withstand the crushing weight of the waves and plumb the dark depths, a submarine of sentient jelly. Finding more oozes as they ventured out of the woods, the submarine grew, thus managing to rescue a large number of undead who had endured the worst of the flood and clung to their magical unlives. Burrows didn't see what happened next, how the battle truly concluded. It fell to Skuggs to inform his fellow councilor.

Oh yes, if you were curious about him, Skuggs was there that day.

He had been there all along.

From a knobby little alcove in one of the tallest trees, he watched events unfold.

You could chart how well and how poorly everything was going by the looks that crossed his pumpkin-skin head. Sometimes merry. Sometimes grumpy. Sometimes enraged. In the end, he was laughing his signature laugh. *Ahehn-hen-hen.*

And, shifting our gaze once more, not far from Skuggs (unaware of him, more's the pity) a daub of mirror glass was still filling out its shape in the tree bark when Cate Jubilee stepped out of it, soaked to the skin with blood and, on the whole, happy as a cat soaked in cream to still be alive.

She surveyed the sweeping immensity of the blood lake with revulsion. At least the liquid level seemed to be sinking, gulped up by this horrid forest. Her Bettys were massive enough to have stood their ground against the flood. The fortresses stood like waders in an ongoing storm, immersed to the hips but unbowed. No pride though. Not while...

Cate caught sight of marmalade wings.

"*Rosemund!*" she bellowed. "Up here!"

"Cate!" The Daethumbrish woman landed next to her. "The undead are washed away. We've won. Doctor John is—"

"Never mind all that. Take Morvran and anyone else we've got that can fly." Cate pointed at the blood lake. "Sweep the surface. Eilandri and I lost one another. She might still be down there."

"We'll find her."

Rosemund dived off a branch and was gone. Cate heard the taut, parachutelike sound of her golden cloak unfurling into wings.

Doctor John is... Rosemund had begun. There was only one way that sentence ended. *Doctor John is about to deploy the terraformer and end the war.* The notion didn't allay Cate's worry for Eilandri, but she was pleased John was wasting no time.

She scanned, hopped from branch to branch to get a closer look, scanned some more, and hoped.

People think hope comes before a battle, staunch and rooted in its proper place. Actually, hope flies like Rosemund Valkyrie, like Ruthven's secret project, like a bird. Hope is the thing with feathers, or so Emily Dickinson once wrote, probably on a quiet, isolated day of her quiet, isolated, somehow elegiac life, a life that was both a funeral of the brain and a party inebriate with things as simple as fresh air, or morning dew.

Hope, that's what unified all the pieces of this post-slaughter picture in the Bloodwood, made it cohesive, made it what it was.

Right in the center of the Bettys' formation, the terraformer sat suspended like a dark geode over the steadily sinking basin of blood. It had been hoisted there by the very long-limbed machines that would lower it to the ground any moment. At the given word.

My word, thought John Isherwood. *The word of a mere man.*

"Doctor Isherwood?"

One of his technicians.

"Yeah?"

"We're ready for... Um. Are you feeling well, sir?"

John Isherwood's brow was wet, his lips dry. His complexion was plum-ruddy, as though he'd been running a marathon in the bitter cold. Behind his spectacles, his eyes had the partially vacant look of someone who has just been handed a letter they know contains a small canister of poisonous fume or a blank check.

"Sir?"

"Yes, I'm fine," said John. "It's the blood. I've never seen anything like it."

The technician smiled, plainly relieved. "That makes two of us, Doctor Isherwood. Shall we proceed with the installation? Everyone's excited about it being the last."

"Is there champagne?"

The technician's smile broadened. "We were hoping you wouldn't guess."

"Toast the end of the war?"

"And you, Doctor. The great mind um... I'm sorry, I don't mean to—"

"No, it's fine. Flattering. Yes, you can proceed."

"Wait until the blood level drops, or..."

John Isherwood looked at the object he'd designed to look so very much like a terraformer.

You might imagine that in that moment, at the apogee of his life, there was a little twist of conscience. Maybe a reemergence of his mother's voice. *Johnny, oh my poor stupid boy. What are you doing? What are you even thinking of doing?* Only there wasn't. Not a spasm of anxiety or regret.

My word, he thought. *What interstitial space is this? What lacuna between the flesh and the fabulous, the skin and the sublime?* Density and divinity. He supposed this was the moment between the bird landing on the balcony and the pen sketching it. Or before it is shot and stuffed. Either way it is transformed.

Completely lost on John Isherwood was that in both cases the bird is captured. "No," he said aloud. "Why wait? Lower it now."

The technician bobbed an exuberant nod. "You got it."

John turned from her retreating back to the sky. It had been blue until only a moment ago. Now it was a startling, atavistic red. Bloody wood, bloody lake, bloody sky, twinkling hemoglobin stars just beginning to come out. As above, so below. Scarlet Citadel. Scarlet army. Crimson business, twelve years of it here in this alien, beautiful world with its... with *her* carmine mind, her cerise lips, her taste like cherries dipped in rosewater, her touch on his cock filling his body and his ravenous mind with amaranth fire. Things were red all over it seemed.

Caterwauls of engineers, scribbles and pencil-chewing mumbles of scientists, giddy gossip of technicians; all of it came to him with the wind that smelled of copper, completing the red tableau. John watched the long-limbed machines begin to lower the object that was not a terraformer. The word had been given.

My word, he thought. *The word of a mere man who is about to become a god.* See the sanguinous thread tying the elements of the picture together?

Not quite?

Maybe this'll bring it home. Through the ashen boughs, toward the site of Cate's victory, flapped Ruthven's secret project, their heart juddering urgently, beating a tattoo like a code whose message was one of irreparable hope.

Elevated as she was, Cate saw the dragon first.

The dragon was about the size of a pony. The dragon was furry-white with red spots like dollops of red paint on a canvas, and the slitted eyes were wide and (scared?) yes, the eyes were full of fear, and when it opened its mouth what emerged was not a roar but a shrill squawk.

"*Rrrrrrnaaaaaa!*"

The dragon was a child.

It flew toward the empty fortress Cate had dropped on Ruthven. There was something terribly deliberate about that.

Movement in the blood lake. Not only marmalade-colored wings but jade-green ones too. Rosemund and Morvran had found Eilandri. They were supporting her as they flew. Big as Eilandri was, it was a wonder they could keep her aloft.

Cate cupped her hands around her mouth. "*Rosemund! Morvran!*"

They looked up at her.

Cate pointed toward the empty fortress, where the dragonling would soon land. "*I'm going to go after that thing. Get Eilandri to the medical center and bring me Steffan Cerulean.*" If she was right, she would need his liquid-manipulation, even if Steffan did find blood tricky.

But as she filled her fingers with mirror-spawning vials, Cate saw Eilandri give her a thumbs up. The gesture said, *I'm okay.*

Cate hesitated, but not for long. "Belay that, you two," she called to her fliers. "Ferry Eilandri to the fortress. We'll take this little horror on, the four of us."

It was a decision she would regret for the rest of her life.

Rosemund and Morvran altered their course, executing a full turnabout and surging toward the fortress at a fast clip. Cate followed, dipping in and out of the fractal realm of endless glass.

The fortress hadn't fallen perfectly, far from it. Its legs had crumpled bonelessly beneath it. The foundations canted. In their topple, the walls had encountered the forest, and though the Bloodwood trees were old and deep-rooted and strong, they were no match for stone. It was only the trunks that brought their crash to a halt. Now the towers and the keep sat at an oddly jaunty angle, the strangest hat worn atop this weird wood. Some of the shattered trees had been tossed over the battlements so fiercely their branches skewered the windows of the Betty's keep, smiting the glass with a heavy crunch like vases being dropped.

Cate emerged from the last unbroken window. Hurriedly she glanced about. There, swerving toward the base of the stricken fortress were Eilandri and the others. Cate sent two mirrors condensing, one near enough in the tilted courtyard, the other about three hundred yards down. She jumped down, choosing to burst out of the second mirror for sheer momentum. The dragonling had looked so scared, moved with such steadiness... it had been like watching a homing arrow punch through a prevailing wind. Time was of the essence, she knew it with a savage surety.

She somersaulted, landed on one of the Betty's legs (somehow it had escaped being crushed, and stuck out like a rogue cigar from a fallen case), dropped with a splash into the blood (by now it was thigh-deep and still sinking), and took in a scene unlike any she had witnessed in all her years of making war.

Ruthven had tried to get out. He'd survived the initial impact. Sinuous fucker that he was, and minus a great deal of his precious red elixir, he must have wound and snaked and slithered through the tiny cracks in the fortress foundations. But he'd been bleeding, jetting, squirting, pumping gallons upon gallons of the stuff. What Cate saw now, half under the fallen Betty and half out, was a glume of what Ruthven had been. He floated in his own insides like a torn paper lantern in a puddle. His fur was a rumpled rug. The one eye that was visible wasn't staring sightlessly. It drifted in the blood, as did his claws and his teeth, all reduced to ribbons. The dragonling had Ruthven's head—or what was left of it—between its jaws. Gently but persistently, it tugged.

Daddy, come out of the pool. I want to go home.

A bizarre thought, disturbing, but stark too. Cate examined it and let it go.

This was nothing like William o' The Wisps' child, the one she'd found in a giant manta ray and spared all those years ago.

Nothing like that, said her confidence.

You still lie to yourself, said her doubt. Sometimes you think you're past that honey, but you aren't. Because it's exactly like the wisp child. You can't kill this creature.

No, agreed her confidence. You can't. But whatever that little vampire is doing, you've got to stop it.

Eilandri landed next to her, dashing Cate's bare right hand with warm droplets. An instant later Morvran and Rosemund were there. Both were drenched in sweat.

"You must weigh five hundred pounds," Morvran groused.

Eilandri held up eight fingers.

"Eight? Buggery."

"What do we do, Cate?" asked Rosemund.

Lie again, said Cate's doubt within her head. I dare you.

Cate made a noise that was part discontent, part resignation. "Bonk it on the bonce and take it somewhere we can muzzle it. It's a vampire but it's also a kid, and that first bit doesn't outweigh the second, am I clear?"

"Crystal," said Rosemund.

"Eight hundred pounds. My back is singing in high C."

"Shut up, Morvran."

Cate looked to Eilandri like a seasoned cartographer checking a trusty map. The Pale Giant put a hand on Cate's shoulder and gave it an encouraging squeeze.

Cate's face said: Well, the war's almost over. Any chance of a smile for your old buddy old pal?

And Eilandri's face said: No.

And Cate's said: Come on. With chocolate truffles on top. Zesty lemon shavings. Daub of mint cream.

And Eilandri's face said: No.

And Cate's face said: I love you.

And Eilandri's face said: I love you too.

Love me enough to...

Still no.

Shit. Well, please yourself.

They began to trudge, quick as they could, toward the dragonling and Ruthven's papyrus-sheaf carcass.

It heard them coming. Cate expected it to rear back on its hind legs, clap wide its wings, and give them a warning squawk. Instead, it looked at Ruthven's body, and it looked at Cate, then back to the Ruthven again. It uttered a sound. Not a squawk. Cate wasn't sure but she thought it sounded like a whine.

That feeling she'd had, a sort of ominous blue discontent, shaded into indigo.

"Close," she heard herself say. "Close on it. Get it *now*. *It's going to do something. Close.*"

The dragonling whined again, high and piteous.

It strained its body. The sudden constriction might have been comical, if only the veins hadn't shown up. They bulged through its fur, invisible to totally vivid, a network of veins crisscrossing the dragonling from claws to the crown of its tapered head. Its whine climbed in pitch, becoming a scream that was all-too human.

"ON IT!" Cate thundered. Her doubt was silent, her confidence a clarion. "GET ON IIIIIIT—"

There was an awful noise. Take a fruit salad, whisk it into a gloop of smoothie, and dump it on a tile floor. That sound would be close to the one that filled Cate's ears as the dragonling first ballooned, then popped.

It was nothing like Ruthven's explosion. Still, the blood fairly fountained. The four scarlet warriors were still charging when it happened. They were doused, not knocked back by the force of the gush but staggered. Wiping ferociously to get it out of her eyes, Cate watched as the blood refused to come down. The majority of it began to spiral. Like a DNA helix it spun and spun in thick strands. And those strands were aiming for one thing, and one thing only.

Cate vented a hoarse shout of pure wordless fury. She bolted, hobnail boots squelching in the Bloodwood's sodden compost, which had reappeared as the blood lake finally drained.

Morvran and Rosemund were too gobsmacked to do much of anything, but Eilandri grasped the situation almost as quickly as Cate had.

Cate could hear her friend storming up behind her. In less than a second Eilandri had overtaken. Her hammer was in her hands.

The blood helix found Ruthven's deflated corpse. And like a gory clown's pump kit, it started to inflate him. At first that collapsed eye filled up and clocked back home in its socket. Then the gums grew plump, and the teeth regained their tactility, their ragged, gnawing edge. Growing, swelling, fattening with the flow of rich blood.

Eilandri lofted her hammer high over her head. She brought it down.

In a shiver too speedy to follow, Ruthven curled around the hammer's handle. His head, grotesquely large compared to the rest of his sagging body, stopped three inches from Eilandri's. His mouth unseamed itself in a sly half-grin.

Cate didn't hear herself cry out.

She didn't hear anything.

Nothing except the inhale.

***

For a second she believed it would be all right.

Eilandri was a colossus. She had survived countless battles, close shaves, even cancer. Ruthven's vampiric inhale, drawing out her blood and pulling it down his throat, wouldn't kill her. Possibly wouldn't even phase her.

Later, feeling numb to her core, a coroner with a quiet, gentle voice told her that in Eilandri's brain, there was a great lattice of vessels, and in response to being sapped so violently of blood, one of these vessels had gone the way of the dragonling. It had swelled. The result was a massive brain aneurysm.

But Cate would only learn that afterward. At the time, she heard Ruthven take a sup of Eilandri. Her body moved of its own accord. As Cate drew near, the dragon disentangled himself and fled away into the trees.

Eilandri fell. No fanfare. The great hero of the war dying here, in a place of quiet evil. Her legs simply went out from under her and there she went.

One little blood vessel.

Sometimes hope turns its face away.

One little blood vessel.

Cate caught her friend, swung herself around so they could face one another, and brought Eilandri down softly to the ground.

If you had told Cate that Eilandri weighed almost a ton, and that the idea of supporting her weight was quite impossible for one person, Cate Jubilee would not have understood you. Her gaze was not catastrophically distant. She knew what was going on. Neither did she weep. But the trees did. The dragon child was dead and the trees were crying again.

Cate spoke tenderly, her tones hushed and steady. Rosemund and Morvran heard the things she said to her Eilandri, her Ella, her friend... and they never told anyone... Perhaps that's where those things ought to stay. Brushed by but not picked at. Enough of Cate's grief has been spilled on the ink of this story's pages. See Cate slip her hand into Eilandri's. See Cate watch the breath slow, and slow, and stop. See her smile the saddest smile, a smile that contains years of a friendship like an assembly in a glass jar, and that same smile sending the glass jar out to sea, never to return, never. See her close Eilandri's eyes. See her kiss her friend's pate and throat, and one kiss each for her closed eyes, sweet as flowers on a warm spring grave. No more. Let's not linger.

Bad as that few minutes was, something worse was about to happen.

Where the shift began, it wasn't clear to Cate. If pressed, she would have said it began as so many wicked things did: with her boots. Unease in the deep earth. Restless, a bitter language of soil under soil, the systems of the land speaking to one another, tongues caked in loam and stone and angry spit, vituperative.

The magic in her hobnails shrank, a cloddy feeling like clay molding around her toes, arches, and ankles.

She looked at Morvran and Rosemund. Their focus was ensnared elsewhere. Back toward the army and the fortresses.

And the terraformer, thought Cate. At once the shifting beneath her made sense. The last terraformer was communicating with the others. Eurydice was about to be undone. *John, give it to her. Give it to her.*

She thought it, not knowing how prescient she was being in that moment.

Cate tried to lift Eilandri, found that with her reverie snapped she no longer could, and groaned.

Morvran and Rosemund rushed to her.

"We need to get back," Cate told them. "This world is about to go the way of the chocolate kettle." She jostled Eilandri. "Eh, Ella?"

Ella said nothing. Ella was dead.

Cate bit back a sob. It plugged up her throat. She swallowed it like a lump of lead. It was hard. Monstrously hard. She looked at the molten red sky, eyes welling, blinking as though in imitation of the stars.

"We need to go," she said again. "Take her back. I'll be right behind you."

They took Eilandri.

Wings rustled in the gathering gloom. A fallen warrior between the fliers.

In one of Hughes' plays, maidens of a one-eyed god guided fallen warriors to the lands of the dead. *Valkyries.* A ghost of that sad smile played on Cate's lips. Alone, she loaded her fingers for the last time that day with portable mirrors.

Hesitation, then a pushing, a certain straightening in her poise.

Forward, her doubt said.

Forward, her confidence said.

How? she asked them. How do I go forward without my friend?

When neither replied, she craned her neck up, bared her teeth in an expression of unspeakable despair, and shut her eyes. Damn things were prickling again. A few more rapid blinks set them right.

"Fuck," she hissed through those gritted teeth. "Oh, you fuck. You fuck."

Who?

No one.

You.

Herself.

Eurydice. Ruthven. The dragonling.

Herself.

"You fuck. God, okay. Okay."

She hopped in place, sucked in the moist, cloying air, hooshed it loose, rolled the clicking stiffness from her neck, and started back to the clumped fortresses—

An insect thumped onto her chest. It was very large, a wiry cricket with staring eyes of unyielding black. Cate swatted it. The cricket was caught in a cloud of midges. The midges molted, becoming caterpillars, changing with a soft shredding noise into a kaleidoscope of butterflies. Their wings expanded. They were finger-sized. Hand-sized. Large as chopped logs for a fireplace. Large as the fireplace itself. Colonies of insects boiled up to join them as they took to the air. Cate stared, her feet bolted in place with rivets of fascination.

Beetles the color of lemon curd, glow worms, pond skaters, gray grubs, hornets, lice and locusts, mosquitos, mantises, and moths of every distortion and hue from regal to pyramid to luna to death's head, chewing bugs and bruise-shaded bugs, they came in a flood to rival Ruthven's bloody detonation. Weevils, ants, and flies, responding to a call, answering the call of... What? Cate cleared that one for herself. *The terraforming. The end of this world. Must be.* They came from the Bloodwood, and yet on some instinctual level she knew that so many of them had come from abroad, a mass migration of silky, milky, smelly wings, feet, and thin twitching feelers. Columns of them rode the currents of the breeze, those with wings carting those who could not fly up and up. Not a cloud but a whole seething tempest of bugs. Millions, no billions of them. Symphonies of chirps, trills, lisps, buzzes, zips and sawing, salt-in-the-shaker noises so ugly they made the skin feel as though it were crawling with tiny skittering life. The intensity of that sound was overwhelming. Even more astonishing was the sound inside that sound, cradled by the bugs. It was a sound Cate recognized intimately; one she had learned to rely upon in times of trouble.

Laughter.

The hair at the nape of Cate's neck whispered up. Along her back her skin rashed out in gooseflesh.

Clots and drifts and landfills and loads-loads-*loads* of insects. They circled one another, a congregation of worshippers at the dung mound of this benighted world, eating the Bloodwood's trees and boring through the wood and filling the night with their insidious chorus.

From their excrement and breeding and blissful sociability came an egg. It wasn't there one moment, and the next it was.

Cate's eyes widened as it hatched.

***

Decked out in his apiary suit, Hughes pulled a shelf from the false hive. He admired the gooey amber-orange runoff. "Oh yeah. Oh, this'll work. Hand me the scraper thingamajig, sweetie."

He held out a hand.

The scraper thingamajig was not forthcoming.

He glanced up. Evelyn was gone.

Hughes would never know it, but right then his expression was a carbon copy of his wife's from twelve years ago, the day he'd gone to meet Death and Evelyn had vanished while she and her mother played a game of Here Are All The Terrible Monsters Mummy Has Absolutely Clobbered.

No one hands you a manual on how to be a father, either.

"Evelyn?"

He looked around. She had been there. She had been *right there*, he'd seen her only a moment ago.

Well, his mind offered, *you are forgetting things lately, aren't you?*

He closed himself from that tom-foolery. She had been there, by God.

"Evelyn?" he said meekly. And then, in a loud, bright bark, "*Evelyn!*"

Because the possibilities (where is she where is she where is she) had waited offstage, and now they drifted onstage to assail him with the brittle-nerved and immediate fear only a parent can know.

Right. He was striding briskly now, roaming the nearby trees and shrubbery, searching, and thinking hard while he searched. *If she isn't here, she must be...*

(got to be here, she's got to be)

(there she was *right there!*)

If she isn't here, the only place she could have gone in such a flash is...

It could only be...

"EVELYN!"

His Performance perforated the vicinity. Couched in it, his very voice could not be denied, not by the severest skulking creature, not by the most choleric or cantankerous opponent.

Nothing. No sign of her.

That was when he noticed that the bees had fallen silent.

Following an impulse (where it came from, he wasn't sure, but it came from his shadowed side, that was certain), he unloaded a canister of smoke on the hive and reefed it open shelf by shelf. He needn't have bothered with the smoke. The bees scurried slow and indolent. Hughes found the queen by searching the dark side of the shelves, the ones facing away from the red evening sun coming into the apiary. The queen bee was dead. Written in globs of honey by her corpse was this:

You complete me. Complete this, while you're on a roll:

There was a young girl who swallowed a fly...

"Perhaps she'll die," he whispered.

He left the apiary at a dead sprint.

***

Fragments of eggshell melted into the throng of milling bugs.

The man born from that egg stretched his arms languorously over his head. He absorbed all the bugs, one trillion and one creepy crawlies. He took them in with the air of collegial invitation. Come on in, boys and girls, the me, myself, and I is *fiiiiiiine.*

The laughter eclipsed the solid droning sound entirely.

The man gained control of himself. Still floating a hundred yards in the air, he grinned down at the scarlet general.

"Hughes?" said Cate, timidly, because she felt as though she'd unwittingly strayed into a dream. "Baby, is that you?"

The apparition shook its head. His hair spread behind it like a dark flail.

"Not little old me," he said, and it was not a *he* at all but a *she*. "Not little old I."

"I know your voice," said Cate.

"Sure do," said Jane. She fanned her fingers and twiddled them. The gesture was coquettish, and so utterly chilling. "See you, Mother."

And saying no more, she faded into a fly, then the imprint of a fly, then a buzz, and was gone.

***

John Isherwood awoke in bed.

It wasn't his.

His bed in Redspire was a miracle of linen. A woman came every other day to change the bedclothes. And there was an electric blanket, Corinthia maintaining one of those climates that can be kind or cruel at the drop of a hat.

These sheets he lay beneath and this pillowcase under his head were stiff and musty-smelling. They were not linen. John wasn't sure he knew what they were made of. He wasn't sure he wanted to know.

What had, to his dozy eyes, appeared to be a curtain around the bed was really a dense mesh of cobweb. Looking up at the canopy of this four-poster affair, he could see a woodcut. The woodcut showed women arising from the forest and feeding grapes to an emaciated man. Sexy little ladies they were too, in John's estimation. Garbed in weaves of green silk and with hair like autumnal leaves or honeycomb, they seemed to not simply be arriving from the forest but a kind of extension of it.

He lay looking at them. The emaciated man was contemptible in a slovenly, banal fashion, but the forest women were really something.

The next time you see a crow, or a robin, watch the fast *shuff-shuff* of its head on its neck, the quick little twists as it peers to and fro. John Isherwood's mind was like that. He educed where he was (the house of Eurydice), and why he was there (she wanted to see him). It followed that his devices had done their work well.

Turned on a spit inside him, pride and lust crisped, crisped and dripped beads of fatty self-satisfaction.

Over the past decade he had (cunningly, and oh-so-discreetly) collected samples from Evelyn Hughes. Inventing plausible circumstances to explain his possession of strange otherworldly phenomena (not hard invention, people were gullible as hell), he'd consulted with several peers from the university. As Hughes brought in more and more scientific talent, filling Corinthia with the best and brightest minds, John Isherwood widened the sphere of his consultancy. Once John would have pitied Hughes for being complicit in his daughter's downfall. Now, it was cobweb, easy to pull apart. Easy to dismiss.

Oh, but the girl. Evelyn was strange, and otherworldly.

Great minds had worked on her without her knowledge. They had seen what she was made of, under John Isherwood's careful guidance. In secret, he had spliced the findings of his peers with his own research on Eurydice. Of particular note were the synaptic pathways along which her thoughts traveled like, hmm, say electrical traffic and call it neurology. The process of merging something into that traffic, reintroducing (in other words) the divergent molecules, the truant protoplasm, *Evelyn*, reintroducing Evelyn into the stream that was Eurydice... that process had overtaken his life. His whole life.

Now, at long last, it had paid off.

His twitch-quick avian brain pecked the rest of him impatiently.

Eurydice wanted to see him.

Maybe even wanted him.

And judging by the stirring he felt, stiffer than the pillowcase, he wanted her too.

He got out of the bed and looked around the room. It was a cramped room, dusty and tenebrous dark but for a lampshade that gave off a nervous yellow light. John knew how it felt. He was always jittery before he saw her. His woman. His world.

There were boxes everywhere, the kind that delivery guys back home would get John to sign for. They were stacked at the foot of the bed, there under the shuttered window, cleaving to every wall, nestled and nooked, piled high before the only door in the room, jumping blue God, five hundred boxes, five hundred *at least*, and all left to accumulate patinas of mold and dust here in this forgotten cubby of a bedroom.

A peck of curiosity in his head.

John thought, *If the door is sealed off by boxes, who lit the lampshade?*

He looked at it. The lampshade offered no opinion. Hey man, I'm just here to shine. This stray bit of anthropomorphism quirked the good doctor's mouth in a wry smile.

You're not a project lead here, he chided himself. *Not a genius, not even a subversive intellect. Only a man emaciated. Let the forest and the goddess of the forest provide.*

His cock was very hard now.

He imagined it would soften by the time he moved the boxes and headed out into the house to find her, (a game of cat and mouse before love). It didn't soften. Not at all. If anything, his erection began to feel like a lump of stone nudging against his trousers. Slightly painful. Oh-so-pleasurable.

He went out of the room, that wry smile transformed into something leering and carnal.

He closed the door behind him, turned... and saw the same room.

The bed with the covers where he'd left them. The cobwebs where he'd parted them (he could still feel their sticky aftermath on the ball of his thumb). The shuttered windows. The lampshade. The boxes. John Isherwood's expression changed a third time. The leer between a frown. Puzzled. Checking behind him, he saw that without meaning to he'd cleared a few steps into the room. The boxes were there, packed up against the door. The door was sealed off and quite shut.

There was a sound.

John's neck jerked round so swiftly it upset his glasses on their perch.

Unsettled as they were, he could see no difference in the room, except for a smudge on the lampshade cover.

He pushed the glasses up his nose. The smudge was gone.

Nothing was out of place.

He went to the window and tried to open the shades. He found he couldn't. Something had glued them shut, or perhaps something in charge of this room and the house beyond simply preferred them not to open and so shut they remained.

What the fuck had the sound been, anyway?

John couldn't seem to place it. It had been just that tiny bit too faint to aptly recognize, just that tiny bit too loud for his ear to ignore. He unstacked a box blocking the door, thought he heard the sound again, looked, saw nothing, and went back to the pile.

By the time the stack was removed and the door stood open once more, he was grimy with sweat. It had been a long time since he'd had to do any heavy lifting, and the muscles in his legs and back were barking.

John peered out, careful not to actually cross the threshold of the door. The hallway beyond seemed ordinary enough. More woodcuts on a stairwell climbing up into the chest cavity of the house, and another descending toward who knew what, the bowel or...

What was he thinking about anatomy for?

It had nothing to do with his libido. His erection had withered almost instantly when he'd stepped back into the forgotten bedroom. It was... yes, it was the goddess at work in him. Grapes to the emaciated. Fleet footed fawners from the forest.

Cut the numbfuck poetry, his mind jabbed him with its sharp, shrewd beak. *Get out of here and find her.*

John Isherwood did just that. As a precaution, he kept his eyes wide open, in case the hall should vanish upon blinking. No stranger to mysticism and dream visitation was he. He also didn't bother to close the door behind him.

On the right the hall ended in a door fashioned with the likenesses of Ruthven, Skuggs, and Burrows. That door was ajar. On the left, a closed door. More boxes. Thin, fat, curved, straight, precariously piled, suitably fitted. *Place is full of them*, he marveled. *Full to bursting.* He wondered what on earth could be inside them all.

He chose the ascending flight of stairs. Shoe heels thumped the carpet as he hurried (his eyes were beginning to water). Near the top he tripped over a flat-topped box disguised as just another step. A grunt escaped him. John splayed his hands out, hoping to lessen the hurt of the fall, he shut his eyes, and...

Landed in musty-smelly bedclothes.

Knowing where he was at once, John vented a series of curses that would be more welcome at a bodega than a science lab. He swatted petulantly at the cobweb and rucked the sheets as he scrambled out. The room was the same. Boxes in front of the door, nice and neat. Panting, he snatched a look at the lampshade.

Ten flies crawled over its dusty green glass.

The sound he'd heard before. A buzz.

The urge to get out of the room—to find Eurydice and tell her that she was good, but maybe a little too good at pulling his chain before pulling his cord— came over him with nauseating force. His belly cramped. A sour-wine emulsion sense, maroon and deep, assured him that this was all according to plan.

The flies went still.

He could feel them looking at him.

John Isherwood gave them a grin that didn't touch his eyes.

All according to plan.

He would get to the boxes, unstack them, head out into the hall, and holler for Eurydice as loud as he could.

But isn't she here?

Isn't this her house?

He was no longer sure.

Also, in order to unstack the boxes, he'd have to turn his back on those flies.

So what? It might be... *No, it* must *be the shadow.*

The bug who had visited him that night twelve years ago.

Jane.

They were crawling again. The lampshade was covered in plump black bodies. Twenty now, possibly thirty. There had been fewer before.

(So what? So what?)

(Things are red all over)

(Flying fuck into a rolling)

(Plan, all according to sour grapes)

(Feel them inside)

(Eggs, they're like)

"Eggs. I can feel them hatching inside me."

That jolted the good doctor. It had sounded like his voice, and he'd felt his lips moving. Only he hadn't meant to say anything.

Irritation with his goddess overtook common sense. He made a dash for the lampshade, picked it up, and slung it at the wall. The bulb inside broke with a bottle-bank *crunch*. The flies scattered in a dark cloud. A hundred, five hundred, one for every box in the room, more and more and more every moment.

One of the flies landed on his earlobe.

Mimicking his mother's voice, it said, "Ready for my big fat terror-former, birdboy?"

Reduced to childhood by so accurate and freaky an imitation, John gave a bleat of fright and ran for the door. He kicked aside the boxes, yanked at them, sent them tumbling. On some level he was aware of the noises they made when they landed poorly (strings whammed out of tune, tinny sounds, thuds), but the strata of that awareness was almost completely focused on the idea OUT as in GETTING THE HELL OUT.

Enough room, he judged, enough now to squeeze through the door. John Isherwood dove for it.

Fingers in his hair, seizing and strong. Twirled like an unwilling ballerina. An elbow in his throat. He gagged. A fist in his gut. Breath gusting out. Spots in his vision.

On the floor he sprawled. He curled in on the pain, trying to will wind past his thin lips. Nimble hands maneuvered him, slapped his face when he resisted, spread his limbs wide as he gasped. The buzzing enclosed him, a cocoon of teeth-chattering dentist drills and spine-stiffening electric razors, even as the shadow straddled his chest, squeezing his aching stomach between her thighs.

"Why?" he rasped. "Eurydice said—"

"So many things about you," Jane said. "Well, one or two. Still counts. *Like being fucked by an ostrich,* I believe were her words. Novel." She tapped the tip of his penis with a fingernail. "But she'd rather you stuck your little head down there in the sand rather than her. Now, are you?"

"What?"

"*Are you, Johnny?*"

"What? Am I what?"

"*Are you ready?*"

"Ready?" He wet his dry lips with his tongue. She was staring down at him, her whole face conquered by a wild, energetic grin. *Grin back*, his avian mind fluttered. John grinned back. "Ready for what?"

She chuckled her spider-skitter chuckle. "Good question! Tell you what, I'll give you a guess."

John thought of the woodcut, the forest women bringing grapes to the emaciated man. And—absurd but true—he thought of Cate Jubilee raising her beer bottle to him. Toasting him.

"The fruits of my labors," he said.

"The fruits of your labors," Jane agreed. "Tremendous guess. Want to see what you win?"

The glittery boyish hope in his eyes grew uncertain as she laughed and laughed and laughed.

***

By her window overlooking The Willows housing estate in Glasnevin, Eurydice sat and thought about her life. It was raining in Dublin. Warm May rain. Slash, slash, slash, pitter patter puddle splatter. Electric scooters zooming under the murmur of the weather. Jogging man hunched under his umbrella. Two girls, one small the other older, leaning out of the top window in their house and fecking toys out into their damp and drowning garden. A dog begging to be let inside. Sky like an inverted ashtray full to the brim with crumbly gray. Raining in Dublin.

Dry in Hughes' world though.

Oh yes. Dry, dry, dry.

Eurydice drank a glass of cordial, enjoying the cool strawberry tang, the sweet hint of vanilla extract.

Had it been raining while he walked away from her?

She couldn't remember, but decided yeah, it must have been.

Sad weather reflects sad times, the mirror is the message is the medium is the... is the...

She was going to think about him. His name was about to appear in her head, and she mustn't let it.

You might be mistaken into thinking she meant Gormon Hughes, but you'd be wrong. The man she was thinking of—the one who'd walked away from her in the rain, or in the sunshine, or in the dark, or in the dry—*that* was the guy whose name she could not bear.

Thankfully, mercifully, she was prepared.

She put the cordial down on her windowsill, reached under her chair, and retrieved a fifteenth-century mandolin. It was ornate, decorated, in mint condition, and tuned to perfection. Possibly worth a great deal of money, but more likely to be deemed priceless by people with degrees that they regretted getting.

With gusto and grace, Eurydice took a butcher knife from her gown and began to saw at the strings. There was a weird, nasty purring sound, but that didn't last long. The shriek those poor strings made as they were ripped apart would have been familiar to Evelyn Hughes, were she still around to hear them.

Eurydice held the mandolin at arm's length. The strings curled and bobbed like the whiskers of some profane catfish. She tossed the instrument over her shoulder, closing her eyes so as to better savor the lumpy thumps of carved wood striking the floor.

She opened her eyes, retrieved her cordial, took a sip.

She felt much improved. No names sneaking up the stem of her brain. No hint of such a name at all.

Eurydice looked out her window. It was raining in Dublin.

Somewhere in the house, John Isherwood was screaming.

That had been going on for a while.

Sometimes it petered out. Moans and whimpers had their time in the spotlight. Invariably they started up again, those long, loud screams.

Eurydice sighed happily. It really was wonderful to have her sister back where she belonged.

Act Six

Golden Slumbers

Chapter Fifteen

In Corinth City, for the first time in twelve years, which seemed unaccountably too short a while for people's liking, the flies were buzzing again. June was just around the bend and it was hot. The flies, and the woman at the epicenter of their filthy cloud, found that grimy slimy heat refreshing. She was so used to this world's December chill, after all.

Jane, powerful and wizened and not sane (and back in business, hoh yes, hoh yes, BACK IN THE GAME), grinned a huge grin. For every tooth, a termite. For every gum, a gnat. Tiny millipedes splintered her eyeballs like blood vessels.

Oh, a little of her had to remain with Eurydice, of course. There was work to do. Oodles of work now the world had regained her shadow.

But in exchange, not a little but rather a lottle of Jane would be allowed to play.

The doctor had been a nice aperitif, one she'd been pleased to take her time in enjoying to the fullest.

What this girl wants now, she thought, rather giddily. *What this girl absolutely craves is her supper.*

***

The ants went marching, two trillion by two trillion, hurrah, hurrah.

The flies buzzed in an orchestra, hurrah, hurrah.

The fleas went jump, and the roaches ran, mole bugs burrowed, and beetles swam.

And they all went marching, insects upon parade!

(*Where...*)

Up and down each hill of thought, hurrah, hurrah.

Through dells and vales of misbegot, hurrah, hurrah.

The maggots squirmed, and the bees bobbed smart, caterpillars crawl, and dragonflies dart.

And they all went marching,

(*Where am I?*)

insects on parade!

They all of them are in the mood, hurrah, hurrah.

In the mood for scrumptious food, hurrah, hurrah.

(*Oh God, oh Daddy Daddy get me out of here*)

They bite and tear and gnash and munch.

They eat your happiness for lunch.

And they all went marching, insects upon parade!

Unnoticed by the heaving mass of bugs, a mass that went from here to there, far as the mind can picture, a moth stopped flapping to the rhythm of the march. It freed itself, flying hell-for-leather, fast as its wings would go.

In a tiny voice drowned out by the song of the insect parade, the moth said, "Have to get away. I've got to, I've just got to get away from here."

The moth's wings were white as snow. As it increased the distance between itself and the parade, it became clear that by any ordinary standard it was a very large moth.

Farther it fluttered. Farther. Now farther still, beyond the pale rim of the bug realm, a horizon that expanded and narrowed, expanded and narrowed, a breath apparatus, a lifeline. Soon, a completely colorless country surrounded the moth, a flat gray plate of a place. The moth made good its landing.

Those snowy wings gave a shiver, and it was clear the moth could remember the trapped, claustrophobic sensations it had felt as it struggled to leave behind the insect parade. It was safe now. Or was it?

The moth stilled. It transformed.

The gray place took no notice.

Evelyn Hughes looked around. To her credit, she didn't panic. There was a moment of overwhelming loneliness, a few squeaks and moans muffled by her palms, but that was all.

She took stock. Nothing to see, very little clues on offer. Still she kept her head, and... she had it.

My head.

My old head and... Jane's new one.

One and the same, and yet simultaneously so completely different.

That's where she was. She was in Jane's head.

What am I going to do?

For a span of time (how much? Impossible to gauge in that place) the matter was insoluble. She decanted her intelligence over it and not a drop of cleverness got through. It defied her. Denied her. Mocked her. But the calmer she forced herself to be, the more it seemed she would eventually muddle through. Her father had, for the inaugural performance of the resurrected Corinth City theatre, starred in a production of Beeflet. Evelyn had been too young to understand it. There was this man who couldn't make his mind up about anything, and poison dripped into ears, and people hiding in curtains and being stabbed, and lots of talking about what she sensed instinctively to be important somehow. It was brilliant. After, in the car home, she'd asked the star of the evening how he remembered all his lines.

"There were lots!" she said.

"Yes, there were lots. Well, you'll find it easy to remember things, if you take after me," said her father. "You could be on that stage someday."

"Could I?"

"If you like."

"Wow! But... Daddy, what if something goes wrong?"

"You must improvise."

"What's improvise?"

"Improvising is going on," he explained. "You are part of the show, and the show must go on. No matter what."

"I see." She'd twiddled her feet. "Daddy?"

"Yes?"

"How?"

He'd simply grinned at her, and suddenly learning about improvising didn't matter because there in the car next to her was the most beautiful person in the world. She'd told him so. And he'd looked around frantically. What was it? Her father said he was searching for the mirror. The one she must be looking in. For she was the beautiful one, not he.

In the gray place, Evelyn grinned. It didn't touch her eyes, but it did remind her that grinning was possible, even here. The muscles worked. As did the muscle between her ears. Instead of concentrating she allowed her brain to explore as it would.

Before long (and this time she really could tell it had only been a short while), she had an idea.

This was Jane's head, true. But remove someone from their home, and a little of them remains. A crumb or two of personality. Hadn't Evelyn always loved insects? Yes, and she still did! That had Jane written all over it.

Following that logic, it stood to reason that a little of Evelyn lingered. She hoped it was a useful part of her, one recently constructed. Her idea relied upon that being the case.

She postulated that running around looking for that part of her would be a waste of valuable time. Better to think her way there. Evelyn closed her eyes, emptied herself clear, and when she was ready, she thought these words: *In case of Eurydice coming into my head, I built a wall. It's green. There's red moss.*

She opened her eyes.

Nothing had changed.

Again, nothing extravagant rose in her, neither disappointment nor fear. Evelyn merely sighed.

Then, against all odds, she grinned. This one did touch her eyes, which were dark and lovely and determined.

"How do you get to The Hippodrome? Practice, practice, practice."

She screwed her eyes shut for a second time, hoping against hope that this time it would work.

***

It came to pass, on the last day of May, which was in fact Cate Jubilee's birthday, in a quiet, crowded fortress courtyard, keeping with the custom of Daethumberland, the scarlet company gave Eilandri Titansgrave's mortal remains to the pyre.

Cate offered her best eulogy. It wasn't enough.

Eilandri was not merely a giant in stature. For a woman who through the intervention of surgery could not speak, she had nevertheless told many soldiers a great deal about themselves. She was known to write (and imposing upon Cate as an orator, an act that parroted her funeral so sadly, give voice to) the most lewd and naughty jokes at any feast. In combination with the seriousness of her countenance upon their delivery, invariably these jokes set the troops to laughing until they could laugh no more. More tellingly still, in instances of battlefield terror when the blood and mud and shit corrugated the souls of weary men and women, almost everyone who had joined up in the last decade had snuck a glance about. Just in case Eilandri Titansgrave were nearby, you understand. Spy her, and immutably they would feel fortified as if they'd drunk a tonic. Suddenly the blood and mud and shit became bearable. They could fight on. The giant was there. Lives, even small ones, were big in her lavender-eyed estimation. Cate had enjoyed a similar role as a kind of emblem. Cate was a red banner, Eilandri pale. With her story at an end, one fold of inspiring fabric was tucked away that May day among the logs, the smoke going up into the pitiless afternoon, and there was a subtraction in every heart and mind. One less warden against terror in a terrible war. The titan was at long last in her grave.

Afterward, when they were alone, Cate told Hughes that she knew how he felt when he believed Hector was dead.

"I can't go to pieces. Our baby girl is... I don't know. Engulfed? Taken over? Shit. It's ludicrous to even... We're going to have to get her back." She looked at him with red-rimmed eyes. Her color was high, her lips chapped, her whole being calling out for something he couldn't give her. "I don't know how, but we have to."

He vowed they would. Later he'd have his doubts, but in that moment, loving Cate fiercely, he meant it.

"Hughes, I'm so low. I didn't think I could get like this again after the baby."

Hughes did not know which of their children she referred to; the one who'd turned magically to glass, or the one who turned their chaotic lives into an orderly art called parenthood.

"I'm here," was all he could say.

"Is there water?"

He got her some. She drained the whole glass. For a second he thought she might fling it at a wall, but she put it on the floor almost daintily, as though it were as fragile as both of their frayed nerves.

"Give me something to do," she begged him. "I think I could be all right if I were busy. I can't focus enough to give myself... to... you know?"

"I know. The scouting parties you sent out before I arrived. When are they scheduled to return?"

"Nnnnext week, I think."

"Plenty of time. Okay. The Bloodwood was brutal and costly for the enemy, but while our own losses were comparatively minimal, the soldiers were expecting a final, you know, a final victory that day. John's betrayal, Jane's return, even Eilandri's death... these disasters look monumental to you and I. I can tell you for a fact that when it comes to the scales within the average troop's heart, all three of those monumental things are outweighed by the simple ache for home. Homesickness doesn't cover it. These people are homestarved. Don't get me wrong, the disasters are disastrous. They know that. But rather than bother them in a constellation, they're contributing to and, I reckon, worsening that homestarved sentiment. If I were you... Yeah, in fact only you *can* do this. You're the only person equipped *to* do it. I'd use this week before the scouts return with news of our enemy to soothe that ache. Make our people angry as hell, if it can be directed. Make them aware of the fact there *will not be a home to return to* if we fail. Shore them up, Cate. Kindle cold ashes. Flex your famous charm. Listen. Talk. Listen some more for good measure. In short, do what you do best." He pulled her close and kissed the crown of her head. "President's orders."

"It sounds more like your bailiwick."

"Our roles are going to reverse. You're going to do the interpersonal stuff and I'm going to get my hands callused with military command. At least for a short while."

"You think that's best?"

"Hector and Cassandra haven't let my blade dull. They've kept me keen."

"No, you think it's best that... You're the one with the Performance, Hughes. Eloquence comes naturally to you."

"Cate, these are soldiers. Whose hand would they rather on their shoulder? A politician they've never even seen or a general whom they see every day and whom they adore because she inspires them with every scrap of courage they never dreamed they could muster?"

She sniffled, then smiled at him. A rueful smile, but earnest nonetheless. "Fair enough, you silver-tongued dickhead."

"It wags for you, beloved."

"Your tongue or..."

"Ah. Why not both?"

"Goofball. President's orders? Get a grip."

"You love it."

"I do. God help me, I do."

"We couldn't help Eilandri. I wish we could've, but... let's save our girl."

Cate sobered at once. She nodded. "Let's."

***

Hereunto a skein of yarn connecting dream to dream came a figure on a quest. Before her, unseen, was an impediment.

"Bugger."

Desdemona Cauldronpot toppled.

Her string of profanity clipped itself short when she recalled her spiritual imperative, namely *oneness*. She gathered herself and spared a look of cosmic conviviality for the blighting little tit that tripped her.

It was a log. A cut log of wood.

She studied the hillock nearby (there were endless rows of them, perfect green hills under a perfect blue sky) and gave the log an experimental roll between her hands. Upon her arms her bangles *ting-a-linged*.

She set off up the slope. At the top she found a house bereft of logic, for the greater part of its red-bricked body stood atop a thin chimney spewing smoke. The smoke smelled wonderful, that enticing, earthy perfume that defies cold and welcomes warmth, and which you yourself may have come across if you've been strolling near a house burning wood kept in and out of the rain for a year or two. In the yard fronting the odd house was a mole. With a chop of his axe he hewed a felled tree into halves, then quarters, and finally eighths of log-length. In fact, Desdemona heard the mole before she saw him.

"Dear oh dear. It hasn't been this bad since that dark-haired fellow came," he complained morosely. "Like a bolt of lightning from the ball of my foot to my lower back, and not sparing my bottom any of the grief."

Thwack, went the axe.

"Agh! Dear oh dearie me!"

"Good morning!" cried Desdemona.

Mole was not astonished to be hailed from out of the green-blue emptiness of day. His pink snout twitched, and his pink fingers fluttered on the handle of the axe. He regarded Desdemona with his shrewd little squinters. "I should say it is not a good morning, Desdemona Cauldronpot."

"You've heard of me? How?"

"Here and there. Deosil and widdershins." *Thwack.* "Now, kindly leave me to make the best of this inarguably bad morning."

"Aren't you curious as to why I've come?"

"If tales of you are true, you probably hope that I'll unlock some sort of mystic nirvana for you." *Thwack.* "Which I won't. Reason one being my sciatica is a beast, and reason two being because I don't know mystic nirvana from a pot of marmalade."

"Please, allow me."

Mole paused. "Pardon?"

Desdemona held out her hand. He considered that hand. He put the axe in it. She chopped some wood.

"What's it all for?" she wondered, tipping her head at the log pile.

"The fire in my house," replied Mole. "If I can send enough smoke into the blue sky, I might trick it into thinking it ought to be full of clouds. My sciatica is a beast in this weather. I need nice chilly rains to tame it!"

"That's unlike any sciatica I've ever heard of."

"A right beast, so it is."

"I'll bet." With a heave of her not unmuscular shoulders (travel offers plenty of opportunity for exercise), she buried the axe in the stump that served for a chopping block. "Many hands, light work, eh?"

"Betimes," said Mole, noncommittally. "Company courts trouble."

"Well, trouble is what I'm about, Mr. Mole. It is exactly what I'm about. And I need your help if there's to be a solution, or an antidote to that trouble, so to speak."

Mole reaffixed his waistcoat, checking the buttons, and nosing pinkly at their golden buttonish sheen. "I wish you well, Desdemona Cauldronpot, but you know as well as I do that I'm no good to anyone with my back in such widdlingly poor condition. What could this task of yours be, that you'd even think to posit its endeavor toward this old mole?"

She told him.

"Give me the axe," said Mole. "We'd best hurry."

As they went up one hillock and down another, and so forth, Mole took an improbably large jar of liniment jelly from his waistcoat. He applied a generous dollop to the lumbar region of his back.

"Dear oh dearie me," he groused, but they made good time and arrived at a door set into the grassy summit of a hillock. They went in. Mole closed the door after them. Down a stair they went, deep under the hill. The stair was made of red bricks, and from the red bricks issued a sweet-smelling smoke.

"Who first?" said Desdemona.

"Badger," answered Mole. "He should be in high health and fine fettle this time of year. The other fellow... Well, we'll have to see about him when the time comes."

Desdemona accepted that without fuss. After a while her curiosity got the better of her.

"Are we walking on your chimney? Red brick? Smoke? It seems like we're walking on stairs made of your chimney."

"Here we are," said Mole.

There was a door.

Passing through it, their shoes splodged in a cream-white substance that was globulous and agglutinated on top and hard as wood underneath.

"Why, it's wax!" cried Desdemona. "And are those trees?"

They were indeed. Crooked-limbed trees totally devoid of leaves. But only the tops rose out of the wax. As for the trunks and roots, they were completely immersed in the wax. Here and there, she could see apples of red and green dangling from a few of the otherwise bare branches.

"Mole!" It was Badger. He emerged from the goo, folding away a sizeable snorkel. "How are you, old chap? Sorry for the mess. Whole place has-has-has rather gone to hell in a crockery drawer, don't you know?"

Mole gave the waxy wasteland a critical look. "You've really let it build up, Badger."

"Don't be too cross with me, Mole. The trouble is... the trouble is, old chap, I can't seem to find the plug."

"The plug?" said Desdemona.

"Yes, yes indeed. The plug to let all this ah..." Badger gestured to the wax. "To let all this flush away. It's a very advanced plug, mind you. Got heating thingy... mechanisms. Heats it all up, melts it you might say, and Bobbie's your aunt, it all drains and the trees and I have a bit of breathing room. Incidentally, hello Desdemona."

"You know me as well?"

"Words, like lollipops, get around."

"Oh!"

"We really ought to keep moving," said Mole.

"Moving?" Badger wiped a gobbet of wax from under his chin. "Moving you say?"

"We really must have your assistance in a most urgent matter," Desdemona implored him.

"Oh no. No, I can't possibly go. If I leave this wax to build up any more, I shall need to root out my diving suit and the damn thing chafes like hell in a wicker chair. No," said Badger crisply, "no I really can't see my way to going anywhere."

Desdemona told him about the urgent matter.

"I'll need my stilts," said Badger. "Hold here a moment."

When he'd resurfaced from burrowing deep into the wax and fitted his feet into his walking stilts, they followed Badger to another door, this one made from apples and standing just above the wax as though victim of a levitation contract.

Desdemona touched a finger to one glossy red apple. It was icy cold, and her nail produced a *tick-tick* noise upon it.

"Tin," explained Badger. He opened the door. "After you, old chap. How's the back?"

"Slants and slights," said Mole.

"Drat."

"Yes."

"I wonder could it be related to..."

"Almost unquestionably."

"We'd better get a move on, in that case."

Desdemona was too busy thinking about their last port of call, the one Mole dubbed "the other fellow." She had heard stories. Word, like a lollipop, got around. Though, come to think about it, she had never shared a lollipop in her life. Perhaps the saying was meant to imply that too many lollipops made you round?

This time the stairs were made of red and green tin. They descended a long way. The dark was lit by something inexplicable, the invisible stage lamps of dreams. No talk between them.

Through the final door awaiting them at the bottom of the stair, they found themselves in a watercolor hall, everything diffuse and elongated as if by strokes of a brush. The hearth was cold. The downy carpet showed a scene of murder, many armies engaged in bloodshed upon a hill dyed red with gore, and they could make it out only because of the gassy light filtering through the drawn curtains of that vile hall.

"He's usually here," said Badger. His stilts made muffled thumps on the carpet. "Here in front of the roaring fire. But the stone is cool to the touch. Where could he be?"

Almost psychically responsive, a tremendous croaking cough came from somewhere nearby.

Desdemona saw her companions exchange a look. They headed toward the sound.

They found the one they were looking for in a bedchamber of despicable decoration: bouquets of fungus, fat sickly flowers, candles of hardened mucus, fixtures carved to look like weapons or the dreadful work of weapons, and as for the bed and its occupant, well, they were most despicable of all. Under the canopy of milkweed, juncus, and bladderwort lay Toad.

He did not look well. His breathing had a damp, rattling quality.

Whether the room smelled abysmally of stomach acid and swamp mug because of Toad or because of his taste in accoutrements, Desdemona could not tell.

"Good morning, Toad," said Badger brightly. "You look a tad worse for wear, old bean."

"Peaky," said Mole. "Very peaky."

Toad blinked at them, one eye slower than the other.

"What the blue blazes are you doing here?" he said with weak yet very puffy indignation. "How many times do I have to tell you two oafs? If I want to see you, I shall pay you a visit or send a telegram inviting you to enjoy my..." He coughed, coughed, coughed, wet as a rainstorm. "My gracious hospitality. Not that either of you pillocks deserve it."

"There are extenuating circumstances," said Mole.

"Extenuating... *extenuating circumstances?*" Toad's throat swelled like a balloon and deflated. His eyes bulged yellowly. "*Brrrrrhuh.* I'll be the judge of that, Mole! The judge and very likely the jury and executioner, you great squinting fool. Can't you see I have an ague? Can't you hear it, or are you deaf as well as damn well bat-blind? And who is this third fool you bring into my home without invitation, this girl gawping at me as though she were lobotomized?"

"Desdemona Cauldronpot," she said. "I take it you have not heard of me."

"Certainly not. I am not in the..." Cough, cough, dribble. He didn't wipe the dribble as it rolled thickly over his warts. "Not in the habit of familiarizing myself with every tart in the sweetshop."

"I happen," she said, "to be a very well-known facilitator of the occult."

"The moment... the instant I begin to give a shit, I shall let you know." Toad laughed, coughed, and laughed some more. "The occult. Crystal balls mooned over and palms crossed. I shall take my ague over derangement of the spirit any day or night!"

Old muscles stirred in Desdemona, muscles of primness, muscles that would rise up in defense of herself and the macabre arts and crash down upon the heads of naysayers, preferably with tomes heavy with secrets and, of course, heavy with pages too.

She restrained herself, just. She reached for oneness. Inner peace slammed through her like a fishhook through a particularly enlightened worm.

She smiled beatifically. "We shall have time to discuss your beliefs, and mine, on the way."

Toad blinked at Mole and Badger again. "What is this jezebel bumbling on about?"

"We're needed, old bean."

"A job. An important job that needs doing."

Again the bulge of the chrysoberyl-yellow eyes. "*Brrrrrrhuh.* A job? Don't be absurd. I have an ague. Can't you hear it? My very breath sounds like a bog's belly winding up to a fabulous fart! I am bloated with coughs. No, I must sleep, recover, get back to one-hundred-and-ten-percent! And you must truss yourselves up with goodbyes because I'll speak no more to you."

"Won't you hear the nature of the quest?" said Mole.

"I won't hear a word," Toad said, and he ribbuted hatefully. "Not a rudely speckled word, mark you."

Desdemona told him anyway.

Toad blinked at her.

"Truly?" he said.

She nodded.

Toad mopped the spit from her immense and wart-clogged chin. "Mole, fetch my uniform. Badger, my sword."

"What about your ague?" said Badger. "Will you be able to manage?"

"Hang my ague! *Brrrrrhuh.* Some things are more important."

Desdemona Cauldronpot made a pleased little sound. "And with that, we are four. It's a long journey from here." A sudden doubt tickled her brow into furrowing. "I only hope we're not too late."

***

So much occurs to you when someone wakes you in the dark. Especially if you're a parent. When more and more people flock to a city it grows to accommodate their humdrum sanity, their unique madness. Creek beds swell and bust their banks when the rains come. Similarly, when you become a parent, your anxiety grows to encompass a whole other person. In times of trouble, times of strife, times of shadow in your life, you must sleep because not sleeping is impossible. But sleeping seems impossible too. And then you do, you slip away to sleep in spite of everything.

Then your lover wakes you in the dark and that anxiousness pierces your grogginess. You're wide awake. Almost instantly the questions come.

Are we safe?

Are they safe?

Who?

The children, your mind babbles. The kids.

Are the kids safe?

Their daughter was not safe, and one night, late in the first week of June, Hughes touched Cate's anxiety-riddled face after he woke her and told her everything was okay. He was sorry. He needed to ask her something.

"Ask me, Puppy."

"Cate." He hesitated. "Do you remember the name of Ernie Wilks' dog?"

"Ern... What?"

"You remember my old neighbor Ernie?"

"Think so."

"What was his dog's name?"

Cate didn't ask him why he wanted to know. She frowned thoughtfully, her eyes vacating the premises of the present, moving back and back, finding the slobbery, stinky dog. Good old Cate. The woman was a storm, but there was bliss and quiet genius in the eye of her hurricane.

I love you, he thought. *I love you so much and I will never stop. I wouldn't know how.*

Cate returned, yawned against the back of her hand, and said, "Boo something?"

"Boochums!"

"You forgot?"

"Yeah."

She gave him a muzzy smile. With no imminent danger, drowsiness had stolen over her. "Need to kiss you more."

"Sorry?"

Cate turned over. "So you'll forget you're president," she murmured. "Post war plan. Save our girl. Win the war. Then kiss you better. More."

"Kiss me?"

She held up a clarifying finger. "On the face. And pizza."

"Eat pizza or kiss it?"

"Mm."

"Ahhhm. Well," he said. "If you'd like."

Sleepy sounds drifted from her side of the bed. Hughes looked at her bare, tattooed shoulder go up and down with her breath. A moment later he heard snores.

"Right," he said.

Careful not to disturb her he slipped out from under the covers and padded out of the room.

Wrapped up warm, he stepped onto the balcony of the Betty. Below him the fortress was cloaked, gloved, socked and shoed in mist, and a bitter cold mist at that. Hughes could pick out spots of red-orange light below, sort of blushing warmly in the pale face of the fog. *Windows*, he thought. *Betty's eyes*. Not much to see, of course. Eurydice had blinded the scarlet army, set them to fumbling over themselves.

He thought about John then. Hughes hadn't enjoyed much free time to ponder the good (traitorous bastard) doctor, but he did now, and his thoughts were not kind. The terraformers had done their duty, resurrecting Jane and killing Cate's hopes of triumph.

John. If you're still alive, which I highly doubt, but if you are... heaven help you. You'll need God to intervene on your behalf. You shook my daughter's hand. Looked her in the eye. Smiled at her. How long had you planned it? Did you look at her and see Jane? How long? To what end? God help you. I won't.

It was easier to think about John Isherwood. Stoking that anger kept his mind off Evelyn. And off the... the other thing.

Boochums. Unusual name. Memorable, or so you'd think. Boochums. Ernie used to call him the Farting Wonder. Boochums-Boo-Boo-Boochums.

Could Hughes picture him? Yes.

Hear his merry, throaty barks? Yeah.

Smell his pungent smell? Absolutely.

He'd been having a vivid dream. In the dream Ernie cackled his witchy cackle, and his dog was just out of the bath, and it was Hughes' turn to use the bath. He couldn't use Sheila Kofatch's. She'd been turned into a bug and crushed, and her bath was a seethe of hornets bubbling with yellow beetles. So he had to use Ernie's, though after the dog, naturally, etiquette demanded no less in the weird logic of dreams, and the dog's tongue lolled pinkly, and his fur was dark and dripping, and his big doggie eyes looked at Hughes with a trust that said, "You know my name, don't you?"

"I do," Hughes replied. Only he didn't.

He'd forgotten the dog's name.

"Boochums," he grumbled on the misty balcony. "Boochums. I've got it now."

Cool, clammy hands of mist explored his skin. They seemed to peruse the railing Hughes was leaning his hip against and to tap their ghostly fingertips and palms against the closed door behind him.

Maybe in mimicry of those windows glowing below him, or perhaps because he was stretched on the rack of stress and being pulled every which way, Hughes took out his cigarette lighter, stopping short of retrieving an actual smoke by sheer force of will.

He lifted the casing lid and rolled the spark wheel under the ball of his thumb. Complex machinery couldn't function in Eurydice. The place was too turbulent for that, but simple mechanisms worked.

A tiny knife of fire snicked out.

The small sound suggested Miss Gleam's magic scissors.

Snicker-snick.

It had been a long time since his mind had found her.

The little fire danced, the mist drawn to it like some dumb white moth.

There had been a white moth. When? Oh yes. The one in Daethumberland. The one Evelyn called as the crossbow twanged and the bolt sailed toward her. Her peril had beckoned the moth then, just as it beckoned her father now. Beckoned him away from his city and into the dungeon dimension, the ever-changing world, the mad queendom Eurydice.

Flicker-shiver, went the little lighter fire. Soft wind. Caressing wind. Somewhere in the pale night, a hacking cough, then nothing.

Hughes looked out into the mist with a desperation, as though he wanted to spool it up and... he didn't know... cure it somehow. Cure was the wrong word. Wrong, shit, he was wrong about so much. Iphigenia seemed to believe he was fabulously right, fabulously suited to meet trouble of every stripe, but she was sick. She needed him. Hell, what was he doing thinking of disease and recovery?

Clotted and blind and hazy. *I'm tired and I couldn't remember the dog's name.*

"Boochums," he said, and smothered in the mist and couched in his expressive voice that jolly name sounded like an ode to despair.

The desire to go back inside and curl up with Cate rose in him. It was very strong.

He closed the lighter, but a restless impulse made him *snick* it open again.

Close. *Snick.*

Some part of him resented Cate her ability to go so far into motherly concern that she came out the other side, practical and staunch. She could sleep deeply and well because her daughter was in danger and Cate needed to be at her best if they were going to save her. Hughes boxed that resentment away and stored it somewhere to be destroyed. He had cast Cate in tones of ugly contempt once, at the outset of their love when she made the whole exercise dependent on his being more open and honest with her. Never again. She deserved his love and his love was what she would get. Especially now. Now more than ever.

Close. *Snick.*

He'd stay out here awhile. Cate would sleep for both of them.

Close. *Snick.*

Healthy exercise, that ought to tire him out.

A wry smile twisted his lips. Jumping jacks on the balcony, eh?

Spring-Heeled jumping jacks.

The smile fell like a snow-frozen bird.

Mental exercise might have to suffice. How far back to go? The day he'd just had seemed a worthy subject of scrutiny. A day of unexpected allies who brought strange promises. Promises that if they were true, they could determine the outcome of the war.

Close. *Snick.*

That sounded good. A jog up the lane of recent memory.

Close.

Just what the doctor ordered.

Snick.

The little fire danced upon a stage of steel.

Hughes closed his eyes and remembered.

***

Earlier that same day, at eight minutes past eight on the dot, the Beldame arrived in Cate's audience chamber.

Cate kept the place austere, and the only decoration was a tinge of color to the window, a pigment of daffodil-yellow tempered into the glass. By that charming light Hughes took in the Beldame as she bent her body so as not to scrape her hooded head on the door frame. It really was a full body enterprise, that bend. Hughes did not think a spine ought to move like that, and he resolved to look askance when she made her way out so as not to watch that movement again. The Beldame was clad in ragged robes. She was thin to the point of emaciation. In her hood her face was smooth as cut marble and unnaturally long. The effect might have been equine, but Hughes found himself thinking instead of a painting he'd seen hung upon the wall of a gallery, a pale, stretched, inhuman face seized forever in a howl that would never end. Staccato and jagged, the Beldame's movements were also like a painting come to life, as though she were quite uncertain as to how to move at all. *But is it the legs under the robe or where the legs are, i.e. here?* Hughes thought it might be the latter. He wondered at the source of such a discomfort, but wonder was all he could do. Isaac Lawless and the rest of the cartographers had never even heard of a Beldame.

"Welcome," he said. "I'm Gormon Hughes. This is Cate Jubilee."

"I am Beldame."

Hughes and Cate had no need of an understanding glance. Their brains sparked along the same current. If the Beldames used no names, instead identifying with their aggregate, so be it.

So without skipping a beat, Cate said, "Would you like a cup of tea? Something stronger? I have vodka from the vault of Lord Burrows himself."

Hughes could not help detecting a teensy bit of unconscious smugness in Cate's tone. Raiding Burrows' dark distilleries several years ago was still a feather in her veritable cap.

"No," said the Beldame. "We are sustained by the bells."

"How nice," said Cate. "Please make yourself comfortable."

"I will be," replied the Beldame, "when I leave."

Not, in Hughes' informed opinion, an encouraging start to negotiations.

Directness, then. Blunt and to the point, to the whole *sword*.

Hughes, positioned by the desk Cate was seated at, picked an object off the mahogany and held it up. Made of a tin-gray metal it weighed surprisingly little and looked to his eye like a cross between a bird and a bug. This, Isaac had copped at once. *That's a flitter,* he'd marveled. *That's how they talk to each other. Skuggs and Burrows and them. Long distance, like. It's their telephone.*

Hughes joggled the flitter in his palm. "Is what you said in this true?" he asked the Beldame.

She inclined her head, the folds of her hood hiding that stretched face for a moment. "Yes. We know Eurydice's weakness. We have been privy to it since the installation of the bell beneath our silver roof at the Rotunda of the Bell Sir. Strike that weakness, and she will be at your mercy."

"Why come to us now?" Cate said. "When we're on the backfoot and not leagues ahead? You've a funny sense of timing, as well as picking sides."

"Our Bell Sir wishes us to join you. He has tasted of the wind. It blows hard for you today, cumbersome and cruel. But the breezes are fickle and will bluster in your favor before long." The Beldame stepped toward him. Hughes kept himself calm and still as she plucked the flitter from his palm. She slid a grotesquely slender finger along it. The flitter came to life and flew into the sleeve of her robe. "When the prevailing wind rushes scarlet, we wish our colors to be consummate with yours."

"Excuse our ignorance, Beldame," said Cate. "Who is Bell Sir?"

The Beldame seemed to consider the question. "When you are thankful for all the good things in your life, whom do you thank?"

"God," said Cate. "In my way. I suppose. Why?"

"Death is our God. Lucy Nowhere, blessed be Her name. The Bell Sir is Her one and only angel."

Cate sat forward. "An angel with a purpose?"

"Yes."

"What purpose? If your colors run scarlet, we'd like to know the shades your dye can run."

The Beldame made no reply.

Cate's eyes glittered craftily. "You know who John Isherwood is?"

"Yes."

"Then you understand why I'm asking."

"Yes."

"Answer me."

The Beldame raised a gangling arm. She pointed at the window.

"The flies are buzzing. Eurydice's shadow runs amok. Your daughter cannot exist while Jane does. We would give her back to you."

Hughes grinned nastily. "You must think we're very new to this. We're keen on an alliance, true. But trust is not akin to a breeze. Think of it as... credit. And tenuous trust is poor currency in this room. We need you, and I think you need us even more. Why? Consider your next words carefully. What is the agenda of your Bell Sir? What does he want?"

There was a pause.

Then, reluctantly, the Beldame spoke.

"When the last autumn comes, as decreed by Death, the Bell Sir will ring our most sacred bell. All life will end."

"That doesn't make sense. What would Death do?" Cate wondered.

Like her voice, the Beldame's face was remarkably inexpressive. When Cate asked what Death would do in the absence of life, Hughes saw a mote of pity wrinkle the Beldame's smooth brow. "She would rest."

Cate opened her mouth, then seemed to reconsider. She looked at Hughes. He could only shrug.

"And your Bell Sir believes that forming an alliance with us will bring you one pace closer to that apocalypse?" he asked.

The Beldame nodded.

"How?"

"You will kill this world. We will speed along your success. In return, we shall require sanctuary."

"In our world?"

"Yes. You will bring our Rotunda there. You will not persecute us. You will help us to ensure that when the time comes, the final bell will ring."

She held a hand up as they made to protest.

"We do not expect the last autumn for many centuries yet. Think of it as... credit." And now Hughes heard the most miniscule iota of amusement in her voice. "A bill that you yourself will not have to pay. A receipt for destiny. For the tolling of the bell is inevitable. We can assure you of that."

Cate touched the red bells tattooed at her throat. Hughes wasn't sure she noticed she was doing it. His wife peered narrowly at the rickety figure looming in the yellow light. "Can you guarantee Evelyn's safety?"

Another hood-rustling nod.

"How?"

"The same way you can guarantee that you will keep your end of the bargain. Trust."

Cate's gaze narrowed further. "Go on then. Eurydice's weakness."

"I think not. An agreement outside the Rotunda would be profane. We must forge a pact there. It will be blessed by the Bell Sir. And for that, we must have Frank Gallant."

"Frank?" This from Hughes. "What's he got to do with it?"

"His mothers were our sworn enemies. An arrangement with him at the core would be propitious."

"There's something more."

"You are percipient," she told him without a hint of admiration. "Yes. There must be a ritual of strings and bell rings. The Bell Sir knows that our two forces cannot align without a holy link. We are a holy sisterhood, you see. Any improper accord would undoubtedly be punished by God, which spells suffering for all. So there must be a fitting bridge between the Scarlet Citadel and the Beldames, and who better than Frank who has one foot in Eurydice and one foot in your world?"

"I'll send for him immediately." Hughes was only irritated that he hadn't brought Frank with him to Eurydice. It had seemed prudent to leave him in Corinth, which would feel the absence of its president like a thorn under the fingernail. Oh well. No use lamenting spilled milk, or unsummoned dream warriors. "Will you stay here in the meantime and escort us to your Rotunda when the time comes?"

"Impossible," said the Beldame. "You are not ordained to enter. Only Frank is permitted to set foot in the Rotunda."

"Can't be helped."

"Can't be," Cate echoed her husband. "Our trust is, of course, an amazing, brand-spankingly-shiny and delightfully firm variety of trust as we've established. But it's too new to put Frank at risk."

"He will come alone, or we shall make efforts to contact other candidates," the Beldame told them. "Yours is not the only world we might choose for our exodus. I bid you farewell now. Think on our offer of aid."

Startled, Hughes gave a placative gesture. "Wait a moment—"

"Think on your daughter, lost as a lamb in the infected, infested woods that is Jane."

"Hold on, just hold on a—"

The Beldame was making good her exit. Her voice rode over Hughes' own. "Our sympathies for your giant. She was formidable. Take heart in the fact that she is embraced by the grave and Death, the mistress of all endings."

Hughes heard chair legs squeal as they were shunted back.

Our sympathies for your giant. Eilandri.

"Cate," he warned. "Cate, easy my darling—"

"He'll be there," said Cate. She was standing, her hands spread flat over her desk. Her voice was full of flame, pushing through her gritted teeth like an inferno pushing through a furnace grate. "Frank will be there. And if you fuck with him, even *conceive* of fucking with him, I will come to your home and violate its every holy aspect. I will smite your relics. Defile every puritanical idol. I will make you watch as I eat your angel alive. I'm sure it'll be terrific comfort for you and him both, the embrace of the grave being so yummy and sweet."

The Beldame stiffened at the threshold of the room. The hood came around, a backward glance, and a dash of dread quickened in Hughes. Because there was no emotion in that stretched face. None at all.

"We look forward to your friendship," said the Beldame.

She turned her back, and Hughes had just time enough to look away before she crouched hideously under the door frame.

***

To recall all of that—the fragrance of the mahogany desk mingling with the dry, musty, somehow sour odor of the Beldame's robes, the words that were spoken, not to mention the cadence of the daffodil-colored light faltering and renewing on the hood and on the Beldame's horrid face—to conjure all of that so sharply, and yet to be unable to think of the name of a dog, a dog with whom he had been familiar for a tremendous portion of his life...

There on the fortress balcony Hughes felt himself confronted.

It took him a quarter of an hour of slow and cautious contemplation to understand what was happening, or at the very least to understand his reaction to it. Here and now was the first real moment of fear about the whole ordeal. That dread, so redolent of cold mist, found like-to-like company with his anxiety, which surrounded him and grasped feebly for Evelyn, whom he missed and yearned to hold so deeply the sea's own fathoms would despair. His mind had always been perfectly capable, an abacus that totted up each sum to come, a hall of mirrors favorable in every way toward the act of reflection.

What did it mean when the beads showed signs of breaking?

When the glass began to crack?

The answer was simple and devastating. It was only fitting that Cate should articulate it, her being the most simple and devastating fixture in his life (true love is nothing if not those because it is infinite as a plane of fog lit up with lanterns).

As he got into bed and lay there in the waning dark, Cate turned over. She put an arm around him, the inky symbols and animals melded by the bedroom gloom into the likeness of unmarked skin, and she nuzzled his neck with her nose. "You're just getting a bit fuzzy around the edges."

"There's white in my beard," he said. "Evie pointed it out. Had you noticed?"

"Yeah."

"You didn't say anything."

"Suits you. 'Sokay. I'm going white too." Big jaw-creaking yawn. "Snow in my fire, whodda thunk it?"

Hughes grunted.

Cate stroked his face, settling steadily back to sleep.

Then, blearily, and without knowing what she was doing, she said, "Getting older."

Presently her snoring recommenced.

Hughes lay awake, thinking.

Chapter Sixteen

By every metric they had won.

The three counselors to Eurydice sat in the dead riddlewood tree that was Skuggs' house. Each of them had their own variation of sitting: Skuggs crouched unobtrusively, Burrows brooded in his bandages, and Ruthven curled like a contemptible ribbon about one of the ceiling beams. The low glow from the lumenfly lamps barely touched any of them. That room was a nest of shadows.

It was June seventh. Outside it was misty as misty could be. It was verging on eleven o'clock and *she* was late.

"She's late," said Skuggs, articulating his displeasure.

No one offered their opinion. Skuggs looked up at the dragon. Feed though he had over the past week, eating gluttonously and often and well, Ruthven was a far cry from his usual self. *Proper squished and pulpest, he was. Flattened like a footnote under Cate Jubilee's deceitsy treat, a whole ruddy scuddy fortress, by the Lady it bottles the brainsteam, yes oh yes oh yes.*

But it was more than that. There had been a child.

And though the death of that surprising, squirmy squirt of a vampire babe had bemused Skuggs very, very much because he was, lest we forget, a despicable little monster, that bemusement of his had drip by drip given way to unease.

For Ruthven hadn't rallied them toward vengeance. He hadn't reeled and writhed and shown his wrath.

As far as Skuggs knew, Ruthven hadn't said anything. A week without a word. And that boded oddly.

Because they *had* won, eh? Eh indeed.

"Burrows?" Skuggs tried.

The necromancer's head tilted slightly, sending a ripple through his black veil. His magic had repaired a great deal of his ruined nose, but his voice still sounded nasally, somehow skewed. "What do you want?" Before Skuggs could answer, Burrows seemed to return from wherever his mind had taken him. "She was always late."

"Stood us up on occasion, if I rememberest right as rain?"

"You remember right. Now shut up."

Skuggs scowled. But he did shut up. No use poking the lich while he was down. That was another thing entirely. Burrows had taken a few buggersome wounds at the battle in the Bloodwood. *Very* buggersome indeed. Only able to watch so much of the fray with his single crystalline eye, Skuggs had tried to pry the facts of those injuries from his fellow counselor, but Burrows was clammed up over the pearls of information, damn his mausoleum-stinking breeches, damn his rotterblock pride.

A nest of shadow and woe, that was his house on this, the eighth hour of the seventh day of the sixth month. Decreasing numbers, declining spirts. Skuggs couldn't even fetch himself a mug of cider because that bastard dead-raiser Burrows had plonked himself in front of the kegs without a by-your-leave.

His scowl gained a few extra dimensions of rue.

He glanced at the mannequin that Eurydice sometimes inhabited when she wished to attend their council meetings. It was inanimate. Limp as a skinned skunk. No help there.

The silence in his riddlewood home grew unbearable.

What was going on? They had won! The moronic doctor had given their mistress the jolt of power she'd needed to get her shadow back and... and... and *she* was back! The agents of the Red Death, Cate Jubilee and Gormless Hughes and slaughtered, stupid Eilandri Titansgrave, and all the rest, they were losers! Skuggs and his lot, well, they were the winner-winner-chicklet-dinners!

How then could the mood be so glum? As though they weren't champions at all, but bottomest of the barrel and fish therein too, skewered by the very shadow they just went to all the trouble of wrenching up from *her* grave, bugs and all. What was a few scrapes in the course of duty? What was one lost whelp?

It made no scabbing sense to him. None at all.

Ruthven struck dumb and Burrows more laudy-lordy-tantrummy than ever.

Skuggs fetched a sigh he was sure neither of them would hear.

Just my guzzlible—

He heard, dulled by the thick and tainted wood of the tree, the growl of a wolf. The sound rolled out of two throats.

A voice followed, sultry and insinuating, like a locust cloud over a field of ripe and swaying corn.

"Is that Burrows' woofy boy? Come here."

The growl intensified.

"Come, come, come."

The double-throated growl became a double-throated whine.

"Gooooood booooyyyy. Yes, who's the gooboy? Yourra gooboy! I missed you. I missed this tree. Skuggs has it looking well. Want to come in with me, boy? No? One kiss before I go. Whose tongue smells like mortified dung? Yours does! Yes, it does!"

By this time Skuggs had hurried to the window and pressed his pumpkinish head against the glass so as to get the full view. The mist was frustratingly dense, but wait... coming up the walkway to the riddlewood house, there she was, hot-dimply-damn! In the flesh and no mistaking her!

This was the first time Skuggs had seen her since May. He turned to gauge Burrows' and Ruthven's reactions, eager to share the moment before her grand arrival with them.

They hadn't moved. Burrows' arms were crossed in a mummified shroud. Ruthven's slitted eyes were faraway.

Genuine amazement seized Skuggs. He could only goggle at them.

One floor below the door was opened and shut with gusto. Tramping up the stairs came Jane, her dark hair mussed and her eyes bright like a black forest full of fireflies.

Those eyes roamed about the room, taking stock of the surly scene in every detail.

Jane caught Skuggs' eye. She tipped him a wink and walked over to Burrows. Standing before him she slid her hands along his shoulders, rising up to cup his chin. Instinctually his thin, supercilious mouth pulled even thinner, then he looked up and seemed to register Jane's presence for the first time.

"May I?" she said.

Silence. Burrows gave the smallest nod.

Slowly and with an almost motherly tenderness, Jane lifted his veil.

Skuggs gagged at the very thought. He had seen under Burrows' veil once, when they were young and the council of Eurydice was freshly formed, and he never wanted to see that face again. Its horror, however, left Jane completely unperturbed.

"You poor thing," she said. "Did Cate Jubilee do that to your nose?"

"She did."

"Want to hear something fun?"

No reply. Burrows was channeling his craft today; solemn and sad as the pile of magazines in an undertaker's toilet.

Jane leaned down to him, her eyebrows hitched high. "Well? Do you or don't you?"

"I suppose I do."

"Ruthven killed her friend. Eilandri Titansgrave. That's fun, isn't it? I'll do you one better, Burrows. I spied on the funeral. Cate delivered the eulogy herself. She could barely keep it together. You remember that Cate and Hughes lost a child? I'd bet that Eilandri was instrumental in helping Cate cope with her grief. And now that anchor in her life is gone forever."

Skuggs couldn't see Burrows' face, but he heard the trace of a smile when the necromancer spoke. "That ah... does buck me up. A little."

"Hey, when we're down, a little goes a long way." She planted a kiss on the spot where his nose had once jutted perfectly, and now slanted to one side. She lowered his veil and evaporated into a sizzling seethe of bugs. The seethe scaled the walls of the riddlewood. Among the raftering ceiling beams it coalesced once more.

Jane stroked Ruthven's spotted fur. "And you, my friend. You're lower than low, huh?"

No response. Ruthven's slitted eyes stared unblinkingly ahead.

Jane looked at Skuggs and Burrows. They shrugged.

"No big speech," she said, turning back to Ruthven. "No glitz or glamorizing things. I'm going to help you. Ruthven, did you know that I was the one who sang to the Bloodwood?"

"How could you?" he said.

Encouraged by the sound of his sibilant voice, Jane broke into a grin. "I was old when the Bloodwood was only a few little saplings pushing out of the mulch. I remember when the wood wasn't a wood at all, but rather a dragon named Carmilla. She died and her memories soaked into the ground and gave birth to trees with trunks as white as snow and leaves as red as blood. When the trees taught themselves to think, they wished they could be a dragon again. And they wept, Ruthven. They wept until I came and dried their tears. I gave them succor. I gave them an egg to fertilize, an egg of song." Her grin widened. "I'm a demon for songs. And that was how you were born. When we've killed Cate, and Hughes, and all the rest of them... you and I will go to the Bloodwood... and we'll sing you a son."

She might have gone on, but Ruthven withdrew from the touch of her hand.

"You misunderstand," he said. "What I mean is: *how could you let yourself be outwitted by mortal men?* The war. The invasion and defilement of our home. The senseless death of..." He could not say it. But they all knew what he had been about to say. Ruthven rose, gazing down at Jane with all his teeth bared in a snarl. "None of it would have happened if you had simply stopped thinking with your belly. I am a cold one, I admit it. You think I do not hear the stories circulating about me? I am not as deaf to them as people think. Yes, I am sinister in my curiosity. Burrows is proud. Skuggs, debased. But none," he hissed, "*none* could accuse us of stupidity." Then, like a flash in a pan, his fury was gone, replaced with the mournful coolness of an iceberg. His head reared up and to the side. His muzzle peeled back in a grimace. "*Sing me a new son.* What does it mean when even Ruthven the Ruthless feels a chill creep up his spine at such a suggestion? Have you an answer for me, Jane? When we needed you most, how could you leave us to our own devices? How can you flounce in here now as if nothing has happened?"

"Listen to me—"

The dragon was quick. He went for her, his mouth drawing wide.

Below, Burrows jolted to his feet. Skuggs' pulled in a lung's worth of holler.

At the last instant Ruthven stopped. From Skuggs' vantage on the scene, the dragon's teeth framed Jane as though they were a wicked portrait frame and she were the subject of some perverse artist.

In Jane's hand, the sword. It was very much like Hughes' sword, Chimera, only insectile, and most exquisitely corrupted.

It's point nicked Ruthven's upper palate. There was no movement. Indeed, there seemed to be the definite impression that should there be any movement whatsoever, the tip of that sword might travel to open air by way of Ruthven's brain.

Inside their lamps the lumenflies flew over the corpses of their dead friends, their wings like cut silk, their upturned legs so much like tobacco shavings, and the live ones ticked against the glass while outside the two-headed wolf howled long, and strange, before lapsing into silence.

Jane let her sword arm drop. She flicked the blade end over end. It landed on the floor, three inches from Skuggs' foot and point-first. There it wobbled back and forth before he steadied it to soothe his spasming nerves.

That brittle silence fell once more.

Gradually, and with a rumble that came from deep within him, Ruthven withdrew to a range in which swift devouring was not so imminent.

"I'll listen. Though I expect I'll not like what I hear."

Jane smiled at him. It was lopsided, cheeky, and so far past madness that it corroded its way back to sanity. "You're the one who misunderstood," she said. "Did I say *new* son? Did I? No, I did not. Ruthven, when all of this is over, you and I will go to the Bloodwood and I'll sing you the *same* son."

"The sap of the Bloodwood is not inclined toward precise reproduction. In fact, resists that." Ruthven shifted, coiling around a higher beam to maintain his downward gaze upon her. "My first effort was cloning, another Ruthven, something I think I would have regretted in the fullness of time. Later I grew accustomed to my alternative: new life. A dragon that was not a simulation of me but one I could raise in my image."

"You don't believe me?" Jane asked him.

"Embodying a miracle does not make you a messiah." His tongue flickered out, not forked like a serpent's but many-tined and barbed like a torture flail. "No, Jane. I do not believe you."

Well, you could have knocked Skuggs over with a feather when Jane began to sing. He bet Burrows wasn't far behind, so unusual an occurrence was it. Odder still (Skuggs had been right about the ominous oddness stewing that day), streaming out of Ruthven came the dragon's very own blood. Not much, only a few tassels. They knotted together to form a skeletal structure, small but sublimely detailed, of a dragon.

Jane stopped, her lips closing on the tune, though it lingered longer than it had any right too, a musical aftersound lacing the air. Those lips quirked with amusement when she saw Ruthven's face. "Believe me now?"

Ruthven's blood returned to him. He said, "It's true? We could... remake the child?"

"In your draconian image, Ruthven. Perfect in every way. And it'll be our secret. Eurydice need never hear about it. You know how she is with music. Hey, look at me. Don't drift away again, sad as a lone stone. Look, I'm sorry I disappointed you. Left you, you know, to your own devices. I'm dogshit, I know it. The fly and the shit. I'm an anti-Icarus who flew too far from your bright suns, and what happened? Condemned, that's what. For twelve years I wasn't me at all, but someone else. Twelve years. Clack up the abacus of that much hell." Her head skitter-jerked on her neck, so like a bug. "Abacus? Not a me word, a Hughes word. He's thinking about it. Time... thinking, memories. A dog's name, boo-something. Oh, don't mind me, that happens. Spend ten minutes trying to kill a guy and over a decade as his daughter and it's bound to tangle your wiring. Anyway, I'm back."

Her words evoked a weird, captivating energy that filled the space, like a tightrope walker that encouraged you to come out with her, out over the ravine, yes. Even the sound of her saying that, saying "I'm back," made Skuggs' pulse race. *Yes,* he thought. *Yes. Yes.*

"In contrition for my sins, I come," Jane said, swooping in a bow, "bearing many gifts."

"I count one, so far," said Burrows but without any pique. He, like Skuggs, sensed Jane's theatricality in motion. Something wonderful was about to happen. "Ruthven's experiment will see fruition, okay. That's one gift."

"Watch, watch, watch!"

Jane crammed her fingers in her mouth and whistled.

"Skuggs!" she cried. "To the window!"

To the window he went. What he saw out there took his breath away.

"No," he said the second he got it back. "No, no, can't be!"

"It is!" Jane burst into fruit flies, flesh flies, and flit flies, their buzz a cacophony. She reconstituting, laughing. "Show them in! Get that rear in gear, you handsome little devil!"

Skuggs rushed to do as she said.

Up he scurried half a minute later. In his wake, they came.

The Old Stony Crow trailing his cloak of petrified feathers.

Yellow-Eye the Gentler with his fat fingers aglitter with rings.

Baroness Wichtera, thin and regal like a cadaverous swan.

Twicesome Eland, who could only be seen from the corner of the eye.

More came, and more, and even more besides.

In they shambled and shuffled and hulked and hobbled and lumbered and strode, in out of the mist to Skuggs' riddlewood home.

There was a great shaking of hands and catching up. Skuggs cracked the cider barrels, and even fetched a keg of deathly-white-liqueur from the cellar he'd winnowed in the hollow roots of the riddlewood. Where was the Troll? Dead! Where was William o' The Wisps? Missing. But the rest of them were there at last. Where had they been all this time? Lost in the changing terrain of Eurydice! The mistress had been set completely off kilter by the loss of her shadow. Jane's return meant that places sealed off or buried or broken could now be accessed once more. And that was precisely what Jane had done. The shadow had been busy over the past fortnight.

"She found us," said Crow. "Told us all about this war you've got on your hands. Caught us up. We were gutted of course, to have missed out on such a thoroughly enjoyable rumpus. Though," he amended, glancing at Ruthven, "we heard it wasn't all roses."

"It is now," said Burrows.

"All roses," agreed Ruthven. His voice, frosty and lurid, slithered unspeakably up every back and every neck. All was right again, all was normal, no, better than it had been before.

"Now we are an army," said Yellow-Eye with a distinctly hungry menace that set every mouth present to grinning. "A true army. One that represents our Lady because all the things she loves can be brought to bear upon all that she despises."

"Hear, hear!" boomed the Baroness Wichtera. "Mount their heads on pikes!" A chorus of hate rose, the drums of war thumping.

"The hounds will fight for their still-warm skin!"

"Birds will fight for their eyes!"

"A rough fight!"

"A rabid fight!"

"One last fight to drive them out of our world forevermore!"

"No," said Burrows with a jollity Skuggs would not have believed possible. "One fight to drive them out, and another on their turf. They've had a taste of our world. Let's take a bite of theirs! What do you say?"

Cheers. Applause. Caterwauls and whistles. Merry slams of fists upon the walls and tables and chairbacks.

"We'll pillage and burn and break and bash!"

"Plunder and pluck!"

"Pester and fester!"

"Ravage and ruin!"

"A war! Crystal against scarlet!"

"A war like no other!"

Jane, the hero of the hour, slipped away from the hullabaloo. She'd seen something she wanted to tend to.

Quite detached from festivities, nursing a mug of cider and with his face turned away, was Skuggs.

"Haven't had the chance to say hello properly," she said. She looked at him. Her head canted to one side. "Skuggs? Are you crying?"

He nodded, unable to speak.

"What is it?" She went to one knee before him. "What can I do?"

"Nothing. *Ahehn-hen-hen,*" he snickered through his tears. "Nothing. You've already done it."

***

Sometime later, when the brightness of pleasant astonishment and reunion had dimmed just a little, Skuggs pulled Burrows aside. Excitement still percolated throughout the riddlewood tree, and the revelry was loud enough to disguise their conversation.

"How long do you reckon it'll take this lot to get mobilized?" Skuggs asked Burrows.

"They're mobilized now," said Burrows. Bemusement tugged his arrogant mouth. "Don't glare, Skuggs. I take your meaning. Could be late June if we're lucky. Mid-July if we're not. That's an approximation, you understand. Whatever mild interrogation I've been able to get in edgeways reveals precious little about the size of our combined forces."

"Not in the form for talking shop, are they?"

"No, I expect not. Can you blame them?"

"Not at all, not at all, Burrows. Pleasure before beheadings, and that."

"Business."

"What?"

"Pleasure before business."

Skuggs thought about it. "Nah, I don't think so. Anyway..." Skuggs grew animated. "The reason I ask is this: how would you fancy a bit of a sumjum?"

"A what?"

"A trip. Bit of a jaunt, like."

Burrows stared at him. "A *sojourn*," he said at last. "Where to?"

"To the Rotunda of the Bell Sir."

"Why should we go there?"

"On account of Frank Gallant."

"Frank Gallant?"

"Yes," said Skuggs, barely able to contain his splendid joy. "What do you say you and I bunk off for a quick rowdy one at the Rotunda? I know you hate that dreamy, stringy creep as much as I do."

"True, but you've lost me. Why should Frank Gallant be at the Rotunda?"

"Don't you know about the plan? The Beldames and suchlike? Eurydice cookeled it up on the stove of her sinistrest thoughts."

"First I'm hearing about it."

Skuggs caught his fellow counselor up.

"Oh," said Burrows, and his voice was water seeping from a fetid river into a graveyard, covering every buried coffin with blue mildew. "Oh, that is juicy. Happening now, you say?"

"Not now. Soon," said Skuggs. "Soonest as can be!"

"Count me in."

"Really?"

"If those four ears of yours stop working, read my fecund lips. Count me in."

Skuggs threw his arms about Burrows.

Of course, height being what it is, he ended up embracing the necromancer's knees.

Quickly realizing what he'd done, Skuggs retreated.

"Pop that in the bin, eh? No one needs to remember. They'll say I've gone soft between the temples."

"Already forgotten," said Burrows graciously. "And you're not soft."

"I appreciate it."

"Mushy."

"Eh?"

"Your head," said Burrows. "Mushy."

"Ahehn-hen-hen. Um." Skuggs glanced about. "When shall we bugger off then? Feels a bit like bunking, but it won't take too long. We'll be back in a week or two, before we're really missed. So when?"

"No time like the present."

The voice came from the nearby stair, where Burrows was already descending. Skuggs hurried after, grinning.

"Any chance of a lift on that wolf of yours?"

"None whatsoever. Frank Gallant," mused Burrows. "All these years turning his back, now he'll walk right toward us."

Outside, he spoke to his two-headed wolf. One head panted and slobbered, the other took the news of their venture with poise and silence. Skuggs looked back at his riddlewood home. Shadows capered with the waxing of the lumenfly light, and through the windows he heard wild, wonderful voices all a'mingled.

"Back in a jiff, Jane," he said, wondering if in her genius she might sense him speaking to her, doubting it, and doing it anyway. "Back well in time for the big finale. Pleasure before beheadings, you know how it is."

"Skuggs."

Burrows had mounted up.

"Coming," said Skuggs.

Glittering pink crystal rose from beneath the ground and swallowed him whole. Flowing through the subterranean gemstone jungle, Skuggs tittered to himself. Being one of the winners really was grand. You got to indulge yourself. You got to do as you liked, and all the losers could do was take it.

Fingers crossed the Beldames don't kill him before we get there, he thought. *Fingers, toes, and a third of my bones. Frank, hang in there. At least long enough for me to have a go.*

***

I'm fenced in by a wall, thought Evelyn. *Four sides. I see every granule on the bricks. Every smidgen of cement. Time has shrunk the wall. I see the moss growing on the shrinking wall. It's red and wet with dew, and from where I'm sitting it looks like dust kitties or pillow fluff or carnival cotton.*

She opened her eyes.

Nothing.

Wait, had there been... had...

On impulse, Evelyn reached out a hand.

For one fantastic instant she felt something solid against her fingers.

Solid as a stone. As *brick*.

Then it was gone.

She laughed herself hoarse, wiggling and flailing and hip-hip-hooraying.

"Stop that now," she told herself. A grin suggested itself on her lips. She hastened it away. "*Stop it.* There we are. Practice, practice, practice. Hm. Okay." What was the line from her father's play, that one about poor thieves stealing fruit from a wealthy farmer... Ah, yes. "Once more unto the peach, dear friends, once more! If we're in luck we may yet pinch some bread!"

She giggled, composed herself, and closed her eyes again.

I'm protected by a wall. Four sides.

***

To President Hughes,

For as long as I can remember, I haven't had cause to write anything other than my signature on paperwork. Bearing that in mind, you'll forgive my handwriting, which to your esteemed eye probably looks like a dog's breakfast.

No way to sugarcoat this, so I shall say it and have done. Jane isn't just back where you are. She's back here in Corinth too. And she's up to her old tricks.

Yesterday there were nine cases, including a decorated chef going berserk with an apple peeler in one hand and a Tursurami Steel dicing knife in the other. Today that number more than doubled. Twenty homicides, all told, and twenty culprits haring up the nearest roof for a jaunt afterward.

You remember how they used to write on the walls afterward? "They are in me," right? Scrawled in blood and human hair and whatever else the killer had to hand. You and I reasoned that whole business was the person underneath the possession making contact as Jane gobbled them up from the inside. Sort of a subconscious thingamabob. You get me. Well now the culprits are writing messages of a different strain.

Again, there really isn't any way to say it delicately.

They're love poems, Hughes.

Jane's making her victims write them for you. I won't reproduce them here. Grisly is one thing. Grisly I can handle like a trowel in a botany shop. What gets under my skin and crawls around is how loving they are. Like you and she were together before and she's never been quite able to let you go. Treacle from a bad potboiler romance, but enough to give me the sours for all their trial at sweetness.

She's stronger than before. Sicker.

We put our heads together, those of us holding the fort here while you and your wife sort out affairs in Eurydice. A few loud voices were staunchly against letting the media go to print with stories about Jane's return, but Hector and I wouldn't budge. The story is out. It's got legs. It's running. Best to get behind it in the hopes of catching up. I haven't a breeze what headline they shall run. The police are making inquiries. I haven't a breeze about inquiries either, aside from the obvious: how could we be so stupid? How did that bastard of a doctor keep the secret under his hat for so long, and so well? Without Estelle Corlum's Perfect Prison, how are we to stop Jane?

If all of that weren't bleak enough, we've got a serious heat wave coming. According to the western seaboard meteorology report I've got here in front of me, it'll hit Champleurs first, move up through the farmland, and hit Corinthia at the zenith of June. Temperatures that'd singe your eyebrows. There won't be people protesting in the streets because they'll be baked into their sofas. At about five o'clock today I went out with my ear to the ground, wondering at the Jane dilemma. I couldn't think with the humidity. A fortnight out from the spike, and it's already like breathing wet chimney fumes. I've been on the telephone to a woman in the Ikahaguan Climate Center, chinning and wagging about temperature dispersal and emergency cooling measures. Infrastructure and that; I won't bother you with the details. Truth be told there isn't time to do a fraction of it anyway. Even if there was, all manufacture efforts are going to The Front.

Mind you, hard as it was to gain an inch on the Jane conundrum, I gained a whole yard in opposition to that boy Oliver Clufp. You remember him? Bugger whose crew blew up a purifier this spring. I think he went by Owly. See, I was walking the beat in Leonidas from half five to seven or thereabouts. And I tell you, Hughes, what our old haunt lacks in fancy drawers and diamond rings, she makes up for in sheer gumption. I ran into a group of lads, one of them the son of a captain in the streetbeaters. They were carrying this dinged-up portabee, the kind you see hauling gadgets and slabs of meat and fish in the bazaar, you know. Short-circuited thing was smattered in rust, and with the legs cut off it looked like a huge bucket. The lads had filled it with water. I asked them where they were taking it. One of them, the captain's son who knew me, said they were bringing it to the apartment complex nearby. Lots of geriatric types there who can't hobble to their own doors, much less a water dispensary. You know me, I'm wise to any crap, even if it's shoveled in a silver packet. I said, Right, right, right, and who would be your first stop at that apartment complex? Missus Doddinger with the gammy knees?

Well, they all stopped grinning and looked at me like I was carved out of the dumbest rock around. Missus Doddinger? No, they said, she was all the way on the fifteenth floor. Why'd they go traipsing up fifteen floors with this bloody heavy a load when they could off it as they climbed? And I said, Ah yes. Sorry about that.

Talk about passing a test with flying colors, eh?

Owly and his lot, they're Leonidas boys, true. But just because they're from here doesn't mean here is from them, if you'll forgive my little indulgence into poeticalness, sir. Those lads dishing out water tonight prove it.

Not to winkle you away from this heat wave disaster round the corner. All I'm saying is we'll last as long as we can. And that moon launch business is doing everyone the world of good. I had my doubts at the get-go, but you were right to invest in it as you have. Drop a mention of the Laurana Project into any conversation in Corinth City, and you'll see a bit of twinkle in the eye of every tired, glum face. Your scientist chum Hiromi has finally stopped pestering Hector and griping to me about this pitfall and that shortcoming. Seems like we're gearing up for blastoff any day now.

Which brings me to the most important part of this letter.

I hope you'll forgive me saying it, sir, because I'm sure you're needed there. You're needed here more. No sense putting out fires abroad while home is burning, that's what I say.

Oh, yes. I feel I ought to tell you: One of Jane's possession victims is Hedley Intrig. I believe she's the principal of your Evelyn's school. She didn't hurt any students, but I can't say the same for her secretary, and a teacher who happened to be passing the office.

I'd say I'm sorry about what's happened to your girl Evelyn, but we're going to get her back with this scheme of yours. The Beldames and Frank, or some other way. We caught Jane once, we can do it again.

Think about what I've said.

H. Thud

P.S. Something about your description of the Beldames (long faces in particular) joggled a memory. Something about a party. I've been racking my brains trying to think what it could be. Any ideas?

P.P.S. I've got our friend Falstaff cooling his heels in the lockup. Never got the chance to tell you. Not that it matters much in the grand scheme. Still, thought you'd like to know.

P.P.P.S. Hettie sends her love. She says she's sure it'll all work out in the end. Artists, eh?

* * *

When he'd finished Thud's letter Hughes checked that he'd committed its contents to memory with a single reading (he had), folded the letter away, and sat alone in Cate's private rooms for what felt like a long time. An appointment with a pair of trimming scissors had cropped his hair short and his beard into a nice, neat frame for his face. Moroseness and exhaustion are the very devil for a comely face, and in the evening moonlight of Eurydice he looked unwell, all the handsomeness and health sapped. If you'd asked him what he was thinking about, he probably wouldn't have answered. Which might inadvertently give you the general gist of his mood. Sometimes the universe plops you into a gravy of emotion and all you can do is stew in it without much thought to the casserole of things getting better or the cracked gravy pot of things getting worse.

As the Champleurs say, *Laissez les temps rouler.* Let the times roll. Good, bad, happy, sad, sane, mad. *Laissez les temps rouler.*

A sound made him look up.

Only a creak of a window left ajar. A breeze moved through the room, realized it was unwelcome, and left as quietly as it had come.

Hughes looked at the window a while, not seeing it. His gaze drifted to his clasped hands. He found himself reaching mentally for Iphigenia. There she was on the very peripheries of his awareness. She was spring-green and warm, but terribly faint in the manner of that last little bit of sunshine before the light vanishes completely and night's coup begins.

To his surprise, she reached back. That was how, at that horribly low point, they held one another, a woman who was a world who was dying and silly old, small old, getting older old Gormon Hughes. They couldn't speak. She too frail. That was war for you. Take take take. Constant ends and precious few beginnings to cozen them. But they could give one another this. And as any wise connoisseur of magic and woman-worlds and so forth will tell you, when the thing itself is almost gone the ersatz, or the shadow, will have to work with all its might to keep from being lost in the gloom.

So when the embrace was over, Hughes got smartly to his feet and did the sensible thing that every leader of his caliber ought to do in a time of crisis. He went to look for his wife.

On his way he was diverted.

First by grief and then by grief's antidote.

Now by this point in events, Frank Gallant had arrived at the scarlet camp in Eurydice, received his mandate, and gone. During their very brief time together, Frank had asked Hughes to watch out for Mr. Glint.

"He's taken Eilandri hard," Frank disclosed. "I don't think he'd ever felt for someone like... like he did about her. Not with anyone. Not even his *former partner*, the crazy diamond herself, Miss Gleam. Take care of him while I'm gone, Hughes?"

Hughes had supplied that he would. Better, he'd promised.

As it happened, that very night, the night of the letter from Hoshrum Thud, Hughes' word would be put to the test. For as he searched throughout the neighboring fortresses for any sign of Cate, he overheard a pair of sentries discussing, "that absolute horror show of a man" who could only be Mr. Glint. One of the sentries had spied Glint lurching down into the lowest reaches of their current Betty, presumably to find something scuttling or furry to eat in her dungeonous bowels. The other sentry disputed this, saying that Glint had emerged after a very short time, probably having given up on the idea of locating supper, only to gain the fortress battlements and leap down into the mist, which while only a fraction of its former self compared to the recent spate of impenetrable fog, was still thick as pudding as one got closer to the ground.

It was to this sentry whom the president spoke, though they believed him to be a curious passerby in the service given his ordinary clothes of black, green, and scarlet.

Hughes made it his business to find Steffan Cerulean, whose hydrokinetic powers made traversing the mist trivial. They found Mr. Glint on a sullen slump of hill. The hill was impaled from the inside by fantastic tusks, as though it were stuffed with the carcasses of mammoths. Mist crept hauntingly among tall stalks of grass, climbing up the tusks and flowing down their curves as though to polish the ivory.

Mr. Glint wasn't writing poetry. Mr. Glint wasn't sleeping.

Mr. Glint was sitting on an ugly hill in an ugly world, thinking about the first person he had decided was beautiful. Little creatures covered him, so motionless was he. They were like mini porcupines, with their snouts, feet, and every spiky bit along their back replaced with quills of light.

The intensity of Mr. Glint's sadness was so great, his moping and mourning so total, he had not tried to eat a single one of them.

Hughes murmured a word to Steffan Cerulean, who drew off to a respectful distance. Hughes went up the hill. He sat by the statuesque figure. The tusks were riddled with coarse, osteal nodes that jabbed and prodded, but the grass was passably comfortable.

After a while Hughes put out his hand. Not making a big hubbub about it. Just putting his hand out, possibly for a stretch... or possibly for something else.

For a while, nothing happened.

With a gentleness heretofore unheard of, Mr. Glint's long fingers closed on that hand.

If your nineteen-year-old self could study, with depth and circumspection, a vision of yourself at forty-two, there is no doubt that you would be repelled. Whether that repellence would be due to exogenous factors like time, or endogenous factors like the choices you made in the intervening twenty-odd years, well, safe to say the constant is the antipathy itself. There are upsides. When you're nineteen there are monsters right in front of you. By the time you're forty-two, you have, for the most part, managed to put them behind you. Or, if you're lucky, you've got the monsters by your side.

From the corner of his eye, Hughes saw a tear roll down Mr. Glint's gaunt cheek.

He squeezed the monster's hand.

And thought of him as monstrous no more.

An hour or two later, squirreling about for Cate in the medical center, he happened to see a face that was marked with a spray of freckles and topped with a mop of red hair. The owner of the freckles must have been on the receiving end of a joke because as Hughes chanced to look at him, he grinned. The man's nose wrinkled. The freckles there were transformed from full moons into half-moons. In that moment, Hughes was nineteen again.

He introduced himself to the owner of the freckles, who recognized him at once.

"Dan Jurdels, sir. Er. Mr. President, I mean. Sergeant Daniel Jurdels. And this is my, er..."

"Senior Surgeon Anissa Jurdels." She shook Hughes' hand. "Damned honored to meet you, Mr. President. Everyone's giving us looks."

"I can back off," Hughes offered.

"Wouldn't hear of it, sir," said Sergeant Dan Jurdels with a hint of a smile. "My wife loves a bit of attention, so she does."

"My husband is pleased to have someone in his inner circle who knows how to sew," said the surgeon tartly. "Wounds and socks."

"And who is this," said Hughes, cocking his head lightly and fixing a charmed look at the cat in Anissa's arms. "I didn't know cats were allowed in the medical center."

"The purring is curative," said Anissa. "Well-known fact."

"I see."

"And it isn't native to this part of the army," she went on. "Scrap is a company cat."

"A company cat? Which one?"

"Ah. Mine, sir," said the sergeant, reddening. "Not strictly according to regulation, sir. Bugger. *Mr. President.* Oh dear. I didn't say bugger aloud, did I?"

"You did, love," said Anissa.

"Piss. Oh dear!"

"Scrap," said Hughes, tactfully ignoring the sergeant, stroking the cat's head and twiddling its ear. She licked his finger. Years of working with Iphigenia's creatures had left him with a fair heart where animals were concerned, and he'd liked cats a good deal to begin with.

"A cute name, isn't it?" said Senior Surgeon Anissa. "It's short for... Hush, Dan. What are you groaning about? Don't be rude in front of the president. It's short for Mr. Scrappalotocus née Scrappybum."

"Mr. Scrappalotocus," said Hughes.

"Née Scrappybum."

The cat was tawny and friendlier than any feline Hughes had ever met. She wriggled round, offering him her tummy. Hughes did his duty.

Then, as casually as he could, he said, "You wouldn't be the Jurdels who own a farm outside Corinth?"

Anissa beamed. The sergeant was too bewildered for pleasure. "That we are," he said. "How could you know that?"

"Would there be... a blackberry thicket on that farm?"

The surgeon stopped beaming. Her husband's bewilderment deepened before Hughes' eyes. "True enough, there is." He opened his mouth, perhaps to ask another clarifying question, but Hughes' face, richly animated with emotion, conveyed that he had something to say and was working his way toward it. So Dan Jurdels shut up and pondered just what on earth was about to happen.

"You were probably never told," Hughes began. To himself, a mutter. "No, why would you?" Meeting their gaze, he forced himself to hold it. "I was responsible for your daughter's death."

Someone was passing them when he said it, a stomach surgeon. His eyes widened at what he heard. He passed on quickly. By morning the words the president had spoken would be on every scarlet soldier's lips. But their significance to popular rumor and speculation would pale compared to what would soon follow.

The Jurdels stood together, Dan with his hands in his pockets and Anissa holding Scrap in her arms. Hughes, adept at untangling the manifold quandaries of the human face, found their expressions cryptic and complex.

Careful that he did not trip or stumble over the detritus of that dark day in his past, Hughes recounted events as he had experienced them. He told them about his desperate plan to join the Scarlet Citadel, about his chance meeting with Laurana and her squad, as well as with a drunken sot named Walter Pillion, whom Hughes impersonated with spectacular success. He told them about his misadventure in Iphigenia, where a two-headed wolf had slain the Citadel unit he had tricked his way into. The beast killed Laurana too. Hughes had been at her side when she went over.

The Jurdels listened in silence. His story cast their daughter as the valiant heroine she was. Resurrected for a few minutes by his eloquence, she shone brave, and bright, and kind.

Aside from the catalyst to tragedy, there was little of Hughes himself in the tale. Though he had known her a scantly short period of time, Laurana was a fulcrum around which Hughes' life turned. His guilt for what had happened was a good amount of the luggage he carried forward from past to future. Some days it felt like an entire case in its own right. That omission was purposeful.

These people didn't need to hear any of that.

They deserved the truth, not a sentence more or a paragraph less.

He finished, adding one final thing, a reluctant concession to the strength of his shame. "She called me 'my guy.' I can't tell you why, but I remember that really frequently. I was asked to name the moon rocket project. I opened my mouth, and before I knew it, I had suggested Laurana's name. Not sure why I, ahm." He gave a kind of close-throated sigh and was overcome for a second. He recovered.

"Actually, to be honest, I *can* tell you why her name seemed a perfect fit. Laurana's freckles went from moons to half-moons when she... smiled at me."

Anissa covered her mouth with a hand. Dan's head was bowed.

"I'm so sorry," said Hughes.

That stirred them.

Hughes hardly noticed. "I wish I could give her back to you. I know you can never... can never forgive me. I'm a dad now, and my girl, she means... So I can under..." He clamped down on that. No one could understand. Even if Evelyn was lost to him, he couldn't. Hurt etches itself as storms etch their white snowflakes, with a craftiness, each cold ache precise and utterly unique. "I'm sorry. I should go."

They put their hands out. Not making a big hubbub about it. Just putting one hand out each, possibly for a stretch... or possibly for something else.

"Here, lad," said Dan Jurdels.

Hughes stared, uncomprehending.

His feet knew what to do even if his head did not.

They stepped forward. Anissa's hand rested on his left shoulder, Dan's the right. He gave it a squeeze, she a pat.

"You're well within your rights to slap me," said Hughes. "I would in your position. I'd curse me and wish all the worst for me."

"You never know," said Dan. "Never know about a thing till you're wrapped up in it. Not really."

"Laurana would be alive if not for me."

"Enough of that now. What's done is done and can't be helped. Besides, Laurie's living again in whatever underworld she found for herself, right?"

"Yes, but—"

"Then I expect we'll see her someday, if we're lucky or stubborn enough so as to leave no room for crap fortune, isn't that the way of it, my love?"

Anissa nodded. "That's the way of it. Isn't that the way of it, Scrap?"

Scrap yawned agreeably.

Hughes did not know what to say.

Independent of one another, the Jurdels gave him a shoulder-shake, as if to inform him that he was making a holy show of yourself, and he was to stop immediately.

"Thanks for telling us," said Dan.

"Our guy now," said Anissa, her voice an impossible concoction of joy and sorrow. "You're our guy now, President Hughes. Our guy..."

Chapter Seventeen

The second thing Frank Gallant thought when he saw the Rotunda of the Bell Sir was, *This reminds me of that poem Livia Massicordesto of Middlewich rattled off one time:* So now my summer task is ended, Mary/And I return to thee, mine own heart's home/As to his Queen some victor Knight of Faëry/Earning bright spoils for her inchanted dome.

Beautiful, but also eerie.

Livia had later told Frank about the poet, who was a sweet, doomed sort of man, and about the weird spelling at the end of the first stanza: inchanted not enchanted.

That funky tidbit was what made the recitation stick with him, indeed what made it resurface now in his mind.

The first thing he thought when he saw the moon glittering on the Rotunda's silver dome and painting the white pillars like radiant spears was, *Frank, oh Frank. Prune your garden all you like, weeds of trouble are ever gonna grow.*

The little crisscross of those two ideas, an inchanted dome and a sense of creeping, invasive danger, fixed him with a resigned feeling about this whole Beldame business. If something was going to go wrong, so be it. He didn't see how it couldn't.

Frank saddled up his miniature Betty (a tiny fortress of leather and organic bio-machinery that one could ride like an extremely rapid, amazingly bow-legged horse) and got going. He allowed his hair to flow into firm curves and fine strings. In a moment a strange hirsute guitar streaked with borealis light floated behind him, playing mellow ditties that would have been right at home within that radio-busting genre, sparking the soundwaves, bopping necks and encouraging free, free love, rock and roll.

Frank smiled as beautifully and, perhaps, as eerily as any poem. Ambling toward the Rotunda, he made a truly peculiar pilgrim. Pretty notes plucked along with his recurring thoughts.

Inchanted dome. Weeds of trouble. So be it, honey boy. Bad shit to come. Moonlight anointing the dome, white for a change in this changing world. Let the waxy light drip the night fandango.

Foreboding. Cool, cool.

Still, some part of him found hope hard to relinquish. The Beldames were an unknown quantity, keeping themselves to themselves, least as long as Frank had been around. The only things he knew about them with acute certainty, and in a sense the only things that mattered to him, were that they were sworn enemies of his mothers, and they said they could help turn the tables on Eurydice. Hey, they'd even save Evelyn Hughes while they were at it.

In order to forge the alliance, Frank was required. Some ritual needed doing.

Well, sign him up. Evelyn called him Uncle Frank, always had done. He loved the girl like crazy.

The structure loomed, closer now. Against a featureless backdrop, it seemed as lonely as he felt.

Huh. Come to think of weeds, where were they? Where were any signs of life? He could make out the snake of a distant river, muslin-soft shapes of distant trees, but they seemed unnaturally... well, diverted. As though they were giving this place a wide berth. *As though...*

What?

Frank couldn't say.

Above him there were carvings on the stone cornice and the gleaming silver. Depicted women bringing bells up toward the dome's summit. They had long faces, set and determined. No genius to surmise who they were: his allies in the making.

And why hadn't Cate and Hughes sent backup? Why send Frank in on his own? Because for better or worse they had no choice but to take the Beldames word at face value. Too much of an unknown quantity, right. Who knew what the Beldames had going on? Not he.

Not anybody.

Unease riding him just as he rode his mini Betty, Frank passed under the lip of the threshold. He realized his own strings were playing the sort of music he associated with horror films in which bad things happened to the ones who went off on their own. He grunted, stilled them, and peered into the gloom. Aside from a great many doors, alcoves, and stairs, there was a long hallway directly ahead of him. Unless his eyes were fooling him, it led to a large moonlit chamber.

Frank powered down his mount and slid himself from the saddle. He collected himself. This took a few minutes. Frank was, as Hughes had noted on more than one occasion, an ocean of a man. There was a lot of him to gather.

"Here goes nothing."

As he neared the central chamber the moonlight made a bid to illuminate him. His outfit need not be described outside of this: it was a suit so gorgeous that a master tailor would be hospitalized just by sniffing it. The situation was serious. Looking his utmost best seemed the least Frank could do.

His shoes *tepped* on the chamber tiles.

There was a loud rushing sound. Everyone went black. Frank was aware of movement all around him. He readied his strings like a porcupine readying its quills. Another rush. Light returned. It punched down from a skylight, flowing over a monstrously large bell.

A great many voices yelled at once. "Surprise!"

Frank blinked at the women. He counted eight of them. They were in a ring around him. Their hoods were up, but inside he could see their long faces. Not particularly sad faces, mind. Quite the opposite. Even jollier than their smiles were the party hats. They were perched atop each hooded head, attached with a length of wire. The hats were pointy. The hats were periwinkle blue. They were definitely of the party persuasion.

Say this for Frank, he was quick to recover from complete astonishment. "What's the occasion?" he said.

"You!" said a Beldame.

"The son of the Nightjar Coven," said another.

"The one who led his allies to the slaughter of his own mothers."

"They gave you their wombs. You gave them their tombs."

"Sure did," Frank said. "I'd do it again too."

"Then it's true?" said one. "You feel no remorse for your role in slaying the very witches who gave you life?"

"Remorse?" Frank shook his head. "Truth be told I hardly think about it. A rare dream. Nothing more."

"Yes," said a Beldame, taller and thinner than her tall, thin sisters. Frank thought she might be the leader. "You are the Dream Warrior. Celebrating your emancipation in dreams is only fitting."

"Yeah."

"Would you like some rum punch?"

"Y... Yes, I would." He waited until all eight of them had gulped theirs to sip from his own clay cup. Even then he only touched the punch to his lips and mimed swallowing. A party was dandy, but caution was candy. "You're too kind to welcome me here. It's a pleasure to meet kindred spirits in the hate department."

"The pleasure is ours, Dream Warrior."

"My mommas always used to say, 'Frank, you steer clear of those Beldames. Nobody good ever prayed to something that goes *dingalingaling*.' Of course, their revulsion only made me think you lovely ladies were knelling my kind of tune."

"The Coven defamed us constantly. They spread rumors about us."

"They did not!"

"It's true."

Frank blew out his cheeks. "For shame, Mommas. For shame. What sort of rumors? Hoh. That bad?"

Their smiles were plastic.

"Forget I asked. Bunch of lies and slander, I expect."

Their smiles were natural again.

"You will have a leg of lamb with mint sauce?" asked the leader.

But Frank hadn't heard her. He had looked up sharply. Into the dark innards of the chamber bell he gazed. Not expecting to see anything, instead waiting for...

"What's that sound?" he said.

"Snoring," the Beldames replied.

"Who's sleeping? The Bell Sir?"

His hostesses made no remark to confirm or deny it.

Ostensibly losing interest in the bell and its slumbering denizen, Frank gave the leader of the Beldames exactly the same smile she was giving him.

"I'm okay for lamb," he said.

She stepped toward him. Her sisters followed suit in a rustle of fabric, their movements like the contortions of dancers whose bones have been broken and poorly reset. "We have researched the food of that other world, the one you chose to be your home away from home. We have roast boar stuffed with orange, goat's cheese, octopus sandwiches, quail, and plucked pheasant basted in a rich and, we are assured, delectable sauce."

"You're kind to have done the research on my account. That sounds extravagant and exactly the sort of dinner during which we might toast the fatal moribundity of my three mothers. One succumbed at the boot of the legend herself, Cate Jubilee, and the other two at the teeth, tongue, and throat of my close associate, Mr. Glint. Cate and Glint are, to afford them the credit they deserve, the true architects of the Coven's downfall. Our toast ought to include them as well, and if our glasses and plates remain occupied, a major token of celebration should go to Gormon Hughes for his part in proceedings, which was substantial. But I think my appetite will keep till we've talked our way into this truce. Does that suit you, sisters of the silver Rotunda?"

"To business then. Drink. Please."

Frank drank, not daring to forego again, and as a consequence daring a mouthful of the Beldames' rum punch. It was oversweet. After years in consultation with Mr. Glint, Frank's knowledge of poisons was quite admirable. One essential element of ingested poisons is that many are unattended by flavor or can be easily masked. Feeling precautionary despite his growing appreciation for his odd hostesses, and in case that cloying sweet taste was a camouflage for something sinister, Frank did something shrewd. He sent a long string of nylon down his throat, absolutely secretly, without so much as a shift in his friendly, charming expression. The string split a thousandfold and separated the mouthful of rum punch into a sprinkling of teensy tiny droplets. These, he kept low in his esophagus, pretty much out of harm's way should any malicious surprise have designs on his stomach or upon a hope of absorption into his bloodstream. "When you spoke to Cate and Hughes, you talked about a ritual."

"Yes," said the tallest and thinnest of the Beldames. "I spoke to them personally about it."

"Permit me to ask about it. You told Cate and Hughes that it was to be a ritual of strings and bell rings. I can provide the strings, you the bell rings, naturally. But what are the specifics?"

The leader answered him. "You will be required to perform a few of our holy sacraments. Are you not even peckish after your long travel?"

"If we can stick to the matter at hand—"

"And you have only drunk a thimble of your punch."

Those faces, so long. And their mouths. They've got no lips.

Frank accepted a plate of lamb with mint sauce. He was polite and debonair, and in his mind a kind of jaundiced understanding began to dawn.

"There's that snoring again," Frank said, fawning over the food without eating a bite. His tone was idle. "Think the Bell Sir might fancy coming down and joining us? That is him up there, right?"

"Such sounds do not concern you."

"You wouldn't have a ladder, would you? I wouldn't mind a look."

Rustle, came the noise of fabric. The bracelet the Beldames had initially formed around him was now shrunk to a ring.

Close as they were, he could peer into the recesses of their hoods and learn the reason for their lack of lips. They had been sawed off. Their nostrils were blotched with burn scars. The flesh of their cheeks was scourged. No. Flayed.

"Do that to yourselves?" he asked.

They nodded, smiling.

He hooked a thumb at the bell. "Because he told you to?"

Nods.

"Do a lot of things because he tells you to, huh?"

Eager nods. Pleased and contented nods.

Frank looked down at the tiles. They were bell shaped, and no matter where his eyes wandered, the shadow of that enormous bell engulfed a little of the pristine picture. When he looked up again, he grinned a sickly, sheepish grin that would have horrified his friends if they'd seen it. It horrified Frank, and he was the one wearing it.

"There never was a ritual, was there?" he asked them.

The Beldames nodded. They nodded in unison. And they were still smiling.

"Hughes and Cate were right not to trust you, weren't they?"

Nods.

"But you knew they would," said Frank. "Trust you."

Amused nods.

"Because they were desperate. Me too, I guess." Frank rubbed at his mouth. When he removed it that meek smile was gone, as if it had been painted on and his palm were covered in benzyl alcohol. "Gonna kill me?"

Nods.

"Gonna tuh—" His throat closed on the word. He swallowed. There was an audible click. His tongue wet his lips. Dry, so dry, when had they... "Gonna torture me?"

Glad nods. They took the party hats off, crumpled them up, nodding to one another, whispering like conspirators: "Torture. Yes, torture. He's a fine guesser. We'll torture him. Yes. Or allow him to be tortured. Yes, yes."

"Why? Why not kill me now and have done?"

"You are of the Nightjar Coven's flesh," said the leader. "Your blood is theirs. As their final act before their death, they turned people into animals. Not because of a fascination with beasts but because they were in love with *metamorphosis*. They were avatars of *transmutation*. Revolting though these words are to me, I feel I must say them. You must know of your mothers' blasphemy before your pain begins."

"I don't understand."

"Of course you are flummoxed. You are an ignorant son of witches. You are not in commune with our master, the Bell Sir. You have no appreciation for the one true change, the only change deemed by Lucy Nowhere and her angel the Bell Sir to be fitting for worship and obeisance!"

"I really don't—"

"Death! Life and Death!"

The sisters of the silver-domed Rotunda took up the cry, the chorus of the one true change.

"Life and Death! Death and Life!"

"But I'm not them!" Frank protested. "I'm not my mothers!"

"You are a mirror in which the hags, should they be grabbed from their graves, would see themselves reflected. Your caprices and desires are the same as theirs were and always have been. Are you not a walker of the roads both real and dreamish? Seldom settling, and never for long? Are you not compelled to move around a problem rather than confront it, as though your heart were deep down a cowardly carousel? Your mothers were lonely, so they fused their wombs together into a girl. Proof in the pudding arises there, for you were not content with that.

You called yourself a boy and then a man thereafter! We honor this, for it reflects your true nature. You are their *son*."

"Hey, fuck you, okay? The sins of the mothers are not the sins of the son."

"Your behavior is an affront to God," said the leader. "You will be punished."

Frank stared at her. His teeth were tucked together in a lattice, grinding, grinding. That dryness cracking his lips had slithered like animated snakeskin into his mouth and down his throat. He wanted to swallow. No spit. Not a drop. He was not aware of it, but the aurora in his hair was a montage of colors that flowed and flashed, foglights over a condemned neon city. That light, and the yellow light of his wide, unbelieving eyes bathed the Beldames, making them members in a disco palace whose very job it was to condemn, and to see to that job with great pleasure.

Frank tried to collect himself and found to his dismay that he couldn't. The worse had happened, and instead of falling back on that cozy bed of calm resignation, he felt as though his stomach had fallen while the rest of him stayed upright. He was more scared now than he had ever been. Even so, his innate sense of style gave a rebellious flicker. "I bet," he said, as mean as he could manage. "I bet your Bell Sir angel is as dumb as a cheese grater. I bet you lot take turns on him while he drools away his days. And I bet he takes it up the ass too."

The look on the leading Beldame's face would not be much comfort to Frank later because when you're in pain it's hard to focus on anything else. But he savored it now. It was sweet indeed.

"What sort of faith tells you deception is okay, anyhow?" he asked her. "You lied to Cate and Hughes. You've lied to me. You've—"

"Not about everything," said the lead Beldame, not even trying to conceal her anger. "We were honest about the surprise. We had one in store. One yet remains."

"And what might that be?"

Agony somersaulted through his skull. Frank fell. When a pink crystal cane turned him over, he found himself squinting at the world through a spreading black mold. Fuzzy. Frantic signals of a consciousness that is about to let go. Two figures stepped into the center of his shrinking vision.

"Us," answered Burrows.

"Us," agreed Skuggs.

The last thing Frank heard before the darkness took him was Skuggs' loathsome little laugh.

***

As incidents of assault and murder increased, as the insect parade marched on, as Spring-Heeled Jane, shadow of Eurydice, bane of gentle deeds and kindness, and maddest of the mad, continued to devour what little happiness could be found in a city plagued with drought, a girl was building a wall.

Evelyn held her hand against the brick. It was green, a stark impossible green, and the moss on the bricks was red. She remembered being very small, and a forest in the Corinthian countryside. Beside the forest was a locked and bolted cottage where, quite recently, a farmer and his wife had lived. Her mother told her that both the farmer and his wife had joined the army, that the farmer was a sergeant and his wife a surgeon of tremendous skill. The walls of the cottage were red brick and the moss braiding them was foamy, scaly, and green. Her mother told her the moss was called goblin's gold, or dragon's gold, because its molecular structure made it luminous in the dank caves where it usually spread.

Evelyn wondered now if she'd been thinking of that cottage, and of goblin's gold, when she suggested to Frank that her wall might be green with red moss. She wondered if she'd simply exchanged the colors for an unconscious attempt at originality, prioritizing her own agency while taking shelter in a cherished memory and the notions of familiarity and comfort. She wondered how often she thought she had something figured out, and how often she had been mistaken without realizing. And if now weren't one of those moments.

For a moment, the solidity of the brick changed. It felt wobbly and gelatinous. It threatened to fall apart or fade, perhaps never to return.

Stubbornness crashed down atop anxiety, flattening it.

I am encompassed by a wall. Encircled, abutted, hedged, wreathed, circumjacented. It's green as green with moss as red as red, tall and thick, and vastly, unrepentantly strong.

The brick hardened. A little.

Evelyn visualized as Frank Gallant had taught her.

She had not had time to construct a trap inside her mind, one which would be sprung on Eurydice should Evelyn's older sister decide to trespass in her head.

I am surrounded by a wall.

Evelyn smiled as the brick grew harder and harder against her palm and fingers.

And what am I?

I am the trap that will be sprung.

***

Warmth is companionable.
You miss it if it's unavailable.
Warmth is a sign of comfort.
You could fall straight to sleep in its presence.
Warmth is delicious.
Get the grub while it's hot!
Warmth is a thing people covet.
Even if you prefer the cold, some part of you cares only to be warm.
Warmth is made specifically for you.
Coats, kindled fires, wooly socks, blankets, radiators, electrically heated water.
Warmth is nursing.
You'll never have an ache that warmth of some kind can't help.
Warmth is medicinal.
Too much of it can kill you.

It was killing Corinth City. Corinthia as a whole was being wrung like a rag for its last drop of sweat. And that country, temperate and mild, had it better than most. In Missicordelia the metropolises yielded up their citizens like sacrifices to the heat. Political centers, schools, streets journaled in neon, sushi parlors, arcades, and the apartments fitted together in Jenga towers; they were baked in an oily, suffocating warmth that slipped through concrete walls and paper Shoji doors alike. Calcifern and Rhönland, land-locked, found themselves reliant upon Corinthia's (and to a lesser extent Daethumberland's) purified water. But Corinthia's rationing was ramping up, and fewer and fewer trucks came, and by

June tempers had flared and diminished, and the people who watched for the coming of the trucks could not entertain their children, who themselves did not ask to be entertained. They were all too thirsty. In Ikahagua, by far the worst affected by the drought thanks to a lack of infrastructure and a young, buckle-legged democratic regime, the warmth meandered sluggishly out of the carob and the cypress. In their defense the jungles tried to placate the warmth, to coax it into staying, and to be sealed harmlessly inside a trillion damp green tombs. The warmth would not be persuaded. It invaded isolated villages with the vigor it used to parasitically feed on towns and cities. You could call cities in Ikahagua jam-packed, they were that densely populated, and the warmth seemed to suck the sweetness of the jam, leaving nothing but the parched packed feeling behind, as well as death. And a stinking death too because heat swells mortifying flesh with the most evil cocktail of smells. The smell attracted flies like a deranged bride to her senseless groom.

This story began in Corinth City, and it spends a lot of time there.

The truth of every story is that for every one person you meet and like (or even fall in love with), there are sixty million you don't meet. You might have liked them just as much as you like Cate, or Hughes, or Frank, or even Mr. Glint.

What can be said for those unencountered?

What could have been done differently?

Not much. Everything.

The caterpillar of spring had finished its metamorphosis.

The butterfly of summer was here. Its wings were dark and unspeakably warm.

Laissez les mal temps rouler.

***

Skuggs was enjoying himself.

No, that was not adequate.

As he paced around the chair into which Frank Gallant was strapped, Skuggs decided that "immensely" was the missing component. Yessum, yessum, yes. He was enjoying himself *immensely*.

The room was small, perhaps the smallest in the Rotunda of the Bell Sir. It was, for the most part, undecorated. Blood spilled long ago was grouted into the tiled floor. Once there had been lashes here, and whips, and flails decked out in thorns, and other tools of flagellation. Now there was only the chair with its straps and a trolley full of things designed to make people scream, both of which Skuggs had commandeered from the Beldames who were most obliging.

And because places retain a little of their purpose even when that purpose is abandoned and they fall into disuse, there was a smell. Only a whiff but distinct as the old blood on the old, dusty tile. It was despair.

Against the wall near the only door in or out leaned the necrotic figure of Burrows, master of the undead and counselor to Eurydice. Smoking an odorless, foul-tasting tobacco from a pipe of bone, Burrows wasn't enjoying himself as much as Skuggs. But it was a close thing.

"Now, Frank, I know what musings are on the march in that head of yours," Skuggs declared. "You're musing about how much of a lead you've got on silly old Skuggsie. Skuggsie doesn't know you're nie-on-invincible on account of you being the Dream Warrior. Only someone proficientest in nightmares could have a go at you, eh? Not slimy, slippery Skuggs. He hasn't got a ice cube's hope in hell of torturing you, eh? Eh?

"May I draw your attention to the *straps,*" and Skuggs pronounced the word like it was some fascinating relic recently located. "The straps, I say, fastened about your feet and wrists. Notice a certain, ahehn-hen-hen... hindering quality to them, do you? Deep in the skin? Right down to, dare I say, the strings? Any guesses what they're made of? I shan't keep you in suspense. Oh, just a smidge then. A guess? No? I'll tell you."

Skuggs paused, turning his face for a moment so it was shielded from view by the trolley, trying to contain a fit of giggles. He succeeded, just. He adjusted the trolley height so it was better suited to his own. His gloved hands wiggled over the implements arrayed in neat rows.

"Twenty-two years ago, Eurydice sent me on a mission. She didn't tell me why I was to do what I did, only deigning to give me instructions which were to be followed to the letter. I traveled a long way, farther afield than ever I've had to go, at least as far as this world is concerned. At the end of my journey was a carousel. There I found the corpse of a witch. Well trampled and stomped, she was. But she was *there.*"

The answer to his own question fairly bubbled in Skuggs. He couldn't bear to hold it in. He jiggled his hideous, compact body and let the truth fly from his lips.

"A Nightjar witch's hair, Frank. The straps are made from your mother's hair. In this room, bound with those straps, you are as helpless as a child."

Eager to gauge how this delicious surprise was being digested by his prisoner, Skuggs glanced at Frank.

Who stared. And said nothing.

Skuggs was not to be deterred. He was only in possession of a single eye, but in his cyclopean cleverness he had, over time, taught himself to dramatically dilate his pupil. He did this now, the white of his eye eaten up by a pool of black. His iris of crystalline pink was also momentary devoured. The effect was, strangely, very much like a wink.

Frank Gallant did not return the gesture.

"If I supposes rightly," Skuggs told him, "I would say you are the most hated person in the world." He craned round to look at Burrows. "Sure as sure you wouldn't like a chair? Going to be a piddlingly long time on your toes."

"I'm fine."

"Suit yourself. Or veil and robes yourself, in your case. *Ahehn-hen-hen.*" Skuggs' smile curdled at Burrows' stony silence, but it replenished its mischief and jocularity in a pinch the moment he returned his gaze to Frank.

"The most hated person in all the world," Skuggs repeated. "Burrows and the undead hate you because you're a traitor. Likewise for the slugmen, the troll-coffin-squatters and their master Old Yellow-Eye, the pecking birds, the wily girls drowning anyone who splashes into the Goose or the Gander, the eelflakes and featherdrakes, the Slenderthing and his fat children, the list rambles on! You name 'em, and know that your name inspires the tastiest hate in 'em. Could be your status as a turncoat is why Eurydice herself despises your guts. Can't be sure on that score. She's... wossname... ineffa-something.

"Me?"

Skuggs pottered over to Frank. He leaned in so that Frank could smell the sour reek of his face, so much like the flesh of a rancid pumpkin.

"I couldn't care which way your loyalty goes. Our side. Their side. Sod it. Frank, I hate you because you're pretty."

The prisoner's stare was unflinching. It gave away nothing whatsoever.

Skuggs' eye roved about that expression, hunting for a crumb of anger, a morsel of fear. There was nothing.

If Frank had spat in his face, smiled courageously, uttered a cutting observation on Skuggs' appearance or manner, Skuggs would have been content that this little prelude to the main event (*foreplay, ahehn-hen-hen*) had been worth the price of admission all on its own.

Instead, those eyes of lambent gold rebuked and denied him, like a sheet of Braille set afire before the fingers could translate a word.

Again Skuggs found himself turning away from the man in the chair. This time it was a sneer he smothered, not a spasm of giggles.

An idea suggested itself. A tactic to regain footing in front of Burrows.

Skuggs selected two gadgets from the trolley, whirled, and fixed Frank with his friendliest smile. The warm saliva coating the tar-black teeth slid over his gums, producing a wet squittering sound. He shook his right hand. "Tweezers for your fingernails." He shook his right. "Tweezers modified with a beautiful needle. When the tips of the tweezers rip the nail off, the needle slides out, jabbing you good and proper in newly exposed flesh, nice and pink and vulnerable, eh? It jabs deep, this needle. Tickles something horrible at the back of your brain and makes your whole soul squeal.

"Look, Frank. You might be too lovely for your own good, but I'm willing to let my prejudice slide and extend my hand in friendship. Granted, there'll be a pair of tweezers in it either way, but the main thing is that the hand is being extended. How about you say, good and loud so myself and Burrows can hear, 'Cate Jubilee is a dirty little bitch, and I hope she shits herself to death.' Say that, and I'll consider my offer accepted. Friends, right? If you were my friend, Frank, I'd be well and truestly generous. I'd use this." He hefted the regular tweezers. "Course, if you don't say Cate Jubilee is a dirty little bitch who deserves nothing more than a bowel disease what makes her shit herself to death, well, I shall have to rescind my kindly-windly offer altogether. In that circumstance, I'd have to use this." He displayed the modified tweezers, closing them and yanking with a twist. The gesture made a vicious little needle burst from the tweezer's mechanism. Its application to the raw flesh under a fingernail would indeed be agonizing.

"Well?" said Skuggs. "What's it to be?"

Frank Gallant did not parrot the repugnant phrase.

He said nothing at all. His stare could have peeled paint.

All four of Skuggs' ears twitched. He'd heard something from the spot where Burrows was standing. Not a cough. The necromancer was a savant when it came to puffing a pipe. Could be it... No, not a bleeding chance. Burrows was a humorless bastard.

Even if he were really seized by the urge, surely he wouldn't... by the Lady, he wouldn't chuckle at Skuggs' efforts at intimidation.

Would he?

"I've changed my mind," Skuggs said, turning to rummage in a compartment under the trolley. Out of its depths he took something he'd intended to save till later. Hurriedly, rage thrumming up his throat, he showed Frank a device that was shaped like a blowtorch. Which, in effect, it was.

Skuggs flicked a node. Flame *whumped* out of the object in a long blue-orange finger.

It pointed at Frank's eyes.

"Close them if you like. It won't matter," Skuggs said. "Let's melt those blinkers into jelly."

***

Hughes knocked at the office door. "Are you there, Kitten?"

"I am, Puppy. Come in. Are you seasick? The pendulous gait of the Bettys is a problem we've never been able to rectify."

"I'm okay."

"Sure? You're not used to it. A little queasiness is expected."

"I'm fine, Cate. You don't need to fuss over me."

Instead of the armchair he usually selected, he passed the wall-hung map of Eurydice (which was so complex with algorithmic sequences accounting for the changeability of the land that it was, in truth, more diagram than map). He sidestepped the tray containing the general's dinner (Cate had not eaten a single bite), came round her desk, and slipped his hands over her waist, interlacing them at the small of her back.

"You don't need to fuss over me either," she told him. "I know you can read people effortlessly. I even come with illustrations. But you mustn't feel obliged... you don't have to love me. Not if it requires work. I don't ever want you to feel that."

"Cate. It's loving you that's effortless. Everything else is a trial by comparison." She kissed him, softly at first, and then with a brief but exquisite passion. He understood her. She retreated from him, leaving the lingering taste of her that still, twenty years on, never failed to make a lepidopterarium of Gormon Hughes. In other words, a home for butterflies.

Beneath the tattoos that now covered her face and body completely, he detected signs of restless, almost petulant anger.

"The scouts returned," he said. It was not a question.

Cate gestured to her desk. "Isaac just dropped in their report. It's there, the blue file in all that clutter. A hundred-and-twenty-five odd pages. I had the short version from Isaac."

"And?"

"We're in trouble."

"How deep?"

"Neck. Possibly jaw. And sinking."

"I see."

"They're marshaling under Jane's auspice. For twelve years, Skuggs, Burrows, and Ruthven have been running around like headless chickens. Before, I convinced myself that it was because they were plotting something. In a way, I was right. With their collaboration, John Isherwood succeeded in pulling the rug out from under us, and as a result Eurydice has her shadow back. But I wasn't entirely right. The reason our enemy looked as though they were fumbling around in the dark is because they lacked a general of their own. I thought Burrows might be it, with Skuggs as his master of communication, and Ruthven as his vampiric, draconic ordinance. It even crossed my mind that Eurydice, insane though she undoubtedly is, might be the conductor at the pulpit of their orchestra. Both of those presumptions were dead wrong.

"It's Jane, Hughes. It's always been Jane. She is the one who has at last united them. It's not base conjecture on my part. The proof is in that blue file. Are you all right?"

"A bit nauseous. It's either the topic of Jane or the aptly described pendulous gait of the fortress. It'll pass. Please, continue."

"That compass I took from Skuggs all those years ago. You remember it? At the outset of the war I gave it to Isaac Lawless and the other cartographers. Following it, they found perhaps two-dozen communities of the vilest character."

"Communities?"

Cate nodded. "Isolated civilizations the Citadel has never even heard tell of, much less encountered in the flesh. They've been sequestered in the hidden inglenooks of this world for God knows how long. We rediscovered them. And here's the interesting part, Hughes. After a period of observation, we concluded that these communities had either decided on a neutral policy, or were, astonishingly, unaware that there is a war going on in the first place."

"If they were as isolated as you describe..."

"Exactly. Skuggs needed the compass to find them. Without it, our enemy has been forced to lead me on what I didn't realize was a wild goose chase. They searched for their hidden allies, I pursued. Occasionally we would pitch ourselves into battle, and it was during these melees that the more important element of their plan would be executed."

"The installation of the terraformers," said Hughes bitterly. "Or the Jane resurrection machines."

"Yes."

"So what are you telling me? That Jane has contacted and rallied some of these hidden allies?"

"Not some," said Cate. "All."

Hughes looked at her. "What are we up against?"

Her fingers drummed on his chest with a cantering equine rhythm. Gallop. Gallop. Still. Her eyes communicated a great deal about how she felt, a depthful, comprehensive fear that was quite absent from her voice. "Some of the saplings in the Bloodwood have, thanks to their shallow subterranean growth, uprooted themselves. They're young, but still bloody massive. If their bone-crushing branches weren't enough, their leaves, the same leaves that make up the sticky red compost of the Bloodwood, have drawn away many of the region's mosquitos. Aside from giant trees wearing crowns of droning bloodsuckers, we have toadish, jumping men with bulging eyes whose stare is capable of inflicting a temporary paralysis, and who are armed with ice picks that do not melt no matter the heat. Isaac fancies they nabbed these from the frozen mucus of dead trolls. What else? We have weird women in soiled rags who seem to bring their rivers with them wherever they go, possibly for convenient drownings. Phoenixes that disgorge a petrol-like fluid, only for a click of their beaks to ignite an inferno. Sinister, sentient clouds that roam in packs and unleash flakes of soot-black snow that, at a moment's notice, transform into serpentine eels with venomous slime and teeth like sabers. A bristling, hairy cavalcade of two-headed bears, leopards, tigers, and other dual-mawed predators presumably taking orders from Burrows' own mount, the wolf. The usual rabble of undead, birds, and gooey pseudopods. What else? That report on my desk has our foes listed. Alphabetically, which is considerate. A for Acidic Oozes, Z for Zeppelins stitched from skin and powered by coals of concentrated hate. Systematizing dread and contempt, how very charming."

"Cate."

"What else?"

"Cate, I understand."

"Do you?" In his dark eyes she saw what he wanted her to see. "I suppose so. You've dealt with Jane firsthand. She's as bad as any army."

"How many?"

"Assembled to her banner? Our scouts estimate one-and-a-quarter-million troops, if you can clump some of these horrors within such a mundane collective. The numbers grow every day."

"I can see why you're in a tizzy," Hughes said. "It's a staggering force." He paused. "An invasion force."

"Right about that," said Cate. "Wrong about me. Shit odds I can cope with. I want you here. Personally, and professionally. The troops are responding to you." She shook her head. A frustrated sound escaped her. "I'm muddling myself. It's nothing to do with that."

"Then what is it?"

Gently, reluctantly, she removed his hands and stood back, regarding him with eyes that were tired, worried, and absolutely resolved.

"You need to go back home," she said. "Your Performance has got to be broadcast right alongside the rocket launch. Because while Cate your wife wants you near, and her people's morale could use you, Cate the leader of your scarlet army needs the antidote to the disease that is Eurydice. I need more soldiers. This is no longer a matter of rescuing Evelyn, though that's still an essential key to our victory in the war. It's about lasting long enough to discover the method of that rescue. What's that?"

"What?"

"That grim smile," Cate said. "What's it for?"

"It's nothing. Just you and Hoshrum Thud are on the same wavelength."

She frowned at him. "He sent you a letter? What does it say?"

"You can read it, if you like."

She stepped forward, the distance she'd created between them crumbling beneath curiosity and, perhaps, an unwitting desire to be close to her lover before his departure.

Hughes handed her the letter.

Cate read. Her face, dimpled and taut, fell almost immediately.

She looked at him with such incredible pity that Hughes, now injected with his own curiosity, looked at the letter. The light from Cate's anbaric lamps rendered it semi-transparent. He could see through to the side on which Thud's writing had been magically transposed.

There were only two lines.

But where had the rest of Thud's letter gone?

"Puppy," Cate said. "Baby, I'm so sorry."

"What is it?"

She handed him back the letter.

Hughes. Sorry to erase the former message but figured you'd have memorized it by now. Your father's had a heart attack. In intensive care. Doing all I can.
Thud

Act Seven

Blue Moon

Chapter Eighteen

Evelyn was not satisfied until she could maintain the wall without conscious effort. If you have ever had to remember something, something absolutely essential to your life which could not be immediately dealt with, but which nevertheless must be delivered upon down the road, then you have a good sense of the green wall and its red moss. Evelyn believed in it, developed that belief into a concrete knowledge, then held the wall's image like an important telephone number, a password, the concept for a new sketch, or poem, or some sublime invention.

Only when she could do that (and it took weeks of constant practice without a wink of sleep) did she allow herself to feel satisfied. The satisfaction, sipped and swallowed in a moment of triumph, was heady and sweet. Only then did she form a chair, a desk, and a lamp out of the malleable brainclay underfoot. Last, and most important of all, she conjured the diary.

It was a special diary. It wrote itself.

And it would never run out of pages.

The contents were truly gruesome, which made sense since they were a manifestation of Jane's thoughts. In inky letters so redolent of bugs, Evelyn watched ideas, perceptions, hypotheticals, and deductions scrawl themselves from one page to the next. She had to turn the pages quickly to keep up.

After meditating on the task ahead, Evelyn did her best to parcel off the bit of her mind that was the most Janeish. This was easier conceived of than done. Even when she thought she might have done it, it was hard to know for sure. It wasn't as if a section of her mind were wriggling in protest at having been carved away from the rest. Oh well. No one to trust in here except herself. She amended that at once.

There was no one to trust in here except the Evelynish bits of herself.

And now that part of her, the Janeish part, did give a paroxysm, as if the game could not help but be given away. It wriggled.

Slow, the rest of her told it. Compelled it. Soothed it. *Slow*.

She glanced at the diary. The scrawl moved as swiftly as ever.

Slowwww.

Slowwww now. Eeeeeaaaaassssyyyyy.

Sllllllllllooooooowwwww.

And it did. The writing slowed. Or had it been her imagination?

"Maybe," she said. "Maybe not."

She conjured a pen with infinite ink, hunched over the diary, and began to write. She didn't pay any heed to sense or lucidity. It was what her father would call "stream of conscious" writing. Words tumbled out of her. The pen nib scratched. In a flash Jane's inky thoughts outpaced her. Evelyn's hand darted, overtaking, only to fall behind again.

Slowww, she thought. *All relaxed. All at peace. A symposium of gentleness, that's just it. Easy to rest. Easy, easy, easy. Slowww.*

Another part of her thought, *Green and red. Four sides.*

And yet another part, a vindictive and ghoulishly grinning part, thought, *The trap is laid and sprung, Jane. Laid and sprung.*

***

Frank had not been awake when Skuggs pried away his fingernails, nor when he was branded, cut, smashed in sensitive places with various mallets and hammers, nor when Skuggs, mumbling and giggling to himself, had brutally removed his right foot at the ankle with a hacksaw.

He had been awake to feel Skuggs burn out his eyes though.

Blind, naked, and alone with his thoughts, a kind of phantom vision replayed the last thing he'd seen over and over. The finger of fire, orange tapering to blue. Pointing at him, weaving as Skuggs brandished it, always pointing where it meant to go. Frank's body, enslaved by pain, was compelled to re-experience the sensation of heat that had washed over his skin. Similarly, the memory loosened his bowels and kneaded his bladder with a greasy, cold tenderness. As they cooked in their sockets under the caress of that hot finger, Frank's eyeballs had smelled like melting plastic.

It was the smell, and the significance of the smell, rather than his blurring, runny-egg view of the world that had induced unconsciousness.

Frank was grateful. He was grateful in the way that the religious offer thanks to God on the receipt of good news. They hope it will come again soon. Likewise with Frank. The pain was incredible. He needed to sleep. This waking world hurt too much, too much, too damn much.

But he couldn't sleep. So he endured, as anyone, brave or cowardly, might have in his place. He whimpered, desperately, and wept like a child. His tears were red, and already streaked in a clear, unsightly pus.

Distracting himself proved impossible. He begged whoever might be listening to end his pain, to heal him, or better yet to kill him, for healing from so extreme a hurt must surely involve singular and taxing suffering of an entirely different species. No one answered. No one came.

And then, just as he was beginning to fade into a beckoning, blissful darkness, someone did come.

A key turned in the lock. The door groaned open. Footsteps, and the uneasy rasp of coarse material dragged over cool stone. The unmistakable feeling that someone was standing over him.

A voice that he recognized, prosaic and feminine, said, "It's too good for you."

That same phantom vision showed him her face as he remembered it, peevish and arrogant, and unnaturally, disturbingly long.

"Only one foot amputated. Fingernails missing yet the fingers themselves remain. Your genitals are bruised and swollen but largely intact. Likewise for your kneecaps, sternum, wrists, and hip joints. These lacerations to your chest," Frank felt the touch of crooked fingertips, and shivered, "are superficial and measly. Skuggs," concluded the leader of the Beldames haughtily, "must be either uncommonly merciful or possessed of a limp and lackluster imagination. It's too good for you, Frank, son of the Nightjar. Much too good."

Frank said nothing. He was preoccupied. It took a tremendous amount of concentration to keep himself from whimpering in front of this dogmatic shrew.

More footsteps. *Rassssp,* sighed the Beldame's vestments as she paced around him.

"We are treating Eurydice's counselors to a feast. The courses are still being served. I stepped away to check on you, and moreover to see Skuggs' handiwork for myself. I must say, I'm unimpressed. I will attempt to drop subtle hints to

Lord Burrows that he ought to handle the rest of your physical atonement from now on. If he cannot be coaxed to it, then perhaps he'll permit my sisters and I our chance at your hide. We can be merciful too, but as devotees of a chastening and censorial angel, we understand the merits of cruelty. And," she rested her hands on his shoulders, "we are possessed of vivid imaginations. Tell me this, Frank. Has your time here in this chair given you a newfound appreciation for your mothers? Has the act of being purged by pain allowed you to meditate on the similarities you share with them, fostering feelings of maternal love and, dare I say it, empathy?"

Blind, naked, and spiritually alone, the Dream Warrior said nothing.

"Very well. Some revelations are personal." Her hands slipped from his skin. He sensed her draw away, those footsteps and their accompanying *rassssp* drifting toward the door. "I shall return. Till then."

The door whispered shut. In the lock, a key clicked.

Furious, and unable to enjoy that fury as it was crushed under an oppressive weight of agony, Frank tried vainly to recover the blissful slumber he'd been so close to.

When he was sure he would not find it, his poor throat throbbing from old screams and new moans and sobs, when he was at the end of hope's raw rope... somehow... he slept...

And wakened to peculiar sounds.

Voices with the volume turned up.

Judging from the bombastic quality of the noise, he supposed it was time for the feast's main course. Skuggs and Burrows were probably scooping their plates full. Skuggs especially. The little fuck had undoubtedly worked up an appetite. The loud stuff Frank was hearing was likely the Beldames toasting Eurydice's counselors. Skuggs and Burrows would be wafting in their praise like perfume. The pair would ladle and fork up their meal, and talk about the war, and about the prisoner strapped to a seat with his own mother's hair. He could almost hear their conspiratorial whispers under the clamor. Burrows laconic and Skuggs quivering with excitement. Possibly planning new vectors of approach to this whole torture gig. The lead Beldame dropping her hints like bombs. Burrows catching on, volunteering to take the reins from Skuggs for a while. Skuggs graciously accepting. The Beldames exchanging sickly smiles.

Frank hoped they all choked.

There was a lull. It went on. Frank had other priorities. Phantom limb syndrome was tunneling through his leg in rampant cables. Those cables of sensation quested in the empty space his foot used to occupy. Where oh where oh where could it be? It was one of the most eerie, horrifying things he had ever experienced.

The voices were back. Louder. Shriller.

That party's really rattling.

A teeth-gritting explosion, full of dimension and gift-wrapped with a pebbly patter-patter noise that followed after.

Really rattling.

A second blast, near identical to the first.

Really, really rattling.

The explosions were only the beginning. Commotion evolved into pandemonium, a riot of mingled sounds in which *booms, crashes, thumps,* and *thwacks* grew indistinguishable.

Frank wondered if the party hadn't been interrupted. *By what?* It was his own voice propping up the question. A skittish, hare-in-the-headlights version of his voice. Hopeless and pathetically afraid. *Interrupted by what?*

Nearby, perhaps twenty paces from his door, somebody was screaming.

A woman. One of the Beldames, Frank guessed. Blind he might be, but his ears were working fine. The Beldame didn't sound scared.

He thought she sounded angry.

Maybe something beyond angry. Cantankerously pissed off. *Outraged.*

"Where is he?" a new voice bellowed. The voice was immense and soggy-sounding, as though a parachute had been inhabited by a swamp and was now being flapped vigorously. "Damn it all, where is he? Tell us this instant, you termagants! You bell-humping harridans!"

There was a whoosh, followed by another explosion. Someone—the owner of the sodden voice, a voice Frank recognized but could not place—was smashing apart the marble of the Rotunda as if it were a packet of stale crackers.

A scuffling. Screams. A door—*his door*—was bashed asunder.

"*Brrrrrhuh.* Fiddlesticks and farthings, there you are, Frank!"

"Toad?"

"Who else but Toad of Lillyhill Manor! In the flesh, warts and all."

"Toad..." For a moment Frank was sure he was the victim of a powerful hallucination, one brought on by the extremity of his anguish. "Toad? Here?"

"I see they've done quite the nasty number on you, the dratted blackguards. You haven't a pupil to behold my majestic form, and I shouldn't wonder if the pain has driven you to a mild or even a severe delirium. Let me say it again for good measure. Yes, it is I. Toad. Here to rescue you, valiantly and quite selflessly, *brrrrrrhuh.*" Distantly, yet creeping closer, more sounds of bedlam. "And I haven't come alone."

With that, Toad's heavy footfalls lumbered away.

Frank opened his mouth, intending to call out to the dream guardian, to beg him to stay. *Wait,* he told himself. He waited wordlessly. *Close it. I'm missing a few pieces, but I will not fall to pieces. Close it.* Reluctantly, he pressed his lips together in a thin line. *Pay attention.* He listened attentively, or as attentively as his pain permitted. It was impossible to tell how well or how poorly the battle for his freedom was going. Encrusted with dried blood, his fingers rubbed the arms of his chair compulsively. He felt flecks of dust on his face, shook from the rafters by Toad's war cries.

"Dis*gusting!*" shrieked a Beldame. "Begone from here, you pests. Rodents! Wrrrretches!"

"Rapscallions," a new voice offered. *Mole?* Could he be here too?

"How *dare* you defile this sacred Rotunda. Begone, begone, BEGONE!"

"Oh, do shut up," said Mole, and with a mighty *thwack* the Beldame's wails and the Beldame herself were chopped to silence.

Silence, ushered in by the blow of Mole's hatchet, now enveloped the halls of the Rotunda.

"Where is he?" someone else.

"Follow me," said Toad. If Toad and Mole were here, then Badger could not be far. For reasons unknown to Frank, two of the dream guardians together was a far less likely prospect than three, as though two were a crowd and three company. But that voice, the one who had asked where he was, did not belong to Badger.

Frantic hurrying noises came to him. Toad's sword was not an ordinary blade. It was sized for its owner, forged from an alloy of dream iron (which is like normal iron, only much harder and slightly more purple) and calcium phantasmagorium (which is a strong catalytic compound derived from the woman o' war, a cousin to the psychedelic jellyfish). When wielded by Toad, the sword had the demolition capabilities of an elephant on mescaline.

It had reduced the stone door of the torture chamber to rubble.

Frank heard a gasp, followed by the sound of boots shooing aside those chunks of stone.

"Those butchers. What have they done to you?"

"Des—"

"Don't speak," said Desdemona Cauldronpot. "Oh, dear, dear Mr. Gallant. Everything's all right now. I'm here."

"Straps..."

"Of course."

She began to undo his bindings. "What are they made of?" she mused quietly to herself as she worked. "Not leather, it's too soft and... and lank, but..."

"My mother's hair."

There was a lump in his throat. His words came out thick and garbled.

"Pardon, Mr. Gallant?"

Frank swallowed with difficulty. "The straps are made of my mother's hair."

He sensed astonishment freeze her solid. She thawed, returning to her task. Under her breath, he could just make out her small, *sotto voce* declarations.

"You poor thing. Poor thing."

"One of them crawled up into the big bell suspended from the ceiling," called Badger, coming toward them along the corridor. "It sounds as though there's something else in there with her. Any ideas, Toad?"

"What's that?"

"Any idea what should be up there?"

"How should I know?"

"You knew about the Beldames."

"So I'm the authority on everything Beldames? Don't be absurd. What about this one who crawled up into the bell, then? Isn't she likely to escape now you've left her unattended, you slovenly fool?"

"Not likely," said Badger. "On account of me sealing the bell's base with a layer of wax."

"She'll break through."

"I doubt she has the strength, old bean. Mole lopped off some of her rather vital portions with his hatchet."

"*Brrrrhuh*, very well, I suppose. Can't you hurry those restraints along, woman?" There was an icy silence. Frank couldn't see what was going on but he heard Toad give a compunctious ribbit. "That is to say, may I, I, ah, offer my noble assistance in—"

"No, thank you," said Desdemona. One hand came free. Frank flexed it. "Can you regenerate your eyes?"

"Not until the straps are gone."

Feet shuffled. "Tripped over your words there, Toad," said Badger amiably. "And your ego."

"*Brrrrhuh*. Be quiet."

The mention of bells set alarms ringing in Frank's head. Exhaustion and relief made him muggy, but he could manage the names of his tormentors without great effort. "Skuggs. Burrows."

"Skuggs and Burrows indeed." Toad coughed stormily, spat, and gave a moist chuckle. "They've got spunk, those two. Almost as feisty as these bloody Beldames!"

"Where are they?"

It was Badger who answered. "Fled. Mole and I delivered a glancing strike to Burrows' nose, or where we presumed his nose to be beneath the veil. Our glancing strike's results were harrowing for the enemy. Evidently Burrows has suffered a recent injury to his shnozz because he howled like that wolf of his chained up outside and staggered about like a drunkard, clawing at his face and cursing us as well as Cate Jubilee, whoever that is.

"And that scampering twit, Skuggs, we got him a spry one too. Ah. *We* meaning Desdemona, of course," amended Mole politely. "She's a demon with her fists."

"The path to oneness is punctuated by many rest stops," said Desdemona Cauldronpot. "Several of them educate the willing student in the efficacy and liberating potential of martial arts."

"You're amazing," said Frank.

"They are absolutely. I'm so pleased you told me about these three, Mr. Gallant. They came through in a pinch, didn't they?"

The second strap loosened and slipped away.

What happened next was very complicated and very quick. Strings perforated the air, flowing, stitching, knotting layer over layer in a tapestry of motion. Aurora borealis light shone dazzlingly—blue, green, red. As it dimmed, Frank Gallant stood. He tested his new foot. Not bad. His fingers closed into fists, relaxed, wiggled. Their nails were perfect.

He opened his eyes.

And put his arms around Desdemona Cauldronpot.

"You. You're who I meant. You're amazing. Thank you," he said. "Thank you, thank you, thank you."

"It was nothing," she stammered.

"Just my life." He pulled away. "That's all." His smile was rich with happiness and full of a beautiful reassurance that told Desdemona she could do no wrong in his reconstituted eyes, no wrong, no way. In any matter she could think of, anything at all, he was her humble servant. This, the smile communicated, simply, earnestly, gorgeously.

"My goodness." Desdemona removed a handkerchief from her expansive sleeve and began to fan herself. "There wouldn't be a window we might open, would there? My goodness me."

Frank swept gracefully past her to shake hands with his old friends. "Toad, Badger, Mole. How are you?"

"My back is in ribbons."

"Wax in my lungs."

"I have an ague."

Frank's smile broadened. "Well, you look good. Now, I don't know about you, but I fancy a chat with that Beldame stuck up in the bell. Wax. Good thinking, Badger. Yes, I want to pick her brain about something. Maybe pick a few other things while I'm at it. Thinking about it is making me tingle in all the right ways."

"Oh my," said Desdemona.

"And after we do that, I'm gonna change out of these clothes."

"Goodness gracious."

"Freedom stokes an appetite, huh? Every appetite. When we're clear and back in safe territory, I reckon I am going to do some bad, bad things in the best possible fashion. I..." Frank turned, frowning. "You okay, Dez?"

"Perfectly well," said Desdemona. "I seem to have fainted for a moment. Thankfully there was a handy carpet for me to break my fall."

"Please get off me," said Badger. "If you don't mind."

Desdemona hooshed herself off the recumbent Badger. She was red-faced and perspiring freely. "I'm quite restored now. Don't mind me."

Frank gave her a slightly puzzled look. His good mood melted through, and with a spritzy little laugh he went out of the room, waving a hand to his four rescuers. "Coming?"

In the central chamber they gathered beneath the bell. Badger's wax must have been fully a foot thick. Muffled, they could hear the trapped Beldame venting her frustration against it.

Badger looked questioningly at Frank. Frank gave him a nod.

Balancing on one of his stilts, Badger lifted the other and whacked the side of the bell, hard. There was no chime. The bell was too ungodly heavy for a stilt to shake. But melted by Badger's magic, the wax splattered to the floor, bringing the leader of the Beldames down with it.

"Frank Gallant," she hissed, dripping wax. "You will rue... you will rue—"

Strings made a lasso round her throat. They tightened.

For a short while there was silence. Except, of course, for the noises of someone struggling very hard to breathe.

"Frank," said Desdemona.

He didn't respond. He was studying the lead Beldame. Her convulsions had thrown her hood back, and her elongated face was going purple. This seemed to interest Frank.

"Frank."

No response.

Mole, Badger, and Toad exchanged glances.

Timidly, Desdemona took Frank's hand.

"You won't rue anything," she said. "You haven't got a bitter bone in your body. And regret? What's regret to you? A stranger, that's who. You're not that sort of person."

Silence. Glottal choking sounds from the shuddering Beldame.

Minutely, without ceremony, Frank looked at Desdemona, who gave him an encouraging smile. He stared into some middle distance, looked back at her, and dipped his head.

The Beldame collapsed as the strings loosened and curled back toward their origin. Frank motioned to Toad, whispered something in his ear. Toad coughed a hacking cough. When he took his hand from his mouth, he was grinning. Her wind returning, the Beldame fixed Frank with a look of incalculable hate. "What now, child of the Nightjar? You want me to thank you? Step away. Don't offer me your hand as though you care. I shall rise on my own and see you out of here with dignity." She yanked her hood back over her waxy, bald scalp. "Bygones will be bygones. I will nurse those of my sisters still alive back to health. Now that our gambit has failed, you will hear no more from the sisters of the Rotunda. But mark my words, Frank, you..." She stopped. When she spoke, there was no authority in her voice. Not a drop. "What is he doing?"

She pointed at Toad, who was tromping cheerfully toward the bell.

"You. Hulking frog. Get away from that. No, no, no, *get away from that bell at once! Your soul will be damned, mutilated, slit, and sundered, away away AWAY!*"

Ignoring her increasingly desperate commands, Toad bunched his muscles and hopped. His feet and fingers gripped the rim of the bell. Moody noises rumbled in his bloated throat.

"Hulking am I? *Frrrrog*, am I?"

To the lead Beldame's evident horror, Toad plunged a hand into the depths of the bell. Earlier, before the Beldames, Skuggs and Burrows had ambushed him, and within those very depths of the bell, Frank had heard a strange snoring. Now, he heard moans and mewls of animalistic distress.

"What have we here?" cried Toad with unabashed delight. "Some shrinking violet anxious to hide away? Not today, you naughty bloom. Come to Toad of Lillyhill Manor and see how the sunshine affects your petals!"

With a fantastic wrench, Toad extracted the thing that lived inside the bell.

It landed by the Beldame in a spray of wax. It mewled like a cat whose milk bowl and litter box have been violated. The Beldame screamed and flung herself to the ground in supplication.

Frank examined this so-called angel of the Beldames' faith.

The Bell Sir was like a man and at the same time like a cat. He was overfed and idiot-eyed. The Beldames had stuffed him into a suit of armor, which had never been changed to accommodate his fattening weight. So his breastplate was underhung by a massive pouting lip of a paunch, smeared in hair and matted with sweat. His black-and-brown hair was a patchwork. His whiskered face, jowly and squinting in the brightness of the chamber, cast about crazily. "Uom?" he yawped. "Uom? Uom?"

"Oh, it's vile," said Desdemona. She hesitated. "Though of course, according to oneness, we are all beneficiaries of equal beauty."

"Uom? Uom?"

"What's it saying?" said Badger.

"Who gives a damn?" Toad replied. "It's clearly unfit to live. Mole, my sword."

The Beldame scrambled in front of the Bell Sir, throwing out her arms.

"You will not touch him!"

"Touch that freakish thing? Not on your life!" Toad ribbited in an offended manner. "I'm quite sure I'd catch something, and I already have one ague to deal with. Now, my sword on the other hand, will touch his head and burst it like an overripe melon."

"No!"

"No," said Frank. He walked toward the Bell Sir.

The Beldame crouched, her expression suspicious, her fingers twitching claws.

Behind her, the Bell Sir shielded his face and went on mewling.

Frank put his hands in his pockets. "We'll go. You'll escort us out with dignity. You'll tend to your surviving sisters, and to him." Frank's chin jutted toward the Bell Sir. "We'll never hear from one another again. Bygones will be bygones. Before all that occurs, however, I want to know about Eurydice. Maybe you don't know about her vulnerabilities. Maybe you do. I think I'll be able to tell if you're lying through your teeth or electing to tell the truth out of fear of what will happen if you fib. And you should be afraid, Beldame. Because some part of me knows you're right about me and my mommas. Some part of me, which I despise and attempt to subjugate, defies that attempt, and goes on, and that is the carousel at work. The carousel of beasts. I can be beastly. I am changeable. When the chips are down, I really can be one nasty son of a witch."

Her suspicion had crystallized into a leery grimace.

Under it, he sensed her indecision.

"It's too good for you, this deal," he told her. "But it's the best you're going to get. So, Beldame. Your answer. Do we sully ourselves with further unpleasantness, or do we give this whole allies thing one more shake?"

Desdemona and the dream guardians held their private thoughts.

The Bell Sir shifted, moaning at the world.

The Beldame glowered.

Frank Gallant waited.

And when the waiting was over, he listened attentively.

***

"Were you saying something, Jane? Sorry. I was watching the rains. Of all the places Lucy Nowhere had to pick for us to be, she had to pick somewhere wet. Cold too. Wallowy wet and crappy cold. There was frost this morning. It made me think of *him* singing to the frost on our wedding day. Sang it right off the grass and the flowers and the leaves on the trees. What'd you say? No, I'm not getting caught up. Hm? No, I don't need anything like that. I'm just watching the rains.

"Frank Gallant got away? Away from where? Oh, yeah. How did he manage that? No, I'm not angry. Should I be? It doesn't matter. I had a thought that him dying would make me happy. I bet it will. Right now I can't be bothered to... can't be arsed as they say here in Dublin... can't be arsed to feel angry.

"You were talking about something before, what was it? Oh, the army. Right. Going good? Good. You take care of all that, Jane. Hey, you see that record player? Put on The Rolling Stones. Just do it. Skip this song. Waitwaitwait. There. That's a good one. Yes, I'm feeling fine. Why do you ask? It must be windy out there. The rain is sheeting. See?

"*Get what you want... get what you need.* That's a lyric and a half. What do you think about the invasion, Jane? Think I'm pushing things too far? Aheh. Thanks for saying so. I missed you. I'm telling you too often. I really did though. How are things in Corinth City? How hot? Wow. Well, I'll bet it's a change of pace for you, with you only being there in winter before. Did I mention the frost this morning? I did? It made me think of *him*.

"Jane? What happened there? What do you mean, *when?* Just now. You started spouting off about... Yes, just now. Your face went odd and you started speaking really, well, oddly. That's what I'm trying to tell you. You said something about... the fact that the girls of Wimples School have a deal worked out with the janitor. That they pay him in pocket money to sneak out messages to his friend, a teacher at the local all-boys-school. That those messages are passed to the boys in exchange for reprieves from their masculine antics, such as gluing teacher's chalk to the blackboard or filling the toilets with shaving foam. You said that there's one particularly popular boy among the girls, and he's named... I thought you said *Skuggs* for a second, but I think it was *Skud?* You don't remember? I don't know, how could I know? You said it. Maybe it was a thought from Hughes sailing in? Oh, that's worn off, has it? In that case I have no idea. Whatever. I'm sure it's just one of your fancies, Jane.

"You can head out for a while. Yeah, I'll check in with you later. Okay. Love you too. Oh, Jane? I didn't mean it. I am arsed. We'll get Frank. We'll get every single one of them. You think so? Thank you. It's good to have you back. Really good."

After Jane was gone, Eurydice sat and watched the rains.

On the record, Mick Jagger and the rest of the Stones did their thing.

Eurydice made it three-quarters of the way through the track before she rose from her chair, went to the record player, and tore it to pieces. There had been frost that morning. It had made her think of *him.*

You try sometimes, but in her mind the fucked-up truth was that you never get what you need.

***

7:31am.

It was the sixteenth of June, a week after Thud's letter, six days after Frank's rescue, when Hughes arrived home.

He would have come faster. The Citadel had travel back and forth to Eurydice down to a fine art, but the portal technicians were not miracle workers.

Hughes spent the time compiling a list of mandates to be sent out by his administration... when he was productive. When he was idle, he chewed his nails down to the quick, fretfully and mechanically.

He doled his commands out at the base of Redspire, with Hector, Cassandra, Montcrieff, and a few other capable agents acting as his interlocutors.

Hector took him aside. "You look terrible, my Lord."

"Friends don't address one another by title, Hector. And I feel terrible."

"Do you want me to come to the hospital with you?"

"No, I'll be all right. Is Jane still, you know—"

"Yes, unfortunately. But funny you should ask. It's slackened off."

"Really?"

"She went from zero to dizzyingly fast and accelerating. Infestation on a grand scale. Cases of assault and murder everywhere, more than a hundred times our police force could cope with. Then, most perplexingly, the rate of increase slowed. Last night the number of incidents was its lowest since her return."

"Something's happened."

Hector nodded. "Good or bad remains to be seen."

Hughes ran the flat of his hand along his stubbled cheek, producing an unpleasant scritching sound. "Is Hiromi ready for the launch?"

"She's asking for a delay till tomorrow morning."

"Make it tomorrow night. More eyes on screens."

"True. Shall I contact Gailfax Marmley?"

"No. I haven't got time."

"How will you test your digitized Performance without him?"

"You don't understand, Hector. The moment for testing has come and gone. I need the solution. Jo, get me Jo."

"Jo? How will she—"

"I've been thinking about the problem in a straightforward fashion for years. Maybe... maybe the time has come for a bit of roundabout, even crooked thinking. At the very least, she's a brilliant sounding board."

"It'll be done. All of it."

"Thank you." A pause. "Hector?"

"Yes, my friend?"

"Do living ghosts ever forget things?"

"What kind of things?"

"Anything? Do you forget?"

"Yes. Why?"

Hughes made that gesture again, passing his hand across his unwashed, inelegant facial hair. *Scrrrritch.* "It's nothing. Forget I mentioned it, since you're able to," he said and left the underground.

8:09am.

When he got himself in front of the chair, Hughes did not sit down so much as subside. Close enough to reach out and touch was a bed. One of six in the small room. Hospitals were efficient enough in Corinth City, but like portal technicians the staff running them were not miracle workers. Sometimes medical problems are complicated, sometimes they're a simple matter of space. Three of the six beds were occupied by people suffering from heatstroke and symptoms of advanced dehydration.

In the bed closest to Hughes—a recovery ward special, complete with metal railings and hard, unyielding pillows—his father looked like a ghost haunting his own body. Never the best-looking man, Gormon Hughes Senior had nevertheless projected a sense of youthful vigor. To call a kettle black, he was downright spry. He still ran his own teashop for God's sake, at eighty-four.

Now his eyes were closed, his mouth was open, and his skin was like sour milk and thin, God, so thin as though something inside him were stretching it, making demands of it. Veins stood out starkly in his arms, blue and purple.

Hughes leaned forward to close his father's mouth. Hesitated. Thought about waiting for a nurse to do it. Did it anyway. He sat back.

The light in the room was the same color as his father's skin.

It was quiet. Tonight, there'd been cacophonous snores, beeps, shuffling crepe-soled-shoe sounds, coughs, small, private noises of large, private ache. But for now, it was quiet.

"Hey, Dad."

His father slept. Only he didn't look like he was sleeping.

He looks...

Hughes stopped that idea in its tracks.

"Things are coming to a head. It's weird. The war is about to end one way or the other, the entire bloody world is going to be saved or conquered, we're going to send two men and a woman to the moon, and instead of things broadening out, I feel as though something important is shrinking, as though cords and strings were yanking tight, I... Narrowing, like. Um. Compressed. I can't talk to you, or Wend... or my mother. I can't talk to Krys, The Mum, Frank, Cate's in a whole other world. Everyone here is doing what I tell them, which is a turnout for the books, but when it comes to meaningful advice... how to proceed... what the fuck I'm supposed to do..."

His father slept. Only, he looked as though he were incapable of dreams, much less listening to his son.

"I want to speak to my daughter. I want to hold her. I want to... I... Oh, Dad. Dad, I know exactly what I have to do. I know what I have to do about everything. Every single stratum, layer upon layer of issues calcified, making up the mountain of my problems. I know."

The monitor over the bed bleedle-bleeped and fell silent.

Hughes hung his head. He put his hands over his face, then lowered them, feeling a mixture of pride and self-disgust.

"I know precisely what to do."

His father slept. Only, he didn't look as though he were sleeping.

"Dad. I just don't know how I can do it."

A doctor came in. Hughes saw her walking straight for him.

"Ida Surries," she said, holding out her hand. "How are you, Mr. President?"

"Better than my father. Is his condition, um..."

"He's okay. Has anyone spoken to you?"

"A nurse showed me in. She didn't tell me anything about it."

"Would you like to come outside with me for a minute? We'll have a chat?"

The corridor was busy, so Doctor Ida Surries took him to what the hospital called a Compassion Room, or a Family Room.

"Your father has suffered what's called a major myocardial infarction." Doctor Surries sat with a forward posture, legs crossed and one arm slung over the other, fingers dangling over her knee. Her eyebrows came up along with her shoulders, as though she were apologizing for deploying the lingo when she ought to be shooting straight. "Heart attack. Basically there wasn't enough blood flowing to his heart."

"Has he had surgery?"

"No. Our resident cardiologist, my colleague Doctor Wodebur, ran a few scans and concluded surgery might help. But it would run the risk of—"

"Right."

"—doing more harm than good, right."

"Has he been conscious?" Hughes asked.

"No."

"Will he be?"

"Comas are tricky. Really difficult to gauge, yeah. They vary from case to case. If I may be completely honest—"

"Please."

"All signs indicate that he will recover. But it's impossible to be sure one way or the other."

"Okay. Thank you, Doctor." Hughes had been looking at her closely for a few moments. "Did you used to work in the Toad... In Taggart House?"

Her smile was tired but genuine. "I wondered if you'd remember me. I'm glad you did."

"Me too." *Especially given recent developments with my memory.* Well, well. Ida Surries. Over a decade ago he'd thought of her as Nurse Perky. A lot had happened in the intervening time. Scarlet Citadel man to president. Clueless nurse to competent physician. Not that nurses were any less sleek than doctors. In Hughes' experience it was the former, not the latter, who actually kept hospitals like this one afloat. Still, Ida Surries seemed utterly transformed. He wished he had time to ask her about the past twelve years, but he didn't.

Back in the corridor he made it his business to shake her hand again.

"Thank you for taking the time to talk to me, Doctor. And for looking after my dad. It means a lot. And something else. I know things are untenable here. I know the medical system is a couple of bad days from a full-blown meltdown. I'm working on it. I promise."

Her grip on his hand, polite but lax, suddenly tightened.

"Thank you, sir," she said. "It's... been pretty horrible. I've got people pulling triple shifts, only sending them home when they're practically zombies. You don't know how much it means to hear you say you're... Do you think it'll end soon, Mr. President? The drought?"

"I'm working on it. Me and the best people I've got. Spread the word, okay?"

"Yes. I will."

He thanked her again for taking care of his father and hurried off. He'd lost some time. Hughes knew he'd have to make it up or make it so each passing second counted for double its worth. Ida Surries had just looked at him like the face of desperation itself. More, in her eyes he'd seen the faces of everyone she'd sent home, everyone she'd kept working, every new patient bustled in, every old one hoping they would not soon be bustled out in a bag. In short, he'd seen the drought propelled toward him at speed. It was already here, already doing terrible damage, and somehow he would have to catch up to it.

Faster, he bid himself.

His body, trained to obedience, responded.

But his mind clung to the truth, the one he'd told his father while the old teamaster slept and did not dream (not even of his son who loved him).

8:44am.

That day he left a list of people who could call him with his communications department. The list was exceptionally short. And from that list, there were very few he wanted to hear from. Hiromi Itsuyuda was one.

"How are we doing?" he asked her.

"What is the phrase you theatre types love? *The show must go on*."

He squeezed his eyelids. "It can't be that crap."

"Not crap. We are ironing out the creases. And as with anything complex, we find that we tend to iron new creases in for each one we eradicate."

"Will you be ready for tomorrow night?"

"We'll have to be. The world is watching."

Hughes snorted, told her she was right about that. They talked logistics. Hiromi was a career woman. She had almost no time for people's personal lives, even her boss'. So in the course of their conversation she didn't ask him how he was. Likewise she didn't offer her sympathies about his father, whose condition she almost definitely knew about. Hughes was grateful.

9:12am.

Jo walked into his office, not having to stoop under the door frame, but close.

"Hiromi, I've got to go. Okay. All right. Keep me posted."

Jo hugged him.

"I needed this," said Hughes. "I didn't know until just now."

"Sorry I'm lumpy."

"You're not lumpy. You're blessed with interesting topography." He held her at arm's length and looked up into her face. "I have a favor to ask."

"Reckoned you did."

"It'll take all day. Tomorrow too."

"Cleared my schedule in advance, so I did."

"Will you lock yourself in a room with me until we figure out digitized Performance?"

"Yes."

"We can order anything you like to eat."

"Yup."

"And raid my secret stash of teas."

"Mhmm."

Hughes pursed his lips. "You really can spare the time?"

"Course not." Jo smiled, a huge vulpine smile that would only be ugly if you did not know her. "But you're more important than anything." She sobered. "I can hear them again, you know. The flies."

"I know."

"Can we solve them after we solve digitized Performance?"

"I don't know. Without Estelle Corlum's Perfect Prison, I really don't know. We'll try. One crisis at a time, and even a mountain of problems will crumble."

Jo took this stoically enough. "Lock ourselves in a room, eh?"

"That's the plan."

"Right. Let's call your cadre of butlers and have them send up brekkie."

Hughes plucked up the telephone.

"Have you pen and paper?" Jo asked him.

"Pen and paper?"

"You'll need it. I'm hungry."

9:35.

A man who loves his city, who will not shower because on some level he knows that to rid himself of his current grime would be to lessen his connection to it, who cares for it, nurtures it, loathes its inadequacies, bitterly resents its immovable faults, and nevertheless continues to love it... a man like that does not only work for the betterment of the city. His work is its work. That is what the word politician means, when it isn't corrupted into a role synonymous with gladhanding, bribery, and hapless shrugging of the shoulders. Things are tough all over. What can be done?

Everything. Everything must be done.

Or else what's the damn point?

When she was finished listening to Hughes' explanation, Jo crunched her toast. "Okay. That's the basic shape of the thing, is it?"

"Pretty much."

Jo's chewing was oddly meditative. "It's a wossname," she said eventually. "A conplumtrump."

"A conundrum," Hughes supplied. "Yeah, it is. One I've been whittling at for too long without consulting you."

"Why would you have thought of me? I'm a blacksmith. A tanner. What you might call a materialist, right? All this 'broadcasting magic'... well... it's hardly swords and shod horses, is it?"

"Fair point," he ceded. And she was right. This was not the day to regret past decisions. *Forward*, as Cate would say. *Forward*.

"Was I right to approach you about it now?" he asked.

"Find out, won't we? Have you got a television?"

Hughes blinked. "I can have one brought up."

"Do that." Jo laced her fingers, stretching them high over her head, and popped her knuckles with a sound like a bag of walnuts being hit with a small mammal. "My hands are better thinkers than my head. Cogitation of the palms, Hughes my darling. Make it five or six televisions."

Hughes ordered ten to be sure.

It would be many more sets than that before the day was done.

12:49pm.

With *The Pear and Princess* temporarily closed on account of the intolerable heat, the friends of Hedley Intrig had resorted to conversation over a shared telephone line. They had been shaken by Hedley's involvement in a crime, but they had read in the newspaper that the perpetrators of similar crimes hadn't been at all guilty, and were in fact victims of a magical attack. This consoled the friends enormously. That day, June sixteenth, Marldorp Wilbecomb called Lilian Dippinswick, who added Thomas Coats using a helpful function of the city's telecommunicog. The three of them made a feeble but hopeful attempt at contacting Andrew, alas with no success. Their fifth member had fallen off the grid. Each of them worried about him, in their way.

Lilian Dippinswick was eager to relate the news of her daughter's exam results, which were glowing.

Marldorp Wilbecomb, whose daughter had the kind of results you would not pick up with pliers, they were that foul, was quick to compliment Lilian's daughter and lament his own.

Thomas Coats, whose daughter was a very good liar, wasn't aware there had been exams.

The friends discussed the strains and merits of leaving their daughters in The Wimples School For Exasperating Young Ladies. The amenities were better, but oh, wouldn't it be wonderful to have her home to watch the rocket launch as a family?

Which of course brought them on to the subject they'd each been dying to discuss.

"In my father's day, they'd never have dreamed of such a thing," said Marldorp Wilbecomb. And for once, the idea sounded like a compliment for the contemporary era rather than an insult.

"Wouldn't have dreamed it," agreed Thomas Coats.

Lilian Dippinswick sighed. "Isn't it wonderful?"

Meanwhile, in Hughes' think-tank room in Redspire...

"What annoys me is that anthropomorphism didn't work." Hughes paced, his feet stepping nimbly and unconsciously between the strewn pieces of the disassembled televisions.

"Anthrop-what?" said Jo.

"If Death is a person, Lucy Nowhere, and Dreams three people, Phobetor, Phantasus, and Morpheus, then deductive reasoning indicates there must be an avatar representing television."

Jo had stopped puzzling over silicon sheets and was, with the aid of a magnifying glass and blackboard-sketched diagrams, attempting to gain a rich understanding of pixels. "I'm with you. And? Is there one?"

"Sort of. There's a woman—or perhaps more accurately a feminine personality with godlike power—named Ephemera. Television falls within her domain, as well as other short-lived phenomena like tastes, smells, and the other quick sensorial cues, not to mention batteries, Tinfrost decorations, New Year's resolutions, and the fruitless application of sun cream in tropical countries."

"I peel."

"Well, we're in it together. Anyway, when I devised the idea of infusing Performance into a broadcast to influence mass audiences and recruit them to the war effort, Iphigenia suggested I meet with Ephemera and see if she had any tips worth considering."

"Didn't go well?"

Hughes shook his head. "While initially fascinated, Ephemera quickly lost interest in the whole thing. I suppose I shouldn't have been surprised. Ephemera is as ephemera does. But in the moment I was surprised, and angry too. I tried to use my Performance on her. I fancied maybe I could isolate our world's broadcasts, or convince her to divulge some secret that might crack the entire problem open like an egg. I was stupid."

"Too complicated a target?"

"Human beings are complicated, Jo. The Performance works well on them. No, it didn't work because Ephemera was far too *vast* a target. My inability to influence her backed up something Iphigenia told me around the time we first met. Trying to influence gods is like trying to influence worlds: it's the equivalent of dropping a few grains of salt in a freshwater lake and believing it will be transformed into a saltwater sea."

"Hold on a tick," said Jo suddenly. "I think I have an idea..."

2:23pm.

When their principal committed a violent crime, hospitalizing a teacher as well as the principal's own secretary, the girls did not flinch. When the acting principal informed them over classroom speakers that—excluding exceptional circumstances—they would not be returning home to watch the rocket launch with their parents and siblings, the girls did not flinch. Months ago, when water siphoned from a gurgling splash to a trickle and rationing was instituted, the wave of bullying and hording of the precious liquid by those girls who were stronger, smarter, or simply more savage than their counterparts, failed to occur. Any sign or hint of bullying or hording was met with a crushing, hideous brutality, not at the hands of teachers, but rather at the hands of their fellow students. They did not love one another, and most of them did not even particularly like even their closest friends. But the philosophy, unspoken yet absolute, held true for all of them. They would not flinch.

Because the girls of The Wimples School For Exasperating Young Ladies were made of sterner stuff.

Daisy Wilbecomb, daughter of Marldorp, convinced her friends to play hooky during sixth period. There hadn't been need for much convincing. Jillie Dippinswick had gone because she was flunking chemistry anyway, and Fionnuala Coats accompanied them because Fionnuala Coats was going through a rebellious period (which for a Wimples' girl was not your standard fare of earrings, tattoos, and boys, but rather experimental drugs, young men rather than old boys, and a tendency toward mascara that did not run so much as perform Olympic sprints). The three girls had met along with their fourth member, the daughter of a man who was not called Andrew, at a parent-teacher meeting in which their parents bonded. Thus, their friendship had been forged in the fires of acute embarrassment.

"What do you reckon these stains are?" said Daisy. The stains in question blotted the roof tarmac. They were probably more than fifteen years old, which, to Daisy, made them practically prehistoric.

"Seagull shit," said Jillie Dippinswick, lighting a cigarette from the pack she'd stashed in her skirt. The shrewd, slightly skittish staff at Wimples had been checking bras using scanning equipment since the electric drill incident a number of years ago. If a girl knew her skirts, they were about as good as a bra for secreting bits and bobs you didn't fancy the teachers finding. Jillie inhaled deeply and exhaled with the expert air of a lifelong smoker (she would be thirteen in August). She joined Daisy by the stains. "Yeah, no, the white bits are definitely seagull crap."

"What about the redder bit?"

Jillie shrugged. "Maybe he had a hemorrhoid. My dad's poo is red when he has a hemorrhoid. Finny. Come here and have a look."

"Seen them," called Fionnuala Coats, who was lighting up something significantly stronger than a cigarette.

"Seen them?"

"Yeah."

"Yeah, well, you've seen it all. Stains of all kinds," said Jillie sneeringly. Her caustic attitude faded as she puzzled over the stains again. "It's definitely blood," she concluded.

Daisy gave her a skeptical look. "Do you reckon?"

"Well, it's not tomato ketchup or strawberry jam. Red's one of them whatjamaccalits."

"Rare natural pigmentations," called Fionnuala, who was not flunking biology, or any of the sciences for that matter.

Jillie rolled her eyes.

Daisy held out a hand. Jillie handed her the ciggie. Daisy dragged, frowning down at the stains.

"I bet Evelyn would know what they are," she said.

Even acidic Jillie had no reply to this. She nodded, somber, almost sad.

Evelyn, if experience was to be believed, knew everything.

"Was Worbs saying something about her?" Daisy asked.

Jillie didn't know, but Fionnuala did. "Yeah. Worbs was listening at the principal's door to see if she could overhear anything worth blackmailing him with."

"Smart," said Jillie. "Worbs has been lousy with detention recently."

"So she's listening away when she hears, you know, stuff about Evelyn."

"What stuff?"

"Just like, bad. You know. Not coming into school."

"Did she hear what the story was? Evelyn being sick or whatever?"

"Not that she said, but it must be that."

"Oh."

Daisy dragged, handed the ciggie back to Jillie, and went on wondering about the stains. She was utterly accurate in her guess: Evelyn knew exactly where the stains had come from. They had come from Mr. Glint. Years ago, on this very roof, Paris of Troy had pierced both of Glint's eyeballs with arrows. Mr. Glint's sclera had run like poached eggs. There had been blood, of course, just as Jillie Dippinswick professed. Blood was Mr. Glint's calling card in those days, his and other people's. To some extent it still was his calling card. And it would be, demonstrably, before the war was over.

To lift their spirits, which had involuntarily slumped, the girls put on a radio that had been stashed in a flaking-paint cubicle behind the rooftop power generator. They played songs and talked about small things until *it* came on the airwaves. *It* being the megahit still topping charts. That day, there was not a single channel refusing to run it at least every hour.

The girls sang along, their high humor restored with an extra helping of rock and roll, enlivening and electrifying them.

"Moo-oo-ooon girl. Buy me a ticket... to the white viewin' room. Moo-oo-ooon girl. Come back to me soon..."

Meanwhile, at the summit of the scarlet tower...

"I wish you wouldn't hum that," said Hughes.

"Pardon?"

"That tune, Jo. It's bloody everywhere."

"Didn't realize I was humming. Sorry, love."

"I'm sorry. I'm getting snippy."

Jo showed him where she wanted him and had him hold out his fingers. These she affixed with copper pegs. Cables snaked out of the pegs, connecting Hughes to a generator not entirely unlike the unit a trio of young women had rooted behind in search of a radio. "What song was it?" Jo asked him.

"Moon Girl."

"Catchy. Pretty tune and nice lyrics. Perfect package of a song, really. No wonder I was humming. Why don't you like it?"

"I don't enjoy rock and roll. The beat gets under my skin."

"Gets in my toes and makes them tap."

"You and half the city."

"I expect Evelyn likes it."

Hughes glanced up at her. As she worked, Jo's face was a portrait of concentration. "She likes it," he said. "Loves it."

"There you are then. It's natural for a dad to hate his daughter's music."

"I resent that. I didn't like it before she was born."

"Sounds to me like you were getting in a bit of crotchety dislike early before the rush."

"I'm forty-two, Jo. I'm a few wrinkles and more than a few grumbles from that. Aren't I? Well, aren't I?" There was a meaningful silence. Hughes grunted, unable to stop it from sounding like the grunt of a crotchety old man. "Explain how this is going to work then. And carry on smiling like a dog lapping a gravy pot."

"Give us your hand there, please. Righteo. I've got you fixed up with copper pegs, which will act as conductors. First you're going to swallow these capsules. Heavy, aren't they? I made them dense. Thermoplastics, silicon, urea formaldehyde, glass, lead, raw gases sublimated, and phosphor."

"I swallow these."

"Exactly."

"Formaldehyde?"

"Urea formaldehyde. It's important."

"If you say so."

"Here's a glass of water to help them go down."

"Thank you."

"It's a big glass."

"Thank you very much."

She beamed at him. "Very welcome. Once you've got those gobbled up, I'm going to use this," she thumped the generator, "to run lots of electricity through your body."

"I'll activate Faethe immediately."

"You'd want to, yeah."

"Should I effectively prevent the materials from killing me, keeping them in a kind of pre-absorption stasis? I shall be chemically comparable to a television. The addition of volts measured to the correct wattage will complete the illusion. All that remains is to project my Performance while immersed in that illusion. This is crooked thinking, Jolene."

"Getting cold feet?"

"Quite the contrary. I think we're on to a winner. Is the camera set up?"

"The little red light is winking."

Hughes drew a breath, relaxed his shoulders, neck, and the taut, tremoring muscles in his stomach. He grinned sheepishly. But inside, his hope was a bounding wolf, more excited than afraid. "Ready."

Ten minutes later, when he had purged his blood vessels, nervous system, and digestive tract, he stripped naked and squeezed the hazardous materials through his skin in a film of gooey sweat. That sweat smelled abominably like burnt plastic. Hughes felt a spasm move in him, harmless revulsion rather than anything sinister. The pendant and chain of his amulet seemed to have dramatically increased in weight, as though what he had just done had taxed the magic within it.

In a corner, facing away from him, Jo was watching the recorded footage on a portable vid screen.

Quietly, Hughes slipped out of the room. In the bathroom he gave in to discomfort's urgings. He would not shower, but he did wet a towel to dab at his body and scrub his face. The lead, complex and poisonous, had been the most difficult to expunge.

Dressed and feeling more Hughesish than he had in a long while, he returned to the think-tank. Anticipation fairly fizzed. If he was outside himself, he would have noticed the swagger in his stride and perhaps would have cautioned himself not to get his hopes up too high.

Too late.

Those hopes teetered precipitously and fell with a howl the moment he saw Jo's eyes. She did not even have to say anything.

"Damn."

"Sorry, Hughes."

"No. It's not your fault." *Scritch, scritch* roamed his fingers in his stubble. "Not your fault. Sod it anyway." He blew air through pinched lips. Smiled anemically. "Back to the drawing board."

8:55pm.

Loen Reddlebate sighed the contented sigh of a man who knows that all is not right in the world, but here, in his little corner of it, they are so close to right as makes no matter. His girlfriend snuggled closer, sleepily and cozily. They were on the couch watching a show about criminals doing terrible things to one another. Now and then, Loen's girlfriend would ask him if he was excited. Loen would always respond in the affirmative. It was true too. He was excited.

He had been a middle-of-the-road musician for fifteen years, trying and failing to establish himself and accrue a glimmer of the reputation his friends and family assured him he was destined for... someday.

Life had not been pleasant during those middle-road years. Surrounded by peers who gradually learned more about the industry, their instruments, and the sleek, oily politics of the music sphere, only to achieve greater and greater success, Loen had begun to feel like a forager for gold whose fellow prospectors had long since upgraded to sifting for platinum.

Then, in November of the previous year, he had been inspired by a telephone conversation between his girlfriend and one of her closest confidants. Their charming (if a little dull) yammering seemed to have one central point of focus: the Laurana Project. What was it all about anyway, that whole rocket-go-boom, we-gonna-land-onna-moon thing? Grinning laconically, Loen had found a crumpled grocery list in his pocket. Next to the note about toiletries, he'd jotted down the opening lines to a song that he had very little sense of, but which he understood somehow would turn out to be good. Maybe very good. A month later, he negotiated an hour of studio time in exchange for a crate of beer. The first song he recorded on the album was "Moon Girl."

The recording technician, recognizing that what he was hearing was not just a goodie but a greatie, pulled a few strings and got Loen's album in front of Rubiola Records. The album made its way to the desk of Joachim Rubiola himself. According to Loen's now-agent, Rubiola had listened to *Moon Girl* twice, back-to-back, whereupon he'd clicked off the album and demanded to see the artist. Loen hadn't known what to wear, how to speak. He needn't have worried. Joachim Rubiola did the talking for him. Handily, he also had suggestions about what Loen Reddlebate ought to be wearing when he was out in public, and more importantly, when he was on stage. Rubiola had many ideas pertaining to Loen Reddlebate.

By Tinfrost *Moon Girl* as an album was slated for major international success. The titular single was number one on every conceivable chart, defiant even in the face of the holiday jingles. Such a smash was unheard of since the very early days of rock and roll, when the genre had come rolling up from Ikahagua, a fusion of the nastiest parts of blues, country, and swing accentuated by, well, something entirely new.

Loen, something of a pining introvert, had no idea what to do with fame now he was in its lap. He became mantric, repeating the same takedown of his own hit. "What's there to like about it? What about it is so special? What, what, what?" To which his girlfriend, Tamy-Lynn, had shrugged and replied, "Baby, it's just a song. Get over yourself and get into the listeners. They want you. So get into them."

Over time, he had come to understand the fullness of her meaning.

There had been parties. Discussions of an important, if difficult, second album. Parties. Glitzy events. Some rather livelier parties. And then... then, things had begun to blur around the edges for Loen Reddlebate.

If not for Tamy-Lynn, he wasn't sure he would have made it. Fame's lap was like quicksand, man. Swallowed you up. Swallowed you whole.

Settled, and reasonably sober again, he had broached the idea of that important, if difficult, second album to Rubiola. Rubiola vacillated. Rubiola hummed and hawed. Rubiola was greedy.

Now according to the news the rocket would launch tomorrow night. Loen's new album, *Astrobought*, would release the day after, June eighteenth.

All in all, Loen felt pretty good. He was, as Tamy-Lynn continued to goad him into saying, excited. For tomorrow, and for what the future held.

If the thing in the room with them had anything to say about it, that future would hold nothing but the screams of the woman he loved, and the buzz of flies.

Crouched in the dark just outside the couple's awareness was Jane. With eyes that scuttled and flitted with a wild insectile energy, she watched them holding one another, limned in the sometimes warm, sometimes cold television light. She was a fan of the tube. It gave the middle class a fuzzy feeling of suburban bliss, the rich sensations of danger and licentiousness so detached from them in their padded worlds, and for the poor, it provided a cornucopia of escapist dreams. Such feelings, to Jane, were a delectable seasoning.

She herself felt drawn to Loen. He excited her. She was thinking what it would be like to have him say something really kind and sweet to his partner. Something goopy. Maybe... yeah, maybe a marriage proposal. Honey, life is so cool, how about we step it up. Next level shit. Together. I mean it sweetie pie. You and me, forever and ever. Jane imagined the look on Tamy-Lynn's face as he told her this. She imagined how that look would change when, during the ensuing kiss, Loen would take a firm hold of her hair, drag her flailing and shrieking off the couch, and mash her head through the TV screen.

Ohhh boy. Oh boy oh boy, but that sounded *awesome*.

(beautiful shade of pink-red lining that man's head dark hair rimmed in light reminds me of sunset in Lelepon Daddy I remember thinking Daddy if you were an angel I'd believe in)

"God," said Jane.

Loen Reddlebate turned around. His eyes surveyed the room behind the couch, pitched in flickering darkness. On the TV a retired gangster was stuck in traffic. Some guys were coming to kill him. This the audience knew. This, the retired gangster did not.

"Everything okay?" murmured Tamy-Lynn drowsily.

"Thought I heard something."

Coffee table. Mug. Coaster. Lampshade like a man doffing his hat. Album shelf. Window with the blind closed. His and Tamy-Lynn's shadows and the shadow of the couch. Loen's eyes lingered on the lampshade, so like a man back there. His expression, intent and severe, grew relaxed. He tipped the dark a wink like an old friend (as a jobbing musician he had, for much of his adult life, been nocturnal), and turned back to see if the retired gangster was gonna get his head blown off.

Jane didn't lower her hands, which were clasped over her mouth.

She didn't dare.

In her brain, a tally card ticked another box. Fifteen. She had been made to speak fifteen times in the past week. Last week the tally had read nine. The week before, seven. Fifteen. And the night was young yet!

Desperate to understand what was happening to her, she made a concerted effort to recall the words that had risen like unweighted bodies from the riverbed morgue of her mind.

Guh, a syllable, just a... guh, had it been "good"? "Gumdrop"? "Gregarious"? A *G* word. Guh...

Behind her clamping hands her lips slid over her gums in a snarl.

As usual the shitting bastard words eluded her. An instant ago they'd been solid enough to shove their way through her lips. An angel? Something about an angel with dark hair?

That held no associations for Jane. At least, none that she could think of.

Hughes? she thought, a message-in-a-bottle sort of thought. *Hughes, is that you? Are you fucking with me? Because you know what happens when you fuck with me. You're fucking with the—*

(there was a girl playing guitar and singing what was she singing on the tip of my tongue what was it sounds like Pharoah Jacket)

"Frères Jacques," said Jane. Muffled against her fingers it came out as, "Fvuh Jkuh."

Music ramping up on the show, masking the noise, but Loen almost looked around anyway, instinct rather than actual sound puckering his ear canal.

The retired gangster was checking his watch, his eyes narrowed into frustrated slits. He had somewhere to be. His killers, black-gloved and black-masked, weaved through cars locked in place by the motionless, sunbaked freeway. Drivers seeing them have no inkling as to what was about to happen, only that something was indeed about to happen. Their fright was upon them before they know it.

(Frères Jacques that's right dormez-vous sonnez les matinnes as in are you sleeping listen to the matins and matins means)

No! Beneath her spiderleg tangle hair, Jane's eyes bulged. *I will not! I won't!*

(right on the tip of my tongue matins means it means it means)

HUGHES IF THAT'S YOU STOP IT BEFORE I—

(it means it means it means)

The killers pulled out their quickbolts. Tungsten-tipped payloads glinted in the sunshine, crossbow bolts designed for piercing thin metal, thick glass, and flesh. The killers lined up on either side of the retired gangster's car, six men in black. A woman behind the wheel of a Calcifern car saw them and screamed. The retired gangster, eyes on his watch, looked up sharply, right as the assassins raised their weapons—

(it means)

"MORNING PRAYERS!"

Loen jumped an instant before the TV parroted the steely squawks of murder.

Tamy-Lynn, roused from her doze by the unfamiliar voice shouting behind them, shot up in her seat like a rabbit. "What was that?"

Loen was up. He lunged for the light switch.

Click.

The musician and his muse looked around frantically.

But the room was empty.

Out in the luminous night, among the rooftops, Jane hovered like a cloud of locusts over a ripe cornfield. The burring, buzzing, rumble of her disturbed vermin and rodents scampering along the shingles and gutters.

It wasn't Hughes.

How could she be sure?

She didn't know. But she was sure.

Consideration resolved the matter further. It didn't... have his fingerprints. It wasn't dramatic enough for Hughes, the showy prick.

What was happening to her was slow. Subtle. Unconscionable.

I am a locust over corn, she thought to herself. And hesitated.

Her lips moved, and in a quiet, unsure voice, she said, "Only..."

(*only you're not hungry*)

"No. I'm not," Jane agreed.

A moment later she wondered who she was agreeing with, and what about.

Two miles away from Loen Reddlebate's scenic apartment, atop Redspire, which had historically been referred to many times as the Tower of the Elegy...

Jolene, formerly and cruelly referred to many times as Ogre Jo, who believed that her physical deformities did not count against her if a man as beautiful as Hughes could care for her, opened the door that led out of the office, spared one final, forlorn look behind her, and left without a word.

The office, still to that day referred to by many with awed and respectful voices as The Dragon's Lair, felt the *clisping* sound of the door as it closed, only to fill its aftermath with an oppressive, physically claustrophobic silence.

Gormon Hughes, son of the late Last Dragon, Wendy Dragontail, and the bedridden teamaster Gormon Hughes Senior, spared a forlorn look at the door through which Jo had exited before succumbing to the silence.

Many times this dark-haired, dark-eyed man had been called intelligent, innovative, exceptional, and even sublime.

He had been called lover.

He had been called man of the city.

He had been called Dad.

The silence expressed to him how unworthy he was of such titles.

He agreed wholeheartedly.

Why, said the silence, which was heavy and elegantly serrated as a headsman's axe, should he be deserving of such aplomb and furor when he could not even solve a simple problem? When he could not crack so easy a code, although he was assisted by so brilliantly jagged a mind as Jo's?

He agreed wholeheartedly.

What he ought to do is quietly resign his position, encouraged the silence. He ought to accept that this, his scarlet tower, was always the Tower of the Elegy. On his first day, its denizens had been preparing for a funeral, the subjects being people whose demise he had a direct role in fulfilling. There was only death here. Only failure. Had he forgotten he was only a street boy? A poor, half-starved, insipid puppy masquerading as a bloodhound, then as master of the pack?

He agreed wholeheartedly.

And he was getting older, the silence reminded him. He was thoroughly against the music his daughter adored. He was out of touch. He was beginning to forget things.

"I remember my responsibilities," he said.

The silence, affronted by its interruption, told him that he had already let everyone down. His responsibilities were so much ash. A breeze would soon come and blow it away, like the smoldering end of a cigarette. Speaking of, why not indulge in one of those? He had failed so fabulously in every other aspect of his life. Why not subvert expectation and actively choose failure, thus retaining agency and a tremendous feeling of self-importance?

He grinned.

"Don't be ridiculous."

The silence embodied itself.

"Good," he said. "Stay that way. Let sleeping dogs lie. This one is still awake."

He went to his chest-of-drawers, located an old friend, swept it around himself, and stalked out of the office.

In the elevator he emptied himself out. When he'd reintroduced Corinth City to its past in the form of a theatrical production, the first of many, he'd played the leading role himself. He trusted no one else with the part, and it had been a roaring success. Here at the forefront of his brain was an old grain of movie star advice from the late William Keaton: *acting is reacting.*

Once you knew the part top to bottom and back again, all that remained was feeling out the action each night. Your fellow actor might deliver a line in a new and interesting way. An element of the scene, heretofore unnoticeable, might cease to blend in and suggest something powerful to you. A cue might be missed. A word skipped, an entire line skipped, a whole scene! You had to be ready, on your toes, prepared. An actor prepares, as Hughes had told Doctor John Isherwood so many years ago. An actor prepares so that when the unexpected happens they may respond appropriately. In other words, the heart of performance, in the theatrical sense, is exploration in charted territory and improvisation in the wild.

The elevator *clunked*, *thunked*, and *rattled*. Its doors trundled open.

A man stepped out, still very much Hughes, only changed.

His mind and his heart were wide open.

Prepared.

Redspire was busy. It was always busy.

When they spoke to him, they were all giddiness over the rocket. Sometimes, when they didn't notice him, he overheard their hushed, rustling gossip. Maybe it would go off without a hitch. Maybe there'd be obstructions. Or maybe, just maybe, something almost divine like luck or fate would intervene. The rocket's engines would explode. There would be a shockwave that would reach the city all the way from the launch pad in the countryside. Windows would burst. The heat would climb ten, no, twenty degrees, roasting people in their homes. No one could tempt disaster by any means more provocative than laying claim to the stars. Mark my words, take ye heed, blahdy blah.

The vessel that was Hughes took it in but had no use for it.

Here was a corridor lined in marble pillars, white and veined with gold. Pitchforks of June moonlight stabbed through the tall windows, piercing the gaps in the pillars and skewering the grove of wilted flowers. In the June of his nineteenth year, he'd walked this corridor for the first time. Falstaff had bid him to mind that step there. They'd discussed the Yi-Shi concept of organic regenesis, the dead buried without coffins in the soil, their bodies embalmed with a nutrient-rich paste that encouraged the earth to eat them, regurgitate them, transform them into new life. *Assholes to apples, men to mulch.*

With resources diverted to irrigation of the agricultural sphere, the drought had withered every hint of green in Redspire. He looked at the withered stalks of foxglove and the brown, lifeless viburnum and thought of Iphigenia.

Spliffy, that was his pet name for her.

If she were less devastated by the war, at the height of her worldly, womanly splendor, would his Performance enjoy a parallel boost in strength?

The notion flowed in and out of him, as useless as gossip.

What was, was. What could have been, never would.

The moonlight drew him one way, the memory of Falstaff another.

He followed the neat, talented sensibilities of the butler for now.

Here was a dark, frowsty, musty, stale place. Dungeons are damper in the winter. He stood with a good view on the steps leading down to the cells. There were anbaric lamps, firefly-orange and dialed dim so that light seemed a dim-witted watchman, helpless while shadows had the run of the place, flickering mischievously. A few citizens hired to guard duty and pinned with icons of a scarlet tower played cards and listened to the radio. Kind of them not to use earphones. The malcontents behind bars listened too. Strange, but the dullness of cell life seemed distant, replaced by an avid delight that shrunken living spaces could not consequently shrink. Then Hughes heard the commentators and understood at once. The channel hosts were chatting rockets. They had a physicist on, filling the role of the expert in residence. Standing near the entrance, a shade among shades, he wondered which of those cells held his old friend. He wondered if Falstaff cared about the whole lunar enterprise.

Falstaff, who had traveled the world to change his stripes. Given his frankly terrifying aptitude for assassination, he was proof that someone set in their ways could change convincingly given the right motivation. Yet given that Falstaff had saved the life of Commissioner Thud due to pure politeness... well, it was proof that even a profound restyling of one's character could not entirely divorce you from who you were at heart.

Hughes thought of Chimera, the name of his broken sword and his most frightful power, the power to effect real transformation in a person.

Over the course of his life, he'd used it a handful of times on a handful of people. Miss Gleam. Tommy Fahrenheit. Brenda Kofatch. There were times he'd wanted to use it, been very close to using it, only to have something stay his hand at the last instant. The times that stuck out most shamefully in his memory were the moments in which he'd almost lost his temper and done the irrevocable to the people he loved most. His wife. His daughter.

There were times he'd been asked to dole it out.

Times he'd doled it out of his own judgment.

So what? Wasn't Brenda happily married to her partner, Rummy Lou? Wasn't Tommy Fahrenheit sober as a stone? Wasn't Miss Gleam...

He swallowed drily.

Wasn't Miss Gleam dead?

But the war effort needed willing recruits. If they would not volunteer, he would coax them into volunteering. They would never begrudge him for it. It would forever seem like their own idea.

"Did you scratch your beard?" one guard asked another.

"No."

"I heard you. *Scritch, scritch.* Sign of manky bristles, that. Shave or wash, that's my advice."

"Not my beard. I use a rinse my niece got me last Tinfrost. Lemony."

"Oh."

"One of the prisoners, probably."

The guard looked around for the offending scratcher of unkempt facial hair. No one was paying any attention to him, their focus solely for the radio.

Out of sight, Hughes took his hand from his chin with some disgust.

Movement in one of the cells. A prim, precise movement of someone putting their ear to the bars of their cell. Listening for what the guard had heard, the *scritching* sound. As a butler, Falstaff had an uncanny quality to hear things from two rooms away.

Hughes moved on.

The moonlight beckoned. He went to it.

Here was the balcony where his mother had died. Overlooking the city, its floor was swept and its balustrade brushed as a courtesy. Deep, reverential quiet. An unlived feeling.

Hughes leaned on the balustrade. He looked at the city. The city was there.

Somewhere in that rambling, glittering crisis was Nikandros District, and in Nikandros, a statue of the last king of Corinthia. The Tyrant. The statue would be in a square, one side occupied by the Sequins Messenger Club headquarters, the other by *The Coconut* nightclub.

A little memory made harbor in his head.

You didn't do that, did you?

Cate. She'd said that on their second official date on the day of his first Triumph. Hughes had told her about his Performance, how he had used it to coax Jo out of a storage compartment at The Foundry, how he had instilled in that gentle giant a tangible feeling of self-worth.

To his surprise, at least at the time, Cate's expression had darkened.

You didn't do that, did you?

He had, and he'd apologized later for all the good that did.

And what are these armies you'd conjure out of the suburbs and shanty towns of the world? he asked himself. *Who are your proposed soldiers but a million Jos? Unobtained by statistical categorization. All Jo. All unique. They haven't volunteered because they can't.*

"Or because they won't."

Open as he was, a taste from that long-ago date crept up his tongue, warm and unpleasant. *I know you,* he thought. *I know your bitter tang well.*

Resentment.

Below him, trains, traffic, and pedestrian lights moved in weird luminous rhythms. Horns mingled with the nighttime city sounds. People were still expected to work, drought or no drought. Was that his city?

Won't. Can't. Do it anyway.

I will make you do it anyway.

That fucking statue. The one of the Tyrant in Nikandros District.

Ah, here, a new scene for his open-minded, open-hearted self to inhabit.

Ready, Hughes?

Ready or not, here it is.

Won't. Can't. Have it anyway.

Consider:

Why hadn't he ordered that fucking statue pulled down to loud public fanfare, officiously demolished, or silently disposed of? Was it because, after his acquisition of the presidency, Hughes had done his own private research into the last man who wore the crown? Was it because he had begun to feel a strange sympathy for that man who was called tyrant, as sailors sharing a grudging respect amid storms?

That acrid taste owned his mouth now. Ruled it.

He stood there, the balmy night wringing sweat from his pores, making his light linen shirt of scarlet stick to the small of his back. The moonlight was silvery, and that new astral geography within human grasp brooded in the black, a scaly white eye peering down on him, on the man they would call tyrant if they knew his plan, recriminatory.

On this very balcony, Wendy had told him something despicable.

Despicable, yes... but resonant now.

My dear boy, what is sovereignty but dirtying your hands in the hope your efforts keep things clean?

"We've got nothing in common," he said. "You're no kind of mother. You're nothing. You're shit. And the city agrees with me, don't you?" The city offered no opinion either way. Hughes' eyes drank its glow, ate its light. "Besides. I'd rather be the dark present than the pale past."

His eyes widened. His head rose a little. Resentment slid down his gullet. Astonishment, still warm and citrus-bitter, only more so, overwhelmed his senses.

He had remembered Evelyn's words. *Your beard's going gray, Father of mine. Could even be white.*

And it was white.

Just like Wendy's.

Dark was supplanted by pale. But first it mixed with it. Inherited it.

Look at where he was. Look at who he was.

He moved on, his tread heavier than before.

Here was a rose hedge, in no better state than the rest of the gardens of Redspire. Under the dead leaves and dead, thorny flowers, Walter Pillion slept eternally. Dead.

Walter, there was a character. He'd once threatened to make Hughes intimately familiar with two halves of a broken wine glass. Truly one of history's charmers.

"Cocksucker," Hughes said, but the voice was not his own. It was a perfect impression of Walter. Which was the second time he'd impersonated the mean, drunken bastard.

Walter had been a member of Laurana's unit. He'd held a torch for Hughes. One hell of a torch. Well, Hughes deserved to be burned some way or other after what he'd done. The impersonation had contributed to Laurana's death. Okay, maybe it hadn't. Maybe she would have died anyway. That was the thing that lost you sleep. You never knew.

A Hughes in one universe, Hughes 1 call him, went into the Iphigenia portal and met the two-headed wolf. Hughes 2 stayed home. He repaid his debts some other way. Or Miss Gleam tore him apart.

You never knew. It was that simple. That complicated too.

You won't remember. You can't. You make yourself do it anyway.

Open mind, open heart, you were screwed right from the start.

He couldn't remember Walter's face.

That was fitting. Hadn't it been his own face for a few hours? Playing a part did that. It masked you, transformed you, put the real you to sleep and woke up the secret stranger.

"Rest well, Walter," he said. "I really am sorry. Laurana's parents say I'm their guy now. *Our guy.* They said that. I wonder if they knew me as you did, would they still believe that? I bet you thought you knew me too. We contain multitudes. Who said that, Walter? The emperor of Mysicordelia? No, I don't think so. Well, I'll let you know if I remember. I'm forgetting an awful lot lately. Cate says I'm getting older, Evelyn says I'm going white, and you told me I was a cocksucker who ought to have died in Laurana's place. Maybe that's true. Laurana would have made a terrific president. I named a project after her, a rocket that'll take off tomorrow night, land on the moon God knows when. I bet you've heard about it. Gossip on the rosevine, eh, Walter? Thorny stories blunted by word of mouth. I'm grateful to be alive about as much as I'm sorry she died. And I'm sorry you died too. I remember telling Hector I probably could have saved you from yourself. Got you off the booze. Would you have wanted that? Would that have made you another Jo? One out of a million volunteers? I see why you couldn't quit. Quitting itself is easy, it's staying a quitter that presents the problem. You wouldn't have a smoke, would you, Walter? No, I guess not." He checked the time. Quarter of midnight. "Okay, I best be off now. Rest well, Walter. Sweet dreams."

Through that desolate once-upon-a-time-but-never-again garden, his last word echoed along with his footfalls.

Dreams.

Something reached out, another impulse.

Hughes followed it, his pace quickening for a reason he couldn't have articulated if he'd tried.

Returning to where he'd started, the eighty-eighth floor, he hurried past his desk and down a hallway with glass cabinets along one wall. Navigating his presidential rooms, shuffling and sorting, rummaging and rooting, and creating all manner of kerfuffle and disorder, he eventually found what he was looking for on a random shelf behind a plastic container of elastic bands and a stack of loose documents, noticeably bereft of elastic bands to keep them together. As they drifted and riffled to the ground, his hand closed around the object of his search.

It was rough, striated, and knobbly-gnarly as a gorilla's knuckle. Hughes couldn't believe he'd crammed it where it wouldn't be seen.

He opened his hand and admired none other than the hunk of willow bark given to him by Phantasus.

"It isn't rotten at all," he mused to himself, turning it this way and that. "Quite unchanged."

This is a bad wood, the Lord of Fantasy had told him. *Impish and evil. But good emerges where you least expect, and even trees have their dreams.*

The impulse to find it had sprouted into a large corona of a desire.

Give it a go. What's the harm?

Smiling at the lengths he was going to in order to solve the broadcast dilemma, Hughes closed his eyes and opened himself further, further, and further still, so his mind could accommodate the dreams of a tree.

The smile did not last long.

Kothbiro

This is how trees dream.

They lack the confidence, anxiety,

Regret, or expansive, elaborate imaginations

To do it the traditional way. They must dream as actors

Perform. Improvising constantly. Reacting. Keeping their jade

Minds and their emerald hearts widely, photosynthetically open.

Wasp nests and hornet hives and bird-twig kingdoms resolve.

And beneath chlorophyll-green spires of amnesiac intellect

You will find brambles and briars, and soil-deep

desires. Enriched with a vascular purpose

of communication. Even for a tree

a dream is still a message.

And to

those who

believe in

palm reading:

No sage or

soothsayer

could tell

the future

from the

vermiculate

lines of

the leaves.

But, a bit ironically, trees dream of the future all the time. From crown to

roots.

Kothbiro

Koth bi ro

Koth   bi   ro

Koth   bi   ro

Koth   bi   ro

Koth   bi   ro

***

Midnight had come and gone. This would be the last morning, the last afternoon, the final dusk of human beings confined to earth. Tonight, the engines would belch forth their fire. Tonight, the cosmic would be achieved.

Sometime during the witching hour between twelve and one, somewhere creative, a telephone began to ring.

It was answered.

"Hello?" said Jo, groggily and muzzily.

"Jo, it's Hughes."

"Hughes. Ow."

"Is everything all right?"

"Whacked my elbow off the headboard. What's up?" She listened. "What do you mean, 'what does cloth beer' mean? You use one for clothes and the other for a piss up. What time is it?"

"Almost one. Jo, I said Kothbiro."

"Don't be silly. Everyone knows that. I'm as thick as clotted cream and even I know what Kothbiro means."

"I don't."

"Well, I suppose I grew up around Jolenes who were born everywhere, including Ikahagua where that word comes from. It's thing. Cultural thing. Did you say one in the morning?"

"Jo."

"Yeah?"

"What does it mean?"

"Suit yourself." She yawned apocalyptically. "Kothbiro means 'the rains will come.' Now can I go back to sleep, please?"

***

"Frank!" Cate threw her arms around him. Taking a night watch patrol to be close to her troops, she'd seen him approaching the fortress, along with his unusual entourage.

"Cathy."

"Oh, Frank."

"I know. You hate when I call you Cathy."

"I do." She kissed his cheek, a big smacking kiss. "I love that you're here to call me by the name I hate. I've been worried sick." She held him at arm's length. Frank hadn't limped into the fortress, but he didn't have to. Blemished or not he was on the mend from some horrendous shit, that was plain to see. "God, what did they... We should never have sent you alone."

"You had to."

"I'm sorry."

"Don't be. First, introductions, then the good news, then the bad news."

To the admiration, speculation, and absolute head-scratching bewilderment of the troops on duty, Cate shook the hands of Badger, Mole, and Toad.

"At your service, madam."

"A pleasure, I'm sure."

"*Brrrrhuh*, I have suspicions about this *woman in charge of the martial forces* business, but I shall keep them under a lily pad, so to speak! Well, you've a good firm shake, to your credit. Vuh... Oh, I see, *very* firm."

Cate wiped the slime on her pant leg while Toad massaged feeling back into his fingers. She hugged Desdemona. "Should I ask how you knew to go to him?"

"The spirit of oneness provides," said Desdemona.

"Beg pardon?"

"Us dreamers must stick together."

"Fair enough. It's good to see you Deniiii... Erm. *Miss* Cauldronpot. Frank," said Cate, turning to her poor, misused friend. "Bad news, good news?"

"The bad news is, Eurydice only has one weakness."

"What's the good news?"

His grin was exultant. "I know what it is."

Chapter Nineteen

On Wednesday, July twelfth, Lord Burrows, necromancer extraordinaire, was feeling mortiferously good.

Earlier that week, around teatime or tomb's time on Sunday the ninth, the last stragglers had arrived. Merriment ensued, for the army of Eurydice was at full strength. Indeed, "strength" was a grievous understatement. With so numerous and skilled a force, they were indomitable, indefatigable, un-bloody-beatable!

Of course it wouldn't do to peacock in front of the troops. But here, in his dismally damp, moldy, sour-smelling, coffin-like quarters, he could be permitted a mouthful of wine and a moment of peaceable happiness.

If he were to glance out his windows, which were dusty, crooked, freckled in weird fungus, and malignantly green, he would have beheld a host unlike any this world of his had ever seen. And that vista would only represent a *fraction* of the true host, which could not be measured with even as observant a pair of eyes as belonged to Burrows.

Within the next few days that insurmountable force would reach the portal to the human world, thus drawing the scarlet crusaders, the Agents of the Red Death, into a final confrontation. One that Cate Jubilee and her allies could not hope to win.

Burrows could see it now. He toasted the good and grotesque times to come and drank deeply.

The vintage was nice with an evocative bouquet, the wine offered as a gift from Jane's own orchard. There the grapes bloomed fat and black and buzzed all the way from vine to bottle.

A nice vintage. Perfectly adequate.

But vodka, ah, would have been a treat to enjoy now.

The first thing he was going to do when the counteroffensive was over; he would reclaim his distilleries. Cate Jubilee had robbed them. If rumor was to be believed (and who knew where such rumors sprang from, though they were invariably true), the red-haired devil sang songs about Burrows' largesse and generosity while supping of his precious alcohols.

Burrows' positive Wednesday attitude developed a few creases of displeasure. His thin, arrogant mouth was one such crease exemplified. His grip on the wine goblet was tighter than he realized.

He would start with her nose. Yeah. When she was at his mercy he would violate her face with his scythe, and when the middle of her horrible, hateful face sported a yawning wet red second mouth and she was screaming, then, yes, *then* the real fun would start.

Afterward he would give what was left of her to his undead servants. After over a decade fighting the woman, those who were still clinging to unlife had well and truly earned a nibble or two of her flesh.

Or, and here was a thought, maybe he would raise her remains. Make her watch as they ravaged her world. The idea held a grand appeal.

Why, he could almost hear her begging for death already.

Burrows snapped his fingers. A white fire burst to life in the nearby hearth. It did not dance but rather writhed, maggotish and pale. He waved a hand. A book drifted from a hidden shelf. It was *Circles Within Circles: Schisms and Unifications Within Modern Necromancy* by Gedmilla Burrows, who was, of course, Burrows' grandmother. In spring, she had been successfully traded for a couple of the Scarlet Citadel's cartographers. Nana Gedmilla was still around, in a manner of speaking. Upon meeting her again in late June, Burrows had declared her in the peak of health. Particularly her nose. How pretty it was, and not crushed or warped in the least.

In the spirit of things, he'd also helped himself to her liver.

Burrows swilled his wine and drank to a new nose to admire when he lifted his veil, a new liver to pollute, and a war on the verge of becoming an invasion. The vile white fire crackled. He heaved a contented sigh.

And was soaked in wine when the room's heavy lynchwood doors slammed inward. Ruthven slithered in, his fur whispering over the floorboards.

"What? What?" It seemed all Burrows could manage.

Ruthven opened his mouth and, rather like a retired scarecrow with an oozing pumpkin skull being evacuated through the rusted teeth of a combine harvester, Skuggs plopped out.

Skuggs shivered.

"Tell him what you told me," Ruthven said.

Skuggs gave Burrows a chagrined look.

"Tell him."

"Back off, snake, I'll tell him." Skuggs' upper lip tucked in and his tongue, lumpy with sores, slid over it nervously. His eye had a scared, stunned cast, and stunned he must have been because in his right mind Skuggs would never have called the vampire dragon "snake." Never. Ignoring the state of his soiled clothes, Burrows listened intently.

"I don't get it. It doesn't make a scum-licking bit of sense." Skuggs seemed to get some semblance of a grip on himself. "I been doing just what Jane said I ought to. Keeping my eye on Cate Jubilee and her lot. She said, Skuggs, it'll be a formality. They've got to follow our army, on account of it going straight for their portal. They've got to defend it. So I restles back on me laurels, thinking, this'll be a doddle. But the formality's not keeping formal, Burrows. It's gone downright casual!"

"What?"

"Our wormy apple's gone banana shaped!"

"What are you talking about?" Burrows cut his gaze to Ruthven. "What's he talking about?"

"They're not following us," said Ruthven. "The scarlet army broke course this morning. They're headed southwest toward Icthland and the Zenicor Ridge."

"But that's terrific news," said Burrows. Skuggs' fear was even more nonsensical now. "Wonderful news. We'll make them regret it. We'll head through that portal, kill whatever we find on the other side, and set a trap for when Cate and her coterie jump through."

"This is nothing to celebrate, Burrows." Ruthven's claw tapped Skuggs. "Tell him."

"I've kept in the habit of eavesdropping. Lashing on a hooded cloak and a false bit of clobber I nicked from a dead Citadel man a few years back. Well, I thought a change in direction would be cause for chat in the red ranks, and I was right. I overheard one toff talking to another, not the soldiery, these were proper bigwiggins with the frippery and finery and that. One said, Come on, cut the 'need to know' shite. Where are we going? And the other goes, I asked Captain Whatshisname whose partner is one of them portal techies what was in the room where the decision was just made. Anyway, the second one says, he says: we're off to someplace called *The Furnace*."

Burrows' heart did not pump blood, in the traditional meaning of the word. Imagine the most diabolical mortician. Imagine the fluid cabinet such a funeral director might make use of. Imagine the toxic, system-clearing sludge such liquids might become if mixed together. That is what oozed through Burrows' veins.

He felt his purge fluid innards go cold. His mouth reverted to its former mantra. "What? What are you... What?"

"We must turn around," said Ruthven. "We must go back."

"But how could they know?" Burrows said. His voice was toneless. "How could they know about that?"

"I been thinking," Skuggs admitted. "It must have been the doddering Beldames. When Frank's friends showed up and made us scarper quickliest as could be, they must have kept one of those scrungly biddies alive. Must have skinned her and scolded her into coughing up the truth about... about our mistress."

"But they don't know about the Crystal Country. Only us three do. Only us."

"We've been imprudent," said Ruthven. "Lamentably distracted. It should have occurred to us that the Beldames are old. As old as the Nightjar Coven, their ancient enemy, who were young when the mountains of our world were beginning to wrinkle. Enough. There'll be time to discuss it later. Burrows, we must alter our plans. Turn back now, and we might catch them before they reach The Furnace."

"Yes." The initial shock had passed. Burrows was a general once more. "I'll send a flitter to each regiment. You and Skuggs can pass the word to Stony Crow, the Gentler, the whole bunch."

"We wretched few," said Skuggs.

"We band of brothers," said Ruthven. "As we do, we might well consider how we are going to pass the word... to our dear mistress."

There was a terrible silence.

"Cross that bridge when we come to it," said Burrows.

"There's something else," said Skuggs.

The other two stared at him.

"It's the bit I've been twisted up over," he confided.

"Not the fact that our foes have found our most vulnerable spot," said Burrows, already turning his mind from Skuggs and weaving a spell to craft the many thousands of flitters he would require. "That left you straight and sound, did it? I bet. I just bet it did."

The dragon coiled round to Skuggs, his slitted pupil like a cavity in the universe. "What has you twisted, Skuggs?"

Skuggs told them.

Ruthven's teeth bared in savage distaste. Burrows' spell faltered.

"Exquisite," he said. In the hearth, his maggot-colored fire snuffed out. Wine-sodden, his clothes adhered to his body uncomfortably. His Nana's book was on the ground where he'd dropped it, equally wet. The moment of peaceable happiness seemed distant, like something that had happened to someone else. Burrows' veil shivered as he gave voice to a sound, not quite a laugh, not quite a hiss either, that would have curdled fresh milk. "Wonders never cease. Eurydice is going to love this. Sincerely, she's going to lap it up like a kitten laps up cream. How many, huh? Skuggs, you sniveling creep, look at me. *How many?*"

***

June seventeenth, three-and-a-half weeks earlier...

If they didn't have tectonic, wafer-thin vid screens, they clustered around ordinary televisions. If they didn't have those, they went to their siblings', distant relations', neighbors' houses. A lot of favors were called in. Traffic the previous night was bad, a mass migration to get the whole family in front of the best display possible. Barring access to a television, or given a paucity of visual platforms in general, they huddled around radios.

A few (and really it was quite a few, only trifling compared to the tens of millions watching and listening at home) pitched camp as close to the launch site as the guys in the hardhats let them do so. Blankets unfurled. Picnic baskets, wicker hampers, Tupperware. Come one, come all. Beers, tiny prosecco bottles on ice, juice cartons, a little water where it could be scrounged. Bandanas, head scarfs, skirts, shirt sleeves; they fluttered at throats, the napes of necks, waists, fluttered and wafted like chrisoms affixed round the child of this noble, propitious, goddamn beautiful evening.

Twenty past six, and where dusk hadn't shaded it lavender and peach, the sky was like a kid's idea of the sky, bluer than blue. It was unforgivingly hot.

But that day, that one day, no one seemed to give a shit.

Parents, hard-bitten and bull-brained, found themselves lenient on the children. For their part children found themselves softening up round the edges. The bullies slank away to hang out with their crews. The bullied assembled crews of their own, bruised but unshakably happy.

And the bluest blue sky, which so often that summer gave the impression of an ozone dome squashed down atop the world, suffocating, looked like it was made of eggshell. Like all you had to do was get up there and you could punch right through to whatever lay beyond.

Which was, folk grinningly agreed, the day's intended outcome.

Tiny close-knit groups. Massive parties laughing and jostling one another for a better view. The poor curled up in the back of their cars, listening to burbled reports on the raucous airwaves. The rich, clinking champagne flutes and chocolate-dusted tiramisu plates as they goggled up at corporate-sponsored, electricity-guzzler superscreens. The middle-of-the-roaders hushing their mums and dads, sons and daughters, surrounded in the subtle hum of the homestead.

Everyone would remember where they were.

For the rest of their lives, they would remember.

Will they? thought Hughes, with no gentleness to curtail the cynicism creaking in him. *Will they remember? And how long will those lives be?*

"Thirty seconds, sir," a voice told him.

Hughes glanced up. In front of him, an altar of bulky equipment designed to capture footage of his speech. Entwined at the camera operators' feet nested a craze of cables meant to deliver President Gormon Hughes to God knew how many people.

I suppose a more pertinent question, he thought, *is how short?*

Hector, somewhere. Where?

Suddenly Hughes felt as though he must speak to his friend.

What about, who could say?

He tried to look as though he were stretching out stiff muscles in his neck.

Hector?

"Twenty seconds."

Hector, remind me, what's the first rule of swordplay? I've got the second and third, but what's the first?

How do you start?

How do you go on after you start?

He was here to deliver a speech, to be delivered unto the breathless masses, the audience too wide to be contained in any theatre, to... But what was that speech?

Where was Hector?

There!

Hector must have felt Hughes staring. He looked over. What he saw in Hughes' face must have given him a start. He frowned and began to hurry over to the chief broadcast engineer. They spoke. The chief shook his head emphatically. Hector gestured to Hughes. The chief gawped. Hector spoke, only to be met with another shake of the head.

"Ten seconds, sir."

Just as sharply as he'd known he must speak to Hector, Hughes understood that what he needed, his old friend could not provide.

The feeling inside him was pendulous. Swooping.

Not dread, but panic.

Dead silence in the recording room. The camera lenses were alien eyes in an observation tank. The countdown guy held up five fingers. Four.

Iphigenia, he begged. *Send your arms to protect me. Guide me.*

Three fingers.

Very faintly, he thought he heard a kind, bemused voice say, *Guide yourself.*

Two.

The first line of the poem shot across his brain.

This is how trees dream.

Accompanying it, heliographing magnificently, was a memory as strong as the roots of the poem, and their sprawling root-word climax: *Kothbiro,* which means *the rains will come.*

That strongest of memories was of a park full of trees. He was nineteen. Cate's head was on his chest. A level up chimed. A game for a boy. A lesson for a liar.

The poem. The memory. The elixir of hope.

One finger.

None.

Red lights winked on. Live, we are live.

Dark hair combed, dark-and-pale beard clipped and pomaded, and hazel eyes shining, Hughes spoke, effortlessly, and collectedly.

The world paid close attention.

"Ladies and gentlemen, people across the globe, my name is Gormon Hughes. For those of you who don't know me, I'm the President of Corinthia. Before that I was a boy who wanted to understand what was going on because I felt as though the world and those in power were keeping secrets from me. Perhaps that feeling was justified yesterday and might be again tomorrow. Today I am in power. Today, I keep no secrets from you.

"Thanks to the ingenuity of the international scientific community, and in particular the astounding genius of Professor Hiromi Itsuyuda, the Laurana Project is about to send three astronauts out into the cosmos: destination, that pale jewel, which I have come to believe is like a diamond in the night sky. The moon is a proposal ring; come, it invites, and explore endless horizons. The moon is also our closest galactic neighbor, and we could hope for no better precursor for this mission than the neighborly and convivial spirit of collaboration assumed by the brilliant intellects that made today possible. These bright minds are solving secrets the universe would keep in the dark, hidden from us. So many secrets, like grains of sand sifting through our fingers every second of every day.

"Yet while we look to the heavens for hope we must also look to ourselves. While three astronauts, a woman and two men, embark on a journey that shall place them in the company of stars, we find ourselves in the company of doubt and trouble. The war with Eurydice has raged for twelve years, but I tell you now, that behind the scenes it has lasted for longer than that. It is and has always been a war of commerce, and magic, and heroes, and villains, and those who are cast as shadows who would like very much to walk in the light. But more than any of those things it is a war of constant aggression, one punctuated by the very drums of hate and resentment. The only thing that counteracts resentment is love. It is for sweet love that we carry out the bitter business of today.

"Good people of the world, I come to you in our hour of need. I come to you in the name of my daughter, your daughters, your sons, nieces, nephews, grandchildren, great-grandchildren, and all the children yet to be born. I believe that this drought which has brought our way of life to its knees was created by Eurydice. She would starve us, make us thirsty, force our children to cry out for the very rains that they have never felt upon their faces.

"I believe too that the rains can return. The Ikahaguans have a word: Kothbiro, a nursery word that brings comfort to the weeping child. Kothbiro. The rains will come. But we must bring them. We must go out and bring the rains home with us. I ask you to contact your local military volunteer office. If you have a strong back, we need you. If you have a sharp mind, we need you. If you have skilled hands, we need you. If you are brave and willing to learn the trade of a master, we need you. I can't compel you. Nor would I wish to. I'm just a father speaking to you now, hoping that one day my daughter will sift through the secrets of the powerful, sorting the lies from the truth, and the bad from the good. I want my daughter to have children of her own.

"This is our darkest hour, an hour of shadows, an hour of need. Let the rocket fires burn, and the moon shuttle land safe, and in the name of God let this call not go unanswered."

Hughes gave an imperceptible signal. Camera operators responded.

Red lights winked off.

Dead silence in the recording room. All heads turned to the monitor on the eastern wall. There, live from the launch site, the day's second countdown began.

Hughes looked for Hector. Hector was crying. And smiling.

The rocket fires burned.

The shuttle slept inside the rocket, soon to be deployed, soon to land safely upon the moon's gray-white wasteland.

And the call, heedless of the name of God, did not go unanswered.

***

July tenth, and a deadly game of cat and mouse was playing out between the two armies. In discord with nature, the mouse was being forced into chasing the cat. Long before it had begun, the results of the game had already been decided. But tired, worn, and weak as it might feel, the mouse could not quit because the prize at stake was the mouse's own home.

Feeling frustrated, desperate, and distinctly mousy (her left eye, for example, had developed a whiskery little twitch), Cate concluded the afternoon's work and went for something to eat. By chance she ran into Lorna Blacktower, who informed her that she was on the way to collect Cate for a special occasion. Today was the anniversary of the Battle of Impfolly Barrow, the first triumphant rumpus of the war.

"Don't say rumpus, Lorna," said Cate. "Scrap I can deal with. I can even stomach colorful expressions like, "barney," "brannigan," or "have a donnybrook," depending on the speaker. But rumpus? I don't think so."

"Someone's grumpy."

Cate relented. "Sorry."

"You're not."

"Yes, I am." Lorna was smiling at her. Cate returned it. Her hand went to the mirolaen bloom she wore, as white against her red hair as fresh snow on a field of blood. "I always forget the tenth and remember the thirty-first. Odd that I should prioritize the major dates of my father's war and not my own."

"I don't think it's odd at all," said Lorna. "Come on, they're waiting for us."

"Who is?"

"You'll see."

Fifteen minutes later, Cate was sitting down to a supper of salt lamb, leeks, and boiled potatoes with most of the original members of her Company when the word came to them.

Leaving their meals to go cold, the Company raced out of the mess hall, along the corridor, up a spiral stair, and out into the central courtyard. Gossip circulated among their group, a skimming birdlike murmuration that erred on the side of caution while sounding closer to glee with every passing moment.

The afternoon was bright and clear. This being Eurydice, however, the ever-changing sky was brown, smooth, and shiny like the skin of an amphibian. In the distance, thunderheads gathered with the makings of a summer storm in them. As the Company crested the battlements, they could just about discern the thunder itself, a chorus of ribbits and croaks.

"This is my kind of weather," preened Toad with his hands on his hips.

Next to him, Badger and Mole adjusted their earmuffs.

Cate rushed forward, throwing herself toward a merlon gaping like an empty gum between the toothy crenellations.

I'm not seeing this. I cannot be seeing this.

She was.

The Bettys were stationed on the lip of a V-shaped valley. A river flowed through the valley. This being Eurydice, the river had not been there yesterday.

Now, the river was joined by a train of marchers. The train snaked by the banks of the river, curving and winding as far as the valley's edge. Scarlet banners flapped and riffled in the early evening breeze. Convoys or carriages, wagons, and carts packed to the brim with supplies straggled in the midst of the armored men and women. Cate couldn't begin to guess at their number. Two-hundred thousand? Three? Five?

Their boots shook up a clamor so loud they rivaled the toadish croak of the nearing thunder.

Instinctually knowing there would be a message for her, Cate snatched from her pocket the sheet of enchanted paper she and Hughes used to keep in touch.

The sheet bore four words:

To my Kitten,
Surprise.

Cate grinned, a huge, feline, and corybantic grin.

She was a mouse no longer.

***

Cate Jubilee's guess was way off, though you ought to forgive her that.

There were more than five-hundred thousand volunteers marshaled to Eurydice to join the fight.

More than double.

More than triple.

Two million strong arrived on the tenth of July, their hearts and their minds closed to the evil of this hostile world, and wide open to the future of their own. A future that glowed like the moon.

Incidentally, that was the answer to Burrows' question, which would arise on the twelfth of July. *How many?* he'd ask.

Two million.

***

"I bring you nurses."
Hughes kissed Cate's left hand.
"I bring you doctors."
He kissed her right.
"I bring you bio-mechanical, structural, marine, and chemical engineers."
Her left.
"I bring you fresh food, fresh clothes, and freshly forged magic items."
He kissed her nose.
"I bring you soldiers to wield them."
He kissed her eyelids, one, then the other.
"I bring you Faethe, Amulet of Dragons."
He kissed her chin.
"I bring you a broken sword named Chimera."
He kissed the lobes of her ears, the hollow of her throat, and the middle of her brow.
"I bring you myself. I am, now and forever, at your command."
She kissed him.
"So responsible," said Cate. "You know what happens to responsible men?"
"Someone comes along and makes them irresponsible."
She drew a line between his chest and hers with a finger, slung her arm round his neck, kissed him again, and said, "If I could marry you twice, I would."

***

As the storm blew in and showered the fortress in stinking, marsh-gas smelling sleet, Cate summoned the following people to the cartography center:

Professor Dianne Bevinshirt was a fit, wiry little woman. She radiated the aura of someone who really liked exercise. When her body grew tired, her mind began to lift the mental weights of advanced physics, bacteriology, genetics, and, most recently, portalology. This rotatory process had repeated itself in cycles since she was three-and-a-half. Now she was thirty-seven. Perfectionist watchmakers would be baffled by the internal gears and springs of Dianne Bevinshirt.

She was here because Cate needed someone who understood Eurydice's geography beneath the geography, so to speak. If a world can shift on the turn of a whim, then what has been presumed safe can quickly become dangerous. As the astronomers at the space station had learned, generally by smashing their amazing minds against the problem until it fell over out of sheer sympathy, mathematics can simplify anything. Even behavior. Even shifts in an unpredictable world.

She was also here because Cate was reasonably sure that Dianne Bevinshirt had no hand whatsoever in John Isherwood's betrayal. After exhaustive interrogations, and as far as Cate could tell, John seemed to have worked alone. Besides, something told her that Dianne Bevinshirt was incapable of betraying anything, not even her diet, which consisted of thirty whisked egg yolks a day and the occasional bowl of carrot shavings.

Burnished Isaac Lawless was almost completely unchanged from the first time Hughes had met him. Oh, that first time there'd been bruises, welts, a torn nostril, a few handfuls of hair torn out at the root, and Isaac had been deprived of his clothes, thus leaving his... well, what Isaac would call his nadgers and his third leg... exposed to the elements.

Today he wore tight-fitting survivalist leathers dyed scarlet, though an enchanted pennant pinned to his shoulder could be activated to alter the outfits color at a moment's notice. This adaptability had proved ideal for the provision of camouflage while traversing the fiercer locations in Eurydice.

But yes, aside from a bill of good health and the fact that he wasn't stark bollock naked, Isaac was exactly the same as Hughes remembered him, in other words a mean and naughty-minded little bastard.

Hector, likewise, was as constantly himself as it is possible for someone to be. As a living ghost the edges of his being had the quality of thin pale curtains with sunshine pouring through them, golden and diaphanous. Today Hughes wrapped his throat in the peony scarf Hector had gifted him long ago. It was a small sign of Hughes' deference and love for his former mentor.

Frank Gallant wore a suit of charcoal-black, Mr. Glint a suit the color of wine, or stagnant blood.

Cate's hair was tied back in a long, elegant braid, exposing her face in all its hard-jawed, characterful-nosed glory. Her tattoos were more extensive than even those of Hughes' old companion, Krys the Painted Girl, and that was really saying something. Over her body of ink and glass, Cate wore an unadorned but striking set of silvery-white armor. This so called "steelish" armor had been intended for Hughes but later redesigned to fit his wife. It was a fair sight heavier than Isaac's leathers, almost as cumbersome as steel plate. But the weight was well worth the shouldering, for the armor's ingenious capacity for turning the claws, projectiles, blades, and teeth of her foes had saved Cate's life more times than she herself even realized. Another general might have donned a humbler ensemble, but Cate was a firm believer in dressing for the job at hand, and you couldn't have a war meeting without capital double-yew *War*.

They stood around a three-dimensional map of Eurydice. The map was equipped with levers and bolts, so that areas of the geography could be amended in accordance with the oh-so-frequent adjustments in Eurydice's terrain. Cate held the position of authority at the head of the map. Frank was on her left, Hughes on her right, the place of highest trust.

Hughes, they all reflected in their own private way, *looks like a man who has just climbed a mountain and has energy for another peak. He looks charming, well-groomed, and immaculately tailored. He looks like precisely what he is: a man who has succeeded in assembling the largest army in the history of... um, history. Catching his eye feels tantamount to catching the eye of a sphinx who knows the secret pleasures of the universe. In essence, he looks tremendously good.*

Everyone mused on this, except Mr. Glint, who despite years of education and a great deal of self-improvement, still thought "handsome" meant someone who has lost a couple of fingers.

"Cate tells me we've got something," said Hughes. "Something big. Obviously, I'm way behind. So catch me up."

Frank Gallant set a credit chit on the map. It sparkled pinkly.

"Somewhere in this world there is a Crystal Country. It is the chink in Eurydice's armor. If we can get there, we've got her."

They all looked at Hughes for his reaction. But he was composed.

"Go on," he said softly.

Frank gripped the credit chit representing the Crystal Country between forefinger and thumb. He moved it to one region of Eurydice. To another. Here. There. He did it swiftly, precisely, and spoke all the while. "Our problem is that Eurydice has control over where it appears. Mr. Lawless, in your opinion as a cartographer, does Eurydice exert control like this over all of her domain?"

"Like hell," said Isaac Lawless. "Eurydice's unstable as a house made of jelly. What are you smiling at, Hughes?"

"Nothing. You jogged a memory. Please, continue."

"Right." Isaac cranked a few levers and manipulated bolts, creating turmoil across the three-dimensional map as it sundered and rejigged itself into a cohesive whole. "If Eurydice could control herself completely, we'd have been buggered from the start. The ground would have opened up and swallowed us whole. She'd have unleashed toxins from every plant she could. The atmosphere and celestial shifts would have condensed so violently, we'd have shit ourselves dry, been blown to bits by a barrage of lightning strikes, or been drowned by the unpredictable tides. As above, so below like."

"How long's your career, Mr. Lawless?" asked Frank.

"Forty years, this summer, pal."

"How much of this world have you seen?"

Isaac perused his ear with a finger, his face contorted with thought. "Reckon I've seen a fair whack. Most, dare I say, and I do."

"And have you ever seen this Crystal Country?"

"Pal, I've never even heard of it till you came with yon Toad, Badger, and Mole. Never even *heard* of it."

"Why should Eurydice have control over this part of her world when she lacks control elsewhere?"

"Why is water wet, mate? Some shite simply is as it is. I just draw the maps and tot down me observations of the culture and that. I'll leave the biospherical psychology to those as get paid for it."

Frank nodded. "Thank you, Mr. Lawless. Prudently put. It doesn't matter how Eurydice exerts control over the Crystal Countryside, though I'm sure the good Professor Bevinshirt can illuminate us later. It matters that Eurydice can. It matters that she does."

"And if we can reach it somehow," said Hughes. "What then?"

"If the lead Beldame told Frank the truth," said Cate. "Then Eurydice will be exposed. We can't say exactly how that'll look, but I'll take exposed over invincible any day."

Hughes seemed unsatisfied. "If the Beldame told the truth. Did she, Frank? How reliable is this information? I don't mean to burst our bubble here. It just seems..."

Frank smiled. "Too good to be true?"

"Yeah."

"The universe hands you a rose but you can't help but fear the thorns, huh? Wise, brother. Wise. There are thorns, big barbed ones. We'll get into that. But the flower, this Crystal Country, is just as real."

How do you know? How can you be sure?

Hughes knew Frank couldn't hear his thoughts. All the same, Frank's demeanor changed. His eyes—so yellow and warm—turned baleful, like the headlights of a car bearing down on you. The aurora fluctuating in his hair went sable-black and tenebrous, strung through with ribbons of red. All at once Hughes believed his friend. Every word. For a moment, he almost felt sorry for the Beldames, who had gotten on the wrong side of this beautiful, dangerous man. Almost, but not quite.

The moment passed.

Frank was charming old Frank again.

"Okay," said Hughes. "So we need to get ourselves inside this Crystal Country. Now tell me about the thorns, as Frank calls them. The most obvious one I can think of is the fact that Eurydice has total geographic power over it. How are we supposed to get to it if she keeps moving it around?"

Cate jerked her chin toward Frank. "Thanks to Frank, we've got the answer there too."

Frank gestured politely to Isaac. "Mr. Lawless, would you mind?"

"You're some slick mick, eh?"

"I try, Mr. Lawless."

"Do you give lessons?"

"On what?"

"Being slick."

Frank grinned. "By arrangement. Would you—?"

"Yeah, yeah."

Isaac grabbed a particularly large bolt labeled "Bloody Everything" and yanked. With a *ruckle-ruckle-blat* the entire map slid, skid, and gyrated, every region coming apart and reassembling somewhere different, some elements blending and mixing as they changed until the whole of Eurydice lay transformed.

Or so it seemed.

Hughes' brow wrinkled.

When the whole apparatus fell still, he walked around the map, tapping a few regions with a finger. "These three," he said wonderingly, "didn't move." He glanced up. No one was looking at him. They were staring at Professor Dianne Bevinshirt.

Hughes joined them, his brows rising expectantly.

"They never move," said the professor. "According to our electroencephalograms, they have never moved."

"Electro... like an EEG?" said Hughes. "I thought those monitor brain activity."

"The psychoanalytical and neurological communities have made a convincing argument suggesting that we in the sciences should only partly treat Eurydice as a world," said Bevinshirt. "In part she should also be treated as a woman, and a mentally erratic one at that."

"Jelly," said Isaac Lawless proudly.

The professor ignored him. She said, "Even in the most unstable psyche, there are usually some areas of a subject's personality that remain fixed. We believe these," she indicated the three immovable regions, "are those stable areas. They are the parts of Eurydice that she cannot control, but which nevertheless remain uniformly regulated and predictable.

"Here, we have a plateau of rock that culminates in this formation. Upon examination, we have deduced that it perfectly mimics the ancient druidic astrolabe, those mysterious stony henges used, at least in some fashion, to chart the progression of the stars. There is some debate, but we believe that this represents

Eurydice's connection with the cosmos and her forever uncertain place in their superstructure."

"How can uncertainty be a constant?" said Hughes. He cursed under his breath and grinned an embarrassed grin. "Because that's how people work. It's truly rare to find someone settled in their own shoes. Forgive me, Professor. Go on. This is fascinating and, I expect, pertinent to the question I posed earlier."

Bevinshirt gave a slight nod, showing that she'd taken his veiled meaning to heart. "Here, a desert in which little to no discernible life is permitted to live. The region's climate actively resists the attempts of flora and fauna to gain a foothold, much less thrive. Yet at the center of the region, a maelstrom of sandstorms, isolated earthquakes, and catastrophic magical detonations, our advanced probes have detected sound."

"Is it music?" said Hughes.

Bevinshirt, a woman who was not easily impressed, looked very impressed indeed. "How do you know that?" she asked.

"Yeah, how do you know that?" said Cate.

"Something Evelyn told my father once. She told him that Eurydice likes when the music breaks." Hughes had moved to stand next to Cate. Still looking at the group and not his wife, he touched her hand under the map's table. "I know what it's like to surround that which you love in resentment. I believe that Eurydice views music as an integral part of herself, and the aggressive wasteland around it is a construct that hints at self-loathing, negation, and yes, resentment."

He felt Cate's fingers squeeze his, lovingly and supportively, before she pulled away.

"What about the third region?" Hughes asked.

"The Furnace," Bevinshirt replied.

"Looks like a fireplace laid out horizontal-like," Isaac observed. "Never been there. Must have skirted it a few times and been deterred, probably by heat."

"No," said Bevinshirt. "Not the heat. This is conjecture, but I believe it was more likely that you and your fellow cartographers were repelled on an instinctual level by the emotion pulsing from this place."

"I think I can guess, but tell us anyway. What is The Furnace, Professor?" said Hughes.

"It is the locus of her rage. The seat of Eurydice's anger."

"And the key to the Crystal Country," said Frank. "The Beldame told me something sleeps under the coals of The Furnace, which are constantly tended by Pokers, Ash Wardens, and Smoldering Sentries. Something keeps the coals lit. Something that connects the fire on the surface to the superheated core of the world. If mastered, this thing could wrest control of the Crystal Country from Eurydice—"

"And give it to us," said Hughes. "I'm with you. What is it, the thing sleeping under The Furnace?"

"A dragon."

Silence. Outside, the sky was dark and overcast like a pond seethed in scum. The noxious winds blew strangely cold. Against the map room's lone window, hail pelted, a billion battering fists.

"A dragon," Hughes repeated. His head, lowered, came up. His dark eyes twinkled. He did not know it, but that twinkle reminded those who had known her of Wendy. "And I, the Last Dragon of our world, will compel it. I'll use my Performance. I'll get us to that Crystal Country. How do we draw it out of its slumber?"

"We stop those who tend it from doing so," said Frank. "Three sites of power. We need to conquer all three and break their idols to rouse the dragon."

"For now, we keep up the appearance of desperation," said Cate. "Follow Eurydice's army toward the portal. Two days from now we'll alter course and head straight for The Furnace. See this pass boring through the mountains?"

"A spot ideally chosen," said Hector. "Provided there *are* mountains there in two days' time."

Isaac Lawless snorted. "Bleeding mad for a last-minuter is Eurydice."

Cate was undeterred. "We'll deal with that if it happens. All being favorable we'll be able to take a decently direct route, see?"

"I see," said Hughes. "What if Burrows splits his forces, some to follow us and the rest toward the portal. We're gambling on exploiting Eurydice's weakness by fronting our own."

"Low risk. If any," Frank said. "Consider, man. They're keeping close watch on us. Count on it. Once they clap eyes on the size of this new army, once they figure out where it's headed—and they *will* figure it out, count *double* on that—

you really think they'll split up? You think Eurydice and Jane will *let* them split up?"

Hughes allowed that he did not.

"I still don't like it," he said. "Low risk is still a risk, Frank. Cate, it's your call. You're the general here."

"All or nothing," she said. No hesitation, a good sign if he knew her instincts half as well as he thought he did. "The truth is we don't have a choice. The numbers arrayed against us are too great. Commit or bust."

"All or nothing," Hughes echoed. "Okay. I'll notify Thud, have him rally as many of the streetbeaters he can spare to guard the portal entrance. Maybe he can scrounge up something from the people who were on the fence as to whether or not they'd join up with the Citadel."

"The prospect of staying home might decide them," said Cate. "Clever, Hughes. Can you live with that as a contingent?"

"I've got to."

"Can you bespell a dragon, convince it to open the way to the Crystal Country, and win the war for us in one fell swoop?"

Hughes' didn't have to look around to know every set of eyes were on him.

He thought about projecting a confident air, but as the seconds crept by his whole *I am the Last Dragon* vibe had seemed less like bravado and more like the sort of chest-thumping that got better men than him into trouble. He decided to opt for that best of policies, honesty. It was working for him so far. Elixir of hope or not, the truth was addictive stuff.

"I wish I could declare it one way or the other. I don't know if it'll work. The Performance is not a fine art. It's let me down before, and it might let us down here." Cate's pinky slipped around his. It gave him heart. He didn't smile, but that twinkle in his eye was on full display. "I can promise you one thing. I'm going to give it my best shot. And if all goes to hell, I'll use my amulet and beat that dragon until it forgets all former loyalties and calls me Sweet Papa Gormon."

There were chuckles. Cate laughed her magnificent laugh. Even Dianne Bevinshirt's lips showed the ghost of a smile.

"Miss Professor?" said a voice like a hot tarmac cooling on the sidewalk of hell. Bevinshirt cleared her throat. "Yes, Mr.... Um..."

"Glint, Miss."

"Yes, Mr. Glint?"

"If all them stable bits on the map are Eurydice's stable bits..." He took the credit chit from Frank and held it up for them all to regard. "Then what is this Crystal Country thing?"

"Well, it's quite complicated, but if I had to describe it simply, I'd say—"

"Is it her preconscious mind?"

Bevinshirt's jaw dropped.

"Or subconscious? Or conscious?"

The jaw remained dropped.

"Only," said Mr. Glint, "I got some experience with them." He turned to Hughes. "I can give you tips."

"Thank you."

"You can have this Eurydice lady. And the fiery dragon. But this Ruthven bloke, the vampire dragon, killed Eilandri Titansgrave. Sucked her blood. Took her away." Mr. Glint's fingers closed into fists. "That makes him mine."

Act Eight

Kothbiro

or

You Are My Stethoscope

Chapter Twenty

Contrary to popular belief, the undead can be run ragged. Such is the compromise necromancy must make for the art of raising the dead: if you salvage some of a life, you must salvage all of a life. That includes mortal tenacity, their appetites, and the ability to overexert oneself and become bushed.

The same went for many other creatures who were never mortal in the first place.

Oozes for example, suffer from an unfortunate tendency to solidify into immense lollipops if pushed beyond their limits. Featherdrakes shed copiously and plummet from the sky, asleep, should they be denied rest. Slugmen become snailmen, who become shellmen, i.e. dead.

So it was that, reluctantly, and vowing that it need only be a brief respite, the forces of Eurydice camped for the evening outside Burrows' mansion of bones.

A select few individuals had access to the mansion itself.

This included Skuggs, who'd have preferred to stay outside, if it was all the same to Burrows.

The thing was, Skuggs had been pondersome on a few nuzzling, puzzling quandaries lately. He liked very much to do his pondersomes in a handy cave or under a lightning-sizzled tree; in other words, in private. Of course, his guzzlible luck prevailed. The flitter came just as the third of the evening's moons swept, wicked and snow-white, into the starry sky. Burrows wanted to see him. Immediately. Skuggs grumbled, groused, but eventually loped to Burrows' dining room. It was, as you might imagine, absolutely macabre-mad with decorative bones. The drawn curtains were flaps of stitched skin, the table glistened like freshly exposed musculature, the chandelier was ribcagey, and Skuggs had his suspicions about the manufacture of the candlesticks, which had a definite... *boniness* about them.

Skuggs' nostrils cringed at the smell of dinner, which had been served and tidied up. Burrows and his top brass stood around the table now, across which a map of The Furnace lay spread.

Muffled but unmistakable, they could all hear the two-headed wolf in the adjoining room, gnawing on something juicy.

Burrows did not look around, but the necromancer must have sewed eyes into the back of his head because no sooner had Skuggs crept up behind him when he said, "Where's Ruthven?"

"How should I know? I'm not his keeper." Skuggs availed himself of a goblet a servant had neglected to remove from the table. The food here might turn your belly, but booze was booze. "Probably with Jane. Speaking of, Burrows, I've been meaning to—"

"I suppose I can waste time telling you both separately. Not like disaster is looming or anything. Cate Jubilee's ranks has swelled dramatically, but we still outnumber them ten to one. The sacrifice is speed. They're outpacing us. At this rate they'll reach The Furnace half a day ahead of our vanguard. Cate, Hughes, Frank Gallant, and their entire host will have unfettered access to the three sites of power. If they summon the dragon, there'll be nothing we can do. Jane's reminded us of Hughes' unique talent. She says it's a tossup between working and falling flat, but she doesn't like those odds and neither do I."

"Too right," said Skuggs. "Thinking of Jane, Burrows me old, wilted crocus, I wonder if—"

"Drastic times, drastic measures." Burrows showed Skuggs three hastily yet evocatively whittled statuettes. "You," a statuette came down on the map with a *click*. "Ruthven." Another. "And I." The third. "We'll set out at midnight tonight, each of us backed by a hyper-mobile troop. We go hell-for-leather, reach The Furnace, and fortify the sites of power. From then on all we have to do is hold off that red devil Jubilee and her cohorts long enough for the main body of our army to smash them in the back." For the first time Burrows turned sidelong. Skuggs could feel those eyes hidden behind the black veil boring into his skull. "I believe you'd call it a tarsty sandwich, me old rotten rose. I'm giving you the biggest troop. Don't say I never do anything for you."

"Me? Defend a site of power?"

"Backed by an elite unit, carefully selected to be efficient, unflinching, and deadly."

Skuggs had to resist the impulse to wring his hands. He set the goblet down, its contents untried. "Defend it for how long?"

"As long as you have to."

"Give us an estimate."

"Could be eight hours. More likely it'll be closer to twelve."

"But I'm no fighter," Skuggs said, a touch desperately. Burrows' top brass had all gone quiet. They were looking at him. He didn't give a bassoon's blue horn if they did or not. "I'll go with you, Burrows. Or Ruthven. Or..." His lower row of teeth clipped out nervously but he pressed on. "Or Jane! I'll go with any of you. Only not on my own. Cate Jubilee's got a warrant for me in her head, and she'll stop at nothing to cross my head off the paper forever. Elite unit or no, on my own I'll be scourged to squelchy bits in no time!"

Burrows' tone did not rise. He was conversational, speaking as if it were only the two of them.

"You're crafty. I know how you won your riddlewood house. Do you?"

"Course I do. But—"

"You're quick. And better with that knife than most would give you credit for. If Cate comes, slit her throat. Give her the knife. Fuck her with it. If someone else arrives, picture her while you give it to them, pointy-end-first. You've a warrant in your head for her too. We all do." He gestured. There were nods and eager mutters of agreement from his high command round the table. Taking their cue, they set back to talking amongst themselves.

An attendant hurried in. "Lord Burrows, Ruthven has arrived. He... erm... he demands you meet him in your solar, where he can stretch out and be comfortable."

"It's a demand I'll acquiesce to. I need him amenable as my fellow counselor here. Skuggs, amuse yourself however you like. At midnight, we skedaddle."

"Burrows, I've got to talk to you—"

"I won't hear any more protests, Skuggs."

"It's about—"

A terribly cold hand closed on his shoulder. "No," said Burrows. "No more."

Skuggs went on dauntlessly. He was sick of slinking off when a thing that needed saying went unsaid.

Quietly as a spider injects venom, he said, "It's about Jane. She's not herself."

"None of us are ourselves. Our Mistress Eurydice is in the greatest danger she's ever known."

Skuggs opened his mouth to retort, but the hand, which had already begun to send tendrils of chill through his clothes and down into the meat of his shoulder, was removed.

"Skuggs," said Burrows, just as quietly yet with none of the venom. "You remember how callously I treated Ruthven when he lost his child? The truth is I was masking my sympathy for him. I felt such a heinous shock of sympathy for him as I had never felt for anyone. When the sibling of my wolf was killed... listen... do you hear the sounds of gnawing? They've stopped. My wolf recalls her loss as intensely as if it happened yesterday. She's attenuated to grief, magically and inescapably. When Ruthven's child sacrificed itself for him, giving up the prospect of its own life for the prospects of its parent, I was reminded sharply of my lost friend, my wolf, who I have had since I raised both he and his sister on the eve of my sixteenth birthday. That wolf, the male, insisted on going to Iphigenia to inflict the damage that needed inflicting because of the caprice of our beloved mistress. She wanted carnage, and my wolf volunteered. The prospect of putting his own life in danger was acceptable, so long as his sister and myself could preserve our own prospects. And when word came of his death, I begged Eurydice to let me seek out any means possible to take retribution. I begged since my mind could think of nothing but the two-headed pup yapping gladly for his new lease on life and showing his love and appreciation by licking my hands and my face. Eurydice denied me. I struggled to contain myself. But I did contain myself and have been biding my time ever since. Or so I thought, but grief unattenuated can sleep, only to wake when you least expect. Ruthven's child died, and sympathy kicked the bedpost in my brain, and roused my sleeping grief. You couldn't have known, though perhaps you felt you knew something. Still, I didn't expect you to have put two and two together. I'm good at masking my emotions, Skuggs. You might say I am practiced in the use of veils." His insidious lips twisted, though of their usual arrogance there was no sign. "And you might also say that while I'm no stranger to feeling that something is wrong—disturbingly and frighteningly wrong—I can recognize when there is nothing to be done to make it right. That sometimes the needs of the many outweigh the anxieties of the few. That though the flies may buzz troublingly, they buzz, and that is what matters.

"Do you understand, Skuggs?"

Skuggs nodded, his one-eyed gaze fixed on his boots.

"Reach out to our mistress if that understanding dwindles. But you know what she'll say."

"It's raining in Dublin. Something like that."

"Something like that. Do you still love her?"

"Say again?"

"Our mistress? I'm asking if you still love her?"

Skuggs' head shot up. He looked at Burrows as if he were the craziest loon in the world.

"I thought as much," said Burrows.

Skuggs fidgeted, embarrassed. "A tarsty sandwich, you said?"

"Us on one side, the rest of the army on the other."

"And Cate, Hughes, and all them mungulous unctuous buggers crushed between?"

"That's the idea."

"I'll go sharpen my knife."

Burrows picked up the goblet and handed it to him. Skuggs looked from it to the necromancer and back again. He grinned, drank the gunky, waxy gin in one great gulp, and handed the goblet back.

"I didn't know. About your wolfie. That is, I knew, but I hadn't the smallest, cursoriliest of clues that—"

"See you at midnight," said Burrows.

"Right."

Skuggs waddled out of the bone mansion, more pondersome than ever.

Yet at the same time, he felt more sure and centered than he had in a long time. The night's fourth moon was rising, sickle-shaped and gray, much prettier than the last, in his opinion.

Not one bit in the mood for snickering, he went looking for a handy cave or the underside of a lightning-sizzled tree, somewhere private to think on today, and midnight, and the stuff that came afterward.

By their cookfires, the undead regaining their strength were treated to a feast of introspective mumbles as he passed.

"Ahehm-hem-hem."

***

Using her carefully built rumor mill, which consisted of trustworthies such as Sergeant Daniel Jurdels to name but one, Cate Jubilee ground out the most attractive loaves of gossip. As she expected, the entire army, from soldiers to cooks to surgeons, gobbled every loaf ravenously.

These rumors consisted of the standard fare of things a general wishes her people to believe strongly before a military offensive.

We, as the forces of good, have not only moral superiority, which goes without saying, but in this instance a battlefield advantage that ought to make our spirits soar to glorious and indeed ballistic heights. We are faster, better equipped, able to avail of the favorable terrain, and poised to strike harmoniously and catastrophically. We're going to win. They're going to lose.

It isn't over.

But it soon will be.

The precipitous decline of morale that followed the battle of the Bloodwood and the death of Eilandri had been plateaued by the arrival of such astonishing reinforcements. Instead of a lull in the heart when one thought of the Pale Giant's lifeless body, there was a rising. Not "poor Eilandri" but "for Eilandri." Let's do it. Let's get to this Furnace and show the evil scumbags the heat, the real heat! For the people on the other side of the portal. For the kids. For ourselves. For Eilandri and all those who'd fallen before her. As the loaves were broken up for sharing and devoured, that improvement only continued.

As the newcomers adjusted to the seesawing, seasickness inducing motion of the Bettys, the experienced veterans helped, offered advice, grinned knowing grins, and winked surreptitious winks. The veterans pointed out the finer applications of magic items. They welcomed, roughly, yet very warmly. In return the newcomers brought hope. And socks. And biscuit tins.

"Why biscuit tins?" Cate asked Hughes.

"It's a reminder of home," he said. "Never underestimate the power of a biscuit tin."

"*You harr vise Hoos. Verrrry vise.*"

"True, eet ees true. Can I've a custard cream?"

"Only if you can take one."

"Cate! Cate, come back here! We've got a strategic meeting in five minutes—*Cate Jubilee you get back here your president demands... oh sod it.*"

From a high balcony, Frank Gallant watched his friend tear off after his other friend, silver-black chasing fiery-red. He dearly hoped that they wouldn't associate their hijinks with the act of play, thereby connoting play with the member of their family unit to whom play came so effortlessly and charmingly. He dearly hoped his friends would maintain the happy vibes as long as possible. Running into either of them these last few days, Frank had felt he was rolling an invisible dice. Maybe Hughes and Cate would be in fine fettle and finer fooling. Maybe they'd be severe. More often than not, they looked like they were on the brink of something, barely gripping the edge.

It was the war, Frank got that. The war and their daughter.

Scratch that.

It was all the kid.

Evelyn, he thought. *Cute as a button, smart as a whip. A kind heart like her daddy and a real firebrand just like her momma. Sweet too, always sweet to her Uncle Frank. Evelyn. What's that freak Jane doing in the pilot seat? How much of it can you see? How much of it feels like you're the one doing it? I hope you're closed off from everything. Hibernating somewhere deep within the monster, within the insect hive. I dearly hope it.*

The wind blew pale strands of hair across his face. He brushed them back. A presence joined him on the balcony, grim and horrifying to many, familiar and wholesome to Frank.

"Mr. Glint."

"Mr. Gallant."

"Coming to the meeting?"

"Are you going?"

"Yeah, I guess so. Just to fine tune some of the details. It's all worked out. Yeah, I'll go."

"Then I will go," said Mr. Glint.

Frank's aurora burned a bemused blue. "You still feel sore about letting me go off on my own, don't you."

Mr. Glint said nothing for a while. Then he said, "I was not in my right mind."

Frank had grasped that at the time. Mr. Glint had been a sad spectacle when Frank arrived in Eurydice. The fate of a certain lavender-eyed woman was the cause there. Simple, folks. Simple, right. And so hideously complex too.

"If I said I forgive you for the umpteenth time, will that make you feel better?"

"No," said Mr. Glint.

"I mean, I chose to go on my own. We knew it was the only way."

"Yes."

A pause.

"That Ruthven better watch his ass."

"Best watch his front too, Mr. Gallant."

Another pause.

"It won't matter."

"Pardon, Mr. Gallant?"

"It won't matter if he watches his ass or his front," said Frank. "Won't matter if he watches at all, will it?"

A deep silence.

"No," said Mr. Glint. "It won't."

In the courtyard, to the hilarity of many onlookers, Cate had vanished into a glass surface holding the biscuit tin. Hughes was now declaring in a loud, distinguished, presidential voice that this was not playing fair, and he would start smashing windows if she didn't at least consent to hand over a ginger nut.

"Mr. Gallant?"

"Yes, Mr. Glint?"

"Got something for you."

"What's this? A book of... Are these yours?"

Glint nodded.

"A book of your poems?"

"Compiled them in a..." Mr. Glint's sour mouth worked as he found the correct word. "In a compilation," he declared.

"That's amazing."

"Yeah?"

"Amazing," said Frank. "Truly."

"If I get scragged in the barney, don't publish them. They're for you." A vision of posthumous literary glory seemed to flash before Mr. Glint's sunken eyes. "Unless you think a publisher might be really keen."

"You? Bite the dust? No way. Don't feel stung. Here, I'll hold on to it for now. But I expect you to add to it when we make it through this thing."

"Right you are, Mr. Gallant."

"Let's get to this meeting. I think Hughes is running out of steam. Maybe Cate'll show mercy. Poor guy just wants a... oh, I see she's pelting him with shortbread. I suppose it's better than the hail. Let's hope that holds off. Think of all that cold hissing down in the hot Furnace coals! Talk about steam. Maybe we'll mosey to the meeting anyway, be punctual peas in a pod, right Mr. Glint?"

"Be a change, Mr. Gallant."

They departed the balcony and their quarters. In the corridors folk gave them a wide berth. Scared. Respectful. Same outcome.

"How do you feel about the teams?" Frank asked his partner. "Hughes and Hector heading for one site of power. Cate and her Company another. You and I heading for the last one."

"How do I feel?"

"Yeah, I'm asking."

The anbaric lamps cast Mr. Glint's face in slanting scarlet light, making his bald head look like a skull drawn by an artist with serious issues.

"I feel inevitable," he said.

Frank howled with laughter. "I bet you do."

***

Being a sister is asking for help.

Jane looked up the short (three chunky steps) flight of stairs. She looked past them at the door. Beyond that door there was a bedroom. One she'd been inside countless times. Her sister's bedroom.

The first step was easy.

The second was hard.

The third...

Silent as a louse under a plant pot, she scuttled back to the bottom of the stairs.

She stood there in the dark space, one of those lightless in-between places every house has lots and lots of, and wrapped her arms tight about her chest.

Jane did not look well. She did not look herself.

Her long, mirthful face, a contrast to Hughes' long, melancholy one, was a war ground. On the slopes of her cheekbones to the planes of her chin, cheeks, and brow, emotions waged ugly battle after ugly battle. As they combed her greasy-feeling hair and fumbled at the buttons and buckles of her clothes, her fingers spasmed and hopped like bugs on a hot pan. Unaware she was doing it, she would hoosh up on tiptoe then rock back on her heels, an asylum patient back-and-forth.

And no wonder.

My head. Her head was a *fucking roadshow of shit.*

With great effort, Jane raised one of her trembling fingers and bit it.

An instant of pain brought delicious clarity. She looked around. Behind her, a bend, and far below through the banister, the house's entrance hall. Ahead, the three steps. And the door. There. Now.

If I try, if I really try, I'm sure I can think in a straight

(*wonder what Daisy Jille and Fionnuala are up to now I can picture them eating chocolates from a box they snuck in who knows how Daisy always offered me the caramels she knows I'm mad for them sometimes it scares me how easy it is to lose friends when making them is so hard wish I had a sister it's harder to lose track of them provided they don't lie to you your entire life ha-ha-ha-ha Fionnuala keeps erotic vids on her portable if she's ever caught there'll be such a scrape she showed me once it was a nude man and I remember thinking goodness he must have a devil of time with his trousers*)

line.

Jane staggered. She dragged her rueful gaze up, her eyes terribly wide.

The first step was hard. The second...

No scuttling retreat this time. Freeze zone. Full stop.

Denial had come and gone weeks ago. Acceptance had overwhelmed her like this. In a freeze zone, stiffening and complete. Jane, full stop.

For days she'd grappled with the idea of asking Eurydice what was happening and what could be done to stop it.

Only now did it occur to her: if she, as Eurydice's one and only shadow, could not guess at her predicament's solution, why should Eurydice herself hazard a better one?

And something else glided up from her, as Mr. Glint would say, preconscious mind.

Through the irrepressible clot of thoughts that did not belong to her, Jane felt it nudge her like an unexpected raft in choppy water and grasped it.

A possibility. A truly horrible and outrageous possibility.

She felt her feet take her, steadily and unhurriedly, to the bottom of the stairs once more.

She still did not look well, for things tend to stay the same. But recognizing that hateful possibility had inspired her, and it showed, for things seldom resist metamorphosis, as the caterpillar to the butterfly.

Jane did not know how she would go about it yet, but she would investigate the possibility.

Thus resolved, she turned her back on Eurydice's door.

Being a sister is knowing that sometimes you've gotta help yourself.

***

Evelyn went motionless. Full stop.

After a while she remembered to breathe. She checked the state of her walls, massaging her wrists. There was no need to massage her wrists. Writing in the diary was not like writing in the real world. She could tell her hands were not subject to cramp, and they would obey, good little hands that they were.

Green and mossy-red, her walls were okay. She checked the floor and the roof, which had been a cunning addition to her fortifications. All normal.

What had she felt just now?

She had a fair idea. She checked the diary to be sure.

Yes. As she'd thought.

"Took you long enough, Jane. I suppose I amn't making it easy for you." She flexed her fingers, gave a final roll of the wrists, straightened her back till her neck popped satisfyingly, then bent back to the diary. "Here we go."

In the gray realm of subconsciousness, the girl wrote.

And closer every moment, the insects were no longer on parade.

They were searching.

***

There are different kinds of armor.

The strongest physical armor is possibly something steelish, such as the reflective set crafted by Jo. Or it might be dragon scales, which stories are rather fond of. In that same vein, it could be the fabled and invisible armor granted by Faethe, Amulet of Dragons, invisible because it could transform one's very skin into a nigh-impregnable barrier.

Philosophers have been known to propagate the sincere belief that ethics, moralism, and critical thinking provides an armor purer and more enduring than anything that girds the physical body (perhaps ignoring the fact that ideas, when left exposed to the elements such as complacency and reinterpretation, may also rust).

Iphigenia would lend her opinion on the matter.

When you become a parent, you become armor. A suit uniquely molded. A carapace. A shield.

It is for love that you protect.

It is for love that you also become a weapon.

On the first of August, the day of The Furnace, Hughes wore red. Light, and bright, and fine. His boots were supple but sturdy, his amulet concealed under his shirt. On his hip, Chimera and his Krys knife kept close company.

His Performance moved in him like a powerful muscle warming up.

That morning, he went out and talked with the troops. Cate's example led him. Listen. Speak. Listen some more. Get to as many people as possible while making each group and individual feel special, seen, and heard. As far as he could tell, they were pleased to get a moment alone with him. Few needed clarification of their orders.

More than once he was asked about the moon launch. Did he know how it was going? Were the astronauts well?

Anticipating this, Hughes had written to Thud. He replied honestly that yes, the astronauts were very well. How was the rocket going? Forward. Without incident.

More than once he was told about the children people were fighting for.

More than once he was asked about Evelyn.

At eleven o'clock the western sky, hazy with smoke, was suffused with a red-orange glow. The stomp of the Bettys mingled with a roar, low but constant, that Hughes could feel in his teeth. It was the sound of a coal fire the size of a city.

By noon they could feel the heat. The scent of the smoke was oddly beautiful, redolent of cozy burning coal on a winter's night. Soon it would shrug off that beauty and grow eye-watering. And the heat would be as bad as droughted Corinth City. In reality it would be much worse. Everyone knew it, but when someone asked if anyone had a bag of marshmallows, the laughter Hughes heard ripple around him was genuine.

Hector joined him on the battlements.

"I can see the mantel. Can you, my apt pupil?"

"I see it."

Jutting from the bedrock in a granite shelf, thirty miles from end to end, it might have been difficult to miss if not for the smoke. But Hughes' eyesight was up to the challenge, and he could trace The Furnace's mantel, as well as the crude shape of the land beyond.

"It really is a gargantuan fireplace," he said.

"Cate's breaking away."

He followed Hector's gaze. Cate's fortresses were splitting off on the right while theirs remained with Frank's. The plan was to go together down the left side of The Furnace as far as Frank's targeted site of power. Then Hughes and Hector would continue to the farthest site at the base, all the way on the opposite edge, fifty miles or so west from the mantel.

Cinders drifted by, carried on the wind like fireflies.

Hughes signaled.

In a wave of movement that ran the length of the regiments, shooting through the air, Betty to Betty, the troops slipped on their faceguards.

The heat was ratcheting up, giving the air a dense, tarry texture.

"Now?" said Hector.

"Not quite." Hughes watched the horizon. The mantel was too tall to see the flames. Narrowing his eyes he could just barely make out their blazing architecture: columns of smoke, fat and forming into cones as they climbed high and melted into the dark, flickering sky.

The mantel neared.

"*Brace,*" an officer hollered. "*Brace, boys!*"

"And girls," a voice called cheerily.

"Erm. Yes. Sorry, love."

"Captain."

"Ah. Sorry, Captain. I assumed..."

"Yes?"

"That is I, um..." There was general snickering. They could almost hear the officer's ears going pink. "Begging your pardon, Captain. I only just joined with the auxiliaries. Fought in Champleurs, so I did. Still getting used to, er, modern developments in the army."

"That's quite all right, Sergeant. I myself am *from* Champleurs. With any luck we shall have your famous Corinthian bravery with us today, and not the infamous Johnny Foreigner cowardice. What is the expression of your country? *We are not at home to Mr. Cockup?*"

More giggles in the ranks. Any moment now steam would begin whistling from the officer's ears. "It is certainly a known saying, Captain," he mumbled.

"So intriguing, your language. Anyway, you were saying?"

"What? Oh, right. *Brace,* buh... ahm... *Look, everyone stop grinning and brace, okay?*"

Hughes joined the soldiery, ready for impact. He could not have stopped grinning if he tried. Corinth Bloody City. You could leave it behind, but it always found you again. Like a dog. Or, he supposed, like a master finding its dog.

Flawed as you are, I bloody love you Corinth Bloody City. Today your faithful hound wears a thousand colors, not just scarlet.

He felt the Betty speed up, crouched at the joints, and launch itself at the sheer slope of granite. There was a tremendous, spine-numbing jolt as the fortress feet made contact with the stone. Unseen by the regiments, the pilot pushed a button in the cockpit. Billions of micro filaments burrowed from the Betty into the granite. A foothold gained, Betty swerved a free leg up and slammed it down.

That was how they scaled the mantel.

A few seconds from the lip, the heat rolling from The Furnace became nauseating.

"Now," said Hughes.

Hector, who was perfectly balanced throughout the ordeal, cupped both hands to his mouth. "*Hydromancers!*"

With a *rush-gush-hiss*, countless gallons of water vapor in the air subsumed the particles of smoke in the immediate vicinity. The effect was incredible; Hughes' breath tasted clean and pure. He felt toasty, a little uncomfortable, but no longer seared.

"Remind me to thank Steffan Cerulean," he told Hector. "Three years ago those misfits couldn't irrigate a sponge. That's what I call training."

At the top, the pall of smoke hung in sheets, thickening into the fantastic jumble of pillars they'd spied before. Ahead lay an arch of wedge-shaped brick, The Furnace lintel. Its presence was senseless, there being no chimney to support, and anyhow no need to lend support if there were a chimney. A colossal fireplace built flat on the land and beneath it a dragon connected to the planet's core. Absurd. Monstrous. Strangely striking. It was so perfectly Eurydice. To either side the granite kept on, and in the middle of it all burned field after field of coals. The coals were black and pitted, each one as large as a bungalow. Red-orange light packaged them, and leaping up into the toxic, billowing, cinder-choked air were ribbons of flame. The sound of so much fire chewing all that fuel was unlike anything Hughes had ever heard.

The other Bettys were coming up behind.

It might have been his eyes playing tricks, but Hughes thought he could spot Cate's contingent scaling the mantel on the right side, like weird acrobatic monkeys climbing a kitchen counter. Weird, the images that occurred at such a moment. Well, the mind was a weird place. Just like the eyes it could play tricks.

"Hector?"

"Yes, Hughes?"

"Doesn't forgetting bother you?"

"My bright student. Are you worried about getting older?"

Maybe Hughes shouldn't have been surprised, but he was. "Am I that obvious?"

"This is the second time you've asked me about it. And your pepper-colored hair has acquired a sprinkle of salt. Men get agitated about hair. Hair thinning. Vanishing altogether. Changing color as though age were a jungle worth being a pale chameleon for. Women have it worse, harried with a myriad of menopausal symptoms. Extremely unpleasant, or so I'm told. As to forgetting. We all cope with forgetting." He smiled at Hughes. It was a sad smile. "Sometimes remembering is harder."

"My memory defines who I am."

"In a literal sense that's quite true, though no more than it's true for the rest of us. And as I often tell myself, there's more to it than the superficial self. You recall my father, Priam, lost the run of himself before he died."

"I do. He thought his own daughter Cassandra was General Ulyssé, ironically come to take his children from him."

"Well, my father might have forgotten important things. But we remembered them for him. Corrected him gently, or left him to harmless fantasy so as not to distress him. Now he's gone, we remember him as he was. Well and unwell. The total picture kept in the photo album and radio of the heart. Someday my family will forget things we once felt important. In which case someone may remember for us. If not," Hector shrugged eloquently, "it is no great matter. Young memories will always take the place of old. Don't discount how lucky you are. You have a daughter. She's in dire straits, yes, but we're going to save her. She'll correct you gently."

"Or leave me to my harmless fantasies. This isn't much comfort, Hector."

"She will be the comfort."

"So you say."

"You doubt it?"

Hughes didn't answer.

Hector lapsed into the same silence, not pushing to get at the truth.

Of course, he already knew it.

When you become a parent, you become armor. The most painful damage comes from within, from that which you protect. A daughter is a dream come true. But she is also a constant reminder that you have joined the same conga line that put your father in the hospital and your mother in the grave.

***

Thanks to the diary she had adequate time to prepare, to shore up her defenses, and dig in deep.

Or so she believed.

Nothing could have prepared her for what happened.

As she wrote stream-of-consciousness style, Evelyn followed along with Jane's thoughts inking themselves across the page in real-time.

Here's a chin-tickler what if what if what if another world has decided to butt in? Getting in while the getting is good, the swagger-hipped opportunist! Claps eyes big as oceans on this war involving three worlds and thinks why not chance the arm? It's a valid theory me, thank you me, so erudite, so sleek, so—wait. Could be a shadow. More likely. More underhanded. Skullduggerous. Right job, right tool. A shadow like Hughes and I would be able to figure out how to pull something like this. Make me question myself. Get around in my equipment. Rearrange the fundamentals. Shitter. Shit-shit-shitter, I hope it's one of us. When I kill Hughes I can do them too. I'll be the shadow that collects other shadows. A palimpsest of repurposed umbra. Pretty sounded, prettier than my stomach, I'm hungry. Once this is nipped in the bloom, stalk, stem, and bud, I'll get back to the menu. My Corinth City, my breakfast, brunch, lunch, dinner, and supper. So hungry, and, oh! And the moon launch ought to have the people painting themselves in a lacquer of joy like garlic butter baste. Yummy, yummy, I can't

The ink stopped there.

In the zone, it didn't click with Evelyn. She kept writing.

Funny how the brain works. Her eyes darted over and saw the dead sentence twice before her head recognized it as an anomaly.

She paused, examining it. The tiniest bit of bewilderment crimped the patch of skin between her eyes. Her back and shoulders straightened. A few seconds went by during which she read it over and over.

Yummy, yummy, I can't

Evelyn touched the tip of her pen to the "t" in "can't" as though goading the thought to hurry along.

Yummy, yummy, I can't

Can't what?

Searching for a clue in the previous chunk of writing, Evelyn could find no clues as to what the amputated phrase might mean.

Yummy, yummy, I can't wait?

Yummy, yummy, I can't begin to imagine how... Oh, but this was ridiculous.

Employ a thimble of logic. Eurydice must have done something to Jane. Or an event had befallen Eurydice and Jane, as the world's shadow was stunned senseless. Maybe Evelyn's father and mother were behind it. She hoped so.

And it did make sense.

She read the sentence, and wondered.

Yummy, yummy, I can't

Evelyn didn't like this. No, sir. She did not like it at—

She looked up at the green brick roof. Had she heard something just now?

A *clitter* of speedy, dexterous legs, perhaps?

I'm paranoid.

She listened. The sound didn't repeat.

Paranoid. She nibbled her lip. The diary itself looked okay. Dust jacket and pages that riffled against her fingers, all was as before. Only that last swatch of thought stood out starkly to her like silk cut with a hatchet.

She made herself laugh, a stilted, modest laugh.

Paranoid.

Why not look up to confirm it? she told herself.

I shan't. There's no need.

Why not do it?

Very well. If it'll satisfy.

Still smiling, she looked up.

Above her, two hands were pushing at the roof. It was like the brick was made of warm plaster mold. Before her eyes they pushed their way deeper into her enclosure. She could see arms. And the fingers splayed wide. Groping. Clutching. Reaching for her.

Evelyn screamed.

The sound of her voice in her own ears acted as a kind of talisman. If Evelyn was there, and she was capable of being so very afraid, then the walls she'd built— so like the walls of a farmhouse she'd visited with her mother, the ones glommed and fuzzy with goblin gold moss—were capable of being real, just as real as a scream.

There was an elastic snapping sound as the invader was repulsed, shot off into the dull dimension of the subconscious. Now it was their turn to scream. The scream dopplered crazily. Its owner was not simply furious. They were livid. Full of stridulous creaks, chirrups, and buzzing, it sounded like a woman being buried up to her neck in nectar, only to have a legion of hairy, hungry, insane bugs dumped over her head.

Movement caught her eye. The diary. Words were racing over the page in oozing, gross-smelling ink.

You bitch you bitch you dirty scheming bitch get out of me

Understanding bowled Evelyn flat. Sickeningly bitter resentment and rage picked her back up again. She snatched up the pencil and wrote as fast as she could.

(Scheming, am I? You tried to trick me. Blanked your thoughts. Well, it didn't work. Outfoxed you, didn't I? Didn't I?)

Get out

Things slammed, struck, and battered themselves against her green wall, shaking the red moss bursting through the cracks. Evelyn knew it was the insect parade, Jane's will given form. She kept writing.

(Really trounced you, didn't I?)

Get out get out GEEEEEEET OOOOOOOUUUUUUTTTTT

(there once was a girl who built up a wall and she had a ball that girl in the wall)

(she knew that the fly could not make it fall)

(she felt very tall that girl in the wall)

(she'd made the fly feel so very small)

I'll eat them the people that you love I'll devour every bite

(you're not even hungry I know you're not)

I'll suck their blood through straws like raspberry malt you fucking nuisance you shitter you

(it feels so good getting one over on you Jane)

(just like my dad)

***

"Something's wrong," said Hughes.

They had reached the first site of power.

Absurdly, amazingly, the site looked like an enormous cake formed out of granite. Stone cherries, stone chocolate flakes, even a glaze and a couple swirls of stone frosting. Slicing knives, also granite, thrust out of the cake, forming weird stairways.

If you do as Professor Dianne Bevinshirt advises and think of Eurydice like a woman, then such an absurdity actually makes a strange kind of sense. The Furnace is Eurydice's anger made geographic and real, and while anger is hot like fire, it can also be terribly sweet like cake.

So Hughes had been thinking anyway. That is until he'd seen the occupants of that unlikely dessert.

Yielding to Frank's persuasive nature, the Beldame had given them a sense of what to expect. Ash Wardens who siphoned the dust from the coals, Pokers to administer the fire, and Smoldering Sentries who generated the coal, dumped it out, and kept the whole operation safe. Janitors, bureaucrats, and muscle. Oddly normal, and yet so abnormally presented.

What the Beldame had not described was the abundance of other monsters, plenty of whom the troops recognized on sight. Hughes heard words like, "featherdrake," "bird," and "slugmen" along with other colorful expressions of astonishment and horror.

"Something's wrong," he said. "They beat us here."

"In reduced numbers," said Hector. "Mobile squadrons designed for pure alacrity. The rest of their army must still be behind us."

"Hector, if they're here, then they're at the other sites too."

Which meant they couldn't stick around and lend a hand. They had to keep going. Frank seemed to have come to the same conclusion. His Bettys were already haring off toward the site.

Knowing he had only a few precious seconds to warn her, Hughes wrote to Cate using his magical letter.

Her pre-battle message to him was on the other side.

Love you, Puppy. Always.

He erased the adoring reply he'd penned earlier and wrote with desperate speed.

Cate—Eurydice maneuver—ambush—small force at sites—rest behind.

He flipped the paper, hoping her message would wipe itself clean and words of acknowledgment would come through.

They didn't.

"Fuck." He growled the word. Its repetition was chased with spit. "Fuck."

"Remember this is Cate's bread and butter," said Hector. "The challenge is high but she'll rise above it. Honor her by doing likewise."

"Every now and then I wish you'd be less... philosophical about things."

"Watch me in the fray."

"Only your back."

Hector smiled. It gave Hughes heart, seeing that.

Frank's fortresses were moments away from engaging the enemy.

As his own contingent proceeded along the edge of The Furnace, Hughes lost sight of the forthcoming battle.

A roar split the smoky air.

"The troops are muttering a name," said Hector. "Too quiet for me to hear."

"Ruthven," said Hughes. "They're saying Ruthven. Frank and Mr. Glint are up against the vampiric dragon. Damn. We didn't have enough time to outfit every soldier with a rapid blood transfusion pack. They'll suffer for it."

"All we can do for them is win swiftly."

"And wish Frank luck, though I suppose he has better support than that."

"I should say so!" said Hector. "His partner is misfortune in a silk tie."

***

"Nothing's changed," Frank told a group of captains. "We'll set down at the site as planned. The hydromancers stay aboard and keep us cool. The rest plough ahead, rout the enemy, and break the draconic idol."

"What about Ruthven, sir?"

"Hunker down. His breath means death. We'll deal with him once we disembark."

"Bugger that," said Mr. Glint, who had been counting seconds and judging distance. He climbed the crenellations and jumped off the fortress, landing exactly where he meant to.

"Ah, a brave passenger," said Ruthven, sibilant and bemused. "Your blood could be drugged, but one dose won't down me. Poor pitiable creature. Bid your sorry life adieu." He flapped his wings, gaining altitude, and inhaled happily. Red helixes of blood spun out of Mr. Glint, flowing down the vampire's eager throat.

Mid-air, his flight path grew jagged. He passed within firing distance of the fortress. A few crossbow bolts soared, though none found their mark.

No one seemed to mind.

For as he passed overhead, the scarlet army was treated to the least likely sound. It was guttural, strained, and extremely pleasant to their ears. Ruthven was gagging.

Meanwhile, moving with that dreadful speediness which had, twenty years ago, frightened Hughes more than anything in the world (saving, of course, Mr. Glint's mouth), Mr. Glint crawled along the white-and-crimson-spotted fur. The wind lashed at his suit. His hat was long gone, lost to The Furnace.

He wrapped his long fingers around the length of cartilage connecting body to wing. He got his feet under him. He gave a few experimental tugs.

And in a torrential burst of blood that sent him tumbling wet and red down into the smoke, Mr. Glint tore one of Ruthven's wings off.

***

Having set down three minutes before Hughes sent his warning, Cate and her Company stormed their site of power, flanked by a full third of the army.

The Smoldering Sentinels—huge, brass golems with bulging bellies—vomited flaming coals, snapped and cracked whips of fire, and succumbed to scarlet.

The Ash Wardens—unnerving humanoids that looked like a cross between anteaters and unearthed victims of a volcanic eruption buried in white, flaking pyroclastic material—performed incantations. They fought. They succumbed to scarlet.

The Pokers—squat, squarish, dark, and very similar to the coals they shifted with their tools of iron—put up something too paltry to be called a fight. They succumbed to scarlet.

Cate's Company were the meat and bones of it, the bloody imperative that the soldiers followed dutifully, awe sparkling in their eyes. They were the stuff of legend.

Cate herself had gone to great lengths to place herself as far from the narratives about her as possible, at least in the eyes of the troops. When she fought with a daredevilish genius, honed over the grindstone of her battle mantra *you try to kill me, I try to kill you*, the soldiers did not feel fanatical.

They felt like dying for her.

Even better, like living for her.

The site succumbed to scarlet, the creed color of the Citadel, the hue of their general's hair and of her fiery spirit that burned with a passion for survival and nonsensical delights of war, hotter than the cinder-coughing, atmosphere rippling, sweaty-skin-tingling heat of The Furnace.

Her boots caked in blood, brains, and coal dust, Cate wasted no time in hurrying to the summit of the site.

Unlike Frank's site, this one was shaped like a jar-contained serving of tiramisu. Cate, inured to the freaky-deakiness of this world, hadn't given this peculiarity a single thought. What mattered was the idol. Break it, and her part in this final conflict would be over.

The idea of checking the letter in her pocket never even occurred to her.

A mere ten paces from the idol the ground behind her fissured. Something came out. It held a knife.

"Cate!" called Xacorca Demon, too late.

No shriek from the general. But a sound halfway between a grunt and hiss escaped her.

Cate looked down in time to see Skuggs wrench his crystal knife from her leg. The wound squirted red. It was cleverly struck. Cate's Jolene-forged steel would have turned a paralyzing blow to the spine, or a killing one to the neck or throat. Skuggs was short and couldn't meaningfully aim for her head. Instead, he had correctly guessed that any armor worn by Cate would perforce be flexible and thinner round her legs, particularly the area behind the knee. The crystal knife was serrated. It took a not-insignificant amount of Cate with it as it left her body. Skuggs grinned up at her. Then he vanished into the stone, leaving a smear of pink quartz like a signature.

"Ambush!" Cate shouted.

From everywhere around the vanguard of the army—Cate's Company and Cate herself—tiny cracks in the mineral voided the things that had been formerly concealed. Oozes, pouchy, burbling, and making grotesque smooching sounds as they jiggled, came up into the flickering light. Above them loomed an ooze fifty times larger than the rest, the Pontifex Jelly, purple-gray and veiny.

"No one say 'just like old times,'" said Cate. "I can't stand cliché."

"Please, Cate?" said Kevlin Paladin.

She sighed. "Fine. Just like old times, gang."

The Company charged.

***

Scoops of ice cream, cold as the coffin, sweet as bed.

Granted these scoops were made of igneous deposits and presented a site of tremendous arcane power, but Hughes found himself glad of the setting.

Evelyn was very fond of ice cream. Mostly this was because of the taste, which was a pretty good reason. But in part her fondness came from a poem Mr. Glint had told her about. Not one of his, but whoever had written it was good at what they did because the words stuck. *The only empress is the empress of ice cream.*

If omens existed—Gormon Hughes doubted it, but if they did—he took those massive unmalting scoops as a good one.

Their Betty, the first to reach the site, pulled up alongside the scoops and canted to one side. Lopsided like that, the army could disembark the fortress. Hughes and Hector were first off.

With the battle cries of the soldiers ringing in their ears, the two men—living and living ghost—broke into a sprint.

And immediately, unhesitatingly began to carve a swathe through the undead.

Sagging bellies spilled their contents. Brown teeth broke. Severed limbs flopped, shuddering like stunned mackerel. Necks twisted. Heads rolled. Filthy fingers showing bone flew like pizza sticks across a restaurant table.

Towering over the horde, the Smoldering Sentries let their hot coals go, drenching friend and foe alike in crushing, flesh-sizzling death. Ash formed tangles of barbed wire, manipulated by the naked Wardens. Iron poked. Men and women choked on fumes and the throat-rawing heat; the hydromancers could only do so much to keep it at bay.

The undead sang as they jostled one another for a chance at Hughes.

At last we meet, dark Gormon Hughes
Your hellcat wife is evidence
That you're the bearer of black news
And so we shall give you your dues
Extending our benevolence
Our claws, our jaws, our recompense!

"Keep singing," he snarled, popping a head between his hands like a ripe tomato. "You just keep singing. I'll harmonize."

Round his neck Faethe felt light, the demands upon its power small. They could not touch him. He was too fast. And when he touched them, they met their true end, usually in grisly and spectacular fashion.

Hughes had not even deigned to draw Chimera or the Krys knife.

They noticed. Their song washed over him, a vocalization of their affrontery and anger.

He harmonized, violently.

At his side, Hector was more sword than man.

They pulled far ahead of their support. That was all right. The soldiers had their orders. Beyond the waves of undead whose pale desiccated wigs of hair were so redolent of sea foam, a massive stone spoon was wedged into the exact middle point of the three ice cream scoops. It pointed up at those heavy, smoggy clouds like an accusatory finger; I tinge thee orange with accusations. The spoon handle was wide, about thirty feet or so, and it sort of leveled out at the top in a platform. The idol was on that platform. As he neared, Hughes could see it.

And he saw something else that took him back to his dumb, reckless youth.

Guarding the idol, silhouetted against the smoke and the clouds and an impossible midday moon, milk-white and threaded red like a blind, bloodshot eye, a two-headed wolf reared back its heads and howled.

Its rider's hair streamed out like cobweb over a tomb, shot-through and aglow with moonlight. His black damask cloak was spidery with gold patterns, and his crown and face-covering veil were rotten.

"Catch up to me, Hector."

"I will."

Hughes tapped a deeper reservoir of Faethe's power. The amulet, nicely cool till now, warmed just a little, and grew heavier until it weighed as much as half a bag of sugar. Bending at the knees, Hughes felt the stone beneath him *crack*.

He launched, aiming for the moon.

The site of power, the battle, and the fireplace with its luminous fuel spread out below him in muzzy canvas.

Moving beyond the influence of the hydromancers, he activated Faethe again. Inhaling, he sorted the harmful chemicals from the smoke, nourishing his body with clean filtered air and expunging the gunky leftovers on the exhale. Poisonous fumes poured from his lips and nostrils. The wind caressed him. He and the sky were acquainted. That glaring moon seemed close enough to pluck. He was bathed in light from above and below, and the fumes he breathed were a halo above him, a crown both royal and toxic. A small, profane dragon he made in that moment, but a terrible one nevertheless.

Gravity snatched him out of the air.

He fell, but it was a controlled plummet. A targeted one.

Burrows cast a spell of shielding. Hughes barely registered it as he broke through. Burrows' scythe was quick. Hughes was quicker. The wolf's backbone was hard. He hit it harder.

There was an instant of unbearable sticky dampness, like being dunked in a flooded butcher shop with all the rotting meat slopping against him, clinging to him, and then—

Two long, masculine arms erupted through the wolf's chest. In their hands, they gripped the monster's heart. The rest of Hughes followed. He rolled onto the stone, momentarily disoriented. He could hear splattering, presumably the wolf' insides spilling from the hole he had made in its torso. He could hear doggish whining, Burrows' rasping voice, the words indistinct, the loathing clear.

In his hands, the monstrous heart beat once, twice.

Once, twice.

Once.

And was whisked out of his fingers.

He was too surprised to resist.

He looked at Burrows. The Lord of necromancy guided the heart back into the cavity left by Hughes' attack. Blood flowed back. Fragments of muscle and bone melded and sealed the wound shut. Fur reknit. The rewind function on the wolf's vid player had been engaged, and the results were ghoulish.

"Monster," Burrows snapped. "You'd try and take both my friends from me? One wasn't enough for you? You and your broken-down spinster of a patron. A botanist and a zookeeper, that's what Iphigenia is. A glorified..." A measure of composure returned. Hughes detected an imperious curve of Burrows' lips. "Eurydice might be capricious, but she's got panache. Surely you can appreciate that as a man of the rostrum? Shh. It's all right, girl." The wolf was growling. Burrows stroked her as Hughes got to his feet. "Your brother didn't have me that day years ago. You do, you've got me. Hughes, do you believe you can subvert the whirligig of life I've built for myself? Undo the cycle by undoing me? You think you can do what Death herself cannot?"

"I think Lucy Nowhere, she who swings the scythe and enjoys the taste of ambrosia fudge, is patient. I think she let you defy the laws of nature with your so-called art because she knew a day of reckoning would arrive for Burrows, grandson, son, and father of necromancers. Inventions become obsolete. Innovators are replaced. The old is born from the new, again and again. That is the only cycle worthy of consideration, and even then only if you've got nothing better to do on a Sunday afternoon."

"The laws of nature. Another mouthpiece for fatalism. I'd expected more from Cate Jubilee's paramour."

"You're boring me, Burrows."

"Am I?"

"Yes. You and your mutt. Once, the sight of you both would have instilled an unconquerable fear in me. Indeed, the nightmares of a wolf with two heads still come now and then. But I'm older. I've taken my place as a spoke in the wheel, accepted it, as you seem incapable of accepting. I didn't do it willingly. But the unwilling wheel turns, Burrows. It turns. And with the vantage point that the turning has afforded me, the new and exciting and frightening perspective, I see that you're not so horrible. You're a petulant boy who wants to play with his toys forever. You've even got a faithful pup. I bet you resurrected her and her sibling with a conviction that you were defying norms and tempting destiny, all the while knowing secretly that you were lonely and in need of doting, sympathetic company, no matter how cold and how foul-smelling it might be."

"Now you're boring me."

"You don't look bored." Hughes let a guileful nastiness creep over his expression. "You look like you're about to tantrum. Has the Lord a favorite blanket I might fetch him? A soother? I can burp him, if he has excess wind. I have experience."

"Insolent pig. I'm going to destroy your wife, raise her, and give her giblets to my slavering kindred. I'll have her scrubbing up what's left of you from this place. She'll feel every moment of grief, understand? And I'll raise that for her too, like a zeppelin of despair, at every feasible occasion."

"Wait there, Burrows. You and that poor violated pet, wait there for me," said Hughes. "I'm coming. The cycle has paused too long for you. Commendably long. Wait there. We'll shove it back into action. Together."

They clashed.

Burrows and the wolf were quite the pairing, one monster symbiotic with the other. Hughes could dismember, decapitate, and generally brutalize the beast, but Burrows' ability to repair the damage rendered his efforts meaningless.

Similarly, whenever Hughes attempted to sidestep his opponent and reach the Lord of necromancy, two lupine heads, one calm, the other insane, would bar his way. Their breath was hot with an underlying stench, like a chemical plant abandoned after some disaster, a reek of rubbing alcohol, putrefaction, and mutated organisms.

Hughes felt exhaustion mount in tandem with his amulet's weight. He had pushed his Performance once already. It had slid off the wolf's mind without effect. Hughes had no inkling whether or not his odds of success and failure had skewed since Iphigenia's decline in health. The percentage values no longer appeared in his head when he called up his power, and the Performance itself lacked its surging elegance. Some part of him whispered that it would never work again after his decision to choose the honest approach for his moon launch broadcast.

He had no inkling whatsoever as to the truth. But he did have suspicions.

Clamping against his chest with an unpleasant heat and weighing a little over thirty kilograms, Faethe was showing that even Wendy Dragontail had her limits. Hughes would reach them himself soon.

Someone was behind him.

Hector. Thank God.

In the depths of his mind, he felt a sororal, spring-green presence yield up a warning.

His eyes flashed wide. He created space by kicking the wolf square in the ribs, drew Chimera and his Krys knife with slender rustles of metal against scabbard, spun on his heel, and threw up a standard block designed to guard as much of the body as possible when caught unawares.

He was lucky.

The sword that met his with a bitter ring of steel—what a sword, so very like his own Chimera, only enameled in beetle-back plating, covered in chelicerae, mandibles, and other insectile paraphernalia. Its blade, unbroken, was hornet-stinger shaped.

Knowing its wielder, knowing what she could do with an opening, Hughes flicked his Krys knife. Yes, he had been right. She would have stuck him with her own if he hadn't defended. Her Chrysalis knife. Metal ground and screeched.

Their eyes met.

"Jane," he said.

"Daddy," she replied.

She convulsed as a blade ripped through her midsection. She looked down at it, astonishment and pain wracking her expression.

"Might I interject?" said a voice like luxurious carrot cake tasted on a day of gentle rain.

Hughes grinned.

Hector.

***

We find solace in the least likely places. Even when we're scared.

Maybe especially then.

As he fought, Hughes found an odd consolation in the idea that Jane was here. If she'd chosen to go toe-to-toe with him, it meant Cate and Frank would have a better shot at their idols. There was another benefit. Doubtful as its current strength might be, he could try his Performance on her. Hell, it worked before, all those years ago at Tinfrost. Why not again?

It was only when he used it and encountered her properly that he discovered the reality of the situation. There was no blip of puzzlement. He understood the implications at once.

Jane was not entirely present. Formidable as she was—abjectly terrifying as she was—he and Hector were only facing a third of her.

The bug bitch was like a plague, spread wide and despicable.

She saw him register it and was just as incisive.

She laughed at him.

Hector parried a strike from Burrows, riposted, fell back as the wolf advanced.

Jane stalked Hughes. Worms dripped in an unguent of white goo from the hole in her stomach. Flies scurried in and out of her smiling mouth.

"You might not believe this, but it's really good to see you," she said. "You empty-hearted angel. Ungh! Fucker. You just love to cut me, don't you? It's okay. I'll let you. I like when you touch me, no matter the context. I've wanted to— hoh! Quick, but not quick enough, mister. I've just been dying to ask you this. Have any sexual fantasies about me entered your head? Like without meaning to, they just WHAM! Appear! Has a piece of you thought 'that's so wrong,' and another piece argued, 'but it feels so right'? Did you ever sneak a peek at your daughter and think... what if?" She looked into his face and could not contain her delight. Her laughter was shrill and wild and so deeply, inescapably crazy. "You're so revolted. Oh, my honeycomb guy. My sad Hughes. I missed you so bad."

***

"Mr. Glint."

"Yes, Mr. Gallant."

"That was a risky, ill-considered, dare I say parlous thing to do."

"Yes, Mr. Gallant."

Frank looked around at the site of power, completely drenched in blood. He looked at Ruthven. The dragon was slipping, flexing its spurting wing stump, trying to comprehend what had just happened. Lastly, Frank looked at Mr. Glint, who had his head lowered apologetically. Frank's features softened.

"Well done," he said.

Mr. Glint's head came up. Seeing hope on his face was like seeing a piñata in a mass grave.

"Thank you, Mr. Gallant."

"Got a wooden stake handy?"

The pair had, after Frank located his partner, fought a number of henchmen armed with coffins. Mr. Glint bent to one of their corpses. He took a coffin, angled it just so, and gave a good hard wrench. There was a brittle crunch. He tossed the leavings aside and held up the crooked length of wood for Frank's inspection. There was a nail sticking out of it.

"This do?" said Glint.

"Yeah, should suffice okay. Vampire first. Idol second."

Ruthven's muzzle wrinkled at their approach. Frank didn't think he factored into that disgusted equation much. As far as Ruthven was concerned, Mr. Glint was the start and end of his problems.

"What is in that offensive gruel you call blood?"

"This and that," said Mr. Glint.

"It is an education in impurity."

"Thanks."

"Are you a human being?"

"I am one of them acquired taste things."

He hefted the stake. Ruthven hiss-growled, a blend of cobra and rabid dog backed into a corner. He jerked at the neck, went still. *Listening*, Frank thought. *What to?* Without a word, Ruthven slid off the edge of the giant stone tiramisu and was gone. Silence fell. Except for the nearby sounds of battle, obviously. This was war, after all.

Frank and Mr. Glint peered over the edge. The dragon was bleeding so copiously the fires below had absorbed it greedily and transformed such a generously donated amount of liquid into a brand-new column of smoke.

"Reckon he'll be back," said Mr. Glint.

"Probably."

"With virgins."

"Come again?"

"Very keen on virgins, your basic vampire."

"Is that so?" said Frank, tickled in spite of everything. "For feeding, like? Enjoy the bouquet of virgin blood?"

Glint shook his head. "Nah. I'd say it's because vampires have a weakness for hobbies. Eternal life and that. Got to while away the time somehow."

Frank frowned. "You've lost me."

"Very keen on hobbies, your basic virgin."

That was when they heard the buzzing.

Stepping back in a hurry, they watched as a frenzied cloud of bugs lifted Ruthven out of the clutches of the flames. The bugs amalgamated.

Jane, aloft on two huge house-fly wings, gripped Ruthven by the intact wing.

"Drown them all," she said.

Ruthven's jaws sprang wide. Something gurgled along the hideous pipe of his body.

Mr. Glint stepped in front of Frank a hair's breadth before the blood crashed over them in a tsunami.

***

High command over the united forces had introduced Cate to every stripe of injury you can imagine. A bleak but undeniable fact was this: despite fantastic advances in modern medicine, that old staple of war, amputation, remained as common a side effect of battle as it was in the days of her father. In his day a lot of men and a few women, not as many in those days, crouched in trenches or rose up like the wrath of nationalism into no-man's-land, brandishing crossbows and swords. Keep low, watch for special artillery. Try not to get your head shot. As a soldier the country owned your head, no good to the country without that. How many people had her father carried back to the mud slick, infection-breeding, pus-smelling hole that passed for a medical ward, people with their arms or legs blown off, or more amputees in the making? She didn't know. Probably more than a few. If she had to guess, it was probably a lot more.

Those who lost a vital piece of themselves had made Cate familiar with the reality of something she had only seen in movies, and that something was called phantom limb syndrome.

It itches, General.

General, it hurts.

Cate, I can't feel it now, but an hour ago it's like it was *still there.*

She had even heard of cases—incredible and difficult to verify but engaging regardless—in which those suffering from phantom limb syndrome had actually manipulated the physical world with the part of their body they'd lost. A glass nudged by a nub of gristle where a finger used to be. A *tap-tap* sound where there was no foot to make it. Bullshit, maybe. But in a life as funky as this... who could say for sure?

The body is a defective cargo claw. Sometimes it just doesn't want to let go. Maybe the mind is the same way.

Helmet and fiery hair scintillating, hobnail boots causing mayhem, Cate went to work against the Pontifex Jelly, its oozes, and Skuggs, and in a very personal level of her mind, she thought: *It itches. It hurts. I can feel her now like she's still here.*

Only Eilandri wasn't there.

Eilandri would never be here again.

Skuggs, tongue jittering grossly over his teeth with excitement, lunged. He'd impaled her leg. Now he meant to finish the job.

Eilandri would never be here again.

But she *had* been here.

And to the person she cared about most in the world, she had divulged many a useful secret.

If Jane hadn't intervened, tackling Cate and showering her in insects and insults, Cate would have coated the toe of her boot with Skuggs' brains.

Jane was overwhelming, her words stinging worse than her blows thanks to Cate's armor. It was like being hit by a bag of wasps on bad methamphetamines. Cate fought to disentangle herself, catching snatches of Jane's poisonous words.

"—from him... scuzzbucket scumbelching bimbo... aren't fit to touch his perfect lumpen pumpkin head... you asshole, asshole, ASSHOOOOOOOOLE!"

Using an old reliable technique, Cate pitched her weight backward, palmed the stone beneath her, and spun her enchanted boots in a corkscrew. An oldie it may have been, but as Hughes often said of music, oldies are still goodies.

A heel connected. Jane's shoulder was whacked out of its socket. She skittered back, resetting the stricken bone with a distinct *pop.*

Jane opened her mouth—

***

—Evelyn's pen scritch-scritch-scratched over the diary page—

***

—and said, "*Mum I'm here I'm inside her I love you so much please be oooooKAAAAYNNNNNOOOOO*, you don't speak for me, kid, this is my ride, minemineminemineMINE!"

"Evie? Evie, I love you too. Mummy's here. Daddy too, he's very close by. Can you speak to me?"

"Stay out of this, tramp. The brat doesn't call the shots heeeeerrrrreee—*yes, Mum. I've a wall between Jane and I. It's quite good. Uncle Frank and Auntie Jolene showed me.*"

Skuggs gawped, his back to a stone cherry, his knife held out before him in a limp hand. His mistress' shadow was being... no squirming out of it... puppeteered. Or perhaps pupated, in Jane's case, given her buggish nature. So Skuggs conjectured as Evelyn's words passed through Jane's quivering lips.

"*Mum, Jane's in three places at once. Here, and with Frank and Dad too.*"

Manifesting in three places at once. Cate supposed a shadow could do things like that when its world was in its prime. If only her Hughes could match it... oh well. Cometh the hour, cometh the girl with the boots, and so forth.

Let's see...

No time! Instinct reigns supreme!

Her confidence sang to blot out her doubt's protests.

"Evie. Can you get Jane in one place? Here, can you unify her here with me?"

Jane retched, screamed, and exploded into motion. Swift as a spider she moved. Her teeth clicked together a millimeter from Cate's nose. Cate stared into her eyes. It was totally incongruous, but as she spoke Evelyn's words a pandemonium of panic and hate showed in Jane's eyes (*God, they're so like Hughes' eyes it's uncanny*).

"I can't, Mum. I'm only able to push Jane so far while I'm inside these walls."

"You have to let her in then."

"I can't. She'll come in and eat me alive. You ought to hear it, Mum. They're all over the place. Slamming against the walls trying to get in."

"What are trying to get in?"

"The buuuuuuggggssSSSSSAAAAAH—"

Jane's mouth, a ravenous cavern of insatiable appetite, stretched.

"—AAAAH'LL EAT YOU ALL, DRINK YOU ALL, KILL Y—"

Cate's hands rose. They cupped Jane's face.

"Evelyn."

Stillness. The sounds of battle, even the ever-beating drums of hate that lingered sub-aurally throughout war, melted away. Jane's face, elongated in a nerve-curdling scream, changed. The change was extremely subtle and unceremonious, almost impossible to discern with the naked eye. To Cate Jubilee, Jane looked younger.

"Evelyn."

Younger. Younger still. Sweeter. Now dramatically older, wicked, hungry, a monster. Now younger again, and the furthest thing from monstrous.

A contest of wills was taking place before Cate's eyes.

"You're your father's daughter," she said.

And saying that, Cate pulled one hand back so Jane and Evelyn could see. She turned it one way to show a tattoo of...

"Lights."

She turned it again to show a tattoo of...

"Camera."

And one last time, to show a tattoo of... her. Of Evelyn Hughes.

Cate winked impishly.

"Action."

***

Under siege, Evelyn read the diary.

She looked at the bricks above her, keeping her safe from the bogeywoman.

She reread the diary.

No.

Lights.

No. She couldn't. Could not.

Camera.

Even if she did, all it would achieve would be, well nothing. Less than nothing. She'd be gobbled up. Another of Jane's victims. Only it would be worse because she'd become Jane. Forever. That settled it. At least here, scribbling away, she could be of use. Minimize risk. Maximize... Dratting maximize the probability of not being dratting-well-eaten. There was no way, no conceivable way that she—

Action.

Without pausing to think she flung the pen aside, clambered onto the desk, smudging the ink with her shoes in the process. She bade a brick to loosen. It did. She took hold of it. Both hands.

Fear—that clever medusa—petrified her.

Her mum's words showed the medusa the mirror, turning fear to stone, and filling her with a charmed, fierce bravery.

You are your father's daughter.

I love you, Mum.

And Daddy. You are an angel. I believe.

Evelyn screwed her courage to the sticking place.

"Lay on, Jane. And God damn whichever one of us cries out first."

She pulled out the brick.

The insect parade poured in, engulfing her.

***

At the cherry-chocolate cake site of power, the river of blood was ebbing to a stream. Then a creek. Then a trickle. Mr. Glint shook bloody drops from his jacket cuffs like an avatar of commercial hell. Frank, soaked to the skin, looked up at the spot Jane occupied. Correction, the spot she had occupied. The bug bitch was gone. Ruthven the vampiric nightmare, had been dropped. He was scrabbling for purchase on the stone to keep from going on a one way trip to flaming coaltown.

Meanwhile, at the ice cream site, there were peculiar developments.

Hughes had listened, fascinated, as Jane—no, as *Evelyn*—held up one half of a conversation. That the other half belonged to Cate was obvious from word-go. The fact that Evelyn had managed to preserve her innate self within Jane, and keep that self separate behind what Frank Gallant would call a mental barrier, was also obvious. Suddenly a recent letter he'd gotten from Thud made a lot more sense. The letter was wary but hopeful. It explained to Hughes that the number of Jane related incidents had fallen, as if off a ledge. Thud couldn't understand it. Hughes now did.

How many lives had his daughter, his brave baby girl, saved?

Unaware that he was echoing a thought his wife had that same day, he thought, *Probably more than a few. Probably a lot more.*

Distracted, perhaps reasonably, he had a moment to register the feel of hot breath on his neck, a moment to smell the gassy, rancid-pork smell before the wolf's teeth closed around him.

A line of pressure ran from his collarbone to his hip, each point a tooth trying to dig into him, and made his guts run like warm jam if only they could. Wisps of smoke unwound past his face. No, that wasn't it. He was passing them. The wolf was lifting him up, presumably bringing its other head around. If it turned him around, would it be the calm one or the crazy one he'd see? Poised canine intelligence or slobbering lunacy. Hughes knew that if given the choice between them, he preferred not to choose at all.

Around his neck, his amulet Faethe hung like a brick of lead. Knowing he was beginning to push his luck, he tapped that wellspring of energy. The amulet knew what he wanted. Its magic was sophisticated as the woman who had worn it before him.

Suddenly *he* was the brick of lead. A bag of bricks. A crate.

The wolf's teeth first cracked, then, as it refused to let him go, its jaw broke and ruptured. Long facial bones rammed through its muzzle. Gums were lanced. Tooth fragments and goopy brownish blood gushed like infected shit. Hughes landed, wondering how long he had before Burrows healed the wolf's high-pitched whines of hurt.

Claws raked across his back harmlessly. Those which the necromancy had failed to supply with enough biotin shattered on impact. A wet and cataclysmic howl shook The Furnace.

Closer to the idol, Hector was keeping Burrows busy.

Hughes' knife was in his hand, but he'd dropped his sword somewhere—where?

The moon went dark, then light, a strange celestial blink that was classically Eurydice. He reeled around. Jane was gone. The wolven stare accosted him, demanded his attention. Both heads.

The crazed one opened its mouth and a raven's head darted out. Its beak pecked him. The blow wasn't hard enough to drive him back, not with Faethe bolting his body in place, but Hughes took a step away nonetheless.

"The other one had wings. Black wings. You've got the bird inside you."

Ridiculous. Zany, wild-eyed madness. But true. There were worms, a huge raven, and who knew what else inside that thing. The creature, a sister to the male wolf he'd met in Iphigenia, was like a testament to the world that had created it. Baleful and grim, the wolf's stare seemed to confirm that. The crazed head licked the blood from the calm's muzzle. The gesture was bizarrely tender, like watching somebody give themselves a hug.

Holding that stare, not even thinking about looking away, Hughes thought of Phobetor, the master of fear he'd met in the dream world around the time Evelyn first disappeared. Phobetor had presented him with the two-headed wolf and asked Hughes if he was afraid.

"I'm not," he told it. "I meant it then and I mean it now. I'm older. Yesterday's monsters don't seem so bad. And you are yesterday's monster."

The crazed head barked. A denial, or a challenge maybe.

Burrows was trying to get to them. Hector denied his attempts. Burrows called out to the wolf in a language that only the undead speak.

"Stay," said Hughes. The wolf stayed. He sheathed his Krys knife. "I won't do this the same way. I haven't got Iphigenia to hand me your heart, and my Performance feels even more sluggish than my amulet. We shall have to improvise. We can devise our own cycles with their own rubrics and idiosyncrasies. Something ends, something begins. Are you ready?"

The calm head studied him. The crazed one snapped around to look at Burrows. It barked in a fusillade, loud as catapult fire. The calm head nuzzled it. The crazed stirred round, saw Hughes, and grinned a feral grin, exposing a factory of needles amidst diseased gums.

Hughes took one step. The second was harder. The third, almost impossible. The fourth?

Easy.

Easy as blackberry pie.

The wolf pounced.

Hughes' world became a kaleidoscope of claws, teeth, a sour reek, and fur matted with gross gunge and active fluids, blood and slobber. It was the world of his nightmares. Frankly, it was a world he was ready to leave behind.

He got under it, Atlas getting ready to raise the unraisable. His chest was cooking, the amulet was that hot, and ungodly heavy. He beckoned its power anyway. Fuck it. The show must go on. He stood, his heartbeat whamming against its casings.

He took the wolf with him.

He lifted it high over his head.

He began to walk toward the lip of the platform.

One foot, then the other.

"No!" Burrows' voice held none of its nobility. The Lord of necromancy had never sounded so human. "Please! I'm *begging* you!"

Hughes wished he were stronger. He wished his arms would stop shaking. That the smell of his own skin charring wouldn't remind him of Sunday night steaks. That Burrows' pleas would glance off him like hammers glancing off something impervious. He wished those things, but enchanted magic only goes so far, and the lovely dark of you lightens to a pale version of itself. Wish away, shadow man. The heart ends up pierced no matter what.

"Mistress! You've got to stop him!" Burrows' wail went unanswered. "Please! Eurydice *pleeeeease!*"

The pommel of Hector's sword knocked the wind out of him. Burrows wheezed, tried to cast a spell, and was forced to use his scythe to parry Hector's onslaught.

The wolf was writhing. Hughes thought, *I'm going to drop her.* He was close to the platform edge. Another step. Maybe two, and he'd—

Two things happened so closely together they were hardly consecutive.

Faethe failed. Hughes managed to get out from under the wolf before its ginormous bulk squashed him, but not, as it turned out, before it could exact revenge for the humiliation it had just endured.

One of her claws, crooked but basically intact, touched his face just under the left eye. It dragged to his chin, down his neck, and would have jagged in his clavicle if momentum hadn't ripped Hughes away. Where that claw touched him, his face opened like a wax envelope.

The pain lit up half his head. It was excruciating. He screamed.

The crazed head yipped and yelped. It was celebrating. Even the calm head had a triumphant gleam in its eye. The wolf got to her paws. A little unsteady, a little hesitant, but more confident by the moment. And besides, the prospect of a meal had just amped up its likelihood. Fresh blood drew it.

My blood.

She padded toward him. Testingly. She suspected a trick. She was eerily quiet, except for the panting of the crazed head.

Hughes dredged the lowest reaches of himself, hoping to snag his Performance and bring it up kicking and yowling like a demon, or a seraph. He needed it.

But it wouldn't come.

The spring-green feeling, the presence of that other world, his big sister, his Iphigenia... it was hardly there at all.

Oh my God. She's going to die.

She really is going to die.

The wolf padded. Drool dripped, clear mucus, and more of that brown mush from the wounded head's mouth. Black snouts sniffed the air. Saliva gathered in a foam at the corners of its lips. Four eyes, it had, and all of them lambent-yellow and fixed on him.

Hughes checked his amulet. Very little tea left in that particular kettle.

Clarity came. Awful, shining clarity. As with his Performance, magic items like Chimera and Faethe also came from Iphigenia. Across the battlefield, soldiers would try to use their weapons, only to find out the enchantments were no longer up to the task. Even Cate's hobnail boots. Shit, Hector's life was tied up in such a revelation. He and his siblings were only alive thanks to a magical tether linking them and the crown worn by their sister Creusa. Hughes pictured all of those arcane objects. Not stripped of their power. Not yet. Simply diminishing.

Dying.

He straightened. Okay, so what?

Dying was not dead. They still had time.

The she-wolf was right to be suspicious. He had a few tricks left. Oldies but goodies.

All his muscles had to do was quit throbbing and remember.

All I've got to do is remember.

Ernie's dog's name was...

"Buh" something. It was...

"Boochums," he whispered.

The wolf heads lunged, a pair of grizzly tongs closing shut.

From his past came the perfume of peony flowers. And his body remembered.

First rule of swordplay, balance.

He ducked, sending a frisson of Faethe's remaining energy to his hands. He dug his fingers through fur, flesh, and wrapped his fingers around tubes of bone. The wolf grunted. He crushed her windpipes.

A squirt of energy fueled his legs. A thimble for his trembling arms. He dragged her toward the edge again. No begging from Burrows. Hughes wasn't sure he'd have heard the undead bastard if he'd roared right next to him.

The wolf bit and was rebuked.

Second rule of swordplay, defense.

*Third rule—*he swung the wolf over the edge—*offense.*

Three subcategories each. His name was Boochums. I remember. I do.

The wolf uttered a snarl. Both heads. Then it was gone.

All but its tail, which slammed Hughes as it slalomed back and forth. He lost his footing. Smacked his head on the stone. Slid on the entrails. Felt his feet dangle over doom.

Hot, he thought. *When did it get so hot?*

He tried to get up and deepened his trouble. The wolf's innards were a sleek trail, slippery beyond belief. He groped for a handhold. Under the warm wetness the stone was smooth.

Someone caught him.

"Hector..."

Hector hauled him up. Hughes smiled gratefully at the hand gripping his. His smile grew plastic and unsure. For it was not the hand of a living ghost. It was human. The nails were neat and beautifully manicured.

Hughes looked up into the last face he'd expected to see.

"I've been impertinent, sir. Worse, I've been rude. It's a disgrace. I shall never make it up to you." Falstaff, wearing a Scarlet Citadel uniform, dusted Hughes off. "But I shall try."

"Falstaff."

"Hand, sir."

"Sorry?"

"Hand, sir."

Automatically, Hughes removed his hand from his facial wound.

Falstaff removed a sterile cloth pad from his pocket and held it hard against the spot to staunch the bleeding.

"Hector needs you," said Falstaff. "You're no use to him drained, if you'll pardon my saying so, sir."

Hughes said nothing. He was looking at the butler turned assassin turned... whatever this was.

"Upon my oath I shall regain your respect, Master Hughes. I know your forgiveness is outside my—"

"Falstaff."

"Sir?"

"You already have it."

Falstaff said nothing. Then he nodded. His face was statuesque, except for a tear rolling down one cheek. Hughes didn't comment on it.

It seemed the polite thing to do.

***

Like a reptile swerving around a cactus to get at the water in an oasis, Ruthven swerved around Mr. Glint and Frank Gallant. Frank retracted the snorkel strings he'd sent above the deluge of blood, breathing huskily and deeply, his lungs inflamed with ache. Mr. Glint asked him if he was all right. He said he was. The same could not be said for the allied forces. Ruthven's flood had driven a lot of them back to their Bettys. Those too slow or too exhausted from the battle to climb aboard a fortress had been swept off the site of power into the coals.

Submerged, Frank hadn't been able to hear their screams as they burned alive. He was glad. And he was done.

Amazingly, irrevocably done with Eurydice, done with her prize bloodsucker and with this whole world that seemed to him like a tapestry stitched out of bad surprises, disappointment, and contempt.

Gorging himself on his own blood and that of the defenders, Ruthven was regenerating his stump, making it a wing again.

Soon he'd be airborne.

Wordlessly, the aurora in his hair lavender-purple and pulsing, Frank broke into a run.

Ruthven, who was perched on a fortress among the dead, simpering to himself about how he would rebuild his child, how Jane in her brilliance would help him do it, how when the invasion of the human world began he would drink as he had never drunk before, a banquet in which the vintages on offer were diverse and sublimely tasty, found himself interrupted mid-tirade by strings.

Expecting the Dream Warrior, he coiled his long body so he could snap his teeth on the strings. They held. He gnawed at them, one slitted eye dilated and glaring at Frank.

Frank lassoed him again. And again. The gnawing was agony. He didn't let go. Done. The word was like a red bell knelling inside him. He thought of the tattoos on Catherine's throat. Cate often changed her tattoos, but the bells were a constant fixture. *Ask not for whom they toll*, she advised her worst enemies. *They toll for me.* Inside Frank's head the word knelled. Done. Done. *At last I am done.*

Ruthven's efforts to sever the strings grew frantic when Mr. Glint arrived and began to climb them. Giving up as Glint neared, the vampire's throat bulged as he unloaded a lake's worth of blood. Mr. Glint was not washed away. He climbed inevitably onward.

His gravelly, graveyard voice rolled over Ruthven. "For her, I will be brave as a comet. Plunging into heights and wordless black eternity. Eilandri. Eilandri. Her name was the best poem I ever heard."

Poisonous or not, Ruthven figured that the blood, which had been the key to the mysteries of his life, would provide the solution once more. He tried to drink Mr. Glint. He gagged, drank, stopped as paroxysms shook his frame, drank again.

Glint climbed on.

"Get him partner," Frank growled. More strings added to the bonds. "Show him what you can do."

There was no way Mr. Glint could have heard that. He was too far away, and besides The Furnace was loud that day with the sounds of things reaching their end.

Hear it or not, Mr. Glint showed Ruthven what he could do.

Crrrrrrrack, went his stretching jaw. His teeth, like weathered tombstones, sliced into Ruthven's eyes, which popped like bath bubbles. The vampire roared as, slowly and deliberately, Mr. Glint's mouth closed on a large slab of his skull and the brain beneath. The teeth met in the middle. Blood and brains exploded into the air. Mr. Glint chewed, swallowed, and went in for seconds.

Frank watched as raptures of miserable pain wracked the vampire.

Those shudders kept going as Ruthven slid off his perch and fell toward cold, hard stone. Impulsively, Frank flung out a length of nylon, got hold of the stake Mr. Glint had fashioned, and sent it toward his partner.

Glint's long-fingered hand caught it. He too was falling.

Ruthven was still alive when Mr. Glint landed on him.

The stake came up. The stake drove down.

Any supposition about vampires and virgins is without credibility. But not every myth is a lie. The stake pierced the vampire's heart.

And just like that the rhapsody of the Bloodwood was over.

***

Burrows didn't understand.

They should have held out. *He* should have held out. Even if he couldn't, Jane was the ace in the hole. Where was she? Where were Skuggs and Ruthven? Where was his wolf?

He didn't know. This ethereal prick was too much of a fucking nuisance.

A good swordsman, a little too good for Burrows' taste.

What was it about him that made the necromancer Lord feel as though he were meeting one of his own servants, upjumped and rebellious?

It was a weird, unbalancing feeling, unacceptable because Burrows needed to be balanced or he was going to die.

The ethereal prick was balance itself.

It was that very quality—the wavy, in-and-out etherealness—that had piqued Burrows' interest.

His spirits sank as Hughes limped over to join the fight. Iphigenia's shadow looked very much the worse for wear, but there was a stubborn twinkle in those hazel-dark eyes Burrows thought boded poorly for his chances here.

"I'm here, Hector," said Hughes.

Hector.

Hector...

"You're the son of Priam King," Burrows said.

Hector didn't let up his attack, not even to nod.

"I make it my business to research those who defy Lucy Nowhere. Who defy Death herself." Burrows' spirits weren't sinking anymore. Things were looking up. "I've heard of you, Hector. I bet you've heard of me too."

He slashed a wild arc with his scythe to give himself room to utter an incantation. Hector hesitated. That handsome face clouded with puzzlement.

"A living ghost is a kind of undead," Burrows explained, his arrogant, gray-lipped mouth twisting happily. "Kill your friend."

His smile vanished as Hector's mouth bloomed in a laugh.

It was a bright, merry sound, and Burrows had no idea how an undead could produce it. He hadn't been wrong. Hector *was* a ghost. Wasn't he?

"I don't understand," he said.

The look Hector gave him was indulgent, almost kind. "I already have a master." With blinding speed, he spun past Burrows' defenses.

His sword flashed white-gold. There was a whispery sound, something parting ways with something else, like a velvet goodbye.

Burrows' head toppled from his shoulders. Across the battlefield, the undead vented sounds of despair and started to wither away.

Where it came to rest, their Lord's head was exposed, the veil lifted.

In Burrows' eyes there were lights.

Hughes watched them flicker and go dark.

Out, out, brief candle.

***

As to what was going on—Jane listening to Cate Jubilee instead of gutting her, worse doing the tattooed wench's bidding—Skuggs hadn't the leastest, flimsiest smidgen of a clue. But he believed he knew how to stop it.

It took courage. He didn't lack for that, whatever Ruthven and Burrows thought. He'd stuck his neck out before, and he would do so again right now. Loyalty made him courageous.

Quietly, surreptitiously, he skulked toward Cate Jubilee.

He needn't have taken such precaution. The red woman was entirely focused on Jane. No wonder. Jane was doing something, a kind of gathering. Fields and forests of bugs teemed out of The Furnace's densely packed smoke. They flowed into Eurydice's shadow. Jane seemed to be doing it against her own will. She was hovering a foot off the ground. Her eyes were rolled back in her head. One of her hands was pawing and jerking at the air, as if she were trying to open a door that had been closed to her. Her other hand held Cate Jubilee's, and that was wrong.

Squeezing his knife tight, Skuggs jumped onto Cate Jubilee, wrenched off her helmet, and moved to put things right.

He met resistance. He pushed. The resistance pushed back, fluttering a pair of snow-white wings.

A moth. It had detached from the bugs just in time to stop his killing blow.

Skuggs watched in bewildered horror as the point of his crystal blade appeared on the other side of the moth's plump body.

With the last of its strength it flapped its wings, taking his knife with it. Skuggs hadn't tried to retrieve the knife. He felt dizzy. Too much was happening too fast.

He raised his single eye to follow the moth's path, and that was when a hand plunged his own knife into his neck. It sawed at him, cutting first one throat, then the other. Skuggs opened his mouth to say "Stop" or perhaps "Why?" What came out was his blood, thick and lumpy, the consistency of pumpkin pulp.

The owner of the hand that did the cutting was not Cate Jubilee.

Skuggs looked at her.

Jane looked back.

Only it wasn't Jane at all.

For once Skuggs wasn't worried about his guzzlible luck. He was worried about what happened after you died. He knew you went somewhere, only he didn't know where.

He had always found death amusing, at least in other people.

Now it was him dying, he felt somewhat obligated to find the funny side.

The world was losing its solidity.

The smoke was taking over. Maybe a darkness blacker than any smoke.

He no longer felt dizzy. He no longer felt anything.

Another thought occurred about what came next: he wondered if he would meet the spirit of the riddlewood tree. If so, Skuggs thought they would meet as friends rather than enemies. Bond over their shared roots.

Ahehn-hen—

***

As Skuggs' body slumped to the stone, a mother and a daughter spoke:

"What's happening, Mum?"

"You're fighting, sweetie. And winning."

"She's so strong."

"Yes. You're stronger."

"What's happening around us? All I can see is you."

"Keep seeing me. I'll tell you what's going on. Oh, Evie, it's okay."

"She's hurting me, Mum. She knows how to hurt me because..."

"Shh."

"... because she *is* me."

"Will I hold you?"

"Please. Please hold me."

"There."

"What's going on?"

"Well, let's see. My Company are making wobbly dessert of the Pontifex Jelly, so that's good. Some of them are destroying the idol at this site of power. And... and over there Frank and Mr. Glint are breaking their idol. And your dad and Hector are taking care of theirs. The idols are important for us winning, sweetie."

"Okay. Can you really see Frank and Dad?"

"Absolutely."

"It's smoky."

"When I say I can see them, I'm engaging in helpful, well-informed speculation. Which is almost as good as seeing."

"I'm sorry for all the times I've lied to you, Mum."

"Don't mind that now. I'm sure you felt you had to."

"And you feel you have to now."

"Yes, sweetie."

"But you believe honesty is the elixir of hope?"

"Yes."

"Like Dad?"

"Yes."

"Mum?"

"Yes?"

"I never saw a dog."

"Pardon?"

"One time I told you there was a dog. I didn't see one. I'm so sorry."

"I see. Well. That's all right, dear."

"This hurts so much."

"Being yourself often tends to. Granted, *your*self is a bit more complicated than most people's."

"What's happening now? I feel really warm all of a sudden and... something's loud."

"It seems I wasn't lying after all."

"What is it, Mum?"

"Nothing, dear. It's only a dragon."

***

It was nothing like he had expected.

When he was a boy, Hughes had liked all kinds of theatrical plays. Though he hadn't been able to go see any, theatre being something of a dead art at that time, he had been able to read about it. For countless hours, he had done just that.

His father, poor as mud but smart as clay, had literally built furniture in his teashop out of pages, both plays and traditional novels. In a digital era this was something of a gimmick to his patrons, but for Gormon Hughes Senior it was more than an affection. The apple did not fall far from the tree. Every story you can think of was represented in those rustly manuscripts, and Hughes Junior had gobbled them up, partly because they kept him warm when his thin blanket could not ward off the winter cold, mostly because he had that special mind some children have, the type that puts them right into the action of a well-told fiction.

His favorite was, and always would be, *A Summer Knight's Stroll*, which was about a man named Gwendle Gardener who got into constant, riveting trouble. The small, self-contained stories in the play were fun, and often hilarious, but there was a somber thread running through them like a belt of ownership cinched around the waist of a princess who longs to be free.

One such adventure concerned Sir Gwendle facing off against a dragon. The playwright had written the dragon like a person with hopes and dreams and fears. Apparently, this was a huge departure from the dragons that had really existed in Hughes' world, which were engines of fire and hunger, and though vastly intelligent in their own way, they were not as adaptable and prone to change as human beings, who overthrew the dragons by sheer force of ingenuity.

Hughes fancied the dragon in *A Summer Knight's Stroll* better.

To his awe and mounting distress, he recognized that the dragon rising from The Furnace was not like a person. It was not an engine of fire and hunger either, though there was a great deal of flame involved—the creature seemed to be built out of burning coals, scorched metal, and pressure-hardened diamonds held together by the *shape* of a dragon.

This dragon was a link between the surface and the tectonic plates and the very core of a world. It was Eurydice's anger summoned out of the ground. As it arched its back and breathed its first exhumed breath, a network of clouds melted and were reborn, melted and were reborn in flame so hot it burned blue, and ton after billowing ton of lung-pumped smoke.

Hughes. The voice that spoke directly into his mind was feeble but still sweet and green as a field in April. *Hughes...*

Spliffy?

He felt her smile. *Once more with feeling. Okay?*

Okay.

She gave him everything she had left, which amounted to a stage.

Hughes, ever the actor, took it.

In the magnificent glow of the dragon, his long, malleable face took on the aspect of a king who knew what he was about. Who was as autumnal as his patroness was springlike. Who expressed as little hatred as he dared and who loved unconditionally. Who got what he wanted. One way or another.

The dragon seemed to notice him, drawn by a silent gravity.

Its town-sized eye bore down on him. Such a little shadow man he was.

"Take me to the Crystal Country," he said.

And for the last time in his life, he pushed his Performance.

Chapter Twenty-One

Hughes opened his eyes, not knowing exactly when he'd closed them, only that he must have.

After forty-two years on his own gray earth, Iphigenia's green one, and Eurydice's whatever-the-fuck color one, there was not much shock left to be had for the wayward son of a teamaster.

The Crystal Country gave him one anyway.

Small-seeming (the word that struck Hughes was "quaint"), it was more a hamlet than a country. A shire of low slopes and wide grassy expanses. A dale of trees, hedges, and wildflowers. Pink gemstone, multifaceted and sparkling, was the chief (indeed the only) ingredient in everything. He brushed two fingers over the stem of a blooming cockscomb. Not pliant at all. Dense. Cold.

The gemstone was the same type that formed from the corpses of Eurydice's creatures. There was no exception. Even Burrows had been crystallizing when Hughes and Hector destroyed the idol and summoned The Furnace dragon. The pretty pink stuff had been introduced into the economic pipeline by the Dragontail family. Slowly, it had taken its place as the forerunner among world currencies, at least in Hughes' world. Seriously macabre, but as Cate Jubilee had pointed out, the crystal was divisible, tangible, and shiny. That last bit carried the most weight with human beings. She wasn't being cynical, Cate lacked the necessary components for dejected outlooks as far as people were concerned. It was how it was: shiny sells, and if it buys, even better.

It explained why President Hughes had such a devil of a time trying to phase out credits and get Corinthia back on the pound and copper penny.

He walked a winding trail between agapanthus hills, his boots *clicking* against the glittering quartz. Now and then there was a teeth-gritting *crunch* underfoot as he broke an errant weed or pebble. *If I'd read about this in a fairy tale as a kid, I'd have thought the author was pushing the envelope of believability too far. A dale of riches. A shire of splendor.*

The sky was lilac shading to blue at the horizon. His nostrils were full of the air's odd gifts, a certain fizzy sweetness like the smell you get before you take a mouthful of pink lemonade.

How long he explored, he wasn't sure, but after climbing one of the taller slopes for a look around, he gazed over the dells and hedgerows and spotted a lane of fruit trees.

At the end of the lane was a pink house.

He didn't think it was wishful thinking to assume its occupant.

An inventory of himself confirmed Chimera had been lost in the battle. The events of it were a whirling dervish in his mind, he hadn't even thought of his sword till now. Still, he had a good substitute.

The Painted Girl's words came to him across a bridge of time.

You keep your Krys knife handy, Hughes.

"I will, Krys." And in his mind he added, *To the very end.*

The fruit trees were of a kind he had only ever seen along the fashionable promenades in Jaenqui-Across-The-River. Pomegranates. Leaves carpeted the lane. There was no avoiding the glassy *crunches* there.

As he lifted a hand to the front doorknob, something *plipped* damply against his wrist. He frowned at the drop of red, vivid against his pale skin. The nasty gash the wolf had given him was still pumping lustily away, so much so that Hughes had bled through his surgical bandage.

Nothing he could do about that.

Or... maybe there was.

Hughes didn't bother to knock. He went in, sparing a final glance at the peaceful Crystal Country, embedding it in his memory as best he could.

Knowing who lived in this house, he might never see a place like this, or any place, ever again.

***

A high-hackle instinct expected Eurydice to jump out brandishing an arsenal of pink crystal weapons. Easing the door shut behind him, Hughes was glad to be disappointed.

The house was eerily quiet.

Adding to the noise-muffling acoustics were the stacks, jumbles, and towers of boxes. All shapes. All sizes. Some of them were encased in transportive bubble wrap, some bare except for the delivery service stickers slapped on the lid.

He didn't quite dare touch one, no mean feat given how many there were. The entry hall was flush with doors, both opposite and underneath a stair climbing to the second floor, and he had no doubt each room was crammed to the brim with boxes just like the ones out here. No lights were on, but from a high window over the front door, a couple along the right wall where the stairs scaled, and another window at the end of the hall, there came a light that made Hughes' brow wrinkle in confusion.

It was a city sort of light, rainy and aglow with the burnished orange blush of streetlamps.

Only the Crystal Country had been dry. There had been no streetlamps.

He climbed a few steps and peered out the lowest window.

There was the Crystal Country all right, and... and somewhere else.

Somewhere rainy and secluded, a city that slipped right under the radar.

Dublin, he thought. *The estate in Dublin where Lucy Nowhere hid the worlds. What did that apprentice of hers, Rupert Prindlee, call it?*

The Willows estate in Glasnevin.

So, the pink house existed in both places at once. Looking out the window, he was glimpsing the Crystal Country and Eurydice's view of Dublin like two photographs superimposed over one another.

Hughes thought about continuing upstairs, then reconsidered.

He'd had an idea as to how to solve the issue of his facial bleed, and checking each room thoroughly was the crux and biscuit of it.

Beginning with the doors to the left of the entry hall, he began a meticulous search. He found enough boxes to flatten a charging elephant, but fuck all else. He wondered what could be in them.

Old investigative muscles spun up in Hughes. Evelyn had once told his father that Eurydice likes "when the music breaks." Not a far cry from saying that the lunatic got her kicks smashing up instruments.

Door number five yielded a sight gruesome and, in a crooked sense, encouraging.

This was a room—again glutted floor to ceiling with boxes—that contained a four-posted bed. Someone had been murdered there. Messily. On the floor, one lens cracked, and both lenses dappled in gore, were a pair of owlish spectacles. Hughes picked them up. He wished he could feel sympathy for John Isherwood, who Jane had most likely eaten alive in this room. A sliver of himself, one he didn't care for, wished he could feel vindicated. John had orchestrated Jane's return, which put Evelyn in the line of fire. Instead, he felt nothing.

Round the side of the bed was a cupboard. Hughes found what he wanted there. See, it wasn't a dramatic leap to conclude that John's betrayal had been a long time in the planning. That meant the doctor had been here before, perhaps in dreams, and if Hughes had learned something about dreams, it was that though their rules were fickle, downright unruly, they held a great power to influence the waking world and vice versa.

Inside the cupboard was a heavy leather bag. Hughes brought it out by the handles, set it on the bed, and flicked open its latches.

Five minutes later he was concentrating in front of a foldout mirror with a basin of sterile solution and a suture kit. Between husband and wife, Cate was the dab hand at combat needlework, but in this, as with so many other things, she had rubbed off on him.

It hurt like a son of a bitch, but when he sat back and examined the results Hughes thought he hadn't done half bad. A little mad scientist, a little patchy amateur, but yeah. Not too shabby.

He returned to the entry hall, weighed up further exploration of the ground floor versus heading right for the stairs, and chose the stairs.

They creaked.

The near certainty of an appearance from the lady of the house compounded with every step. She might come at him head on. She might creep up as her shadow crept up behind the unsuspecting. She might use magic. He might have caught her at supper, so a fork might be in store, or a carving knife. She might scream or unleash peels of loony bin laughter. She might speak his name with such cold perversion that his own sanity would snap, and then there would be two patients in this pink asylum. She might do things to him he couldn't even think of, and that was when Hughes realized it was his ignorance—the fact that he did not know what Eurydice even looked like—that was making his heart gallop, his palms greasy, and his throat dry.

He climbed two sets of stairs. Two more went by. With no one to impress with his courage, Hughes' face was a picture of unease. There had not been four stories to this house, at least not from the outside. Two more went by.

Furnishings drew his eye, especially the ones that might conceal her.

Aside from the never-ending piles of boxes, he saw carpets redefining shag, for they were stitched to show images of what a religious leader would call deplorable fornication and what Hughes called scenes of interesting affection. The figures depicted were not exactly animals, but not exactly human either. Their bodies contorted in ways that sat strangely with him. Not bad. Strange.

On the curtains he saw embroidery—fields of flowers, dancers, leaf crowns, birds, a marital bed in the open wilderness by a stream, a wedding in the heart of nature.

Some of the ceilings were fitted with lights. More often than not when Hughes tried the lights the bulbs gave off a tiny fizzle of spark and shined no more. But occasionally the electricity worked, and Hughes could get a look at the ceilings. There were murals up there. The kind painted on laid lime plaster. Frescos, they were called.

Like the carpets and the curtains, the frescos on the ceiling showed images of a party, though this one was not set in nature and it did not involve sex, contortionista style or not. The party stretched from ceiling to ceiling, using the walls running along the upper portions of each stair to connect them. One big jamboree. Not one Hughes would want to rock up to any time soon. The party in the fresco was thriving in a dark world, a world of teeth that smiled too widely and eyes that peered too intrusively, a world of tempers that flayed the skin off bone, of drinking fountains that rotted you from the inside out, or made you a twisted kind of angel, or blew out your brains and transformed the fragments of your skull into roses worn in the hair of women. Hughes could practically hear the chuckles of those women who mercifully hid their faces behind fans. Their chuckles would sound like the crazy hysterical cries of hyenas. The party was a rager that went on and on, with barrels broken and the fluid that came gurgling out—not alcohol—was lapped up with greedy tongues. He saw a three-headed dog. He'd believed Burrows' two-headed wolves were the worst canines he would ever clap eyes on. In that he'd been wrong.

It got to be that when he tried the lights and the bulbs fizzled but didn't come on, he felt relieved.

Soon he stopped trying the lights altogether.

There was a secret detail to everything he saw. Had he been a less observant man (one who was not familiar with the first rule of policework), he might have missed those details. Had he not spent as long as he had in the company of Hoshrum Thud, he might not have assembled those details into a pattern. But Hughes had, and he did.

He folded the secret away in case it came in useful later and trudged on.

Boxes rambled. He nudged one, almost spilled the stack it was balancing, breathed out shakily when he got it steadied.

Where was Eurydice? What was her game?

The unthinkable might happen now.

Or now.

Or now.

On the ninth floor, the stairs came to an abrupt end.

Just to see if he was going nuts, he found a window and peeked out.

He saw the Crystal Country overlayed by Dublin. It was exactly the same view as he'd gotten on the ground floor. No change at all.

Which makes me mad, or the house mad.

Hughes wanted to believe the latter. But the former nettled him. If he was losing his beloved memory, why not his mind too?

No. I'm not crazy.

I can't be.

The highest floor in the pink house began with a floor of checkerboard tile—white and black. The black tiles were massive, the white teeny. Hughes recalled one of Miss Gleam's malevolent pearls of conversation. She'd been *snicking* those scissors of hers in front of him, turning his bowels to water.

She was, she told him, a woman of large black truths...

Snicker-snick, went the scissor blades.

... and little white lies.

The rest of this wide, tiled area was dominated by furry curtains, furry as a certain draconic vampire had been furry. In the middle of the area was a table of necrotic flesh. On the table was a lampshade made to look like a single cyclopean eye.

No boxes.

Instead, there were wooden stands on which instruments had been hung, everything from flutes to bassoons to guitars. The instrument stands were arranged in a perfect circle. And as if someone had gone from one to the next in a fit of extreme pique, a couple of the instruments were wrecked beyond repair. It was concentric. Whoever had smashed that lute, those bagpipes, that harp, they were doing it one at a time. The scene gave the impression that once this circle was all scrap and flingers, a few boxes would be opened, and a new set of instruments would take their place on the stands. Next on the chopping block, so to speak.

On the far side of the room, Hughes spied a short flight of steps curving round to who knew where on this uppermost floor. He made for it, giving the room's accoutrements as wide a berth as possible. The flight didn't curve for long. Here, now, were three steps.

And a door.

Now, he thought firmly. *Now it'll happen. She'll fling that door wide and storm down here, a terrible homunculus of changing human features, a woman who reflects her world. She'll be intent on treating me as she treats her weird purchases in the boxes, but I'll be ready. Any second now it'll happen.*

But nothing did.

Hughes wet his lips. They were chapped, almost as dry as his throat.

Nothing.

He mouthed the words, "Get it over with."

Nothing.

Hughes started up the flight. All three steps were impossible to confront. He confronted them. And pressed on.

It is for love that you put one foot in front of the other.

Evelyn's question: How am I a stethoscope, Dad?

His reply: You remind me that my heart is still there.

For love. All for love.

He opened the door and there, at last, Eurydice.

***

The bedroom was like yours. Your mother's. Your sister's. Your daughter's.

There were picture frames. Chests-of-drawers. Cabinets. Shoes under the bed. A laundry basket. A bed and an end table with a fuchsia-shaded lamp. Books.

Magazines. A triptych of casement windows overlooking Glasnevin. It had been raining. Not now. It would again. There were clouds. Not threatening. Promises. One thing you could be sure of: Glasnevin, Dublin, and Ireland would never be without rain. Just as The Willows housing estate would never again be without worlds to foster, to protect, and to keep hidden from prying intelligences.

The bedroom was like yours.

Eurydice was like a woman you have met before or might very well meet today.

She was a tanned brunette whose good complexion and better hair went to waste cooped up indoors. She wore blue jeans, sandals, a halter neck top the color of sunset. Hughes couldn't see her face, only its distorted reflection in the rain-stippled glass.

He drew his Krys knife and walked toward her. His steps were hushed on the plain creamy carpet. When he caught his own reflection in the window, he froze. She'd see him. Eurydice, however, passed no remark. The reflection of her face didn't change one iota.

Either she hadn't spotted him—possible but damn unlikely—or she *had* spotted him and didn't care he was there.

He found that hard to accept, though he managed it after a moment.

Everything he knew about her suggested a turbulent character, which meant that the anger and joy could as easily spin due south, becoming blissful calm or sadness.

Hughes' gaze strayed to his reflection again. His reflection gazed back. He was, even to the uncritical eye, an assassin sneaking up behind an ordinary-seeming woman. A blatant cutthroat. That was the role he was playing, the part he must needs cast himself as in this shadow drama. He tried to square his knowledge of Eurydice and all the horrors carried out at her command with this woman sitting in front of him, found he could, and at the same time found that his role was about to undergo a rapid rewrite. Right or wrong, call it improvisation. A gut move. Acting is reacting.

He put his knife away. He walked another couple steps and leaned against the window so he could see her properly.

Her face wasn't a carbon copy of Jane's. No huge surprise. Hughes didn't resemble Iphigenia in the slightest. He decided he didn't like that face all the same. It was an echo of the scenes depicted in the furnishings on the lower floors—pretty on the surface, even beautiful, yet concealing secrets.

"Do you regret any of it?" he asked her.

She glanced his way. She gave a small, flat whistle. "Wowee. You're the spit-and-polish of her."

"Who?"

"Who do you think?" said Eurydice. "Jane."

"It's fairly uncanny, I'll concede as much. I suppose all shadows of worlds share a genetic heritage. It follows we look like brothers, sisters, or close cousins."

"She'll never be yours."

She meant Evelyn.

"True," Hughes agreed. "But if you think she'll be yours, you're mistaken."

"I don't think that."

"Good."

"There's cordial if you want some."

"No, thank you. It occurs to me that you may have given up on it as of recently, but there was a time when you thought Evelyn was yours. You wouldn't have lured her away from her real family if you didn't deeply believe you were owed a false sister."

"You deprived a world of her shadow."

"Justly. I'd do it again in a heartbeat. You haven't answered my question. The invasions. The intense, fanatical, consuming violence. The war in which the majority of banners flew your colors and the greatest host of voices chanted your name. Do you regret it, Eurydice? I expect an answer before I decide what happens next."

"You can't kill me. Lucy wouldn't allow it."

"Ah, confident, are you? After what you've done to Iphigenia, a fellow resident of this estate, you're truly convinced of your immunity?"

Eurydice reached under her chair and brought out a machete.

"I'm confident. And if Death lets me down, which she won't, there's always this. I'll mount your head as a trophy display and show Jane when she visits next. She'll be tickled. I've never heard her talk about someone the way she talks about you. It's like you cursed her by existing. It's an unhealthy obsession, but she wears it well."

"Maybe that's a case of like adoring like," said Hughes.

She glanced at him. This time that glance was a mirror for the clouds over Dublin. Beyond threat. A rumbling dark promise.

"What do you mean by that?"

"Nothing that isn't blindingly obvious. You're a junkie for music and powerfully ashamed of it. It's such a strong emotion that it's seeped into the decorations of your house. In your carpets, sexually explicit orgies provide camouflage for figures dressed piously and self-consciously. These figures all carry instruments, as do the demonic minstrels in the ceiling frescoes, and—"

"Don't."

"—as does the man in the wedding scene depicted in the curtains. A man with his face defaced by hooked fingernails. I can't help but notice your fingernails, which are scuffed and ragged. Does the man's face return to the picture, I wonder? How often do you have to scratch it away?"

"I'm warning you."

"Warn away. It's a melody I'm particularly deaf to. Is he a man you yearned to marry, or was that wedding bed by the stream—"

The final word of his question—"yours"—went unspoken.

She swiped at him with the machete.

He avoided it narrowly, dove over the bed, and came to his feet again as she tore open a nearby drawer. She had dropped the machete. Her hands emerged from the drawer carrying something far more insidious. The chainsaw was rusty-bladed. The chainsaw had worn handle grips. The chainsaw spluttered to grinding, buzzing life on the first pull of the ignition.

Eurydice smiled at him. "Sounds like flies, doesn't it?" she shouted over the clamor. "Are you going to push me again, you little shit?"

He shook his head.

"Okay then."

She compressed a button. The chainsaw *chugga-chugged* and fell quiet.

Hughes relaxed, though not much since she kept hold of those worn handle grips.

"Not one," she said.

"Sorry?"

"The answer to your question. Have I any regrets. Not one. Which is more than I can say for *him*."

Hughes did not ask who she meant by "him." The rust-flecked teeth of the chainsaw were sterling motivation to embrace caution. Besides, he thought he could take a reasonable shot at who Eurydice was talking about.

She was watching him, her smile a stretched elastic band, capable of snapping fatally should he misjudge her again, should he push.

"May I ask about the fresco?" he said.

"What about it?"

"Is it a real place?"

"Illustrated, you mean? Yeah. It's real."

"I'm sorry to hear it."

She raised a brown brow. "I'm sorry to know it." She said no more.

It was something.

Hughes' mind, in overdrive and accelerating, hazarded a guess. An excellent one, as it turned out.

"Is it an underworld?" he said. "Perhaps the one you were meant to venture to after death in the mortal world?"

"Hades." She pronounced the word, and the walls grew soft and spongy with a cadaverous black mold. "*Hades.*" She spoke the word, and the end table and lamp began to ooze like scabs ripped away and infected wounds beneath squeezed. "*HADES.*" She spoke the word, the windows smashed, and the night reached in, smothering, choking, strangling.

Hughes' back thumped the door to the bedroom's adjoining en suite. His clothes rippled and his beard bristles shivered in a sudden gale. Both arms jounced up, shielding his face and body.

The wind left. He took a breath and tasted the room's gentle air. He brought his hands down by his sides, his eyes scanning with a sage cunning, for he knew that trouble, like lightning, can inarguably strike the same place twice. But the room was normal. It was as though the malefic name of the underworld had never been spoke. The only change was Eurydice, sitting in her chair. It faced Hughes now, with the three windows framing her. The chainsaw was nowhere to be seen.

"I've been told it's changed. Hades, I'm talking about. Complete renovation. Lord Hades himself is reformed from his wicked, wicked ways. His wife, Persephone, has sworn off every vice under the moon. Cerberus the three-headed hound is, by all accounts, a cutie. I find it hard to believe, but Lucy says it's true, so..." Eurydice made a noncommittal sound. "All I remember is the feeling... like every moment I spent in that place demanded I laugh until I screamed and scream until I laughed. Maybe I've deleted the worst of it. Do you think our brains are like computers?"

"I think the brain of a world could be like that. Human beings are analog. Where you, vast and vibrant Eurydice, have storage and a predisposition to constant updates and innovations, we have notebooks."

"Sounds flimsy."

"I agree."

His compliment had not gone unnoticed. Hughes was sure that if he'd complimented her a moment before he did, or a moment after, the effect would have been minimal or nonexistent. Eurydice was leaps and bounds more unpredictable than anything he had ever encountered.

She gave him a shrewd look, couched in pleasure. "Vast and vibrant. I like that. Yummy to say out loud. Has anyone ever told you that you're really flattering?"

"I tend toward an observation and truthful approach, which tends to be well received."

She fanned herself, mockingly, but still obviously pleased. "Starry, starry night. More flattery, this time circumambulatory rather than straightforward. You remind me of... What?"

"I didn't say anything."

"Didn't you? Maybe it's the thunder. Can you hear thunder? I can. And... you can ask me something else, if you want to."

Hughes wanted to ask about the man with the scratched-away face, the one she kept sidling up to as their conversation progressed, the one she had fetched a chainsaw rather than talk about directly.

Are you going to push me again, you little shit?

The chainsaws buzz had indeed sounded like flies.

If Hughes could avoid a replay of that harrowing spectacle, he would.

So instead, he asked the other question he needed answered.

"What will you do now, Eurydice?"

"Rebuild. You and your scarlet army can set up outposts. Colonize me. You can stick around with my blessing and permission. I doubt you'd respect my privacy if I asked kindly, pretty please, with cherries on top. And because I am vast and vibrant, my plasma, my primordial sludge, and my organically rich oceans will... I don't think the word is "generate," I... think it might be inspire. They'll inspire with new life. I'll inspire them."

"You'll accelerate the evolutionary process."

She shrugged. Rolled her fingers into her hair. Shook it vigorously. Smoothed it back from her face.

"You'll attack again," said Hughes. It wasn't a question.

Eurydice looked at him.

Hughes came around the bed and sat on its window-side edge. This brought him three feet from her, well within chainsawing distance should it make a miraculous reappearance.

"Forgive me, mighty, garrulous, and life-conjuring Eurydice. I am only a man. It may not be for me to understand, but your approach, while observational and truthful, doesn't seem conducive to the same peace you and I are embodying now in this very moment. It seems actively aggressive."

"As a man, you know very well that it's aggressive. Justifiably so. After all, your people were the instigators of this war. Do you deny the charge that for decades now your Scarlet Citadel has plundered my citizens, the way a miner would plunder a vein of mountain ore? I don't use that word lightly. *Plunder.*"

"I don't deny it."

"They may not look like you do, or obey the same laws and strictures, but they think. They feel. They have culture, including that closest-knit culture: family. And for the sake of your royal mint and the possibility of economic sovereignty, you've delivered slaughter and genocide to my children."

He held up his hands, mollifying. "I'm not arguing with you. It's an unforgivable thing. I've attempted to move my world away from the use of credits."

"You never used your Performance for it. You could have."

"You're right. Moreover, I should have. Bearing that in mind, I think you know I've tried. I can see it in your eyes. As to instigators of this war, as you say, that isn't us. Not me or mine. Everything you said about that is horseshit."

That was a push, calculated but risky. He'd come closer to her to mitigate that risk. Outwardly he was friendly, cool as a patch of shadow on a sunny day. Inside, he tensed, ready for an evil swing of pendulum Eurydice.

She stared at him, gravely.

Then she burst out laughing. Hughes breathed easier.

"Feisty boy," she dubbed him. "Who'd have thought Iphigenia could have gumption like that?"

Her face went terribly slack. "You weren't calling me a liar, were you?"

"Aren't you?" he said. "My daughter thinks you are."

"She's right. But you don't call me names, or I'll make you sorry, Hughes. I'll make you wish Jane were here to kill you. I know what it's like to want to die. We're old pals, that feeling and I. I could introduce you."

"No, Eurydice. I'm sorry."

"What'd you say?"

"I'm sorry."

She stood and loomed over him, smiling humorlessly. "You bet you are. Horseshit. A crock of horseshit. That's very funny." She pinched his cheek, hard. "I say your people started the war. You say horseshit. Go on and tell me what stinks."

"My mother once told my wife about her theories on the creation of the portals between worlds, otherwise known as the doors of fire. My wife told me. The rumor is that Diedrich Lutz was daydreaming as he sketched the blueprints for the portals. In that daydream he scribbled two names, circling them, and adding notches and crosses for good measure. The two names were Iphigenia and Eurydice. Wendy Dragontail described it as an instance in which a portal of a different kind, a so-called thought-vortex, opened in Diedrich Lutz's mind. He thought to himself, what shall I name these big doors, and both you and Iphigenia replied." Though his cheek was throbbing where her fingernails dug into flesh, Hughes matched Eurydice's smile. His was truculent, taunting. "I am only a man, and in dangerous times men are prone to suspicion if they want to live to see tomorrow. I suspect Diedrich Lutz didn't merely daydream the names for each portal. I suspect he daydreamed the portals themselves."

She pinched harder. It hurt almost as badly as the stitching poking through his other cheek. "Suspicions aren't evidence."

"Do you see a judge? What about a jury? This isn't a court. Just us. You're a woman, Eurydice, but you're also a world. Your inhabitants are complicated. Some would be battle hungry by nature, but some would resist an unprompted invasion, which is what you secretly desired. Compromising, and after researching my world and Iphigenia's, you decided that the latter would be easy to take, and the former would try and take you. At least on the surface of things. And with the invention of the portal, human beings, intrigued, naïve, and fabulously avaricious as we are, couldn't resist crossing the doors of fire, discovering the sparkling pink deposits left by your dead, and cruelly plundering those spoils. It was a masterstroke by you, wise warmonger Eurydice. Galvanized by the prospect of extinction, your naysayers would be silenced. Your isolationists would become your most fervent supporters.

"Only you didn't count on Iphigenia casting her shadow on my world. Creating me, a little brother crafted to pick up the slack and rush to the defense of his older sister. Iphigenia read you like a pamphlet, quickly and comprehensively. So when Lutz dreamed of his magnum opus, he dreamed of two portals instead of one. And it would mean the plunder of Iphigenia too, until contact between she and I could be established. A price my sister was willing to pay. Ultimately, it was of little consequence to your plan, which went off without a hitch. You showed us the way. We followed. The good, logical course of things inverted so that daughters no longer buried fathers. Fathers buried their daughters. The war happened.

"That's what stinks, reproachfully, hideously. I'm not absolving us of our role in it. I'm pointing out yours. Incidentally, if you don't take that hand off my face, I'm going to make it so you wish you never had a hand in the first place. I may not have as grim a collection of old pals as yours, Eurydice, but I've a knife given to me by a friend. It's sharp. I could introduce you."

There was an awful silence.

"Gumption," she said.

"Lots."

She let him go. His cheek sang painfully, but her nails hadn't broken skin. She sat back down. That imposing emptiness was gone. The way she knuckled her chin and looked at him, why, she could have almost passed for human.

"You're easy to talk to."

He inclined his head graciously.

"My wedding day... nobody talked," continued Eurydice, looking past him now as if gazing directly at the past. "We were too busy to talk."

"Weddings are chock-full of diversions."

"Right? My mouth was too busy smiling, or... or full of wine or singing to talk. You know how the elderly have a photo album, and maybe when it's raining and the joints are chiming like church bells they take down the album and remember ye olde days of sunshine? I don't keep an album like that. I don't need to."

Sensing that this was an opportunity worth pushing her on, just a little, Hughes pitched his tone nice and casual and said, "I expect you, the lovely bride, were the best singer that day."

"You expect wrong. I was good. Stunningly good. But Orpheus was a million times better than me. A *billion*."

He nodded as though that were interesting in a nicest, most casual sense of the word. "Right, right. And this Orpheus. I bet he wasn't half bad on the lyre, either, eh?"

"Not half bad?" She snorted cheerfully. "He was a *genius*. Whatever artistic realm lies beyond genius, that's where he hung his laurels. He could play to the winter and persuade it to let spring come six weeks early! He could sing to a waterfall and make it flow back on itself. I know, Hughes! I saw him do it."

"Quite the troubadour. I wouldn't be surprised if it was melodies composed by Orpheus that renovated Hades, changing it for the better."

The light of joyful nostalgia flickered in her eyes, guttered, and went out. When Burrows' candles had snuffed, his eyes had looked finally, irrevocably dead. Eurydice's eyes looked very much alive. And furious.

"You tricked me," she said, that weird spooky emptiness stealing over her again. "Fooled me into saying his name out loud. I haven't done that in... I don't know how long. A long time. You made me."

"Eurydice. I didn't mean to offend y—"

"Shut up before I shut you up. Youuuu... You *wouldn't be surprised if Orpheus' melodies changed Hades for the better...*" She smiled, and it was like invisible fingers pushing at the mouth of a plasticene model, that was how unnatural that smile looked. "If only you knew how stupid that sounds. How fucking *mortal* it sounds."

"I don't understand."

"It's okay. You'll get it when you're dead."

She stood up, her face frighteningly vacant, and started toward the drawer. Hughes knew exactly what lay inside that drawer. He rocked to his feet in a hurry, grasping her arm.

A new tack was required.

"*Orpheus!*" He yanked her round and roared into her face. "His name prickles your sensibilities that much, have it! *Orpheus, Orpheus, ORPHEEEEEEEUUUUUS!*"

What happened next was almost as worrying as her absent-minded savagery. She flinched. No, it was more intense than that. She *quailed* from him.

"Why are you wincing? What's so bad about your husband? Tell me!"

"I can't!"

"You can. God damn it, you will because I'll make you."

"Lucy keeps us safe here!"

"Yeah, well, I don't see her. Do you?"

She pushed him. He grabbed her wrists. "Oh, so you can push and I... Listen. I won't kill you, but I'll give as good as I get. You'll turn like a coin, this meekness'll vanish and I'll see your wrath, your *Menin*. First here's mine."

"How do you know that word?" No shrinking scaredy-cat routine. She'd turned like a coin, only she was bewildered, not angry. He let her go. She didn't massage her wrists—his fingers hadn't even left marks. "*Menin.* How do you—"

"Iphigenia taught me."

"Wrath." Eurydice tasted it on her tongue. "First word of Iliad, you know."

"The what?"

"Never mind. Iphigenia taught you? That adds up. She comes from the same place I did, before we became worlds."

"Greece?" said Hughes.

"Yeah. I haven't heard the name of my home in ages. Did she tell you, by the way? How she became a world?"

"Yes. Her father sacrificed her to appease the wind, or a God of the wind."

"Sounds about right. Even though we're sure they'll catch us, dads can let us fall. They can be the ones who fail us."

"So can husbands," said Hughes.

She glanced at him, and as if her glance really were connected to the clouds over Dublin, it began to rain. Drops stippled the window glass. There was thunder and it filled the silence in the room like poison filling a cup.

"I hear buzzing in your future," she told him.

"And I music in your past," he replied drily. "Let's stop dancing around one another, Eurydice. I know your story already. There's beauty, and betrayal, and a vow of revenge against not only the perpetrator, but everything and everyone. It ends with the formation of a world. In my heart, so mortal and fallible, I suspect it begins with a meeting, followed by a pledge of eternal fealty and a proposal of marriage. All I lack is the details. You might as well tell me, or dash to your drawer, chainsaw the heads from both of us, and have done."

"I could."

"You could. But you'd lose out on my famous gumption. And in spite of the obstacles between us, I feel a door has opened that was shut before. I find you easy to talk to."

He watched as her face shifted like a landscape fast-forwarded. Dubious. Indignant. Bemused. Scornful. Bemused again. And there her expression stayed.

She gestured. He sat on the bed. She joined him.

Side-by-side they looked out the window at Dublin.

"I said yes, of course. When he asked me to be his and his alone. How could I refuse Orpheus of Thrace, the greatest musician and vocalist in Greece? How could I. You know he sang me a better relationship with my parents? No kidding. Mother, Father, and I used to bicker all the time, things would settle then— boom—tempers flared up again. Orpheus said he could sing to Dad until he didn't want to drink his monthly wages, and if that weren't enough, he further swore he could make Mum less vainglorious and stubborn. And the wild thing? He was right. A little ditty, and hey presto, Daddy never touched a drop of booze again. Mum threw her gilded mirror in a creek bed. You've gone still, Hughes."

"It's nothing to worry about."

"Say."

"Well... I see similarities between Orpheus' power to transform personalities and my own abilities."

"I don't think he was the shadow of a world. Maybe your Performance isn't as unique as you think."

"Maybe."

"Anyway, we got married and that was that. At least I thought it would be."

"Trouble entered paradise?"

"Faster than you'd believe," agreed Eurydice. "His tours of neighboring towns became tours of neighboring cities, then neighboring countries. He'd lavished me with songs, poems, and instrumental arrangements. They dried up. It was amazing how quickly my life went from passionately warm to cold."

"However did you cope with this drought?" he said bitterly.

Eurydice frowned at him. Her frown evaporated.

He didn't have to ask if the drought that had put the squeeze on his entire world was her handiwork. They both knew the truth. Like her subjugation of Evelyn, his daughter's replacement with Jane, the fact of that deadly dry time lay between them. But Hughes had not lied to her. Certain doors, formerly closed, were now wide open. It was thanks to these that Eurydice went on.

"I coped by sitting him down and explaining my feelings. We were growing apart. I didn't want to. He sat there, his sensitive face sort of taking it in, and when I was done he didn't hesitate. Said he felt the same way. Would I come on tour with him?"

"Interesting. Did it work?"

"So well you wouldn't believe. We were closer than ever. He had me climb the stage and take a bow after the completion of his every show. He introduced me to the crowd as his true muse, the one who waked in him the deepest, most exciting passions. The crowd clapped as we kissed. Shit, it was a lot bigger than clapping. It was louder than that," she said, pointing toward the window as thunder rattled the sky. "Best days of my life. Shame it was the touring that doomed us."

"How so?" said Hughes.

"I attracted the attention of a God. Okay, a Lord of an underworld. They're basically Gods. They make a world at the height of her strength look meek. Pathetic."

"This Lord who took an interest in you. Was it Hades?"

"Got it in one. These were different days, when the governance of the underworlds was municipal, or metropolitan in the case of the larger settlements such as Hades. Before Lucy Nowhere took up the mantle of Death and set protections in place.

Hades and the other Lords and Ladies of the underworlds had free rein, or close. They could take a fancy to mortals, for example. Mortals could take fancy to them.

"I suppose you're going to call me fickle, but while I was still in love with Orpheus, Hades earned a healthy heaping of my affection. He appeared to me in visions that lasted a few seconds. Then, as my desire grew, the visions lasted longer. Hades told me that his wife, Persephone, spent half the year with him and half with her Olympian side of the family. Why not enact a similar arrangement? Spend half my time with Orpheus in the lands of the living and half in the underworld called Hades with its eponymous master for a paramour?"

"You were tempted."

"You can say that again. Orpheus was sweet but Hades had a... I guess you could say a *swarthiness* about him. It was sexy. I consulted Orpheus. He said he was open to it, so long as he could take other muses when I wasn't around. He also asked me never to forsake our marriage or to tell Hades that I loved him outright. I thought that was a fair deal."

"The plot thickens. Tell me, headstrong and romantic Eurydice. When did you discover," said Hughes, "that you were dead?"

Eurydice clicked her tongue and made a glum noise.

"You're quick on the uptake. When? Oh, as soon as I arrived in Hades. I felt this vital... thing within me giving, and tugging, almost an umbilical cord sort of sensation... and then my remaining lifespan was chopped by the reaper woman, and I was dead. I felt thinner, unbearably spread out. All at once I became a spirit and I felt better at once. I was shocked, but there's an explanation behind what happened to me. You see, the living can visit the underworld and be fine, but Hades fooled me. A compact made with a Lord of an underworld can condemn you to die before your time. Again, these were different days. Lucy would never allow that now."

"I see. I'm not, by the way."

"Not what?"

"Not calling you fickle." Hughes smiled comfortingly. "I've been in love with two people at once. One conquered the other in the course of things, but it didn't happen overnight."

"Huh." She gave him an appraising look.

"You were dead," Hughes prompted. "I can't imagine Orpheus took it well."

"He took it as he ought to have taken it. As a violation, a manipulation, and a challenge. He sang that he would have me back, plunged the countryside into winter with a nocturne in D minor, and spread word far and wide that spring would never come till a door opened for him that led directly to me."

"I like this lover of yours."

"Brilliant, wasn't he? So dramatic. Obviously the world couldn't cope with such a transgression against its own natural laws. Rather than bear the perverse winter it relented instantly, sending a rapidly germinating tree to Orpheus. Its roots formed a door, guiding him to Charon, the ferryman of Hades, who under distress from my musical love, was forced to escort Orpheus to the underworld. There Hades doted on me, adored me despite my refusal to reciprocate his sexual advances, and generally swaggered about like an erect phallus trying to attract as much attention as possible. He never took advantage in that way, but I still hated him with every fiber of my being."

"I don't blame you. Judging by the fresco on the ceilings, Hades was a nightmare. Screaming and laughter."

"Screaming and laughter, yes. Orpheus arrived. He played his way to me. It was... breathtaking. Hades would have squashed Orpheus, but half the underworld would have risen up against him, so popular was the musician from Thrace. Hades grinned a golden-toothed grin, and said, well, well, well, isn't this a turnout for the oracles. Why, yes, Orpheus could take me back to the lands of the living, but there was a catch. If Orpheus turned around while he led me out, if he lost faith that I would follow him into the dark and out the other side, then I would stay in the underworld forever."

"It sounds simple." Hughes grimaced. "Anything but. I've got a vivid imagination. I'm picturing it now. Having to walk an uncertain path with Cate behind me. Unable to see her face, take courage in her smile? It'd get to me. I like to think I wouldn't turn, wouldn't give in to the voices whispering to me in the language of doubt. I'd like to believe it." He watched the rains trickle from the roof gutters. "But I can't be sure."

"I can." Her voice—the clench-jawed rage in it—jerked his head toward her instinctively. "If you love someone, you'd do anything for them. Right? Well, say something."

"Anything."

"All right then. Looking ahead of you is not a tall order."

"I agree. But looking ahead and walking ahead, knowing that you are dealing with trickier, older, nastier people than any you've met? Unsure as to whether or not your enemy is using each precious second to draw your love further and further away from you? That is a tall order. It's bloody vertiginous."

"You're overdoing it."

"Doubt is articulate, Eurydice. It speaks in a formal, practiced voice where hope is awkward and bumbling. But we're diverting ourselves. Orpheus turned, and, I take it, you became a world almost right away."

"Nothing almost about it."

"Iphigenia described it as a wonderful experience born out of a traumatic one. She wanted to live, her father had ordered her killed in a degrading and excruciatingly manner, and suddenly she was expanding like a green wind. She had become, in essence, the first springtime of a new world."

Eurydice got up off the bed and went to the window. The pads of her fingers pressed to the glass, as though trying to line up with the droplets on the other side.

Hughes watched her posture for signs of a bad swing of the mood pendulum.

He detected nothing wrong. Other than the ostensible. He spoke to it.

"Your experience wasn't like that."

She shook her head. "No."

"Your experience was purely a traumatic one."

"Yeah."

"We don't have to talk about it."

And they didn't. Hughes was glad.

Pitter-patter. Trickle-plip-rivulet-run.

The rain spoke. It sounded like doubt whispering.

"Those were different days," said Hughes. "Your Orpheus has passed on. He's followed the call of his own underworld."

"He travels them all. Most recently he played the radiantly luminous court of the sun herself, Amaterasu."

The fact that she'd kept up with his movements so diligently made Hughes bold.

"Have you ever thought of inviting him here?"

Crickle-crunch.

Where the pads of her fingers touched it, the window was now lined with cracks.

"Never even crossed my mind," said Eurydice.

"But war did?"

She took her hand from the glass and turned back to him. The cracks were gone. "It did. Do you want me to be... what? Contrite? Read my lips, Hughes. I have zero regrets. Zilch. I'm going to rebuild, and I'm going to finish what I started."

"I think you have so many regrets that they spill through your fingers. I think they nag and niggle you so bad, you have to shove them into a box and tamp them down like the busted scraps of a broken instrument."

"We can go back to dancing."

"Oh, cut it out. You're as ashamed of yourself as you are of Orpheus. You've doubled down on a road bricked with blood. Doing a U-turn now would tear you to pieces, or so you've convinced yourself." Hughes was up by then, right in her grill. "And that shadow of yours, she must have riled you up over the years. Made you think you were in the right even after you came to understand you were wrong. You want to throttle me, do it!"

He snagged her hands and locked them round his throat.

"Here, see. We're dancing again. I can hear the rev of the saw, the flies will gather on my eyelids. Keep them there and pay close attention. I'm gonna tell you something. Hold it. I heard you out, so you do the same now. I was like you. Insofar as a man can be like a woman and the world so vast and so forlornly vibrant. Okay? I was so like you it gives me grief!"

"What are you talking about?"

"I was in love," he told her. "I was in love and I got kicked into the dirt. Betrayed so completely I thought I was a goner. I thought my life was over. And there was no sign of me becoming a world. You exchanged your hardships, I get that. But she tore my guts out, and I had to sit in what was left of myself and stew in it. I was hungry and desperate. I did some stupid things. Made what was terrible even worse. How could I. Easily, that's how. The young stumble around because the map of their lives looks good, you know, easy to configure. It's only when you get older that you realize you're lost. And you've got to accept that.

"And accepting is hard. It's embittering as hell. I'm with you there. I feel it close, here in the pit of my stomach and at the back of my mind just waiting for me to let my guard down. This is the resentment. God, I can't tell you how resentful I was. Can't *begin* to tell you."

There was a knock at the door.

They both started.

Another knock. Gentle. Almost apologetic.

"Cripes, I hope I'm not disturbing."

"I know that voice," said Hughes, gently removing her hands from his throat. "Eurydice, can I..."

He trailed off. Her face had resumed that off-putting blankness. Keeping one eye on her just in case fireworks were on the fizzle, Hughes went to the door. He opened it. He'd been right. The voice was familiar.

"Rupert?"

Death's apprentice beamed. "Good day to you, Mr. Hughes!" Up along the flight of steps came the grumbles of well-honed wallowing, meaning a certain mopey bear had accompanied her rider.

"Rupert, what in God's name are you doing here?"

"Well, Mr. Hughes. I'm not here in an official capacity. Off duty, you understand. Attend! Yesterday I had an apprehensive, ummm, premonition. On a hunch, I checked my honey pot. I must tell you the shock I got when I saw what the stickiness had to tell me, well, it gave me a belly-blueing turn and no mistake! Going as fast as I could, I hurried to the court of Amaterasu where I found an individual whom I knew I must bring right here to Eurydice's house." Rupert Prindlee called over one shoulder. "You can come up now."

A man appeared at the bottom of the stairs.

"Hi," he said.

Behind him, Hughes heard an intake of breath.

Wait a minute, he thought. *The court of Amaterasu...*

"Hi, yourself," said Hughes. "I take it you're Orpheus."

"Ah." The man grinned. "My reputation precedes me."

***

Romance is a jelly house. Delicious, exciting, but delicate. So very delicate. Cate Jubilee taught Hughes that, and now he did the thing that all great lessons demand.

He passed it on.

***

"What is *he* doing here?" Eurydice had bypassed anger and gone straight to incandescence. Veins stood out in her neck in thick cables. "What does he think he's doing here now, after all this time? That charlatan. That *traitor*."

Hughes murmured that Rupert Prindlee ought to take his bear and make himself scarce. As Rupert hurried off, Hughes signaled to Orpheus to be quiet, left the bedroom door partially open, and rushed to Eurydice.

"I don't know," he said. "You'd better ask him."

"Ask him? I ought to kill him!"

"A little late, the man's dead."

Eurydice threaded her fingers through her hair. Instead of shaking it out as she'd done earlier, she dug her nails into her scalp and vented a sound between her snarling lips that made Hughes' back rash out in gooseflesh.

"I can't believe this," she said. "The gall of him would be admirable if it wasn't so—"

"Charming?"

"Suicidal."

"Oh."

He watched in alarm as her personality pendulum swung. She fixed Hughes with a plaintive look that was utterly sincere.

"What do I do?"

"Do the opposite of your wedding day," said Hughes. "Talk to him."

"There's nothing to say. He hurt me so deeply, and I've spent my second life as a world meting out retribution for it."

"There's plenty to say. Start with the second most beautiful word in any language."

"What's that?"

"Hello."

She scowled at him. Wrung her hands. Lashed out at the window, smashing it to glimmering smithereens, letting the wind and the damp canter in. The glass reformed at once. Eurydice giggled; the laugh lined with mania.

Her face went vacant. Then sad. Then dolorously sad.

"You can't expect me to put it behind me. I've got to walk forward, always." Shaking hands covered her face. "All he had to do was walk forward."

This is it.

Hughes stood as close to her as his famous gumption let him.

"Eurydice. Look at me."

She did.

"I don't expect a thing from you. Not contrition, not forgiveness for the slights my people made, not a thing. But I'm telling you now, from someone who stared off the edge for too long, who let the resentful view drag him forward, you never stop walking. If you can't turn and try things the other way, you never stop. The good times never roll again." He took her hands in his own, kissed them, and held them to his breast. "Not if you won't let them."

A funny thing happened then.

No, not funny. The other one.

Remarkable.

Hughes watched awestruck as Eurydice, the woman and the world, tried to put the pieces back together. Her pieces. They didn't fit. He could tell from the exertion and anguish writ large in her eyes. But she tried. And he got the impression that while it didn't work—not completely—something had happened inside her.

As though the act of trying might just be enough.

Without speaking, Hughes turned and went to the door. Orpheus was on the other side. He was of an age with Eurydice, at least appearance wise, and handsome in a rumpled, scruffy sort of way. Hughes ushered him in.

Eurydice said that second most beautiful word.

Orpheus said it back.

Hughes left, leaving the ex-lovers to talk in privacy.

But after a minute or two, he couldn't resist a look.

Through the keyhole he saw them holding one another. Orpheus was crying, Eurydice sobbing. And she was laughing. She looked up at him, pinched his cheek, said something Hughes couldn't hear, and pulled Orpheus to her.

Hughes grinned. Maybe not ex-lovers after all.

At the bottom of the curvy flight of steps was Rupert Prindlee and his bear.

Hughes gave him a nod.

They headed for the lower floors, toward the entry hall, and home.

"Cripes and jam, I can hardly stand it. You must tell me, Mr. Hughes. What are they doing?" said Rupert Prindlee.

Hughes scratched his beard thoughtfully.

"Making music," he said.

<u>Ending At The Beginning...</u>

On the day he was to meet Death (the real Death, this time) Hughes asked himself a very important question: *Am I sure about this?*

The answer arrived at the same time as his traveling companion.

Yes. He was sure.

They left together, and at the graveyard by the ruins of Saint Mauritius' Cathedral, Hughes closed his eyes and pictured a dream. It was the dream of a tree, leafy crown to deepest root. He was having that one frequently. Almost every night in fact. Kothbiro. That was the dream's name. Kothbiro. Rains will come.

He and his traveling companion opened their eyes in Dreaming Jija. They journeyed through the black vapor, the tusky mountain pass, and under the sleeping cloud child toward the lank-haired woods. Partway there, they met Rupert Prindlee, who cripes-and-jammed repeatedly about how all of this was an amazingly rare occurrence, that Rupert had in fact *never heard the like of it before*, at least not during his tenure as Death's apprentice.

Rupert led the two travelers along safe, hidden paths to an underworld called The Hollow of Baron Samedi. The Lord of that community was a debonair fellow who insisted that Hughes and his companion call him Mr. Saturday. Rupert explained the situation. Mr. Saturday was happy to oblige.

In the heart of the Hollow there was a room called the Pathetic Fallacy Chamber. From it, there came the unmistakable ruckus of a storm. Mr. Saturday informed Hughes and his companion that they should wait here, and with this pronouncement made, he took Rupert Prindlee by the elbow and whisked him away for the time being.

"Are you ready for this?" Hughes asked his traveling companion.

"No," said Mr. Glint.

The Pathetic Fallacy Chamber shut down. The storm sounds dissipated.

Out of the chamber, wearing a wetsuit and toweling off her soggy, shimmering blue hair was an old friend.

"As I cogitate and crow! Could that be the foremost exemplars of our race, the insurmountable and decadently concise Mr. Glint, esquire?"

"Yeah," said Mr. Glint.

"Then come to my arms and embrace me, man!"

They embraced.

"You're wet," said Glint.

"I am fresh from the Chamber of Pathetic Fallacy, dear fellow. That means—"

"Pathetic Fallacy is when nature is ascribed behavior that is distinctly human," said Mr. Glint in his tombstone tones. "One of them literary phenomenons."

The woman shrieked happily. "I couldn't have said it better myself! Ah, estimable, exquisite Mr. Glint, you haven't let your enviable intellect accrue rust."

"Mr. Gallant has kept me sharp as a whetstone."

"I do not doubt it. No, I do not doubt it! But I am neglecting my manners, yes indeed. I have another embrace to offer, not to you, sweet Glint, but to an old friend who has emerged like a divinely lovely louse from the woodwork of the afternoon. Hughes. Brother who is not, in actual fact, our brother, but who nevertheless occupies a brotherly inglenook in our conjoined adulation." Miss Gleam held out her arms. "Hug?"

Hughes looked from his former tormentor to his other, slightly taller former tormentor. Miss Gleam looked genuinely keen, Mr. Glint expectant.

He sighed.

And hugged Miss Gleam.

"I assure you I have undergone rather comprehensive a change," she whispered into his ear. "I am quite metamorphosed, and... do I bravely exclaim it? I shall! Reformed. Reformed, brother Hughes!"

This did not bring Hughes much comfort, probably because her whispering had brought her lips and teeth within nipping distance of his jugular vein. Those teeth, he couldn't help but notice, were still filed into needle-like points.

"I'll leave you to it then," he said when he was released.

"Nonsense! Ludicrous! You will have tea at my studio."

"Your studio?"

"It's like a room," explained Mr. Glint. "Only fancy."

"My associate continues to roast the notion of brevity over the hot fire of his wit like a Tinfrost chestnut. Though in this case, he hasn't got the whole nut, mine being a special kind of studio. Come along!" said Miss Gleam. "I won't hear a word of protest."

"Only, I've got other obligations—"

"Not a word."

Reluctantly, Hughes followed.

The Hollow's architecture defied explanation. It was like a suburban town, only imbued with a zany spirit of oddness that was so typically underworldish. Streets zigzagged into the air and down into the dark beneath hills of witchgrass, pedestrian crossings were guarded by enormous bronze chickens that laid eggs that sprouted legs and graduate hats, a jumble of shops, supermarkets, and, strangely, carnival tents. The air smelled of jambalaya and aromatic, spicy gumbo. Hughes was glad of Rupert Prindlee, who was probably still around somewhere. Without Rupert, he'd never find his way out of here.

Miss Gleam's studio was slanty roofed (Hughes found this ironic and very fitting), but otherwise ordinary. Inside she vanished to change out of the wetsuit.

While she changed Hughes got the lay of the land, sometimes shooting glances at Mr. Glint, who waited with the patience of a stone, thinking God knew what in that sunken-eyed head of his. The studio was axed into two sections, one livable, the other designed for work. Though what sort of work, Hughes was temporarily at a loss to figure out.

Sedentary, certainly. The spacious room was mostly glass, showcasing the furniture with dazzling, glitzy sunshine. There were two chairs, both plush and stocked with ample pillows. A table with a notepad and pen sat beside one of the chairs. The other had a reclining feature, so its occupant could lie down if they wanted to.

An unbelievable possibility formed in Hughes' mind.

No. There's no way...

Surely nobody can reform that *much.*

Gleam reappeared in a suit, chic and ornamented with stripes, silk flourishes, and diamond cufflinks.

"I've called off all clients for the day. No visitors either. No exceptions. Hughes, you will not object to my brewing the tea? I'm no master, nor even a journeywoman, but an amateur has her enthusiasm."

"I don't object. Miss Gleam—"

"Ah, you've examined my set up here in the Hollow and extrapolated my ongoing pursuit into the field of psychoanalysis."

"I have."

"Do you approve?"

Hughes wasn't sure what he thought. "It's a worthy calling... It's just that... Well. You? A therapist?"

Miss Gleam's grin was like nothing so much as a tangerine full of razorblades.

"And what about you, Mr. Glint? Are you the very soul of stupefaction at the mere prospect of Mad Miss Gleam offering counsel, advice, and sympathy to a growing list of hopefuls?"

Mr. Glint grunted. "Not really. The dead aren't the same as the living. Point of pride, I bet. I'd also put a crisp note or two on this: the dead have different priorities."

"Call us spirits, noble comrade. *The dead* sounds so humdrum. *Spirits* has a certain... mysticism. A certain thrill about it. Spirited spirits spiriting spiritedly! HaHA!"

"Haha," said Mr. Glint with all the joviality of an electrocuted penitentiary inmate. "Right you are, Miss Gleam. I shall rephrase. Spirits have different priorities."

"That we most unambiguously do." Miss Gleam caressed the headrest of her therapist chair. Her touch was loving. "When I died, I came here. Mr. Saturday acquainted me with my afterlife, then left me to my own devices. I decided to turn over a new leaf, though to tell you the truth, I believe the leaf was three-quarters turned for me, requiring minimal effort on my part. Don't mistake me. I am still Miss Gleam. I have a vindictive side. A temper. A naughty streak. That last, you'll remember well, Hughes."

"How could I forget?"

"And I still, as you observed when you arrived, have a penchant for storms. Yet here... with the lands of the living so distant... it's hard to evoke the reasons behind the benchmark moments of my life with any clarity. The anamnesis is a photograph of a photograph. Little of it matters. Though..." She cast a fond smile at Mr. Glint. "Some memories linger. And thank goodness for that. But my inherent Gleamness has been rearranged so the shine at my core illuminates the unexpected. As a therapist I can sort through the oversimplifications and get to what truly matters."

Hughes couldn't believe what he was hearing. "You're talking about gray areas, aren't you?"

"Yes."

"But you *loathed* gray areas. You were a woman of large black truths."

"And little white lies," said Mr. Glint. "But not anymore. Things change."

Miss Gleam clapped her hands together. "I've postponed the tea too long! Mr. Glint, I know your favorite. Hughes, cardamon and fennel, is it?"

"No, thanks. I'd best be on my way."

"Won't you stay?"

"I wish I could." This little white lie seemed achingly obvious to him, but Miss Gleam seemed to recognize the truth shading it. Maybe there was something to this underworld reformation business.

"Some other time," she said. "One for the road?"

He consented to another hug. Mr. Glint's arms enfolded them, making it a party. Hughes thought about Hughes 2, that alternate universe version of himself who lived a pleasant, boring life without a scrap of adventure or trouble. He wondered what Hughes 2 would make of Hughes 1's transience; from beggar boy hunted by these two monsters to a world leader engaging in snuggle time. The two monsters weren't monsters either. By all accounts they were people, muddling as best as they could in the uncertain gray of life, or afterlife, same as everybody else. He decided Hughes 2 would shrug his shoulders and go back to reading the newspaper. *Poor guy,* thought Hughes as Glint and Gleam squeezed. *Doesn't know what he was missing.*

Miss Gleam hurried off to put the kettle on. He heard her open the teabag box with a pair of scissors.

Snicker-snick.

He couldn't keep the darkly amused smile off his lips.

Some things change. Some things stay the same.

As he gathered himself to leave, Miss Gleam seemed to recall something fantastic. She came out of the kitchenette, slapping her brow. "How scatterbrained I am!

It's the excitement of seeing you both, it must be! I have canceled all my clients and warned away all visitors, except one."

"Who?" said Mr. Glint.

Gleam winked cryptically. "She called me almost the moment we arrived. The grapevine is extremely quick in the Hollow. She's heard about your arrival, Mr. Glint, and has expressed... let us say an acute interest in seeing you at your earliest convenience. I suspect your earliest convenience means hers, in this case. Acute may not summarize her anxiousness in the matter."

"Don't get it," said Mr. Glint. "Who would want to see me? You're the only person I know here."

"Untrue, dear man! Untrue! You are also familiar with our soon-to-be-visitor, who, let me arouse your deductive reasoning, is possessed of a pair of purple eyes... *lavender-purple* eyes, might I add..." Miss Gleam waggled her brows meaningfully.

Mr. Glint's mouth fell open. "But she... she said even if my poems were the best things since slice bread, even if I was the last bloke in the world, I wasn't her type. She said I'd only be wasting my time."

"And yet she is coming to visit. Not to see me, but to see you."

"Why?"

"Didn't you say it yourself, old boy?" Miss Gleam chuckled. "Spirits have different priorities."

Hughes took that as his cue.

Before he closed the studio door after him, he caught sight of a thing that would have scared his younger self shitless. Today, it made him happy.

Mr. Glint was dancing for joy.

***

Unlike Miss Gleam—a woman responsible for many a bout of queasy collywobbling terror throughout his life—Hughes' mother did not offer him tea. No offer of a hug either.

He thought that was appropriate.

Stubborn old Wendy. Like mother like son.

They were on a beach. Populated but not crowded. A red sun was setting in a sky the color of fresh peaches. A little breeze moved in the dunes and along the soft surf. Parasols threw long mushroom-shaped shadows across the sand. The air was redolent with the smell of tanning lotion, recently laundered bathing suits, popsicles, and salt.

"Sit, Hughes. As it so happens, there's one here next to me."

"I prefer to stand."

"Your mother prefers you sit."

"Your bloodhound."

"Suit yourself. I'm not sure why you bothered to come and see me if you're going to give me guff. Please yourself. I don't mind."

A bark of unhinged, ferocious laughter rose in his throat, as well as a litany of words he'd have loved to spill out into this picturesque scene like pollution straight from the dumping valve.

He swallowed the bark and the words.

He sat down in the foldout plastic chair next to his mother.

"You have to think things through before you say them," said Wendy.

Hughes debated telling her to take a pill of her own medicine and again let it go. The beach was stunningly pretty. Everyone was having a good time. He wondered idly if Wendy had somehow calculated their meeting to be like this, idyllic and peaceful, a setting that would make harsh words or an outburst next to impossible. It seemed irrational, but he wouldn't put the idea past her.

"Let's be nice to one another," she suggested. "All right?"

"I'll do my best."

"That's all I ask. Ice cream?"

"Why not. It's the only empress."

"Wallace Stevens. He's a sensation in these parts."

"The underworlds?"

"Mhm."

"No kidding."

"I kid you not."

Wendy reached into a picnic basket standing by her parasol. She took out two cones, dipped them in the sand, and handed one to Hughes. "Chocolate orange."

"This is sand, Wendy."

A twinkle in her eye told him otherwise. He tasted it and stared at the cold crystals of chocolate in naked wonderment.

"Son of a bitch," he said.

"I hope no one calls you that."

"What? No, of course not."

"Good."

Hughes ate his ice cream. Somewhere along the shore, his guide Rupert Prindlee was probably jawing contentedly with the Lady of this domain. Surprisingly that Lady was not Wendy Dragontail, who had ruled Corinth City and the country surrounding it with an iron fist clad in a diplomatic glove of velvet. Instead, this lovely underworld's boss was a fair-haired woman named Áine, a queen of fairies and a sovereign of summertime. Hughes had been introduced to her briefly. Áine had smiled at him from the back of an unsaddled red mare.

Now he and his mother were alone. Though her attitude was the same (no amount of existential relocation could knock Wendy Dragontail on her heels), a discombobulated feeling persisted in Hughes. A little of it had to do with her age. When he'd known her, Wendy was in her late fifties. On the night of her death, she was creeping toward seventy. Here, in the underworld that hosted her afterlife, Wendy was twenty-five, possibly younger. Her hair was still as white as snow, but of the wrinkles, sunspots, and loose wattling flesh, there was no sign. That explained some of the off-kilter feeling, but not the majority. For the most part Hughes thought it came down to the setting of this family chat.

The sand, the parasols, the unhurried sigh of the waves. It all existed in stark polarity with Corinth City, a city that was just as much bite as it was growl. In life, Wendy devoted herself to the running of that place. If you asked her if she'd ever taken a holiday, she'd glare at you quizzically and say, "Certainly I have been on holiday. Where? It is a fabulous realm known as 'sleep.' Its gentle oblivion provides me with a respite from many things, including silly questions."

And yet here she was. Lounging. Loafing around with a paperback novel within easy reach and a whack of hazelnut ice cream in her gob.

This topsy-turviness established a link between Wendy and Miss Gleam. It formed a pattern in his conception of the afterlife, a subtle cohesion in the abundant weirdness, almost a theme.

"How is Estelle?" said Wendy.

"She's well. Took up writing short fiction."

"Fiction?"

"Hm?"

"She writes fiction?"

"Fiction, yeah."

"She's certainly read enough of it to sustain her imagination." Wendy held out her cone. "Hazelnut?"

"Is that all you have to say?"

"About hazelnut?"

"About Estelle."

Her mouth quirked, exasperated. "The past is the past. Did you expect me to be punished for my sins? I remember them. I confer with them. They were sitting in that chair before you took it. Always close by. Besides... there's protocol."

"What protocol?"

"I'm telling you that there are systems in place to... how to put it..."

"Wendy—"

"Don't interrupt, Hughes. You asked a question and I'm answering you. There are systems in situ that account for one's wrongdoings and misdeeds and what have you. You think the most vile, perverse killers pop their clogs, are buried, and begin to push up the daisies, only to skip merrily to an underworld and carry on blithely as though death were a gate to be pushed through, 'last one through locks up' style? Use your head, lad. You've run Corinthia for twelve years and much more besides. Rehabilitation and the other maxims of crime and punishment don't wax and wane with the lunar cycle. Things move on. So do people. What is the theatrical aphorism? *The show must go on.*"

"Give it a rest."

"Well, forgive me or don't. I'm sure Estelle has."

The worst thing—the infuriating thing—was that she was right... about Estelle, if nothing else. In a café, six or seven years ago, Estelle admitted to Hughes that she'd finally let go of her bitterness. Wendy had tricked her, abused her, but Wendy was dead. She, Estelle, was still alive. His wonderful friend sipped her coffee, shrugged, and called it justice. Hughes called it time, and he didn't think time was just. Not even a little.

"I wouldn't know the first thing about forgiving you," he said. "Maybe it's something to do with the fact that you've never said sorry."

"I did. On the balcony. Before Estelle came, I asked you to forgive me."

Had she? Hughes didn't think so. Some days his memory was as flawless as ever. Some days (more and more often or so it seemed to him) little explosives went off in his head. Not fire. Smoke and mist.

Today had been a good day, he'd been sure of it. Now... Well, now he wasn't so sure...

"Hughes?"

"Yeah, Mum?"

She looked happy he'd called her that, though he hadn't meant to. It just slipped out.

"You were away with the fairies," she told him. "Granted in this realm the fairies are not very far, but even so. I was saying that I did apologize. I've been to see Idris Corlum and his wife in their underworld, and I apologized to them for what I did. When Estelle's moment comes, I'll do the same with her. My list of malfeasance is comprehensive, but the names will be ticked, the words spoken, the reconciliatory actions undertaken. Satisfied?"

"Give me a munch of hazelnut."

She handed him her cone. He ate. Handed it back.

They listened to the seaside ambience. Relaxing. Hughes didn't feel particularly relaxed. He felt keyed up. His mother had a way of doing that. Always had.

"Why didn't you tell me?" he asked her.

She knew what he meant. "You know now. Do you honestly give a damn?"

"You know, Mum? I really do."

"I thought it would change our relationship. I thought you'd believe your advancement was nepotistic—a lie—rather than meritorious—which was the truth. I thought you'd ask insipid questions like, 'Why weren't you in my life? Why am I only finding out now? Why is my father languishing in poverty while you live in luxury,' as if I never built a safety net should your father ever need one. Not that he'd have taken a handout. Your father is as proud as I am. It's what drew me to him. And his smarts. And the tea, good God the smell of it drove me wild. Talk about a man who knows his way around crushed leaves!"

"Not to snap your reminiscing in twain or anything, but none of this adequately explains why you never told me," said Hughes.

She threw her eyes toward the peachy sky. "Have it your way. Come to your own conclusions. I was ashamed. Lofty-minded. Stubborn old Wendy, yes? Smarmy, conniving, stubborn old Mum. I showed you I cared about you, though I never quite stooped to telling you that you were loved. I'm sorry for that. Once I came close—"

"The day of the Rotbloom Carnival of Bright Oddments and Dark Delights," Hughes cut in. "I remember. I was six. You were going to say it, that you loved me, then you offered me a piggyback so I could see the carnival stage. A butterfly landed in your hair. It was so red, though your hair is good for that." He scratched his beard. "I've inherited your premature paleness as well as your bloody city."

"Forty-two is hardly premature, Hughes."

"True."

"Would you have said it back?"

He frowned at her. Sunset had slipped under the parasol. She was shading her eyes with a flat hand, looking at him. "If I'd told you I loved you that day at the carnival, would you have said it back?"

Now it was Hughes' turn to roll his eyes. His expression was withering. When he spoke his voice came out even harsher, not withering but scathing.

"What do you think?" he said.

A shadow fell across them both.

"Nana, can I go for another swim?"

It was a girl. A redhead. She was cusping puberty, more than ten, definitely not a teen.

"If you keep to the shallow end. The tide plays hoodlum just before sundown," said Wendy. "Frankie, this is—"

"I know, Nana." The girl (*Frankie, her name is Frankie*) held her hand out. Not to shake. Braceleted and tanned, the hand was upturned. Asking for a response. Hughes responded.

He formed a fist. He tapped the fist gently against her palm. His hand made a rock. It made paper. It made scissors.

Frankie's laugh was awesome. It got Hughes grinning right away.

She shook her head and showed him her palm again. Hughes pouted, earning some more of that amazing laughter. Relenting, he held her hand, which resembled nothing so much as a seashell.

He couldn't speak. His tongue felt glued to the roof of his mouth.

Frankie squeezed his hand so hard he could feel it in his wrist. The gesture spoke more than a volume of words. It said she approved of him in a million ways. It said she was enjoying herself here. It wasn't living, but it was good.

"They didn't throw me out, Dad," she told him. "They were respectful. I wasn't recycled. Doctor Lanmoor took me to a crematorium, where I was melted down in a big oven. He saw to it personally. I think he wanted me to be treated as if I'd been born. Like I was a regular baby. He got the liquid glass and poured it into the sea. I think that's why I came here, to this underworld, only Nana thinks there's more to it than that. Please tell Mum, okay? I'd better go swim while the tide is playing hoodlum. Nana turns her nose up at them, but I like the wild waves best."

Saying no more, she planted a peck on Hughes' cheek and pelted off over the sands.

A little while later, Wendy rummaged in the providing granules of the beach and produced a handkerchief. This, she handed to her son.

"Have a good hard blow, there's a good lad."

He honked his nose.

"Dab your eyes."

He did.

"You're a brilliant chap. Bore up well, considering."

"Is she... ageing at the normal rate?"

"Until she wants to stop, yes. Perks of the afterlife."

Hughes folded the handkerchief in his lap and took a shuddery little breath and let it go. He felt better.

He also felt full to brimming point with questions. The most pressing of these wrangled to the top. "Why Frankie?" he asked his mother.

"Because when Frank Gallant stumbled out of the door of fire, he laid hands on my father Walsingham and put him into a sleep. My father never woke up. He died dreaming. It took my own death for me to change my mind about that day. Frank was in a tizzy. He'd only just escaped the petty tyranny of his hag mothers. Now here he is in a new world and a man is approaching him, he doesn't know the man, hasn't got the wherewithal to explain himself, so he does the only thing he can think of, mechanically and disastrously. It was an accident. While I grew accustomed to my afterlife I ran into that fiery young thing and knew at once she was my granddaughter. Don't ask me how, I couldn't tell you. But I *knew*. I asked her for her name and she said everyone called her Red. She didn't like that. She said if she dyed her hair someday she didn't want people to call her Teal or Beige. She was forthcoming with me. I think she knew who I was just as quickly as I knew her. Naming her seemed an opportunity to atone for being a stubborn lump of beeswax."

"Spirits have different priorities," said Hughes.

Wendy was pleased. "That's it. That's it exactly."

Silence. With her group of friends dunking one another in the low surf, splashing, and making mischief, Frankie swam. Plastered to her cheeks was that distinctive red hair, courtesy of her mother, the one and only Cate Jubilee.

Hughes watched her for a while. At length, and without looking at Wendy, he said, "Mum. I've thought carefully about what I'm going to say next. I don't forgive you. That might change. It might stay the same. I'm not being glib when I say you shouldn't ask me how a change might come to be. I couldn't tell you. Maybe our ignorance is tallied alongside our sins. There's a system. Protocols. I haven't a clue about any of it. But I'm grateful. For what it's worth I'm in your debt, and while I abhor so much of what you've done, I love many of your actions with all my heart. It might not sit well with you, but your son prefers it that way."

"So I gather. Well. Thank you for saying that, Hughes. I see that funny little creature with the bear and the honey pot is waving to you."

"I see him. I need to go."

"Will you come again, do you think?"

"I'll do my best."

"That's all I ask."

***

The bear's gait was somnolent. Hughes nodded off for a while.

When he awoke, Rupert Prindlee was shaking him gently.

"We're here," he told Hughes.

Hughes got off the bear, thanking it for carrying him, and looked around. They were in a meadow of mulberries. There was a cottage. The cottage was sunstone, its chimney a yellow finger pointing up at the moon. In its garden of well-kept flowers, a griffon statue curled around a hunk of stone that bore an engraving: *Cottage Aguilonia.*

"Thank you, Rupert," said Hughes. "Really, I can't tell you how—" He turned and discovered he was talking to himself. Rupert, his prodigious honey pot, and his doleful bear were gone.

Without warning, a scent wafted in his direction, and Hughes was reminded of those cartoon animals floating comically toward kitchens, drawn by the scent of apple pie, casserole, or some other delicacy. The scent was that alluring.

When he looked back at the Cottage Aguilonia, he saw the front door was open. A young woman stood on the threshold. She was doughy, dark-haired, and smiling. She was striking, the way a night out in a foreign country is striking. Her smile was genuine, big as she was, and very beautiful. Her dress—or was it a robe?—was sewn out of shadows.

"Usually," she said, "I'm the one people are expecting. It's a nice change, the shoe being on the other foot. Come in out of the cold."

It *was* cold, now she mentioned it.

Hughes walked among the green garden buds and the bright blooms and went into Death's cottage. The interior was as comfortable as the outside was charming. A fire was going, sending out a spirited warmth, and there were hundreds of candles blazing sweetly. There were all the things you might expect in a cottage, including oil paintings, photographs, large chairs, a little kitchen, etcetera. There was also a staff, which had the shape of a washpole, made of bone. It leaned in one corner of the room. When Rupert Prindlee wielded it at their first meeting, Hughes hadn't found the staff all that interesting. In the presence of its true wielder, Hughes thought it very interesting indeed, and not a little eerie.

Lucy Nowhere, who some called The Angel of Mercy, The Scythebearer. Outwitter of the Tarot Troupe, Lover of Lainey, Dark Pilgrim, The Kindly Reaper, or Old Scratch, closed the cottage door.

"I must thank you for setting things right with Eurydice," she said, pottering in the direction of the kitchen. "I wasn't sure sending Rupert to fetch Orpheus was the right move, but I needn't have worried. You're a born mediator. Her anger was a dragon and you tamed it, didn't you?"

"I suppose I did."

"There's no need to be modest."

"I wondered how Rupert's honey worked," said Hughes. "But I thought you were prevented from interfering in mortal affairs?"

"Prevented?" A neat clatter of cups and saucers arose. "No, that's not true. I'm limited, though my partner, Lainey, would disagree wholeheartedly. Of course she's right, as usual. Say then that I limit myself. Death doesn't pick favorites."

Hughes gave her back a shrewd look.

Lucy seemed to feel it. Her shoulders slouched. "There's no need to give me the eye, Gormon Hughes."

"Sorry."

"What matters is that things turned out all right in the end."

"Yes, Lucy."

"And you can wipe that grin off your face whenever you like."

Hughes did so, with difficulty. He thought it would be hard to dislike his hostess. Anthropomorphic personification of ruination and entropy she might be, but she had a way about her. At her invitation he sat in one of the plump-cushioned chairs. She gave him tea. Now Gormon Hughes Junior was no stranger to a cup of tea—far from it!

Safe to say this unassuming, steamy cup was the finest of his life. Scrumptious, perfectly balanced, and tailored to the setting (as all great tea is), it was also the source of the amazing scent that had wafted to him when the cottage door first opened.

Unable to contain himself, Hughes begged the recipe from Lucy, who dashed his hopes with a regretful smile. "I'm afraid none of the ingredients can be found in the lands of the living. You'll just have to wait."

Instead of looking dejected at the macabre implications of this, Hughes perked up.

"That's what I came to speak to you about. First, I have an offering for you."

"Ambrosia fudge!"

"Even if you don't pick favorites, they pick you."

"Frank Gallant tipped you off. He's friends with many of the in-between folk like Tookus Argyle and Livia. Those codgers. Well, I've a fondness for them. I trust you've figured out by now that the in-between folk, also called the midwayers, have my permission to traverse the lands of both living and dead."

"I had, Lucy. I've also reasoned that it was the gift of ambrosia fudge that sealed their chances of becoming midwayers in the first place."

He was confident of it. She surprised him.

"Ah. I see how you'd come to that conclusion. You haven't missed the mark, but you're an inch shy of its bullseye. The midwayers satisfied a very particular list of conditions to become as they are. It isn't for you to know—I mean no offense! At times the road least expected sends us just where we need to go. Likewise the road we set all our hopes on might get us lost. Regardless, thank you for the lovely treat. You shouldn't have. Would you like a piece?"

"No, thank you. I've come seeking something else."

"You and many before you, Hughes. Go ahead and ask me, but fair warning; you'll be disappointed."

Since the war's end, the victory feasts, and the surreal aftermath of Eurydice's pink house, Hughes had rehearsed this moment many times. He spoke deliberately, and with a weight that accentuated each word, lending them a persuasive and articulate power.

"Iphigenia is dying. I can't speak to her. There's barely a connection. She's dying, and her death means mine will follow. Parts of my body, formerly silent, are making themselves known to me with lamentable shouts and groans. There's white hair in my beard and more at my temples. Like weeds in a maintained garden, more of it seems to crop up every day. I'm forgetting things. A person's memory is the mirror they consult to remind themselves who they are. When the glass fogs because age has labored one's breath, they lose sight of who they are.

"It's an important time for my city. The war is over, but history and human sociology dictates that when something ends, something begins. It's a formative time for my daughter. She needs me. I can't simply be present. I have to be at my best. In short, there's too much to do, and it doesn't take a great brilliance to know that I haven't got time to do it. I want to make a deal with you, Lucy Nowhere, Angel of Mercy and Kindly Reaper of the Last Harvest. I need more time."

Lucy listened patiently. When he was done, she stowed the ambrosia fudge away and sat down in the chair opposite. She set down her tea, thought better of it, had a splendidly long gulp, and set it down again on an oval-shaped table laid with doily cloth. From the hearth the fire sent out tentacles of light that merged insolently and captivatingly with her raiment of midnight.

"May I reassure you of a few things before we return to the subject of you wanting more time?"

"Needing, not wanting. And this is your house, Lucy. Your bailiwick too. We go as you steer."

"To begin with, you look great."

Hughes blinked. He was sure he'd heard wrong.

"Really terrific," she said, proving he had heard exactly right. "You're in good shape. The lines in your brow are comely, no, rugged! And what's a few white hairs? What's a whole head of them? You won't be a frail dandelion but a vigorous, pale-whiskered rover. I think you'll be a ringer for some of the great actors of your world. Energy will lag, but keep fit and you'll hardly notice. The winter of you, Gormon Hughes, will be indistinguishable from early autumn.

"Moving on, your perfect memory was never perfect. It was really good. Now it's really good minus a few wires, and on occasion the wires that remain get tangled. To use your analogy, I contend that a few clouds of fog is part of owning a mirror. The only one who forgets nothing is me. I remember everything, even the things that haven't happened yet. That's my load to carry. Not yours, and if you saw eternity for a moment it would be a moment too long.

"The last thing I'll say is this: Iphigenia may very well be dying, but she has not enjoyed her last good day. There's more to come. You can visit her on those days, just as you used to."

Hughes waited in case there was a coda. There was none.

Lucy sipped her tea and looked at him imploringly.

"You're nothing like I expected," he told her.

"Really?"

"Really."

"And what did you expect?"

Hughes thought about it. "Someone less human."

Lucy made an amused noise that emanated from the entirety of her, as if her mouth could not handle a noise as lovely and wholesome as that. The fire danced happily, responding, as did the candleflames, the pages of several books, and the kettle, which rattled on its hot hob appreciatively.

"I've been on vacation. The longer I stay with my dear Lainey, the more ordinary I become. It takes a while for me to become extraordinary again."

"Who is Lainey?"

"A knight. You've seen her handiwork."

Hughes wondered how, then understanding dawned. "The hill in Dreaming Jija, the hill that was once the guardian of that realm! Lainey was the knight in the story."

Lucy smiled the smile of a woman in love. "My silver knight was on top form that day. I can't say the same for myself, though again, she and my friends from that time in my life might disagree."

"How did you fall in love with Lainey?"

"Oh! I like that question! I used to think it was little by little, but now I know it was all at once. Instantly. The moment she looked at me."

Hughes thought of Cate. "I know what you mean. And do you always look like this?"

He had to stifle a yelp as she transformed:

She was a rosy-cheeked child with jackal-heads instead of hands, each tooth an hourglass sifting seconds of life.

"Not at all."

She was a tall woman with golden hair and wings of celestial light.

"There are as many ideas of what I look like..."

She was an enormous spider with a scorpion's tail and swaying cow dugs.

"... as there are people in the universe."

She was a crow, a scarecrow, a field of sighing corn under a dead star.

"I do my best..."

She was Lucy Nowhere, smiling.

"... to accommodate."

Sometime in the past few seconds, Hughes didn't know when, he'd tipped his chair over and fled to the far wall of the cottage. There he cowered.

Lucy motioned. The chair tipped upright. His teacup, spilled and chipped, reformed and filled perfectly.

"I'm unworthy," he said, not knowing why he would say something so meek, but unable to stop himself. "I'm small."

Lucy looked astonished.

She hurried to him. After much soothing and an explanation that she thought he was one of the worthiest people she'd met and was a fair sight taller than the average fellow, Hughes allowed himself to be drawn back to his chair. A swallow of Lucy's miraculous tea restored him the rest of the way.

"I don't know what came over me," he said. "I only saw a few of your incarnations, but my mind created countless alternatives."

"A strong imagination can be a bother," Lucy said sagely. "On the whole, I'd rather that than none at all! Are you sure you're all right?"

"For now, yes. For tomorrow, I can't tell."

"Very layered, Hughes. *Very layered.* Is that your way of telling me you're still set on this 'give me more time' business?"

"I am."

"But—"

"Maybe I will be disappointed," he said firmly. "Still, I've got to try. There's too much to do, Lucy. The show must go on."

"You know it can't."

"Even so."

"Listen to me. You might be a poor player who struts and frets your hour upon the stage and then is heard no more. But you signify something. To the people around you and to me. That's what I'm for," Lucy said. "Why I take different forms. Why I arrive when the curtain falls. You end and then it's on to the next show, whatever that may be. But when I come, when the scythe is swung and everything you were and are and ever will be moves on... you get to see how people remember you. And that is your bow. Are you listening to me, Hughes? The performance ends, yes. But if you're kind, and good, and honest with yourself and with others, then it ends with applause."

Her words moved him. He opened his mouth and stopped himself in time. Lucy waited. Hughes said nothing.

Lucy fetched a sigh. "So be it."

She stood and held out her hand. The staff of bone slammed against her palm. Instantly the shadows forming her ensemble boiled up blackly. A hood covered her hair. Peering into the hood's depths, Hughes no longer saw Lucy's mild, benevolent face. He saw a skull, and in the skull's sockets he saw a darkness, and in the darkness was a scarlet-red sky holding court over a wasteland.

The staff was no longer a staff. A blade extended from the head. The scythe had one blunt side, and one *sharp*.

Hughes heard Death speak straight into his mind.

"You will remain in this cottage for seven days and nights. Take no sleep. You may help yourself to anything else you require. Take no sleep. I will return."

The shadows multiplied, engulfing the room.

Hughes felt himself prickle coldly all over, as though a goose had walked over his grave. When the worst of the unpleasant feeling passed, he shot to his feet, his gaze cutting all around. Save for him, the cottage was empty.

***

Stay awake for seven days and nights? That wouldn't be too much trouble.

He'd stayed up three or four days straight when the going got tough. That had been a doddle. A groggy, at times grumblesome doddle, but a doddle nonetheless.

He remembered he'd had a kip on the back of Rupert's bear. That was a bonus, and one Lucy wouldn't have counted on, perfect view of eternity or no.

Seven, eh? Only seven?

It must be the first test of many. No problem. He'd pass it, Lucy would return, and he'd be on to test number two. Come what may, it was worth it. Evelyn, Cate, and to a slightly lesser extent the city they called home, were worth it.

Seven days. Seven nights.

Right.

For starters how would he pass the time? Plenty of books. He went to find something to eat. There was a ton of supplies—fully stocked pantry, fridge, and freezer. Excellent. Grub was a surefire way to give the system a jolt. No booze, that was good. Alcohol would be soporific. Coffee. Plenty of that. Gooood. And tea, save the best for last.

He made himself a sandwich and another cup of Lucy's finest to wash it down.

Start as you mean to go on, that's the ticket.

A cursory examination of the book spines got his brain zipping. He hadn't read any of these, and there were lots of plays. A doddle, he thought cheerfully. He munched his sandwich, slurped his tea, and selected a play at random.

Here goes.

***

Something nudged him.

"Nurh?"

Nudge-nudge.

"Wassat?"

He blinked mushily and glared up at the nudging article, which was a scythe.

"Damn," he said. He mopped his greasy-feeling face with his hand. "How far'd I get?"

"*Five days, four nights,*" said Death.

Hughes scowled. He had vague memories of jogging around the cottage and feeling what could only be described as a perpetual full body twitch. He thought he'd never be able to look at coffee again. He would even need a trial separation from tea. From *tea*!

"I'll have to try again," he said. "Either that or... Come on, Lucy. There's got to be another way."

The shadowy hood melted back into its dress shape. Lucy ruffled her hair and tucked it behind her ears.

"Well?" he demanded. "Maybe I could... I don't know... challenge you to a game or something."

"That would come after the sleep trial."

"Right. Erm. I don't suppose we could skip that one?"

"No. Sorry."

"I'll have to try again," he repeated.

Lucy offered him a hand.

Hughes took it. Pride was a luxury of the well-rested.

She dusted him down. "A bath would do you good," she said kindly. "And the comfort of your own bed."

"I can't go home. Not until I've secured more time."

"Iphigenia is alive. So are you. That's what I've been trying to tell you. You've already got time."

He gave her a miserable look. "How much?"

"Enough," she replied.

"Enough for what?"

"That's up to you."

"Lucy—"

"No, Hughes. I've said my final word. Go home. Think about what I told you. And mull this over too: if you can't defeat sleep, how do expect to defeat

ME?"

***

Kothbiro means *the rains will come.*

They did.

These are the rains. And this is Corinth City.

Hear them. See it.

Once more, with feeling.

Fake plants drip and judder, and the gutters gossip to one another while spilling their damp worries on the ever-consoling street. The street funnels every liquid gem to its proper place. Sometimes those places involve infrastructure. Sometimes they involve rats, bats, mice, and other quiet survivors of this oddball city. Sometimes the water goes deeper than the sewer system, and Knickerbocker toasts his information network with a tinfoil chalice that is as full as his heart.

Nightclub signs, pharmacy signs, signs above dive bars, salons, waxing and massage parlors, tidy signs hung over offices and messy neon signs below eye-level where they will not offend sensibilities, boutiques, bazaar stalls, shops, stands, and sundry; all the indexes of go here, go there, beckoning, and begoneing, are enshrined in rain, sanctified in their electric purity.

Tommy Fahrenheit sticks to places that serve juice. He is still uncomfortable showing his face here since his disgrace at The Hippodrome over a decade ago, but the city shares none of its discomfort. Twelve hours is a long time in a city, never mind twelve whole years. He drinks a concoction of pears, ginger, and Calcifern yogurt at a bazaar stall. Leonidas was never his haunt, but he can see it has changed a great deal in the last few months. It's got something to do with new policing, variable taxation schemes, investment, stuff that goes in one of Tommy's ears and out the other. He has considered joining up with this police force but wonders if they'd have him with his checkered history. He decides to try his luck. What could it hurt? If he fails, there's always his origins, always Champleurs. He is approached by an attractive pair of women, one of whom seems to be a support, one who seems intent on attacking him, so long as the location he falls is a bed, preferably with her underneath him. He's interested. That's something he used to lack; interest in both things and people. Now he's got it in spades. As for his physique, it is superb. Not what it once was, not *splendif*. He doesn't mind.

The rains scatter and skim over the motorways, every lane congested with rush-hour traffic. A subtle vexation frizzes up like headlights, but it's okay. The anger of the commuters is only a sign pointing elsewhere. To home.

Brenda Kofatch beats the traffic by virtue of sheer forward thinking. She and her girlfriend, Rummy Lou, have date plans tonight, and she needs time to get ready. Recently, Brenda was approached by an old friend of her mother's for the second time in her life. He admitted to something strange, something he wanted to beg her pardon for. Brenda gave it, wondering if it was all some convoluted joke, but the man accepted her forgiveness as if it were deadly serious and left before she could ask him if he was who she thought he was. Brenda has since dismissed the whole event as a fugue, possibly the result of a lack of sleep. She and Rummy have been working hard, saving harder. Weddings aren't cheap, after all.

Real trees and flowers are less and less of a luxury nowadays, but change comes slow as the rain running down the grooves in bark. The trunks of the trees are scored and veined in water, and the flowers bursting from the soil seem to weep with joy.

Far away, though not too far, a Painted Girl and a Ringmaster Woman sit in their carousel house, bickering amiably over what they're going to do when the rains let up. Because it's pouring in a lot of different worlds, not just the one that contains Corinth City.

Rills of rain pattering on their coat, a member of the Sequins Messenger club cycles down a street, one overlooked by a teashop full of manuscripts. The teashop has undergone some expansion in recent days. It's busy. The patrons sip from cups, make satisfied sounds as their taste buds light up, and go back to reading. The teamaster works assiduously. He dislikes his pacemaker but admits to his son that most of the time he forgets the thing is even there. He never has to remind his son to visit because in that great dance called the Autumn Waltz, he has stepped in all the right places. He looks forward to those visits, mostly because his granddaughter always has something new to tell him. Her excitement is contagious, and when you're old a little vicarious excitement is a fine thing.

Tenement roofs, semi-detached roofs, standalone, slanted, canted, tile, brick, corrugated metal, every kind of roof cries out the name of each cloud rolling up there in the sky, and the clouds answer in the only way they know how.

Hoshrum Thud is off the cigars (he has had a stern talking-to from his doctor and, more pressingly, his wife), but he still has his ways of cutting loose. A company in Jaenqui-Across-The-River ships him a box of thirty tobacco-free smolderers each month, one for every day. They're packed full of picked herbs, and they taste like dishwater, but it's the act of smoking he enjoys, not the flavor. From upstairs he can hear the hearty whacks of something heavy being hit with something else. No doubt Hettie is on the brink of another artistic revelation. Heaven help the critics should they go against the will of her adoring public. Thud grins, puffing away as he watches the downpour through his parlor window. He is dog tired. He stands anyway because his ass is sick of sitting. He has spent all day on it while his ears listen to a host of jargonistic plans and his mouth advises on how these plans can be made at least semi-functional. Coalition government. He'd call it a joke, but he'd be consigning himself to the punchline. Head of National Security. Not too shabby, as titles go, but the ins-and-outs of the job were still bafflingly new to Thud. Paperwork had not disappeared so much as transformed. As commissioner he'd dealt with patrol routes, run-of-the-mill operations. This new stuff was... He sought for the word, found it. It was *bureaucratic*. The rain sieved and sloshed. Thud watched it, the herbal cigar poised in his fingers.

Bureaucratic. He supposed that was his life now. He would sit on a complaining bottom, listening to Prime Minister Hector or one of the other people who actually seemed comfortable in their appointed role, and he would speak when spoken to, offer his opinion, do the tricks they needed him to do. The dog is elevated, but he is still a mutt.

With a flurry of motion he reefs open the window, crushes the cigar, and flings it into the early evening gloom. The rains suck it away, smoke, herbs, and all. A minute later Thud is pulling on his coat. No. That is not his life. Not now. Not ever. He will do his duty, and he will do it with diligence and wisdom, but he will also do things like a copper. Sniffing out trouble. Dealing with bad people on behalf of the good ones. There are more good than bad, but the bad are industrious, so he shall be too. And it couldn't always be done the coalition government way. Sometimes what was needed was the *city's* way, and that meant *his* way. They still belonged together. The cobbles call to his shoes and the rain-soaked alleys to his very soul. The door slams. Upstairs, Hettie Thud smiles to herself and goes on designing visions of the future.

The rain explores. It has adventures.

There are no more portals, so the city is full of ex-Scarlet Citadel and ex-army. All civilians now. All exploring themselves and the world. All adventuring.

Things are better since the drought and the war came to an end.

A lot better.

It'll take work to keep them this way. It'll take something more to improve. Something this city has in amazing quantities.

The rain comes down, but the city is on its way up.

It soars.

It is the thing with feathers.

And as for Hughes...

***

In the city there loomed a tower.

In the tower there was an office.

In the office there sat a man.

His hair and his beard had once been pepper-dark and lush. Now they were well-salted, his hair thinning at the peak. His clothes had once been moth-eaten, more hand-me-aways than hand-me-downs. Now his clothes were tailor made to his body, which was not as lithe and elegant as it had once been. Even his face—equine like his father's and foxy like his mother's—seemed stretched somehow over time's relentless rack.

Yesterday he had been young.

Today...

He huffed and fought the encroaching September cold by kindling a fire.

On his television, footage of the lunar landing played, grainy yet enthralling.

In his mind, footage of a more personal kind played.

He remembered:

(Hooyou?)

(Our guy)

And Laurana in her afterlife, playing volleyball on a sun-kissed beach, fresh blackberry juice on her mouth like lipstick.

He remembered:

(I'm as thick as clotted cream)

(You are the chamber itself)

And Jo befriending Estelle Corlum at a banquet, the two agreeing to travel the world together.

He remembered:

(Stringy bits)

(I'm still a puppet who has been handed his own strings)

And Frank Gallant leaving the city with his partner, Mr. Glint, traveling who knew where but promising to return someday.

He remembered.

(witchy cackles)

(a small bathtub and big dog)

"Boochums," murmured Hughes. "The pooch's name was Boochums."

Last night, he'd visited Iphigenia.

Nothing to report there. It was a visit to his older sister. She'd had a good day. She was happy to see him. He'd missed her so much it ached.

Nothing to report. Nothing out of the ordinary.

The fire wasn't helping his joints much. They were still barking lustily at him, those hellish hounds from the kennel of age. He shuffled closer to the flames and watched the astronauts. They were still up there, well provisioned for the long haul, thrilled out of their minds to be collecting samples. See this moon rock, folks at home? We do! We do!

Hughes supposed it was pretty cool. Only a grouch would resent the broadcasters and the folks at home their good time, and a grouch he refused to be, white hairs or no white hairs.

He watched an astronaut wade around as if through soup. Another appeared in the distance, bending to collect another jaw-dropping sample no doubt. They'd be home soon. There'd be a tornado of press, a few glamorous events, a few opportunities for socialites to rub elbows with the spacefarers. Hughes would be called on to put in an appearance. His name still carried weight, a flourish of celebrity, even if his political career was over.

Retiring the presidency had been the right call.

It was the prospect of what to do with himself now that nettled. The Citadel was basically an arm of the government, its resources diverted to handle a swathe of Corinthia's (say it with me now, folks at home) bureaucracy. Who had seen that coming? And with magic items losing their potency in concord with Iphigenia's fluctuating health, Redspire had been demoted to a kind of bemusing relic. A useful if rather outmoded featurette of Corinthian culture. Yesterday's news.

He had never recovered his sword, Chimera. His Krys knife gathered dust somewhere in his chambers. His Performance was a thing of the past, a thing he'd done during that tantalizing span of time that beckoned him and forbade him access—yesterday.

Yesterday he'd been young.

Today...

Voices. He heard them. Loud, coming closer. Someone hammered on the door of the Dragon's Lair, his office at the top of the tower.

"Ser Gardener! Ser Gardener! Good ser, there is a demon upon my heels!"

Hughes' heart leaped. He called in a voice profuse with gallantry and courage, "Why, such a voice harkens, as sweet as honey! Could it be a fawn at my door? In! In at once!"

The door flew open. Evelyn rolled in, displaying a dexterity that made Hughes' creaky hips flare and his mouth flower into a grin.

"You are most gracious, ser," she told him, her cheeks flushed, her hair a wild mop. "The demon is of the most sordid and despicable variety. Of the bloated bum species, I believe."

"The bloated bum species?"

"The better to hold in her noxious toots, ser."

"Egads! Well, never fear, gentle fawn of the green woods. The laws of hospitality now shield you, and my sword is sworn to your service!"

"*What eez thees?*"

Cate advanced through the door, her fingers hooked fiendishly, her expression mangled with demonic wroth.

"You theenk you cen escape me by seeking senkchoo-hairy?" She threw back her head and roared laughter that would have caused the most malefic of hellspawn to quiver and spoil their clean trousers. "Thees knight haz white in his beard! He eez too old for acts hoff nobb-hillity!"

"One is never too old to do the right thing!" cried Evelyn the fawn. "The right thing in this instance being bashing your bloated bum with the flat of his sword!"

"Seelee child, I see no swort."

"Here, demon." Hughes raised his left shoe menacingly. "Silver, forged in the fires of Mount Minglepig by Pringus the Jinglesmith and blessed by Clarence the mushroom familiar, he of fungal fury!"

Cate's face dropped. "You harr lyink!"

"I am too old to lie. But not too old to slay thee!"

They charged.

Tickles ensued.

Not wanting to be left out, Evelyn jumped on them, which did not improve matters. Or it vastly improved them, depending on how you looked at it.

Outside a curtain of rain fell upon the day's drama, only to lift once more for night's big entrance.

Inside, it was dry.

Inside, there was laughter, Evelyn's loudest of all.

Hughes thought he could hear the sound of that laughter passing from today into tomorrow.

It sounded like enough to him. More than enough.

"What shall we do tonight?" Cate asked when they could laugh no more.

"There's a concert on in Nikandros." Evelyn deflated. "Oh. Never mind actually. It's rock and roll."

"I can take you," Cate offered.

"We'll both take you."

They both looked at Hughes, incredulous.

"Are you feeling all right, Father of mine?"

"I am, Daughter of mine."

"But... but you hate rock and roll."

Hughes smiled. "I think I'm ready to give it a second chance. Who's playing?"

"Loen Reddlebate."

Evelyn and Cate's astonishment hiked up another notch when Hughes nodded and said, "I'll book the tickets. See if I can score us some VIPs. Would you like to meet the man himself, honey?"

The look on his daughter's face did what the fire in his hearth had failed to do. It warmed him all the way through.

At the concert, he found he knew none of the words to the songs, except one: Loen Reddlebate's megahit. Hughes remembered all of the lyrics to that one.

He sang with his wife and his daughter, all three of them wearing VIP passes.

He sang with a kiss from Cate tingling on his cheek.

He sang with Evelyn's hand clutching his.

The song was "Moon Girl."

THE END

ARISE ALPHA

By Jez Cajiao

When you steal a hundred grand from some very bad people, the best way to survive is to stay small and quiet...

Possibly its not to save a pair of drowning girls, not go 'viral' on social media and certainly not to let the local police take your passport, trapping you on a small 'party' island in the middle of the Mediterranean Sea.

But Steve isn't the average guy, he's ex-military, ex-enforcer and ex-human. He's a one-man nanite fueled nightmare for those that cross the line, and he's decided that it's time to clean up his act. He's going to make up for the things he's done, and save 'the little guys'.

It's a nice fantasy, but even he has to admit, it's really just a justification, because he's a very bad man, with horrifying abilities, and he's only just learning what he's capable of. He needs a reason to not go to the dark, and if that's hunting down the creatures of the night and beating them to death with their own femurs?

Well, he's just the man for the job.

Stolen money. Greek Islands. Werewolves and Enforcers...
What could possibly go wrong?

https://www.amazon.com/Arise-Alpha-Dark-LitRPG-Adventure-ebook

THEFT OF DECKS BOOK ONE

By Lars Machmüller
When the deck is stacked against you? Change the game!

In the frontier town of Isarn, Chase will never be more than the lowly Darkborn thief he is. Banned from training, banned from acquiring better cards, if the Lightborn had their way, he'd be banned from life itself.

He's not alone though, and the one thing he and his friends have is determination. Losing a hand to a brutal punishment only fueled his obsession to get access to his own amazing, reality-bending cards.

That is the path to power and a future for them all. Nobody cares where you came from when you're rich enough. For now, though, they're facing both established powers, churches and age-old prejudices. It's time to get to work, and if the Lightborn won't share and play nice?

Sometimes the only way to get dealt a better hand is to steal the whole damn deck!

D&D meets Magic the Gathering in this epic fantasy deckbuilding LitRPG

https://mybook.to/TheftofDecksbook1

QUEST ACADEMY

By Brian J. Nordon

A world infested by demons.
An Academy designed to train Heroes to save humanity from annihilation.
A new student's power could make all the difference.

Humans have been pushed to the brink of extinction by an ever-evolving demonic threat. Portals are opening faster than ever, Towers bursting into the skies and Dungeons being mined below the last safe havens of society. The demons are winning.

Quest Academy stands defiantly against them, as a place to train the next generation of Heroes. The Guild Association is holding the line, but are in dire need of new blood and the powerful abilities they could bring to the battlefront. To be the saviors that humanity needs, they need to surpass the limits of those that came before them.

In a war with everything on the line, every power matters. With an adaptive enemy, comes the need for a constant shift in tactics. A new age of strategy is emerging, with even the unlikeliest of Heroes making an impact.

Salvatore Argento has never seen a demon.
He has never aspired to become a Hero.
Yet his power might be the one to tip the odds in humanity's favor.

Buy on Amazon

WANDERING WARRIOR

By Michael Head

A divine quest to deliver justice.
One year to accomplish his mission.
After nineteen planets, there's something different about this one.

James Holden has reached the maximum level there is for a human. That's perfect, since he's the only one of his kind. A wandering warrior, without control of his destination, tossed between universes by gods who've failed to tell him why. James is the lone Judge on a new world in need of someone to balance the scales. He isn't afraid to do so with extreme prejudice. As the Chief Justice, he has to right the wrongs the innocent can't fix themselves.

As James quickly discovers, the roots of corruption run deep. Guilds choose to protect themselves rather than the people. Monsters roam the wilderness unchecked. Judgment is usually a decision between right and wrong, but nothing is ever that simple. This time, being the strongest human won't be enough to punish the guilty. James might have to recruit some new blood, even if he prefers to work alone.

On his twentieth world, he is going to win, no matter the cost. James will have to find a way to break past the limits of the system if he's going to have a chance at making a difference.

Buy on Amazon

KNIGHTS OF ETERNITY

By Rachel Ní Chuirc

When Zara awoke in chains she thought she'd gone mad.

She was Zara the Fury - mistress of flame and fear. Her name was whispered across the land, from ramshackle taverns to the royal court. Even the heroic Gilded Knights thought twice before crossing her path.
She was feared—*respected.*
Now she was curled up on a dirt floor on her fiancé's orders. Valerius, leader of the Gilded, mocks her cries for help. And the kingdom is on the brink of war over the missing Lady Eternity...
But that wasn't why Zara thought she had gone mad.
The reason why is that the last thing she remembered was blood, an arcade screen, and the gun that changed everything.

But no chains can hold the Fury, and when she gets out?
The world is going to *burn*.

Buy on Amazon

SOCIAL MEDIA

Jack Fields Author Page
https://www.facebook.com/JackFieldsAuthor

LitRPG Legion Page
https://www.facebook.com/groups/litrpglegion

LITRPG!

To learn more about LitRPG, talk to authors, and have an awesome time, please join the LitRPG Group.

https://www.facebook.com/groups/LitRPGGroup

FACEBOOK

Here's a few wonderfully active Facebook groups I'd recommend, as you'll get to hear about great new books and new releases.

https://www.facebook.com/groups/LitRPGlegion/

https://www.facebook.com/groups/GamelitSociety

https://www.facebook.com/groups

https://www.facebook.com/groups/LitRPGforum/

RECOMMENDATIONS

If you liked this novel, you might also like...

Creation's Bane by Kevin Sinclair

Knights of Eternity by Rachel Ní Chuirc

Quest Academy by Brian J. Nordon

Somnia Online by K.T. Hanna

The Good Guys by Eric Ugland

The Ten Realms by Michael Chatfield

UnderVerse by Jez Cajiao

Wandering Warrior by Michael Head

World of Chains by Lars Machmüller